CHARLOTTE LAMB

Charlotte Lamb was born in London in time for World War II, and spent most of the war moving from relative to relative to escape bombing. Educated at a convent, she married a journalist and now has five children. Charlotte Lamb has written over one hundred books, most of them for Harlequin Mills & Boon.

MARGARET ST. GEORGE

Multiple award winner Margaret St. George, who also writes as Maggie Osborne, is the author of more than thirty novels, in categories ranging from historical to mystery to romantic romp. Margaret is a native of Colorado where she lives with her husband.

JACKIE WEGER

For Jackie Weger, writing romances is a way to put magic in her life. Having had five children before the age of twenty-two, she suspects she missed out in the fantasy department. It wasn't until she was forty that Jackie tried her hand at writing, completing her first novel in only three weeks.

Snowbound

Charlotte Lamb
Margaret St. George
Jackie Weger

Harlequin Books

TORONTO • NEW YORK • LONDON
AMSTERDAM • PARIS • SYDNEY • HAMBURG
STOCKHOLM • ATHENS • TOKYO • MILAN
MADRID • WARSAW • BUDAPEST • AUCKLAND

HARLEQUIN BOOKS

by Request—SNOWBOUND

Copyright © 1998 by Harlequin Books S.A.

ISBN 0-373-20143-5

The publisher acknowledges the copyright holders of the individual works as follows:
SHOTGUN WEDDING
Copyright © 1991 by Charlotte Lamb
MURDER BY THE BOOK
Copyright © 1992 by Margaret St. George
ON A WING AND A PRAYER
Copyright © 1988 by Jackie Weger

This edition published by arrangement with Harlequin Books S.A.

Printed in U.S.A.

CONTENTS

She'd run out on him once—
but Mother Nature wouldn't let her run again.

SHOTGUN WEDDING

Charlotte Lamb

CHAPTER ONE

JULIET NEWCOME was just leaving her Chelsea flat when the telephone rang, and she almost did not go back to answer it because she had such a busy day ahead of her, but she had never found it easy to ignore the shrill insistence of a ringing phone, so she sighed and went back.

'Julie? It's me,' said her mother in a husky rush. 'I'm glad I caught you, I thought you might already be on your way to work, and I have to leave at once if I'm to get the London train, and then it will take ages to get to Heathrow from the railway station… oh, I do hate travelling.'

Frowning, Juliet said, 'Slow down, Mum—what are you talking about? Where are you going?'

'Well, that's just it. I only heard myself this morning…well, last night, well, in the middle of the night.' Shirley Mendelli's incoherence did not surprise her daughter, who was quite accustomed to it. It was one of the traits Juliet was glad she had not inherited. She knew she looked very like her mother; they were both tall, slim, with thick chestnut hair and blue eyes, and they both had good skins and oval faces, but in temperament they were very different. Juliet was calm and capable; Shirley was impulsive, impractical and volatile.

'Heard what?' Juliet patiently asked, but she should have remembered that you couldn't halt her mother's flow. Shirley would only tell the story her way—you threw her if you interrupted.

'I'm trying to tell you! Do listen, Juliet!' Shirley plaintively said. 'They rang at three o'clock this morning, which seemed like the dead of night to me, I was half asleep when I picked up the phone. Well, I couldn't book a plane then, of course, everything was closed for the night. I went back to bed but I couldn't sleep, so I got up again and packed my case and made sure the cottage was tidy, and I booked the first available flight to Italy…'

'Italy?' Juliet guessed then, her face sobering. 'It's Giorgio? He's been taken ill?'

Her stepfather had been in Italy for several weeks on a buying expedition, a task he undertook twice a year for the chain of shops they jointly owned. They sold luxury, handmade shoes, bought from various countries, but Italy was one of their main suppliers. Juliet had spoken to him only yesterday morning, when he had been in the best of spirits, so she knew that whatever had gone wrong must have happened suddenly.

'Arrested!' Shirley said dramatically, and Juliet gave a little gasp of shock and incredulity.

'Arrested? Giorgio? But whatever for?' Giorgio was the last man she would ever have expected to break the law. He simply wasn't the type; he loved the good life too much. *La Dolce Vita* was what he lived for, in fact: nice clothes, a comfortable home, a good car, a wife who adored him and fussed over him, elegant food, a little wine, a cigar after dinner. Giorgio had always seemed to Juliet to be one of the happiest men around. Over sixty, he was still a very handsome man, with silvery hair and dark eyes, a wonderful tan and a charming, endearing manner. She knew her mother thought the sun shone out of him, and he seemed to love her mother very much, too.

'Oh, I don't know, Julie,' her mother wailed. 'I couldn't make it out. I spoke to a policeman first, who said something about a driving offence. He had a thick accent, and in the shock of hearing the news my Italian deserted me—I didn't understand half what he said. Then they let me speak to Giorgio, but only for a little while and all he would say was that he was innocent, he didn't do it. He was almost in tears. He's gone to pieces—you know what he's like.'

'Do I not?' Juliet was smiling ruefully because Giorgio was one of those men who always needed a woman to look after them. His mother had been a fierce, dominating Sicilian who had given birth to twelve children, most of them girls, loved them possessively and ruled them with a rod of iron, which was why Giorgio had managed to reach the age of forty-five without ever marrying. His mother would not hear of it. Her other son, the eldest, had married a girl she had picked out for him, but Giorgio, her youngest child, was her favourite, and she would not let go of him. Giorgio had been too affectionate to fight her. He couldn't bring himself to hurt her feelings.

When her death had finally freed him, though, he had married the first woman he had met soon afterwards. The really surprising thing has been that he had married a foreigner, a visiting English tourist. It might so easily have been a disaster, that astonishing, unexpected marriage, but it hadn't, it had instead been a blazing success, and they were still happy over fifteen years later.

'So you see why I must get to him as soon as I can!' said her mother.

'Of course—poor Giorgio! He must be in quite a state. Would you like me to come, too? I'll have to rearrange a few appointments for today, but that won't be hard. I could book a late afternoon flight, I'm sure there must be one…'

'No, no, dear, I can manage on my own. I'd rather you stayed here, then if I need anything—money, legal help—I can ring you. We can't all three of us be away or who knows what might happen to the business?'

Juliet smiled wryly. 'Oh, I think it would stagger on for a few days, but I'll do whatever you want me to, you know that. Anything I can do now?'

'Just one thing—will you go down to the cottage at the weekend and make sure everything is OK? The workmen should have finished work on the new kitchen extension and be out of there—I meant to drive down to make sure they had done the job properly. Mrs Cottman, who comes in to clean the place for me, you know? Well, she was going to keep an eye on them, but her daughter has had a baby and she's gone to Leeds to look after them both, so I don't know what sort of state the cottage is in, and it's on my mind, so if you could...'

'Sure! It's Thursday, isn't it?' Juliet stared at the wall, mentally checking off her weekend plans. 'I don't have anything important on this weekend.' Just a date with the man she was currently seeing, but that would have to be shelved. It was more important to set her mother's mind at rest. 'Look, I'll drive down tomorrow night. Just remember, if you need to speak to me after five tomorrow I'll be driving down to the cottage, so wait and ring me there after nine.'

'Oh, dear, it is a long drive, darling. Are you sure you don't mind?'

'Quite sure! In fact, I'll enjoy a break from London for a couple of days,' Juliet soothed. 'Don't worry about it. Just concentrate on Giorgio, give him my love, and make sure you get him the best possible lawyers. As soon as you arrive, get in touch with the Lazaro brothers—they've known him for years, and they're such good friends; I'm sure they'll be happy to help. And Mum...keep in touch, won't you?'

'Of course, darling. I must hurry or I'll miss my flight... bye, talk to you soon.' Shirley Mendelli flung the phone down and Juliet smiled wryly as she replaced her own. Really, she should be going with her mother. Mum was bound to get flustered and into a panic, and although she now spoke pretty fluent colloquial Italian, after her years with Giorgio, it would probably desert her faced with a worrying situation. Juliet hesitated, then decided to wait and see how her mother sounded next time she rang up. If Mum got out of her depth no doubt she'd ring tonight and she could always catch the next flight to Milan and join her.

She had a busy day ahead of her, visiting three of the London stores in turn, so she pushed all thought of her mother and Giorgio to the back of her mind for the moment, and hurried out to the garages adjoining the block of flats in which she lived, to pick up her small red estate car. It was a useful vehicle; she could carry quite a large amount of stock in the back of it if necessary, but it didn't take up too much room if you had to park somewhere in busy London streets.

It was typical of Juliet that she should be so practical in her choice of car, just as it was typical of her mother that she should have named her only daughter so romantically. Juliet disliked her own name: kids loved to make fun of classmates, and, everywhere she had gone at school, she had been greeted with falsetto shrieks of, 'Romeo, Romeo wherefore art thou Romeo?' or even, 'Who let you off the balcony, Juliet?' Fortunately, in time, most people had begun to call her Julie.

Except her father, she thought suddenly, grimacing. He had gone on calling her Juliet. Typical of him to be obstinate and unyielding in that, as in everything else. Jack Newcome's mind had set in concrete long before she was born; he had never changed while she knew him, and no

doubt he never would. She had never been able to understand why her mother had ever married him.

Traffic was heavy that morning. It was nine o'clock by
the time Julie reached her first call of the day: the Bond
Street store. She parked in the alley at the back, but walked
round to inspect the window display, standing on the pavement, her chestnut head to one side. Yes, it caught the
attention, and, from the look of it, had cost very little,
which was a big plus.

She was delighted with that spring's colours: daffodil-
yellow, leaf-green, sky-blue. They lifted the heart as you
looked at them, and the window-dresser here had produced
an alluring effect with some clouds of pink gauze, a few
sprays of artificial apple blossom, a brilliantly painted
landscape background. The delicate handmade shoes
seemed to float above the clouds, among the blossom—
you felt they must be as light as air and a joy to wear.

This new girl was talented; they must keep her. Julie
made a mental note to tell the manageress to give the girl
a small rise. It was a mistake to underpay talented staff,
Giorgio had told her when she began managing her first
store. She bit her lower lip, thinking about her stepfather.
What could have happened? He wasn't a careless driver;
on the contrary he was a very experienced one with a
blameless record.

'Something wrong?'

The voice made her jump, swinging round, but she relaxed when she saw the young woman standing next to
her. 'Oh, hello, Sandy. Sorry, I was miles away.'

'I thought you were hating the window display!'

'Good heavens, no! I love it,' said Juliet, and Sandy
Carter gave a relieved grin, her brown eyes brightening
again.

'Oh, good! I was pleased with it myself. Karen did it, the new girl. She's good, don't you think?'

'Very,' agreed Juliet, nodding. 'In fact, I was just deciding to give her a small rise. We must keep this girl, Sandy. She's the most promising window-dresser we've had for ages.'

'I'll do my best to keep her happy!' promised Sandy, and Juliet smiled at her.

'And your best is pretty good!'

Sandy had been managing the store for several years, and was very good at her job. Staff and customers liked her, yet she was very efficient; this branch had run like clockwork ever since she took over.

She grinned back at Juliet, pleased with her comment, and in a friendly mood they walked together through the front of the shop and into Sandy's little office. Juliet smiled and nodded to the two girls busy tidying the racks of shoes, but didn't linger to talk to them. 'I have a lot to get through today, Sandy,' she explained. 'I'm having to do my mother's job as well as my own, for the moment. She has had to go to Italy—something has happened to Giorgio…'

Sandy listened while Juliet told her all about Shirley Mendelli's phone call that morning, looking as startled as Juliet had felt, and expressed much the same disbelief. 'Giorgio, of all people! He can't have been drinking? Well, I know he likes the odd glass of *vino*, but he doesn't overdo it, does he?'

'Giorgio isn't given to extremes,' agreed Juliet. 'That's probably why he and my mother get on so well. It takes a man as easygoing as Giorgio to put up with her mood swings.'

'How did your own father…' began Sandy, then hesitated, because Juliet rarely mentioned her father. 'Sorry, that's not my business!'

Juliet made a wry face. 'Oh, it's no secret. My father never understood my mother, she drove him crazy. Their marriage was a disaster from day one, I imagine.'

She would never have told anyone else that, but Sandy was probably her closest friend; they had got to know each other while they were both working in the Oxford Street store, seven years ago. At that time, Juliet had been shy, self-conscious and unhappy, and would never have made friends with anyone if they hadn't done most of the work. Sandy was so different; cheerful, casual, friendly, she had been so easy to get on with that Juliet had got to know her almost without realising it.

A pocket Venus with brown eyes and gingery fair hair, Sandy was married to a travelling salesman who was often away for half the week, which Juliet knew she would hate, but which did not seem to bother Sandy.

She was always happy to see her husband, Tom, back again, but when he was away she didn't seem unhappy, maybe because she had an absorbing career of her own, and a great many friends. She and Tom lived in a modern block of flats, mostly occupied by young people, none of them with children. Sandy had rapidly got to know most of them, and her social life was a busy one, but she was a big success in her job and Juliet hoped they would keep her.

The trouble was, they were a small chain; just half a dozen shops so far, mostly around London, although they had opened one in Manchester recently. Shirley and Giorgio had moved up there for a few months, to see it launched and monitor its progress. If it was a success, they would open another next year, but they couldn't pay as much money as a bigger chain might be able to offer Sandy. If they continued to expand, one day, no doubt, there would be room for Sandy to move up into an executive position, which was what she wanted, Juliet was aware, but that was all very much a future dream, and not likely to happen for some years since they could not risk expansion until it became easier to borrow money at manageable interest rates.

'You never see your father, do you?' Sandy asked, breaking into Juliet's abstracted thoughts, and with a start of surprise Juliet shook her head.

'No,' she said in a flat, harsh voice, then hurriedly picked up the accounting sheets for the previous month, which were lying on the desk in an open folder. 'Well, we must get on, Sandy!' she said, her eyes on the neat rows of figures. 'Sorry, but not only have I got my mother's work to do; she wants me to go down to Cornwall this weekend. She's had some building work done, but hasn't had a chance to inspect it, so I promised to pop down there tomorrow.'

'Pop down?' repeated Sandy, half aghast, half amused. 'It will take you hours! And it's bound to be freezing down there.' She made Cornwall sound like the Arctic and Juliet laughed.

'I can't say I'm looking forward to that long drive, especially on a Friday evening, after a full week's work, but I don't want her fretting over the cottage while she's so upset over Giorgio.'

'But weren't you going to some posh ball with Adam?'

Juliet pulled a face. 'Yes, and I'm not looking forward to telling him I can't go.'

'Can't you drive down to Cornwall today, and get back in time for the ball?'

'No, I have several very important appointments; I can't put them off, and, anyway, I want to be near Heathrow just in case my mother rings up and says she needs me urgently in Milan. By tomorrow night she should have found out exactly what's wrong.'

Sandy nodded sympathetically. 'Yes, of course. Oh, well, Adam will understand; family has to come first.'

Juliet gave her a wry smile. 'Let's hope so. But it's his firm's annual party, all his bosses will be there, and Adam wants to make a big impression. He even came with me to buy my dress, to make sure I looked suitably ritzy, so he isn't going to be too pleased when he hears I'm going down to Cornwall instead, but I don't see how I can get back by Saturday night. I shall be exhausted after the drive down there. I doubt if I shall be able to face driving back almost at once.'

'No, I should say not,' agreed Sandy, but when Juliet talked to Adam York that evening he was by no means as understanding. In fact, he was furious. He went red and stiffened, his blue eyes flashing sparks at her.

'You can't be serious! You must come! I can't go to the ball alone, people will think you stood me up! I'll look a complete fool!' Nothing could horrify Adam more than the prospect of looking a fool. Juliet knew that and looked at him ruefully. She realised why his dignity meant a great deal to him. He was a man from a poor background who was climbing the ladder of success so fast that it occasionally gave him vertigo, made his head swim and made him afraid of falling. He felt the need to appear completely in control, completely at his ease. He used dignity as an armour. It was his inner uncertainties that had attracted her, in fact, not that Adam would be too pleased if she told him so. He could be rather sweet and helpless, when he stopped pretending to be a big, tough executive.

'I'm sorry, Adam. I know how much it means to you, but it's a matter of priorities...'

His face tightened angrily. 'I see. And I come second to your mother's cottage, do I?'

'I didn't mean that.'

'Oh, yes, you did. Your mother asks you to drive hundreds of miles to check on her cottage, so you dump me and our date without a second thought. My career doesn't matter a damn to you, does it? I've explained over and over again how important this occasion is…the Chairman will be there! He always dances with a couple of the prettiest women—he might have picked you.'

'He might not even have noticed me!' Juliet muttered.

Adam snapped back, 'The wives and girlfriends of executives always get noticed! The higher you go in the company, the more important it is to have a presentable woman.'

'Oh, thanks. So that's what I am, is it? A presentable woman?' Juliet was seething, too, now, and had flushed bright pink. 'I'm not a possession of yours, Adam. You can't trot me out to be assessed by your boss once a year. Do I get marks out of ten? How do they work it out? A mark for clothes sense? A mark for good legs? What else do they judge a woman on? You'll be asking me to cook dinner for the whole board of directors, soon, to prove to them I can cook, too.'

'Oh, don't be so ridiculous!' he snarled, his hands screwing into fists as if he wanted to hit her, although Adam was far too polite to do anything of the kind. 'You know what I meant. It's vital for you to be with me this one evening of the year. It isn't too much to ask, is it? Everyone will be there—the managing director, my head of department, everyone! I've talked about you, they're expecting you…'

Their eyes met and she read his expression, frowning. Adam had boasted about her, she realised suddenly. Her family firm had been getting big publicity lately, with their expansion out of London. She was a very useful girlfriend for an ambitious man like Adam; if she didn't show up his pride and his ego would be dented. It wasn't that he would miss her; it was merely that he wanted to show her off. She hesitated, not knowing what to say, both irritated and sorry for him.

'Isn't there anyone else you could take?' she suggested at last, and he looked at her as if she was mad.

'Another woman? You really want me to take another woman?'

She fell silent, realising suddenly what she had said, and all that underlay the words. Adam sounded outraged, as if she had suggested some heinous infidelity, had told him to betray her. There was a fraught silence while they both stared at each other, and Juliet tried to say something, anything, to cover the discovery she had just made, they had both made.

Adam had been having a light supper with her, just a warm quiche with salad followed by fruit. He got up from the table, pushing back his chair with a violence that made it fall over, and walked, stiff-legged like a stork, to the door. Juliet followed him and watched him collect his expensive camel-hair overcoat, put it on and turn towards her, drawing on his tan leather gloves.

'There's nothing to say, is there?' he said. 'Either you come to the ball with me, or you don't, and we're finished. Let me know by tomorrow evening which way you decide.' He opened the front door and paused, his flushed face struggling to be polite. 'Thank you for supper—it was delicious.'

As the door closed she felt a bubble of hysterical laughter in her throat. How typical of Adam to become formal and courteous after issuing her with an ultimatum. Then she stopped laughing. Why hadn't she realised until now that she wasn't serious about Adam? Her mouth indented wryly; but *hadn't* she known? Had she ever thought of herself as serious, committed to him? She had drifted into the relationship gradually, not intending to get seriously involved—it hadn't entered her head that Adam thought she was serious, or that Adam himself might be serious.

She curled up on the carpet in front of the electric log fire which glowed on her small hearth, trying to sort out her thoughts, Adam's feelings. What exactly did she mean by... serious? What was she saying? That he was in love with her? The idea made her frown, then laugh shortly. No. Not that. Adam was not in love; he felt nothing so overwhelming.

He had probably decided, though, no doubt after careful thought, because that was Adam's way of reaching any important decision, that she would make a suitable wife for a rising young executive; and perhaps that was the right way to consider marriage—as a partnership. What, after all, had love to do with it?

No sane person would marry for love—that was no basis for choosing someone to live with, to bring up children with, was it? Juliet didn't trust love. Love was messy and explosive, it made you vulnerable, betrayed you and it didn't last; worst of all, it left you feeling like hell. She had been in love once, and the wound still ached on certain days, like the scars of some old battle. She never intended to let love happen to her again, and, luckily, so far she had never been in the slightest danger of caring that much for anyone else.

She had felt quite safe with Adam, she liked him, but not too much. He was no threat to her emotions, and yet he was good company. They had a lot of friends in common, and everyone felt that they made a nice couple; their mutual friends approved, and, although she had ignored the fact until now, so did their families. She should have guessed, meeting the smiles, the knowing looks, the little hints, from his mother, her own.

Why on earth hadn't she realised the way the wind was blowing? How had she stayed blind for so long? She could kick herself. Had she preferred not to know? It was so convenient to have a representable male as an escort, someone her mother and Giorgio liked, someone who knew most of her friends and had a busy career of his own, so that he understood the demands her job made—and also, admittedly, she did like Adam.

She bit her lip, her frown deepening. Yes, she liked him—but not enough to think of spending her life with him, surely? Her blue eyes were troubled. It was just as well that this had happened. She had been warned, and now she had to make a very important decision. She was too tired tonight, though. She looked at her watch, and got up. She would sleep on it, decide tomorrow.

She must have been more tired than she realised, because she slept through her alarm and woke with a start to find that it was gone eight and she was going to be late for work.

It was a bad start to a difficult day; she was in a hurry from then on and had to shelve any thought of Adam and whether or not she wanted to end their relationship. It was only as she drove out of London, heading west along the motorway, that she admitted to herself that the decision had been made without her needing to think. She had not rung Adam, and silence was an answer in itself. He would know what it meant. If she had rung him, he might have tried to persuade her, or flown into another rage, and she was too tired to face either reaction. Adam would have no problem finding someone to take; he was not good-looking, but he was attractive—a tall, slim man with a thin face, smooth brown hair, and pale blue eyes. Sometimes she had had trouble conjuring up his face in her memory, it was true; Adam was not memorable. But he dressed well, he was very eligible and she knew other girls noticed him; he would soon find someone else.

I'll miss him, she thought, pulling a face. They had been seeing each other for months; he was a habit with her.

Oh, well. She sighed, making herself concentrate on the road. There was no point in regret for what could not be helped. Life wasn't easy, that was all. The motorway wasn't crowded, at least, that was something, and the news from Italy that afternoon had been comforting. Her mother's panic was over; Giorgio had been involved in an accident and had been accused of causing it but his lawyers had found witnesses who swore the other driver had been responsible for the crash. Giorgio and Shirley would be coming home in a few days, with any luck.

Some time later, after crossing the county line into Devon, she glanced at the dashboard clock; not too long now. She didn't enjoy driving long distances at night. It was March and the weather had taken a turn for the worse during the afternoon. The sky was cloudless, an icy wind blowing from the east. She was doing a steady seventy miles an hour and at this rate she should get to the cottage before nine. She decided not to stop for a meal. There was plenty of food in the store cupboard at the cottage; tinned or frozen. She would be happy with whatever she found.

Night had fallen, but there was a strange light in the sky—not the sulphurous glow of street lighting, something very different. Juliet screwed up her eyes in puzzled surprise, staring—what was it? It looked positively eerie.

Then she saw the first soft white flakes blowing across the windscreen and her heart sank. Oh, no! Not snow! She hadn't bargained for that when she had agreed to drive down here.

As she drove on westwards, the gentle drift of snow became a howling blizzard, and she began to think she wasn't going to make it, but the roads were not yet impassable. An hour later she finally reached the isolated little cottage at the edge of moorland, within earshot of the sea.

It had been built for a shepherd, nearly two hundred years ago; a simple little dwelling, two rooms downstairs, two up, flint walls, a slate roof. It had been modernised now, of course, and much extended. There was a bathroom, a cosy country kitchen, even central heating, and Juliet pulled up outside the front door with a long sigh of relief. Her gloved hands seemed to be frozen to the wheel, and she was cramped and shivering. She found the front door key, dived out, unlocked the cottage, then ran back to fetch her suitcase before gratefully slamming the front door behind her.

It only took a short while to make the place a warm and welcoming home; she put on lights, turned on the oil-fired central heating, made up her bed, switched on the electric underblanket in it, unpacked, opened a can of tomato soup, heated it, cut some of the new loaf of bread she had brought with her, toasted it, and sat down to eat her supper at the kitchen table.

Her first spoonful was on its way to her mouth when the phone rang, and she dropped soup all over herself with a cry of shock.

Jumping up, she dabbed herself with a tea-cloth while she was running to snatch up the phone. 'Hello?' she breathlessly said, expecting to hear her mother's voice.

There was a silence, then a husky male voice said, 'Mrs Mendelli?'

Disappointed, Juliet said flatly, 'No, I'm afraid she isn't here at the moment. She's in Italy, with her husband. Would you like to leave a message?'

There was another silence, then he said, 'Who is that?'

For no reason she could have explained, that voice made a shiver run down her back; an instinctive, atavistic shudder. She didn't recognise the voice, yet she almost didn't answer, which was crazy.

He had only asked who she was! A perfectly natural question, wasn't it? What is the matter with you? she asked herself.

'I'm her daughter,' she slowly said, and got a second shock when she heard the phone click, and realised he had hung up without another word. After a surprised pause, she replaced her own phone, frowning. How rude.

She went back to the table and sat down. Well, at least her soup was still hot. She finished her meal hungrily, but couldn't stop thinking about the phone call. Who could it have been? They had no near neighbours here; the nearest house was a mile off, nearer the sea, but if it had been someone she knew he would have said so—he wouldn't have hung up without a word.

She hadn't felt nervous about being here alone until then, but as she washed up and tidied the kitchen before going upstairs to bed she felt distinctly jumpy. Every little noise made her nerves prickle. She kept freezing, listening—was that the wind rustling the trees, or the sound of someone creeping around the house? Was that the crack of a twig underfoot outside, or the noise of the central heating in the pipes?

She was here to check up on the building work her mother had had done, so she went on a tour of inspection, telling herself it was not because she wanted to make sure there was nobody else in the house. She liked the new extension, which was to be a dining area leading out of the kitchen. The pine panelling and floor looked wonderful, and it had all been left very neat and tidy.

The doors and windows were all securely bolted, there was no sign of anyone outside, the snow glistening, pure and untrodden in the lights of the house, and so, wryly making a face at her own reflection in a mirror as she passed, she turned off the downstairs lights at last, and went up to bed just before ten. How could she have let herself get so jumpy over a phone call, and the rudeness of some total stranger?

She had a bath, her weary muscles relaxing in the warm, scented water, and then she put on the warm, blue-striped pyjamas she had brought with her, knowing how cold it could be in the cottage, even in March. Her bed had warmed up nicely, though, so she switched off the electric blanket and the bedside lamp and snuggled down with a sigh. She was exhausted; she fell asleep within minutes.

She woke with a jolt some time later, and sat up, eyes wide yet blank with sleep, trembling as if from a nightmare. She didn't know where she was for a second and stared around, slowly recognising the shadows of the furniture, remembering why she was here.

The room was filled with the eerie light she had seen on her drive; the reflection of the moon and stars on the snow outside, a magical, disturbing light which made her shiver.

She was about to lie down again when she heard the creak of a floorboard outside, on the landing. Her heart crashed into her ribs; she stared fixedly across the room—there was someone there, outside her room.

Before she had time to think the door began to open

and she saw in the strange white light of the snow a shape appear in the doorway, a tall, looming shape. The outline of a man.

CHAPTER TWO

JULIET wanted to scream, but she couldn't—her throat seemed numb, her mouth was open but no sound came out, although inside her head she was screaming, and the moment stretched like a tortured nerve, on and on, while she stared and the dark shape in the doorway did not move.

Then suddenly he did, taking a long, silent stride towards the bed, and that seemed to free her voice. She did not scream, but she gave a high, shaking cry, shrinking back against the headboard of the bed, her wide eyes watching him like the terrified eyes of a trapped animal watching the predator, unable to flee because of its own fear. He was wearing black from head to foot; a leather jacket which shone with wet snow, black trousers, black boots. His head was black, too; she saw the sheen of his jet-black hair. If she could only see his face she might not be so scared, but the pale snow light did not illumine his features—it merely shimmered across his face in an unearthly way.

He was only a few feet away by the time she had managed to start thinking. What was she doing, sitting there, waiting for him? She had to get away.

She scrambled off the bed and began to run towards the open door, but he moved faster, launching himself at her like a rugger player, his hands reaching for her. Juliet screamed then, and went on screaming as she fell, with him, their bodies hitting the carpet together and rolling over and over.

'Who's going to hear you?' he whispered hoarsely, and

28

he was right, of course. Nobody would hear her, because there were no houses within earshot—this was a very isolated cottage, deliberately chosen because it stood a mile from any other habitation, a place out of the rush of modern life, a place to be safe and peaceful. There was irony in that thought now.

'My husband will be back from work soon, he'll be here any minute...' She tried to sound convincing, but he laughed.

'Oh, I'm really scared,' he whispered in that deep, husky voice, and she recognised it, she realised that it had been familiar from the start.

He was the man who had rung earlier. He must have been checking to see if anyone was in the cottage, and when he knew she was there alone...

Who was he? she thought desperately. She had this strange, disturbing feeling that she knew him. Her heart pounded against her ribs; she couldn't bear it, the thought of what he might plan to do to her. She suddenly rolled away, meaning to get up and run, but he was more quick-thinking than she was, his arm shot out and clamped her by the waist.

She lay on her side, facing away from him, trying to push his hand down, struggling violently, and he moved closer, forcing her into intimate body contact, his chest against her back, his thigh touching hers, his other arm sliding under her to hold her even tighter.

Juliet was breathing so rapidly that it hurt, and she was sobbing soundlessly, tears hot in her eyes. With another shock of fear she felt one of his hands move up. Her pyjama jacket had come undone in the struggle and he pushed it softly aside, slid a hand inside and touched her bare breasts with his fingertips, stroked her hard nipples, a light, caressing slide of flesh on flesh which made her jack-knife in recoil, trying to get away from him, while she moaned, 'No!'.

This time, though, he didn't try to stop her. He let her break free, let her struggle shakily to her feet, always expecting to be dragged back, like a mouse which a tormenting cat allows to escape only to snatch it back a second later.

He just sat up and watched her, as she ran for the door, trembling and uncertain, her mind in panic.

She had to get away from him; her head whirled with hurried plans and fears. If she could get a head start she could get to the car, but then she realised that her car keys were in her handbag, which was in the bedroom, and in this weather to try to run across the moors, or even along the road to the nearest village, would be suicide. The snow cut them off as effectively as if this cottage were an island in the middle of a frozen sea.

'There's nowhere to run to, Juliet,' he said behind her, reading her mind.

She froze in the doorway, her feelings chaotic. She had thought she was going crazy, that the strange, tormenting familiarity she had felt had all been imagination, but now she knew it hadn't been.

'You…you…' She looked back and he was on his feet, but he wasn't chasing after her. He simply stood there, a tall, black shadow in the snowlit room, staring at her, and she stared back, beginning to glimpse features beneath the cap of thick black hair.

A long, straight nose, a firm chin, wide, hard mouth, and his eyes…those eyes…grey, cold, disturbing… She took a long, appalled breath. It was him.

'You can't get away, not this time,' he said, and again the words echoed in her mind.

'This time?' she repeated aloud, beginning to shake again.

'Even if you could start the car, you wouldn't get far. The snow is already wall-high. I had to abandon my own car half a mile from here and walk the rest of the way, and I thought I might not make it. And the telephone lines are down locally. That wind has caused all sorts of damage, and the snow is causing more.' He sounded so matter of fact—how could he talk that way, seem so at ease, while her ears rang with memories she had tried to bury fathoms deep years ago?

'Who are you?' she whispered, but she knew, she had recognised him when he'd spoken her name. Perhaps she had even recognised his voice when he'd rung earlier. Something in the timbre of that voice had made the hair stand up on the back of her neck, sent dread spiralling through her. She hadn't quite put it all together—her subconscious hadn't told her conscious mind what it knew—but somewhere inside her head she had known, she realised that now.

'You know who I am,' he said with derision, reading her mind again, and that disturbed her even more. She did not want him reading her mind, guessing at her thoughts and feelings, all her reactions. She needed to put a mask upon her face and hide herself from him.

'I don't,' she lied, hoping it would be true and knowing that it wasn't.

He reached out a hand to the bedside lamp and she broke out hoarsely, 'No, don't put on the light!'

She didn't want to see his face, she didn't want to know for sure, because in this strange snowy light there was something dreamlike, mysterious, unreal about being here with him, and if he put on the light he would break the spell, bring them both out into the real world.

'Afraid of facing me, Juliet?' he asked in icy mockery.

She angrily snapped back, 'No!'

'You prefer it in the dark?' His voice held double meaning; she felt heat rise in her face.

'I'd prefer you to go away...now!'

He laughed softly. 'Don't you want to see how much I've changed? You've changed, you know. Even in the dark I could tell that. When you were seventeen you were downright skinny, flat as a boy, front and back...' He paused, and then went on, his voice mocking, 'Nobody could say that now. You have a very sexy body.'

'Shut up!' she broke out.

He talked on over her. 'Beautiful breasts...'

'Shut up!' Her face was burning now. His words conjured up the vision of his hand inside her pyjama jacket, the cool brush of his fingers on her bare flesh, and she was so angry she shook with it.

'Y-y-you had no right! T-touching me like that!' she stammered, her throat rough. 'You scared me senseless. I thought... I didn't know, did I? That it was you. I thought it was someone who'd broken in...any minute, I thought, I might be killed.'

'I didn't intend it to happen that way,' he began, and she gave a furious laugh.

'No?'

'No,' he said impatiently. 'Look, I had to see you, and there was no answer at your London flat, or at your mother's, so I rang here, and when you answered I decided to drive down here right away.'

'And break in and attack me!' she accused.

'I did not attack you!'

'What do you call it, then? You knocked me off my feet—'

'I had to stop you running away—you were in a stupid panic!'

'You knocked me to the ground, and then you…' She put her hands to her flushed cheeks, trying to shut out the memory. 'You…handled me!' she spat at him.

'I'm only human—you were too close for comfort; as soon as I touched you my curiosity got the better of me,' he said without any sign of contrition.

'You mean you enjoyed terrifying me!'

There was a little silence, then he laughed shortly. 'Yes, maybe I did. I was angry, and…yes, maybe I did, and I'm not apologising, Juliet, not after what you've done to me.'

She was the one to fall silent, then, biting her lip. For a moment, neither of them said anything, then he began talking again in that soft, mocking, conversational tone.

'Even your hair is different. You wore your hair in a long tail, right down to your waist, I remember. When you walked along it swung about behind you, like a squirrel's bushy tail. I was always tempted to pull it. You've cut it off, haven't you? I felt how short it was…and it curls; it never did that. I hope you haven't changed the colour, too. I loved it; conker colour, a bright, shiny chestnut.'

Juliet couldn't bear any more. Shakily, she said, 'I don't know why you're here, or what you think you're doing, but I don't want you here—go away!'

She had hardly finished speaking when he said harshly, 'Did you know my father had died?'

The shock seemed to knock the breath out of her. It was at least a minute before she said, 'No…' The word was half denial, half grief, because she had loved his father, far more than she had ever loved her own.

'A month ago,' he said, sounding as if he didn't believe her. '*The Times* carried an obit. You didn't see it?'

'No. I rarely read newspapers, except trade Press. I don't

have the time.' Her mother couldn't have seen the news, either, or she would certainly have said something. She, too, had been fond of the old man, and she knew how close he and Juliet had been. Taking a deep breath, Juliet quietly said, 'I'm very sorry to hear he's dead…you'll miss him.'

He laughed angrily. 'I could hardly miss him more than I have for the last eight years. He hasn't spoken to me since the night you left.'

She was stunned into silence, and, before she could say how sorry she was to hear that, he turned abruptly and switched on her bedside lamp. The sudden brilliance blinded her for a little while, then her eyes focused on him, seeing him properly for the first time. He looked even taller, a lean and hungry man, and dangerous with it, his face so familiar that she wondered how she had not known it even in the dark, those chiselled features and cold eyes, that wide, passionate mouth.

He was assessing her, too, from head to foot, with raking insolence; and she hurriedly buttoned up her pyjama jacket under that stare, making his mouth flick upwards at one corner in silent derision.

That smile made her angry again, and she burst out, 'Don't try to make me feel guilty about your father. Have you forgotten what you did to me that night? How could I stay there after that?'

His face was hard. 'You had led me to believe that that was what you wanted, remember?'

Her flush deepened. 'I was seventeen! I didn't know what I was doing!'

His grey eyes lashed her. 'Oh, I think you did. You wanted to marry into my family, you wanted to be the next mistress of Chantries. You'd had your sights set on me for months—you followed me everywhere I went; every time

I turned round, there you were, as clinging as a limpet. My God, you chased me relentlessly.'

She wanted to burst into tears, and at the same time she was angry enough to kill him, because it was true and yet it was all lies. She had followed him around everywhere, she had clung like a limpet, but not because she wanted to be mistress of his family estate. That hadn't entered into it. She wasn't the ambitious type. She wasn't a social climber, or a fortune hunter. She had been half child, half woman, head over heels in love and unable to hide it. All she had wanted was to be close to him, to be able to see him, watch him, listen to his voice. She had been infatuated, obsessed, almost possessed, and she hadn't thought about any future with him, or realised where her wild pursuit of him might lead.

'I didn't want Chantries!' she muttered, glaring at him. 'That part isn't true. I won't have you accusing me of that! You were the one who misunderstood... I was just a silly teenager who was having her first crush—it wasn't real.'

His eyes flashed, electric, deadly. 'Not real? A first crush?' She heard hatred in his voice. 'And for that you ruined my entire life?'

She paled, drawing a painful breath. 'I didn't—'

Harshly, he broke in on her, 'My father's last will only turned up a few days ago. He had locked it in a drawer in the library, nobody knew it was there. His lawyers didn't have a copy of it—they believed the last will was one which left everything to me, but then last week the executors were going through his papers, and they found a later one.' He paused, staring bitterly at her. 'He didn't leave Chantries to me.'

Juliet went quite white, her eyes horrified. 'He didn't? But...then, who inherits?' Simeon had been an only child, but she knew that his father had had a brother, who lived up north in Scotland, somewhere, and that he had had several sons. Had old Robert Gerard left his estate to one of his nephews? How cruel and unfair. It was so unlike him; she wouldn't have believed him capable of it. No wonder Simeon was so angry; he had every right to resent this.

He was staring at her fixedly, his skin dark with rage, his jawline clenched. Suddenly he said in an icy voice, 'The whole estate, money, land, everything, was left to our children.'

The shock was so intense that all the blood seemed to leave her body; she swayed, shivering, as if in a high wind, and for a moment almost fainted. He took two strides to get to her, caught her as she slumped, and put her on the bed, but she struggled against his hands, trembling, pushing him away, unnerved by his touch, and sat up on the edge of the bed looking dazedly at him.

'You didn't mean that.'

'Yes,' he bit out through tight lips.

'He couldn't have!'

'He did.'

'It can't be legal!'

'Perfectly legal, it seems,' he snapped. 'He knew what he was doing, he had made other wills, only this time he didn't inform his solicitor. But he followed the formula that had been used with his previous wills, and the wording was all perfectly correct. He left everything in trust for any children—'

She interrupted shakily. 'Oh! To *your* children, you mean.' Her mind scrambled ahead, guessing what he had come here to say. 'I see why you had to find me. You want to marry again, have children, and so you need a divorce.' She felt a stab of odd feeling as she said the word, maybe of pain because their strange, brief marriage had caused her such misery, and its ending would be as strange as its beginning. She forced a smile which wavered uncertainly. 'I wouldn't have thought you needed to get my agreement, not after all these years. It must be a straightforward procedure, surely?'

'No divorce!' he snarled, and she shrank from the look in his eyes. If anything, he had grown even angrier while he listened to her. 'You didn't let me finish. Just shut up and listen. The children must be ours, yours and mine.'

She gave a gasp. 'What?'

'You heard me. He was quite specific; only our issue counts. If we have divorced, or if we don't have children within two years of my father's death, the estate goes to my eldest cousin, Tony.'

'Simeon,' she whispered, appalled. 'Oh, I'm so sorry! How could he do it to you? It isn't like him to be so unkind.'

'You ran away,' he said fiercely. 'He blamed me for that. He never forgave me. I was his son, his only son, but I never mattered the way you did. You were always his pet, he doted on you from the minute you were born.'

It was true, she couldn't deny it. There had been a very strong affection between her and Robert Gerard. He had been that sort of man—he had loved women and enjoyed their company far more than that of his own sex, although he had been a very masculine man, big and broad and energetic. A real countryman, always out on his land, working at something, and in his leisure time riding, fishing, shooting the rabbits and pigeons which raided his fields.

He had got on well with his farmworkers; he had been a kind-hearted man, generous and impulsive, in spite of a notoriously hot temper. He had never sulked, though, she thought, half smiling at the memory. He had flared up, roared and raged, and then tried to make amends as best he could to his victim, and people who had known him had usually loved him. He had never forgotten, though, that his family had been farming that land since the time of the Normans, or that his house stood on the site of an ancient motte and bailey castle, battered down during the Wars of the Roses. The present house had been built in 1700, after a fire had destroyed the Tudor building, but Robert Gerard had taught Juliet to be aware of the other dwellings which had stood there, and whose remants still littered the grounds and he, himself, had taken enormous pride in his family history.

It had been his wife who had first taken an interest in the small Juliet; indeed it had been Mrs Gerard who had suggested that name for her, although it had been enthusiastically accepted by her mother. Mrs Gerard had longed to have another child, a daughter, but after the birth of her first child, Simeon, she had developed complications and had had to have an emergency operation which had made it impossible for her to have any more babies. Juliet's father had been gamekeeper on the Chantries estate and his wife had worked part-time for Mrs Gerard in the house, taking the baby with her after the birth.

Simeon had been nine when Juliet was born, and had just gone away to boarding school. His mother had been lonely—having another child around the house had made it easier for her to bear her son's absence. She had been a tiny, delicate woman with a very sweet face, and already suffering from the wasting disease which had killed her some ten years later. Simeon had been at university by then, and Robert Gerard had been left quite alone in the beautiful old house set among tall oaks looking down over a slow-winding river. That had been when his deep affection for Juliet really began; he had clung to her, at first, because his wife had loved her, and then for her own sake.

'I loved him, too,' she told Simeon now, her blue eyes wide and defiant. 'He was more a father to me than my own ever was! Your father was a wonderful man, warm and generous and thoughtful. A pity you aren't more like him!'

'Oh, yes! It was very thoughtful and generous of him to leave me out of his will!' he said with vitriolic sarcasm, and she had to see his point.

'Yes, he shouldn't have done that,' she agreed huskily, looking down yet watching him through her lashes with confused uncertainty. She had many reasons for hating Simeon Gerard—she hadn't imagined that she would ever feel any sort of sympathy for him again—but obviously it must have been a terrible shock to him to discover that his father had changed his will. There had never been an instant's doubt that Chantries was to pass to Simeon; why else had he gone from university, where he had taken a science degree, to agricultural college to complete a specialised course in farming and estate management? He had spent years training to run Chantries, and now his father had snatched it away from him. It was grossly unfair. She frowned, watching his hard, unsmiling face. 'But can't you challenge the will? Contest it?'

'On what grounds? That my father was out of his mind when he made it? Do you really think I'm going to do that? I told you, the will is perfectly legal.'

'Isn't there a loophole anywhere?'

'None. If we don't have children, the estate goes to my cousin.' He fixed glittering, steely eyes on her. 'And that would be a disaster because Tony would probably sell it. He isn't a farmer, nor does he want to be…he likes living in London, having a good time, spending money, and as soon as he can liquidate the estate he will settle down to spend every last penny of it.'

She believed him; Tony had always been a spendthrift, wild and undisciplined, brought up by a rather silly mother to be spoilt and selfish. Robert Gerard had known just what sort of man Tony was—why on earth had he left Chantries to him, instead of to Simeon?

'It doesn't make sense,' she said aloud, her eyes puzzled. 'Why did he do it? He always talked as if nothing would make him happier than to know that you would one day run Chantries.'

'My father changed after you left,' Simeon muttered, scowling over her head. 'He grew bitter, and he blamed me for everything that had happened. He was lonely, but he wouldn't have me in the house—I wasn't welcome at Chantries any more.'

Juliet was shaken. 'You left, too? But maybe that's why—'

'I didn't leave. I was thrown out. I lived with the MacIntyres in Rose Cottage for some months, until I realised I would never be allowed back home, then I moved into one of the farm cottages which happened to fall vacant when old Ben Smith died.'

'Oh, did he? I'm sorry,' she instinctively said, her mind's eye at once conjuring up the old man with his brown, weather-beaten face and stooped shoulders walking across the fields, his black and white sheepdog loping at his heels. They were the figures of her childhood, these people: old Ben and Mr Gerard and all the others she had known as a little girl. She had tried to shut the door on them all, for years, but Simeon had pushed the door open again and was forcing her to remember everything.

'He was ninety,' Simeon said in a gentler, half regretful tone. He had known Ben all his life, had gone around the countryside with him, learning country ways. She suddenly recalled one night when they had both gone with Ben to lie in bushes in a copse and wait for a badger family to venture out to hunt. It had been a magical experience; she could almost smell the damp earth, the crushed grass on which they had lain.

Simeon's voice broke through her memories. 'Yes, he had a good innings, and he'd enjoyed his life, which is more than we can all say. Even after he retired, he was always busy; he poached, of course, although I turned a blind eye and pretended never to guess.' He grinned and under her eyes became younger, more carefree, the way he had been once. Simeon had been a reckless, exciting boy, a teasing, protective man, until… Juliet winced and stopped thinking.

'The trouble is,' Simeon said, 'the Bens of this world have no place in modern farming. We have machines to do everything he did.'

'More's the pity,' she muttered, and he sighed.

'Yes. He was quite a character.'

'When you left Chantries, did you have to stop working on the estate too?' she asked, and he shook his head.

'No, I still worked on the estate. In fact, I've been running the place for the last few years, because my father's health began to deteriorate and he more or less gave up the estate management to me.'

She gave him a bewildered look. 'So he did start speaking to you again?'

'No,' Simeon said curtly, bitterness in every line of his face. 'We communicated in writing. I sent him notes and letters, and long memos, and he replied in kind. It was absurd.'

She bit her lip. 'Doesn't it sound as if he was sick? Mentally, I mean. It's not like him—his illness may have made him confused, might have changed his personality. Couldn't you make that the basis for contesting the will?'

'I'm not having my father's name blackened in some courtroom!' Simeon snarled, and she took a nervous step away from him. He had always been a dominant character, even as a boy, but since she last saw him he had become a formidable, alarming man. She wouldn't want to cross him, or find herself opposing him.

'I didn't suggest—' she began to stammer.

'That was what you implied—that I should challenge the will on the grounds that my father didn't know what he was doing. And I won't have it. I'd rather see Tony let loose on Chantries than have my father's reputation blackened like that.' His rage was disturbing, yet she was touched by it because of what it meant: an affection for his father which he had rarely allowed to show but of which she had always been certain.

There was a brief pause, then Simeon went on quietly, 'In a sense, I think he was mentally ill, at the end. He never went out, never saw anybody—he brooded on the past all the time, I gathered from Dr Manners. He kept me in touch with my father's condition, and he was worried about his mental state—oh, he didn't think he was going crazy, but he knew Dad was in severe depression, and he kept trying to talk him into seeing me, but Dad wouldn't listen.' Simeon shot her a sideways look, his brows lowering. 'There were photos of you and my mother everywhere around him, but none of me, of course.'

Was he jealous of her? she wondered suddenly, her blue eyes wide with shock. Had he always been jealous of the affection between her and his parents? He had been sent away to school and she had somehow moved into his place in the family—was that how he saw it?

Simeon grimaced. 'He pretended I no longer existed. He wouldn't let Dr Manners talk about me. Even when he wrote instructions to me about the farm, he was impersonal, as though I was a stranger, just an employee. He never wrote "Dear Simeon". He just headed everything "To The Farm Manager".'

'Oh, Sim,' she said, instinctively putting a hand on his arm. 'I'm so sorry...'

He stiffened, looking down at the slender, pale fingers touching his black jacket, and she went pink and snatched her hand away, asking hurriedly, 'What was wrong with him physically?'

Simeon gave her an odd look, his black lashes flicking down against his brown, weathered skin. 'At first the doctors weren't too sure—one of them even came up with some crazy theory that he was trying to give himself the disease my mother died of. I think they believed it was psychosomatic, but it turned out to be some obscure disease of the liver. I suppose he would have died of it, but actually what killed him was a heart attack. It was very sudden.' He stopped short, brooding for a few seconds, then added, 'And I never said goodbye to him.'

'Maybe he never meant that will to stand, maybe he would have changed it,' she suggested, trying to think of some way of comforting him, and Simeon looked harshly at her.

'It hardly matters what he might have meant. The legal consequences are all that matter, and they are very clear cut, aren't they?'

'I'm very sorry, Simeon,' Juliet whispered unhappily, meeting his angry grey eyes. 'I know how much it will hurt you to lose Chantries.'

'I don't intend to lose it,' he said through his teeth, holding her gaze insistently. 'You are going to give me a child to inherit the estate.'

For a long, dazed moment she didn't understand—she stared at him blankly, trying to grasp what he meant, and then what he had said sunk in, and her mind reeled with appalled realisation. A flame of red swept up her face, and then she went white, trembling violently because the very idea made her sick; it terrified her, the thought of letting him touch her, ever again, impose his body on her, the way he had once before, on their wedding night.

'No!' she whispered, the one word carrying all her re-action—the shock, the dismay, the sick recoil.

Simeon couldn't have failed to hear it in her voice, read it in her stricken face, but he watched her impassively, a hardbitten man who had been toughened and hardened by years of bitter estrangement from his father. This was no longer the man she had known all her life, but then she was not the starry-eyed adolescent he had known. She had become a woman literally overnight, and the years since then had changed her radically, too. They had both been through a sort of hell since they'd last met, and she ached with regret as she looked at him, because she knew that what had gone wrong between Simeon and his father had been her fault, although she had never meant to separate them.

Almost pleadingly she said, 'You weren't serious?' She couldn't believe he had meant it. Nobody could be that ruthless and cold-blooded, could they?

His lips hardened, then parted just enough to bite out the one word, 'Yes.'

'No,' she denied, panic beating up inside her.

'I'm not asking you to do this for nothing,' he said coolly. 'You'll get a generous allowance from the estate once there's a child and everything is settled. I can't see that I'm being unreasonable. The whole situation is your fault—it is up to you to solve it in the obvious way.'

'I can't believe this is happening,' she said wildly, 'I can't listen to any more.' She stumbled towards the door again, but Simeon caught her arm and his touch made her cry out. 'Don't! Don't touch me!'

He didn't let go, he just bent towards her and said softly, 'This time will be different—you're not a virgin teenager any more, after all. You're a woman, and no doubt there have been other men in your life since you ran away.'

She felt herself flushing again, and her lashes dropped to hide the expression in her blue eyes. 'That has nothing to do with it,' she said huskily. 'I couldn't sleep with you in cold blood, I just couldn't.'

There was an odd silence and she glanced through her lashes at him, slightly alarmed to find him smiling crookedly.

'In hot blood, then,' he said, and there was a tormenting gleam in his grey eyes now. He let his eyes wander down over the supple curve of her body, and to her shame she felt heat growing inside her, felt a pulse begin to throb in her throat. She might hate him, but he still did something to her.

'No,' she refused again, her voice high-pitched, feeling as if she might faint any minute. 'Please, leave me alone, can't you? I'm sorry, but what you're asking is impossible, I couldn't do it!'

Simeon considered her face, his brows together, then shrugged. 'Well, it's the middle of the night and we're both tired after that long drive from London, so we'll leave it for now, and talk about it in the morning.'

He let go of her and turned towards the door and Juliet watched him with desperate uncertainty.

'What do you mean—talk in the morning? You can't stay here, you know. I won't let you.'

'Throw me out, then,' he said with casual arrogance, because he knew she wasn't up to doing that. He went out of the room and she heard him walk into the big master bedroom. 'Very comfortable,' he called back to her. 'This will be fine.'

She stood there indecisively for a moment, wondering what to do, and then chose safety first. She locked her bedroom door as noisily as possible, so that he should hear her.

'Goodnight, Juliet,' was all the response she got, in an amused voice, and then the muted sounds of him moving around the room, visiting the bathroom, the soft creak of the bedsprings and then the click as he switched off the light.

Juliet lay in her bed staring at the dark ceiling for half an hour, her mind in utter confusion, before sleep finally overcame her, and then her dreams were chaotic.

CHAPTER THREE

JULIET woke up with a start and didn't remember, for a moment, what had happened last night. She lay looking at the ceiling with a blank expression, noticing the play of icy light across it, hearing the wind outside howling across the moor, and wondering why she felt so tired and flat, almost depressed. Her head ached and she didn't want to get up. Was she getting a cold? Or was it the arrival of snow that had upset her?

Then she heard a faint sound in the cottage and it all came back to her in a blinding flash. She sat up with a gasp, staring at her bedroom door.

He was here. In the cottage, on the other side of that door, moving about, whistling softly. Simeon. Her pale lips framed the name silently. Simeon. Her husband.

She had pushed the memory of her brief marriage to the back of her mind so many years ago that she found the fact of it incredible now, just as she had found it the day she'd stood beside him in a register office, going through the civil ceremony which made them man and wife, looking sideways at him through her lashes in dazed disbelief. She might have tried consciously to suppress those memories, but she found that she had forgotten nothing. Everything about that day must have been burnt into her unconscious mind; she could summon up even the tiniest detail now.

She had been wearing her best dress, but it had hardly been suitable—a simple blue dress meant for a schoolgirl to wear at weekends, nothing special or very pretty. Her father didn't believe in spending good money on anything he felt was unnecessary, and pretty clothes for his only daughter came into the category of 'unnecessary'.

He had been there, to make certain it really happened; a grim, hostile presence in his only suit, a heavy country tweed he had had for years and wore at all formal occasions, even funerals, although for those he added a black armband around one sleeve of his jacket. She had almost expected him to have his shotgun over his arm, but Jack Newcome was too conventional for that. He had left it at home, although the threat of it smouldered in his sullen eyes every time he looked at her and Simeon.

He had found them together, after the harvest festival dance, lying in each other's arms, in the sweet-smelling, long grass under the heavy-laden apple trees in the orchard behind Chantries, and he had had his gun then. He had levelled it at Simeon, murder in his eyes, and Juliet had screamed, believing he meant to shoot.

'No, Father!'

He had looked at her, skating a disgusted look over her, silently commenting on her unbuttoned blouse, the glimpse that gave of her tiny, pale breasts, the way her skirt had ridden to her upper thigh, leaving her long legs bare. His face contemptuous, he had spat out an insult, called her something vile that had made her flinch, turning a shamed scarlet, and that had brought Simeon to his feet, his face dark with rage.

'Don't use language like that to her!'

'What else is she, then?' Jack Newcome had said, his mouth distasteful.

'Nothing happened, man!' Simeon had angrily protested, and her father had given a sneering laugh.

'Don't bother to lie to me. I know what I saw before you heard me coming.'

Simeon's flush had deepened. 'Look, Jack—' he had
begun and the older man had snapped at him.

'Mr Newcome to you after tonight!' Then reproach had
shown in his eyes. 'I never thought you'd do this to me,
Mr Simeon. Not your father's son. As for her, well, I can't
say I'm surprised. She's her mother's daughter, after all. I
knew it would come out in her sooner or later, but I'd
hoped to get her married off first. I won't be shamed in
front of the whole county again, Mr Simeon. I had enough
of scandal and gossip when my wife ran off with her fancy
foreigner—I won't be made a laughing stock a second
time.'

He had still had the gun pointed at Simeon, and his
finger had been on the trigger, crooked as if to squeeze.
Juliet had been so terrified that she had begun to scream
again, and that had brought old Robert Gerard from the
house, hurrying down the rough grass of the orchard path,
his breathing noisy.

'What in heaven's name is all this noise? What's going
on?' he had asked, staring in stunned surprise at the tableau
he found under the trees; the heavy-set gamekeeper, the
trembling, sobbing girl, and finally his own son.

Simeon and Jack Newcome had begun to talk at once,
and Robert Gerard had broken in on them, impatiently. 'I
can't listen to all of you. Jack, you tell me, and for God's
sake lower that gun—is it loaded?' He had read the answer
in the other man's grim face and gone on gruffly, 'What's
the matter with you? You know better than to point a
loaded gun at someone.'

The two older men had known each other all their lives.
Her father had worked on the Chantries estate since leaving school; he was an excellent game-keeper, he knew
every aspect of his work, and he was temperamentally
suited to it. He was up before dawn and out in the woods

and fields, each day—and then after a few hours' sleep at night, he was always out again, on the alert for poachers after pheasants or partridge or even rabbits. The energetic lifestyle had seemed to suit him; he was a tough and physically wiry man, even though he was fifty; could walk miles without tiring.

Even the necessary solitude in the woods had seemed to suit him because he was quite happy alone; indeed was usually silent when he was in company, with one exception. Robert Gerard. The two men had seen each other most days and Jack Newcome was usually quite relaxed and easy with his employer, but not that night.

'I just caught them at it,' he had muttered, without lowering his gun. 'Did you know what was going on? I've had my suspicions lately, you must have had yours—why didn't you tell him to leave her alone?'

'What are you talking about?' Robert had asked incredulously, and Juliet had closed her eyes, tears rolling down her face.

Her father had bitterly given his side and Robert Gerard had turned on his son with angry questions. Simeon had shouted back at him, and then the three men had all snarled and shouted at each other across and around her while she'd just stood there, shaking and terrified.

She had never heard her father speak like that to Robert Gerard. Her father had always respected his employer. She would have said Robert Gerard was as close to being his friend as anyone in the world.

That was why he had been content to allow Juliet to spend so much time up at Chantries, especially after her mother had gone.

Juliet had been eleven years old when her mother had run off with Giorgio after a holiday she had taken in Sicily with her aunt. Aunt Dora had always dreamt of seeing

Sicily but had been afraid of going alone, her head full of tales of bandits and kidnapping, so she had invited Shirley Newcome to go with her. It had only been for a fortnight, the first real holiday Shirley had had since her marriage. Jack Newcome didn't believe in holidays, especially abroad, and he hadn't wanted his wife to go, but for once she had had the courage to insist on her own way, and that holiday had torn their lives apart.

Her mother had met Giorgio and fallen madly in love, and hadn't come back. At the time, Juliet had felt betrayed, abandoned, but now with adult hindsight she could understand why her mother had chosen the man she loved rather than her child. When they talked about it, later, her mother had said frankly, 'After twelve cold, empty years buried in that place with your father, being with Giorgio was like coming alive again. I was so happy, darling. I couldn't bear to go back to Jack. I agonised over leaving you, and I know it must have hurt you, but I badly wanted you to be with us, and I kept hoping I would get you back once the divorce went through. I didn't believe he would be allowed to keep you. After all, he was never home, and he had never shown any interest in you. My lawyer was so confident that I would get custody of you. We didn't reckon on Mrs Gerard taking you over altogether.'

'I think Dad kept me simply to spite you,' Juliet had wryly said.

'I've no doubt about it! He was such a hard man!'

The court had decided to leave Juliet where she was, granting custody to Jack Newcome, but her mother had had the right to see her at least once a week, if she chose.

'Once Giorgio and I were living in London, I suggested that I should come down to Devon every other week, and you should visit us alternate weeks, but your father wouldn't co-operate. He wouldn't let you go out with us when we came to you. He made us sit in that cottage, with him there all the time, staring at us, like some horrible great basilisk, terrifying the life out of poor Giorgio.'

Juliet had giggled. 'Oh, I remember those visits!' They had been difficult and embarrassing for her, too.

Her mother had sighed. 'And as for you paying us any visits, he wouldn't hear of it. He said he couldn't spare the time to take you to London, and he would not let you travel alone. I felt so guilty, but we couldn't afford the time and money for weekly visits then, darling.' She had given Juliet a wistful, pleading look. 'Did you hate me?'

'No, of course not,' Juliet had said, knowing that that was what her mother wanted to hear, and after a while it had been true because her father had made her so afraid of him that she had gone over to her mother's side in their feud. 'I didn't blame you for wanting to get away fom Dad.' Her mother had written often, had always remembered her birthday, and Christmas. To be fair to him, her father had never suppressed those letters and cards, or held back the gifts her mother had sent her. It was true, too, that he had rarely said a word against her mother, but then he had never mentioned her at all, if he could help it.

It was as if he had expunged his ex-wife from his memory, beginning with the day he had had everything she'd left behind her cleared out of the cottage and burnt on a huge bonfire in the garden.

Juliet had watched from her bedroom window, pale and frightened by the destruction. She could still remember the smoke curling up, the grey sky through bare branches, the smell of autumn leaves, her father's grim face as he moved around the bonfire. Even at that age Juliet had felt the obstinate, unyielding nature behind his actions, and been disturbed by it.

The night he had found her in Simeon's arms he had

looked just like that, a cold, grim man who never forgot or forgave, and all their denials and attempts to explain had made no impact on him.

Robert Gerard had been almost as angry, in a very different way. He had put an arm around Juliet, muttering roughly, 'That's enough, Jack. Can't you see, you're terrifying the child? Take her home now. We'll talk about this in the morning, when we've slept on it.'

'I'm not having her in my house again,' Jack Newcome had grated. 'I'm finished with her.'

Juliet had given a small, shuddering cry, and Robert Gerard had tightened his hold on her, putting his chin down against her tumbled hair.

'Jack, for heaven's sake!' he had protested, but her father had already turned to walk away, as if having said his final word.

Then Simeon had suddenly said, 'I'm going to marry her!' and both older men had stared at him in waiting silence.

Simeon had stared back at them, his face pale and grimly set. 'But she has to be married from her own home, not from ours, or there would be gossip, and that's what you want to avoid, isn't it?'

Her father had considered him for a long moment, then had given Robert Gerard a questioning look.

As pale as his son was, Robert had stared at the clear, autumn night sky, his brows together as he thought it over, then he had looked back at Jack Newcome and given him a sharp nod.

And so it was settled, and Juliet had gone home that night, with her father, in unforgiving silence, to wait for her wedding day, after which she was to move in to Chantries. Simeon and his father had decided that a honeymoon was essential, to give a more normal appearance to that hurried, hole-and-corner wedding, so the bride and groom had driven straight from the register office to a hotel in Taunton, to spend a few days, but the very next morning Juliet had got up early, without waking Simeon, and stolen out of the hotel and out of his life, leaving a brief note.

It is all a mistake, I couldn't bear to go through last night ever again and I don't want to be married. Please divorce me, or have the marriage annulled or whatever you like, but don't come after me because I couldn't bear to see you again, not ever. I'll be OK—I'm going to my mother.

She had had just enough money for a coach to London, and had sat in a tense silence all the way, feeling like a fugitive, and afraid all the time of being caught and taken back. It had been an enormous relief to reach her destination. Shirley and Giorgio had welcomed her with open arms, if a good deal of surprise. They had not heard about the marriage, and she hadn't been able to bring herself to tell them anything of what had happened.

'Have you left school?' her mother had asked, and she had nodded.

'And I want a job,' she had said.

'You've got one!' Giorgio had cheerfully agreed. 'A job and a home—with us, Julietta.'

Tears had come into her eyes. 'Are you sure I won't be any trouble?'

'Trouble?' Giorgio's dark eyes had been liquid with emotion; he was a very affectionate, soft-hearted man. 'Oh, my dear girl, no. We have always wanted you—this is your home. It makes us both very happy to have you with us.'

'We've got plenty of room,' her mother had said with

her more practical approach, but she had been beaming. 'Come and see, darling.'

She had taken Juliet to see her new bedroom, a pastel-painted room which was light years away from the austerity of her bedroom in the cottage where she had grown up. Alone, Shirley had asked her shrewdly, 'What's wrong, darling? We're delighted to have you, but what exactly pushed you into coming? A row with your father?'

She had longed to confide in her mother, but she had been afraid that her mother would be aghast and furious at what she heard. What if her mother thought she was to blame? She remembered the disgust in her father's face when he had confronted her and Simeon—she couldn't have born it if her mother looked at her like that.

So she had lied, and nodded. 'Y-yes, he…I…'

Her stammering had aroused her mother's protective instincts and Shirley had put her arms round her, hugging her.

'You poor kid! What did he do? He didn't hit you?'

'Oh, no!' Juliet had said. 'He's never hit me…' She had whitened, remembering her father's face. 'He just talks to me… looks at me as if I was…' She had broken off, biting her lip.

Her mother had made a face. 'I know just what you mean. Your father is old-fashioned. I suppose he didn't want you to grow up? I wondered how he would cope with a teenage daughter! Well, don't you worry, I'll look after you, he isn't bullying you with me around!'

'What if he comes after me?' Juliet had whispered.

'If he does, he'll have me to deal with! He's had you long enough—now it's my turn to look after you. I'd never have left you with him if I hadn't thought he loved you.

I'd have fought to the death to keep you. Don't you worry, it will all be sorted out, and you needn't see him if you don't want to.'

'I never want to see any of them again,' Juliet had said.

She had begun to work in the shop which Shirley ran, while Giorgio was busy with a second store he had opened in Knightsbridge, not far from Harrods. For a few months Juliet had been haunted by everything that had happened, had kept expecting Simeon, or her father, or Robert Gerard, to turn up, but they had never come, and she had gradually pushed it all to the back of her mind. Her new life had occupied her every waking thought. She was young and living in London, one of the most magical cities in the world. She had refused to be unhappy.

Eight years had gone by without anything disturbing her busy days, but now, out of the blue, Simeon had turned up again.

She was dazed by the news he had brought. Robert Gerard's death was a grief to her, but even more of a shock was the news about his will. It had been unjust of him to leave Chantries away from Simeon, but even so Sim surely couldn't really have expected her to take his proposition seriously? Could he?

A sharp rap on the bedroom door made her jump, her nerves shredded.

'Up you get, Julie. The coffee's made and I'm just going to cook some breakfast,' his deep voice said, and she managed a husky reply.

'I'll be five minutes.'

He laughed shortly. 'I'll believe that when I see you.'

Challenged, she raced through her washing and dressing, and made it downstairs in about seven minutes, just in time to see Simeon put a dish of grilled bacon and mushrooms on the table.

He sat down then, raising a black brow at her. 'Amazing! You made it!'

She ignored that, accepting the cup of black coffee he had poured her. 'Where did you get the bacon and mushrooms?'

'I stocked up at a garage shop en route last night, in case you didn't have much fresh food,' he said, offering her the dish of food.

'Thank you, they smell delicious,' she said, feeling very hungry.

They ate in silence for several minutes, then, as they both took toast and spread it with marmalade, Simeon said, 'The snow is knee-deep this morning—did you notice?'

She hadn't and threw a startled glance at the window. All she could see of the garden was a white desert, crisp and untrodden except for a few tiny bird footprints scattered here and there. The snow was banked up to the top of the garden wall. That meant the roads must be blocked.

Nervously lowering her lashes, she watched Simeon. He was no longer looking quite as sinister as he had last night in his black leather jacket and black thigh boots. He had clearly shaved, and showered; his black hair was smoothly brushed and he was wearing jeans with a ribbed white sweater over a thin, powder-blue cotton shirt. He looked relaxed and casual, but Juliet didn't trust him any more than she would trust a basking shark. He looked across the table at her with an expression in his grey eyes that made her tense.

'We won't be able to leave, so we have plenty of time,' he said, and she unguardedly repeated the last word, her face bewildered.

'Time?'

'Time to…talk,' he murmured, lazily assessing her from head to toe in a deliberately tormenting fashion. 'And other things.'

Her colour rose again. The talking wasn't that alarming; it was the 'other things' that bothered her, but she didn't say so. She was going to have to watch what she said to him; he was in a mischievous and dangerous mood. He might be smiling and relaxed on the surface, but she knew that underneath that sunny façade the same anger and hostility simmered, and at any moment he might unleash them.

'Some more coffee?' he offered.

She absently took some, murmuring a stiff, 'Thank you.' She couldn't stay here with him—but how was she to get away?

'How is your mother?' he asked politely.

'Very well,' she told him, staring at the window with dismay. A flurry of snowflakes was whirling past. Simeon caught her look of consternation and followed her gaze. He smiled.

'Oh, dear, snowing again. We may be stranded here for days.'

'The snow ploughs will come out to clear the roads soon,' she thought aloud.

'The main roads,' he corrected. 'They won't clear this road yet—I'd imagine very few people use it in winter.'

She gave him a sharp look, frowning. 'How did you know about this place, anyway? How did you find it?'

He shrugged. 'I made a lot of phone calls late yesterday afternoon, after I got to London and discovered that you had left work and that you weren't at your flat. I rang your mother—no reply there, either—I rang all your shops and finally got on to someone who said you were in Cornwall.'

A suspicion crossed Juliet's mind. 'Was that the manageress of the Bond Street store, by any chance?' He nodded and she thought aloud, 'Wait until I see Sandy again! She knows that it's a company rule never to give out any personal details about a member of staff to a stranger!'

His eyes glinted with amusement. 'Maybe she forgot.'

Juliet viewed him witout any answering spark of humour. 'You didn't tell her…anything…did you?'

'That we were married, for instance?' he mocked, watching the colour rise in her face.

The very idea of Sandy knowing her long-buried secret made her want to scream, and he knew it. He held her in suspense a moment longer, grinning in a way that made her want to hit him, then shook his head.

'No, I didn't need to. I just said I urgently needed to talk to you about a death in the family, and for some reason she seemed to think I was in Italy, so she told me you were in Cornwall. She muttered something about your mother, so I wasn't sure if you were there with her or not, and she didn't know the address or phone number, but getting both didn't take me long.'

'I bet!' she said bitterly, and he looked even more amused, as if she had flattered him, which certainly had not been her intention.

'Well, Mendelli is hardly a common name in England. I just went into a reference library and looked up the telephone directories for Cornwall, then rang this number to check you were actually here. You answered, so I got in my car and set off. I had a detailed map, so finding the nearest village wasn't difficult, either, and I stopped at the garage there, for petrol and food, and they told me how to find the cottage. Of course, they thought I was mad, driving in such terrible weather.'

'You were!' she retorted, and he eyed her quizzically.

'What about you? Why on earth are you here, at this time of year?'

She explained about the building work which had been done, and why her mother had wanted to know the cottage had been left in good condition, and he gave her a cynical look.

'So while she's on holiday in sunny Italy you had to drive all the way down here, in a blizzard?'

'She isn't on holiday!'

'Why is she in Italy, then?'

She hesitated. 'Business.' She wasn't going to tell him about Giorgio's problems; he would only leap to the conclusion that the poor man had brought them on himself.

His black brows flickered upwards in wry comment. 'It's quite incredible to think of her turning into a successful businesswoman. I remember her as a quiet little woman always in the background. It amazed me when she ran off with that Italian. My father always thought she would come back—he said it was just a middle-aged fling.'

Juliet's blue eyes glittered with anger. 'Giorgio was the best thing that ever happened to my mother, and I don't blame her for grabbing him after years of living "in the background", as you put it. Why do you think she was so quiet? Living with my father was slowly killing her. She always says it was like living on a desert island alone with someone who didn't seem to notice that she was there. Her natural personality was bubbly and lively, but my father was so withdrawn that he managed to smother her.'

He leaned back in his chair, a hand roughly thrust through his hair, grimacing. 'Yes, your father's a hard man to live with, I can believe that.' He stared challengingly over the table. 'Don't you want to hear how he is?'

She met his grey eyes, her chin up. 'Did he send me any message?'

He shook his head, still watching her.

There was bleakness in her face. 'Well, I don't want to hear about him, either. The day I left Chantries I made up my mind to forget he existed.'

Simeon's sharp eyes probed her features like a lancet, looking for some weak point, then he shrugged. 'He's pretty fit, actually. The life he leads, I suppose. He hates my guts, of course, and doesn't bother to hide it. Oh, he takes any order I give him, without a word, and if we pass each other he gives me a nod, but somehow he makes it clear that he blames me for everything.'

'That makes two of us, then,' she muttered, looking down.

'What?'

His voice made her jump, but she stubbornly repeated what she had said, in a louder voice.

'You blame me?' he snarled, then laughed in a harsh, unamused way. 'How like a woman. It couldn't be your fault, could it? You didn't throw yourself at me, day after day? You didn't make it very plain what you wanted—'

'I didn't know what I was doing—I was too young,' she defended. She had been crazy about him, the wild, uncontrollable infatuation of first love, her mind and heart possessed by a desire she had never felt before, and hadn't known how to handle. If he had repulsed her she would never have let it show so openly, though. She had been much too shy and unsure of herself. Simeon could have averted what happened. He could have discouraged her, gently. But he hadn't. On the contrary, he had let her believe that he felt the same intense attraction.

'That night,' she accused, 'you could have sent me away, but you didn't. You should never have kissed me that night.'

'I kissed you?' he repeated fiercely, and her colour burnt higher.

'Well, maybe I started to kiss you first, but you didn't have to kiss me back. You weren't a teenager, you were an adult man.'

'And I was the one who had to pay,' he ground out. 'They made me marry you, remember. It was a high price to pay for a few kisses.'

She laughed bitterly. 'Oh, I remember. And to get your own back, you made *me* pay on our wedding night, didn't you?'

Dark colour swept up his face, his hands clenched into fists. For a second she tensed, afraid that Simeon might lose control. After all, he had lost control on their wedding night.

'I was angrier than I had ever been in my life before,' he muttered, his face moody.

'You didn't have to be so brutal!' she accused, and his eyes flashed.

'Juliet, heaven help me, if you don't stop saying things like that I'll—'

'What? Hit me?' she interrupted and he breathed audibly, staring at her.

'I've never gone in for hitting women, although for you I might make an exception! If I was less than gentle with you that night it was because I was furious at being forced into marrying you!'

She bit down on her lip, flinching, and he caught that reaction and frowningly sighed.

'I'm sorry, Juliet, but surely now you can see why I felt that way? You're not a schoolgirl any more. If your father hadn't made me feel so guilty, practically accusing me of rape, calling you vile names…my God, what else could I do but say I'd marry you? And then I felt I'd been a fool,

I felt trapped. I kept trying to think of a way out, but there was none. My father and your father had made up their minds by then—even it I could have convinced my own father that you were still a virgin, that I'd never had you, your father was going to insist on the marriage. Well, that was what I believed, and I still think his pride would have made it too hard for him to back down. I had to go through with it.'

'Don't talk about it any more!' she broke out, shivering. Simeon was right; she could understand how he had felt—maybe she had even felt the same way? Her father had destroyed something that night. The distaste in his face had made her ashamed, her love for Simeon had turned sour and shrivelled as she faced her father's accusing eyes. She had tried to convince herself that she was happy to be marrying him, that it was her dream come true, but even before he was so cruel to her on their wedding night she had been dreading the future.

'We have to talk about it sooner or later!' Simeon snapped. 'What happened that night made my father change his will, and wrecked my life!'

'What do you think it did to mine?' she retorted.

He fell silent, then abruptly got up from the table, and began to clear the breakfast things.

Relieved, she began to help him carry them into the kitchen and stack the dishwasher. When everything was tidy, Simeon wandered around the sitting-room looking at the photos and ornaments, his face thoughtful. She watched him uneasily, curled up like a small, nervous cat in a deep armchair, her legs under her, wondering what he was thinking and what on earth to say to get through to him that he had to leave. A glance at the window told her that the snow was still blowing in the wind she could hear howling around the house. There was no chance of being able to get away for hours yet, but she was nervous of being here alone with him.

'You seem to have had a pretty successful life since I last saw you, in fact,' he drily commented at last, throwing himself down on the couch beside her chair, and staring at her with his hands linked behind his head. 'Running away to join your mother gave you a new start. I should have gone away, too, but I felt I couldn't just walk out on my father. I had to stay and face the music. It wasn't easy, believe, me.' His mouth twisted. 'Especially with your father treating me like a pariah. He was at my father's funeral, and he didn't speak to me, even then, just walked away afterwards.'

'I don't know how my mother stood it for as long as she did,' Juliet said absently, noticing how the cold sunlight gleamed on his thick black hair. There were one or two silvery hairs among them now, she suddenly saw for the first time. Time was catching up with him. He would be forty in a few years. It seemed incredible.

'She must have loved him once,' said Simeon.

'Only because he was so unlike anyone she had ever met,' Juliet said. 'She told me once—she married him because he was so hard to fathom, silent and mysterious, a mystery man. She thought she would be the one to get past his wall of silence, she would understand him—but she didn't. What she didn't realise was that he didn't need her, need anyone. I wonder what would have happened to her if she hadn't met Giorgio. He's a lovely man, he makes her so happy. She's quite different. You wouldn't know her. They've built up a very successful business together. They are real partners, they make all the decisions together, see each other all day, work happily together. It's all the complete opposite of her years with my father.'

'I read an article about them once,' he surprised her by

saying. 'They were opening a new store in Manchester, and there was a photo of them. I recognised your mother, even though she had changed so much. She looked terrific. I can see what you mean; she looked as if she was happy. I had had no idea how successful they were, until then. You were mentioned—"their daughter, Juliet, who works for the company in London". An elegant brunette, they called you.' His eyes flickered over her in gleaming assessment. 'Elegant? Hmm…not quite, not this morning.'

Because of the freezing weather, she had put on the warmest clothes she had with her; they had been left behind that autumn, after her last visit, when she had helped to paint the old barn behind the cottage. She hadn't bothered to pack these things up afterwards, just washed them and put them into a drawer, where she had found them that morning, smelling slightly of a lavender-perfumed sachet she had packed in with them: old, well-washed jeans, a yellow-striped man's shirt, from Italy, which she had borrowed years ago from Giorgio, during a phase when she had loved to wear men's shirts, waistcoats and jackets, and a comfortably thick yellow lambswool riding sweater. She had had another motive for picking this outfit. These were the least attractive clothes she had with her. She was wearing them as an armour against Simeon.

'You look down-to-earth, practical and ready for whatever comes,' he said, and she didn't think he was flattering her. Perhaps he had even guessed she had worn these clothes to put him off. He paused, watching her, then asked softly, 'Are you?' and she stared, confused.

'Am I what?'

'Ready for whatever comes,' he said and watched with a smile as a flush crept up her face. 'You know, I hardly recognise you,' he suddenly said. 'If I'd walked past you in the street I probably wouldn't have known you.'

'You never did,' she said, head lowered, mouth stubborn. 'Any more than you knew my mother.'

'Well, here we are, quite alone—this time we will get to know each other.' He got up and she went into a panic and scrambled up, too, knocking over her chair.

'Don't touch me!' She had been pushing his threat to the back of her mind, trying to convince herself that he hadn't meant what he said, but fear suddenly swamped her mind and she began to tremble violently. 'I couldn't bear it if you touched me,' she whispered, staring at him.

'You'll have to bear it,' Simeon said in a low, harsh voice, and his eyes held a disturbing insistence which warned her that he meant precisely what he said.

CHAPTER FOUR

'I'M GOING for a walk,' Juliet said desperately, heading for the door, and hoping he wouldn't stop her.

He didn't. He came after her in long, unhurried strides. 'Good idea. It seems to have stopped snowing and the sky is as blue as your eyes.'

She blinked, taken aback by the simile, but didn't risk looking at him, just grabbed her sheepskin coat from the cupboard in the little hallway, buttoned herself into it, found some shabby old boots, and put on Fair Isle woolen gloves and a matching woollen hood which she had bought on a trip to Scotland with her mother and Giorgio several years ago, and which she kept here in Cornwall because they were the perfect things to wear on long walks across the moor on cold days.

She gave Simeon a glance, noting that he had put on his leather jacket, those high black leather boots which looked like the sort of boots motorcyclists wore, and leather gloves. Offhandedly, she said, 'There are some warm scarves in here, if you'd like to borrow one.' She pulled out a long red wollen one which belonged to Giorgio.

'Thanks,' Simeon said, bending his head. 'Put it on for me, would you, please?'

She hesitated, then quickly threw it round his neck, trying not to touch him, but in her haste her fingers brushed his cheek and she only just managed not to give a cry of shock at the electric buzz that brief contact gave her. He looked down at her with a crooked little smile.

'Thank you.'

She quickly turned away and pulled open the door and they both looked out, their eyes narrowed against the brilliance of sunlight reflected on mirror-like snow. The wind had dropped; it was nowhere near so cold. The landscape looked marvellous; great, rolling acres of untrodden snow, white and dazzling under that blue sky. It was so beautiful it caught the breath, but it was so empty. Not another house or human being in sight. Juliet stared at that emptiness, biting her lip.

'Changed your mind? It is cold!' said Simeon drily, and she gave him a resentful look, banging the door shut behind her.

'Certainly not.' She began to walk briskly and he fell in beside her, easily keeping step because his legs were so much longer than hers. She saw his black shadow moving on the glassy snow beside her own, fantastical, elongated, rather disturbing in all that empty landscape, as though he haunted her. Or hunted her, she thought, with an inward shudder.

'Did you really want to cross the moor? Remember, heather isn't easy stuff to walk through,' she said, being deliberately patronising.

He gave her a glinting smile, aware of the challenge. 'Oh, I expect I can cope.'

'OK, don't say I didn't warn you,' she said sweetly, and they turned off the road on to the open moorland, their pace slowing once they were struggling through snow-covered heather, then they came out on to a grassy slope which the snow had turned into a frozen slide. Juliet felt her feet go from under her, and careered downwards with a cry, her arms flailing in an attempt to retrieve her balance. She landed with a thump on her behind, and heard Simeon laughing above her.

So he thought that was funny, did he? She felt stupid, especially after warning him against the moor, and that made her aggressive. Very flushed, her bones aching from the jar of the fall, she scooped up two handfuls of snow, firmed them into a ball and turned to hurl it in his direction.

She got a direct hit, right on his head, the black hair suddenly dusted with powdery snow, and sat, open-mouthed with surprise, because she had never been a particularly good shot. She should have got up and run on, because sitting there she was a perfect target, and Simeon moved faster than a rattlesnake.

He bent, straightened, and a second later a snowball hit her and snow showered around her. She grabbed another handful herself, and leapt to her feet, firing off her ammunition before she took to her heels. She heard Simeon set off in pursuit, and ran faster, her breathing rough and ragged in her throat. It was only a game—but that wasn't how it felt to her.

He caught her a moment later, both arms going round her, and she struggled wildly, panic in her face. 'Let go!' she cried, her body arching away from him as far as it could while he held it in the powerful circle of his arms.

'Stop fighting it,' he murmured, looking down at her, his grey eyes very bright and watchful, and despite her fear she noticed that he had not said 'Stop fighting me', and that that was deliberate. 'Stop fighting *it*,' he had said, because he was hinting that she felt some drag of attraction, that she wanted him to kiss her even though she resisted.

'I don't want it,' she lied, staring at his mouth with a confused feeling. She didn't know what to call it, only that it couldn't be desire, yet her mouth had gone dry and she felt strangely dizzy. 'No,' she tried to say, but her lips moved without making any sound, while he watched them intently, as if lip-reading.

'Yes,' he whispered, and then his gloved hands came up to frame her face between their palms.

She couldn't escape his mouth—he held her head just where he wanted it. His lips were icy with snow when they touched hers at first, and she gave a little indrawn gasp. As her lips parted in that involuntary sound Simeon's kiss deepened, grew fierce, invading her mouth, forcing back her head so that she had to grab him to keep her balance, her hands gripping his wide shoulders. She shut her eyes because the blue sky seemed to be spinning above her and her head was swimming too. His mouth moved in hot demand and she helplessly met it, hanging on to him, her body trembling, no longer even making a pretence of fighting. She had had a number of boyfriends over the past eight years, but none of them had ever made her go weak at the knees with one kiss.

It was Simeon who broke off the kiss, just as it had been Simeon who began it. He lifted his head and she felt him looking down at her while she clung to his shoulders, shaking, her eyes closed and her lips burning from the demands he had made on them.

'Next time you're tempted to chuck things at me, remember what the consequences are likely to be, and think again,' he said softly, with mockery, and her eyes flew open, her face very flushed as she met his amused gaze.

'Thanks for the tip! I won't forget,' she said furiously. 'I certainly wouldn't want that to happen again!'

His eyes taunted her. 'Sure about that? I got the impression you were enjoying it.'

'Certain!' she snapped, even angrier because he was quite right and the last thing she wanted was for him to realise he could get her that way. Physically, he attracted her, she couldn't deny it even to herself, but that meant nothing. Her body could make dangerous mistakes, her body craved pleasure, was easily tempted—her mind was a much more reliable guide.

She pulled away from him, avoiding his shrewd, narrowed eyes, and began to walk fast, back towards the cottage, aware after a pause that Simeon was following her, his booted feet crunching on the snow. Ahead of her stretched the double line of footprints, hers and Simeon's, showing the way they had come. A strange sensation hit her, a superstitious quiver along her spine while she stared as if at an omen, and tried to avoid crossing that track.

'Why don't you walk in our footsteps, like King Wenceslas?' Simeon asked behind her, but she pretended not to hear, and went on walking a little to one side of the line.

Simeon halted a moment later. She didn't look back, just plodded on, until he called out to her, 'Look, just coming over those pines…a hawk…what is it, can you see? Sparrowhawk?'

Juliet paused, shading her eyes with one hand while she stared at the blue sky. A dark shape was skating on the wind, pinions spread, but so far away that she couldn't identify it positively.

'I thought I caught a flash of white on the rump,' Simeon said.

'That would be a sparrowhawk,' she agreed, watching to see if she could see the tell-tale blur of white, but at that moment the hawk swooped in descent and they lost it until it soared upward again, carrying something between its talons. Juliet gave a short sigh. 'He's killed.'

Simeon caught up with her, giving her averted profile a hard stare. 'He has to kill to live,' he reminded.

'I know,' she snapped, glaring. 'You were always telling me that when I was small. I hated it then, I hate it now.'

His face was unyielding, a hard mask. 'Hate it or not, it's the way the world works, and there's nothing you can do about that, Juliet.'

'I don't have to like it,' she said confusedly, her mind filled with the image of something small and soft, helplessly struggling against the cruel talons carrying it away.

Simeon caught hold of her chin and lifted her face, his cold grey eyes hunting over it remorselessly while she tried to hide what she was thinking. 'Nature is "red in tooth and claw",' he said coolly. 'You can't change that, and fighting it would only lead to disaster.'

She looked angrily into his eyes, her face obstinate. They weren't only talking about the hawk and its prey, and they both knew it. 'It's cruel,' she said and he shrugged.

'Hawks are rare and beautiful birds, but nature did not intend them to be vegetarians. You can't change the law of their nature, Juliet. They have to be ruthless or die.'

He had to be ruthless or lose Chantries, he was telling her, and his hard mouth and merciless eyes warned her against trying to escape the fate he had planned for her.

'No!' she cried out in protest, pulling her head free and turning to run. Simeon let her go, and didn't even try to catch up with her. Breathlessly stumbling over the deep snow, her legs shaky under her, she heard his unhurried footsteps on her heels, always coming after her, not to be shaken off, as certain as death, making her heart knock like a premonition against her ribs.

Reaching the cottage at last, she unlocked the front door and stamped the snow off her boots outside before she entered. She left her boots on the doormat in the hall, pulled off her coat and hood, and her warm Fair Isle gloves, before hurrying into the kitchen to put on the coffee percolator.

She heard the sound of Simeon scraping snow off his own boots, and then the slam of the front door as he came inside. That bang seemed to echo in her head, shutting them in together, shutting out the world.

Once the coffee was on the stove, she ran upstairs to the bathroom, calling out, 'The coffee is on!'

'Can I help?' Simeon asked from the hall.

'You could put out the cups,' she replied casually, without looking back down at him.

Washing her hands a few moments later, she stared at her reflection in the mirror above the basin. Her skin was glowing a warm pink from the cold air and exercise, and her eyes were bright, as if with fever. She eyed herself with alarm and anxiety.

He had only been here a few hours, and already he had done something drastic to her. She hadn't looked like that before.

Like what? she asked herself angrily, drying her hands roughly with a peach-coloured hand towel. Like what, for heaven's sake? What *did* she look like? What was she afraid of? Simeon wouldn't...well, he wouldn't... It was hard even to put her worst fears into words. She hesitated even to think it, but she had to. Simeon wouldn't use force.

She met her own eyes in the mirror again, and glared at herself. No, that was unthinkable. Simeon wouldn't. Whatever else he might be capable of, that was not possible. She was certain that he wasn't the type to rape a woman.

But that didn't make her feel any better, any less nervous, because that was not what she was afraid of, was it? What was really bothering her was that Simeon might not even need to use force. Force wasn't going to come into his strategy. She had been given a glimpse of how he meant to get his own way, and she was scared stiff now. He meant to seduce her. And he might well do it.

Look at you! she said to her reflection, her blue eyes accusing. Well, just look at you! One kiss and he sends you into a daze, your knees give way and you look feverish.

What is going to happen when he turns on the heat? As he will, make no mistake about it. He has come here determined to get you into bed, and you can't get away, so what are you going to do? How are you going to keep him at arm's length?

She had so many questions—but not a single answer.

Turning away with a helpless sigh, she reluctantly made her way downstairs. If only the cottage were not so remote. Now that the snow had stopped, the snow ploughs would be out, clearing the main roads, but having been out for that walk she knew just how deep the snow was, and there was no chance of her car making it to the main road. She was a prisoner here, with Simeon, for the moment. She had to think of some way of dealing with him, but she hadn't a clue how.

Just as she reached the hall, the phone began to ring, making her jump.

'Shall I get it?' called Simeon from the kitchen, and alarm shot through her.

'No, that's OK, I will,' she hurriedly shouted back, running to snatch up the phone in the sitting-room. It was probably her mother with the latest news of Giorgio, and she certainly didn't want her mother to hear Simeon's voice and start putting two and two together and making a hundred and three.

Simeon appeared in the doorway and watched her, his

grey eyes narrow and alert. She turned her back to hide her expression.

'Hello?' she said, expecting her mother's voice.

'So you did go,' said a curt male voice, and for a moment she couldn't even place it, so much had happened since she left London. 'I didn't really believe you meant it,' the angry voice added, and that was when his identity dawned and she took a deep breath.

'Oh...Adam...'

She felt Simeon move closer, his whole attention on her.

'Will you be back by tonight?' Adam asked in a way which threatened and yet had a pleading note.

'I'm sorry,' she said, wishing Simeon would go away, would stop eavesdropping and watching her. It was hard enough to talk to Adam without having an audience.

'Julie!' Adam broke out. 'You know how important this is to me! Don't be stubborn—you can get back if you leave now.'

'Isn't it snowing in London? It snowed all night here—the roads are totally blocked, I couldn't possibly get back, even if I set out right now.'

Adam said something violent, so loudly that she sensed Simeon picking the words up. She shot him a look over her shoulder and found him far too close, and listening intently. She gave him a furious stare, frowning, and waved him away with a peremptory hand. He had no right to listen in to her private calls.

He didn't move, just lounged negligently against the wall nearby, his expression bland.

Turning away, she said softly into the phone, 'I'm really sorry, Adam, I'd get back if I could.' And because Simeon was listening, she went on, 'I wish I hadn't come, I wish I was back in London with you, safe and sound.' She meant it, too, her voice husky with sincerity, although for very different reasons than those she was implying, not that it mattered, because Adam was too angry to pick up any nuances in her tone.

'It's a bit late for regrets now, though, isn't it?' he snapped. 'What am I supposed to do? I can't go to this affair alone—I have to take a partner.'

'Yes, I know, I'm sorry, Adam.' She felt Simeon's eyes boring a hole into the back of her head and fumed. Why didn't he have the decency to go away?

'Sorry? You walk out on me at a time when I really need you, for no important reason, either, and then say you're sorry?' Adam was shouting now, almost deafening her, and she held the phone a little away from ear.

A second later it was snatched from her hand, and she gave a gasp of shock as she looked up at Simeon's taut face.

'That's enough,' he snarled into the phone while Juliet desperately tried to take it back from him, only to be held off by one hand. 'I won't have any man shouting at my wife down a phone. So clear off.'

She heard the confused sound of Adam reacting to the terse male voice, then Simeon slammed the phone down and cut him off.

'You...' Juliet stammered, so angry she couldn't speak. 'You...'

Simeon stared down at her, his long, lean body very still, but his face grim. 'All right, who is he?' he asked, his lips barely parting to let the sound out.

'You had no right to do that!' seethed Juliet, trembling with resentment.

'Did he have a right to yell at you down a phone?' Simeon snapped, his eyes bleak.

'If I'd wanted to hang up on him, I would have done!' she threw back, glaring up at him.

Simeon bit out, 'So why didn't you? Is he your lover?'

Her colour rose even higher, but she held his contemptuous stare, throwing back that contempt at him. 'If he is, that's my business, not yours!'

Violence glittered in the grey eyes, and he grabbed her by the shoulders, shaking her. 'Is he? Tell me, damn you!'

'I'm not telling you anything!'

'You will!' There was threat in his voice, but she defied him, her chin lifted and her blue eyes obstinate.

'Nothing would make me!'

'No?' he said tersely, and a shudder of panic ran through her at something in his hard face.

He began to pull her towards him, his strength more than a match for her, but then the phone began to ring again and he swore under his breath, one hand immediately moving to snatch the phone up.

'Yes?' he grated.

'Give me that phone,' Juliet said, struggling to take it, but Simeon shifted, his head averted so that she couldn't quite reach.

She heard Adam loudly demand, 'Who is that?'

'I'm her husband. Don't ring again, because I shall just hang up on you,' Simeon said and slammed the phone down again, cutting off Adam's angry spluttering.

Juliet wanted to hit Simeon—she was so angry she was shaking with it, muttering hoarsely. 'How dare you? Who do you think you are? You're...' Words jammed up in her brain, she couldn't form sentences properly, she was so furious. She just spat out words incoherently, glaring up at him with enraged blue eyes. 'High-handed, arrogant...the most...interfering, insolent, laying down the law... You force your way back into my life and start trying to dictate to me! I'm not putting up with it.'

'Shut up!' Simeon suddenly bit out, and pulled her violently towards him, her writhing body helpless against his powerful grip.

When he had kissed her earlier, out on the snowy moorland, his mouth had been quite gentle at first before heat came into the kiss, but this time his mouth was cruel, angry, not caring if it hurt, and she fought against him, trying to pull her head away.

In her struggle, she lost her balance and began to fall, letting herself go in the hope of escaping, but he came with her, holding on to her, although he had stopped kissing her, and they landed on the couch, then rolled, still struggling, on to the floor.

Juliet found herself lying on top of him, her eyes inches away from his. She looked away, and tried to get up but Simeon rolled her deftly over until she was underneath, and he was on top, his powerful body anchoring her down. His weight seemed to crush all the breath out of her body. She lay very still, her skin suddenly pale, pulled tight over her cheekbones, her blue eyes as open as they could stretch, staring up at him in fear.

He stared down at her, lying equally still, hardly seeming to breathe, either. In the charged silence she heard the deep hammer-beat of his heart and hardly knowing what she was doing she put a shaky hand on his deep chest to feel the vibration under her palm while he watched her.

His mouth twisted. 'You can't help it, can you?'

'Can't help what?' She was moved by the sensation of having that heartbeat throbbing into her own body through her palm. Simeon was so alive, so vital. She couldn't imagine that heart ever stopping; a man with a heartbeat like that would live for ever, she thought, half smiling.

'Flirting, being provocative,' he accused, and she snatched her hand away.

'I wasn't!'

'What were you doing, then?' He picked up her hand and put it back on his chest, held it there, staring into her eyes. 'What else was that, but pure provocation? You touched me of your own accord, don't pretend you didn't, and that's how it happened in the first place, and you know it. That summer, it wasn't me who did the chasing—it was you.'

Her eyes fell, she bit her lip. It was true, she couldn't deny it, and she had felt guilty about the consequences ever since. Simeon certainly hadn't chased her; at first he had been amused, quite indulgent, still thinking of her as a child. He had let her tag along with him when he went for walks or played tennis or swam, but there had been no shadow of sexual interest in his behaviour. He had acted like a friendly big brother, which was not what she had wanted at all, and her pride had been galled.

She had been seventeen—a woman, in her own eyes, and the sea tides of adult sexuality had been flowing back and forth in her veins, making her confused and unsure of herself. She acted and reacted without knowing quite what she was doing; it was all instinctive, involuntary.

Oh, yes, she had flirted with him, become provocative and inviting, but she had been playing at it, as a kitten with a ball of wool played at making its first kill. Her real mistake, her folly, had been in picking someone outside her own age-group to experiment with—if she had chosen a boy of seventeen it would have been an exciting summer romance which could have ended gently, but on which one could have looked back with pleasure all one's life. It wouldn't have wrecked two lives.

But she hadn't been interested in boys. Maybe she had always liked Simeon a lot—who could say? She only knew how she had felt that summer; the wild, burning excitement, the drag of need in her body.

So she had made him look at her in a very different way. She had made him see her as a woman. Passion had given her cunning, taught her a woman's skills. She had left the top buttons of her shirts undone, giving glimpses of her small, high breasts; she had bought some new clothes which had changed her whole appearance, made her suddenly very grown-up. Very short shorts, a silky, clinging dress to dance in, a very revealing bikini, in which she had lain about in the sun, her slender little body becoming golden brown and, she hoped, sexy.

Most of all, she had looked at Simeon through her lashes with smouldering invitation, and after a while he had stopped looking amused and started looking back at her in a way that had sent feverish shivers through her whole body.

'Admit it,' Simeon said now, his voice biting, and she gave a long sigh.

'What do you want me to say—that I'm sorry? I am, but that doesn't change anything, does it? OK, I had a crush on you, and I flirted with you, and it all ended badly, but I didn't know what I was doing, none of it was intentional and it was all so long ago. You should have divorced me years ago, married again, then your father wouldn't have made that stupid will.'

'But he did, and we aren't divorced, we're still married, and you are going to give me a child to inherit Chantries.' His voice was brusque—it hit her like a blow.

She trembled, her blue eyes opening wide again, her lips parting on a gasp of rejection. 'No, I won't!'

He stared at her mouth, his grey eyes cruel and insistent. 'You will,' he assured her, his head coming closer, his mouth slowly lowering towards her own.

'No,' she whispered, staring at his mouth and shaking. The hard-cut lines of it fascinated her; there was generosity there, and sexual promise, but held under rein, firmly controlled. It was almost touching her lips now, and the beat of her heart deafened her.

Then the phone began to ring again and Simeon swore, his head lifting, his face darkening with irritation.

'Not him again! Doesn't he know when to give up?'

She laughed almost hysterically. 'No, giving up isn't something Adam is good at. He likes to win.'

She got a hard stare, a grim frown. 'Well, this time he isn't going to, so he had better get used to the idea.'

The ringing went on and on, seeming to get shriller by the minute. 'We must answer it,' Juliet said, and Simeon angrily got up and strode to the phone.

'Right,' he began, while Juliet was getting to her feet. 'Look here, you…'

Then his voice broke off and he listened, his mouth twisting, before turning to hold out the phone to her.

She had an instant's premonition and groaned as she ran to take the phone from him.

'It's your mother,' he told her, quite unnecessarily, because she had known that when she saw his expression change.

'Hello, Mum,' she said huskily and almost held the phone away from her ear as Shirley Mendelli burst out with agitated questions which she did not give Juliet time to answer before gabbling another one.

'Who was that? What's going on? Darling, is something wrong? Why is there a man with you at the cottage? It isn't Adam, I would know his voice and this is quite different. Nasty, I'd even say threatening, the way he snarled at me just now…who is it? And why did he answer the phone that way? Julie, are you all right? Would you like me to ring the police, or—'

'Mum! Mum!' Juliet broke in on her loudly, and at last

Shirley stopped and drew breath. 'Mum,' Juliet said with a sigh, 'it's Simeon—'

'Simeon?' repeated her mother blankly, then, with astonishment, 'Simeon? Do you mean Simeon Gerard? Robert's son?'

'Yes…'

'What on earth is he doing there? I haven't heard anything about that family for years. I didn't know you still kept in touch, you've never mentioned him to me. I never liked him much, he was such an arrogant boy—I don't suppose he's changed.'

'Not much,' Juliet admitted wryly, giving Simeon a brief, sideways glance. 'Mum, he brought me some sad news—'

'Your father?' Shirley's voice changed, sharpened.

'No, his,' Juliet said quickly. 'He died a few weeks ago.'

'Oh, I'm sorry, Robert was a nice man,' her mother said soberly.

'Yes,' Juliet agreed, then changed the subject. 'Why did you ring, though, Mum? Anything wrong? How's Giorgio?'

'Oh, he's fine, there's nothing wrong here, but I rang London just now and heard about the weather down in Cornwall, so I was worried about you. Is it the snow really heavy there? Will you be able to drive back to London today? Now, I don't want you killing yourself trying to drive on icy roads, just to get back to work, darling.'

'I couldn't if I wanted to,' Juliet said heavily. 'The roads are completely blocked around here for the moment. We're hoping the snow ploughs will be able to get out and clear the main roads but unless the weather changes overnight I shan't be able to get back to London for a while, but I shall ring the office in the morning and tell Helen to hold the fort.'

'Your secretary can't run the business, though,' Shirley said. 'I had better fly back.'

'Wait until tomorrow morning, and check with me again, Mum,' Juliet said firmly. 'If I can get back to London, somehow, without killing myself, I promise you, I will. You stay there with Giorgio. How is he now?'

Shirley sighed. 'Calmer, thank heavens. Poor darling. But, Julie, don't you think I ought to come back, just in case…?'

'No, I think your place is with Giorgio, and, anyway, there's nothing urgent happening for a few days. Helen can cope, and I am sure I'll be able to get back to London somehow. I can always take a train.' If I can get as far as the nearest railway station, seven miles away, she thought wryly, but didn't say to her mother.

Shirley suddenly asked, 'But why did Simeon Gerard come all the way to Cornwall to tell you that his father was dead, darling? And why was he so nasty when he answered the phone just now? Really, he scared the life out of me—I thought I'd got a wrong number for a minute.'

'Oh, well,' Juliet said, desperately thinking of some excuse without explaining how angry Adam was because she knew that her mother would feel guilty if she knew that he resented Juliet coming down to Cornwall to check up on the cottage. 'Well, you see, I'd had a couple of funny phone calls…you know the sort, heavy breathing.'

'Oh, how frightening!' Shirley gave an audible shudder. 'Ugh…I am sorry, darling. But how lucky Simeon turned up this morning and could answer the phone instead of you! Knowing there's a man there should put a stop to that! Did you ring the police? Oh, you should, Julie. He may be dangerous.'

'OK, Mum,' Juliet said.

'You still haven't explained why Simeon came all that way, though,' remembered Shirley. 'Were you mentioned in the will? You aren't going to be very rich, are you?'

'Afraid not, nothing so exciting,' Juliet casually said. 'But I am mentioned in the will, and that is why Simeon came down here. Just something Robert wanted me to do... I'll tell you all about it later—this call must be costing a fortune. Keep in touch, Mum, love to Giorgio.'

'Bye, darling,' Shirley said, and Juliet hung up.

She turned to face Simeon, who was eying her with dry mockery. 'So,' he said. 'You didn't have the nerve to tell her the truth. Does she even know we're married?'

She lifted her chin with defiance. 'No, and I'd rather she never found out, I don't want anyone to know. What I want is for you to divorce me—'

'After you've had my child,' he promised, and his face was relentless.

CHAPTER FIVE

JULIET stood there looking at Simeon dumbly, wondering how she was going to make him understand that she couldn't, it was impossible, the very idea made her blood run cold; and he watched her—without expression now, his grey eyes cool and alert.

Then his face changed and he groaned. 'The coffee! I switched it off and poured two cups.'

She had forgotten the coffee too. They both ran for the kitchen, but the coffee in the cups was cold, and there wasn't enough left in the percolator to make two good cups.

'I'll make some more,' Juliet said but Simeon shook his head, glancing at the kitchen clock.

'I'll have instant—I'm quite happy with that, especially as it is almost lunchtime.' He filled the kettle and put it on and found a jar of instant coffee granules in a cupboard.

'Lunchtime?' She looked at the clock, too, amazed to see that he was right. It was almost one o'clock, and as soon as she realised that she began to feel hungry. 'What shall we have?' she thought aloud, opening cupboards and looking in the fridge. There wasn't that much choice. She would have to fall back on something from her stock cupboard, and a tin or two. 'How do you feel about rice or spaghetti with a tomato sauce?' she asked him and he shrugged.

'Fine with me. There are some mushrooms left, too, and I bought onions.'

'Then we're in business,' she said, and began to prepare

the meal while Simeon made the coffee and sat down at the table with his, apparently to watch her work. Blandly, Juliet asked, 'Can you chop onions, or do they make you cry?'

'Nothing makes me cry,' he said, grinning at her, and she wondered how true that was. It could be, from what she knew of him—he seemed impervious enough to her. But what did anyone know about another human being? He could get angry, but could he be hurt?

She handed him a kitchen knife and a large onion, and went to look for a pan in which to make the sauce while the water for the spaghetti boiled.

When she looked round, a pan in her hand, Simeon was already chopping away with quick, deft movements.

'You've done that before,' she said, and he nodded without looking up, his attention on what he was doing.

'I cook for myself, although I have someone in to do the cleaning. I stick to plain cooking, mostly—preferably something I can grill or leave to cook in the oven all day while I'm out. Casseroles, or steak, or maybe fish. I bake potatoes in the oven, too, or make a salad.'

'Good heavens, chef of the year,' she mocked, and he laughed.

'Well, I did eat out a lot at one time, but that gets boring, and once a woman starts cooking for a man she gets ideas.'

He had finished; there was a neat little pile of chopped onion on the wooden board. He turned to ask, 'What about the mushrooms?'

'I'll wash them and just halve them,' she said, wondering how many women had offered to cook for him over the past eight years. He was a sexy man, no denying that; there must have been plenty of women buzzing around that particular honeypot, and she felt a niggling little jab under her ribs at the images forming in her head. Sharply she told herself that it was none of her business; she wasn't a lovestruck teenager any more, she was a sane, sensible woman and Simeon Gerard's love-life was his own affair.

The water was boiling—she fed the spaghetti into it, and turned all her attention to making the sauce. Simeon laid the table, and then began opening cupboards and investigating their contents while she worked.

'Look what I found!' he exclaimed, producing a slightly dusty bottle of red wine. 'Nothing exciting, a cheap plonk really, but it should add a little sparkle to the meal.'

Juliet stared doubtfully at the bottle—was it wise to let him drink over lunch? Wine in the middle of the day always made her sleepy—would it have that effect on him? Now, that might be a good idea.

'Fine, will you open it?' she said.

He gave her a quick, dry glance, and she wondered if he had read her mind, but he made no comment, just set about finding a corkscrew and opening the wine, which he tasted himself and pronounced drinkable.

Juliet concentrated on her sauce, the kitchen filling with a rich aroma of tomato and onion, then she drained the spaghetti and divided it between the two plates waiting for it, adding the sauce on top. Simeon had poured them each a glass; there hadn't been time to let the wine reach room temperature but they warmed their glasses in their hands before drinking, and it wasn't at all bad, with the spaghetti, although Juliet merely sipped hers.

She watched through her lashes while Simeon drank several glasses, hoping it would make him lethargic for the rest of the afternoon. So far it didn't seem to be having any effect at all.

'I enjoyed that,' he said, as he ate the last mouthful of the meal. 'You're a good cook.'

'Anyone can cook spaghetti,' she disclaimed.

'You must teach me, then. It looked easy enough.' He got up, clearing the plates from the table, but put a restraining hand on her shoulder as she moved to rise. 'No, I'll make the coffee. You sit there and admire my technique.'

She relaxed, smiling, and watched him operate. It was an object lesson in economy of effort, and it told her a lot about him. He dealt with the coffee first, and only when that was percolating did he put the plates and cutlery into the dishwasher, then lay out a tray for the coffee, after which he washed up the saucepans by hand and left them to drain on the draining-board. He moved swiftly and neatly, and she felt a little shiver run down her spine, because the man was far too organised—he worked things out before he acted, he had it all planned like a military operation, and that cool, logical brain frightened her.

'Shall we drink our coffee in the sitting-room? It would be more comfortable,' he suggested, and before she could argue he had carried the tray out of the kitchen, leaving her with nothing to do but follow him.

He placed the tray on the low coffee-table and gestured to her to seat herself on the couch, but Juliet didn't trust him, so she chose a chair.

He threw her a mocking little smile, commenting on her wariness without a word, then he sat down on the couch and said, 'Would you pour the coffee, please?'

She hesitated, biting her lip, because to do so she had to get up again, and cross over to him, but she could hardly refuse, so she obeyed and poured coffee into both cups, offered him sugar and milk, then handed him his cup before picking up her own.

He caught her other hand as she straightened. 'Sit here.'

She gave him a derisive glance, shaking her head. 'I'd feel safer over there,' she bluntly said, and he laughed.

'Do I bother you that much?'

The soft implications of that made her colour rise, because it was too true—he did bother her, increasingly, and the last thing she wanted was for him to know that.

'You don't bother me at all!' she snapped, and his eyes teased.

'Then why are you afraid to sit next to me?'

She crossly said, 'I haven't forgotten the way you behaved an hour ago, you know!'

'I had provocation, don't forget that,' he taunted, but he let go of her and she went hurrying back to her chair.

Simeon drank some coffee, watching her with brooding eyes, and she drank some of her own coffee, feeling nervous. What was on his mind now? Why was he looking at her like that?

'So, tell me about this Adam,' he said abruptly. She almost dropped her cup, hot coffee splashed on her hand and she gave a sharp exclaimation and put the cup down on the floor and rubbed her skin, where it was reddened.

'What have you done to yourself now?' Simeon demanded with impatience, watching. 'Did you scald your hand?'

'No, it's fine now. You just made me jump, suddenly snapping at me like that.'

'I didn't snap, I just asked a simple question,' he drawled. 'And if I'm to judge by your guilty expression and the way you jumped I suppose I got my answer. He is your lover, isn't he?'

She was afraid to answer that, because if he believed Adam to be her lover it might make him back off; surely he would think again if he knew she was involved with somebody else? In any case, she needed some sort of protection against him. She certainly couldn't rely on herself; they had only been here alone together for around twelve hours, and already she knew that her resistance to him was low, to say the least. She must be losing her mind—she had very good reasons for hating and despising him, didn't she? He had made her very unhappy; the memory of their wedding night still hurt if she let herself dwell on it. Even now, at this instant, to give it a passing thought made her flinch inwardly, and yet he only had to move close to her for her whole body to burn with a desire so fierce that it terrified her.

It was a chemical reaction, she kept telling herself, a violent physical attraction to his body, not to the man himself. Simeon Gerard, she hated; but unfortunately her stupid body apparently had no memory—her pulses went into overdrive at the sight of him, her skin craved his touch, her mouth went dry and she trembled.

'I refuse to discuss my private life with you,' she said, her eyes lowered and obstinacy in every line of her.

'So you admit he is your private life, then?' Simeon promptly said. 'How long has it been going on?'

'I've known him for a year or so.'

'Does he work for this shoe store chain your mother and stepfather started? Is he hoping to marry into the family and one day control the store?' His tone was derisive, chilly, and she resented it for Adam.

'No, he's an executive with another company, a much bigger one, and any ambitions Adam has are centred entirely on his own firm. He isn't interested in shoes or selling. He's a company man, he likes working for big international firms, jetting about, having important business meetings…' She broke off, suddenly realising that the portrait of Adam she was painting was not a very flattering one. Simeon met her eyes, his face gleaming with amused irony.

'He sounds fascinating.'

She went pink with temper. 'He's very good-looking, as it happens!'

'Good-looking, but boring,' mused Simeon, but before she could snap back at him that Adam was not boring he added, 'Which company did you say he worked for?'

'I didn't.' But she did tell him then, curtly, and saw that he wasn't impressed. Simeon was no businessman; his whole world had always been centred on Chantries, on farming and forestry, on the life of the countryside in which he had grown up. His interests were those of a countryman: he loved horses and dogs, rode every day, fished in the gentle river which ran through his land, and shot the rabbits which preyed on his fields of grain.

A man like Adam had such very different attitudes— they were poles apart. Adam had grown up in a poor home, with everything to fight for; if he ever met Simeon, he would undoubtedly think that the other man had been born with a silver spoon in his mouth. Adam resented men like that; he met them every day, he had to compete with them in his company, and often lost out to them because of the school they had been to or who they knew. She had often heard Adam complain angrily about the old boy network, the inbuilt bias towards men from a wealthy background.

'We wouldn't have a thing in common,' Simeon thought aloud, and she laughed shortly.

'No.'

'Except you,' he added, and then, 'But I have no intention of sharing you with him. He's out.'

She gasped incredulously. 'I don't believe you said that!'

'I did, and I mean it,' he coolly underlined. 'You won't see him again.'

'You have absolutely no right to give me orders, or tell

me who I can see and who I can't. I'll do what I please!' she told him furiously, her face burning.

'No, you'll do what I please,' he drawled, and his grey eyes moved with deliberate slowness over her from her chestnut hair down to her feet, missing out no part of her and sending her heart into her mouth. She felt as if he had touched her and shuddered, then leapt up to flee, to get away as fast as she could from those tormenting eyes.

She expected him to pursue her, but there was no sound of following feet, as she ran through the hall and headed for the stairs and the safety of her bedroom, and her heartbeat slowed a little. It was only as she was on the top stair that she heard him behind her, and looking down she saw him coming up. That sent a wave of panic through her, and she started to rush across the landing, only to trip over her own feet and stumble against the wall. By the time she had recovered her balance Simeon had caught up with her. She felt her feet leave the ground and clutched at him with a cry of alarm.

'What are you doing? Put me down!'

He carried her into the main bedroom, although she fought angrily and uselessly against the strength of his arms, kicking and pummelling him until he put her down on the silk-quilted double bed. She tried to scramble off the other side, but, laughing, he caught her again, his hands closing on her waist. He was like a cruel cat, she thought, playing with a mouse, allowing her to think she might escape only to capture her again. He was on the bed, too, now, pinning her down with an arm over her, one leg moving to anchor her too, and fear almost swamped her mind.

'I hate you!' she cried out, and he laughed again.

'Do you? That *is* going to make this exciting,' he said softly, and her heart plunged in shock. He lowered his

mouth and she turned her head aside to evade his kiss.
'You have a lovely neck,' he whispered, kissing it, his lips
moving down in silky exploration, and then with another
stab of shock she felt him undo the top button of her shirt,
then, swiftly, several more with those deft, experienced
fingers. She had observed his economy of movement earlier, with alarm, and now she experienced the same dismay.

'Stop that!' she muttered, trying to push his head away.
The feel of his hair under her fingertips was too intimate,
though; she wanted to stroke it, she felt his vitality spark-
ing between her skin, his hair, which made her swallow
and pull her hand away, her heart beating even faster with
an explosive mix of desire and rage.

What is happening to me? she thought wildly, and then
his mouth was moving down inside her open shirt, against
her naked breasts, and she closed her eyes with a sharp,
helpless cry of pleasure.

Her hands came up to touch him, too, one plunging into
the thick, warm hair, caressing the powerful nape of his
neck, while her other moved over his shoulders, down his
back, up his chest, exploring his body. She had forgotten
all sanity; she had abandoned any idea of fighting him,
was given up entirely to the sweet, erotic sensations running through her.

He lifted his head from her breasts and looked down at
her, and Juliet's eyes reluctantly opened, dazed by the
light. Simeon ran a fingertip over her lips, and they parted
for him. Still staring into her passion-darkened blue eyes,
he slowly lowered his head and this time she did not try
to evade his searching mouth or fight. She arched to meet
his kiss, a husky little sound escaping her, and closed her
eyes again. This was how she had felt that night, in the

orchard, under the stars, before her father had found them and all hell broke loose.

She had forgotten until now exactly how she had felt, how piercing had been the emotion inside her when Simeon had held her in his arms. She sighed heavily against his hungry mouth, her arms around him, her hands moving up and down his back, clenching on him, and he groaned with husky intensity.

'Juliet…I want you…badly…'

Her stomach twisted in fierce excitement and her breathing roughened. He meant it, her whole body knew he meant it. His skin was burning, his body tense with arousal. She recognised the symptoms because they matched her own. She wanted him, more than she had ever wanted anything in her life before, but she was dumb, she couldn't admit it, because last time she had been so naïve with her confession of love—she had poured it out to him wide-eyed, believing he felt exactly the same, only to have her illusions shattered on her wedding night.

Simeon had not been in love with her, he had kissed her because she had thrown herself at him and once he had started making love to her he had got carried away, only to find himself trapped into a marriage he hadn't wanted. He had blamed her for that, and he had been violently angry, although she hadn't suspected that until they were married and alone in that bedroom, and then his rage had broken out, horrifying her.

She could never forget the shock of discovering that behind the cool mask he had worn until their wedding night itself, he had bitterly resented having to marry her. She should have known, of course; only a silly, blind schoolgirl would have dreamt that a man like Simeon Gerard might want to marry her—let alone believed that they could actually be happy together! Well, she had grown up, acquired a little more sophistication, and she knew a lot more about life now.

Simeon had very good reasons for wanting her to lose her head over him, and he could be very devious. How much of his passion was real? How much a charade, a mimicry of desire, intended just to get her into bed, and make sure she had his child?

She stiffened, her blue eyes opening wide, staring at the ceiling as if she saw pictures there, a film of that long-ago night, of her humiliation and misery. That time, she had made a fool of herself—well, Simeon wasn't going to do it again.

She put both hands on his shoulders and shoved Simeon away, at the same time rolling sideways, off the bed, landing somehow on her feet.

Her sudden escape had taken Simeon completely by surprise. By the time he realised what was happening Juliet was running out of the door. She got to her own bedroom before he caught up with her although she heard him coming at a furious run. She slammed home the bolt and leaned on the door, breathing raggedly, tears in her eyes.

'Juliet!'

His voice was hoarse, and made her jump away, half afraid that he could reach her, touch her, even through a bolted door. Then she stopped and stared at the door panels, running the back of her hand over her wet eyes. She was safe in here. She was safe so long as he couldn't get too close to her. Away from those seductive hands which made her brain stop working, she could actually think. Hadn't she cried enough over him eight years ago?'

He snarled her name again. 'Juliet!'

'Don't shout at me!' she muttered, backing towards her own bed and sinking down on it.

There was a silence, then his voice changed; she could

almost hear him thinking, that twisted mind of his working
out a new strategy to deal with this changed situation.

'Why did you suddenly run away, Juliet? Did I frighten
you? I didn't mean to—I went a little crazy.' His voice
went husky, intimate with laughter. 'Your fault again.'

Oh, of course, it would be, she thought, her mouth tight.

'Every time I touch you, you go to my head,' he said,
and she bit down on her lower lip.

She refused to be taken in by his flattery, but she
couldn't help reacting to it, even though she knew he was
surely lying. He had only been acting just now, when he
had breathed like that, kissed her with such passion, but
he had fooled her while she was in his arms, and if she
wasn't careful he would fool her again, because she was
vulnerable to him, and he knew it.

'I'm sorry if I frightened you,' he said in a gentle voice
which might have fooled her if she hadn't remembered
how he had deceived her in the past. 'I suppose I was
expecting you to be more experienced than you are.' Another pause, then, still gently, 'You aren't, though, are
you? Experienced, I mean. There must have been men,
though. You're far too attractive to have spent the last
eight years in a city like London without meeting any men.
But if you did, they didn't get very far with you, did they?'

He sounded infuriatingly complacent, even smug, and
her teeth met. She wanted to lie, tell him he was quite
wrong, she had had a string of lovers, but that might make
him even more determined to get her into bed. Would in-
experience be a wiser card to play? If she told him the
truth, that there had been no other lover since their wedding night, what would be his reaction? She moved uneasily and caught sight of her reflection in the dressing-
table mirror. Her face was pale now, her blue eyes haunted,
unsure.

The trouble was that in spite of everything she knew about him there was this ceaseless drag of attraction, this feeling flowing through her every time she heard his voice, saw him. She had to kill that emotion. But how?

'This Adam, for instance,' Simeon said, his voice toughening, 'tell me the truth about him—is he your lover?'

She bit her lip. Should she say yes? No, best to say nothing. Silence was her only defence. Let him think what he liked.

Simeon waited, then bit out, 'Whether he is or not, you aren't seeing him again, Juliet.'

She couldn't stay silent, then. Her anger made her snap back, 'I've told you once already—I'm a grown woman, not a child, and I'm not your possession. You aren't giving me orders or telling me who I can see and who I can't.'

His voice changed, grew coaxing. 'At least you're talking to me now— Juliet, open the door, we can't shout at each other through it! If you're so adult, start acting like one!'

'And give you the chance to get at me again?' she scornfully retorted. 'Not on your life. I feel safer with a door between us!'

She picked up the vibrations of his temper, even through the door. She couldn't be sure, but she thought he was grinding his teeth. After a moment, he said tersely, 'Just so long as you understand that you can't see your boyfriend again. I'm deadly serious about that, Juliet. You must see why. I'm not running the risk of losing Chantries because of some question mark hanging over our child. There are to be no other men in the picture until after the birth.'

'I'm not even listening to this!' she muttered furiously.

Simeon went on as calmly as if she hadn't said a thing,

'And to make sure of that, you'll come back to Chantries with me as soon as this snow thaws.'

'I'll do nothing of the kind!'

'You must live with me until the child is born,' he said in a patient voice, as though that was obvious.

'No!' She was getting desperate now; he was so obstinate in refusing to take her seriously.

'You don't have to be afraid, Juliet,' he murmured in that deceptively gentle voice. 'I won't force you. We have plenty of time to get used to each other again.'

He hadn't been gentle on their wedding night. Why should he be any different this time?

'Juliet!' he said sharply, after a while. 'Are you listening to me? Juliet, we can't talk like this. I want to see your face—open the door, I promise I won't even touch you.'

'Go away!' she muttered. 'You must be crazy, even suggesting it. You may be cold-blooded, but I'm not. I'm not sleeping with you, I couldn't stand having you touch me—and I'm certainly not having your child. I'm not going back with you, either. For one thing, I like my job, and I'm not giving it up, and for another, I never want to see Chantries again, so just go away, and leave me alone.'

She was so angry her voice was raw with it, and she picked up a book lying on her bedside table and threw it at the door. The violent gesture was some relief to her; she sagged afterwards, breathing thickly.

'You're overwrought,' Simeon said.

She shouted back at him, 'Don't you patronise me! I'm angry, that's what I am! And I have good cause!'

'Lie down and have a rest,' he merely said in a soothing voice which made her even more furious. 'We'll talk again later, when you're calmer.'

'I won't change my mind—I've nothing else to say,' she snapped, and this time he didn't bother to reply. She heard him walk back down the stairs and into the sitting-room, closing the door quietly.

Juliet threw herself full-length on to the bed and stared at the ceiling, trying to think clearly, but all that happened was that she drifted into a waking daydream about Simeon. She kept getting images of him: smiling at her, mocking her, kissing, caressing her. She tried to force her stupid imagination to remember other moments—Simeon looking at her with icy hostility, Simeon snarling at her, threatening her. It was useless. She remembered only what she secretly wanted to remember; her body was trembling with sensuality, and she despised herself for being so weak. It wasn't as if he hadn't told her with brutal honesty just why he was here! He had announced his intentions last night and only a few hours later she had been in his arms, ready to let him do as he liked with her. What sort of idiot was she?

She winced, closing her eyes. Don't answer that! she told herself. Think about something else. Work, think about work. How long will it be before the roads are clear enough to get back to London? She began devising ways and means of getting out of this cottage, getting back to London. Instead of counting sheep, she counted ways and means of escape, and began to yawn. She was very tired. It had been a disturbed and disturbing night, and she was mentally and physically exhausted. After a little while, she went to sleep, woke up as the room thickened with twilight.

Almost at once, Juliet remembered everything; she sat up with a little gasp and turned to look at the clock, taken aback to see that it was nearly seven o'clock in the evening.

She slid off the bed to look out at the moor. It seemed much lighter outside than it was in the house. The stars showed like the glittering points of swords in the midnight-blue sky. It was cold again, but the snow did not seem as deep. It had been as high as the garden wall, but now it had sunk and she could see plants showing through it. She peered out, frowning—was it her imagination, or was the snow melting?

She leant on the windowsill, staring out, for several minutes, but couldn't say for sure whether or not the thaw had begun. Maybe in the morning she would be able to drive back to London?

She seemed to have been here for days, so much had happened to her—yet it wasn't even twenty-four hours since she had arrived. She would be glad to get back, she told herself. She had to be glad. It was the only sensible view to take.

She sighed and drew her curtains together, then went over to switch on her bedroom light, before walking into her bathroom to shower. She felt hot and creased, for one thing, and for another she needed to wash Simeon out of her hair.

The water cascaded down on her, deafening her to all other sounds. When she had finished, she turned off the overhead jet, and slid into her white towelling robe, lightly towelled her hair and dried her bare legs and feet before going back into her bedroom.

She was padding across the carpet when she heard the sound of a car engine.

Juliet stopped dead, her heart plunging sickeningly. For a second she almost believed she was imagining the noise, and then she knew she wasn't, and ran to the window. Headlights cut through the dusk and illumined the lane, showing her the large black Land Rover slowly drawing up outside.

Who on earth could it be? she wondered, staring at the

vehicle as it parked beside the wall. A local farmer, calling to enquire if she was OK? One of her mother's friends who had noticed the lights?

Then the driver's door opened and someone climbed out and turned to stare up at the cottage, and Juliet drew a sharp breath, hardly believing her eyes.

It was Adam.

vehicle as it parked beside, the way it stood for a moment calling to enquire if she was OK? None of you noticed —? It was you who had noticed the lights.

Then the driver's door opened and someone got out and mused to stare at the car, and Juliet could see a strong, silent figure, darkly outlining her body.

CHAPTER SIX

FOR a second Juliet was too stunned to think, and then her mind worked like crazy. Simeon was downstairs. He would open the door when Adam knocked, and she hated to think what might happen then! There was something aggressive in the set of Adam's shoulders as he began to walk towards the house. He and Simeon were going to clash, that was obvious, and she would love to watch Adam knock Simeon off his perch, but she somehow didn't feel optimistic. The most likely outcome of a fight between the two men was that Adam would get the worst of it, and since she was the reason for his being there it would be her fault if he got hurt, or humiliated any further, so she had to stop it happening.

She didn't stop to put on any clothes; there wasn't time. She just ran for the stairs and took them two at a time, but she was too late to stop Simeon opening the front door and eying Adam with disfavour.

'If you're looking for Mrs Mendelli, she isn't here.'

'I know that.' Adam was equally brusque. He was staring at Simeon coldly as Juliet reached them, and then his eyes moved to her and flicked up and down from her damp hair to her bare legs and feet, not missing the short white towelling robe which, more or less, covered the rest of her. His mouth hardened. 'So there you are, Juliet,' he said in a tone edged with ice.

Simeon gave her a sideways look, then did a double-take, his black brows meeting harshly.

'Go back upstairs and get dressed!' he snapped.

She glared back at him. 'Will you please go back into the sitting-room, and mind your own business? This is a friend of mine.'

'I've already guessed who he is,' Simeon drawled, giving Adam a brief, disparaging glance. 'And you aren't talking to him while you're half naked, so go and get some clothes on!'

'Stop giving her orders!' Adam intervened, scowling, and taking a step forward with the obvious intention of using his wide shoulders to barge Simeon out of his way.

Simeon laughed and Juliet's nerves leapt at the sound of that laughter, because she knew what was going to happen, and it did. Simeon's whole weight met Adam as he tried to push past into the cottage, and Adam was thrown backwards.

'No! Don't...' Juliet broke out tensely, then sighed with relief as she watched Adam land, not on the stone path, but more comfortably in a thick laurel bush which cushioned his fall.

Simeon began to shut the door on him, but Juliet grabbed the handle too, struggling with him, her flushed face turned up towards his in an angry stare.

'Will you stop acting as though you own everything? You don't own this house and you don't own me—and you don't have any right to throw my friends out!'

Adam had got back on his feet. Very red and absolutely furious, he lurched back towards them both, snarling, 'You wait till I get you, you lunatic!'

'Oh, I'm scared,' mocked Simeon, his lean body poised for action, but Juliet moved swiftly in front of him and faced Adam, her eyes dark with apology.

'Adam, I'm so sorry about that, but you shouldn't have tried to force your way past him. He has a filthy temper.'

'I have nothing of the kind!' Simeon denied, his hands closing on her waist as he tried to lift her out of the way.

She slapped his hands down. 'Don't manhandle me, Simeon! Go away.' She gave Adam a pleading look. 'Adam, you shouldn't have come down here—what on earth made you do it?'

'Who's he?' Adam grated, staring past her at Simeon. 'That's what I came here to find out. Who is he? It was him on the phone this morning, wasn't it? What did he mean, he was your husband? He isn't your husband, is he, Julie?'

'Yes,' Simeon said.

At the same time Juliet said, 'No!' then Simeon laughed and she gave a cross little sigh and said, 'Well, yes and no, actually, Adam. It is a long story, and this isn't the time to explain.'

'Oh, I've got all night,' he said in a clipped voice. 'I'm certainly not driving back to London until I know the whole truth, and, anyway, I'm tired—I'm not doing that return journey until tomorrow, and it is far too late to get a hotel room somewhere, even if I knew a hotel, so I'd be grateful if you would let me stay here tonight. Anything would do—a couch, if there's nothing else.'

'Not on your life!' Simeon said, but Juliet had had time to think and she realised that Adam's arrival was the miracle she had been praying for, so she eagerly nodded.

'Of course you can stay, Adam.'

'No! Let him go to a hotel,' said Simeon.

'Will you stay out of this?' Juliet smiled at Adam. 'We can do better than a couch—there's a very comfortable bedroom free.'

'Thank you,' he said rather stiffly. 'I've got an overnight bag in my car, but I'll get it later.' Something in his expression told her that he was afraid that if he went back to his car now he might find the front door locked against him on his return.

Nodding, she stepped back and waved him into the sitting-room. 'Come in here, it's much warmer. Do sit down.' She was nervously talking politely, as though to an acquaintance who had called socially. 'Can I get you anything? You must be frozen, after that long drive. Would you like a hot drink? Coffee? Tea?'

Adam stayed on his feet, facing her, his expression belligerent. He was clearly in no mood to make polite conversation. All he replied was: 'First, I'd just like the truth, however long it takes. Is that guy your husband, or isn't he?'

Simeon lounged in the doorway, listening to them both, and she was very aware that he was there although she didn't look that way.

'Well, yes, in a way,' she huskily said, and Adam's face tightened. Hurriedly, she went on, 'Adam, I was seventeen, we were married for one day, then I left, and I haven't seen him since, until he turned up down here. That's why I said we weren't really married, and, believe me, we'll be getting a divorce.'

'No,' said Simeon coolly. 'We won't.'

'Take no notice of him,' Juliet crossly said. 'I should have started divorce proceedings years ago, but I didn't want to marry again, and I was reluctant to get in touch with him to make arrangements, even through a solicitor, so I kept putting it off.'

Adam's brow was furrowed. 'I don't understand this—you got married and left the same day? Why? What happened?' He shot Simeon a hostile look. 'What did he do to you?'

She was tempted to tell him, but decided it would only

lead to another fight between the two men, so she just said shortly, 'It didn't work out.'

Adam's jaw dropped. 'Didn't work out?'

Simeon answered him because Juliet had gone pink, realising how that had sounded, and was temporarily lost for words.

'No, she didn't give it much of a chance, did she?' he drawled, his face ironic. 'She panicked on our wedding night and ran out on me. My fault, I suppose; I should have realised she was by no means as adult as she seemed, but she had done quite a job of covering up before the wedding. She acted like a woman until the time came to prove she was one, and then she chickened out.'

'I was only seventeen!' she muttered rather resentfully. 'If I acted like a woman around you until we were married it was because I was trying out the role. That's what we do, isn't it? Whether we're men or women, we practise being adult long before we actually are...'

'Well, you had me fooled,' he drily said, and she looked down, biting her lip, knowing there was nothing she could say to that.

'You might have told me,' Adam said, his face sullen. 'You knew I was thinking of marrying you. You should have told me you weren't free—it was very unfair of you to date me all this time without making your situation clear.'

'I'm sorry, Adam,' she said, looking at him regretfully. 'You're right—of course I should have told you, but, you see, it never entered my head because I'd almost forgotten I was married.'

'But you are,' Simeon bit out, his eyes threatening. 'And you're staying married, so you can forget any idea of divorce.'

'Take no notice of him!' Adam said scathingly. 'He

can't stop you getting a divorce, and he knows it. A marriage that only lasted one day? And then eight years' separation? It's a foregone conclusion. That adds up to irretrievable breakdown of the marriage; you couldn't have better grounds for divorce. As soon as we're back in London you can contact your lawyers and start the proceedings, and there'll be nothing he can do about it.'

'And how will you live with yourself afterwards?' Simeon conversationally asked her, his face cool. 'When my cousin and his family take over Chantries?'

She stared back at him, biting her lip, her face uncertain and disturbed.

'What?' Adam asked, looking from one to the other of them. 'What's he talking about now?'

'None of your business,' Simeon said. 'Why don't you go and get your bag from your car and take yourself off upstairs?'

Juliet pulled herself together and gave Adam a pleading little smile. 'Yes, maybe you should do that. You could probably do with a bath, you must be frozen and that will make you feel much better. I'm afraid you'll have to have a scratch supper, we don't have much fresh food and we're living mainly out of tins, but I'll do my best. It should be ready in an hour or so.'

He hesitated. 'If I go out to the car, will he try to lock me out, though?'

'No,' she promised. 'I'll make sure he won't, don't worry.'

Adam shrugged, nodded, and walked out, and Simeon gave Juliet a cool look which moved over her from head to foot, making her very conscious of her nakedness under the short open-lapelled robe.

'Go upstairs and get dressed, will you? It's very distracting having you standing around in almost nothing at all, and I don't like the way he was staring, either.'

She held her lapels together with one hand, giving him a resentful stare back.

'I'll go once Adam is back. I'm not having you lock him out.'

'He's just as you described him,' Simeon observed conversationally. 'Boring, conventional, small-minded. What on earth did you ever see in him?'

She ignored him, watching the door for signs of Adam's return while Simeon watched her like a cat at a mousehole, but this cat could wait all night, she thought, it wasn't going to get what it was waiting for. She knew he was trying to taunt her into a flare of rage, and she knew why. He didn't want her staying calm and collected, in control of herself. Well, she did—and she had every intention of staying calm until she could get away from him.

'Surely he wasn't the best you could find?' drawled Simeon.

She ignored him, but she wished he would stop assessing her with those flicking grey eyes, lingering on the long, smooth bare legs visible below the hem of her robe, the way the damp towelling clung to her hips and the indentation above her thighs, or the deep V-neck where her lapels met. She was still holding her lapels there, trying to hide the glimpse of her breasts he might get, but his eyes kept coming back upwards, making her feel uneasily that he could see far more than she wanted him to see.

'He isn't in love with you, you know. He's possessive, maybe, and he may see you as one of his possessions, but he hasn't lost his head over you. It doesn't go very deep with him.' His brows curved sardonically. 'I would even doubt if anything did.'

She still didn't give any sign of having heard him, but

she was very relieved to hear Adam coming back, closing the door behind him. She walked out to meet him in the hall, smiled at him placatingly.

'I'll show you to your room.'

'I'll do that,' Simeon said behind her.

'This is not your house—you're as much a guest as he is!' she snapped, suddenly at the end of her tether. 'It's my mother's house, and I'm going upstairs anyway, so I'll show him.'

Adam didn't smile but he had a certain smugness as he followed her up the stairs, and, contrarily, that irritated her because she knew he had been delighted to hear her put Simeon in his place, and Adam had no right to smirk about that.

But she didn't want to quarrel with Adam, because his arrival had probably saved her from making a disastrous mistake. If he hadn't come when he did she might have ended up in bed with Simeon and her whole life could have been blighted. If she had become pregnant, she would have had to spend the next nine months at Chantries, waiting for his child to be born, and then, of course, he would want to keep the baby there with him, which would have left her with a terrible decision to face. Should she stay with her baby, and Simeon, knowing that he only wanted her as the mother of the child—or desert her baby and divorce its father? Whatever she decided there would be grief and pain ahead for her, and she had had enough of that eight years ago when she ran away from him and their brief marriage. She was very grateful to Adam for coming all this way.

Opening the door of the third bedroom, which was the smallest of the three, Juliet gave Adam an apologetic look. 'It isn't very spacious, I'm afraid, but it is warm and comfortable, I think.'

He looked around the little box-room, his mouth wry. The furniture was all made of golden pine: just a single bed, with a box cabinet next to it on which stood a glass table lamp, a small chest of drawers, a narrow wardrobe. The curtains and carpet were a spring-like green, the walls painted glossy white.

'It's very pretty,' Adam politely said, although they both knew that it wasn't what he was used to and that he did not like this rural style of furnishing. Adam was an urban man; he liked well-cut suits, elegant décor in his home, French restaurants and city streets. There was nothing for him in this bleak, moorland setting.

'I'm sorry you had this long journey for nothing,' Juliet said, and he shrugged.

'So am I. God knows why I came. I should have my head examined, but that phone call worried me. I couldn't believe you were married, but that fellow had cut me off, and when I rang back he did the same thing again, and I began to think maybe something was seriously wrong here, that he was some madman who had got hold of you and...' He broke off, grimacing, his face darkly flushed. 'Oh, well, you know. I started imagining what could be happening to you, and...'

He stopped again, swallowing and looking sheepish, and Juliet was suddenly touched, and smiled at him.

'That was nice of you, Adam, coming to rescue me!' Then her blue eyes widened and she gave a gasp. 'Adam! It's tonight, isn't it? You're going to miss it!'

He inclined his head without saying anything, and she stared at him, quite speechless for a second. It was a sacrifice she would never have expected him to make, and it amazed and moved her.

'Oh, Adam...and I'd forgotten all about it, I'm so sorry.' She bit her lower lip guiltily, realising she should have thought of it at once when she first saw him. He had talked of nothing else but the firm's ball for weeks. 'I know how much it meant to you to be there!' she murmured apologetically. 'Adam, you shouldn't have given it up for me, you really shouldn't! It was wonderful of you to be so worried about me, and I am very grateful, but you should just have rung the police and asked them to check that I was OK.'

He gave her an odd look, hesitated, then said rather offhandedly, 'Well, I did ring them, actually, but it took me ages to get anyone to talk to me—first of all they just said I should leave a message. Their operator said they were very busy, because of the snow; there had been lots of road accidents. I insisted on talking to someone, and a sergeant came on the line, but he didn't seem to be taking me very seriously. I explained that you were here alone, but that when I rang up some man answered the phone and was very aggressive with me, said he was your husband, which I knew couldn't be true...' Adam was very flushed, his eyes furious. 'But this policeman seemed to find it rather amusing. He didn't laugh, but he sounded as if he might be grinning. He said you could have lied to me, been married all the time. He said it sounded like a domestic matter, and they didn't interfere in domestic matters. I could tell he wasn't going to do anything about it, so in the end I decided I had to come myself.'

'That was very kind and thoughtful of you,' she soothed, quite moved by the realisation that he had thrown away the chance to impress his bosses at the firm's annual celebration, just to come and rescue her from what he had imagined might be terrible danger.

Adam gave her a sideways look, scowled, and burst out resentfully, 'Yes, and now I find the police were quite right, all along—you were lying to me, you are married, and I've been a fool.'

'It isn't like that,' she burst out, going pale. 'I didn't lie…at least, not deliberately. I had forgotten I was married—'

'How could you forget a thing like that?' he demanded in a biting voice, his face hostile.

'It was so long ago, and I was so young, and it didn't seem real, any of it. It was like a dream I had had, and escaped from. I didn't tell you because it simply didn't occur to me, not because I was trying to pull the wool over your eyes.'

Adam fell silent, his face brooding, then said grimly, 'Even if that's all true, I'm surprised your mother, at least, didn't say anything. I'd made it clear I was planning to marry you—she might have warned me—'

'She didn't know! I never told her. I never told anybody. I just wanted to forget all about Simeon, the wedding, everything. I blotted it out—I suppose I wished it had never happened.'

'I'm not surprised,' Adam said, his jawline belligerent. 'That guy is a nasty piece of work, if ever I've seen one. What was he threatening you with just now? Something about a chantry, and you being sorry if you divorced him? What did he mean?'

She hesitated, looking down, her dark lashes lying on her pale cheek. She couldn't face telling Adam about Robert Gerard's will, or the demand Simeon had made in consequence.

'Chantries is his family home,' she said vaguely. 'He wants me to go back there with him.'

'Oh,' Adam said, frowning. 'I see. Family home? Does that mean the fellow's rich?'

'His family are very wealthy,' she admitted. 'They've

owned the estate for generations, and there is a lot of land attached to the house.'

Adam grunted dissatisfaction. 'That explains a lot. Born with a silver spoon in his mouth, was he? Arrogant swine. I can't stand men of his kind.'

She was tempted to smile, but somehow managed to keep a straight face, knowing that Adam disliked men who were born into wealth and power, and yet dreamt of one day acquiring all the things they inherited by birthright. His dislike of men like Simeon was not ideological, it was simple jealousy; he wanted what they had.

Gently, she said, 'Well, thank you, anyway, Adam, for coming to my rescue. You're looking very tired. Why don't you lie down and rest for an hour while I go and get dressed, then cook supper?'

She slipped out of the room, closing the door behind her, and went into her own bedroom, only to stop short on finding Simeon waiting there for her. He was lying full-length on her bed, his hands behind his head, his lean body totally relaxed, and her pulses began to go crazy at the sight of him, which made her even angrier at finding him there.

'What do you think you're doing in here?' she spat at him, keeping her voice down so that Adam shouldn't hear them. She did not want another scene between the two men.

'Isn't it obvious?' drawled Simeon. 'I've been waiting for you to come out of his room. What took you so long?' His tone was light but his eyes were deadly and she was not fooled by the smile curling his mouth. Simeon was at his most dangerous when he looked this casual and laid-back.

'We were talking,' she said curtly. 'Look, I want to get

dressed. Will you get out of here and give me a little privacy? If you want to talk to me, you can do it downstairs.'

He stayed where he was, still smiling with his mouth while his grey eyes were dagger sharp. 'Talking? All this time?' He lifted an arm, glanced down at his watch, his black brows lifting. 'You must have had a lot to say to each other. Why did you have to say it in his bedroom? Why not downstairs, where I could hear you?'

'That's why not!' she bit out, her blue eyes icy. 'We didn't want you standing there, listening to every word, and interrupting whenever you felt like it! Can't you get it through your head that I have a life of my own, and you don't control it?'

He gestured that aside arrogantly, his face hard. 'Well, from now on, you don't go into any bedrooms alone with him, is that clear?'

'From now on, you don't walk into my bedroom, is *that* clear?' she furiously threw back. 'And stop giving me orders. Get off my bed and go away so that I can get dressed!'

'I've seen you naked before,' he said, a glitter of cold mockery in his grey eyes, and watched, smiling, as hot colour ran up her face.

'Get out!' she snapped.

He swung his long legs off the bed and stood up, and she backed, nervous of him even now that Adam was within earshot if she did need to scream for help.

Simeon began to saunter towards the door, then twisted sideways without warning and caught hold of her, his hands closing on her arms, pulling her ruthlessly towards him until their bodies touched.

She began to tremble at the intimate contact, but her head went back and her chin lifted defiantly. 'Let go or I'll call Adam!' she threatened.

He laughed under his breath. 'And what do you think he could do?'

'He—' she began angrily, only to have her voice stifled by his mouth coming down against her lips. She tried to go on talking, but the movement of her mouth merely gave him the chance to deepen the kiss, and she moaned in a sort of anguish, torn between pleasure and rage. He had discovered her vulnerability to him and he didn't scruple to take advantage of it, but she knew his emotions weren't involved, so why was she allowing him to do this to her? He was using his head, not following his heart, and if she let him seduce her into going back with him to Chantries, living with him again as his wife, in every sense of the word, she would be insane.

He stopped kissing her and smiled down at her flushed, confused, uncertain face. 'You're lovelier now than you were at seventeen, you know. Oh, you were sexy then— you were a very precocious adolescent and I wanted you badly, but you were too skinny and wide-eyed to be really sexy. Your figure has improved beyond recognition, you know how to dress and wear make-up, and you're far more sure of yourself, more sophisticated. I think a woman needs the glitter of sophistication to make her really sexy, don't you?'

'I...' she began, stammering because the way he was looking at her made her shudder, made her throat beat with a hunger which terrified her. Did he really find her sexy? Or was he just telling her that to trap her?

He brushed his mouth down her throat, murmuring huskily against her skin, 'I want you far more now than I ever did eight years ago.'

Her heart missed a beat. He's lying, she thought desperately. He must be lying. But common sense couldn't stop her body from reacting violently to what he was doing to it, his hands slipping intimately inside her robe, softly caressing her neck, her shoulders, her naked breasts.

She wanted to push him away, but she couldn't, because she loved it, she ached for the touch of his hands, and she wanted him with an intensity she hadn't even suspected she could feel eight years ago. The teenager who had had such a crush on him simply hadn't had a clue about love.

'We made a bad beginning, Juliet,' Simeon said, looking down at her with a darkly brooding face. 'We made a mess of it all, both of us. I know I was a swine to you that night, and I've bitterly regretted it since, but we have a chance to start again, don't you see? Don't throw it away.'

She stared at him, silenced, her face pale and uncertain, and after a moment he let go of her and stepped back. 'I'll go down and start work on our supper, shall I?'

Huskily, she said, 'Thank you.'

He was gone a second later, and she bolted her door after him, then stood there, her mind in a state of total confusion. How much of all that had he meant? She no longer knew what to believe—he was driving her crazy, and she didn't know how much more of his bewildering, disturbing behaviour she could stand. Thank heavens the snow had begun to thaw and in the morning she would probably be able to drive back to London. Even if the roads were still icy, she could leave her car here at the cottage, in the locked garage and go back with Adam in his Land Rover, which could handle bad road conditions rather better than her own car. One way or another, though, she was determined to get away from Simeon and back to the hectic bustle of the city, which would seem so restful after the so-called calm and tranquillity of the countryside, if Simeon was there.

She pulled herself together; there wasn't time to think about this, she had to get dressed. She did so without really thinking much about what she was putting on, brushed her hair, put on a little light make-up, and went downstairs to help him with the supper.

He was stirring something in a saucepan, and turned to eye her speculatively from head to foot. 'Very neat,' he mocked. 'I'm quite sure the boyfriend will approve.'

She caught sight of herself reflected in the little mirror on the kitchen wall and knew what he meant, although she refused to admit it to him. She had automatically put on a black skirt, a demure white blouse and a warm black V-necked pullover, returning to the safety of city formality.

'Did I say you were sexy? I take it back,' Simeon said, turning down the heat under the pan of vegetable soup he had ready. 'Very tame tonight, aren't we? For his sake?' His grey eyes taunted. 'Or mine? Are you making sure I don't find you quite so sexy while he's around?'

Unconsciously, she might well have been, but she just shrugged, trying to look impatient. 'I simply put on the first thing that came to hand. You're reading too much into it.' She lifted another saucepan lid; he was boiling water. 'What is this for?' she asked.

'Rice,' he said. 'I've found some more tinned tomatoes, a tin of mixed beans, and a tin of tuna…that should make a reasonable meal for three, with this soup to start with, although that only comes out of a packet, I'm afraid, but it smells good and it will help fill us.'

'I'm starving,' she confessed. 'This seems to have been a very long day, and I'm mentally exhausted.'

Simeon put a friendly arm around her and smiled into her eyes. 'You slept all afternoon, and you're still tired?'

'So much has happened since I woke up,' she complained, leaning on him and feeling her body slacken and give itself up to his support.

'It has been an eventful day,' he agreed, then his glance

skated over her head towards the kitchen door and his face iced over. 'Oh, there you are—supper is nearly ready,' he said coldly, and Juliet stiffened and looked round, too, moving out of the circle of his arm.

Adam came right into the room, scowling. 'Sorry to interrupt!'

'You aren't interrupting,' Juliet hurriedly said. 'Simeon has cooked us a terrific pot luck meal, so let's eat now, shall we?'

The meal was not exactly *cordon bleu*, but it was very warming and filling, and Juliet would have eaten it even if it hadn't been, because she was very hungry. They all washed up together, making stiff polite small talk about the weather. Outside the melting snow dripped from the roof, from trees, and water ran somewhere in a gutter, or down a path. It was much warmer, too. They drank their coffee in the sitting-room, still trying to be polite, then listened to a play on the radio for an hour.

When the play ended, they listened to a news bulletin, with the two men commenting on some international news on which they, naturally, disagreed violently. They had nothing in common, especially not their opinions, and Juliet was weary of their sniping at each other, so she got up, said goodnight and left them to fight without their audience.

She fell asleep almost as soon as her head hit the pillow, and woke in a pale, cloudy light which turned out to be morning. Looking at her watch, she found it was half-past seven, so she got up. When she was washed and dressed, she looked out of her window and saw that the snow was almost gone—the road still had a few icy patches, but she was certain she could safely set out for London.

She packed and went down to find Adam already up,

drinking coffee and eating some rather dusty-looking corn-flakes.

'This was all I could find,' he gloomily said.

'That's OK. We can stop on the road,' she said. 'I've decided to leave my car here and go back in yours—is that OK?'

He put down his spoon and stared at her. 'Fine—have you told what's his name?'

She shook her head. 'I'd rather leave before he gets up, if you don't mind.'

'Running away?' Adam said drily, but he didn't ask her any more questions, just finished his coffee, offered her some, and, when she refused it, went off to get his over-night bag. Juliet quietly went out of the cottage and stared across the moorland which glimmered with opalescent mist, praying that Adam wouldn't wake Simeon.

Adam came out, carrying his packed bag, and she softly closed the door behind them, hearing it automatically lock. 'Should you leave him alone in the cottage?' Adam asked, frowning. 'Do you think that's wise?'

'He isn't a criminal,' Juliet said impatiently. 'When he leaves, the door will lock behind him, and he won't be able to get back in, anyway, so there's no problem.'

'Don't you think your mother would object, if she ever finds out, though? I mean, leaving a stranger alone in her cottage?'

'He isn't a stranger. She knows him, she's known him since he was a boy.'

Adam stopped in his track and stared at her. 'But you said she didn't know about the marriage.'

'She didn't, but she knows Simeon. I told you, my parents were divorced and I stayed with my father, who has always worked on Chantries, the Gerard estate—he still does, in fact, he's the head gamekeeper. My mother knew the Gerard family, including Simeon—but she left years before…before we were married.'

'I don't understand any of this,' Adam said, and she threw an anxious look back at the cottage, afraid she might see a curtain stir, a face appear. If Simeon saw them leaving, he would come after them, and urgency churned in her veins.

'Come on, Adam! There isn't time to argue. Let's get away while we can!'

Adam caught the nervousness in her voice, and walked hurriedly over to the Land Rover, unlocked it, and threw their luggage into the back, while Juliet climbed up into the driver's cab. Adam slid behind the wheel and started the engine, then they began to move off. Juliet glanced anxiously into the wing mirror but there was no sign of movement in the cottage. Simeon must be sleeping like the dead.

Adam was driving carefully—the road conditions were still icy—but slowly the cottage vanished into the distance, and Juliet sank back, sighing with a shaky mixture of relief and painful regret. She couldn't have agreed to go back to him, but leaving hurt as much, if not more, than it had hurt her when she ran away from him after their wedding night.

'Is that it, then?' Adam asked suddenly. 'Are you going to divorce him, or not? I mean, it all seems very confused, a real muddle. Don't you think you'd better regularise it? Especially as you seem scared of the fellow.'

'I'm not scared of him!' she denied resentfully.

'It looks like it to me!' said Adam, and of course it did, she knew that, and it was true. She was scared of Simeon; wary of him, too, the way any sane person would be wary of a wild animal out of its cage and prowling around looking for prey.

'Obviously I shall divorce him,' she said in a flat tone, angry with herself because just saying that made her feel depressed. Their marriage had never been a real one; why should it upset her to think of ending it?

'But will he make difficulties?' Adam thought aloud, and again he had hit the nail right on the head.

That was just what Simeon would do—make difficulties. And he would start making them the minute he woke up in the cottage and discovered she had fled. He wasn't going to let her escape without making some sort of effort to get her back. He had too much to lose. He would come after her, and fast, and Juliet felt her nerves crackle like a forest fire at the very prospect of Simeon on her trail, stalking her remorselessly until he managed to corner her.

She looked at the speedometer, her blue eyes feverish. Adam was doing a calm and steady forty miles an hour, and no doubt that was wise, on these slippery roads, but panic had set in now and Juliet was desperate to get to London before Simeon caught up with them.

'Can't you go any faster?' she snapped, and Adam gave her a startled, sideways look. 'He'll be coming after us any minute now,' Juliet warned, and Adam's skin paled, he swallowed convulsively, abandoned caution and put his foot down on the accelerator.

CHAPTER SEVEN

JULIET was asleep when Adam eventually pulled up outside her flat. He touched her arm, and she woke with a start, blinking sleepily up at him. For a few seconds her face was blank, then everything came back to her and she sat up, brushing her chestnut hair back from her flushed face.

'Where are we?'

'Your place,' Adam said in stiff, offended tones. It had not been an easy journey; for the first hour he had fired questions at her and disliked all her answers, and she had been too impatient and irritable to be diplomatic—she didn't see that he had any right to sit in judgement on either her or Simeon, and had said so, which, of course had led to a nasty little row. At last she had simply refused to speak to him at all, had closed her eyes, turning away, and gone to sleep.

'Already?' she said, with relief, looking out of the car at the familiar building, the quiet street. 'You made good time.' He must have driven like a maniac. A glance at her watch told her that it was only one o'clock, lunchtime—and immediately after that she began to feel hungry.

'There wasn't much traffic about.' Adam shrugged. 'The snow must have kept most people off the roads.' He got out and lifted down her luggage and Juliet joined him on the pavement, warily contemplating the curtained windows of her flat. Simeon couldn't have possibly have got here first; Adam had driven far too fast. No doubt he would be hard on their heels, though.

'Shall I come up with you, to make sure everything is OK?' Adam asked politely, apparently reading her expression, and she shook her head.

'No, I'll be fine. It is broad daylight, after all.' She picked up her suitcase. It wasn't heavy and she could manage it perfectly well. 'Thanks, Adam—' she began politely and he inclined his head, interrupting.

'Not at all. Goodbye, Juliet.'

He strode back to the Land Rover, slid behind the wheel, and a moment later was gone, leaving her on the pavement, staring after him. Adam had meant that farewell; finality had echoed in his voice.

He had threatened to end their relationship if she didn't go to the ball, yet he had driven all the way to Cornwall because he was worried about her, and she was grateful to him for that, and felt guilty, because it meant that Adam did care about her in his own way. Would she have done the same, in his place? She considered that wryly, then smiled. Yes, of course she would. She hadn't been in love with him, but she had liked him, she had cared enough to help him if she thought he was in trouble. He was a friend, and she was sorry that she was unlikely ever to see him again.

But she wasn't going to cry. It had been a lukewarm affair from the beginning and she was grateful to him for walking away without further recriminations. He could have been much nastier. Adam's pride was hurt; so was his self-esteem. He had had her tagged as a suitable wife, and he had made a mistake about her; he felt she had made a fool of him. He had lost his chance to impress his bosses at the firm's ball, on her account, only to discover that she had been married all the time, and married to a man like Simeon Gerard, exactly the type Adam most envied and detested.

She looked over her shoulder, suddenly nervous. What was she doing standing around out here when Simeon might roar up at any minute? She hurried into her flat and bolted the front door behind her, then went round the rooms, refusing to admit that she was checking that she was alone there.

Reassured about that, she unpacked and put all her clothes into the washing machine. She needed to wash everything she had worn at the cottage—the shirt Simeon had unbuttoned, the jeans he had unzipped, the towelling robe his hand had parted to explore her body. All her clothes seemed to her to be covered by his fingermarks. She almost felt like throwing them all away, never wearing them again, but that would be crazy; it would be admitting something she wasn't ready to admit.

She started the machine a few moments later, then hunted through her freezer for something simple to cook for lunch, deciding on a fish pie, cod and prawns under a potato lid.

She had almost finished eating it when the phone rang. She jumped up, her nerves going haywire. Was it Simeon?

Maybe she shouldn't answer it? But she wasn't capable of ignoring that shrill, insistent sound, so at last she picked it up.

'Hello?' she almost whispered.

'Oh, you *are* back!' her mother's voice said, and Juliet sagged, her heart slowing.

'Yes. Where are you? Still in Italy?'

'Just about!' Shirley Mendelli cheerfully told her. 'If you hadn't answered this time, I would have booked the next flight over, though. I've been trying to get hold of you all morning. First I rang you at the cottage for ages without getting a reply and then I rang here, then the cottage again, and I was so worried I was going to fly home today, but Giorgio said maybe you were on your way back to London, and not to panic...'

Juliet smiled, imagining the scene, typical of both of them—her mother always did go to extremes and Giorgio always soothed her down, as calm as a millpond and taking the common-sense point of view.

'Then I realised that if you were driving back you would leave around breakfast time, so I waited a couple of hours before starting again and got you right away. I tell you, I'm very relieved to hear your voice! How was the drive back to London? Were the roads tricky?'

'No, we had no trouble. The thaw is well under way now, and there wasn't much traffic.'

'We?' repeated her mother curiously. 'Did Sim Gerard drive you back?'

Juliet hesitated, realising how much of what had happened that weekend she couldn't tell her mother. 'No, Adam did, actually.'

'Adam? You didn't say he had gone down there with you.'

'He didn't come with me, he drove down to bring me back to town, in a Land Rover he had borrowed from a friend...'

'Why a Land Rover?'

'Good in bad road conditions,' Juliet brusquely said.

'Oh, yes. Well, that was thoughtful of him. Darling, do you want me to come back at once? Giorgio has to stay here for a few more days, but I could come alone—if you need me?'

'No, Mum, don't be silly! There are no problems here. You stay with Giorgio; he needs you more than we do!' Juliet urged, hoping she sounded convincing. She didn't want her mother to suspect she had anything worrying her; there was nothing she could do to help, after all.

'Sure you can cope with everything at work?'

'Of course I can! I'm looking forward to being in charge!' Juliet said lightly, but in a way she meant it seriously—being fully occupied in dealing with the business would stop her brooding over Simeon.

Her mother laughed. 'Well, in that case—have fun, darling, and thank you. It's such a help to know you're there, looking after things. But if you need me, I'll fly back at once—you only have to ask, you know that.'

'I know,' Juliet said, knowing she wouldn't ask, couldn't ask. There was too much she had hidden, too much she had never told her mother, and when Shirley heard the whole story she was going to be hurt at being excluded. Would she understand why her daughter had never felt able to confide in her? Why she had only wanted to forget her marriage and what had led up to it? One day, soon, Juliet knew she was going to have to tell her—but not while she was so far away, with worries of her own to fret about.

Juliet was on tenterhooks for the rest of the day, waiting for Simeon to arrive, or ring, but there was no sign of him, and by ten o'clock she had stopped expecting him. That was when she went to bed, but not to sleep. She lay there wide awake for hours, her mind working in ever-decreasing circles.

Her mother had had no reply when she rang the cottage, so Simeon must have left there, and he must have done so early in the morning. Where was he? It was obvious, she decided; he must have driven back to Chantries, not come to London. Why had he done that, though? She had been so certain he would follow her.

Had he abandoned his plan? Had he given up because she had fled with Adam? She couldn't believe it. Simeon wasn't that easily beaten. He had too much at stake; he had put his whole life into Chantries and he wasn't going to lose it if he could do anything to stop it.

Even when she fell asleep she kept waking up. She would sit up in bed suddenly and look dazedly, wildly, about her, as if there was someone or something in the room with her. It was like being haunted. Each time she would realise she was alone, sigh heavily, lie down again and go back to sleep.

Her alarm woke her at seven-thirty and she felt like death as she staggered out of bed and went through her usual routine before setting off for work. She looked out of the window before she left her flat; there was no sign of Simeon's car or of him, so she hurried out and got into her own car.

Her secretary looked up quickly as she walked into the office. 'Oh, good morning. How did your weekend trip go?' Helen knew she had had to drive down to Cornwall. 'I saw that they had snow in the west—did you have any problems down there?'

'I was snowed in for a day, but it soon thawed,' Juliet said, picking up the pile of letters waiting for her on her desk and flipping through them. 'Any messages?' she casually asked, not looking at Helen. He wouldn't have rung here, though—or would he? It would be the last thing she would expect, and so he might have done it.

'I left two on your desk—the Italian suppliers, ringing up about the next delivery.' Helen paused, her brow furrowed, then said in a faintly anxious voice, 'Oh, by the way, somebody rang to ask for you on Friday evening, just as I was leaving. He said it was urgent that he speak with you, but I thought I'd better not give him the address or phone number of the cottage. I hope that was OK?'

Juliet gave her a grim smile. 'Yes, you were quite right.

Never give that sort of personal information out without checking with me first.'

Helen nodded. 'Well, that's a relief. He got quite angry, and kept saying he was a relative of yours, and I wasn't sure I'd done the right thing.'

She was a thin quiet girl with luxuriant brown hair and dark eyes. Her smile, when it came, was gentle and sweet-natured, but she didn't smile, or talk, easily. Helen was shy. She was very capable, and worked hard, but it was difficult to get her to talk about herself.

Juliet knew very little about her life outside the office. She liked her, and trusted her implicitly, but she often wondered why Helen was so secretive. She knew better than to ask direct questions, though, and now she just smiled encouragingly at her secretary and said, 'Well, we'd better get on with some work, hadn't we? Where are those balance sheets I was working on on Friday?'

Helen produced them from the files she kept in such excellent order, and the usual busy silence settled down over the small office. Juliet had been promoted to having her own office and secretary a year ago, after having worked in the various shops, taken a business course, and then shared an office with her mother's secretary, so that she could understudy her mother's job before Shirley and Giorgio moved up to Manchester to open the new shop there.

There was an increasing amount of administration in-volved in running the various shops, and they all knew that more secretarial staff had to be taken on sooner or later, but Shirley and Giorgio had a deeply rooted instinct to keep the firm a family one. They were afraid of ex-panding too fast, in spite of the advice constantly urged on them by their accountants. She suspected that they thought that if the company got too big it would get out of control, or, at least, out of their control, and she could sympathise with that. A strong part of the fun of the job, for everyone who worked for them, at all levels, was the very personal style of management.

Since the workload had doubled over the past couple of years, however, that had left Juliet with a great deal to do, but although she had sometimes complained about that she was glad of it that week because it kept her too busy to think about Simeon.

She was very on edge as she worked in her office or drove around the stores, constantly wondering if and when Simeon was going to appear. He didn't, which should have been a relief, but somehow wasn't. She was sleeping badly, and the tension was eating at her nerves.

Was that why he was doing it? Was he trying to rattle her? If that was it, he was doing a great job. Whatever she was doing, half her mind was on him.

If he knew that, he would be triumphant, she thought angrily, handing a pile of letters she had just signed back to Helen with a glare which made the other girl look very worried.

'Did I make a mistake?'

'What?' Juliet pulled herself together and grimaced. 'No, they were perfectly typed. Thanks. Sorry, Helen, I was thinking about something else.'

'Is anything wrong?' Helen uncertainly asked, watching her. 'You seem very…edgy…'

It was as rare for her to make a personal remark as it was for her to offer a confidence, so Juliet looked at her in surprise, then smiled.

'It's a personal problem—I shouldn't have brought it into work with me! Sorry, take no notice, Helen.' It was a relief to know that Helen wouldn't ask any more questions. At once, she nodded gravely and went back to her desk with the letters to be posted.

That evening, Juliet's mother rang to say that she and Giorgio could fly home at last, and would be on a flight next morning. 'We should be in Manchester by the early evening. I'll ring you when we get back home, darling. We'll probably come down to London in a couple of days to see you, and catch up with everything you've been up to. I suppose it's the usual horrible weather back there? Any more snow? Brr...I wish we could stay here, actually. We've been sunbathing and swimming, and it is going to be hell leaving.'

Juliet laughed. 'I believe you! But the weather has warmed up quite a bit over the last day or so. The sun came out today, and spring looks as if it is happening at last. Manchester isn't the Italian Riviera, but I don't think you'll freeze to death.'

She felt more cheerful as she went to bed. With her mother and Giorgio safely home, her life could get back to normal and she might stop looking over her shoulder all the time, or tensing every time the phone rang. She might even stop thinking about Simeon every waking second of the day, and wondering why he hadn't come looking for her. If only she knew why he had given up, she might be able to forget the whole strange episode.

She had another troubled night, and only fell asleep towards dawn, so deeply that her alarm didn't wake her. Luckily, a neighbour's radio did, playing pop music at a level that made her sit up, yawning, quite disorientated and almost believing the radio was in the bedroom with her. Pulling herself together, she looked at her clock to check the time and realised with a groan that she must have slept through the alarm. She was going to be very late for work this morning.

She stumbled out of bed just as the pop music stopped and a news bulletin began. Juliet was on her way to the bathroom, already pulling her white silk nightdress over her head, when she heard a familiar name through the thin walls.

'Chantries…'

Juliet froze in her tracks, half thinking she had imagined it, but the newsreader continued, 'One of the oldest houses in England, which has been in the possession of the same family since the Middle Ages.'

Why on earth would a news programme carry an item about Chantries? Juliet thought, frowning.

Then the newsreader went on, 'The cause of the fire has not yet been determined.'

Juliet gave a cry of shock, her hand going to her mouth. Oh, no! Oh, my God, no! she thought wildly; he set fire to the house to stop his cousin inheriting it!

'In the blaze, Mr Simeon Gerard, whose father, the previous owner, died last month, was taken to Granville Hospital suffering from burns after being trapped in a bedroom and overcome by smoke. There were no other casualties and…'

The voice broke off and a gabble of other voices and music came through the wall as her neighbour switched restlessly from channel to channel. Frantically, Juliet ran to her own radio and switched it on, her hands shaking as she searched for the right station, but it took her a while to find it, and by the time she did the newsreader was dealing with another story.

Juliet tried other channels, switched on her TV, but no other news bulletin gave the story.

At last she gave up and hurried to shower and get dressed, her mind whirling in fear and anxiety. How badly had he been burnt? It sounded serious. What had the news-

reader said exactly? Taken to hospital, suffering from
burns after being trapped in a bedroom and overcome by
smoke? That could be dangerous, even if you didn't get
burnt. People often died from inhaling smoke.

She had to get to him, as fast as she could. What if he
was...? She couldn't even think the word. Simeon was
tough; he was a survivor. He wouldn't die. He mustn't,
because if he did she'd want to die too.

She closed her eyes, trembling, white-faced. She loved
him. She had always loved him, as long as she could remember. She hadn't just had a crush on him, or lost her
head over him. She had kept telling herself that that was
all she had felt; a teenage infatuation. But it had been far
more than that. She had loved him, the way a woman
loved—deeply, passionately. She had tried to kill her love
after their disastrous wedding night, she had tried to hate
him, but love like that was not so easy to kill. The minute
she had seen him again, it had flared up as fiercely and
hungrily as before. She loved him so much that at times
she had almost hated him, had felt like killing him.

Her blue eyes opened, enormous, their black pupils di-
lated and glittering like dark stars in her white face.
Simeon loved Chantries like that, she thought, with a pang
of fear. A line of poetry came into her head. 'Each man
kills the thing he loves.'

She flinched. Oh, but Simeon couldn't have set fire to
Chantries. He wouldn't do that. He loved the house too
much, it meant too much to him. The idea was crazy; why
on earth had she ever let herself think such a thing?

Simeon could be obsessive, he could be as unpredictable
as a hurricane blowing out of nowhere, a possessive man
whose emotions ran deep below the cool surface he
showed everyone else, but he was also a very strong man,
a man of integrity and honour. Why else had he felt bound

to marry her although he had never intended to in the beginnng?

No, Simeon would never do anything to harm Chantries, even if he was going to lose it.

She rang Granville Hospital once she was sure her voice was steady, and was put through to the ward to which Simeon had been taken. The ward sister spoke to her politely. 'Are you a relative?'

Juliet hesitated, then said for the first time, 'I'm his wife.'

'Oh, yes, Mrs Gerard,' said the sister warmly. 'I have you down as his next of kin. He said you were away on holiday, touring, or we would have rung you to tell you. I hope it wasn't too much of a shock to hear the news. Did the police find you? He told them not to bother, but I expect they felt they should. He's quite comfortable. When do you think you'll get here?'

'Some time today, I can't say for sure exactly when,' Juliet said huskily. 'Sister, what does "quite comfortable" mean exactly? How serious are his injuries?'

'Don't worry, we're keeping him under permanent observation—shock can be a problem in these cases, and inhaling smoke can have after-affects which don't show up at once, but I think I can promise you that there is no need to be seriously worried.'

Juliet saw that she wasn't going to get a clear, factual answer; the ward sister was being far too carefully diplomatic. She would have to wait to know for sure how Simeon was when she could see for herself.

She rang Helen next, and warned her that she wouldn't be in to work. 'A friend has been in an accident, I'm going to see him in hospital, and it will take all day. Hold the fort, would you? Cancel any appointments, make new ones, and if any problems come up try to sit on them until

I ring you later. My mother should be back this evening, thank heavens. I'll talk to her and, if necessary, ask if she can get to London tomorrow to take over for me.'

Helen was politely incurious. 'I see. I'll do my best—don't worry. Is there a phone number where I could reach you today?'

'Not yet,' Juliet said. 'I'll ring back later when I've got an address and phone number to give you.'

'Right,' Helen said, then quietly added, 'I hope your friend isn't too badly hurt, Juliet. I'll keep my fingers crossed for you.'

'Thanks,' Juliet said, and rang off.

Before she set off, she made a final phone call—to her mother's Manchester home. Of course there was nobody there, but she left a message on the answering machine, explaining what had happened and saying that she would ring with more news when she had any. Her mother would be puzzled by her dash to the hospital to see a man she had never mentioned once during the past eight years until last weekend, but Juliet had no time to explain yet. That was something she must face soon, and it was going to come as a terrible shock to Shirley Mendelli, but for the moment the only thing Juliet could think about was getting to Simeon.

CHAPTER EIGHT

THE hospital stood among green lawns and formal circles of rosebeds on the outskirts of a small town some five miles from Chantries. It served not only the town, but the surrounding countryside, and Juliet could remember coming there when she had been just five years old to have her tonsils taken out. It had seemed vast to her, then, a towering threat of a building which had terrified her. That morning, as she walked towards it from the car park where she had left her car, the hospital seemed to have shrunk, yet she still felt a pang of fear, a nervous tremor, looking up at the place. She was afraid for Simeon; what if he was badly hurt? He was such an active man, with lots of energy—how was he going to bear to lie in bed for any length of time?

With the eyes of an adult she saw that the hospital was a ramshackle collection of buildings, of various periods and styles, which had been added on to a central Victorian house which had obviously been the original hospital, and which did have a certain solid style, almost a smugness about the way it stood there, with its rows of flat, unrevealing windows. Perhaps she should have found that complacency reassuring, but she didn't; it worried her, made her feel she was approaching a hostile place where nobody cared if you lived or died.

She walked under the massive portico, between the two huge stone pillars supporting the canopy, through the open double doors into a large hall full of wooden benches on which were seated outpatients waiting to see the casualty officer. She stood there, hesitating, feeling very out of place. Nobody looked round at her; the faces had a glazed patience, a lack of expectation of ever being seen by a doctor, which was vaguely depressing.

Juliet crossed to the porter in his little office and asked for directions, then set out to find the ward where Simeon had spent the night. It was a long walk; the corridors, with their smell of disinfectant and floor polish, seemed endless, but at last she pushed open the swinging door and saw a sister sitting a desk in a glass-walled little office.

'You want to see Mr Gerard?' The other woman gave her a quick, sharp look, then smiled soothingly. 'Are you Mrs Gerard?'

Flushing slightly, Juliet nodded, and the sister said, 'Well, it isn't visiting hours but under the circumstances… he's in the side-ward at the very end. Please, don't stay too long, it's nearly lunchtime.'

Under the circumstances? Juliet thought, her heart squeezed in the grip of fear as she walked through the busy ward. What had the woman meant by that? What circumstances? Was Simeon so ill that they were waiving ordinary hospital rules? Was he… Her eyes closed briefly because she couldn't bear the thought that had slid like a deadly snake into her mind. He couldn't be dying, he mustn't be.

'Are you all right?' asked a young nurse, halting beside her with a searching look, and she started, her eyes opening and a faint flush crawling into her face at the way the girl was staring.

'Yes, I'm fine—I'm looking for Mr Gerard. Sister said he was in the side-ward.'

'Turn left at the end, and you'll see him. He's the only patient in the side-ward at the moment.'

'Thanks,' Juliet said, walking on. Why was Simeon the

only patient in this other ward? Because he was danger-
ously ill and needed absolute quiet?

She turned the corner, a chill finger of fear trailing down
her spine, and looked quickly, urgently, at the only bed
which was occupied. She was so anxious that her eyes
blurred for an instant, and as she paused there, her
breathing ragged, the man in the bed turned his head and
stared at her.

Then her eyes cleared and she could see him, her blue
eyes running over him in a rapid search for clues about
his condition. His face was pale, his hair looking very
black against his colourless skin, but the only injuries she
could see at first did not look serious: a few dark-coloured
bruises on one cheek, where the skin was shiny and highly
glazed, a cut on his temples just over one eye, a bulky
bandage over the palm of one of his hands. Relief made
her legs turn rubbery and she leant on the nearest solid
object, which happened to be a chair.

'Hello,' she said in a shaky voice, trying to smile, but
Simeon did not smile back; in fact he glared at her with
what felt like hatred.

'You!' he grated. 'What on earth are you doing here?'

She had been so obsessed with fear that he was seriously
ill, or even dying, that it hadn't occurred to her to wonder
if he would want to see her. She certainly hadn't expected
to be looked at with bitter hostility, and it cut the ground
from under her feet.

'I...' she stammered, biting her inner lip. 'I h-heard
about the fire on the radio this morning, and...'

'And thought I might be about to join the Choir
Immortal, leaving you with everything I owned, I suppose?' he coldly mocked. 'Sorry to disappoint you—I'm
not about to die.'

'What a pity!' Juliet snapped, anger sending a flow of

adrenalin through her. What on earth made her care so much whether this man lived or died? 'I needn't have come, then!'

'No, you wasted your journey,' he muttered. 'I'm perfectly well.'

'Then why have they kept you in hospital?' She slowly walked over to sit on a chair beside his bed, and noticed something else—that the hair along the right side of his face had an oddly scorched look, as though the flames had leapt past without actually touching.

He grimaced impatiently. 'Oh, they're afraid of shock, mainly—and the after-effects of inhaling smoke. There's nothing seriously wrong with me. In fact, I'm fit enough to leave hospital but they insist on keeping me in for what they laughingly call observation, which entails waking me up every time I drift off to sleep and shining lights in my eyes and banging around my bed shouting questions and offering me food I wouldn't eat if I were going to be hanged in the morning.'

She laced her trembling fingers together in her lap, flushing a little as she realised that he was watching her do so. 'I should think they know what they're doing,' she gently said, and his mouth twisted in derision.

'You must be the perfect patient. You would just do as you're told and not question anything, would you? That isn't the way you behave when I'm around. You never stop arguing with me.'

Her lips parted, a furious retort on her tongue, then she noticed his pallor again, and the dark shadows under his eyes, and she mentally counted to ten before she spoke, changing the subject.

'What about Chantries? Do you know how serious the damage is?'

He leaned back against his piled up pillows with a faint

sigh, his expression ironic. 'Nothing irretrievable, thanks to your father.'

'My father?' she repeated, blue eyes wide and dark.

'He was the one who noticed the smoke coming out of my bedroom window and raised the alarm. He was just setting out on his usual prowl around the grounds, in the early hours, looking for poachers, when he spotted the smoke. He raced up to the house, but couldn't raise any-one, so he broke in through the kitchen window, ran up the stairs and apparently found me unconscious on the floor of my bedroom. He dragged me out, then got a fire extinguisher from the wall and went back to put the fire out, but it had too much of a hold, and time was running out, so he shut the door again, and rang the fire brigade and the ambulance service. I knew nothing of all this; I was barely conscious. But I've been told this morning that they managed to contain the fire—because he acted so promptly, it didn't spread any further, and the only damage was to my bedroom. That's pretty extensive, but it could have been a great deal worse.'

Her throat hurt, and she swallowed painfully before she could get out a few husky words. 'A great deal worse,' she agreed. He could have been killed. The thought stabbed like a knife and her eyes glistened with unshed tears so she looked down, hiding that from him.

There was a long silence, then Simeon said coolly, 'Well, as you're here, you might as well be useful. I've had enough of this place and I'm going to sign myself out tomorrow morning, whether the doctors agree or not. I want you to go to Chantries, fetch me some clothes and drive me home tomorrow morning.'

Juliet frowned. 'I don't think you should do that—I'd advise you to—'

'I didn't ask for your advice!' he bit out, and she fell silent.

In any other circumstances, she would have yelled back at him, told him not to give her orders or snarl at her, but she couldn't shout back at a man who looked the way he did. She had never seen him looking ill, or, in fact, even under the weather. She found it deeply disturbing. Until this moment, if anyone had asked her what sort of man Simeon Gerard was, she wouldn't have hesitated to say, tough, impervious to most human feelings, and even dangerous, if you crossed him. She lowered her lashes and studied him uncertainly through them, tracing the weariness in the way his body lay, slack and still, under the white hospital bedcover, noting the taut white line around his mouth, the way his hands clenched on the sheet. Simeon might not have been burned in the fire, but something disastrous had happened to him—or was this just the effects of shock? But shock could be dangerous, couldn't it? she anxiously reminded herself. Simeon shouldn't leave hospital unless his doctor agreed, she was sure of that.

'Well?' he impatiently grated, lifting his black head from the pillow in an angry movement. 'Will you do as I ask, or won't you?'

She looked up and their eyes met; hers blue, nervous, uncertainly shifting, his a hard, silvery grey. Juliet felt her stomach plunge with painful feeling, a love she could barely conceal, and to distract him from discovering her secret she hurriedly nodded and said, 'Yes, if you insist.'

He gave a little sigh, his head fell back against the pillow and his hands unclenched from the sheet. He closed his eyes, his black lashes lying against the pallor of his cheeks. 'Come around eleven—the specialist will have seen me by then, and I may have permission to go home.'

He didn't add that whatever the specialist said he was

going home, but Juliet was left in no doubt about that. She had no time to try again to persuade him against it because just then a nurse walked up to them with a rattling tray, gave her a polite smile and said, 'I'm sorry, but Sister says could you go now? It's lunchtime, and we don't allow visitors at mealtimes.'

Juliet got up. 'Yes, of course—' she began, but before she could move Simeon's hand shot out and grabbed her wrist in an iron lock.

She looked down, her lips parted on a silent intake of air, and his grey eyes glittered up at her. 'Don't forget!'

She nodded, and his hand fell back, leaving her free. She huskily said, 'Well, I'll see you tomorrow, then.' Inside, she ached to kiss him, to smooth the line of pain away from that taut male mouth, but Simeon had closed his eyes again and seemed to have forgotten she existed, so she turned to go, giving the watching nurse a polite smile.

The other girl gave a little chuckle, her eyes dancing with mischief. 'It's OK, you can kiss him, don't mind me!'

Juliet flushed a little and gave Simeon a startled look, finding his grey eyes open again, fixed on her face with a sardonic irony in them that made her stiffen.

It would have been embarrassing to walk away after that; the nurse knew she was Simeon's wife and must have been surprised to see her about to leave without kissing him. Juliet saw she had no option, so she bent quickly to kiss his cheek, but Simeon moved faster. His head shifted on the pillow and her lips touched his mouth instead. He put a hand up to clasp her head and hold it in place while his mouth moved hotly against hers, then he let her go and Juliet shot upright again, her lips trembling and her pulses beating wildly.

She briefly met his eyes, saw the mockery in them, and turned stumbling away. 'Well...bye...' she muttered.

'See you soon, darling,' Simeon called after her, but she didn't look back. He had been tormenting her deliberately, knowing she couldn't do anything about it. She was angry and humiliated, but helpless, and that amused Simeon even more. She heard him laughing as she turned the corner into the main ward and her teeth met.

She passed the sister as she left the ward and the other woman asked her, 'How did you think your husband looked, Mrs Gerard?'

'Not at all well,' Juliet said. 'He's talking of leaving hospital tomorrow—is that advisable?'

'I wouldn't say it was likely that Mr Stephens, the consultant, who will be seeing him tomorrow, would send him home so soon,' the sister answered warily.

It was impossible, of course, to warn her that Simeon intended to leave, with or without the specialist's permission. Juliet knew he would kill her if she betrayed his conficence, and, anyway, she couldn't conspire against him with the hospital authorities, however much she might disagree with what he was planning.

The ward sister was watching her expression, her smile wry. 'Don't worry, Mrs Gerard, men are always restless and uneasy in hospital.'

Juliet met her eyes, wondering if she knew Simeon's intentions, and the sister calmly said, 'I'm sure Mr Stephens will persuade him to be patient.'

'I hope so,' Juliet said, without much optimism. The other woman did not know Simeon very well if she imagined he was easy to persuade.

Leaving the hospital, she found herself driving in a gentle sunshine through poignantly familiar winding country lanes whose hedges were just coming into leaf. Every turn in the road brought back another memory, and she began to feel unreal. Time slipped backwards in her head. She was a girl, again, suffering the pangs of first love and having no idea how to deal with it.

She would soon reach Chantries. Her stomach plunged with sick reaction to the idea. She had never thought she would see it again. It was crazy to think of going there. He must have someone looking after the house, who could take him his clothes, drive him home. It didn't have to be her.

Yet she kept on driving, as though unable to turn back to London, and safety. Here and there beneath the hedges she glimpsed buttery pale primroses among the grass, spring was well under way in this milder weather, she thought, her eyes following a blackbird taking off from a field with nesting material in his beak: straw and twigs and moss. He had gathered too much, his flight was unsteady and she kept expecting him to crash land, but he vanished into some trees.

She wished it wasn't spring; it made her feel restless, frustrated. But it was more than that, she admitted to herself. Spring was a lovely time of year; the air was warmer, the light more brilliant. It was a time to be happy, not to ache with pain as she did.

Simeon bewildered her, baffled her. Why, if he seriously wanted her to go back to him and give him a child, hadn't he followed her to London when she'd fled from the cottage? Why hadn't he been in touch with her since, either?

He had come down to the cottage in a mood of overbearing determination, so set on getting his own way that she had almost given in—what had happened to change his mind? She couldn't believe that he had found Adam a threat. She had seen no sign of it. In face-to-face confrontation Simeon had been very sure of himself, coolly derisive. It had been Adam who had lost control of his temper without making any impact on Simeon, not the other way around.

She bit her lip, angry with herself for her own contradictory feelings. She had run away, had told herself she wanted to get away, yet all the time she had expected him to follow her; she had been on edge day and night because he hadn't. She ought to make up her mind what she did want, not vacillate back and forth.

She was still arguing with herself when she crested a hill and got her first sight of Chantries, the spring sunshine lingering on warm red brick, great decorated chimneys, uneven, faded tiles, rows of high sash windows. Even from this distance the house pulled at you, beckoning like an alluring hand. It was not one of those houses built to be a stately home, to impress and overawe. Chantries had been intended to be a family home, welcoming its master back from hunting on winter evenings, or from work on the farm, or guests coming to dine or stay. The chimneys told of huge fireplaces in which logs would burn with a crackle, of shadowy, comfortable rooms with shutters at the windows and lamps glowing when night fell.

The house lay within a small park: a sea of green turf on which she could see sheep grazing. A few oaks and elms were scattered around the park, in summer making dark pools of shadow where the sheep lay when the sun was high. Beyond the park stretched the woods, which her father patrolled, but Juliet's eyes were drawn towards the little orchard she could just glimpse at the back of the house, and beyond that to the cottage where she had been born and grown up, and which was still her father's home.

She had never forgiven her father for what happened that night, in the orchard, for the expression on his face, the cruel things he had said to her. The last thing she wanted was to see him.

If he knew that she had arrived, out of the blue, at Chantries, what would he do? Ignore the news? Carefully avoid her? Or would he come to the house to see her?

Her pale mouth moved in a cynical curve. No, not that. Her father was a man who didn't forgive or forget. He wouldn't want to see her again. If she kept out of his way, he would keep out of hers, she could be sure of that.

She drove through the open decorated iron park gates, with their elaborate scroll-work set around linked initials, a finely wrought 'G' for Gerard and 'R' for Robert, the initials of the eighteenth-century Gerard who had had the gates made. From there the drive wound up to the house, flat turf on either side. Juliet drove slowly, staring at the upper floor and seeing for the first time visible evidence of the fire: charred and blackened window-frames, the smoke-darkened red brick around them. A tarpaulin had been erected inside the glass-less window, to keep out the weather, so that it was impossible to glimpse the interior of the room and see what damage had been done internally.

She parked on the gravel in front of the house, got out and looked uncertainly at the great oak front door. It was the original one: massive, studded with iron, with tongues of thick iron running across it from each hinge. Bolted inside, it would withstand a battering-ram.

She stared at it, at the blind windows, and felt panic flood through her. She couldn't go through with it. She couldn't go into that house. She had to get away.

She was about to get back into her car when she heard footsteps grate on the gravel and swung around just as her father came round the corner of the house.

Juliet went white with shock, and Jack Newcome

stopped dead, his head lowered and his body as tense as that of a bull about to charge. They stared at each other without moving or speaking for what seemed an eternity.

Her eyes were dazedly taking in impressions, though, realising all sorts of things that startled and confused her. He had aged more than she had expected, for a start. His hair was quite white, his shoulders had a heavy stoop, he had lost a lot of weight, almost shrunk. He's an old man! she thought, with a stab of shock.

Jack Newcome was staring at her, too, his grizzled brows drawn in a frown that was incredulous.

'Juliet?' His voice was low and rough, as if he didn't quite believe his eyes. 'Is that you?'

'Yes,' she said huskily. 'How are you, Father?' The name came out instinctively, but with a blurred sound.

Her father moved closer, slowly, still staring. 'You… you're so different…'

'I'm eight years older.' It was only to be expected that she would have changed a great deal—after all, she had been a teenager when she'd run away. Now she was a full-grown woman. But she hadn't expected her father to change so much. He had seemed to her to stay the same all through her childhood and adolescence—he had hardly altered, except inwardly, even when her mother had left. Jack Newcome had become bitter, had hardened, turned in on himself, after that. But physically he had stayed the same: a man toughened by years of outdoor life, muscled, wiry, very fit. Now, though, he was no longer the man he had once been.

He came to a standstill, right in front of her, and she realised that they were almost the same height, which startled, if not shocked her. He had once seemed to tower over her. Now she could look straight into his eyes.

'What are you doing here, Juliet?'

'I heard the news on the radio…about the fire, Simeon—' she began in a confused voice and her father's face darkened, his mouth twisting.

'Oh, I see! And you came to find out if you were a wealthy widow, I suppose! Well, you can stop hoping, because—'

'Stop it, Father!' she angrily interrupted. 'I came because I was so scared when I heard, I was afraid Sim might die, and I…'

She couldn't put into words, even to herself, but the truth of how she felt came out, clear and simple. Jack Newcome listened to it, his brows drawn, his face grim.

'If you care for him, why did you go away?'

'That's our business, not yours!' She was still angry, her head thrown back defiantly, and her blue eyes telling him without words that she was an adult now, not a child, and he had no right to bully or even question her.

'It was me who was left here after you'd gone, to face everyone!' he accused, scowling. 'Folk talked of nothing else for months. Everyone I met stared at me—oh, they pretended to be sorry for me, sweet as sugar to my face, but I knew they were all grinning and whispering behind my back. Nothing better to do, most of them. Kids, too, peering over hedges, or round trees at me, calling things, then runnng off!' He broke off, swallowing convulsively. 'First my wife runs off, then my child… Can you wonder they all thought it was my fault, I was to blame?'

She had hated him for years, had blamed him, thought it was all his fault, but a strange mixture of pity and regret made her say gently, 'No, it wasn't your fault, Father. I ran away from Simeon, not you. He knows why I ran away—it had nothing to do with you.'

Jack Newcome fixed his eyes bleakly on her face. 'Then why haven't you been in touch with me since?'

'I'm sorry—I was unhappy, I just wanted to forget...' She made a sweeping gesture that took in the house, the grounds, him. 'Everything! I closed the door because I couldn't bear to remember.' She gazed into his eyes, a look of pleading on her face. 'You can understand that, can't you, Father?' His marriage had been a disaster, and he had had to survive its break-up somehow. He hadn't gone away physically, but she remembered how he had been during the years when she was growing up, and she knew that he had gone away in spirit, closed the door on everyone around him, including her.

Jack Newcome stood very still, his eyes blank as they stared at her, and for a moment she thought he would reject her appeal for sympathy, then a deep sigh shook him and he nodded. 'Yes, I can understand...'

It was the first time they had ever talked as adults, made any sort of real connection, and the surprise of it made them look away, falling silent. Juliet bit her lip and looked through her lowered lashes at him, not sure what to say now. The one thing about him that was familiar was his clothes; he still wore his rough, shabby old tweed jacket, a faded khaki shirt, which as a child she had imagined he wore because it reminded him of his time in the army, his worn corduroy trousers, the wide leather belt around the waist. Now, though, they all hung on him; the body inside them had withered, and she felt a prick of tears behind her eyes. She didn't know this man, had never known him, and soon it would be too late.

Huskily, she said, 'I've been to the hospital. I saw Simeon, he sent me here...he told me you saved his life...'

'Nothing of the kind!' her father gruffly interrupted. 'I just happened to notice the fire before it got a hold. Some local reporter was here an hour or two back, trying to build it up into something heroic, but all I did was wake Sim up.'

'He thinks he wouldn't have woken up,' she said, smiling at him. 'He thinks he would be dead now if it wasn't for you.'

'Nonsense!' Jack Newcome had gone a little red and was scowling again. He was a brave man who hated to have his courage talked about. He had never been one for talking much. He spent his days mostly alone, out in the open, with animals and birds for company, and had little contact with his own kind, which was how he apparently liked it, but Juliet watched him, wondering if that was now as true as it had once been. There were lines of loneliness in his face, a bleakness in his eyes. He was an old man now and he was always alone.

Shrugging, he changed the subject. 'Are you going to stay at Chantries while you're here?'

'He asked me to come and collect his clothes,' she said and her father exclaimed in surprise.

'They're never sending him home so soon! He was in a bad way. when I dragged him out of that room.'

She hid a smile at that admission of his courage in saving Simeon from the fire.

'I doubt if the hospital will approve, but he's determined to come home, whether they like it or not.'

'The fool!' muttered Jack Newcome and Juliet laughed shortly.

'You know Simeon.'

'Oh, I know him—stubborn as a mule and twice as stupid! Can't you talk him out of it?'

'I tried, but he just yelled at me to do as I was told and bring him his clothes. I suppose they weren't all burnt in the fire?'

Her father shook his head. 'Not so far as I know! All

the furniture that wasn't ruined has been moved into the next room—only the stuff on the side of the room where the fire started was badly damaged.'

'What caused the fire?'

'The electric wiring—it's as old as the hills, it all needs replacing.' He looked at her uncertainly. 'Are you nervous of staying overnight in case another fire breaks out? Maybe you had better sleep on the ground floor—the housekeeper had a little suite of rooms next to the kitchen, and the wiring in that was done when the suite was modernised. You'll have to make up a bed for yourself, I'm afraid.'

'No need, I'll probably go to a hotel,' she said, nervous of even entering the house, and he frowned.

'Why pay good money when you can stay here for free? After all, you're Sim's wife—you've the right, I'm sure he must have meant you to...'

'Maybe he did, but I don't think I can face a lot of stares and questions! I suppose he has a housekeeper?'

'There was one, but after his father died Simeon told her he didn't need her any more, as there was just him in the house. Now, he has a woman from the village come in on weekdays, to clean and cook for him, but she went an hour ago, when she'd done all she could in his bedroom—so there's nobody here to ask questions or be curious, don't worry.' He turned towards the front door, producing a bundle of keys from his pocket. 'I have the key, I can let you in.'

Juliet felt very odd as she stepped over that threshold again, for the first time in eight years. The whole weight of the past seemed to descend upon her shoulders.

She almost cried out against all those bitter memories, and then the sun shone past her into the old, shadowy, panelled hall, revealing the beauty she had forgotten. The sunken red-flagged floors shining with years of loving polish, the high beamed roof, the great stone fireplace in which stood a tall vase of spring flowers, their scent sweet on the air, and she realised that somehow she was free of the guilt and resentment and misery she had been carrying around for so long.

CHAPTER NINE

'IF YOU'RE determined to be foolish, I can't stop you,' the ward sister said coldly. 'But I must warn you—'

'I've had all the warnings! Skip the repeat dose and show me where to sign.' Simeon's tone was firm enough to silence the woman, whose lips set thinly before she pushed a form at him, silently indicating where he should put his signature.

Juliet stood beside him, flushed, very conscious of the sister's irritated, reproachful gaze. Nobody had noticed the case she'd carried into the ward; Simeon had taken the clothes and vanished into a bathroom to re-emerge fully clothed in grey trousers and a thick blue roll-necked sweater which gave his grey eyes a warmer colour. He was still pale, the burns on his cheek angry-looking, but dressed he seemed much more himself, almost normal.

'My father chose those for you,' she had told him. 'He could have brought them here, too. You didn't need me.'

'I'll decide what I need,' he had said casually, and her colour had risen. She fought with her stupid feelings, terrified of him seeing and understanding them, but she needn't have bothered. He wasn't there to observe her. He was already going, walking away through the ward and startling the young nurse who was giving out pills to some other patient. Her mouth had dropped open, and she had squeaked after him, 'Oh! Mr Gerard…what…where…?'

Juliet had scuttled after his long-legged, striding figure and tried not to think about what he had just said. He might 'need' her to have his child, but that was a purely material necessity; it wasn't the sort of need she felt for him.

Sister had barred their way, astonished and furious at seeing him fully dressed, and had begun a long argument with him that Simeon had just ended in a peremptory tone. She had tried to draw Juliet into the discussion, but Simeon had said curtly, 'Leave my wife out of this! She just did what I told her.'

Juliet had been glad to stay out of the squabble, but she had been on the ward sister's side, although she'd said nothing. Simeon had no business leaving hospital so early; he couldn't possibly be fit enough. She knew him too well to try to argue with him, however, so she tried to look quietly submissive, no ally for the sister's defeated army, and got a scornful glance from the other woman for her pains.

The necessary form signed, they walked out of the hospital to where Juliet had parked her car. Simeon made for the driver's seat but Juliet slipped past him at the last moment, her hand seizing the door-handle, her chin up in defiance.

'I'll drive, thanks. It *is* my car.'

He considered her expression, his eyes speculative. 'If you insist!' he said at last.

'I do.' She unlocked the door, pushed the empty suitcase into the back and got behind the wheel, slightly unsteady after that little confrontation, but triumphant, too, because she had won, he had backed down. It had been a very minor victory, but it was a victory, all the same.

Simeon slid into the seat next to her, stretching his long legs with a sigh. 'You don't know how glad I am to get out of that place!'

'I expect they're glad to see you go, even though they

felt duty-bound to try to stop you,' Juliet said, starting the engine. 'You aren't exactly the ideal patient.'

He was watching her, his head turned sideways against the back of the seat, and she found his stare unnerving, wondering what he was thinking. 'What happened with your father?' he asked quietly at last.

'We talked.' There was no way she could explain to anyone what had happened when she met her father again; it had been unexpected and disturbing to realise that they were in a sense meeting for the first time, two total strangers. Eight years had made such radical changes in them both; she had come to maturity and her father had grown old. Time had burnt away their differences, resolved all their anger. They had come to terms with themselves, and the past, and with all that out of the way they had been free to get to know each other at last.

'Well, well,' Simeon drawled. 'Who would have thought it?'

'Thought what?' She knew what that amazed tone meant, but she kept her eyes on the road, watching a little white sports car which had come up behind her out of nowhere and was trying to pass her in spite of the zigzag bend just ahead which made the manoeuvre both dangerous and stupid.

'I'm not quite sure, actually,' Simeon murmured thoughtfully. 'Does it mean that you've really grown up—or that your father has finally seen some sense?'

'Both, maybe,' she conceded, a half-smile curving her mouth.

'And how does it feel?' he enquired, and she considered her reply a moment.

'Disconcerting.'

He laughed. 'I'm sure.'

The white car shot past with a roar of tyres and a snarl

of acceleration, and narrowly missed being flattened by a juggernaut bearing down on it from the other direction. The juggernaut blared angrily, the sports car hooted back, and then both disappeared, leaving the road to Juliet's car.

She whistled under her breath. 'I really thought he'd had it, the crazy idiot.'

'It was a woman,' Simeon said.

'You weren't even looking at the car! That's pure male chauvinism.'

'No, it's observation,' he said, his smile infuriating. 'I recognised the car. She lives near Chantries. Andrea Jameson; she works as a freelance designer and goes up to London quite often.' He slipped Juliet a sidelong glance. 'A very sexy little blonde, too. I'd bet on it that every male for twenty miles has noticed her.'

'Well, if she always drives like that she won't live long,' Juliet snapped, angrily aware of a jealous ache behind her ribs. How many women had there been in his life since she'd left? Eight years was a long time. He wasn't the celibate type, either. He had too fierce a sex drive. Were any of the women still around, was he seeing anyone? In many ways, he was a stranger to her—she knew almost nothing about him or his private life, although he had been her husband now for eight years.

'Which bedroom did you use at Chantries?' he asked, breaking into her thoughts, and she jumped so violently that she lost control of the steering-wheel. The car swerved across the carriageway, and a car coming towards them angrily sounded its horn.

Juliet dragged on the wheel, righting the car, and drove on, very flushed and furious with herself.

She darted a look at Simeon, who was heavy browed, and snapped, 'Don't say a single, solitary word!'

'OK, just stop the car,' he said grimly.

'Don't be ridiculous. What are you going to do, hitch a lift?'

'I'm driving the rest of the way, Juliet. I want to get there in one piece.'

'You can forget that!' she said, putting her foot down, half afraid he would grab the wheel. The car leapt forward and Simeon's frown deepened, but he couldn't risk a fight over control of the car while they were doing that speed, so he had to sit there, glowering at her, his long, lean body poised and menacing whenever she glimpsed it out of the corner of her eye.

Ten minutes later they pulled up outside Chantries and Simeon slid out of the passenger seat, came round and opened the driver's door and caught hold of her arm with iron fingers.

'Get out of there!'

She got out but dragged herself free of his grip. 'Don't manhandle me!'

'You risked both our lives!' he accused, and she knew it was true, but she certainly wasn't admitting it to him. The hostility she felt burnt like a fire in peat; deep and slow and unreachable. Her blue eyes smouldered with it and Simeon stared down into them, his face taut.

'You shouldn't have made me jump like that, shouting at me!' she muttered and his mouth twisted.

'I didn't shout. I spoke quite quietly, in fact. That wasn't what made you so jumpy, and you know it. We both know it. Just being alone with me in a car makes you as nervous as hell—do you want me to tell you why?'

'I know why! Because I hate the sight of you!' She got the keys to the house, which her father had given her the previous evening, out of her purse, and offered them to Simeon. 'Here, you let yourself into the house. I'm going.'

'Still running away, Juliet?' His grey eyes glittered

scornfully and she bit into her inner lip, forcing herself to calm down, to sound perfectly confident. She must not let him see any sign of weakness, of uncertainty; he would seize it and use it to his own advantage.

'I have to get back to London—I want to see my mother and stepfather when they arrive there,' she said in a quietly rational voice. 'They flew home last night, but I haven't been able to get in touch with them yet, and we have a lot to discuss.'

'So do we!'

She shook her head, somehow managing a little smile. 'We've said all we had to say, Simeon. I don't want to...' She broke off, a jab of alarm hitting her, as he closed his eyes and swayed back against the car, his skin very pale. 'Sim!' she said, her arm going round him to support him. 'What is it? Do you feel faint?'

He leaned on her, the weight of his lean, muscled body quite surprising, and murmured incoherently. 'Mmm...'

She looked around in desperation, in the hope of spotting her father, or the woman from the village who worked in the house and who had arrived that morning just as she was leaving, but there was no sign of anyone around.

'Can you walk to the house, if I help you?' she asked him, wondering if she should get him back into the car and drive him back to the hospital.

He seemed to force his eyes open, his body still heavy against her. 'What? Oh, yes, I think so.'

'Maybe I ought to drive back to the hospital!' she thought aloud, not knowing quite what to do.

'No, I'll be fine soon, I'm better already,' he said, and he was beginning to look better, it was true, so she slowly guided him towards the house, took the keys he limply held, and unlocked the front door. Simeon managed to stagger, with her help, into the sitting-room and collapse

on to a couch. He still had an arm around her, and somehow he managed to pull her down, too. She was startled
by that, a little gasp escaping her, and was too late to stop
herself tumbling down beside him. He took her unawares;
for a moment she didn't understand, her blue eyes wide
and confused as she stared up at him.

It was she who was lying on the couch—it should be
Simeon, but he was leaning over her, and she couldn't
fathom how that had happened. Only as his hands pressed
her down among the cushions on the couch did it begin to
dawn on her.

She searched his face, suspicion now a certainty. The
weak, helpless look had completely vanished. This was the
face she knew only too well, the hard, determined face of
the man who had wrecked her life once before already and
was apparently intent on doing it again.

'You aren't feeling faint at all!' she accused him, flushing to her hairline.

Simeon watched her back with a mockery that made her
feel like screaming.

What a fool she had been! Hadn't she learnt by now
never to trust him an inch? He wasn't ill. He hadn't been
feeling faint; it had all been acting. It had all been a trick
to get her into the house, on to this couch, all alone here
with him, and it had worked perfectly.

'I wasn't standing outside my own house arguing the
point with you,' Simeon said, quite unashamed of his
cheating.

'You lied to me!'

'I didn't tell you anything! I shut my eyes and leaned
on you and you jumped to conclusions.'

'You meant me to!'

'I had to talk to you. You were going to run away again,
and I couldn't let you.'

'I am not making some cold-blooded bargain with you just so that you can keep Chantries and I can make some money. I don't need money that much. I don't need it at all.'

'And I don't need Chantries,' he said in a deep, harsh voice, making her eyes widen in shock and disbelief.

'What do you take me for?' she burst out, trembling with rage, white with it. 'What sort of fool do you think I am, if you imagine I'm going to believe that for one instant!'

'I'm more of a fool than you are,' he said, his smile bitter with a self-derision that made her wince. 'If I wasn't I would have come after you when you drove off with your London boyfriend. I'd have crashed into your flat, beaten the living daylights out of him, and dragged you off down here by the hair and made you give me what I wanted!'

'Nothing would have made me!' she furiously insisted.

His eyes were wry. 'Be honest with yourself. You know I could have got you into bed, and I wouldn't have had to use force.'

She went crimson, her lips parted to shout a denial at him but no words came out; she was unable to lie but not prepared to make any dangerous admissions.

She didn't need to; he read her expression and smiled crookedly. 'Yes. You and I have always felt that attraction, haven't we? Our minds may not always understand each other, but our bodies seem to. But I didn't follow you, because I was paralysed—just as I was when you ran out on me the first time.'

She seemed to stop breathing, she couldn't swallow, her mouth dry and her ears deafened. What did he mean? Was this another lie, another scheme to make her weaken, give in to him?

'The morning after our wedding, when I woke up and found you gone, it was like being pole-axed,' he said slowly, grimacing. 'At first, I was going to go after you. I wanted to get you back, and I felt like a swine after the way I'd treated you the night before. I knew why you had run. Of course I did. And I felt as guilty as hell—'

'You were!' she muttered, and he didn't argue, just frowned, nodding.

'Yes—I was old enough to know better, I have to take all the blame. But it was more complicated than that. I sat in my car arguing with myself for hours, in a country lane a few miles away, trying to make up my mind what to do, but there was something holding me back, stopping me from moving. It wasn't just the guilt, or the anger, it was worry over you. You were so young, too young to realise what marriage meant.'

'I knew what it meant! I was young, yes, but not that young!' she said huskily. 'That wasn't what made me run away. You've admitted it yourself—you drove me away, you were never in love with me! You hated me. You wanted to hurt me, you were furious with me because you felt you had been forced to marry me.'

'I was angry because we had been forced into a shotgun marriage,' Simeon said roughly. 'I didn't think you were old enough, or in any way ready, for a real marriage.'

'You didn't want to marry me at all!' she cried out, the deeply embedded hurt of it in her blue eyes.

'I hadn't thought of marriage,' he admitted in a heavy, reluctant voice. 'That's true. For heaven's sake, you were a schoolgirl! I was feeling guilty enough because I knew I wanted you like hell and you were just a kid. I kept telling myself to keep my hands off you, but you had other ideas, and I lost my head every time you came close to me. Have you any idea how much that made me despise myself? I tried to stay away from you, but I couldn't, you were the sexiest thing I've ever seen. Sweet seventeen and dying to be kissed, and I was dying to be the one to do the kissing. Only I was no teenager, and a few kisses weren't enough for me. Once I started touching you, I wanted more. I wanted everything. And it made it worse that I soon realised you wanted it, too. You were damnably erotic, Juliet; sensual and sweet and generous—and you drove me wild.'

She had begun to shake, her whole body aching with desire and a wild, uncertain hope. If he meant it…if he loved her… But he hadn't mentioned love, had he? He had talked about wanting her, about passion, never love.

'Then it all exploded around me,' he grimly said. 'And I had to make a choice there and then—what else could I do but say I'd marry you? I hadn't had the time to be certain that was what I wanted, but it had crossed my mind now and then that one day…maybe…when you were older, and knew for sure you wanted me, we might get married. On the other hand, you might fall out of love with me in a month or two. I guessed you were just infatuated with me.'

He looked down into her blue eyes and Juliet hid their expression by letting her lashes droop. She wasn't sure how she had felt eight years ago; whether the explosive mix inside her had been pure chemical reaction, teenage infatuation, or real love. She knew what she felt now—her love for him was tearing her apart—but she wasn't going to let Simeon guess that.

'That was all it was, wasn't it, Juliet?' he asked in a quiet voice and she answered, still without meeting his eyes.

'I suppose so…' Then she looked up at him. 'We should

just have been to bed together and made sure we didn't get caught.'

His mouth twisted. 'That was just the trouble—I couldn't do that, either, not to you. You meant too much, and that's why I lost control on our wedding night. No excuse, I know. I regretted it bitterly next day, but I was full of rage because I felt trapped and yet I still wanted you, even though I blamed you and your father. I didn't mean to hurt you, I meant to be gentle, to make that first time easy for you, but once I started making love to you it all got out of hand.'

'You frightened me!' she broke out. 'I hadn't expected it to hurt, nobody had told me…what it would be like…' She had had no mother to talk to, and what she had learnt in school had been a mix of boring sex lessons with drawings she couldn't quite follow and found ugly, and the half-baked versions whispered by friends. Her confused emotions about Simeon hadn't seemed to have any connection with all that.

'I know,' he gently said, frowning. 'Do you think I hadn't realised that? You were so young, I should never have…' He broke off, sighing. 'But I lost my head. I wanted you too much, Juliet, I couldn't keep myself on a lead once I'd started to touch you, but when I woke up and found you gone I knew what I'd done and I felt sick. That was why I didn't follow you and make you come back. If I had, we might both have been hurt a damn sight more. I had to let you go then, to find yourself, to grow up—and so I went home and my father rang your mother to find out if you were there. Once we knew you were safe, I settled down to wait. I thought that if you had any real feeling for me you would be back. At first, I thought it would just be months, at most a year or so—and then as time passed I had to admit you were never coming back and I almost hated you.'

'I could see that, when you turned up down in Cornwall,' she said with a wry grimace. 'And there was no almost about it. You hated me, especially after your father died and you read his will.' She looked into his grey eyes, searching them for the truth. 'And that's what this is all about now, isn't it? Chantries. You said a few mintues ago that you didn't need Chantries, but that isn't true. You love the place, you always have, and you'd do anything to get it.'

'No,' he said curtly.

'Oh, I think so!' Her face was bitter with accusation and distrust.

'When I said I didn't need Chantries, I meant every word!' Simeon bit out. 'I may have talked cold-bloodedly, down in Cornwall, but do you really believe I'd have forced you to sleep with me, have my baby, if I thought you hated the idea? After I read the will I was blazingly angry, it's true. I·thought about it, and it occurred to me that, whatever else you might have got up to since I last saw you, you hadn't got married again. You were still my wife. That was when the idea hit me. I couldn't lose anything by seeing you, telling you the terms of the will. You might even come back to me. Eight years was a long time—I thought it was worth trying, and...' His mouth twisted. 'And I wanted to see you again. As soon as I'd started thinking about it, I liked it more and more, especially after I'd tracked you down in Cornwall and realised you were ten times sexier and lovelier than you had ever been. And I thought you were attracted to me, too.'

He was watching her closely, eyes narrowed, but Juliet evaded his gaze, looking down, her lashes brushing her flushed cheek.

He sighed, and said, 'Well, then the other guy turned up, and you ran out on me again, for the second time, and knocked me for six. I thought it meant I'd got it completely wrong; you didn't give a damn for me. It looked as if you preferred the other guy, after all. I found it hard to believe, but then women are baffling creatures—they seem to pick the oddest men. I wasn't running after you, just to get slapped in the face again—my pride wouldn't let me. I went back to Chantries to lick my wounds and got in touch with my solicitor, told him I wanted him to start divorce proceedings at once.'

She stared up at him, hardly breathing.

'You did?'

He took the quesiton for disbelief, and snarled at her. 'Yes, I did!'

'OK, OK,' she said mildly. 'No need to shout!'

'Then stop querying everything I say!' His grey eyes glittered into hers, his face as hard as planed wood. 'Lawyers take their time, but your solicitor should hear from mine in a month or so.'

Her mouth was dry. If it was true, why had he done it?

Simeon's mouth indented. 'My solicitor thought I was mad, of course, knowing the terms of my father's will, and tried to talk me out of it, but I told him to mind his own business and get on with the job. By now he has probably begun the long drawn out process. It takes ages for a divorce to come through, you know.'

'Well, after eight years, who's in a hurry?' Juliet huskily said, and his eyes flashed in rage.

'Don't make jokes about it, damn you! I don't find any of this funny. I came back to Chantries feeling like death. Why do you think I didn't wake up when my room caught fire? I rarely drink these days—what happened on our wedding night cured me of drinking much—but the other night

I was going out of my mind. I couldn't sleep, couldn't think about anything but you, and I had to shut down somehow. I hit the whisky for a few hours, fell into bed and slept like the dead. That was why your father had to drag me out of the room.'

She had paled, biting her lip. 'Sim, I'm sorry—'

'Don't say that!' he said hoarsely, and then he swooped down on her, his lips clamping over hers, stifling the little cry she gave. Her mouth parted under the heated possession of that kiss—she couldn't fight him, or the sensual fire which he was lighting deep inside her body. Her arms went round his neck and she yielded, kissing him back hungrily, her fingers in his hair. His hand moved between them, slipped inside her shirt to find her warm flesh, softly caressed her breasts, making her shudder with desire.

It had been so hard to stop him, to run away from what she wanted desperately, but this time she knew she wouldn't stop him; this time, at last, she was going to let it happen. She loved him, she had loved him for years, ever since she had been a very young girl and not quite ready for love. Simeon was right; she had been too young. The overwhelming force of her own emotions had drowned her and she had been right to flee. He had been wise not to come after her, too. Love had come too soon. It had not been the right time for them. Now was their time, and she clung to him, her mouth igniting his desire while she moved against him wildly, restlessly, passion taking over her whole body.

When Simeon broke off that kiss, it almost sent her into shock, her blue eyes opening wide, startled, her bruised mouth parted in a cry of protest. She still clung to him, her hands dragging at his hair, trying to pull him down to her again, but he shook his head, his mouth wry with regret.

'No, darling. Not yet. We aren't being stampeded into it this time, not even by ourselves. We're going to start again, and do it properly—we'll get married again.'

'What?' She was half dazed with passion, and couldn't understand what he was saying. His grey eyes gleamed in sudden, warm amusement and he dropped a light kiss on her eyes.

'Wake up, darling! Don't you see? If we sleep together now, this minute, you'll start suspecting me again—you won't believe I want you, you'll think it was all for Chantries. But it isn't, Juliet.' His voice deepened, dark with a feeling which made her go weak. 'I love you. I don't know quite what I felt eight years ago: a pretty unstable mix of sexual attraction and affection, I think; but I do know it didn't die because you went away. It just smouldered on, right down inside me, and when I saw you again it burst into flames.'

She ran her fingers through his hair, smiling into his eyes, her lips trembling a little. 'Oh, Sim…I know…I felt exactly the same. I'd thought it was all over, and then there you were, and I was lost.'

He kissed her fiercely, held her close, murmuring husky words of passion. 'I want you so much, Juliet. You don't know—'

'I do,' she said, her voice shaky with laughter and desire. 'Oh, yes, I do…' She stroked his flushed face, feeling the heat in his skin and excited by that evidence of how he felt. 'Sim, when I think that it so nearly went wrong—you might have divorced me, we might never have met again, if your room hadn't caught fire!'

He laughed softly. 'Thank God it did! If there had been no fire, you wouldn't have come back here, and I would never have discovered that you did care!'

She gave a little shiver, frowning. 'Frightening, isn't it?'

Every time she thought about it she felt she was staring into a black abyss.

'I'm trying not to look too closely,' admitted Simeon, his expression grim. 'Such a narrow margin—between losing you, and being happy! But there was a fire, and you came. Maybe if you hadn't heard about the fire, fate would have come up with something else. Who knows? We have a second chance, that's all that matters—let's take it and this time make it work, Juliet. That's why I want to go through a second ceremony—this time we'll do it in church, have our marriage blessed. And we'll take a honeymoon somewhere romantic and start married life the right way.'

She loved the idea; she smiled, already working out what she would wear for the church blessing—not white, but a soft cream lace and silk dress she could wear again for parties. Her mind was busy, imagining it. She would insist that her mother and Giorgio came. Her father would have to meet his ex-wife again some time—once she and Simeon were living together, he couldn't ignore her mother when she visited, and once there were children Juliet knew she would need her mother around as often as possible.

A little frown caught her brows together. 'Sim…what am I going to do about my job?'

'We'll have to work something out, won't we?' he said without urgency, and she looked up at him and relaxed again, smiling.

There were going to be problems; they would work them out somehow, together. There would be a solution, and they would find it—she had no doubts about that, any more than she had doubts about Simeon's love for her. He had hit the nail right on the head when he'd said they were fated—it had always been meant that they should come together, and now that at last they had they would be able to make it work.

She'd never stopped loving him—
but could she trust him with her life?

MURDER BY THE BOOK

Margaret St. George

Chapter One

"Each of you has a reason to want me dead." Tillis Morgan smiled at each of the diners seated at the long table, then raised her wineglass in a salute to her abruptly silent weekend guests.

Meg Sandler heard her aunt's statement, but the words didn't penetrate. From the moment Meg had come downstairs and discovered Steven Caldwell standing beside the cocktail cart, she hadn't been able to think of anything else. First came the shock of seeing Steven; a rush of adrenaline sent her heart pounding. And then joy, sheer joy that forgave everything. She had actually rushed toward him, her heart in her eyes, before she spotted Suzanne Halverson standing at Steven's side and realized she was about to make a colossal fool of herself. At the last moment Meg had stopped short, had given Steven a cool nod as she veered toward the fireplace.

Now Steven was seated across the dinner table from her where it was almost impossible to avoid meeting his eyes. Biting her lip and beginning to feel frantic, Meg wondered how she could get out of this weekend. She was a writer, surely she could invent an excuse for leaving that Aunt Tilly would accept.

Ignoring Steven, she looked at Aunt Tilly seated at the

head of the table and resisted an urge to roll her eyes toward the shadows webbing the vaulted ceiling. Aunt Tilly was in fine form tonight, Meg noticed, from her needling comments to her flamboyant costume.

Tillis Morgan wore black, of course. It was her trademark. Meg assumed the funereal color was calculated to suggest mystery, or perhaps menace. Both befitted one of the world's premier mystery writers. Or perhaps Aunt Tilly always chose black to emphasize her creamy porcelain skin, still smooth and handsome at age fifty.

Whatever the reason, Tillis Morgan was famed for her unconventional attire. Tonight she wore a jet-black gown with a scattering of blood-red beads sewn onto the fabric. The beads formed a spider across her breast. With every movement, the spider expanded and glittered in the candlelight, appearing to reach for the black feather boa that alternately adorned Aunt Tilly's shoulders, arms or pale throat. Meg had no idea where Aunt Tilly purchased such singular gowns. She couldn't imagine there were hordes of women demanding feather boas, black crepe and beaded spiders.

"Really, Tillis," Candida Ripley said impatiently. Candida flicked her jeweled fingers in a gesture of annoyance. "Have you nodded off? We're all breathlessly awaiting the punch line."

Meg released a breath. It appeared she hadn't missed much by drifting into thoughts about Steven, not if the dinner company was waiting to hear a punch line. Because she sensed Steven watching her, she focused a determined smile on Candida.

Candida Ripley was no slouch herself when it came to flamboyant attire. Tonight she wore scarlet satin, which until moments ago had been covered by an iridescent feather cape that had to be seen to be believed. Ruby and amethyst flashed at her ears and throat; diamonds glittered on every finger. A feather plume swept up from the luxuriant mass of auburn hair gathered at her neck. Meg suspected Aunt Tilly was not pleased by the way the candlelight shimmered and glowed across her rival's scarlet satin bosom, drawing the eye to Candida and away from the head of the table.

"There is no punch line," Aunt Tilly said. With slow deliberation, she subjected each of her guests to an intense scrutiny as if she could read their minds if she applied herself diligently. "As I was arranging this board meeting it occurred to me that each of you would be pleased to see me in my coffin. Each of you will benefit when I die."

"What?" Meg jerked upright and a ripple of shock traveled down her spine. "You aren't joking," she realized aloud, forgetting Steven for the first time since she had discovered he was here. "Aunt Tilly, surely you can't think that I—"

"Well, dear, you are my principal heir. When I die you'll inherit all this." Tossing back the black feather boa, Tillis waved a hand to indicate Morgan's Manor and all its varied treasures. "Plus my research library, my notes and any works in progress. If something happened to me, you'd be a fool not to complete my current project, it's certain to be a bestseller."

Suzanne Halverson's blond head lifted and she narrowed her gaze on Meg. But everyone had turned to look at her. Meg was acutely conscious of Steven Caldwell's dark-eyed appraisal and felt a burst of heat color her cheeks. She would never have come to Colorado for the weekend if she had known Aunt Tilly had invited Steven and Suzanne.

"That isn't fair," she protested, leaning forward to see Aunt Tilly past the silver candelabra. "I didn't know I was your heir until this minute.'' The faces studying her registered polite disbelief. Not for the first time Meg cursed Aunt Tilly's eccentricities. It was just like Tillis Morgan to invite Meg and Steven for the same weekend. And trust Aunt Tilly to announce the contents of her will in the most dramatic fashion.

"I doubt Tillis's revelation can be much of a surprise," Candida drawled. "Even in her youth Tillis was too frigid and juiceless to have children of her own. She certainly isn't going to start producing them now. You're her only niece, Meg, therefore...plus you're a mystery writer, primed to follow in your aunt's faint footsteps." The candlelight falling from an old-fashioned chandelier gleamed on Candida's satin shrug.

Aunt Tilly's eyes narrowed. The mascaraed spikes of her lashes quivered like tiny black daggers. "How very like you to deduce the obvious, Candida. Perhaps this newfound facility with logic will improve your writing. I understand your latest book is such a bomb the distributors can't even give it away."

"That is a lie! You wish that were true because you're so jealous of me that you can't stand it!"

Dennis Parnham, seated on Meg's left, cleared his voice with a self-righteous sound. "*I* have no reason to wish you dead, Tillis." Dennis leaned closer to Meg so James, Aunt Tilly's manservant, could remove his soup bowl, then he shot his cuffs with a satisfied gesture.

"You smarmy slug," Candida hissed. The plume curving over her auburn hair trembled with intensity. Her eyes narrowed and blazed on Dennis Parnham. "You shouldn't even be here. Worms like you shouldn't be allowed membership in MAIMS."

"Need I remind you that MAIMS stands for Mystery Authors and Interested Mystery Supporters? I'm certainly interested in supporting the genre as my literary agency handles the top names in the field. I have as much right to a seat on the board as you do.'' He gave Candida a reproving look across the saltcellar and silver butter dish. "MAIMS isn't the problem, my dear. But let's resolve our little spat in private, shall we?''

"There's nothing to resolve. The instant I return to New York I intend to shop for a new agent!''

Although the exchange was embarrassing to everyone present, Meg listened with interest. She was also disgusted with Parnham and his practices and she, too, wanted a new literary agent. Eight months ago she would have solicited Steven's opinion, but now...how in the world was she going to endure this weekend?

"I'm sorry, darling. Your agency agreement is iron-clad.'' Smug was the right word for Dennis's smile. Everything about him projected an air of self-satisfaction, from his perfectly coifed silver hair to his exquisitely tailored Bond Street attire. "Take your agency contract to your attorney if you don't believe me. You won't be free to shop for agents, as you so charmingly put it, for another four years.''

Meg's heart sank. If Candida was stuck, then she thought it probable that she was, too. The prospect depressed her.

"For once you and I agree, Candida.'' Aunt Tilly aimed her salad fork at Dennis Parnham. "As for wishing me dead, Dennis...have you forgotten how you tricked me into signing an agreement that assigns you the copyright ownership of my first four books in the event of my death?'' Frowning, Aunt Tilly gestured to James to remove the salad plates.

"That's common practice, dear girl. Many agents—''

"That explanation worked years ago when I was young

and green, but I'm years beyond such swindles now. Everyone at this table knows reputable agents do not steal their client's work. I deeply regret that I didn't stop Meg before she signed with you.''

Meg also regretted that she hadn't sought Aunt Tilly's advice. She was tied to Dennis Parnham for another five years, paying a twenty-percent commission instead of the usual fifteen, and discovering just how miserable an agent could make a writer's life. She hadn't sought Aunt Tilly's advice because she didn't know her famous aunt all that well, didn't know if Aunt Tilly would welcome another mystery writer in the family and, stubbornly, she hadn't wanted to trade on her aunt's name or advice.

She should have swallowed her pride and telephoned Aunt Tilly the moment Parnham approached her. It would have spared her a great many problems and much frustration.

''Let's see now, where were we?'' Having grasped the possibilities for character assignation, Candida cheerfully returned to the topic at hand. The feather arching over her head dipped toward Meg. ''We know about you—with Tillis dead, you inherit everything. And with one of the contenders removed, you'd be a step closer to winning the mystery series assignment.''

Once again Meg was the center of attention, agonizingly aware of Steven and Suzanne watching her. Suzanne was unmistakably enjoying the sight of Steven's former lover being embarrassed in front of the dinner company, but Meg thought she glimpsed a look of sympathy in Steven's gaze.

The last thing she wanted was pity from Steven Caldwell. Her chin lifted. ''This is an idiotic discussion! I came here to attend a board meeting, not to...''

Then she noticed Aunt Tilly. Aunt Tilly was enjoying

the conversation enormously, leaning forward, beaming and smiling. It was Tillis who had set the pot to boil, stirring people up, playing one of her famous pranks. It was no accident that Aunt Tilly had assembled such a volatile group for the weekend. Tillis Morgan loved drama, adored potentially explosive situations.

Meg drew a breath, feeling outmatched. "You're also competing for the Macabre Series, Candida. You, too, would benefit if the list of contenders became shorter." She felt Aunt Tilly's amused approval as strongly as she felt Steven's steady gaze.

All evening it seemed that Steven had been trying to catch her attention. Meg exhaled slowly and wished she had stayed home in New York City. Aside from Aunt Tilly, she didn't care about any of these people. Seeing Steven again upset her. The bad weather made her nervous. And she didn't like the forbidding atmosphere of Morgan's Manor. Discovering she would one day inherit the house caused her more dismay than pleasure.

"I'd like to win the series assignment," Candida agreed pleasantly. "But we aren't talking about me. Everyone knows I loathe Tillis. We're discussing why all of *you* want to kill her."

Meg started. "No one said anything about wanting to kill—"

Candida tilted her wineglass toward Dennis Parnham. "You really are a slug, Dennis. Did I understand correctly? When Tillis goes to the big publishing house in the sky, you'll own her first four books? You stand to make a bloody fortune, don't you?"

Dennis Parnham smoothed back a wave of silver hair and cocked an eyebrow. "If anyone here wants to dance on dear Tillis's grave—" he nodded a faint apology toward Tillis who rewarded him with a thin smile "—it's you, Candida. You've always been jealous of Tillis. Plus, your sales *have* fallen off. Meg and Tillis aren't the only writers desperate to win the Macabre Series. You're counting on the series to revive your career.''

"You're fired, you toad! Do you hear me? Fired! I don't care what the attorneys say, I'll find a way!''

"Now, now,'' Tillis interjected when it appeared Candida might fling herself across the table at Dennis. "We all know manners aren't your strong suit, darling, but I really must insist that you don't throw yourself, your food or your utensils while dining at my table.'' To the others, she purred, "Lovers' spats can get so ugly, can't they?''

No one looked at Candida's husband, Howard Clancy. Everyone present was aware of the romantic attachment between Candida and Dennis, but it seemed churlish of Tillis to refer to it in front of Howard. An uncomfortable silence as thick as the deepening shadows spread through the room.

"You miserable no-talent bitch, Tillis.'' Candida's bosom heaved. "You can't stand to have an uneventful board meeting. You always manage to turn it into a dramatic fiasco because you don't know the meaning of the word professional. I didn't come here to be insulted. In fact, I can't imagine why I came at all!''

"You came because you lust after my position on the board and you hope to bludgeon the board into placing you on the new slate. You hate it that I'm president and you're not. You always want what I have.'' Enjoying Candida's outrage, Tillis waved her fingertips at James. "Please serve the prime rib.''

Howard Clancy, the man who had been married to both Tillis and Candida, raised his glass. He had refused the dinner wine and continued drinking undiluted Scotch. "I must take exception to Candida's statement that Tillis is a no-talent bitch. We all know Tillis is talented.'' Dennis Parnham was the only person who laughed at Howard's failed attempt to lighten the mood.

Meg thought the contrast between Howard Clancy and Dennis Parnham was striking. Dennis was suavely handsome; Howard, who was balding and overweight, was a pleasant man but only mildly attractive. Age and alcohol had blurred the good looks that had once captivated two of publishing's most beautiful and flamboyant mystery writers.

When Steven spoke, Meg lowered her head and pretended to examine her prime rib. Steven wasn't a member of the MAIMS board. She didn't know why Aunt Tilly had invited him.

''I think this conversation has gone far enough,'' he said quietly.

''Really?'' Candida leaned forward to glare at him. ''At the risk of offending my publisher who, by the way, has done nothing whatsoever to promote my new book, I'd like to learn why *you* want Tillis dead. Does it have anything to do with Caldwell Publishing's recent slump? Gossip has it that sales are down.''

''That's nonsense,'' Steven said. He glanced at Meg, then back at Tillis. ''I have no reason to wish you anything but a long life, Tillis.''

Tillis lifted an eyebrow. ''Aren't you forgetting a certain half-million-dollar life-insurance policy naming Caldwell Publishing as beneficiary?''

Dennis Parnham stared at Steven, then at Tillis. ''Whatever possessed you to take out a policy payable to your publisher?''

''I apologize,'' Steven said stiffly. ''I did forget.''

Candida's penciled brow soared toward the feather over

her hair. "You *forgot* a half-million-dollar life-insurance policy?"

"Fifteen years ago," Tillis explained to Dennis, "when Steven's father was president of the company, Caldwell Publishing was experiencing financial difficulties. I wanted to help out." She shrugged. "Brice Caldwell sold me five percent of the company's stock with the proviso that I would sell my shares back to the company at a later date for the same price I paid for them. Any dividends earned in the interim were, of course, mine. In the event that I died before the company recovered financially, I agreed to a life-insurance policy payable to Caldwell Publishing so the company would have the funds to redeem the shares."

"We should have bought back those shares years ago," Steven said, frowning.

"Your father tried, but I wouldn't sell them." Tillis smiled. "It's been a good investment."

"So," Dennis said, staring at Steven. "If Tillis dies, Steven gets half a million dollars to buy back shares now worth three times that much. Very nice."

Steven's expression of contempt eased when he looked at Tillis. "Why did you invite me, Tillis? I thought I was coming to Colorado to discuss the new book and the explosive revelation you promised. Now I'm not sure that's the entire reason."

For a fleeting instant his expression froze as if he had committed a blunder. A glance of dismay passed between Steven and Aunt Tilly, gone before Meg could be certain what she had seen.

"It appears this weekend was originally scheduled as a MAIMS board meeting," Steven continued smoothly. He nodded at Howard Clancy, then at Suzanne Halverson who had not spoken. "But since you've included guests who aren't members of the MAIMS board, perhaps you have something different in mind.''

"Isn't it obvious?" Tillis asked.

While everyone pondered what was supposed to be obvious, Meg studied the snow melting down the long gothic windows that lined the back wall of the dining room. Observing the worsening weather was preferable to looking at Steven, who seemed to be watching her whenever she risked a glance in his direction.

Damn him. The romance between herself and Steven Caldwell was as dead as a corpse. It shouldn't hurt this much to see him again. But it did.

Maybe she was just fooling herself. If it was really over, if Steven was out of her life and out of her heart, then why was the handsome sexy detective in her latest novel a dead ringer for Steven Caldwell? If Steven wasn't on her mind, then why had she created a detective who was tall, broad shouldered and athletic, with dark curly hair and chocolate eyes? Why had her heart flip-flopped when she walked down the staircase and saw him standing in Aunt Tilly's living room? Why did his deep baritone voice still send seductive shivers down her spine? Damn him.

She stared at the thickening snow and remembered things about Steven Caldwell that were better left forgotten. Like the thrilling pressure of his lips exploring hers. Like the night of passionate lovemaking when they celebrated her second book making the bestseller list. Like…

"I get it." Howard Clancy interrupted her reverie. "This weekend is a re-creation of the pivotal scene in *Murder at Eight*."

"Good boy." Tillis beamed.

"I wouldn't know." Candida tossed her head, sending the feather plume into spasms. "I don't read Tillis's trash.

I prefer mysteries where you can't deduce who did it on page ten.''

Even Tillis smiled at so patent a falsehood.

"Have you forgotten the complete set of Tillis Morgan's work in our library?'' Howard reminded her.

Candida shot him a look that dripped venom. "Those books belong to you, not me! A sentimental reminder of your ex-wife to hold over my head when you're mad at me.''

"*Murder at Eight* is the book where the main character assembles all his enemies on a Caribbean Island,'' Suzanne Halverson supplied. It was the first time she had spoken since they entered the dining room. She fixed a thoughtful look on Tillis. "One by one the host murders his guests.''

"That's correct,'' Aunt Tilly said, not looking at Suzanne.

"Good God.'' Howard Clancy's eyes widened. He tried to focus on the snowstorm building outside, considered aloud the excellent possibilities for being marooned in the storm. "Is that why you invited me, Tillis? To have your final revenge?''

"I'd say it's you who have cause to seek revenge,'' Tillis replied softly. "I made your life hell while we were married, then dragged your name through the tabloids during the divorce.''

"Let's not rehash old history, shall we? *Murder at Eight* is shot full of clichés.'' Candida sniffed and flicked a jeweled hand toward Meg. "If you haven't already, my dear, you will eventually write a novel where the suspects are marooned at an isolated site and corpses start dropping like flies. Agatha Christie did it, Tillis did it, even I did it. Of course *I* added a fresh twist.''

Tillis smiled. "Indeed. In your book the corpses fall like hippos, and the reader knows the murderer's identity on page two. But Suzanne has the right idea,'' she informed the table.

Meg frowned, her thoughts jumping to the plot of her work in progress. The book was set in an isolated station in the Australian outback. Perhaps she should rethink the story line. When she glanced away from the snow beginning to pile against the windowpanes, she noticed Steven's dark eyes twinkled with amusement as if he had guessed what she was thinking. Her chin rose and she swiveled toward Dennis Parnham.

"Oh?" Dennis asked lightly. "Then you intend to murder us all, Tillis? Did you poison the mousse?" He spoke with determined amusement, but he pushed his strawberry mousse to one side. Ignoring Tillis's disapproval, he twisted a cigarette into an ivory holder, lit it, then blew smoke toward the chandelier.

"Don't be silly," Howard Clancy said, digging his spoon into the mousse. "Poisoning would require Tillis to enter the kitchen." He winked and blew Tillis a kiss, pretending not to see Candida's murderous scowl. "Take it from a man who was once married to her—Tilly wouldn't recognize a kitchen if someone tied her to a stove."

"I'm flattered that at some point during our marriage you were sober enough to notice where I went or what I did," Tillis said.

"And with whom." The smile on Howard Clancy's lips turned sad. "Let's not forget that, Tilly. With whom."

"It's you who flaunted your infidelity, Howard. You and Candida popped in and out of bed practically under my nose."

"If it's any comfort to you, events have traveled full circle. Now it's my turn to play the jealous fool." Howard glanced at Dennis and Candida. A flush spread across Candida's high cheekbones, and Dennis developed a sudden interest in the ash growing on the end of his cigarette.

Meg cast a desperate glance toward the snow flying past the windows, wondering if Steven and the others felt as uncomfortable as she did. If this evening was any indication, the weekend was going to feel like a year.

Sneaking a peek at her watch, Meg wondered if she could concoct a decent excuse and escape immediately after the brandy. She'd need five minutes to pack her luggage, twenty minutes to drive down the mountain, an hour and a half for the drive to Denver. That would put her at Stapleton Airport in time to catch the red-eye flight to New York City.

She had to decide soon since the storm appeared to be gathering force. Wind hummed in the chimney, rattled the panes. Snow piled against the windows. If she didn't leave almost immediately, the eight-mile stretch of road from Morgan's Manor to Breckenridge would drift over and she'd be stuck.

Slowly, and skipping past Steven, her gaze moved around the table as she contemplated spending the weekend with these people.

She knew Candida Ripley from reading Candida's books and from having run into her in Dennis Parnham's office. They were both on the MAIMS board of directors. And they had both been invited to compete for the Macabre Series, a plum assignment that could revive Candida's career or boost Meg toward wider recognition and readership. Candida had wasted no time letting her know that Meg was an upstart of limited talent who should never have been a contender for the series in the first place.

Then there was Dennis Parnham, famed in mystery circles as an agent who routinely obtained lush advances for the writers he represented. Maybe he did so for established writers such as Candida, but he hadn't done much for Meg except make promises, request endless rewrites and offer lame explanations why he hadn't read her latest submission or sent her royalty checks yet. When she expressed frustration, Dennis offered a practiced smile, patted her shoulder in a condescending manner and reminded Meg that she was in her growth years. She needed to be patient.

Everyone in the industry knew Dennis and Candida were having an affair. A rather stormy affair if gossip could be believed. That's why Howard Clancy's presence at Morgan's Manor was such an awkward surprise. Aside from the relationship between Candida and Dennis—which appeared to be in one of the stormy periods—there was also the tension of ancient history. Meg felt the undertow of hostility flowing between Aunt Tilly, Candida and Howard. It was clear the others felt it, too.

Years ago, Candida had stolen Howard away from Aunt Tilly, whereupon Aunt Tilly had stolen him back again. But in the end, Candida won the prize: Howard. Afterward, murderesses appeared in each writer's books bearing remarkable resemblances to each other and a flurry of lawsuits had followed accompanied by lavish tabloid coverage. The tabloids pondered in gleeful headlines why the queens of mystery, both beautiful women, battled for the affection of a mild-mannered insurance salesman.

Howard became a figure of ridicule from coast to coast. In the end he lost his job, his pension and possibly his self-respect because of the publicity. Meg considered him with a degree of sympathy, wondering what on earth had induced Howard Clancy to return to Morgan's Manor.

Next, she straightened her backbone and studied Suzanne Halverson. If Meg had to describe Suzanne in a novel, she would have depicted her as the type of remote blond beauty who invariably attracted tragedy. Men often found such women irresistible. Perhaps it was their vulnerability, an image of being buffeted by unkind fate, the implied need for a safe haven and a protector. However one labeled the force, men seemed helpless before it; they felt compelled to rush to the rescue.

A year ago Suzanne's husband, Whitney Halverson, had been murdered. Whitney Halverson was found shot to death, slumped over the wheel of his Mercedes. Less than a week later, Suzanne's maid had committed suicide.

Naturally the double shocks had devastated Suzanne. And naturally Suzanne had turned to Whitney's friend, Steven Caldwell, for comfort. In the beginning, Meg had even encouraged Steven to spend time with Suzanne.

She lowered her head and looked away from Suzanne's blond perfection. And felt the scorch of jealousy.

When she glanced up Steven was watching her, wearing that same judgmental expression she knew so well. Anger flared in her eyes. How dare he judge her? Whatever they had together was over.

And yet… She gazed into his dark eyes and her body tightened and her breath quickened. The chemistry was still there even if the affection was not. Her gaze touched his firm wide lips and strong jawline, paused at his tie to imagine the hard muscled chest beneath his striped shirt.

She didn't need this. Biting her lip, Meg wrenched her gaze toward the head of the table and willed her thoughts to cool.

As soon as it was decently possible, she would leave. The other MAIMS board members could propose a slate of officers without her.

Howard Clancy finished his mousse and surrendered his empty dish to James. "Tillis, you really can be an annoying woman. Just what is so damned obvious?"

"You've let this silence go on so long that I've forgotten the question. If it was a question," Dennis Parnham complained.

"Tillis is about to solve the great mystery of why we're all here." Candida rolled her eyes. "Obviously we don't need Mrs. Halverson, Howard or Steven for a board meeting."

Tillis drew out the moment, enjoying the drama she had created. The beaded spider swelled across her breast. "I've received three death threats." She paused. "I have reason to believe one of you sent them."

They stared at her in silence.

The darkness in the room had deepened to the extent that when Tillis stood it was as if a disembodied head floated up from her chair. Pinpoints of candlelight shone in her bright eyes when she smiled.

"Shall we take our coffee and brandy in the living room?"

Chapter Two

"Meg, I need to talk to you."

Meg sensed Steven's presence behind her before she heard his voice and had been praying that any conversation between them would be banal and strictly superficial.

"There's nothing to discuss," she said in a low voice. If she looked at him she was afraid she would humiliate herself by bursting into emotional tears. Suddenly it was all there again, the confusion, the pain. She was glad when the table lamps scattered about the cavernous living room flickered, sputtered a moment, then blinked back on and steadied into a dim glow. The momentary distraction allowed her to move away from him.

"Oh, for God's sake, Tillis. Isn't this pile of rock spooky enough without you playing pranks with the lights?" Making a face, Candida threw herself on a Victorian sofa and arranged a fan of scarlet satin over the stiff cushions. She glared at Dennis Parnham when he moved toward the seat beside her. Instead, he chose a wingbacked chair beside the fireplace and pushed a cigarette into his ivory cigarette holder.

"This place is an antique," Meg murmured, moving farther from Steven. Morgan's Manor had been built in the twenties by Aunt Tilly's father, Meg's grandfather. He had purchased the stones in Germany, had them shipped to the United States and then to Breckenridge, Colorado. Out-of-work miners had hauled the stones up the mountain to a craggy overlook where they were reassembled into something that looked like Dracula's castle.

Crenellated balconies jutted here and there. Narrow-paned leaded glass overlooked steep valleys and soaring peaks. Inside, the house was a rabbit warren of twisting corridors and odd rooms that made little sense to a logical mind. Some rooms, like the living and dining room, were massive. High ceilinged, chill and shadowed even on bright days. Other rooms were undersized, lending themselves to no discernible purpose. It was as if Theodore Morgan had designed the manor for a household of giants and dwarfs, attempting to accommodate each.

"Don't act like more of a fool than you already are, Candida." Aunt Tilly accepted a snifter of brandy from the tray James offered, then seated herself on a gilt-backed thronelike chair the rest of them had avoided. "How do you suggest I manipulated the lighting? I dashed to the basement, toggled the switch, then dashed back upstairs? In seconds? Without anyone noticing?"

Meg experienced difficulty following the conversation. All she could think about was Steven Caldwell. After her curt reply, he had moved into the room and reluctantly seated himself in an ornate armchair. Suzanne perched on the arm of his chair, her fingertips moving over his shoulder.

"One of your prankster stooges could be in the basement," Candida complained. "A hundred people could be creeping around this place and none of us would know it!"

"The lights are effected by the storm, madam." James inclined his head toward the windows. Frost spread fernlike patterns across the panes. Snow collected on the sills. "The electricity has been flickering for the past hour. It's very nasty outside. Hilda heard on the radio that most of the major roads are closed—drifted over with snow."

"You see what I mean?" Candida threw out her hands. "Who the hell is Hilda? This is the first I've heard of any Hilda."

"She's my cook," Tillis said. "James's wife. You didn't think I cooked the prime rib, did you?"

Meg accepted a snifter from the tray. "James, are you saying we're snowed in?" Thoughts of catching the red-eye to New York evaporated when James nodded. She was stuck here for the duration. There would be no escaping Steven and Suzanne.

"I'm afraid so, miss. If the major roads are closed, it's certain our road is impassable."

The moody silence that followed suggested others besides Meg had considered departing immediately instead of remaining for the weekend. As a single body, they turned to consider the frosted windows and the snow flying out of the blackness.

"If I didn't know it was impossible, I'd think you personally arranged this storm, Tillis, so we'd be trapped here." Candida sighed, then tasted her brandy. She offered a grudging nod of approval. "Your taste in liquor is infinitely superior to your taste in fashion. I must say that spider is grotesque."

Rather than watch Suzanne's fingers curling idly through Steven's hair, Meg gripped her brandy snifter and turned to the fire popping in the grate. How could she still feel jealous after all this time? What was wrong with her?

Aunt Tilly cleared her throat. "There's something I wish to confess," she said.

"There's poison in the brandy?" No one smiled at Dennis Parnham's lame attempt at humor.

Tillis ignored him. "As I was planning this weekend, I realized I was eager to see each of you again."

"Even though you believe one of us sent you death threats?" Howard asked. Lamplight gleamed on his balding head.

"In your own way, each of you has added spice and zest to my life. It occurs to me that I've enjoyed loathing my enemies more than I've enjoyed caring about my friends. You've been more exhilarating and infinitely more irritating and interesting."

"Good God." Howard stared at her. "How much have you had to drink, Tilly? Are you taking those threats seriously?"

"I just wanted you to know that I've—appreciated you over the years. That isn't the right word, but it's close."

Candida crossed long shapely legs, then turned her hands in front of her, watching the firelight sparkle across her rings. "If I were the person threatening your life—and I only wish I had thought of it first—I would not be deterred by that sentimental little bit of sop, Tillis. You would have to do much, much better to make me reconsider wringing your scrawny neck."

Tillis laughed, the sound as charming and girlish as it had been in her youth. She smiled at Candida with an expression almost of affection.

"You're unique, Candida. Nasty, ambitious, greedy. Jealous, vain and reckless. A cat in heat possesses a greater sense of loyalty than you do. You have made an exemplary enemy and a challenging adversary. And you prove the old adage about beauty being only skin-deep."

Candida's smile melded glistening teeth and cold eyes. "A skunk smells its own tail first, Tillis dear. Every slanderous word you uttered applies to yourself before it applies to me.''

When Steven spoke, Meg looked up from the fire, the reflex one she instantly regretted. In the dim light his brown hair looked almost black; his hard jaw was shadowed. He was breathtakingly handsome. As Meg tried to squelch such unwanted thoughts, Steven moved away from Suzanne to stand beside the suit of armor guarding the archway.

"Tillis, you still haven't explained why I was invited for the weekend. Or why Suzanne and Howard are here."

Meg's eyebrow arched and she frowned. His phrasing made it sound as if he and Suzanne had not arrived as a couple.

"There's no mystery." Aunt Tilly wandered to the card table set up by the fireplace near Meg. "I've assembled the people who might wish to see me dead."

"You're being overly dramatic," Steven protested. He sounded annoyed. "No one here wants to see you dead."

"You couldn't be more wrong. But we'll leave that point for a moment. I asked you to come because I wished to review my notes for the new book with you."

Everyone present knew Tilly's new book was to be a nonfiction account of Whitney Halverson's murder.

Meg should have remembered Aunt Tilly was gathering facts and background information regarding the murder. Though it was tactless, her gaze involuntarily darted to Suzanne. Suzanne's aristocratic profile was turned toward the windows, away from the group gathered before the fireplace. She wore an expensive silk blouse with heavily padded shoulders, and a slim cashmere skirt. Her blond hair fell in soft waves toward the pearls glowing against her throat.

Meg admitted Suzanne looked tragic and fragile. What

woman could hope to compete with a beautiful and wealthy young widow? Even one with curiously cold eyes. Suzanne turned those cool eyes from the window and followed the conversation between Steven and Aunt Tilly.

"Do I sense reluctance in your voice, Tillis?" Steven asked. "Have you changed your mind about discussing the Halverson book?"

"I've changed my mind about writing the book. The timing doesn't seem as fortuitous as I originally believed." For the first time Tillis looked directly at Suzanne. "As you know, there isn't an ending. The murderer was never apprehended." Aunt Tilly ran her fingertips across the card table. "Without an ending, the project isn't worth pursuing." Again she met Suzanne Halverson's steady gaze. "I've destroyed my notes. Everything is gone."

"Oh, no, you haven't," Candida said briskly. "You're lying. Less than an hour ago you referred to your notes and advised Meg to use them to finish the book if you croaked."

Tillis shot Candida a poisonous look that would have felled a lesser woman. A hint of alarm flickered behind Tillis's lashes.

"I know what you're doing, Tillis—you're playing coy." Candida rolled her eyes toward Steven. "Don't you get it? First she dangles the bait until you're salivating to get your hands on the new project, then she bats her false eyelashes and says, oh never mind. You're supposed to up the ante, dear Steven. The next move is yours and it's going to cost you plenty."

"Shut up, Candida," Tillis muttered.

Steven's expression turned thoughtful. "Has something happened that I should know about?"

"Only that I've decided not to do the book." An odd

urgency charged Aunt Tilly's voice. "Steven, please. This isn't the proper moment to discuss business."

"Of course." He hesitated. "I understand."

"I'm sure you do," Candida said. "It's going to cost a fortune to change Tillis's small mind and put her back to work again." She waved at the smoke drifting her way from Dennis's cigarette. "If we're not going to be enter- tained by sitting in on the negotiations for Tillis's on-again off-again book, and I use the term loosely, then what is the plan for this evening? Shall we conduct the MAIMS board meeting and get it over with?"

Aunt Tilly shook her head. "There'll be time for MAIMS later. Tonight we'll relax and enjoy ourselves. Perhaps cards, conversation..." She touched Meg's shoul- der. "I wonder if I might have a word with you in my office?"

"Of course." Anything to escape Steven.

Dennis eyed the card table and sighed. "Oh, very well. If we're forced to enjoy ourselves...anyone for bridge? Suzanne? Howard?" He grimaced. "For heaven's sake, Howard. We're civilized people. Surely we can share the same bridge table."

"Like we share everything else?"

Dennis stiffened. "Honestly Howard, can't you give that tiresome subject a rest?"

Eager to escape, Meg followed Aunt Tilly down a long shadowy corridor, wishing she had a flashlight. The wall sconces were placed at infrequent intervals and the corri- dor was dark and smelled faintly of dust and age.

Aunt Tilly laughed when Meg muttered that she felt as if she were wandering about in a late-night mystery rerun. Entering her library-office, Tillis moved around the room turning on low table lamps. The bulbs flickered, then steadied.

"When your grandfather built Morgan's Manor, electricity was still new in these parts. I have an idea he believed the supply was limited, that one was allotted a finite amount. So he spaced the outlets rather far and few between. This house really is a monstrosity, isn't it?" She smiled at the room with affection.

Floor-to-ceiling bookshelves covered three walls, ran up and around a small fireplace, threatened to enclose the windows. Behind Aunt Tilly's massive old-fashioned desk was a door that led into a room too large to be a closet, too small to be anything else. Aunt Tilly used it to store office supplies. A full skeleton hung from a hanger on the coatrack. A plaster of paris skull served as the base for a table lamp. Another skull had been sculpted to serve as a pencil cup. Several bottles labeled Poison were scattered here and there.

"A bit outré, I admit, but amusing." Tillis laughed when she noticed Meg examining the skulls and bottles. "The poison bottles contain bath salts, I believe."

Meg seated herself in a comfy worn leather chair and placed her brandy snifter on the table next to her. "Aunt Tilly, I don't want you to think I'm unappreciative regarding Morgan's Manor—"

"But you really don't care for the old place." Tillis took the seat behind the desk and folded her hands on the blotter with a smile. "Morgan's Manor grows on one. It's a perfect site for a mystery writer. Inaccessible, filled with secrets and possessing a certain brooding charm." When she spread her hands the beaded spider flattened across her breast. "Your inheritance doesn't come with strings attached, Meg. If you don't want Morgan's Manor, give it to someone who does, sell it or tear it down if you like. But when the time comes, give the old place a chance. Live here awhile. Maybe you'll find you enjoy having a home away from the city—even a Gothic monster like this—some place to run away to when flight seems the best solution.''

Meg smoothed her hands over her wool skirt. There had been times when she had longed for a hideaway, when she had yearned to escape the heat and pressures of New York City. Aunt Tilly had guessed correctly. But Morgan's Manor?

''I regret that you and I have never really had a chance to know each other,'' Aunt Tilly said suddenly. ''I have a feeling we would be good friends if time and proximity allowed.''

''I'd like to know you better, too. I've admired you for years. From the time I read my first Tillis Morgan novel, I wanted to be like you. I wanted to write wonderful mysteries.'' A blush heated Meg's cheeks, deepened at the suggestion of moisture glistening in Aunt Tilly's eyes. It surprised her to discover Aunt Tilly possessed a streak of sentimentality.

''Oh, my, will you look at me,'' Aunt Tilly said, managing a smile. ''I'm getting weepy in my old age. What would Candida say?''

The dining room had been illuminated by flattering candlelight. Here, with the desk lamp shining full on her face, Aunt Tilly looked tired, thinner than the last time Meg had seen her. She looked achingly vulnerable, a state Meg usually did not associate with Tillis Morgan.

''Aunt Tilly, are you feeling well?''

''Thank you, Meg, for the sentiments you just expressed. I'm very proud of you, you know. If I'd had a daughter, I would have wanted her to be as lovely and bright and gifted as you.'' Aunt Tilly drew a deep breath. ''That's why I'm so distraught that I may have placed you in danger.''

"I beg your pardon?" Meg stared and her eyebrows rose.

"I committed an unforgivable blunder. I made that impulsive statement at dinner and I shouldn't have." Shaking her head, Tillis pressed her hands together until the knuckles whitened. "Lately my brain seems to be running three sentences behind my mouth. I can't think properly."

"I didn't notice any blunder. What did you say?"

"I announced that you're my heir, that you'll inherit everything, including my papers. It was stupid to blurt it out like that just to score a dramatic point."

Meg frowned. "I'm afraid I still don't understand. How is that dangerous to me?"

"I can't say for a fact that it is—and I tried to repair the damage. But it *might* be. It might be very dangerous." She gazed at Meg, but it was clear her mind had jumped to another topic. "I've solved it, of course. The proof is in the photos. I should have telephoned someone immediately, I see that now. But the storm blew up, and it seemed too dangerous to risk being snowbound if..." Her voice trailed and her brows came together. She examined a point in space, working something out in her mind.

Confusion wrinkled Meg's brow. "Aunt Tilly, I'm sorry, but I'm not following this conversation."

"You need to remember that Morgan's Manor has secrets." Tillis looked at Meg, as if recalling she was present. "Your mother is very good at ferreting out secrets. Did you know that? We used to spend our summers here when we were girls. It was Helen who discovered the manor's secrets."

"What secrets?" Meg felt baffled by the skips and jumps in the conversation.

"All in due time." Aunt Tilly's gaze softened. "You remind me of Helen. The curly dark hair, bright green eyes, slender figure. You're as beautiful as Helen was at your age. I could never fool your mother for long. She always saw right through me.''

Meg would rather have discussed the secrets of Morgan's Manor, but Aunt Tilly seemed to have abandoned the subject. "Mother says you used to pull the worst pranks…"

Tillis laughed. "I do love a good prank. The problem is sometimes you can't be present to enjoy the denouement. It would spoil the whole thing. Your mother can sniff a prank almost from the outset. Can you?"

Meg was feeling more puzzled by the minute. She didn't understand the swift topic changes or where the conversation might be leading.

"I'm not sure. Frankly, I'm beginning to suspect this weekend is something of a prank," Meg said finally, feeling her way. "I don't think you intend to murder all of us," she said, smiling. But maybe one of the guests is primed to do a little playacting. Like those role-play mystery weekends she occasionally read about. "I suspect the reference to *Murder at Eight* was no accident—the isolated site and a gathering of enemies. Am I on the right track?"

"I won't deny it." Tillis Morgan smiled.

"So you're confirming there's a prank in the making and you've given us the setup. Therefore, I'd guess the death threats are part of the prank. You made them up and at some point one of us is supposed to find them."

"You're wrong on that point." Aunt Tilly's slim hand dropped to a desk drawer. "The threats are very real. It's also true that any one of my guests could have mailed them. All the postmarks are stamped New York."

Meg stared. Until now, she had assumed the threats were the product of her aunt's fertile imagination. The revelation that they were genuine shocked her. "Have you taken the threats to the police?"

Aunt Tilly shrugged. "The police would read the notes, mutter a bit and advise me to contact them at once if something concrete develops."

"You can't possibly suspect that I..."

"No, dear, of course not. I apologize if I embarrassed you tonight. Benefiting from someone's death and wishing it are quite different things. But the others..."

"Are you including Steven?" Meg asked in a low voice. She hated herself for asking, but couldn't help it.

"Tell me something—is there any danger that Steven is actually involved with Suzanne Halverson? I know their association began innocently enough, but..."

"I wouldn't know," Meg answered stiffly. The familiar and hated jealousy bit into her. "I no longer keep track of Steven's social affairs."

"He hurt you, didn't he?" Aunt Tilly asked softly.

For a moment Meg considered lying, then gave it up. She didn't have the complexion for lies. A fiery blush gave her away every time. "The breakup was my fault," she said finally. "I drove Steven away." Closing her eyes, she passed a hand over her forehead, finding the admission terribly difficult. "I don't know what's wrong with me. I smothered him. I never thought of myself as possessive before. But with Steven..." She spread her hands in a helpless gesture. "I was jealous of everyone he spent time with. I...I drove us both crazy."

A full minute passed before Aunt Tilly responded. "Jealousy is a lethal poison, my dear Meg."

"I know! I just...I couldn't help it."

"There are other names for jealousy. One is fear. Another is self-doubt. You know, of course, that jealous people bring about their own worst fears. You can't continue this, Meg. Jealousy burns up the person who feels it and the object of jealousy is driven away.''

"I wish I could stop it, but I don't know how. Even now, when our relationship is over, I look at Steven with Suzanne and I feel terrible inside.''

Sympathy filled Aunt Tilly's eyes. "So much heartache has been caused by jealousy.'' For a long moment she watched the snow pelting the windowpanes. Then she sighed. "I can't tell you how to believe in yourself or how to trust. You'll have to work that out for yourself. But I can tell you that it's the loose tie that binds, not the hangman's knot.''

Smiling, Aunt Tilly rose behind her desk and slipped an arm around Meg's waist when Meg joined her at the door. "You can beat the jealousy if you really want to. The process will be painful, but you can win. If you try, and if you really want to.''

Meg swallowed the lump in her throat and told herself she absolutely would not cry. "I'm afraid it's too late for Steven and me,'' she whispered.

"Maybe. But maybe not.''

"That wasn't the only problem. Steven's a workaholic, we didn't communicate as well as we should have…''

Aunt Tilly laughed. "And you're not a workaholic? By now you surely know that most men put their work above everything else. Steven is a publisher first. He was the one who spotted the bestseller potential of the Halverson murder. He's been an enormous help.''

"I imagine he has been, being so close to the widow.'' Meg bit her tongue and moaned. "You see?'' she said to Aunt Tilly. "It's like a sickness.''

"It is a sickness, dear.'' Aunt Tilly pressed Meg's hand, then kissed her cheek. "The cure begins with believing in yourself.''

Meg embraced her aunt. "I know you're trying to help. Thank you."

"There's one more thing I want to say to you. Dangerous people do exist outside the pages of the books we write, Meg. And they can hurt you. Never overlook the obvious."

"You're talking in riddles again." But she was glad the conversation had shifted from more personal problems.

Tilly pressed her cheek against Meg's, leaving the scent of an expensive French perfume. "Just remember what we've talked about."

When they walked into the living room, both women stopped short. Howard Clancy looked up from the wing chair when Tillis asked, "What on earth happened here?"

Steven paced in front of the fireplace, pausing to cast a murderous glare at Dennis Parnham, who sat pressed into the corner of the sofa, smoking furiously. There was no sign of Suzanne Halverson or Candida Ripley. Someone had overturned the card table and cards and score tablets lay scattered over the carpet.

Howard pulled himself upright in the chair and passed a hand over his balding head. After looking around he wet his lips with the last drops in his glass. "Someone ought to shoot Dennis," he muttered, then focused on Tillis as she moved to stand over him. "First, he made a pass at Suzanne Halverson—"

"I did *not* make a pass at Suzanne Halverson," Dennis snapped.

"Then, cool as ice, Dennis announces he's taking his writers out of Caldwell Publishing." Howard squinted at Steven. "That's when we lost the happy family atmosphere, so to speak."

Dennis glared at Steven. "Caldwell Publishing is no longer a major player—"

"I'll sue you, Parnham," Steven said, his hands in fists. "Your writers have contracts. You can't break those contracts on a whim. And you can't deny Caldwell's authors a legitimate market for their work."

"Caldwell Publishing is in a slump. You can't expect my authors to follow you down on a sinking ship. As to a legitimate market, there's a dozen legitimate markets." Dennis waved his cigarette. "You haven't done one damned thing to promote Candida's book, and—"

"That's the heart of this threat, isn't it? You're trying to patch things up with Candida by promising her that if she'll stay with your agency, you'll get her a better deal with another house." Steven glanced at Howard. "Forgive me, Howard, I wish you didn't have to hear this. But, Dennis, you are not going to solve your romantic squabbles at my expense!"

"Is that a threat?" Dennis asked, standing.

"If it comes to that, yes." Steven's mouth settled in a grim line. "I'll take you to court if you try to pull your authors out of Caldwell Publishing. And I'll see that every shady trick you ever pulled is exposed."

Dennis's face flushed an unhealthy red. "Fine. File your suit. Spend a fortune. I'll make sure that any court case stretches into years. And in the meantime, I'll take my writers to Ghost House or Shadow Days. You'll be bankrupt before you ever take the stand."

Meg drew a breath and stepped between them, hoping to put a stop to the argument. "Where are Candida and Suzanne?"

Steven stared at her as if she had materialized in front of his eyes. "I don't know. I think they went to bed."

"Maybe all your authors don't see you as God, Dennis," Howard said. He appeared to have followed the exchange with greater acuity than Meg would have believed in view of how much he had drunk. "Maybe they won't want to break their contracts and go trucking off to Ghost House or that other place just because you say so."

Dennis flicked him a contemptuous glance. "If you're referring to Candida, Candida will do as I say."

Meg turned so she couldn't see Howard's face, embarrassed for him. He blustered and mumbled, then sank back into his chair. Tillis bent over him and spoke quietly in his ear.

"I won't do as you say, Dennis," Meg stated quietly. "I don't break contracts. I won't renege on my agreement with Caldwell Publishing." From the corner of her eye, she saw Steven's look of gratitude.

"We'll talk about it."

"No, Dennis. There's nothing to discuss." Although it was early, Meg decided to go to her room. An hour in the company of Aunt Tilly's houseguests felt like two days in a war zone. The hostilities exhausted her.

"Meg, wait." Steven touched her shoulder and a wave of electricity jolted through her body before she hastily stepped away from his hand. "I need to talk to you. Will you take a walk with me?"

The suggestion caught her unawares and was so outrageous that Meg laughed. "In case you haven't noticed, there's a blizzard raging outside. One of the worst storms in ten years according to James. Believe me, this is no night for a walk."

"We won't go far. We'll stay near the house."

It was exactly the kind of silly idea that usually appealed to Meg. Good sense, however, insisted she decline. She and Steven had nothing more to say to each other. There was no point opening old wounds.

"Good God, listen to him! The man's a lunatic." Dennis Parnham stared at them. "Meg, I won't allow you to go out in a damned blizzard with this idiot! It's too dangerous.''

"You won't *allow* me?" Incredulous, Meg stared at him. "Dennis, you're my agent, not my father or my keeper. Ours is strictly a business relationship. You don't decide where I go or with whom." To emphasize her point, she turned to Steven. "Give me two minutes to change into a pair of jeans and find my boots."

Turning sharply, she headed toward the staircase, already berating herself for giving in to a knee-jerk reaction. She knew she was making a mistake.

"IT PAINS ME to admit this, but Dennis was right." Steven pushed his gloves into his pockets and ducked his head against the sting of flying snow. "Coming out here really was a stupid idea."

They huddled at the bottom of the veranda steps, their backs braced against the force of the storm. Meg could see only a few feet in front of her, and what she saw was dismaying. A sea of white rolled under the black night. Giant drifts, sculpted by the wind, floated across the grounds like foaming waves. The road had disappeared.

"We could be stuck here for days," she said, then sank her chin back into the folds of her scarf. She had overheard James discussing the worsening situation with Aunt Tilly. The county plows would clear the highways and major roads first. Then, because area economics depended upon the tourist trade, the plows would clear access to the ski areas. Then the town streets. Private roads figured last on the list of priorities. James had promised to try to locate someone willing to clear Aunt Tilly's road. He hadn't sounded optimistic.

"Maybe being stuck isn't such a bad thing," Steven said. "It's time you and I talked."

Meg watched the white flakes accumulating on Steven's dark brows and lashes, the dusting of white that covered his ski cap. And she remembered another place, another snowy evening. Only they had been laughing then, chasing and pelting each other with snowballs like breathless children.

"There's nothing to talk about."

"Now who's refusing to communicate?" He looked into her eyes. "You didn't return my calls."

She hadn't seen any point. Then after a few weeks the messages he left on her answer machine had stopped. And the silence stretched into months.

"Look, Meg. Suzanne needed a friend." He moved slightly to shield her from the force of the wind. "Her husband was murdered, her maid jumped off the balcony of the hotel's twentieth floor—"

"Suzanne went through a lot—she had a rough ordeal. I've never disputed that. I just...oh, Steven, let's not re-hash this." Stepping away from him, she moved up one of the stone steps, wondering how long she had to remain outside to prove to Dennis that he didn't order her life. She drew a frosty breath and said the hardest words of her life. "I wish you and Suzanne every happiness. Let's leave it at that, okay?"

"Will you listen to me? It's not like that." He followed her up the steps. "If you could get past this stupid jealousy, you'd see the truth."

"What do you want from me, Steven?" She had an awful suspicion that melting snow was causing her mascara to run and her hair to stick to her forehead. She was crazy to have agreed to this lunacy.

"I want you to be reasonable. It's not really so difficult."

"Oh, come on. It was obvious from the first that you

and Suzanne were more than just friends." She had to shout to be heard over the wind whistling around the veranda posts. But that was all right. The anger she had been keeping inside suddenly overwhelmed her. Shouting felt good. And Steven's interest in Suzanne was not an example of stupid jealousy. The most reasonable woman in the world would have been jealous. "You brought Suzanne here. She can't keep her hands off of you. And I don't notice you resisting too strenuously. If you're trying to tell me you don't have a relationship with her, save your breath. I'm not blind!"

"I didn't bring Suzanne to Morgan's Manor. She was here when I arrived."

Meg halted with her boot on the next step. When she turned, she stood at Steven's eye level, close enough that the vapor from his breath bathed her lips and made her feel weak in the knees. His unexpected nearness sent her pulse racing, and she realized if she took one step forward she would be in his arms. Quickly she stepped backward. "I thought Suzanne came with you."

Now she remembered Aunt Tilly inquiring how involved Steven and Suzanne were. Would Aunt Tilly have asked that question if Steven and Suzanne had arrived together?

Steven observed the change in her expression. "Meg, you're wrong. You've been wrong about this from the beginning. I didn't know Suzanne would be here this weekend. But I did know you would be. One of the reasons I came is because I wanted to see you."

"Have you…are you sleeping with her?" Helplessly, Meg listened to the appalling words fall out of her mouth and she was powerless to halt them.

Hating herself, hating the poisonous jealousy that drove her, she clenched her teeth and looked at her feet, wishing miserably that she would blow away on the wind. She would have given anything to withdraw the question. And yet...

"I hoped things had changed," Steven said, closing his eyes. The wind lifted and fell, the howl swelling, then dropping to a whisper. Snow swirled around them. "I haven't slept with Suzanne," he said finally. "But you won't believe that, will you? You have to torture yourself by imagining the worst."

"I want to believe you," she whispered.

"What if I did sleep with her, Meg," he said angrily. "What if it really is a flaming affair? You and I are free to see whomever we please. You made that choice when you broke it off, when you refused to answer my calls and wouldn't take my messages. You made it damned clear that whatever you and I had together, it was finished."

"It is!"

He caught her glove. "Whitney Halverson was my friend. I couldn't turn my back on his widow." Stepping up beside her, he caught her shoulders between his hands. "You had no reason to be jealous."

As if jealousy needed a reason. But the words poured out of her traitorous mouth. "You continued to see her far beyond any duty to Whitney, Steven. Suzanne was using you. Coming on to you. At the end you were spending more time with her than with me." She sounded small and petty, pathetically insecure. "What's the point of fighting about this again?"

His hands tightened on the shoulders of her parka, preventing her from going inside. "Because there's so much you don't understand."

"Then tell me. You seem to think I can read your mind, but damn it, I can't!" She shouted against the wind. "If you and Suzanne aren't lovers, then tell me why she's all over you. Tell me why everyone here believes the two of you are a couple. Make me believe you're only playacting when you look at her or take her arm.'' Oh God, she couldn't stop the accusations from pouring out of her and she was making a fool of herself, unreeling her pain like an old movie. "Let go of me, Steven."

"You're always saying I won't communicate. Maybe the problem is you won't listen. Meg, I started seeing Suzanne because of Whitney and because I believed she needed comfort. But it quickly became something else."

"That's obvious." She tried to pull out of his arms, but he wouldn't let her.

"Damn it, Meg! You get one idea in your head and you won't allow the tiniest possibility that you may be wrong. The thing with Suzanne and me is not what you think."

Tears gathered in her eyes and she thanked heaven for the storm. With luck, Steven would believe the moisture on her cheeks was melting snow.

"If there's something you think I should know, then for heaven's sake just tell me."

Frustration darkened his eyes and she winced as his fingers dug into her shoulders. He said something, but the wind tossed his words away. "...wish I could, but I can't. Not yet. Please, Meg, trust me. This is almost finished. When it is, maybe you and I can start over."

"Trust me." Her laugh spun away in the wind and snow, sounding like a sob. How could she trust him when she didn't trust that he could choose her over someone like Suzanne? Meg Sandler was no one special. She wasn't blond and beautiful. She wasn't witty or profound. She was just...just Meg Sandler.

It had been a dreadful mistake to come outside with him. All the pain came rushing back. The hurt, the ache of losing him. An image of Steven's lean muscled body lying next to Suzanne rose in her mind, a torturous stupid image, and Meg winced. Why did she do this to herself? And she had been crazy to think she no longer loved him. Stupid, stupid. The pain, the sense of betrayal, was as raw now as it had been eight months ago.

"Let go of me, Steven, I mean it. I'm frozen, I'm upset and I want to go inside."

His hands dropped from her shoulders so abruptly that she stumbled and almost fell. Anger heated his eyes. "All right, Meg. Run away. Believe whatever the hell you want to believe."

For a moment she stared into his eyes, as angry as he was. Then she threw open the door and blew inside, pushed by the wind. James glanced outside, waited a moment, then closed the door against a whirl of flying snow. He took her wet cap, parka and gloves.

"Is Mr. Caldwell remaining outside, miss?"

"I don't know." And she didn't care. Wiping the snow from her cheeks and eyes, Meg ran up the stairs, almost colliding with Suzanne at the first landing.

Suzanne made a point of noticing the wet ends of Meg's hair, the smudges of mascara beneath her eyes. "Have you seen Steven?"

"He went for a walk," Meg muttered, examining the woman who had bewitched Steven. Light from the candle sconce gleamed in Suzanne's shining blond hair. A sapphire-colored Scottish wool bathrobe hugged her slim figure. Despite Suzanne's beauty, she reminded Meg of a baked Alaska, pale and luscious on the outside, remote and cold inside.

Observing Suzanne's elegant perfection, Meg became depressingly conscious of her own ordinary "cute" nose, her unmanageable hair, the embarrassing suggestion of freckles scattered across her nose. She would never be tall and willowy; she would never possess a patrician nose or a cool detached attitude. She would always be ordinary Meg Sandler from a small town in Iowa. A down-to-earth unglamorous tomboy with an inquiring mind and a lack of confidence. She was not the type of woman men like Steven Caldwell fell in love with.

"Steven went for a walk?" One of Suzanne's perfectly arched eyebrows rose in disbelief.

"Yes." Meg brushed past her and hurried toward the heavy carved door of her room. Head down, she ran pell-mell into Aunt Tilly.

"I'm sorry." She pressed her hand over her eyes and peered through her fingers to see if Suzanne had witnessed her clumsy display.

Aunt Tilly frowned and watched as Suzanne descended the staircase. "That is a dangerous woman," she said softly.

"I know."

"Did Steven tell you…?" Aunt Tilly gave her a sharp look. "No, he wouldn't. It would only place you at greater risk."

"Communication is not Steven's best talent," Meg said irritably. "Aunt Tilly, I'm in no mood for mysteries. If you think I'm in some kind of danger, then stop beating around the bush and tell me what's going on. I'm entitled to an explanation."

"You're right, of course. But I want to speak to Steven first," Aunt Tilly said, still watching the staircase.

"Okay, have it your way. You and Steven decide what's best for me." Meg threw up her hands and reached for the door latch. "I give up. I'm going to take a hot bath and go to bed."

"Did you and Steven have an argument?"

"It's just not going to work out for us," Meg said in a

low voice. "Even if Suzanne wasn't in the picture..."
When she looked up Aunt Tilly was rubbing her temple.
"Are you all right?"

"Just a headache. I've been having a lot of them recently." She brushed back a strand of Meg's damp hair
and tucked it behind her ear. "You really are quite beautiful, you know."

A protest formed on Meg's lips, then she laughed. "It
must be the dim light. Or you're losing your eyesight."

Whenever someone referred to her as beautiful, Meg
shied away from them. She was pretty enough, she supposed, but nowhere near beautiful. Her hair was too curly,
her mouth was too wide. Her features were too determined
to be beautiful. And at five foot four, she was too short.

Tillis smiled. "I recognize a beautiful woman when I
see one. But I have an idea you don't. Maybe that's part
of your problem."

Meg leaned to kiss her aunt's cheek. "Good night, Aunt
Tilly," she said fondly.

"Good night, my dear." Aunt Tilly placed her hand on
Meg's cheek and looked at her for a long moment, then
she moved down the dim corridor and rapped at Candida's
bedroom door. Meg shook her head and smiled. Even Aunt
Tilly's satin bathrobe was done in the trademark black.

Then Steven came up the staircase. He and Meg stared
at each other, then Meg slammed into her bedroom.

Sometime near midnight someone knocked at her door.
Meg glanced up from the book she was reading, but she
didn't climb out of bed. She had nothing to say to Steven
Caldwell.

Chapter Three

"Good morning, everyone." Stifling a yawn, Meg poured a cup of coffee from the silver service on the sideboard.

Everyone but Aunt Tilly had assembled in the dining room for the breakfast buffet James laid out. Meg wore jeans and a heavy lemon-colored sweater. She noticed Steven had chosen jeans, too. Candida still wore her pink satin bathrobe trimmed with dyed pink fur, though she'd made up her face before coming downstairs. The others wore casually elegant clothing *Town and Country* would have approved as suitable for a country weekend.

"Are you in a more reasonable mood this morning?" Steven asked, stepping beside her to refill his coffee cup.

"If that's supposed to be funny, it isn't." His after-shave teased Meg's senses. He looked fresh and handsome, his hair still damp from his morning shower. Meg looked at him and her heart sank. Already the weekend was a torment. She didn't know how she was going to get through the rest of it. "Did you knock on my door last night? About midnight?"

"Were you expecting someone else?" he asked, looking down at her.

"I wasn't expecting anyone."

"I've spoken to Tillis and she agrees it's time to tell

you everything.'' Steven's gaze brushed her lips, then moved upward.

A helpless feeling sent Meg's spirits plummeting. He had such wonderful eyes. Warm dark brown flecked with tiny green specks. Thick long lashes that any woman would envy. ''All right,'' she conceded with a sigh. ''Tell me 'everything.'''

''Not here.'' He cast a pointed glance at the people in the dining room.

Meg lifted an eyebrow. ''Not in front of Suzanne, you mean?''

''Meg, give it a rest. We need to talk privately.''

Pink flooded her cheeks. But anger was easier to handle than regret or pain. ''Anything you have to say to me you can say in front of everyone,'' she said sharply.

He frowned. ''You couldn't be more wrong. And you're making a big problem worse. When I knock at your door tonight, let me in. I mean it, Meg. Don't fool around. There's a situation involving Suzanne and it's imperative you know about it.''

''Involving Suzanne.'' She hid her face by bending over her coffee cup. ''An announcement of some sort?''

''Do you have to personalize everything?'' Anger flickered in his eyes. ''This doesn't have anything to do with you and me.''

''There is no you and me, Steven. So don't come to my room tonight.'' Lifting her chin she walked away from him, thinking this was a woman's worst nightmare come true. Here she was with no new man of her own, trapped with an old love and his new lady friend, and discovering the pain of loss was as fresh as yesterday. And discovering that Steven still had the power to turn her into jelly.

Trying to put him out of her mind, she approached

James. "Where's Aunt Tilly? I thought she'd be down-stairs by now."

James straightened behind a salver of scrambled eggs. "Madam has not come down yet." The frown he flicked toward the doorway expressed surprise and growing concern.

"That's strange." Meg looked toward the doorway, too. "It isn't like Aunt Tilly to sleep in. She prides herself on being an early riser. Perhaps someone should check?"

"As you wish, miss." James gave the buffet a quick glance, then hurried out of the dining room.

Meg glanced over her shoulder at Steven who was watching her, frowning over his coffee cup. Moving as far away from him as possible, she joined Dennis Parnham at the windows.

"At least the storm has ended," Dennis commented. Sipping his coffee, he watched a pale sun wage battle against an advancing bank of leaden clouds. "It finally stopped snowing at about five this morning. But it looks like more is on the way."

"You were awake at five?" Looking strangely naked without her jewels and plumes, Candida buttered a slice of raisin toast. For morning wear she had limited herself to one diamond ring on each hand. It wasn't the lavish display of last night, Meg noticed, but enough of a showing to remind onlookers they were dealing with a person of consequence.

"I'm surprised you have to ask," Howard commented in an acid voice. "Couldn't you just roll over and notice the empty space in your bed?"

"Don't start, Howard." Candida glared at him. "I can't deal with jealousy on an empty stomach. At least wait until after breakfast."

When Candida mentioned jealousy Meg felt another

burst of heat in her cheeks and carefully avoided looking at Steven. Instead she studied Howard, who was clear eyed and steady of hand this morning. If Meg hadn't known better, she would have sworn he hadn't had a drink in weeks.

"For your information," Dennis snapped, turning toward the table. "I slept in my room and Candida slept in hers."

"Do you know that for a fact?" Howard drawled. "Maybe my wife slept in my room last night."

"Don't be silly." If Dennis's attempt to embarrass Howard was deliberate, it was also effective. An angry flush infused Howard's cheeks. Dennis's smile was nasty. "Everyone knows the two of you don't sleep together anymore. That's why Tillis assigned you separate rooms."

"That's enough, Dennis," Candida snapped before Howard could react. "You're mad at me. Don't take it out on Howard."

Steven seemed to reach a decision. He pushed away from the sideboard and walked toward Meg, bringing the scent of English soap and that damned sexy after-shave.

Before he could speak, Suzanne glided forward and slipped her hand through his arm. "I was so glad when the wind finally stopped. I hate windy weather, don't you?"

"It was still noisy last night. There seemed to be a lot of traffic in the corridor," Meg said, not looking at Steven. She glanced at Suzanne's hand possessively linked through Steven's arm and she escaped toward the buffet, blindly reaching for a plate. Although she never ate breakfast, she picked up the bacon tongs and selected two strips of bacon.

"Excuse me." James reappeared in the archway, his forehead pleated in worried lines. "Madam does not answer a knock at her door. I tried the latch, but the door is locked.''

Meg dropped the bacon. ''Why wouldn't Aunt Tilly respond to your knock?'' Unless something was wrong. ''Do you have a key?'' she asked uneasily.

Reaching into his vest pocket, James produced a key ring. ''I opened the lower lock, the actual door lock. What I should have explained, miss, is the upper bolt is in place. The door is bolted from the inside.''

''And Aunt Tilly didn't respond when you called to her?''

''I'm a bit concerned, miss. I've never known Madam to sleep beyond six or to neglect her guests.''

''Well, don't you get it?'' Candida's bright laughter rang across the room and everyone turned to look at her. ''The whole thing's clear now.'' She waved the slice of raisin toast. ''This is a prank, of course. Tillis set us up last night. That was step one.'' Mimicking Tillis Morgan, she lowered her voice and announced in a dramatic tone, ''Everyone here has a reason to want me dead.''

''Oh. Yes, I see.'' Dennis Parnham smiled. ''So now we're supposed to fly into a panic and think, *Tillis doesn't answer her door, therefore she must be dead. One of us took the bait and murdered her in her sleep.* Is that the idea?''

''Well, of course it is.'' Candida peered around the room. ''Most likely the old sneak has hidden a tape recorder somewhere so she can play it back later to embarrass us. I imagine we're supposed to fly into a frenzy, then start hurtling accusations at one another.'' Opening her mouth, she munched into the raisin toast. ''The woman is absolutely incorrigible. The rest of you can run off in panic if you wish, but I'm going to stay right here and enjoy my breakfast.'' She raised her voice to the corner of the room, speaking for the benefit of any hidden recorders. "You don't fool me, Tillis Morgan. This prank is as transparent as your silly books."

Steven moved up beside Meg. "How can we get into Tillis's room?" he asked James.

"There's a row of windows...I could fetch a ladder."

"You're certain the door is bolted from the inside."

"Yes, sir."

Tillis was Meg's aunt, Meg should take charge. And she needed to build confidence in her decisions. "Fetch the ladder at once, James," she said firmly. "Candida is probably correct. This sounds like a prank. But just in case..." They would most likely discover Aunt Tilly reading in bed, waiting for her "body" to be found, and very pleased by the uproar she had caused. Still, the situation was worrisome and unpleasant.

"Maybe she really is dead," Suzanne suggested.

Offended, Meg responded in a sharp voice. "You almost sound as if you'd be pleased if she was."

Smiling, Suzanne stepped to the coffee urn and freshened her cup. "Obviously we're supposed to think she is."

Disgusted, Meg followed Steven and James into the foyer where they pulled on caps and coats. Even though Meg knew in her heart this was just one of Aunt Tilly's silly pranks, she was feeling more nervous by the minute. Howard joined them, his expression as grim as her own.

He pressed Meg's shoulder. "How can I help?"

"I don't think we'll need you," Steven said. He turned to James. "If you'll hold the base of the ladder, I'll climb up." As Steven was by far the younger man, it seemed the most sensible suggestion. "Thanks anyway, Howard."

"I'll come along just in case."

James opened the front door. "I'll fetch the ladder from the garage, then meet you at the back of the house."

Steven met Meg's gaze as he tugged on his gloves. "Don't worry. This situation has all the earmarks of a prank."

"Of course it's just a prank." She wrung her hands and followed Steven to the door. "I...be careful. I'll wait upstairs. And after Aunt Tilly has her laugh, I plan to give her a tongue-lashing for scaring everyone half to death!"

She rushed up the staircase and hurried to the end of the corridor, halting before Aunt Tilly's door. "Aunt Tilly?" There wasn't a sound. Nothing but silence. Meg's knock sounded overloud in the deserted hallway. When she tried to open the door it caught against the interior bolt.

One by one the others appeared and Meg ceased pounding on Aunt Tilly's door. "I thought you were going to ignore the fuss," she said to Candida.

"Oh, if everyone else is willing to play along..." After tightening the sash of her bathrobe and flicking toast crumbs from her bosom, Candida cast a look of envy at Suzanne's coffee cup. "I wish I'd thought to bring my coffee, too."

Dennis gave Candida his cup, then patted his pockets. "I want a cigarette."

"Did you hear something?" Suzanne asked after several minutes had passed.

"Nothing. You're imagining things." Shoving back the fur-trimmed sleeve of her robe, Candida peered at a watch face surrounded by diamond chips. "What's taking so long?"

"What difference does it make? We're not going anywhere," Meg said, thinking of the drifts blocking the road and the mounds of snow Steven and James had to climb over to reach the back of the house.

Howard came up the staircase, his wet pant legs trailing

clumps of snow. "It shouldn't be long now." He rapped hard on the door. "Tilly? You've had your joke, now open this door."

Following another silence they finally heard footsteps inside the bedroom, then the bolt scraped back and Steven filled the doorway.

"Aunt Tilly?" Meg tried to see around him, but Steven stepped in front of her. When she tried to push past, he caught her arm and blocked the entrance.

"Don't go inside, Meg." He drew a breath and touched her cheek. Now she noticed his face was ashen. "Tillis is dead."

Everyone froze, staring at him. Then Meg shook off his hand with a furious gesture.

"Stop it," she said angrily. "I don't know what instructions Aunt Tilly gave you, but this prank has gone far enough! It's over, do you understand?" Eyes flashing, she stared at him. "This isn't funny."

"I wish to God it was a prank, miss. But it's not." James appeared directly behind Steven. He, too, had climbed the ladder. Moisture glistened in his eyes, and his voice was thick and choked. "Madam is dead."

"Oh, the hell she is!" Elbowing forward, Candida pushed Steven aside and ducked under his arm. "I'll have to see her scrawny dead body with my own eyes before I— Oh, my God!"

Meg dashed inside behind her and halted when Candida did. A gasp sucked the breath from her chest and blindly she grabbed Candida's sleeve. Her fingernails dug into the dyed pink fur. "Oh, no. No!"

Tillis Morgan was dead. To Meg's horror, it was not a prank. Aunt Tilly was unmistakably dead. She lay sprawled on the floor in her black-and-white flannel nightgown almost directly beneath the window; a dusting of snow powdered her hair and forehead.

Turning blindly, Meg reached for Steven. When his arms closed around her, she pressed her face into the collar of his parka and released a sob.

Dennis Parnham stared at Tillis's still figure. "Oh, Jesus."

Swearing softly, Howard covered his face with his hand. After a moment he lowered his fingers and murmured. "Bless her heart. She put up a hell of a fight. Look at this room."

To say a struggle had ensued was to wildly understate the case. A large wing chair lay on its side. A side table and two lamps had toppled. Books had been knocked from the bookcase. The mattress was slightly askew. Loose papers littered the floor like confetti.

"I'm sorry, Meg," Steven murmured, his lips in her hair.

Embarrassed that she had automatically turned to him, Meg disengaged herself and, feeling sick, she watched James pull a sheet from the bed and gently draw it over Aunt Tilly's body.

Candida had bent to peer at something on the floor. "My, my." She pointed but didn't touch. She was too seasoned a mystery writer to disturb evidence. "What have we here? A broken ashtray, a broken cigarette and an ivory cigarette holder. Now who do you suppose these items belong to?"

Dennis flushed under the sudden unpleasant attention. He patted his jacket pockets as if searching for his cigarette holder.

"Obviously you were here last night," Howard accused. "Right in the thick of things from the look of it."

"Now wait just a minute. I stopped by for half an hour.

I admit it. Damn it, stop looking at me like that. Tillis *asked* me to stop by. But I swear I don't know how that ashtray and cigarette got here. I didn't smoke while I was here. Tillis wouldn't permit it.''

When Dennis realized this statement indicated he must have returned at a later time or that he was lying, he wet his lips. "No, wait. I…I did smoke. Yes, I had a cigarette. And I must have left my cigarette holder here. I wondered what happened to it." He spread his hands. "Why are you all staring at me? I did *not* kill Tillis! She was alive when I left this room!"

"It seems someone else was here, too," Suzanne said, kneeling beside Tillis's body. She directed their attention to a ruby-and-amethyst ring lying a few feet from Tillis Morgan's outflung hand. "Candida was wearing this ring last night."

"What?" Stepping forward, Candida stared down at the ring. "That's mine, but it's impossible! I swear I was not here last night. I've never been in this room until now!"

Dennis cocked an eyebrow and spoke in the same sarcastic tone Candida had used to point out the ivory cigarette holder. "I suppose your ring just walked in here."

"Don't give me that oily smile, Dennis Parnham!"

Suzanne lifted an eyebrow. "How do you explain your ring ending up a few feet from Tillis's dead body?"

"I have no idea how it got there." Extending her hands, Candida showed them how loose her rings were. "Maybe the ring dropped off when I ran in here just now. Then it rolled over—" she pointed but couldn't bring herself to look at Tillis's sheet-draped body "—over there."

"Nice try, but you weren't wearing this ring at breakfast," Suzanne pointed out. "Besides, there's snow on it from the window. This ring has been here as long as the body has."

"What the hell are you implying? I was not in this room last night! Wait—I know. Tillis came to my room, she must have stolen the ring off the bureau top or off my finger and—"

Steven interrupted. "Tillis didn't enter your room, Candida. I came up the staircase as she was talking to you in the corridor. Tillis never touched you. She didn't take your ring."

"Now look at that," Dennis said. "The broken glass near the brass lamp. Isn't that the glass Howard used last night?" Malicious pleasure curved his lips. "Howard was the only person using a monogrammed tumbler."

Meg gripped Steven's arm and leaned against him again. Tears flowed down her cheeks. "Please. Can we go downstairs?" she whispered. "It doesn't seem right to stand here arguing, not with Aunt Tilly..."

Suzanne stooped to pick up some of the loose papers scattered over the floor. "They're manuscript pages. From *First Guess,* one of Tillis's old books."

"Meg is right. We're disturbing evidence." Steven's arm tightened around her, then gently he nudged her toward the door. "Everyone out." No one had to be urged twice. "James, lock the door, then telephone the police."

"At once, sir." Bending, James pulled out his key ring, then turned a key in the bedroom lock.

"Before you do another thing, James," Howard said. "I need a drink. Either serve drinks or tell me where Tillis has put the liquor now."

"The liquor cabinet is concealed behind a panel in the dining room, Mr. Clancy. You'll notice a cherry-wood panel to the left of the sideboard. Slide it toward the windows."

"Trust Tillis to find different hiding places for the liquor," Howard grumbled. "She was a lovely woman in many, many ways, but she felt compelled to make a mystery out of damned near everything.''

''Suddenly she's a 'lovely woman'?'' Jealousy flared in Candida's eyes. ''Last night she was a lousy cook, a neglectful wife, a harridan who dragged your name through months of tabloid mud and cost you your job and your pension. But now that a glass with your fingerprints all over it is found at the murder scene, she's a 'lovely woman.' You're so transparent, Howard.''

''You know I didn't murder Tilly.'' First in to the dining room, Howard walked directly to the cherry-wood panel and slid it to one side. ''Well, I'll be damned. It's a whole room. And nicely stocked, too.'' He emerged brandishing a bottle of vodka. ''Bloody Marys anyone?''

Meg's stomach churned and she sat down abruptly. When Steven pushed a handkerchief in her hand, she accepted it gratefully.

''Are you all right?'' he asked, pressing her shoulder.

''No. Aunt Tilly's dead!'' She couldn't accept it. Slowly Meg looked around the room. ''And someone here killed her.''

Howard broke the silence that followed. ''I'll admit there were times when I wanted to wring Tilly's neck.'' After pouring vodka into a tall glass, he added a splash of spiced tomato juice, then swallowed heavily. ''Better.'' He sighed and blinked at them. ''But the truth is, I'll miss the old girl. Tilly and I settled our differences way back when.''

''Apparently Tillis didn't think so,'' Suzanne commented.

Howard narrowed his eyes. ''I beg your pardon?''

''Last night Tillis indicated you were among those who wouldn't grieve much over her death.''

''I've changed my mind. I would like a Bloody Mary,

Howard." Meg hoped it would settle her nerves. Her hands trembled and tears continued to well in her eyes. When she could control the quiver in her voice, she raised her head and studied Suzanne. "Aunt Tilly said *everyone* at the table had a reason to want her dead. We haven't heard your reason, Suzanne."

Immediately Steven's fingers dug into Meg's shoulder. His meaning was plain. But if Steven hoped to spare his precious Suzanne any awkward questions, he was going to be disappointed.

Meg shook off his hand. "Well, Suzanne?"

"You know," Candida said, leaning back in one of the dining room chairs. She tilted her head in a thoughtful expression. "I believe Meg's right. Tell all, Suzanne. Why did you want Tillis dead?"

Suzanne shrugged her padded silk shoulders. "Tillis didn't include me in her accusations."

Dennis raised a hand. "Tillis said *everyone* at the table. For the sake of discussion, let's say Tillis did include you. So how do you benefit from her death?"

"The only possible reference is so thin and flimsy it isn't worth mentioning."

"Mention it anyway," Meg said. She gave Steven a defiant look, not caring that he looked angry.

Suzanne also glanced at Steven. "I suppose it's no secret that I was initially opposed to a book about my husband's murder. But as it seemed Tillis planned to write the book with or without my consent, I dropped my protest and cooperated in every way."

Dennis lit a cigarette. "But you object to having the book published?"

"I did in the beginning. I dreaded the fresh publicity the book would generate. I'd prefer to put all that ugliness behind me. Plus, it seemed a waste of time and effort.

Tillis herself admitted there was no satisfactory ending for the book as the murderer was never apprehended.''

"If I were writing that book," Candida said, thinking out loud, "I'd have been searching for the ending. I wouldn't have relied solely on the police investigation, I'd have conducted an investigation of my own. I'd have discovered who murdered your husband."

"I believe that was Tillis's intention. She was gathering evidence, sifting through paperwork, interviewing people…"

"And Tillis failed," Steven said, moving to stand beside Suzanne. "That's why she abandoned the project and destroyed her notes."

"Surely you of all people can't honestly believe Tillis destroyed her notes." Candida smiled. "Name one writer who ever destroyed his or her notes. It simply doesn't happen. All of us are secretly convinced our notes possess some kind of magic power. We regard our research as sacred. If the magic doesn't work for this book for whatever reason, it may work for the next. Every writer I know would rather run through Bloomingdale's stark naked than destroy a single jot that might form the basis for next year's bestseller. Every set of notes, every scrap of research that Tillis ever compiled is right here in this house."

Knots of frustration formed along Steven's jawline. "Thank you, Candida, for enlightening us." He clenched his teeth, then drew a breath. "However, Tillis insisted she destroyed her research on the case and I believe her."

"Maybe." Dennis blew smoke into the air. "Or maybe Tillis dug up some damaging scandal that Suzanne's afraid of."

"Well, well." Candida's eyes sparkled. "Could we be talking blackmail here?"

"Don't be stupid." Suzanne's expression turned to ice. "Do you really think Tillis Morgan was a blackmailer?"

Candida's sparkle faded into disappointment. "Tillis had a lot of disagreeable qualities, but, no—regrettably I can't visualize her as a blackmailer."

"There is no evidence to suggest I was in Tillis's room last night because I wasn't," Suzanne said. "Each one of you has a motive to kill Tillis Morgan. But I don't."

James returned then and one glance at his expression told Meg something else was terribly wrong.

"What's happened?" Steven asked.

"The telephones, sir. The wires have been ripped from the wall."

"You can't telephone the police?" Meg stood.

"No, miss. I can't telephone anyone. And there's more." James pressed his hands together. "It seems the cars have been disabled. The tires are flat."

"On *all* the cars?" Dennis stared.

"Do you have an air pump?"

"It appears to be missing, miss."

"Howard, you'd better fix me a Bloody Mary, too." Candida sighed. "I suppose it's silly to ask this considering the way things are going, but, James, did you reach anyone last night about plowing out our road?"

"Yes, madam, I did."

Everyone brightened.

"Jim at the service station promised he'd get to us as soon as he could. He predicted it wouldn't be before the day after tomorrow, though. And that's only if there's no more snow."

Meg's shoulders dropped. "Have you heard a weather report? Is more snow expected?"

"I'm afraid so, miss. The radio forecaster predicts scattered snow beginning this afternoon and continuing through the evening."

Steven carried his coffee cup to the windows and gazed up at the swollen gray sky. "It looks like we're going to be stuck here awhile." He gave Meg an I-have-to-talk-to-you look.

"With a dead body!" Candida shuddered.

"Oh, for heaven's sake." Dennis made a face. "You deal with dead bodies all the time. Why should one more disturb you?"

"Shut up, Dennis. The corpses I deal with are fictitious. This one is *real*. And it's personal! That's Tillis up there dead as a mackerel! I didn't like her, but…but I'm sorry she's dead." Candida dabbed her eyes with the sleeve of her robe. "I hate to admit this, but I'll miss the old fraud."

Dennis rolled his eyes. "If you believe that, ladies and gents… Come on, Candida. You've been jealous of Tillis for half your life. You were worried to death that she'd win the Macabre Series and you'd be seen as the has-been you are."

"You heard her, Dennis," Howard growled. "Shut up."

A wave of disgust overwhelmed Meg. "Aunt Tilly made the Parnham Agency a lot of money before she found a new agent who wouldn't steal her work. She made your reputation, Dennis. Can't you feel a little sympathy that she was murdered?"

"Parnham has never forgiven Tillis for leaving his agency," Steven said. "Plus, he's too busy anticipating the money he'll make from Tillis's first four books to waste any time on sympathy."

"Keep it up, Caldwell. I'm keeping track of every slanderous remark. Of course, you can afford a long court case, can't you? Now that you're half a million dollars richer and can buy back a million and a half dollars worth of company stock.''

Meg touched her fingertips to her forehead. "I'm going upstairs to lie down. No one seems to care that Aunt Tilly was murdered, all you can think about is accusing one another. Candida's right—this isn't fiction. This is real. But none of you seem to care."

Steven followed her out of the room. "Meg, wait." He caught her arm and she told herself the resultant tremble she felt had nothing to do with him. "I'll go with you."

She raised her eyes to his wide mouth and to her shame she wanted his arms around her, wanted the comfort Steven could have given her. "Oh, Steven," she whispered, tears filling her eyes. "I wish things could have been different."

"Why can't you believe in yourself?" he asked softly, looking down into her eyes. His hands moved up her arms. "That's the root of the problem, isn't it?"

Immediately she stiffened. "Excuse me. I do want to lie down." She pushed his arms away. "And I need some time alone."

Meg felt his gaze on her as she walked up the staircase, felt his anger and frustration. She felt the same emotions, too. Plus confusion. She didn't understand the conflicting messages he was sending. And right now she was too upset to think about it.

JAMES KNOCKED at Meg's bedroom door about two o'clock, waking her from a fitful doze. "Sorry to disturb you, miss. But Mr. Caldwell wants everyone downstairs in the living room."

Mr. Caldwell could go jump in Dillon Reservoir. Meg bit her lip and sighed. "I'll be along in a minute."

She found her shoes, splashed water over her face and

pulled a comb through her unruly curls. Actually Steven was probably right; it was time for a meeting. They'd all had a few hours to consider the situation. There were things that needed to be said, questions that needed answers.

The others had already gathered when Meg entered the living room. A cheerful fire crackled in the grate. James had set out a light repast for anyone who wanted sandwiches or coffee. Steven sat at the card table with Candida beside him poised over a legal-size pad to take notes.

"Now that everyone's here," Steven said as Meg seated herself on the sofa between Dennis and Howard, "I want to bring the group up to speed on what James and I have been doing." Meg noticed that Suzanne had chosen Aunt Tilly's thronelike chair. "We need to discuss our situation and what happens next."

"Who appointed you our leader?" Dennis demanded.

"Someone needs to take charge. Do you want the job?"

"I was just asking, that's all."

"If no one else objects, we'll proceed." When no one spoke, Steven continued. "James and I have searched the house. We wanted to rule out the possibility of an intruder. There's no sign anyone was here last night except us."

"I doubt an intruder would have hung around to be discovered," Meg pointed out. "If he left after...after he did what he came to do, the snow would have covered his tracks."

"Possibly. But I don't think we're dealing with an intruder. However, you've raised an important point. I think we can agree the snow stopped about five o'clock. It's reasonable to assume it began to taper off about an hour earlier. Therefore, judging from the small amount of snow on Tillis's bedroom floor, I think we can infer she was killed between four and five this morning."

"We know Dennis was awake at five." Having flung this dagger, Candida noted the information on the pad of paper.

"I saw no intruder leaving the premises," Dennis said, choosing to misinterpret Candida's implication.

"James and I walked around the premises and we found no footprints in the snow other than those we made taking the ladder around the house." Steven looked at each person. "So. Who was the last person to see Tillis alive?" No one answered. "Come on folks, we're going to have to do better than this. We can try to figure it out, or we can wait for the police. Either way, we're going to need some answers. I saw Tillis about eleven, eleven-thirty. Did anyone see her after that?"

Howard waved his Scotch. "No one wants to admit being the last person to see Tilly."

"Let's put that question aside for a moment," Meg suggested. "There's something else puzzling me. Steven, you just mentioned the snow on Tilly's bedroom floor. How did it get there?" With an extraordinary effort, Meg kept anything personal out of her expression when she looked at him.

He did the same, answering in a forthright manner. "James and I probably scraped some snow inside when we came in the window. But that's not the entire answer. The window was open about four or five inches when we arrived. There was snow on the carpet beneath the window before I climbed through."

"Open?" Meg's eyebrows lifted. "That explains why the room was so cold. But why on earth would Aunt Tilly open the window during a blizzard? That doesn't make sense."

"The killer opened the window." They all looked at Howard. "The corridor door was bolted from the inside.

So how did the killer leave? Obviously he went out the window."

"Don't be an idiot." Dennis spread his hands. "That's a two-and-a-half-story window. Anyone dropping out of that window would be injured. He'd break his neck."

"The snow would cushion his fall."

"But there's another problem," Meg said slowly. "If the killer opened the window wide enough to crawl through, then he somehow managed to lower it behind him. How?"

"How wide is the sill?" Candida asked.

"Not that wide," Steven replied. "Maybe three inches on the outside. Not large enough to stand on. Meg's right. No one going through the window could then lower it behind him."

"Therefore, the killer could not have escaped through the window," Meg concluded. "So how *did* he get out of the room?"

Steven met her eyes and she realized they were thinking in tandem, working together. For the moment at least, it felt like old times. And she saw in Steven's dark eyes that he recognized it, too.

"Everyone is referring to the murderer as a 'he,'" Suzanne observed from the depths of the thronelike chair. "But if I recall correctly, there are a couple of ladies present who wanted to see Tillis dead."

"Are you accusing me?" Candida demanded.

"If the shoe fits..."

"How dare you!" Candida sprang out of her chair and went for Suzanne.

Chapter Four

It took both Steven and Howard to wrestle Candida back into her chair, and several minutes passed before Candida calmed down enough that the discussion could continue. Meg decided she would have disliked Suzanne Halverson even if Steven were not involved with her.

When Candida stopped shouting, Meg asked Suzanne, "Why did Aunt Tilly invite you for the weekend? If she had abandoned the book, why did she need you here?"

"I wasn't invited. I came to Breckenridge to ski. Once I arrived, I decided to pay Tillis a call. Coming to Morgan's Manor was strictly an impulse. I had some questions about the book." She shrugged. "While I was discussing the book with Tillis, the rest of you arrived. At some point someone mentioned the road had become impassable. Shortly thereafter I discovered James had taken my luggage to a room and I assumed I was welcome to stay."

"When you and Tilly came out of her office, it looked as if you'd been arguing. You were both angry." Howard gestured with his drink. "What was that all about?"

"It's none of your business."

"The hell it isn't," Candida snapped. "There's been a murder here, and *you're* one of the suspects, too!"

Suzanne lifted a cool eyebrow. "Did anyone observe

any blood? Any crushed bones? Are we absolutely certain that Tillis didn't die of natural causes?''

"If she did, it was a pretty damned violent natural cause." Dennis blew a smoke ring and made a sound of irritation. "Have you forgotten what her room looked like?"

"We can definitely rule out natural causes," Candida said with a look of disgust. "At the risk of being indelicate, we only saw one side of Tillis. There's a possibility that Tillis's down side is bashed in. The fireplace tools were scattered around. Maybe she was struck with the poker, but the damage won't be evident until she's moved. Or she might have been strangled, in which case there wouldn't be blood or obvious damage. There would be marks beneath her collar that we didn't observe. But we can state with absolute certainty that Tillis did *not* die of natural causes.''

Meg stood abruptly and went to the buffet for a glass of ice water. Standing with her back to the others, she fought to get control of herself. Instinct told her that Tillis would have been the first to briskly advise her to put her emotions aside. Emotionalism impeded intellect. Aunt Tilly had said so a dozen times and Meg agreed. Aunt Tilly also would have expected her to approach the facts in a cool professional manner. Meg needed her wits about her. She couldn't afford to go queasy every time someone referred to the murder scene. She would never discover the murderer's identity unless she resolved to approach the puzzle with detachment.

"Are you all right?" Steven asked when she returned to the group. Genuine concern warmed his dark eyes.

"I had a bad moment, but I'm fine now. Where are we?"

"There's something else no one seems to have consid-

ered.'' Suzanne tented her long fingers beneath her chin.
''There were *eight* people in the dining room when Tillis
said everyone present had a reason to want her dead. She
didn't say, 'Everyone here except James has a reason to
want me dead.'''

Startled and hating to admit it, Meg had to concede Suzanne's point. Without speaking, Candida leaned to tug the
pull rope and after a few minutes James appeared. Clearly
uncomfortable, Steven explained the issue in question.

Meg sympathized with Steven's reluctance because it
was apparent that James was shattered. Red-rimmed eyes
suggested he had been weeping. He looked ancient and
tired. And startled when he learned the nature of his sum-
mons.

''I didn't think Madam included…but I understand you
must inquire.'' He straightened his shoulders and looked
steadily out the back windows. His voice emerged sounding like the rattle of old parchment. ''Madam gave me to
understand that Hilda and I would be remembered in her
will. That's all Madam said. I don't know if she intended
a sum of money or a memento of some sort.''

''Did you or Hilda go to Tillis's room last night?''

''I stopped by Madam's room about thirty minutes after
Miss Meg returned from her walk outside. Madam and I
spent about five minutes discussing the menus for today.
Then my wife and I tidied the kitchen before we retired to
our quarters on the third floor. We watched television and
went to bed after the news.''

Steven nodded, thanked James and told him that was
all.

''I can't believe we did that,'' Meg murmured after
James left. She shook her head. ''That poor old man is
devastated.''

''And we are getting exactly nowhere,'' Candida stated.

She drummed her fingernails on top of the legal pad. "Before we try to ferret out who did it, perhaps we should figure out how it was done. Agreed? What we have here is a classic locked-door mystery." Her bosom lifted in a tremulous sigh. "Tillis would have loved this, absolutely loved it. Well. We've all read or written locked-door murder mysteries. So how was this one done? How did the murderer get out of Tillis's room? That's the problem, isn't it?"

Dennis was first to offer a theory. "How about the old standby solution—the killer locked the bolt from outside the room."

Steven stroked his jaw and stared at Meg. "Maybe the killer doesn't get out. He hides in the room until the body is discovered, then he appears during the confusion arising at the body's discovery. It appears that he rushed into the room with everyone else."

Meg met his gaze. "Suppose the first person on the scene is the murderer. He commits the murder, then pretends the victim was dead when he found the body." She didn't flinch from Steven's startled frown. "It only appears like a locked-door murder."

"Maybe the killer is never in the room in the first place," Howard said when it was his turn. "I read this story once—I forget the exact details—but the killer shoots an icicle through the window. It looks like the victim was stabbed, but the police can't find a weapon because the icicle has melted."

Candida muttered under her breath. "That's so far out, Howard. And here's another long shot. The killer slips into Tillis's room through a secret door and leaves the same way. I used this idea in one of my books."

"It was one of her best," Howard informed them.

"I'm not an expert in murder like the rest of you,"

Suzanne said when Candida coldly inquired if she had a possible solution.

"So *you* say! Maybe you're more expert than anyone here."

When it appeared that Candida and Suzanne would go at it again, Steven held up a hand. "It's time we took a short break. Let's have some coffee and sandwiches, then we'll discuss each possibility and see if any of them fit the facts."

He followed Meg to the windows, away from the others, and handed her a cup of coffee. Outside, blue shadows crept through the snow-shrouded pines. Meg was thinking it would be dark soon when she spotted the first snowflake.

"Oh, no. It's snowing again!" Her heart dropped to her toes. And Steven was standing too near. She could smell the after-shave he always wore, and she remembered his arms holding her in Aunt Tilly's bedroom. She warned herself to keep the conversation impersonal. "We have to talk about who disabled the cars and the telephones. And the delay additional snow will cause in getting help."

"I doubt anyone is going to admit anything." Steven's sweater was the same chocolate shade as his eyes. Meg felt the disturbing tug of his solid athletic body. "For a minute, it felt like better days, didn't it? You and me thinking along the same lines."

"Why do you say things like that? It only makes it harder for both of us." Anger flashed in Meg's eyes. "Look, Steven. We tried to have a relationship, but it didn't work. I was too possessive, you were too uncommunicative. Nothing's changed. I can't tell you to go off and have a good time with Suzanne. And you're still talking about talking without saying anything."

"If it had been up to me, I would have told you everything from the beginning." He stared at her. "On second thought maybe that's not true. Maybe for once I wanted you to just trust me. Do you know what it feels like? When the person you care about doesn't trust you?''

"I *do* trust you. Or I did." It was just so damned confusing. Was there any rational way to explain jealousy? "I just…it's just that…" She threw out her hands, upset. "I can't explain it. I just cared so much." She wished to hell she hadn't admitted that.

Steven's face revealed a frustration as deep as her own. "You're one of those aggravating women who drive men crazy. I don't know whether to hurl you out a window or make love to you." His gaze focused on her lips and an electric tingle exploded down Meg's spine. Her stomach tightened. "I'd like to do both. Instead I'll try to talk to you. But it has to be in private, Meg. Tonight."

No other man affected Meg the way Steven Caldwell did. He could leave her weak-kneed and shaky inside with just a look. The realization left her feeling helpless and dejected.

"We're ready to resume," Candida called. She consulted her notes with a show of importance. "While the rest of you were eating sandwiches, I tested Dennis's theory about the murderer locking the door from outside Tillis's bedroom. There is absolutely no way to slide that inside bolt from outside the door. I tried it every possible way and it can't be done."

Steven took his seat at the card table. "To demolish another theory—we're agreed there was no intruder, and the rest of us were in the dining room. So no one could have been hiding in Tillis's room. Everyone is accounted for."

"And we can scratch Howard's dumb theory about someone firing a projectile into the room," Dennis said. "The killer would have to be perched at the top of a two-

and-half-story pine in the middle of a blizzard. He'd have to hope that Tillis would open the window, then he would have to fire through a four-inch opening at the exact moment Tillis happened to pass by.''

''That window bothers me,'' Meg said at the instant Steven said the same thing. She looked at him a moment, then dropped her gaze. ''Regarding the theory of the first person in the room being the killer...'' She drew a breath. ''There wasn't time. Steven went up the ladder first, but James was right behind him. Plus, those of us waiting in the corridor would have heard the struggle and the furniture being overturned. For this theory to work, Steven would have had to murder Aunt Tilly and vandalize the bedroom before James appeared—in less than a minute. There's no way.''

Flipping a page of the legal pad, Candida traced a red fingernail down her notes. ''How about secret entrances? Did anyone ever hear Tillis mention a secret door?''

''Really, Candida,'' Dennis smiled. ''You've been reading too many of your own novels.''

''Pig.'' Sulky mouthed, Candida rang for James and put the question when he appeared.

A ghost of a smile appeared on James's lips. ''I've worked here for twenty years and never discovered any secret passages.''

''That doesn't mean there aren't any,'' Candida insisted stubbornly.

''I suppose there could be secret passages and I failed to notice.'' The ghost of a smile took on a little flesh.

''Aunt Tilly mentioned Morgan's Manor had secrets. Do you know what she meant by that?'' Meg asked.

''Well, the liquor room is a secret unless you know about the sliding panel. And there's another room where we keep the silver and another where Madam stores her furs." James gave Meg a look that said he would show her the rooms later in private.

"There you are," Candida crowed. "Secret rooms! Is there another secret room opening off Tillis's bedroom?"

"I'd be most surprised if there were." When no one said anything further, he added, "What time will you be wanting dinner served, miss?"

It startled Meg that James deferred to her as the mistress of the house. Tears clogged her throat. "The sandwiches were...I think we'll dine late. About eight?" The others nodded. "Something light. Please tell Hilda not to go to any trouble."

"This is embarrassing." Dennis stubbed out a cigarette with an irritated gesture. "We have two of the best mystery writers in the field today, the best agent working in mystery and a mystery publisher. And we can't come up with a workable scenario."

"Why would Aunt Tilly open the window?" Meg wondered aloud. She could see the same question was worrying Steven. "Why would the killer open it, for that matter? It's a frigid night, snow is blowing—but someone opened that window. Why?"

"The body is lying almost directly beneath the window," Steven said, thinking aloud. "Maybe someone wanted it to appear that Tillis had been dead longer than she really was."

Meg looked at Dennis. "You said you smoked a cigarette in Aunt Tilly's room. Did Aunt Tilly open the window when you lit up?"

"I really don't remember if I smoked or not. But I do know Tillis did not open the window while I was there."

Howard sighed. "I hate to admit this, but I saw Tillis after Dennis did and I didn't see an ashtray and the window was not open. But I think Dennis is the killer." His eyes narrowed. "I think, you killed Tilly, Dennis, because you wanted to make sure she didn't win the Macabre Series. You want Candida or Meg to win so your agency will get a piece of the money."

"That's a damned lie! Maybe you killed Tillis so Candida would have a better chance at the Macabre Series! Your meal ticket's sales haven't been so fat lately, have they? You have a stake in who wins the Macabre Series, too!"

Steven stepped between them. "I know everyone is on edge and upset, but let's try to keep personal grievances out of this."

"Are you sure about the window, Howard?" Meg persisted. "You were drinking heavily last night. Can you trust your memory?"

"I drink too much, I admit it. But because I drink a lot, I have a high tolerance for liquor. Believe me, I wasn't so foxed that I'd fail to notice an open window."

"Dear Tillis had quite an evening, didn't she?" Candida sniffed. "Three men in her room. Saying your goodbyes, were you, gentlemen?"

The question stirred something deep in Meg's mind, but she couldn't pull the reference to the surface.

"I've had it, folks." Standing, Dennis placed his hands in the small of his back and scowled at Howard. "We've been at this for hours. It's six o'clock now. I'm in favor of taking a break until dinner."

Suzanne smothered a yawn. "This was a waste of time, wasn't it? About the only things we know for a fact are that Tillis is dead, no one could possibly have killed her, everyone is lying about being in her room and Steven was very likely the last person to see Tillis alive. Otherwise we've learned nothing."

"I am *not* lying, damn it!" Sparks blazed in Candida's eyes.

"Your ring got there by itself." Suzanne smiled as if at a private joke, then excused herself. Before she went upstairs, she asked Steven to accompany her. She wanted to talk to him.

Meg watched them go and felt her heart twist.

Candida promptly vanished, Howard headed for the hidden liquor room and Dennis settled himself in front of the television to watch the evening news.

"Tillis's death will make all the national channels," he commented to Meg. He was practically rubbing his hands together. "The media is going to eat this up with a spoon. Famous mystery writer murdered in secluded mansion surrounded by enemies old and new. A classic whodunit. I'd trample my grandmother to get to a telephone right now!"

"You really are a slime, Dennis. The minute I can get out of my agency contract, I'm gone."

"Sorry, darlin'. The agency agreement is ironclad. Meanwhile we're going to make a lot of money together. With Tillis out of the running, I predict you're a shoo-in for the Macabre Series. Candida's a has-been. She's lost it."

"You didn't think so a few days ago."

He shrugged and lit a cigarette. "Things change."

Because she couldn't stand spending another minute in the same room with Dennis Parnham, Meg marched out of the living room. Not until she stood in the foyer pulling on her cap and gloves did she realize where she was going.

The crisp frigid air outside was exactly what she needed. Closing her eyes, Meg stepped onto the veranda and drew a deep breath of icy, needle-sharp air and held it inside.

Last night's wind had swept the ground almost clear of snow along the front side of the house. After pushing her gloves into her parka pockets, Meg walked as far as she could before the drifts became too deep to negotiate.

The early-evening snow was lovely, falling in thick fat flakes that called to mind romantic skiing vacations. Tilting her head back, Meg caught a powdery snowflake on her tongue and tried not to remember the ski trip to Vermont. With Steven.

It wasn't as if she hadn't tried to forget him. She hadn't fallen into the trap of moping by the telephone for eight months. There had been other men, other enjoyable evenings.

But Steven was a tough act to follow. Many people didn't understand writers, but Steven did. He understood the stress and pressure of a looming deadline, didn't complain during those awful times when Meg ignored him and worked around the clock to finish a manuscript on time. He understood the spikes of despair when she was positive she would never have another salable idea, and he could tease her into laughing and admitting she was being silly. He sympathized with her bereft feeling when the manuscript was finally finished. And he understood the lump-in-the-throat joy she experienced when she stood in a bookstore and saw her book—*her* book!—in front of her on the shelf.

He knew her life history, had listened as she described growing up on a farm in Iowa, knew that she had followed her dream to New York City before she understood a writer didn't have to live near the presses to publish a book.

And he knew the intimate things. That she hated having freckles, that she wished she wore a larger bra size. He knew she never felt she was dressed right and that she turned shy meeting people for the first time. He knew about Mark Braden, the man she had almost married, and how it had shattered her when Mark eloped with her best friend. Steven knew she loathed Greek and Chinese food. He knew that kissing her breasts drove her wild.

Meg stared up at the snow tumbling out of the twilight sky and wished she was not thinking these things. But she was. And she knew Steven as well as he knew her.

She knew business compelled him to attend publishing parties that bored or irritated him, knew he had to entertain sulky writers at lunch and stroke their egos when what he really wanted was to shake some humility into them. She knew the panic and long hours a breakdown in scheduling could cause, or a foul-up in the artwork department. And she knew how he felt when he lost out in the auction of a book he loved and truly wanted to publish.

And she, too, knew some of the intimate things. She sensed that Steven still battled some lingering conflicts over following in his father's footsteps, that he didn't fully trust his judgment about choosing the right tie for the right suit. She knew he laughed at cornball jokes and was secretly addicted to sitcoms. She knew he sang in the shower and scattered wet towels everywhere.

She knew that she still loved him.

But she'd been hurt once by a man unworthy of trust, by a man who pretended to be open but wasn't. It struck her as ironic that she was in the same situation again. Mark had told her that she misunderstood his relationship with Sandra, just like Steven was telling her she misunderstood his relationship with Suzanne. Right up to the moment he eloped with Sandra, Mark was telling her she had no reason to be jealous.

A sigh sent white vapors spiraling among the snowflakes. It was almost dark. Time to return inside.

Shaking free of old and bitter memories, Meg gazed up at Morgan's Manor, now hers. What on earth would she do with it? Three odd-shaped stories of Gothic design. An anachronism. She started toward the veranda, then something occurred to her and she turned around.

Unless it was a trick of the fading light, it appeared the windows on the third floor were boarded from the inside. Surely James and Hilda had not boarded the windows in the servant's quarters. But that was what it looked like. She would have to remember to ask James.

When she returned inside and hung her parka and cap in the foyer, no one was around. The TV still blared in the living room; she thought she heard Steven and Howard talking in the dining room.

As she wasn't eager to run into Steven, she turned down the back corridor and ended before the door to Aunt Tilly's office. Feeling like an intruder, she hesitated, then pressed the latch and stepped inside.

"Oh. I'm sorry, I didn't realize anyone was in here."

Candida looked as startled as she did. "You scared me to death!" She fanned her face with the book in her hand, then pushed the book back on the shelf. "I wanted to see Tillis's research library. I didn't think anyone would mind."

"If you mean me—I wonder about other writers' resources, too."

Biting her lip, Candida stepped into the lamplight. "Meg, I want you to know—I didn't kill your aunt. There was a lot of bad blood between us, and it's true I want the Macabre Series and I'm a step closer with Tillis out of the running. It's also true I'm not crying my eyes out that she's gone. But...I've been thinking about what Tillis said last night. You know, about how much she enjoyed her enemies, and I understand what she meant. I'll miss Tillis. Life is going to be pretty damned dull without her. She was my favorite person to hate."

Meg sat on the arm of a chair. "May I ask you something personal? About you and Howard and Aunt Tilly?"

A smile curved Candida's full mouth. "You're wondering why Tillis and I both wanted a balding, rather overweight insurance salesman."

The color deepened in Meg's cheeks. "Something like that."

Candida shrugged. "Who can explain why one person falls in love with another person? I can tell you that once upon a time Howard didn't drink like he does today. And I can tell you that he's a genuinely nice man. It didn't bother me a bit to cuckold Tillis, but Howard went through agony. Howard is weak, but—" she spread her hands "—but he's—nice. I know that's a pallid word, but it's also the best description. Howard Clancy is a nice man. A thoughtful, loyal man. I was so damned jealous that he belonged to Tillis. And maybe she was jealous when I won him. I can't explain it any better than that."

"Jealousy," Meg said softly, covering her eyes. Then she looked at Candida again. "But you and Dennis...I'm sorry, this isn't any of my business."

"Sometimes nice isn't enough," Candida explained. "Sometimes we need drama and thunder and lightning. Sometimes we can't help hurting nice people just because they are nice. Or maybe we feel compelled to push them to the limit until they can't be nice anymore, until they turn as mean and small as we secretly believe we are ourselves. Well." Candida cast a self-conscious look toward the door. "Enough of that. I think I'll join the others for cocktails. Are you coming?"

"You go ahead. I'll be along in a minute or two."

When Candida had gone, Meg looked around the room. There was something exceptionally intimate about a person's office. This was the room that held the greatest emotional charge. Here one triumphed or collapsed in defeat. This was the dream site, and this is where one came to lick wounds and hide from the slings and arrows of the world. This was the room that contained a writer's pulse beat.

Clasping her hands behind her back, Meg walked slowly along the bookcases, as interested as Candida had been to read the titles on the spines of Aunt Tilly's books. Meg owned many of the same volumes, but her library was not nearly as extensive as Aunt Tilly's.

When she reached the skeleton hanging from the coat-rack she paused and smiled as she realized it had a rubber knife taped to its ribs. After examining the photos on top of the mantelpiece, she sampled the contents of the poison bottles and discovered they were indeed filled with bath salts. Finally, having circled the room, she gingerly sat on the chair behind Aunt Tilly's desk.

In daylight the view would be wonderful. The windows opened to a sweeping vista of pine and spruce and mossy mountainside.

For several minutes Meg sat quietly at the desk, her fingers folded on top of the blotter, her thoughts engaged in a moral battle. Should she open the desk drawers and inspect the contents?

It seemed an unforgivable violation to rifle Tillis's desk while the room so strongly bore Tillis's imprint. Meg would hate it if a stranger went through her desk drawers.

But she wasn't a stranger. This house, this room, were hers now. And certainly Tillis would expect her to search for clues.

Still it was with reluctance that she opened the top drawer. There was the usual paraphernalia, loose paper clips, staples, rubber bands, a roll of stamps. Two bankbooks Meg simply could not bring herself to open yet, and a pile of bills and receipts.

The death threats were in the third drawer. Hands shaking, Meg withdrew the envelopes and confirmed the New York City postmarks. The envelopes had been mailed about a week apart, the most recent being a week ago yesterday.

Each of the threats was pasted together from newspaper clippings, the words different sizes and different type sets. Each carried the same message.

If you don't stop poking your nose into ancient history, you will die. You know this is not a joke.

Meg could understand why Aunt Tilly had not taken the pages to the police. There wasn't enough information. "Ancient history" could refer to events far in the past, or it could be someone's idea of yesterday. Still, someone had taken the trouble to paste the threats and mail them.

And now Aunt Tilly was dead.

Gooseflesh rose on the back of her neck and on her upper arms. Hastily Meg folded the threats back into their envelopes and pushed them into the drawer. Then, standing, she rubbed her arms briskly and gave herself a shake.

All right, get serious she commanded herself. This is a real-life murder mystery, not a ghost story. She'd just take a peek into Aunt Tilly's supply room, then she'd hightail it back to a noisy room full of people. She would save further exploration of Aunt Tilly's office for a bright sunshiny day when every creak didn't sound so idiotically sinister.

Meg opened the door to the supply room and reached inside for the light switch. Then she sucked in a hard breath.

Every box of stationery and envelopes had been torn open and emptied on the floor. So had the envelopes of carbon paper. Reams of typing paper lay thick on the floor in front of the file cabinet. Every drawer of the cabinet was jerked open and files strewn helter-skelter atop the rest of the mess.

Bending—Meg refused to think of it as collapsing—she reached a shaking hand and picked up an empty file folder. The label read, *Death Drums*. Presumably the folder had held Aunt Tilly's notes for that book. She picked up and scanned a loose sheet, recognizing a page from an early draft of *The Conroy Case*. It was going to be a daunting task to reassemble the files. Who did this, she wondered, pushing upward on shaky legs. What were they looking for?

Candida's image rose in Meg's mind as she stared at the chaotic mess covering the supply room floor. She remembered the guilty look on Candida's face when Meg found her in Aunt Tilly's office. Shortly before she was discovered, had Candida been searching for a copy of Aunt Tilly's proposal for the Macabre Series?

Two weeks remained until the proposal cutoff date. Maybe Candida hadn't yet submitted her proposal. In that event, it would be enormously helpful to know what the competition had proposed. Even if the strongest competitor was now dead.

And that, of course, was the most helpful circumstance of all.

Chapter Five

Once again Meg found herself seated across from Steven at the dinner table, trying not to meet his eyes.

"Will it ever stop snowing?" Sighing heavily, Candida looked away from the dark windows and returned her attention to the apple pie. She pushed her plate aside. "I can't believe we're actually living the oldest cliché in the mystery-novel business. Trapped on an isolated mountain, cut off from all communication. There's a dead body upstairs and one of you is a murderer. If I wrote this, my editor would die laughing before she had time to scribble a rejection letter."

It was the first time anyone had spoken in several minutes.

"I'm sure you'd write it in such a fresh way that everyone would love the book and it would be a runaway bestseller."

"Oh, Howard." Candida sighed again. "You're always so loyal and so...so damned nice." She spread her palms in a gesture of helplessness. "Such a genuinely nice man. What's wrong with me that I hate it that you're so nice? Why do I always push you to be nasty? And you so seldom are."

"Oh, please." Suzanne pushed back in her chair.

"We're all on edge here. Must you choose this moment to analyze your husband and yourself?"

"I was just making a comment, for God's sake. Why are you so edgy anyway? You aren't one of the invited enemies, you weren't in Tillis's room, you swear you had no reason to kill her. This is all according to you, of course. But if any of it is true, then what do you have to complain about? All you have to do is wait for the plow to rescue us, then you can waltz off and resume your skiing vacation."

"Frankly, the company is becoming tedious."

"Oh my heavens!" Meg sat up straight and blinked. "Skis."

Steven understood at once. "Why didn't we think of this earlier? Damn it."

Meg stared at him. "One of us could ski down to Breckenridge and get help!"

There was a beat of silence, then a rush of excited voices.

"Suzanne," Steven leaned forward, his pie forgotten. "Did you bring your skis? Are they in your rental car?"

"No. I decided to rent equipment here rather than go through the aggravation of checking everything on the plane, then having to collect it and—"

Candida flew out of her seat and jerked the velvet rope to summon James. "James! Are there any skis on the premises?"

"Skis?" Sudden understanding followed. "Of course. I should have thought of it at once. There are two sets in the garage."

Everyone at the table leaped up and ran for the coat closet. They all pulled on parkas and hurried out to the garage.

James halted in front of an empty rack against the back

wall. He put his hand against the wall, blinked, then slowly turned. "The skis are gone."

"Gone? What do you mean they're gone?" Candida demanded. "How can they be gone?"

James shrugged helplessly. "I don't know, madam. There were two sets of skis here a day or two ago. Now they're gone."

"Were the skis in the rack when you came into the garage to get the ladder?" Steven asked finally.

"I don't remember." James wrung his hands. "I was worrying about Madam. All I could think about was fetching the ladder and hurrying. I didn't even notice the tires were flat on the cars. All I could think about—"

"So no one can say when the tires were flattened or when the skis vanished." Dennis made a sound of disgust. "Some detectives you are."

"Wait a minute," Meg said, watching her breath plume out before her. "Give me a second to think about this. Okay, let's assume the murderer punctured the tires, and the murderer took the skis, all right?"

"Who else?" Dennis flung out his hands.

"Why did he do it?"

"What an idiotic question! He did it to keep us here, of course. So he'd have a full complement of suspects to obscure his own activities."

Staring at Meg, Steven nodded his head. "I'm following you. And it's an excellent point. We knew early last evening that we were snowbound and marooned. No one was going anywhere."

Candida pursed her lips. "I see where you two are leading. Stealing the skis and disabling the cars seems redundant. It wasn't necessary because of the storm."

Stepping to Aunt Tilly's car, Steven inspected the flattened tires. "The murderer knew we couldn't go anywhere because of the drifts. By morning the murder had been committed so there was no reason to flatten the tires then. So why do it?''

''There has to be a reason,'' Meg said. ''There must be some benefit to the killer to keep us here.''

Candida nodded. ''Maybe the killer has to delay the arrival of the police for some reason. He had to consider the possibility that maybe one of us could bash our car through the drifts last night or this morning. To make sure we can't, he flattens the tires. And to make doubly sure that no one can go for the authorities, he hides the skis.''

''This is all fascinating speculation,'' Suzanne remarked, ''but could we continue the discussion inside? It's freezing out here.''

For an instant Meg met Steven's eyes, feeling the warmth of knowing they were sharing the same thoughts, that their ideas dovetailed beautifully. He smiled as if he were thinking the same thing before Meg hurried outside.

She fell into step beside James during the trek back to the house. ''What are the chances that your friend at the service station will plow us out anytime soon?''

James frowned at the tumbling snowflakes. ''Not encouraging, miss, I'm sorry to say. We haven't had a weekend storm this severe all season. The plows will be working around the clock, but we're at the bottom of the list.''

''Surely this isn't the first time Morgan's Manor has been snowed in. Who usually plows out the road?''

''Jim or Ed from the service station. But when I spoke to Jim last night he already had two dozen calls. At that time, we weren't anticipating an emergency. Everyone planned to stay for the weekend, we had plenty of supplies...there was no urgency.'' James's breath released in a sigh. ''I told Jim to put us last on his list.''

It was a subdued group who gathered in the living room for coffee and brandy.

"Well? Now what?" Dennis brandished a cigarette and turned a brooding expression toward the fireplace. "Do we just sit here and wait to be rescued?"

"Do you have a better idea?" Candida grimaced. "All you've done is complain, Dennis. Too bad the killer didn't murder you while he was at it!"

"You would have liked that, wouldn't you?"

Candida narrowed her eyes. "Maybe I would!"

"Oh, spare us." Suzanne sighed, then wandered to the coffee urn. Tonight she wore a blue silk designer dress. The petal hem fluttered attractively against blue silk stockings.

It was the kind of dress Meg longed for in her heart, but would never have bought. She glanced down at her jeans and lemon-colored sweater. A small sigh lifted her breasts. Tomboys never thought to buy blue stockings.

"Is anyone up for a rubber of bridge?" Breaking the silence, Howard ran his fingertips over the surface of the card table.

"Bridge! How civilized. Having completed his work, the murderer now sits down to a relaxing game of bridge. Well, count me out." Dennis stood and placed his empty brandy snifter on a side table. "I'm going upstairs. I'd rather read a briefcase full of dreadful manuscripts than sit around playing card games with a murderer."

Meg's first impulse was to agree with Dennis. But on second thought, she decided bridge might be a good idea. It would give them something to concentrate on that wasn't connected to Aunt Tilly's murder. And at least they wouldn't be hurling accusations at one another.

"I'm game," she said, taking a seat at the card table.

"Come on someone, Howard and I need two more players."

"Make that three more players," Howard said. "Now that I think about it, I've had too much to drink to make a decent partner for anyone. I believe I'll go upstairs, lie down awhile and finish Ludlum's latest thriller."

"Actually Dennis and Howard are doing us a favor," Candida announced, taking a seat at the card table. "Neither is a skilled player. Come on, Steven and Suzanne. There's nothing interesting on TV and you aren't doing anything else. Sit down and shuffle the deck. Although I don't like to play cards with a left-handed player," she said, squinting at Suzanne.

"It does *not* affect how I play," Suzanne snapped.

They played in silence, concentrating fiercely, playing a cutthroat game. No mercy offered; no prisoners taken. Meg and Steven were both strong players and they knew each other's game. Each was determined to beat the other. They had been playing for almost an hour when the front door slammed.

"Who was that?" Steven asked.

"Dennis." Suzanne looked up, then back down at her cards. She sat facing the archway that opened onto the foyer. "Bundled up like an Eskimo, but still smoking. I loathe smokers."

Meg shifted to see wisps of cigarette smoke slowly dissipating in the foyer beyond the archway. She glanced at the clock. "Where on earth is he going at this time of night?"

Steven shrugged and returned his attention to his hand. "Dennis is a big boy. He doesn't need us to watch over him."

"It is odd," Candida commented with a frown. "Dennis detests fresh air. He goes from office to taxi to his apartment with scarcely a breath of air that hasn't been heated, cooled or treated in some manner. I've never known Dennis Parnham to seek out fresh air of his own free will. As for—''

"Are you going to play that hand, or talk?" Scowling, Suzanne stifled a yawn. "It's hard enough to concentrate. This altitude makes me sleepy. If Candida will deign to finish that hand maybe we can all go to bed."

A few minutes later Meg lifted her head. "Did anyone besides me hear a noise?"

"Hear what? I don't hear anything but the stereo."

"I thought I heard something, too," Steven agreed, laying down his cards. As he started to rise from his chair Howard appeared from the direction of the staircase. "Oh, it was you."

"I thought you went to bed," Candida said. But Howard didn't look as if he had been to bed. He still wore the clothing he'd worn to dinner. A gray jacket, navy tie and dark slacks.

"I've been thinking," Howard said, studying Candida. "I don't like the idea of you being alone tonight." He shrugged an apology toward the others. "No offense, but there's a murderer among us. I'd feel better if you slept in my room tonight."

"That's just—" Then Candida's expression collapsed and her eyes filled with gratitude. "Thank you, Howard. I don't want to be alone, either." She managed a thin smile. "As Howard said, no offense but I don't want any of you murdering *me* tonight."

"It's ten-thirty. Are you ready to go upstairs?" Howard asked, looking at his watch.

Candida glanced at the scorecard, noticed she and Steven were lagging behind. "I think so. I'm tired, too."

Meg had an uncomfortable idea that if she hadn't been

so tired and upset from everything that had happened to-day, she could have put her finger on something slightly askew. She couldn't bring the thought forward enough to identify it.

Then she did. Or maybe it was something else that was awry, but she suddenly realized if Howard and Candida went upstairs, she would be left alone with Steven and Suzanne. Quickly she pushed back her chair and stood. "I believe I'll call it a night, too."

"Steven, will you join me in a nightcap?" Suzanne asked, calling Steven back when it appeared he would follow Meg.

"I really don't...well, just a quick one."

Meg met his expressionless gaze, then glanced at Suzanne before she turned away. Judging from the predatory interest in Suzanne's cool eyes, Meg doubted Steven would turn up at her door tonight, after all. She tried to tell herself she didn't care.

WHEN A KNOCK SOUNDED at her door, she almost ran to answer it, surprised and embarrassed by how glad she was that Steven had remembered her, after all.

"Oh." She blinked at James, then hastily apologized for her look of disappointment. "I was expecting someone else."

"I came about tomorrow's menus, miss."

"Whatever you and Hilda decide will be fine. I'm sorry, James, I'm just not up to planning menus or making decisions about the house yet. I hope you understand. It's not that—"

"Quite so, miss. Hilda and I will manage."

"Before you go, there's something I've been wondering." She stepped into the corridor beside him. "How many telephones are in the house?"

"Five, miss." He listed their locations.

"I see." Meg hadn't guessed the existence of the phone on the third floor. "You're saying someone went into your quarters and jerked the phone wires out of the wall even there. But who knew about that telephone?"

"I can't say, miss. All Madam's guests have visited Morgan's Manor before except Mrs. Halverson." James's expression indicated he didn't hold Suzanne Halverson in high regard. "It's possible everyone knows where all the telephones are."

Obviously someone did. "You and Hilda were occupied downstairs most of yesterday, weren't you?" He nodded confirmation. "So someone could have disabled the telephones then?"

"Not in the afternoon, miss. The phones were in service after dinner when I phoned the service station about the plow."

"I'd forgotten that. So pulling out the wires had to happen later in the evening."

"As far as I know, the call to the service station was the last telephone call made and that was about nine o'clock. The vandalism could have happened anytime after that."

"There's something else I'm curious about. It appears most of the windows on the third floor are boarded up. Could that be true?"

The faintest smile touched James's lips. "Yes, miss."

As Meg's bedroom was nearest the landing, she saw Suzanne appear at the top of the stairs, and she stopped speaking until Suzanne had passed them in the corridor. Suzanne gave her a lengthy speculative look that Meg couldn't decipher.

"Don't the boarded windows make your apartment as

dark as a cave?'' she asked, returning her attention to James.

"Only the back half of our apartment lacks windows, miss. It was a bit strange at first, but in twenty years we've gotten accustomed to it. We don't spend much time in our quarters anyway, and when we're there, we're usually in the living room.''

"But why were the windows covered over?''

"Years ago, before Hilda and I came to Morgan's Manor, Madam's father remodeled the servants' quarters and other parts of the house. As I understand it, the original servants' quarters were a collection of small sleeping rooms. Then, when modern conveniences made it possible to manage a large house without so many servants, Mr. Morgan tore out the sleeping rooms and remodeled the third floor into one apartment for a live-in couple. As Madam explained it, the original configuration didn't align with the new apartment. New walls ended smack in the middle of a window and so forth. So the windows were boarded over and the interior walls resurfaced. There are a few boarded windows on the second floor, too.'' James coughed into his hand and phrased the next sentence as tactfully as he could. "It's said Mr. Morgan always chose the least expensive way to do things.''

"He was too cheap to do the job properly, is that it?''

"As you say, miss.''

They smiled at each other.

"Thank you, James. Right now I'm seeing mysteries in everything.''

"It's a terrible, terrible thing that's happened here,'' he said in a low voice. "Madam's loss will be keenly felt.''

After James left, Meg walked to her window and gazed out at the falling snowflakes. Their intensity seemed to be diminishing. Lost in thought, she started when another knock sounded at her door.

"I didn't mean to frighten you," Steven said, stepping into her bedroom. "Had you forgotten our date?" Smiling, he carried a brandy bottle and two snifters to her bedside table.

"This is hardly a date." But his phrasing underscored the mistake she had made. Allowing Steven into her bedroom brought a rush of memories, and invited intimacies Meg did not wish to encourage. "I'm not sure this is a good idea."

"Are we going to start that again? I thought we agreed we had to talk."

"Look, *someone* murdered Aunt Tilly..."

"Good God." He straightened abruptly and turned to face her. "You mean you're afraid to be alone with... Meg—" his broad shoulders stiffened and his dark eyes stared into hers "—do you really suspect me? Can you honestly think I could murder anyone?"

"You seem to have been the last person to see Aunt Tilly alive." She stared at him, testing the thought. Then her shoulders dropped and she sighed. "No, of course not. The trouble is, I don't think the others are murderers, either. But someone is." After a pause, she looked up at him. "Who do you think the killer is?"

Before he answered, he handed her a snifter of brandy and sat down on the edge of her bed. "I think enough accusations have been tossed around, don't you?" He smiled when she walked away from the bed and took the chair by the window, tucking her feet up under her body.

"There's something you should know." Rolling the snifter between her palms, Meg related her conversation with James. "Did you know there was a telephone in the servants' quarters?"

"No. I didn't."

"I'd be willing to bet no one else did, either." Meg frowned. "I hate to say this, but I have an uneasy suspicion that James and Hilda are the only people who knew the location of all the telephones."

"Are you suggesting James or Hilda ripped the wires out of the wall?"

"I just can't believe that." Meg looked away from the lamplight playing over Steven's strong chin and jawline. His hair was rumpled and the suggestion of a new beard shadowed his cheeks. "But no one else has spent enough time in this house to know James and Hilda have a phone in their quarters."

"Meg, the reason I wanted to talk to you—"

"Wait. There's something else." She told him about the supply room in Aunt Tilly's office. "At first I thought Candida was the culprit, searching for Aunt Tilly's Macabre Series proposal. But on second thought, I'm not as convinced. It seems hard to believe that Candida would rip apart the supply room, then calmly start browsing through the library. But who else would be looking for something?"

Swearing softly, Steven bent forward and rested his elbows on his knees. He ran a hand over his face. "I'll bet you a lobster dinner it wasn't Candida who tore through Tillis's files. It was Suzanne."

Meg's eyebrows soared. "Okay, Steven. You wanted to talk about Suzanne, so talk. After hearing that, I want to hear what you have to say."

What she really wanted was to halt the flood of memories. Meg kept remembering the last time they had been in a bedroom together. With another man she would have felt shy and awkward about conducting a conversation in a bedroom. But not with Steven. It struck her as remarkable how quickly they had resumed old habits. Steven had pushed off his shoes, plumped up the pillows and stretched out on top of the quilt. She had kicked off her own shoes and curled into the corner of the wing chair. They had enjoyed a hundred stimulating conversations sitting in these exact positions. And afterward...

"Oh, God, where should I begin?" he said.

"Tell me why you think Suzanne might have vandalized Aunt Tilly's supply room."

"The story starts long before this weekend. You remember when Whitney Halverson was murdered. Whitney was found shot to death in his car while Suzanne was in Los Angeles. I started seeing Suzanne shortly afterward—as a friend," he added. His gaze challenged her to protest.

"It's your story. Tell it the way you see it. But I'll concede you started seeing Suzanne as a friend. In the beginning."

Tilting his head, Steven studied the circles of color rising on her cheeks. "The relationship with Suzanne was never what you thought it was, Meg."

"Let's omit any personal references, okay?" Meg turned her face to the window. Her cheeks felt hot.

"That's impossible," he said bluntly. "You and I—our relationship—is twisted into the events of this weekend whether we like it or not."

"What are you talking about?"

"We're one of the triangles that make up this weekend, at least the way you see it, we are. You, me and Suzanne. Then there's Suzanne, me and Tillis—the Halverson book triangle. And there's Howard, Candida and Tillis—an old triangle that still vibrates. And there's Howard, Candida and Dennis—that triangle is sending off powerful signals. Then we have you, Tillis and Candida—the Macabre Series triangle. And we have Tillis, James and Hilda—the

Morgan Manor triangle. Finally we have publisher, agent and writers—the industry triangle.''

Meg stared. ''All the triangles interlock,'' she whispered. ''They each have a dynamic that's crashing up against another dynamic.''

Steven nodded. ''The triangle I want to talk to you about involves Suzanne, her maid and her husband—the basic elements in the Halverson case.'' He drew a breath and met Meg's eyes. ''In the beginning I probably did spend too much time with Suzanne. I felt I owed something to her because of my friendship with Whitney. I felt he would have expected me to offer support to his widow. Plus, the story fascinated me. An older wealthy man, a beautiful younger wife, a violent death, the double tragedy of the maid dying shortly afterward. After a few weeks it occurred to me there was a book in Suzanne and Whitney's story. I asked Tillis if she would be interested in writing it.''

''Aunt Tilly would have loved jumping into the middle of a real murder case.''

''She accepted the offer at once.''

Swinging his legs from the bed, Steven took the brandy bottle to Meg's chair and freshened her drink. His nearness made her feel dizzy and she didn't breathe again until he returned to the bed. A sinking feeling stole over her. He was so intense, so steady and solid. And she was so willing to believe whatever he told her.

''As Candida pointed out, any book about the Halverson case faced an insurmountable problem. It had no ending. While trying to find an ending, Tillis studied the police reports, the newspaper accounts, every scrap of evidence she could pry out of the authorities. And she managed to get copies of everything the police had. As you know, Tillis could be very persuasive. Plus, she conducted interviews with just about everyone who had known Whitney or Suzanne and she made hundreds of telephone calls tracking down loose ends.''

An uneasy sensation opened in the pit of Meg's stomach. She leaned forward in her chair. "Did Aunt Tilly realize how dangerous conducting her own investigation might be?"

"To Tillis, the investigation was an exciting challenge. She and I agreed I would continue to see Suzanne on a social basis. My task was to try to discover if there was anything Suzanne hadn't told the police."

Meg put a growing suspicion into words. "Were you looking for clues—or did you and Aunt Tilly suspect Suzanne was somehow involved with Whitney's murder?"

A long minute passed before Steven answered. "In the beginning there seemed to be no question that Suzanne was in Los Angeles at the moment Whitney was shot. The airlines checked out. A woman answering Suzanne's description used her ticket to fly to Los Angeles, then checked into the Royal Palms Hotel."

"But?" Meg didn't take her eyes from his face.

"But Tillis discovered Suzanne failed to sign the hotel register. No sample of her handwriting proves it was actually Suzanne who checked into the Royal Palms, although the description matches. At least from what the hotel clerk could see of her."

Meg frowned. "What does that mean?"

"The woman who registered at the Royal Palms wore dark glasses, a slouch hat and a scarf. She was bundled up."

"In *Los Angeles?*"

He smiled. "It was enough to raise a question mark in Tillis's mind, too. Suzanne explained the muffling by saying she had a mild case of the flu, chills and so forth. Then

I discovered Whitney had been planning a divorce. Suzanne confided he had spoken to his attorney. That's why she was upset about Whitney's murder but not devastated. As Whitney's widow, she inherited his considerable estate, as his ex-wife she would have inherited nothing.''

"I'm starting to track this." Meg leaned forward again. "At some point, you and Aunt Tilly concluded Suzanne murdered her husband. You couldn't prove how she did it. But you had a theory."

"Right on target. And I have a feeling you can guess the theory."

"I think so, but tell me anyway."

"The theory didn't hold much water as Tillis couldn't produce a shred of supporting proof. She hoped Suzanne might let something slip to me. But aside from the information about the divorce, it didn't happen."

This was the kind of puzzle Meg loved. Her eyes sparkled as she thought it through. "For Suzanne to be the murderer, then she couldn't be the woman on the plane. She had to be in New York City when Whitney Halverson was shot."

"You're doing fine, keep going."

"It could have been the maid on the plane masquerading as Suzanne. Suzanne stays in New York, kills Whitney, then flies to California under an assumed name." Meg pulled her lower lip between her teeth. "This puts a new light on the maid's suicide. Did you and Aunt Tilly conclude that Suzanne covered her tracks by pushing the maid over the balcony?"

"There isn't an iota of proof. None. Just speculation on mine and Tillis's part. Except…"

Meg was starting to feel like a fool as the implications of the conversation filtered to a personal level. She had done Steven an injustice. His interest in Suzanne had been tied to a book and to discovering his friend's murderer. He thought it was possible Suzanne had murdered *two* people. And all this time Meg had believed it was a romantic entanglement. Shame colored her throat and cheeks. She had allowed her jealousy to poison her thoughts.

"Except what?" she asked, her head down.

"Except Tillis telephoned me a couple of days ago. She was very excited. She said she had found the ending to the book and she had enough proof to take to the authorities. She asked me to fly to Colorado and confirm what she had found. She didn't want to risk the material in the mails. Suzanne told the truth about how she arrived here. She wasn't invited. Tillis was definitely not expecting her."

"I think I owe you an apology."

"We'll return to that in a minute." He held her gaze for a long dizzying moment. "There's more you should know."

"Go on." Meg's hands were trembling and she felt as if a weight had lifted from her heart. It was as if she had stumbled around in the darkness for a very long time and suddenly emerged into the sunshine. He wasn't in love with Suzanne.

"Tillis said she and Suzanne had a terrible argument shortly after Suzanne arrived. Suzanne demanded that Tillis drop the book and stop prying into the murder. Maybe Tillis hinted that she knew who had committed the murder, I don't know. Tillis was vague on that point. But she admitted some regrettable things were said. Eventually Tillis realized the situation could be dangerous. She knew the storm was worsening and the roads were drifting over. She suddenly realized Suzanne might be unable to leave Morgan's Manor. Not knowing how dangerous Suzanne might become if she believed she was cornered, Tillis pretended to be persuaded. She told Suzanne she would abandon the book and had, in fact, already destroyed her research.''

''But that was a lie.''

''Absolutely. Tillis would not have asked me to fly to Colorado to examine her research if she had destroyed it.''

''When you went to Aunt Tilly's room last night, did she show you the new evidence?''

''No,'' Steven said after a pause. ''We discussed the material only as it applied to you.''

Meg stared at him. ''I remember now.''

''Yes. At dinner Tillis announced you were her primary beneficiary and would inherit the notes and research for her new book. I made the situation worse by mentioning a new revelation in the case.''

''Earlier, Aunt Tilly tells Suzanne the research has been destroyed,'' Meg said slowly. ''Then at dinner she gives the very same research to me. And you announce there's explosive new material.''

''If Tillis could prove Suzanne murdered her husband—which was the implication of the new material— then Tillis also understood she was in danger. By stating that you would inherit her research, she feared she had placed you in danger, too.''

''And Candida kept insisting Tillis would never have destroyed her notes.''

Steven nodded, his expression grim. ''Now you tell me someone has rifled through Tillis's files.''

''Suzanne.'' Meg stared at him. ''The next question is did she find what she was looking for?''

''My guess is she didn't,'' Steven said after a pause. ''Tillis said she hid the material. I doubt she hid it in as obvious a spot as her file cabinet.'' He studied Meg. ''Tillis also said she told you how to find the material.''

''What?'' Meg straightened. ''But that's...no, Steven,

she didn't. Maybe she intended to and was murdered before she had a chance. But Aunt Tilly didn't talk about the Halverson case at all. No, wait a minute.'' Frowning, she tried to remember. ''No, she never said a word about hiding something or where it could be found. I'm sure she didn't.''

''Meg, try to remember. When I spoke to Tillis at eleven-thirty, she said you would know how to find the material if you needed to. She didn't exactly say she had revealed her hiding place, but she displayed no doubt that she had pointed you in the right direction. She felt confident you would know where to look.''

''That's crazy.'' Meg spread her hands. ''Steven, I don't have a clue!''

''Tillis agreed it was time you knew what she was working on. Her death makes it imperative that you know.''

''Steven…'' It had to be said. ''Do you think Suzanne murdered Aunt Tilly?''

For a full minute he didn't speak. ''I think Suzanne has the strongest motive,'' he said finally.

''Should we tell the others?'' The minute Meg spoke, she knew she was wrong and she waved the words away. ''No, we can't let Suzanne know what we suspect. Not while we're trapped here.''

''I absolutely agree. Plus, we have to remember there isn't a shred of proof, nothing, Meg, until Tillis's notes are found. And the notes won't prove anything about Tillis's murder. But right now, the possibility that the research notes exist places *you* in danger. If Tillis was murdered because of those notes…''

''Then I'm next on the list,'' Meg whispered. Her hands started to shake and she held them out in front of her. ''Oh my God. I don't think I'm as brave as I thought I was,'' she said in a small voice.

Steven knelt beside her and took both her hands in his. "I'm not going to let anything happen to you."

"Oh, Steven, I was wrong about everything. I'm sorry."

"You were wrong about Suzanne," he said, bringing her hands to his lips. He kissed her fingertips. "And you were wrong about my secretary, and that new writer, what's her name? Ellen Prather. Meg, you've been wrong about all of it."

Slowly Meg pulled her hands away. "You haven't helped much. You could have told me all this before. It would have spared me a lot of pain if you'd explained all this months ago."

He rocked back on his heels and examined her expression. "Is that true? If you had known I was seeing Suzanne because I was trying to learn more about Whitney's murder, can you honestly say you would have advised me to continue seeing her?"

"The point is, you didn't tell me." She drew back in the chair. "Just like you didn't tell me until we were arguing about it that there were problems with Ellen Prather's contract and that's why you had to keep seeing *her*. You could have spared us a lot of problems by communicating more openly."

Standing, Steven looked down at her and his brows met in a frown. "Communication isn't the problem. The problem is trust. For a relationship to work, both parties have to trust each other. You can't build a solid relationship by always assuming the worst."

She stood, too. "Aunt Tilly trusted Howard and he had an affair with Candida. Howard trusted Candida and she's openly sleeping with Dennis Parnham. I trusted Mark Braden and he eloped with my best friend."

"I'm not Mark Braden, damn it." Steven glared at her,

his frustration evident. "How long do I have to continue paying for Mark Braden's sins?"

Meg drew back as if he had slapped her. "Is that what you think I'm doing? Punishing you because I can't punish Mark?"

"That's part of it, yes. Each time I spend time with a woman you decide a painful experience is about to be repeated. Finally, with Suzanne, you decided to reject me rather than wait for me to reject you, which is what you feared would happen again." He caught her by the shoulders and gave her a shake. "And damn it, Meg, that's exactly what might have happened. You can't expect me to go on being accused whenever I happen to smile at another woman. That's not realistic. There *are* other women in my life. My secretary, authors, friends I knew before I met you. Just like there are other men in *your* life. But I don't make you feel guilty about them."

"That's because I don't see them anymore. I don't rub your nose in other relationships." Meg twisted away from his hands.

He swore. "You're missing the point. I don't *care* if you see other men. If you want to have lunch with an old friend, fine. Do it. Because I *trust* you. I trust our relationship. At least, I did. You're the one who can't trust. And without trust, there can be no relationship!"

"And without communication, there can be no relationship!"

"If you'd open your eyes, you'd see that we communicate better than anyone else we know. But your idea of communication is having me explain and justify every word, every smile, directed to another female. And, Meg, I'm not going to do that."

"Fine. No one's asking you to. Because you and I don't have a relationship, not anymore!"

Meg realized they were shouting and she lowered her voice. The instant she did, they both heard voices in the corridor. The sounds in the hallway broke the tension flashing between them and gave Meg an excuse to move away from him. She tiptoed to the door and pressed her ear to the wood.

"It's Candida and Howard," she whispered.

Steven looked at her a moment, then joined her at the door.

They heard Candida's voice as clearly as if she were standing a foot away. "Honestly, Howard. You really should seek help. Go to AA or something."

"All I want is just one more, that's all. To help me sleep. I'll only be a minute. You stand here on the landing, right under the sconce."

"Why can't I wait in the bedroom?" Candida grumbled.

"Because if someone tried to murder you in the bedroom, I wouldn't hear you scream or get there in time to save you. This way, if you scream, I'll hear you and so will everyone else."

"How long is this going to take?"

"Just long enough for me to pour another Scotch. Not long. There were two bottles on the serving cart in the living room. I'll dash in, fill my glass and be back in two minutes. Now stand right here and don't move. I want the light shining on you. Okay?"

"Just hurry up, will you?"

Meg heard footsteps receding down the staircase. She gazed at Steven's dark head pressed to the door beside hers and suppressed an urge to giggle. "If we opened the door right now," she whispered, "we'd scare Candida out of her wits." Straightening, she rubbed her ear.

Her smile faded as she suddenly realized how close she and Steven were standing. Inches away, she could see the shadow of his new beard, responded to the electric warmth and excitement of his body near hers. An earthquake began in the pit of her stomach and trembled outward. She wanted to move away from him, but she couldn't. Helplessly she gazed up into his intense dark eyes and found he was staring at her mouth. A tremble began at her toes and swept upward.

And then he kissed her. One instant they were standing together looking into each other's eyes, the next instant Meg was in his arms crushed against his body. It was a hard angry kiss, a kiss explosive with the passion they had once shared. A kiss that punished and flamed with desire in the same moment.

Meg's lips opened and her fingernails dug into his shoulders. She felt his hands on her waist pulling her hard against his thighs, felt the heat of his need and passion. She felt her own nerves kindle and surge to the surface of her skin, was aware that her pulse raced and pounded in her ears.

When he released her, she stumbled backward, breathless and wide-eyed.

"Maybe someday I'll get over you," he said in a low voice, his eyes traveling hungrily over her face. "But it hasn't happened yet. Maybe our relationship isn't what it once was—but it's still a relationship whether you and I like it or not."

The door opened, and he was gone.

IN THE MORNING after a sleepless night of tossing and turning, Meg walked down the staircase and entered the dining room. "Good morning," she said, heading straight for the silver coffee urn.

"What's good about it?" Candida asked in a sour tone. Once again she wore the furry pink bathrobe. Strands of auburn hair dripped over her collar. "We're still trapped in this gloomy pile of stones and we still have a dead body upstairs." She turned brooding eyes to the windows.

Meg slid a wary look toward Steven, as confused now as she had been after he left her room. He looked as tired and out of sorts as she did. "Where's Dennis?" she asked, turning to James.

"Mr. Parnham hasn't come down yet, miss."

A terrible sense of déjà vu tightened Meg's skin. "The same man who was up at five o'clock yesterday morning isn't up yet at eight o'clock?"

Candida lowered her fork. "Oh, no," she whispered. "Surely you don't think..."

"Did anyone see Dennis return last night?" Steven asked, approaching the coffee urn as Meg left it.

"Return from where?" Howard asked. After Steven explained, Howard said, "Maybe he's still wandering around outside." He didn't sound upset by the suggestion.

"That isn't funny, Howard," Candida said sharply.

Steven touched Suzanne's shoulder. "What was Dennis wearing, do you remember?"

Pushing up from the table, Suzanne walked to the doorway and checked the coatrack in the foyer. "He came back inside. Dennis was wearing a blue parka and a ski cap. They're both hanging on the coatrack."

"Oh my God." Candida raised wide eyes. "He's dead. I just know the killer got Dennis, too."

After a moment of silence, everyone rushed for the staircase.

Chapter Six

Suzanne was the last person up the staircase, carrying a cup of coffee and a slice of buttered toast.

"God forbid that something as trivial as another murder should interfere with your breakfast!" Candida's contempt was magnificent to witness. Her bosom thrust forward, her chin pulled down, her upper lip curled.

"And how interesting, not to mention incriminating, that you automatically presume Dennis has been murdered," Suzanne replied. "May we assume you have prior knowledge?"

Candida narrowed her eyes and leaned forward. "You may assume I have a brain in my head since he was the only one missing from the breakfast table. However, I can't imagine why anyone would murder Tillis or Dennis when they could have the pleasure of murdering you!"

Suzanne's smile was so supremely superior that only Meg's intervention prevented Candida from slapping her. "Please, not now," she said, stepping between them.

"You publishing people are so dramatic and excitable," Suzanne murmured, continuing forward to stand behind Steven.

It occurred to Meg that although she spent most of her professional life creating murder mysteries, she had never been remotely connected to a real murder case. Until now. A chilly ripple of unease and fascination swept over her as she watched Suzanne finish eating her toast.

Had Suzanne Halverson actually cold-bloodedly murdered her husband and her maid? In the dim corridor light Suzanne looked so normal, so reasonable. It didn't seem possible she could murder anyone.

But it didn't seem impossible, either. And maybe Suzanne hadn't stopped at two murders...

Steven pounded again on Dennis's bedroom door. "Dennis? Are you in there?"

"See if it's locked," Howard advised.

The door opened easily and swung inward. Someone gasped.

For one terrible moment no one uttered a word. They stood immobile in the doorway, staring inside the room at Dennis Parnham's slumped body.

"You see?" Candida whispered. She straightened to her full height. "What did I tell you! He's as dead as last year's bestseller. So now we have two dead bodies we're stuck with. This isn't just frightening, it's appalling!"

"Stay in the corridor," Steven ordered in a gruff voice. After passing a hand over his face, he shook his head, then straightened. "All right. This time we won't all go rushing into the scene. One person will enter the room. Suzanne?"

"Why Suzanne?" Meg asked, surprised.

"Suzanne is the only person here who did not know Dennis and presumably had no reason to kill him."

"I loathe smokers...but not enough to murder them," Suzanne drawled, smiling at Meg.

Placing his hand on Suzanne's waist, Steven guided her forward. "Do you have any objection to examining Dennis to determine if he's as dead as he looks?"

Suzanne answered with a shrug, then stepped into the

room. Without hesitation she walked to the chair where Dennis sat slumped, his silver head hanging to one side at an unnatural angle. She placed two fingers beneath his ear.

"No pulse. I'd say his neck is broken. He's cool to the touch as if he's been dead for a while."

Candida leaned into the room. "Stand right where you are. Don't touch anything. But take a look around. Do you see anything suspicious?"

"You can see for yourselves there's no evidence of a struggle. He's not wearing his jacket or tie, but otherwise it appears he's wearing the clothing he wore last night. White shirt, dark slacks." Bending, Suzanne examined the typewritten pages scattered around the base of the chair. "He was reading a manuscript titled *Death, Death, Death* by someone named—" she tilted her head "—Beth Poppins."

Candida rolled her eyes. "That's overkill, overkill, overkill. Beth Poppins, whom I've never heard of, is definitely a novice."

"You can see that his briefcase is open." Kneeling, Suzanne looked inside. "There are two or three more manuscripts, an expensive-looking pen set, business cards, what looks like a set of agency contracts and three unopened packages of cigarettes."

"That reminds me—check the table beside his chair," Meg called from the doorway. "The ashtray. Was Dennis smoking when he was killed?"

"What a peculiar question. If you have to know, there's one crushed butt in the ashtray. A couple of spent matches. Very little ash."

Meg frowned. "Is there another ashtray in the room?"

"None that I can see. Why, are you planning to take up smoking?"

Meg pressed her lips together. "Can you see if there's anything in the wastebasket?"

"It's empty."

"That helps with the timing," Steven nodded, following Meg's train of thought. To Suzanne he said, "Can you tell if he has any blood or tissue under his fingernails? Did he put up a fight?"

Suzanne bent beside Dennis's dangling hand. "Nothing unusual that I can see." She smiled. "I'd guess he knew his killer, probably trusted him. Or her."

"Thank you, madam detective, none of us would have thought of that," Candida snarled. "I'm going to get dressed, then I'll meet all of you downstairs." She leveled a grim look at Howard. "I'd like to have a Bloody Mary waiting. A strong one."

After beckoning Suzanne out of the room, Steven instructed James to lock the door. Without speaking everyone filed down the staircase and back into the dining room, glad for the bright sunshine falling past the heavy velvet curtains. Howard walked straight to the sliding cherrywood panel, pushed it open, then emerged with vodka and spiced tomato juice. Howard mixed the drinks and James served them around the table.

Meg had an absurd idea everyone was waiting for someone to make a toast. Howard cleared his throat, opened his mouth, then he muttered something and swallowed half his drink. Meg tasted hers tentatively and was relieved to discover it wasn't as strong as she feared it would be.

"We can't just sit here any longer, waiting to be rescued," Steven said, his tone somber. "It's time we talked about someone walking down to Breckenridge."

James shook his head. "Forgive me for interrupting, sir, but that's a perilous idea. It's stopped snowing, but the wind has whipped up again. Taking the windchill factor into account, the temperature outside is minus fifteen. It could be fatally dangerous to attempt an eight-mile walk in this temperature and altitude.''

Howard agreed. ''I read a story once where a guy tried to do something like you're suggesting. He exhausted himself wading through drifts, then became delirious. Hypothermia, I imagine. Anyway, he wandered off the road, got lost, and they found his body in the spring. I don't think walking to town is an option.''

James inclined his head in agreement. ''I hope none of you will attempt it. I feel certain Jim will reach us with the plow by tomorrow.''

''By *tomorrow?*'' Candida came into the dining room and flung herself into a chair, then downed half her Bloody Mary. ''By tomorrow someone else could be dead! The murderer is picking us off like ducks in a shooting gallery. One per night. So what are we supposed to do? Just sit here and wait until we're all dead?''

''If anyone has any ideas, now's the time to speak up.'' Frustration tightened Steven's jaw. He drummed his fingertips on the tabletop. No one spoke. ''If the plow isn't here by noon tomorrow, I'll walk into Breckenridge to get help. Regardless of the weather. We can't wait much longer, we have to take the risk.''

Howard's reference to hypothermia continued to reverberate in Meg's mind. She looked at Steven, picturing him delirious and freezing and her chest tightened. Clenching her teeth, she carried her drink to the windows. ''At least it's stopped snowing.'' The sky was clear and cold, so dazzlingly blue it hurt her eyes to look up. Wind teased long tails of snow off the top of the mountain peaks in the distance, but there were no clouds.

''Whichever one of you is the killer,'' Suzanne said,

"*you* should have to make the walk into Breckenridge. Any volunteers?"

Candida's glare threw off sparks. "Whichever one of you is murdering people, would you do everyone a favor and kill that smug bitch next?"

"Oh, dear, now I've made you angry." Suzanne smiled, then gave Candida a thoughtful look. "First, you want Tillis dead and—what do you know?—Tillis dies. Then you mention it's a shame the killer didn't murder Dennis—and how lucky can you get?—Dennis turns up dead. Does anyone recognize a pattern developing here?"

Howard grabbed Candida as she started around the table, her fingernails reaching. With effort he wrestled her back into her chair.

"Let's all calm down," Steven cautioned. "Insults and accusations won't get us anywhere."

Meg discovered her shoulders were tight, her chest constricted. Drawing a breath, she held it, then expelled the tension. "Should we discuss Dennis's murder?" she asked Steven. "Assuming we can do so in a rational manner?"

"We can try," Steven said, glancing at the others.

"There are certain facts we probably can agree on," Meg began.

Candida nodded, still glaring at Suzanne. "The bed wasn't slept in. Dennis was wearing the same clothing he wore to dinner. We can reasonably assume he was murdered last night."

"We can also assume he was murdered relatively early in the evening."

"Because of the cigarette," Steven agreed. Once again he and Meg were thinking along the same lines.

She nodded. "Dennis was a heavy smoker. But there's only one cigarette butt in the ashtray. And that's not because he emptied his ashtray. Suzanne reported there was nothing in the wastebasket."

"I see." Grudging admiration lit Candida's eyes. "If Dennis had been sitting there reading for any length of time, there would have been several cigarette butts in the ashtray."

"Wait a minute," Howard interrupted. "I don't like the direction this conversation is heading. You're suggesting that Dennis was murdered almost immediately after he went upstairs. That means you're saying I did it. All of you were downstairs watching each other and playing bridge. Except me. I went upstairs right after Dennis did. And no one saw him alive after that."

"Don't be silly, Howard. You couldn't murder anyone." Candida made a face. "Plus, Suzanne *did* see Dennis after you went upstairs. Dennis returned downstairs and went outside. He was outside when you came down to get me for bed."

Howard looked puzzled. "I still don't get it. Why did he go outside?"

Standing, Suzanne went to the sideboard and refilled her coffee cup. "He didn't stop to chat. We don't know why he went out."

Howard followed her. "Are you sure it was Dennis?"

"Who else could it have been?" Suzanne spoke with exaggerated patience. "Steven was with us, you appeared a few minutes later. That leaves Dennis. Of course it was him."

"If Dennis was killed shortly after he returned inside, then the question becomes, 'When did he return?'" Steven looked toward the breakfast buffet. "Did anyone see Dennis after he went out? James?"

"No, sir. I wasn't aware that anyone went out after we returned from the garage."

"I didn't hear him come in," Candida said. "Howard and I read for a while, then we went to sleep around midnight. Dennis Parnham was a slug and whoever killed him did the world a favor. But it wasn't me and it wasn't Howard. We were never out of each other's sight."

"I didn't see him return, either," Steven said without looking at Meg. "I had a brandy with Suzanne, then went to my room."

Meg waited. When Steven didn't mention going to her room, she released a tiny sigh of relief. Eventually the police would have to know the truth, but for the moment Suzanne didn't have to know.

"James came by my room to discuss today's menus and we stood in the corridor. But I didn't see Dennis return."

James jogged her memory. "You mentioned you were expecting someone, miss."

"Did I?" A fistful of butterflies were released in her stomach. "I can't think why I'd say something like that. I wasn't expecting anyone."

When she glanced up, Steven was watching her with a frown. She gave a tiny shrug of her shoulders and looked away from him.

"Someone isn't telling the truth here," Suzanne commented.

Meg felt her cheeks turn pink and knew she sounded suspicious as hell. "If James says I said that, I must have." Flustered and trying to look innocent, she spread her hands. "I don't remember. But I don't know why I would have said I was expecting someone when I wasn't." Feeling guilty for lying, she didn't dare glance at James.

"It occurs to me that everyone who had a motive to kill Tillis also had a motive to kill Dennis," Steven mentioned. Meg appreciated his effort to take the attention away from her.

"Which leaves me out," Suzanne observed.

In Meg's mind Suzanne was the most likely candidate to have murdered Aunt Tilly, although she couldn't figure out how Suzanne had done it. But she couldn't think of any reason why Suzanne might want to murder Dennis Parnham.

"It's obvious whoever murdered Tillis also murdered Dennis. Surely no one imagines it's a coincidence that Tillis and Dennis just happened to be murdered at the same house on the same weekend surrounded by the same suspects." Candida uttered a snort of exasperation.

"Well, that takes us off the list of suspects," Howard announced cheerfully, pouring another Bloody Mary. "Candida and I were together when someone broke Dennis's neck. We can alibi each other."

"But you weren't together every minute," Meg objected. "I happened to overhear the two of you in the corridor last night. Candida waited on the upstairs landing while you went downstairs."

"Oh, for heaven's sake. Howard was only gone two minutes."

"Out of curiosity I stood on the landing under the sconce before I came down to breakfast," Meg persisted. "From that particular spot you can't see the bottom of the staircase. So you don't really know where Howard went or what he did."

"He went downstairs to get a drink. He returned two minutes later with a drink." Candida lifted her shoulders in a shrug. "Where's the mystery? Besides, Dennis wasn't murdered downstairs, he was killed in his bedroom."

Suzanne smiled at Candida. "I believe the point Meg is trying to make is that you two were *not* together every minute. If you'd lie about that, what else are you lying about?"

"We're not lying about anything," Howard said, placing his hand on Candida's shoulder to keep her in her seat. "Besides, didn't we agree that Dennis was killed early in the evening?"

"At a time when no one could have killed him." Steven pushed a hand through his hair. "We seem to have two murders that no one could have committed."

"But someone did," Meg replied quietly. "The question is—what do we do now?"

No one had an answer.

THE AIR WAS FRESH, cold and wonderful, perfumed by the strong tangy scent of pine. Meg stepped off the veranda and drew the crisp air deep into her lungs.

When she opened her eyes she noticed a movement about sixty yards from where she stood and turned to discover a liquid-eyed deer poised as still as a statue, watching her.

"Oh, Steven, look!" Then Meg remembered she was alone and felt foolish. A sigh lifted her chest as she realized how deeply Steven was ingrained in her life and thoughts.

In less time than it would have taken to describe her delight, the deer whirled and darted through a stand of pine, then disappeared into a shallow gully. After a moment Meg spotted him again, bounding up the rise on the far side of the gully.

She watched with pleasure, glad to be reminded that lovely things still inhabited the world. A few miles from where she stood, laughing vacationers zipped down crowded ski slopes. Couples were ice skating, frolicking in condominium hot tubs, enjoying a leisurely lunch inside one of the trendy restaurants lining Breckenridge's main street. Elsewhere in the world, and not that far from here, business proceeded as usual.

Responding to the needle-sharp wind, Meg tugged her cap down over her ears, then glanced back at the house, relieved to be free of the oppressive atmosphere inside. Then she ducked her head and walked around the house until she stood nearly beneath Dennis's window. She didn't approach close enough to disturb any possible evidence beneath the window, but close enough to observe there probably wasn't any evidence.

Disappointment altered her expression. She had half expected to discover the murderer had emptied Dennis's ashtray out the window. That would have suggested the murder occurred later than they assumed it did. But the snow beneath the window was as clean as a flow of marshmallow sauce.

Next, she trudged around the house to stand beneath Aunt Tilly's window where she gazed up at the gigantic fat icicles hanging from the eaves beneath the stone sill of the window.

Why had Aunt Tilly opened the window the night she was murdered? Meg felt positive the opened window was significant. But in what way? No answer came to mind.

Frustrated, she directed her attention to the ground directly beneath the window. Yesterday's snow had not been thick enough to obscure signs of activity. She could see where the ladder had been, where Steven and James had trampled the drifts. In front of the ladder marks were holes in the snow where icicles had fallen from the roof. The holes ran the length of the house, some with broken icicles still protruding above the surface.

If there were clues here, Meg couldn't spot them. Keeping her head down against the piercing wind, she started back toward the veranda, reluctant to return inside.

If she hadn't paused to look at the mountainside in the hope of spying the deer again, she would have been seriously injured.

An enormous thick icicle shot past her shoulder like a dagger and buried itself in the snow at her feet with a heavy sound.

Heart pounding, Meg gaped at the shattered pieces a moment, realizing if she had taken one more step the icicle would have struck her head or her back. Howard's story about using an icicle as a murder weapon flashed through her mind and she quickly raised her head.

Sunlight skittered across one of the second-floor windowpanes.

An icy chill constricted Meg's flesh. Light flashed across the pane because the window moved. Someone had just closed it. Her gaze fastened on the stump of an icicle beneath the stone sill and her stomach did a slow roll.

She was willing to wager everything she owned that the window opened into Suzanne Halverson's room. And she had a blood-freezing suspicion that the hurtling dagger of ice had been no accident.

The upsetting icicle incident unnerved Meg enough that she almost missed noticing something peculiar when she passed the windows to Aunt Tilly's office. Here the tracks made by Steven and James widened and curved beneath the windows. One of the stone sills seemed to have accumulated less snow on the ledge than the others. As she watched, a flurry of wind swirled more snow off the ledges.

Shaking her head, she continued toward the veranda. Sinister implications popped up everywhere, probably meaningless.

But she had not imagined the daggerlike icicle.

PASSING CANDIDA on the sofa, Meg proceeded directly to the coffee service and poured a cup with unsteady hands before she returned to warm herself in front of the fireplace. "Where is everyone?"

"What happened to you?" Candida tossed aside the book she was reading and studied Meg's pale expression. "You look like you've seen a ghost." A mirthless smile curved her mouth. "It wouldn't surprise me if we have a few ghosts around here."

"Candida, if you weren't in Aunt Tilly's room, how did your ring get in there?"

Candida dug her fingers into the twist of auburn hair arranged on top of her head. Nature had never created that particular shade of auburn. "I've thought about that a hundred times and I can't come up with an answer. I could swear I put that ring on the top of the bureau with the others."

"Could the murderer have come into your room while you were sleeping and stolen the ring?"

"I wish I could say yes. That would explain the mystery. But I locked the inside bolt before I went to bed. Unless our murderer can walk through walls, he couldn't have taken the ring while I was sleeping."

Still tense, Meg sat down and sipped her coffee, letting the heat warm her. "There are too many incidents in this situation that defy explanation," she muttered.

"At least one mystery is solved." When Meg raised an eyebrow, Candida explained, pleased to have figured it out first. "Now we know why the tires were flattened and the phones disabled."

"We do?"

"Obviously it was done to prevent us from summoning help and from leaving the premises. Because..." She paused dramatically. "The killer had to keep us trapped here because he wasn't finished! Dennis was still alive."

"Good God," Meg whispered. "Yes. Of course."

"If I were you, I'd sleep with one eye open tonight. I know I'm very glad to have Howard. I don't want to be alone in this house after the sun sets. It's fatal." After looking over her shoulder, she leaned forward and spoke in a conspiratorial whisper. "On another subject—what's going on between you and Steven? I thought that was over."

"I beg your pardon?"

"Oh, come on. We're mystery writers. We notice things. I'd have to be blind and a fool not to notice the tension between you two. The air quivers with it when you're both in the same room."

"I think you're exaggerating, don't you?"

"Hardly. I'm not exactly a stranger to this kind of awkward situation." Candida smiled. "Look, this isn't any of my business—"

"That's right."

"But during the past two days I've come to respect you. At least a little. So I'm going to say this. When we arrived at Morgan's Manor, you and Steven were circling each other like bulldogs. Now something's changed. You're still circling, but the hostility has disappeared. I'd say you've progressed to wary but warm."

"Candida, I really don't want to discuss this."

"Whenever a man does that kind of turnaround, you have to ask yourself why. What changed? If I were you, and thank God I'm not, I'd be asking myself what have I got that Steven Caldwell has suddenly decided he wants? Or that his great and good friend, Suzanne the snow queen, wants."

Ice accumulated in Meg's veins. She stared at Candida

without seeing her, but Candida's words rose like glaciers in her mind. It hadn't entered Meg's thoughts that Steven might have an ulterior motive. She hadn't asked herself if he wanted something from her.

And of course he did. Steven had told her up front what he wanted. And what Suzanne wanted.

They both wanted to find Aunt Tilly's research notes.

And it appeared they both believed that Meg knew where the material was hidden.

"Did I strike a nerve?" Candida purred, observing Meg's expression.

"I don't know what to think anymore." Rising abruptly, Meg turned her hot face to the fire. Was it possible that Steven was toying with her, hoping she would lead him to Aunt Tilly's notes? Closing her eyes, confused, she pressed a hand to her mouth.

Maybe Steven was so bewitched by Suzanne that he didn't care anymore that Suzanne might have murdered Whitney. Maybe he wanted to find Aunt Tilly's notes and destroy them to protect Suzanne. Maybe...

She bit her lip hard. No, she was letting the jealousy interfere again, letting it rule her thinking. Steven wasn't like that. He was a good man, an honest man. He wouldn't protect a murderer. But love did strange things to people.

"Stop it!" she whispered, shaking her head. "You have to trust."

"I couldn't disagree more." Candida sniffed. "You can't trust anyone. Trust at your own peril, that's what I always say. By the way, has anyone found the alleged death threats Tillis claimed she received?"

"I found them." Gazing into the fire, Meg repeated the message pasted on the threats. "The part about ancient history could refer to anything."

"Not really. Let's think this through. A love triangle

could be ancient history. Howard, Tillis and myself. But that particular piece of ancient history was put to bed long ago. So to speak. That can't be the reference. Did Tillis have any ancient history with Dennis?''

"I think we can rule out Dennis since he was murdered, too.''

"How about Steven?'' Candida asked. "Any ancient history there?''

Steven. Meg's stomach hurt when she thought about him. "I don't think so.''

"Which brings us to Suzanne.'' Candida's eyes gleamed. "Ancient history—murdered husband. Poking about—researching a book. Plus the threat says 'You know this isn't a joke.' How would Tillis know the threats aren't a joke unless she knew that whoever wrote the threats had committed murder before and was capable of doing so again? Maybe whoever murdered Suzanne's husband discovered Tillis was investigating the case. If we knew who the suspects were in the Halverson case, we'd probably have a good idea who sent the death threats.''

"I know a little about the Halverson case,'' Meg said quickly, hating herself that she was about to jump in and turn suspicion away from Suzanne. "If you're thinking Suzanne is on the Halverson suspect list, she's not. She was in Los Angeles when Whitney was murdered.''

"Of course I was thinking about her,'' Candida said bluntly. "If I know Tillis, the thought crossed her mind, too. Maybe Dennis wasn't so far offtrack when he suggested Tillis had dug up something embarrassing to Suzanne. Murdering your husband would be considered embarrassing in some circles.''

Meg's expression was sober. "You're building a scenario out of whole cloth, you know that, don't you? There's no evidence connecting Suzanne to her husband's murder.'' Not yet. ''And how about Dennis? If the same killer murdered both Aunt Tilly and Dennis...''

''Dennis is a problem. But you know what a sleaze he was. Maybe Dennis found out something about the Halverson case and was blackmailing Suzanne, so she broke his rotten neck.''

''Candida, that's absolute fiction. You're getting worked up over thin air. Personally, I'd love to agree with you. But there isn't a whisper of evidence to support anything you've said. The police did not implicate Suzanne in any way. And she didn't know Dennis Parnham. You're speculating based on personal dislike.''

''You're right.'' A sigh lifted Candida's bosom. ''It's just that I'd enjoy it immensely if Suzanne turned out to be the killer. I want it to be her.''

So did Meg, but she couldn't believe Suzanne had killed Dennis.

''Everyone had a motive to kill Tillis,'' Candida said, pacing beside the sofa. ''Don't look at me like that. It's true. Except maybe—*maybe* Suzanne. And Howard, his motive is thin on Tillis's murder. Dennis is the problem. It's too bad Tillis is dead. She would have been a damned good suspect. She hated Dennis for years.'' Candida stopped and her eyes widened. ''Oh my God.''

''What's wrong?'' Meg asked. Candida's face had turned a snowy color, then flashed crimson. She swayed on her feet. Alarmed, Meg stepped forward, but Candida shoved her aside.

''I've figured this out!'' Her voice spiraled upward toward hysteria. ''Didn't you read Agatha Christie's *Ten Little Indians?* Of course you did. Everyone's read that book. Remember? The host is the first person killed, only he isn't really dead. He fakes his death so he can murder everyone else without suspicion. No one suspects him because they all believe he was the first victim!'' Trembling shook Candida's body and her voice rose to a shout. ''So he goes around killing all the enemies that he's invited to his isolated island!''

''Candida, please. Calm down. You're worrying me.''

''Don't you get it? Don't you see? Tillis invites all her enemies up here for the weekend, just like in Christie's book. And now Dennis is dead! Tonight, she'll get another one of us!'' Candida's voice had risen to a shriek.

''What's going on in here?'' Steven asked from the doorway.

''Am I glad to see you! Candida is hysterical. She thinks—'' Howard appeared in the doorway behind Steven, looked into the room, then rushed to his agitated wife's side.

Whirling, Candida beat her fists against Howard's chest. ''Tillis is alive. *She's* the murderer! Tillis is killing us off one by one!''

''Sweetheart, that isn't possible.'' Catching her fists, holding her, Howard spoke in a low soothing voice. He tried to stroke Candida's forehead, her heaving shoulders. ''You saw Tillis, honey. She was dead.''

''No! No, she isn't! I tell you, it's the same as Christie's book. She's going to kill us off one by one!'' Great sobs racked Candida's body. She spoke in shuddering gasps.

''Meg?'' Speaking quietly, Steven touched her arm. ''What happened here?''

''I don't know,'' Meg answered helplessly. ''We were talking and she got more and more worked up, then suddenly...she's convinced Aunt Tilly isn't dead.''

In mounting consternation, they watched as Candida went out of control. She screamed, she wept, she shouted and cursed. She insisted that Tillis was alive and the thought terrified her.

"Why won't you believe me?" Mascara flowed down her wet cheeks. "You're setting us up for another murder! Oh, God! It's like that book. Tillis could be creeping around right now setting up tonight's murder! And you won't do anything! You're going to let her murder me!"

"What do you want me to do, sweetheart?" Tense with anxiety, Howard followed her frantic pacing, trying to calm her. "What will help you?"

"Go see if she's still dead!" The scream seemed to deplete Candida's energy. Collapsing on the sofa, she curled into a ball and sobbed. The fright and desperation in her weeping set everyone's nerves on edge.

"Steven?" Howard looked at him and cleared his throat. "I think we should...I don't know what else to do..."

Incredulous, Meg also turned to Steven. "Surely you aren't considering...Steven, that's crazy!"

"Meg, look at her," Steven said quietly, nodding toward the sofa. "She's hysterical and frightened out of her wits. If this is a performance, it's a convincing one." Leaning, he pulled the rope to summon James, then instructed James to accompany them upstairs and open Tillis's room. "Howard, if this shock treatment is going to work, Candida has to see for herself."

Without a word, Howard scooped Candida off the sofa and carried her toward the staircase.

"Meg?" Steven asked, his expression grim. "Are you coming?"

A shudder convulsed her shoulders. "No."

When they returned fifteen minutes later, neither Howard nor Steven spoke a word. They walked directly to the serving cart and poured tumblers of straight Scotch. Ten minutes later Candida returned to the living room. She had washed her face, combed her hair and donned a subdued wool jersey dress for dinner.

"I apologize," she said stiffly. Crimson burned on her cheeks. After a brief hesitation, she accepted the drink Howard silently offered. "I don't know what came over me. I just…"

"We understand," Meg said gently. "This situation has placed everyone under an unbearable strain. If we can just hold out until tomorrow…"

Above Candida's shoulder, Meg exchanged a long look with Steven. Earlier she had objected to his decision to walk into Breckenridge to summon help. Now she thought of the icicle incident and Candida's breakdown of nerves. She thought about Howard's steady drinking and how she herself had doubted Steven's integrity. She met his gaze and tried to signal that she supported his decision. They needed help. They needed to be rescued before someone else died.

They looked at each other for a full minute and Meg wondered what he was thinking. She had an idea Steven was trying to tell her something, too.

"I think I'll go upstairs and change for dinner," she said, dropping her gaze. Trying to read minds was futile. Once upon a time she had believed she could guess what Steven was thinking, but she wasn't sure anymore. Too much water had passed under the bridge.

As she walked up the staircase she thought about what had happened to Candida. And although Meg wouldn't have admitted it to a soul, for one terrible minute Candida's belief that Aunt Tilly was alive had made a crazy kind of sense. Everyone at Morgan's Manor hovered on the edge of hysteria.

MEG CHANGED into a navy-and-crimson sweater dress and freshened her lipstick, but she didn't return downstairs at once. Sitting beside the window, which she had opened a crack, hands folded in her lap, she watched the sunset flare into icy streaks of orange, then fade to lavender. She made herself think about Steven.

She forced herself to examine the worst possibilities. That Steven was in love with Suzanne and was conspiring to help her. That what he really wanted was Aunt Tilly's research notes. She made herself take a long speculative look at the two murders and she asked herself if Steven Caldwell could have committed either one.

The answer to all the questions was yes. All Meg's worst suspicions *could* be true. But were they?

"Trust," she whispered. In her heart she knew that Steven's statement about trust being the foundation of a relationship was true.

But trusting was so hard, it didn't come naturally to her. Ashamed of what she had been thinking, Meg was glad she had kept her thoughts to herself. Steven Caldwell could not be guilty of deceit, conspiracy or murder. It wasn't possible.

A tiny residual of doubt surprised her. But then she was new at trusting. Still, she had to begin somewhere.

Feeling a little better, she checked her hair in the mirror, then stepped into the dim corridor and closed her bedroom door. At the landing, she paused, looking up at the sconce Candida had stood beneath last night. There was something troubling about the incident...

Footsteps rushed over the carpet behind her. Before Meg could turn to see who was running toward her, a hand flattened against her back. And brutally shoved her forward.

Arms pinwheeling, she pitched down the dark staircase. The last thing she heard was a woman's scream. The voice sounded like her own.

Chapter Seven

Regaining consciousness, Meg found she was lying on the living room sofa, surrounded by anxious faces. She struggled to sit up, but the movement unleashed galloping horses in her head. The room spun in front of her eyes. Gingerly reaching a hand to her forehead, she eased back on the pillows. "What...what happened?" she whispered.

"Hold still," Steven instructed firmly. Now she felt his strong hands moving gently over her ankle. She knew she wasn't injured too severely because his touch sent a tingle though her body. "I don't think it's broken," he said.

Meg managed to open one eye and saw James hovering over her holding a tray of bandages. Everyone had gathered around to watch.

"This may hurt a bit, Meg. I'm going to tape your ankle." Steven's dark eyes met hers. "I think it's sprained."

The genuine concern in his gaze confused her and she lay back and closed her eyes. She no longer knew what the relationship between them was, or what it meant. Nothing was clear-cut anymore, except the chemistry that still operated in full force. His touch affected her like an atomic reaction. Even now.

"You have a cut on your forehead, miss," James said, kneeling beside her. Gently he bathed a spot near her hairline, then applied antiseptic and a padded bandage. When Meg moved her arm, she discovered her elbow had been bandaged, too.

"A scrape, miss."

"May I have an aspirin?" she requested. "My head is pounding."

"I'm not surprised," Steven said in a level voice, glancing up from the end of the sofa. His hand was warm on her leg, almost a caress. "You took a header down the staircase. You gave everyone a bad scare."

"I thought you were dead," Candida announced with an elaborate shudder. "You were just laying there, all crumpled up and not moving."

"For once Candida's prediction was wrong," Suzanne commented. "But of course the evening is young yet." Sipping coffee, she watched Steven wind tape around Meg's ankle. "It's swelling a little. That's going to hurt."

"I can't believe I was so clumsy." There was something about the fall that Meg felt she should remember, and that she wanted to remember, but she couldn't pull the memory through the headache banging the inside of her skull. "This is so embarrassing. I haven't fallen down a flight of stairs since I was a toddler."

"It was your high heels," Candida guessed, nodding toward the navy pumps someone had retrieved and placed on the coffee table. "Writers don't wear heels to work. We get out of the habit of walking in them. Believe it or not, I've tripped a dozen times on my stilettos."

Even if her head hadn't felt as if the top were ready to fly off, Meg could not have imagined Candida Ripley working in sneakers as Meg did.

"Is the aspirin helping, miss?"

"I think so. Thank you, James." This time she managed

to sit up, and after a moment the room steadied. She ached all over.

Steven kept his hand on her leg even after he secured the tape around her ankle and lower leg. "You cut your forehead, banged up your elbow, scraped your knees and I think your ankle is probably sprained. I imagine you have a dozen bumps and bruises we don't know about, but nothing seems to be broken."

"That's nothing for a tomboy like me," Meg said, managing a wobbly smile.

Steven's answering smile didn't reach his eyes. "When you wake up tomorrow morning, you're going to feel like you were run over by a truck." He glanced at James. "You mentioned a cane?"

"I'll fetch it at once."

Steven went to the bar for a drink. "That does it. We have two dead bodies and a person who requires medical attention." He glanced toward the darkness pressing against the windowpanes. "At first light, I'll walk to Breckenridge."

"I don't like the idea, but I think you're right. Let's hope you're alive to do it," Candida muttered.

"We can't wait any longer for the plow to get here," Howard agreed.

"Perhaps we should discuss what we're going to say after we're rescued," Suzanne suggested, moving away from the sofa to the thronelike chair.

"What is there to discuss?" Howard shrugged. "We just tell the police what happened."

"Suzanne has a point," Steven said, still watching Meg. His gaze lingered on her taped leg, then traveled up her body and settled on her face. "Tillis's murder will make the national news. Swarms of reporters are going to descend on Breckenridge. And on us."

"We aren't going to be permitted to leave," Candida said, thinking out loud. "The police are going to insist that we remain in the area."

When he realized he was staring, Steven moved away from Meg and stood in front of the fireplace. Thoughtfully he studied the faces in front of him. "The media is going to hound us for statements, for the inside story. A lot of accusations have been flung about in the past couple of days. I think Suzanne has raised a legitimate question. Are we going to use the media to continue insulting and accusing one another?"

"I'd hate to have that happen," Howard mentioned.

Candida broke the ensuing silence. "Despite everything that's been said here, about motives and who wanted to kill whom, there's something about each murder that makes it impossible for any of us to have done it. Someone here *did* murder Tillis and Dennis. But the truth is—based on what we know right now—none of us can point a finger and say with any certainty, 'You did it.'"

"Much as I hate to agree with anything you say," Suzanne murmured, "I do agree."

"Then can we also agree that we'll let the police make any necessary accusations and we will refrain from doing so?" Steven's glance told Meg that he hoped she would keep their speculation about Aunt Tilly's notes confidential until they had the evidence in hand. "If a reporter asks our opinion about what happened here, we'll merely say the police are investigating."

Everyone pledged to honor the agreement.

"I've found Madam's walking stick," James said, placing the cane within Meg's reach. "When would you like dinner served, miss?"

"I imagine dinner is ready now, isn't it?" When James nodded, Meg reached for the cane, let her head settle, then with Steven's assistance she stood. The walls bounced forward and back before her vision steadied. "The rest of you go ahead. I think I'll have a tray in my room. Maybe soup and something cold to drink if it isn't too much trouble, James."

Before she could protest, assuming she would have, Steven swept her into his arms. "I don't want you placing any weight on that foot," he said, his mouth inches from hers.

Meg suspected the dizziness that overwhelmed her had little to do with her ankle. Steven's arms felt safe and good. Hesitating only briefly, Meg wound her arms around his neck and rested her head on his wide shoulder. Usually she didn't feel comfortable surrendering her problems to someone else, but right now it was a relief to have Steven take charge. She closed her eyes and relaxed in his strong arms.

"How heroic," Suzanne commented, watching Steven carry Meg effortlessly toward the stairs. "Will you dress her in her jammies, too?"

"I'll do that," Candida announced firmly, following Steven up the staircase.

After Steven placed Meg on her bed, he leaned over her and gently touched his fingertips to her cheek. "How are you feeling? Honestly."

"I feel like hell. Honestly."

"I thought so." He smiled. "I'll stop in later." With reluctance, he moved toward the door.

"Oh, go on, get out of here." Candida made a shooing motion with her hands. "The best thing for her right now is rest. And she isn't going to rest with you looking at her like that."

At the door Steven gave her a thumbs-up sign. "Hang in a little longer. Help will be on the way soon."

"Looks like things are heating up," Candida commented when Steven had gone. "Is that wise?"

"I don't know." Biting her lip, Meg sat up and carefully swung her legs over the side of the bed. "For the moment, everything personal is on hold."

"Good. I hate to be negative, but *everyone* is a suspect until these murders are solved." Fists on hips, Candida gazed at Meg. "Steven's right about one thing. Tomorrow you're going to ache every time you move."

"I can't believe I was so clumsy."

"Well, let's get you out of that dress and into your nightgown." Sitting beside Meg on the bed, Candida carefully unzipped the back of the sweater dress, then gingerly helped Meg ease it over her head. Candida stared. "You're covered with bruises." She shook her head, dislodging an auburn curl. "You're damned lucky you didn't break your neck."

Like Dennis. That disturbing thought tumbled through Meg's mind nudging other thoughts that frustrated her in their elusiveness.

"Flannel," Candida noticed, commenting on her nightgown. A smile curved her lips. "That answers one question. You didn't come here looking to patch things up with Steven."

"Steven likes..." But Meg didn't finish the sentence. A blush warmed her cheeks and she looked away. Once she was settled under the quilt against a mound of pillows, she swallowed another aspirin and urged Candida to join the others for dinner. "I'll be fine."

"I hate to leave you alone," Candida said uncertainly. "Someone could—" She bit off the words.

"I'd say the excitement is over for tonight," Meg insisted, hoping she was right.

A few minutes after Candida departed, a knock sounded

and Howard pushed the door open with his shoulder. He was carrying a bed tray.

"Dinner is served," he announced in a cheerful voice, "and I've come to keep you company."

Meg inspected the tray after he placed it over her lap. The soup smelled heavenly, but she had no appetite. "The Scotch must be yours," she said, smiling at Howard who had pulled a chair close to the bed. Because she knew she should eat something and because Howard urged her, she tasted a spoonful of the soup. "Are you really here to keep me company, or did Candida send you to protect me?"

"A little of both."

She did feel better having him with her. "Thank you."

Before lapsing into companionable silence, they spoke of inconsequential safe topics. Books they had enjoyed, films they wanted to see, Colorado versus New York weather.

After a while Howard told her that he remembered Meg as a little girl. Meg apologized that she retained no memory of him.

"Don't know why you should. It was a long time ago. You were just a cute little kid wearing pigtails and braces. Tillis and I stopped by your folks' farm on the way to New York City." He smiled at the memory. "It wasn't all fussing and fighting the way the tabloids made it sound. Tillis and I had our good times, too."

"I'm sure you did."

A sigh lifted Howard's chest. "But Tilly drove me crazy with her jealousy."

Meg started and the soup spilled across the bed tray. "Aunt Tilly was jealous?"

Howard laughed. "Lord, yes. You wouldn't think she would be, would you? Considering her enormous ego. But she was. Oh, yes." He looked into his Scotch. "After a while, a man starts thinking if he's going to be blamed for something, he might as well do it.''

Dropping her head back on the pillows, Meg closed her eyes. When Aunt Tilly said jealousy was poison, she had known what she was talking about. But she hadn't told Meg how to make the feelings go away.

"Do you ever feel jealous?" Meg asked. Immediately she thought of Dennis and regretted the question.

"I suppose anyone in love experiences flashes of jealousy," Howard said slowly. "The immediate urge is to lash out at the people who are hurting you. But I can tell you that doesn't work. It only makes the situation far worse for everyone." He poked at the ice in his glass. "I guess the best solution is to be honest. Tell the person you love that you need reassurance. If you think about it, she doesn't know she's hurting you unless you tell her. If she knew you needed reassurance, she might give it and then you wouldn't feel so wild inside when she smiled at another man."

The conversation had passed from general to personal and Meg shifted uncomfortably. "I miss Aunt Tilly," she said softly.

Howard emerged from his personal reverie. "Who do you think killed her, Meg? I go over and over it in my mind, trying to figure it out, and I can't. I know enough about mystery writing from having lived with two mystery writers that the killer ought to be someone who did *not* leave something behind in Tilly's room. That's how it would unfold in a novel."

"I suppose." Then Meg grasped the implications of what he was saying. "You mean you think Steven, Suzanne or I murdered Aunt Tilly?"

"That's how it would be resolved in a novel. But I like you and Steven. I don't much care for that Suzanne person, but I can't think she killed anyone, either. We've got an unsolved murder and no reasonable suspects.''

"Two unsolved murders," Meg reminded him with a sigh.

There was another knock on the door, and Steven entered. Howard stood and stretched, then picked up Meg's tray. "Well, I enjoyed our visit. Try to get some rest."

Meg tilted her head and raised an eyebrow. "Did Candida send you, too?" she asked Steven. "Are you the next shift?"

"I thought I'd check in on you before you went to sleep," he said, taking the chair Howard had vacated. "Are the aspirins helping?"

"You know, I keep thinking there's something about this tumble that I'm not remembering, something hovering around the edge of memory." Lifting a hand, she touched the bandage on her forehead and tried to concentrate. "I came out of my room. I walked to the landing. I paused to look at the sconce that Candida stood under last night. Then..." Meg's eyes widened and she sat up so suddenly that her head reeled. "Steven! I remember now. Someone pushed me!"

He stared. "Meg—are you sure?"

"Yes! I heard footsteps, but before I could turn around...where was everyone when you found me? Who was upstairs?"

"I didn't find you, Candida did." He frowned, trying to remember. "I think everyone was upstairs dressing for dinner. If you were pushed—it could have been anyone."

"What do you mean, *if* I was pushed?" Meg asked after a minute.

Taking her hand, he stroked it between his fingers. "Please don't be offended by what I'm about to say." Meg agreed, but she was already bristling, having guessed where this was leading. "We've all been under tremendous strain." Glancing up at her, he frowned uncomfortably. "You remember what happened to Candida this afternoon. For a short while she honestly believed that Tillis was still alive. When we were upstairs she swore she glimpsed Tillis sneaking through a doorway. Candida genuinely did not believe she was imagining anything."

"Are you claiming that I imagined someone pushed me down the staircase?"

"I'm not claiming anything, Meg. I'm merely suggesting it wouldn't be surprising if you did imagine something. We're all nervous and on edge, seeing suspicious shadows where there may or may not be shadows."

"There's something else," she said in a tight voice, then she told him about the icicle incident. Even as she spoke, Meg realized how farfetched the whole thing sounded. That someone might try to injure her by flinging an icicle. Narrowing her eyes, feeling defensive, she stared at him, searching for signs of amusement or outright dismissal. "It was a huge icicle. Shaped like a dagger. Steven, it could have killed me."

"You didn't actually see a person at the window?"

She studied him another minute, searching for any hint that he thought she was exaggerating or overreacting. But he kept his face carefully expressionless. "No, I didn't," she answered reluctantly.

"So you can't say for certain that Suzanne threw the icicle. Or that she was even in her room at the time it happened."

Meg stared at him. "Why are you defending her?"

"I'm not. I'm just pointing out how the mind can play tricks when people are laboring under a great deal of stress. Maybe the window was open, or maybe you only thought it moved when the sun came out from behind a cloud and flashed across the pane. Maybe someone broke off the icicle and hurled it at you. Or maybe it broke off and fell of its own accord. It's possible there's a natural explanation for what happened. That's all I'm suggesting.''

"You're saying that I'm imagining things.''

"Meg, that *isn't* what I'm saying." He dropped her hand. "But it's possible, isn't it?''

With an effort Meg erased the scowl from her brow. "All right. I concede it's *possible* that I let my imagination run away with me.'' She opened her eyes and examined his expression. "But I don't believe it, Steven. I know what happened.''

"Look, I don't want to argue with you.'' Standing, he leaned to kiss her forehead. "I'll let you get some rest now.'' His fingertips brushed her lips, then lingered on her cheek. "The next time I see you, I'll have a policeman and a medic right behind me.''

"Be careful,'' she whispered, meeting his dark eyes. "I wish you didn't have to walk down the mountain. I wish there was some other way.'' Suddenly she couldn't imagine her life without Steven. She hadn't seen much of him during the past eight months, but at least she had known he was alive. And in some dim corner of her mind, she had hoped that maybe someday...

"I'll be fine. Don't worry.'' But she saw that her anxiety on his behalf pleased him. He paused at the doorway and smiled. "By the way, did I mention how sexy that nightgown is?''

Meg's laugh made her head ache and she touched the bandage on her forehead with a moan. "You're the only man I know who thinks flannel nighties are sexy.''

His steady gaze held hers. "Good,'' he said quietly.

Good heavens. Was it possible that Steven occasionally felt a twinge of jealousy? Before she could say anything, he touched his fingertips to his lips and blew her a kiss, then he closed the door behind him.

Meg stared at the door for a few minutes, then she carefully climbed out of bed, gripped the cane and hobbled forward. She locked the inside bolt, then wincing and grinding her teeth against the pain, she returned to bed and collapsed against the pillows and closed her eyes, forcing herself to concentrate on what happened.

Damn it. She hadn't imagined a single thing. Someone had thrown the icicle at her. And someone had shoved her down the staircase.

IN THE MORNING, Meg felt as stiff as a poker. Every muscle in her body ached and protested when she tried to move. Her head was no longer throbbing and aching, but everything else was.

Groaning, she glanced at the morning sunshine, then dragged herself out of bed. It took forty-five minutes to dress, put on some makeup and do her hair. The effort exhausted her. She was secretly glad when Howard appeared, swept aside her halfhearted objections, then lifted her in his arms and carried her downstairs to the dining room.

"Thank God," Candida breathed. "We sent Howard up to see if you were alive. When you didn't come downstairs…"

As soon as Meg was seated, she scanned the faces in the room.

"All present and accounted for," Candida announced. "No new murders."

"Did Steven leave for Breckenridge?"

"James said he set out at dawn," Suzanne answered. "How's the ankle this morning?"

"Sore. But I'll live." She didn't look at Suzanne when

she answered. If Suzanne didn't want her alive to find Aunt Tilly's notes, then Suzanne might have pushed her down the stairs. But then Candida might have done it, too. With Meg out of the way, Candida would win the Macabre Series by default.

After breakfast Howard insisted on carrying Meg into the living room and settling her on the sofa in front of the fire. Candida snapped on the television and they watched the morning soaps. No one was really interested in the soaps, but no one felt like talking, either.

They waited. Minds drifting, the television merely a focal distraction, they waited, straining to hear the sound of an engine in the driveway. Meg wished Howard hadn't told them the story of the man who had succumbed to hypothermia and died in the snowdrifts.

"WAKE UP," Candida said, shaking Meg's shoulder. "They're here!"

Blinking, Meg pushed up on the sofa. After rubbing her eyes, she leaned forward to peer through the living room windows. An enormous orange plow filled the driveway. As she watched, both doors opened on the plow's cab and Steven emerged. Relief raced through her body and now she let herself realize how worried she had been. A half-dozen police cars turned into the driveway behind the plow.

The ordeal had ended.

Within minutes two dozen people filled the house. A stream of uniformed men flowed up and down the staircase. Others spread throughout the house. Someone retaped Meg's ankle and examined the cut on her forehead and elbow. James laid out a buffet with coffee, sandwiches and small finger food. The sheriff's department arrived, then the Colorado Bureau of Investigation. A photographer dashed up the staircase followed by a fingerprinting crew. After a long while, two collapsible gurneys came down the staircase. Aunt Tilly and Dennis Parnham were carried outside.

Meg watched through the windows as the coroner's wagon slowly pulled out of the driveway and turned down the road to Breckenridge. Tears glistened in her eyes.

One of the sheriff's deputies took Howard into the dining room to record his statement; Candida went to Aunt Tilly's library. Steven gave his statement upstairs; someone took Suzanne into the kitchen. Meg gave her statement from the sofa in the living room. Twenty minutes later Sheriff Conner came into the living room and sat on the thronelike chair across from her.

"_____ your aunt, Miss Sandler. Tillis was our local celebrity. I'm confident I speak for the entire community when I say we'll all miss her."

If Meg had met Sheriff Conner out of uniform, she would not have guessed his profession. He was a large man, raw boned, with a ruddy, benign face. Only his eyes gave him away, intelligent blue eyes that missed nothing.

As she returned Sheriff Conner's smile, it suddenly occurred to Meg that she faced a daunting task ahead. There were arrangements to be made, people to be notified, a dozen things to do, all of them unpleasant. She reached a trembling hand to the bandage on her elbow, wondering how she would find the energy to proceed. Now that the terrible weekend had finally ended, she felt drained and tired.

"I've read over your statement, Miss Sandler, and there are a few points I'd like to clarify."

"I want to help in any way I can."

"To your knowledge, did anyone besides yourself actually see the death threats?"

"I doubt it, Sheriff. Unless someone searched Aunt Tilly's desk." She shrugged. "You saw the supply room. It's possible the same person who trashed the supply room also rifled through Aunt Tilly's desk."

"The person who vandalized the supply room—what do you think he or she was looking for?"

A flush of color tinted Meg's cheeks. "I don't know."

He studied her expression. "Deputy Merrit didn't find the death threats. We have only your word that they existed."

"What?" She sat up straight and blinked. "The threats were in the third desk drawer!"

"They aren't there now, Miss Sandler."

"Then whoever sent them must have taken them out of the desk and destroyed them," Meg said, speaking sl Turning her head, she glanced at the fireplace. The envelopes would have burned to ash in an instant. "But I promise you, Sheriff. The threats did exist. And the wording was exactly as I reported in my statement."

Sheriff Conner indicated her taped leg and focused a pointed glance on the bandage on her forehead. "What happened to you?" When she finished explaining, he studied her in silence. "You're absolutely sure that's how it happened, Miss Sandler? You lost your footing on your high heels and fell?"

She hadn't mentioned that she was pushed. After thinking about Steven's reaction, she was no longer absolutely certain about anything. Maybe Steven was right. Maybe her nerves were in such a state that she had only imagined a hand against her back. The memory had begun to blur. As for the icicle incident, Meg had learned her lesson. She'd heard how farfetched and outlandish the story sounded.

"The thing is, Miss Sandler—we've got two dead bodies here. And an accident, if you will, which could have had serious consequences. You're damned lucky it didn't. If I understand this correctly, you came within an inch or two of being body number three.''

"I..." She bit her lip. "I'm sure it was just an accident.''

Sheriff Conner didn't look persuaded. One bushy eyebrow lifted. "Is there anything you want to tell me?'' he asked gently.

Oh, yes. Meg wanted to tell him about the icicle and about the hand shoving her down the staircase. But she would have felt foolish mentioning either when she had absolutely no proof that either incident was anything more than an overwrought imagination.

And she yearned to tell him about Suzanne Halverson, that Suzanne had murdered her husband and probably her maid. But Meg had no proof of that accusation, either. All she had was Steven's belief that such proof *might* exist. But maybe it didn't. Maybe it never had, or maybe the research material was lost forever.

Probably she should tell the sheriff that only James and Hilda knew where all the telephones were located. But she didn't because she didn't believe James or Hilda had disabled the phones despite that damning piece of information. She didn't want to point the authorities in the wrong direction.

Finally, she wanted to discuss all the vague formless thoughts floating in disconnected strands through her mind. She longed to discuss everything with someone whom she could trust. But it was pointless until she made sense of her thoughts herself. And until she had proof.

"No," she said at length, feeling the color deepen on her cheeks. Which Sheriff Conner's sharp eyes did not miss. "There's nothing else at this time.''

"If you change your mind," he said quietly, "if you think of anything you might have forgotten…" He placed his card on the sofa beside her and Meg picked it up, turning it between her fingers.

"Sheriff…" She bit her lip and made herself say the words. "About Aunt Tilly…"

Sheriff Conner anticipated the necessary questions. "Breckenridge is a small town. We don't get many murders here. Therefore, both bodies will be taken to Denver to be autopsied." When he observed Meg's grimace, he added in a gentler tone, "An autopsy is standard procedure in a murder case."

"I know. It's just…how long…?"

"There's no way to guess. It will depend on the medical examiner's caseload, on a half dozen things that are outside our control. Some families hold a memorial service in these circumstances instead of a funeral. Some just wait. Sometimes a delay isn't all that bad."

Meg nodded, thinking about the reporters that would soon descend. Perhaps it was a good idea to delay the funeral until the sensationalism had abated.

"That about does it for now," Sheriff Conner said, standing. "We've notified the telephone company about the telephones. They'll get someone out here this afternoon. We'd appreciate it if you wouldn't leave the county without letting our office know where you're going." He didn't say she had to request permission, but his expression made it explicit. To soften the implication, he smiled. "Standard procedure."

"I understand." Meg shook his hand. "Thank you."

By four o'clock only one police car remained in the driveway. The plow had departed hours ago. Jim from the service station had repaired the flattened tires. A repairman was upstairs working on the telephones. James served coffee to those assembled in the living room.

"No thank you," Howard said, declining coffee. "No offense, but Candida and I are eager to get out of here." He smiled at Meg and shrugged. "We'll be staying at Hunter's Lodge if anyone needs to contact us."

"I hope that's not where you're staying," Candida said to Suzanne.

"I haven't decided yet."

Candida's auburn eyebrows soared. "You came here at the height of the ski season without making reservations? One might be tempted to think you never intended to ski at all, that you planned all along to visit Tillis, murder her, then get out of town."

"What a pity that your gift for fiction doesn't translate to your novels."

When Steven stepped between them, Meg watched with gratitude. She lacked the energy to play hostess or peacemaker. Aside from his ruddy, wind-burned cheeks, Steven appeared to have suffered no ill effects from the trek down the mountainside. He wore a tweed jacket over a white turtleneck and Meg decided he had never looked more handsome.

For a brief instant she considered asking Steven to stay at Morgan's Manor. Then she decided against it. She needed to be alone for a while. Plus, she wasn't sure if they had resolved anything in their relationship, if it could be called that at this point, or if they were back to square one.

Suzanne glanced at the staircase. "Well. If James will bring down my luggage, I'll say goodbye to you people. I can't say it hasn't been entertaining..." She tossed back a wave of blond hair and raised an eyebrow in Steven's direction. "You arrived by shuttle, didn't you? Can I give you a lift into town?"

He looked at Meg as if waiting for her to say something. When she didn't, he asked, "Do you need any help notifying relatives? Making arrangements?"

"I don't know yet. But thank you." Conflicting emotions pulled her in different directions. She wasn't ready for personal confrontations. But she hated to watch him go off with Suzanne.

"I'll phone you," he said. There was disappointment in his tone as if Meg had somehow let him down.

An awkward silence opened and deepened. In different circumstances they would have shaken hands, perhaps embraced, would have murmured polite goodbyes and promised to get together soon. But no one knew the proper etiquette for parting from fellow suspects, one of whom was a killer.

"We never held the MAIMS board meeting," Candida said, glancing at her wristwatch. "Now don't look at me like that, Meg. Life goes on, you know. That's why we came here, after all."

"Maybe in a day or two." Suddenly Meg was eager to see them go. Yesterday she had felt as if she and Candida might develop a friendship in spite of being competitors for the Macabre Series. Today, everything had changed. The distance had reappeared in Candida's cool gaze. She looked at Meg and saw a rival, a young upstart.

Steven was last to depart. Before he followed Suzanne to her rental car, he paused on the veranda and placed his hands on Meg's shoulders. She pretended his touch didn't send her heart crashing against her rib cage.

"I'll phone you as soon as I know where I'll be staying." He looked into her eyes. "Let's have lunch tomorrow. I think it would be good for you to get out of here for a while, too.''

"I…call first. Let's see how I'm feeling then."

Suddenly she felt awkward with him. They could no longer avoid discussing personal issues by concentrating solely on the circumstances at Morgan's Manor. The moment was rapidly approaching when they would have to confront the changes this weekend had brought. They would have to decide where they went from here, backward or forward. Meg wasn't sure she was ready for that confrontation.

For an instant, she thought Steven intended to kiss her. His fingers tightened on her shoulders, his gaze traveled to her parted lips and lingered. Then Suzanne leaned on the horn, and his hands dropped to his sides.

"I'll see you tomorrow," he said as he turned down the steps.

Meg stayed on the veranda, leaning on her cane and watching until Suzanne's car curved out of sight, then James helped her across an icy patch and back into the house.

Writers not only work in solitude, eventually they learn to appreciate and almost crave solitude. Meg stood in the foyer, her eyes closed, enjoying the silence in the house and the knowledge that she was alone. Too long a time had passed in the company of people and she looked forward to a few hours all to herself.

Then she remembered the calls that had to be placed. Someone—herself—had to notify Aunt Tilly's agent about Aunt Tilly's death. And she had to telephone her mother and father. And Aunt Tilly's attorney and accountant. And all the friends listed in Aunt Tilly's thick address book. The dreaded task would not become less onerous by delaying it.

After asking James to serve a fresh coffee tray, she gripped the handle of the cane and limped toward the telephone in Aunt Tilly's office.

But no matter what she did or how she occupied herself, there was no escaping the question that dominated every thought.

Which of them had murdered Dennis and Aunt Tilly?

Chapter Eight

The next day was cold but bright and invigorating. A brilliant blue sky curved overhead; winter sunlight sparkled across the snowfields. The spruce and pine looked as if they had been dipped in sugar frosting.

Even Morgan's Manor possessed a storybook quality today, Meg thought, looking back at the house through the rear windshield of Steven's rental car. Icicles draped the eaves like a crystal necklace. Snow hugged the rooftops and sills in picturesque folds. Frost glittered on the stones as if the house had been strewn with diamond chips.

"This was a good idea," she said, turning on the seat to smile at Steven. "Thank you for inviting me."

Today Steven appeared well rested and relaxed. A wave of dark hair swept his forehead above his dark aviator glasses. He wore a cream-colored sweater over a chocolate turtleneck and dark slacks. The lines between his eyes had faded. No one seeing Steven or Meg would have guessed they had endured a nightmarish weekend. Realizing this, Meg flexed her shoulders and let the last remnants of tension drain away, determined to enjoy the outing. And the pleasure of having Steven all to herself.

"I'm sorry to have phoned so late," Steven apologized, smiling at her, then looking back at the road. With the snow banked high on both sides, the road reminded Meg of a broad sled run. "I tried to call last night but your line was continually busy. This morning I had to rent a car, telephone my office...I called as soon as I could."

"I know my phone has been tied up. I've been notifying people of Aunt Tilly's death."

The hardest call she'd had to make had been to her parents. Meg's mother, Aunt Tilly's sister, had been at a Friends of the Library meeting and had not been home. But informing her father about Aunt Tilly's murder had been almost as upsetting as speaking to her mother would have been. His shock and grief had been palpable. Next she telephoned Aunt Tilly's agent, Marcella Brass, and that, too, had been an extremely difficult conversation. Aunt Tilly and Marcella had been friends as well as business associates. Then came the names in Aunt Tilly's address book. Meg hadn't finished until after eleven o'clock.

"Where are you staying?" she asked, changing the subject.

"Good timing," Steven said, pointing to the Poles, a hotel complex at the bottom of Aunt Tilly's road. "I'm staying there."

Meg studied the sprawling complex and warned herself not to say a word. But the question came anyway despite an effort to bite back the words. "Is Suzanne staying at the Poles, too?"

"Suzanne rented a unit on the first floor. I took one on the fourth floor," Steven said. He didn't look away from the road.

"I see." Her old enemy, the green-eyed monster, gripped her chest and squeezed. Instantly Meg pictured Steven and Suzanne checking in together, and later sitting head to head over a candlelit dinner, laughing, gazing into each other's eyes, fingers intertwining. Don't do this to

yourself, she pleaded silently, don't think about it. But the image of Steven and Suzanne flickered in front of her mind.

Steven's hands tightened on the wheel. "Look, Meg. Suzanne gave me a ride into town. She was looking for a place to stay. I was looking for a place to stay. What was I supposed to do? Tell her, yes, there are several vacancies at the Poles, but you can't stay here. You'll have to find another place because...I don't know the reason, Meg, you fill in the blanks."

"Of course you couldn't say that." Dots of hot color rose in Meg's cheeks. Hearing it stated that way made her feel foolish. "You don't have to explain anything."

"The hell I don't." Anger tightened his expression when he glanced at her. "Did you hear your tone of voice? It's the same old thing. Explain this, justify that. I told you why I was seeing Suzanne, I explained there's no romantic involvement, but that doesn't mean anything to you, does it? Either you haven't been listening, or you don't believe me. Neither possibility is very pleasant."

"Steven, I'm sorry."

She was more sorry than he knew. In an instant the rapport between them had changed to anger and defensiveness. And Meg was to blame. Closing her eyes, she tried to remember how many times she had done this. How many times had she taken a nice moment and let her jealousy turn it into something unpleasant? A feeling of helplessness overwhelmed her.

Neither of them spoke again until Steven parked in the lot across from the Bell Tower Mall and helped her out of the car. "I feel so silly about my foot," she murmured, leaning on her cane and hoping to start over with an uncontroversial subject. The swelling around her ankle had diminished considerably, but she still couldn't wear a shoe comfortably. To accommodate going outside, she had pulled a pair of James's wool socks over her house slipper.

Steven made an effort, too. He smiled and took her arm. "This is a ski town, remember? Here a banged-up leg is a badge of honor. Everyone will assume you earned it while executing a fantastic maneuver on the area's most wicked slope."

"Actually, the sprain isn't as severe as we first thought. The medic said I'll be as good as new in a couple of days."

But Steven had guessed right. Nearly everyone who passed gave her a good-natured, knowing grin. A few murmured, "Better luck next time" or "Hope that happened at the end of your vacation and not on your first day here."

The hostess at the Horseshoe II on Main Street seated them near the window at a table where no one would accidentally bump Meg's foot. Meg glanced at the restaurant's brass-and-tulip-glass appointments, the stylish mauve-and-emerald color scheme, then she leaned forward in her chair to watch the steady flow of vacationers streaming past the large front windows. It was wonderful to observe flushed cheeks, bright eyes, laughing happy people who weren't involved in a sensational double murder, people whose only thoughts were to enjoy themselves.

"How soon do you think the reporters will begin to arrive?" she asked after she and Steven had been served steaming mugs of hot mulled wine. They sat close together in order to hear above the laughter and conversation in the room, close enough that Meg was aware of Steven's breath on her cheek, his mouth inches from her own. She tried to concentrate on what he was saying, finding the task difficult.

"The story made the Denver TV channels last night," Steven replied. "The details were sketchy, but the reporters played up the sensationalism. Life imitates fiction, famous mystery writer murdered in classic locked-door case—that kind of thing. I imagine the national media will arrive by this afternoon.''

Sunlight streamed through the window, teasing red highlights from Steven's hair. When he looked at her, he did so with his characteristic intensity, focusing his full attention. Anyone watching might have guessed they were lovers without a care in the world, totally absorbed in each other. Looking at him, Meg thought how handsome he was, how self-assured and at ease wherever he was. And how incredible it was to realize they were both involved in a murder case.

She also realized their conversation had trickled away like sand out of an hourglass. Steven was looking at her, but she recognized that shuttered expression. He was turning something over in his mind, examining it, approaching a difficult decision.

''A penny for your thoughts,'' she said softly. Instantly she regretted speaking. An uneasy feeling warned her that she didn't really want to know what he was thinking.

For a moment it appeared he hadn't heard, then he said, ''I was thinking how beautiful you are. I like the way you're wearing your hair now. Short and curly. And red is a wonderful color on you.''

Meg glanced at her red sweater and dark slacks. Nothing fancy. But her taste didn't lean toward designer items. An unreformed tomboy, her choices were as simple and as practical as she was. Sometimes, like today, she wished she could be different. It would have been nice to open her closet and find something special to wear to her lunch with Steven. Instead she had tried on and discarded three slacks outfits before deciding on this one.

''I appreciate the compliments,'' she said, telling herself

to stop right there. But her mouth wasn't obeying her mind today. "That isn't really what you were thinking, was it?"

He hesitated. "Let's not spoil today by getting into problem areas, okay?"

Everything sensible warned her to accept what he was saying and change the subject. But the same undefinable impulse that drew people to disaster sites pulled her forward. "I thought you said you weren't uncommunicative..."

Steven frowned at his wine, moving the mug in tight damp circles on the tabletop. "All right. That's a fair comment."

Hating herself for not letting it drop, Meg watched him with a powerless feeling that she had stepped on a roller coaster of her own creation and it was too late to step off.

Lifting his head, Steven stared out the window as if gathering his thoughts. "Look, Meg, when I agreed to come to Morgan's Manor for this weekend, I didn't know Suzanne would be there. But I knew you would be. I didn't know if you were involved with someone else or not. I hoped you weren't. I had a half-baked idea that we would talk, that we'd discover we missed each other and recognize that what we had together was something special. I thought maybe things had changed during the time we were apart, enough that..." He met her eyes. "But they haven't. You're still possessive, you still make me feel guilty as hell over nothing."

At the back of her mind, Meg heard Howard's wistful voice saying that if a man is continually accused of something, after a while he starts thinking he might as well do it.

But this was a scene they had played before and Meg dropped into her role with habitual helplessness. The best defense was an offense, and she fell into it automatically.

"If you had only told me what you were doing with Suzanne, that it was business, I would have handled the situation better. But the way you chose—anyone would have felt jealous."

"I'm sorry, Meg, but I don't believe that. The point is, Suzanne isn't the problem. If you weren't jealous about Suzanne, you'd be jealous about someone else. The problem isn't me being uncommunicative." He spread his hands. "I don't know how I could be more open than I have been. I've been trying. The problem is your possessiveness, your jealousy. And I don't know how to deal with it."

Being with Steven this week had been upsetting in the beginning, but it had also been exciting and wonderful. The closeness of sharing common dangers, common problems, the joy of discovering they still thought along the same lines, the physical attraction that hadn't diminished. Now Meg looked at him and her heart constricted. She was doing it again. She was driving him away, and with him went the only future she had ever really wanted.

The man she wanted was rejecting her. She was causing it to happen and she didn't know how to stop it.

"You don't know how terrible this jealousy is from my end," she said in a low voice, looking down at her salad. "I wind up feeling so small and petty and ugly. But I see you with someone else and the world falls out from under me. Then I look in a mirror and see nothing but flaws, real or imagined. I tell myself if I were prettier, or if I didn't have freckles, or...it's self-destructive and awful. I can't concentrate on writing or anything else. I keep seeing you and someone else in my mind, and it's torture." Lifting her head, she looked at him with misery-filled eyes.

Frustration tightened Steven's jaw. "I can't understand it, Meg. You're a beautiful woman, you have a successful career, lots of friends, a man who would love you the rest of his life—if you would just let it happen. But you make a relationship impossible!''

He had never mentioned love before. Hearing it now, in this context, was like a dagger to Meg's heart. ''I know, I know,'' she whispered. Leaning forward, she covered her eyes. ''Oh, Steven, don't you think I'd change if I could?''

''Then why don't you? Meg, no one can change for you. This is something you have to do yourself. Put this crazy jealousy out of your life! You're tearing yourself apart for no reason.''

''I want to! Do you think I *like* torturing myself? I hate it. But damn it, Steven, you could help by—''

He stared at her, then shook his head. ''No, Meg. Trust doesn't come with strings attached—I'll trust you if you'll explain every smile, every little nuance. I won't do that, not anymore. It doesn't work. And it doesn't solve the problem.'' He leaned back in his chair, away from her, his body language closing her out.

''Maybe this isn't the right time to be discussing personal issues,'' Meg said. She heard the hint of despair in her voice, felt herself grabbing at straws. And she felt the approach of an inevitability that she couldn't bear to think about. ''We've just been through an intense and highly emotional ordeal, maybe we're—''

''The part that's so hard to accept,'' he said, interrupting, ''is how right we are for each other in so many ways. We have the same sense of humor, the same view of the world. We're both in publishing, we like the same books, the same things.''

''Except for Greek food,'' she said automatically. Suddenly Meg felt a lump rise in her throat and recognized the sting of tears behind her eyelids. He was saying goodbye.

A brief smile touched his lips. "Remember the first time I took you to a Greek restaurant? What a surprise it was to discover a passion we didn't share?"

"I remember everything," she whispered. "Coffee and brioche in bed surrounded by the Sunday *Times*...burnt hot dogs and the sunset at the beach house." She closed her lashes, hoping to conceal the moisture welling in her eyes.

"Arguing about the book reviews...you slaving over a hot word processor while I read manuscripts or worked on contracts."

"You laughing at *Murphy Brown*...fixing dinner together on Sunday nights...the long phone calls during the week."

Neither of them mentioned the times Meg had quizzed him about his secretary, or about a pretty new author. They didn't bring up the imagined hurts, the angry explanations. They lapsed into silence, remembering the past, increasingly aware there would be no future.

"Let's get out of here," Steven said in a gruff voice.

Fumbling behind her, Meg found her cane, then Steven helped her into her parka and to the door. They didn't speak again until he stopped the car in front of the veranda at Morgan's Manor.

Meg stared at a point in space, hoping she could hold back the tears until she got inside. This time the relationship was truly over. There would be no more second chances. Meg realized she hadn't genuinely believed it before. Somewhere in a secret corner of her mind, she had believed they would work out their problems someday and she and Steven would be together again. A magic wand would slay the green-eyed monster and everything would be all right.

Now, sitting so close to Steven that she could feel the

magnetic warmth of his thigh next to hers, could smell the
tweedy scent of his jacket and the intoxicating fragrance
of his after-shave, she tried to tell herself that she would
probably never again be alone with him. Would never
again melt into his body as he took her in his arms and
kissed her. Would never again awaken to his dark head on
the pillow next to hers. Tears glistened in her eyes as she
reached for the door handle.

"Meg." His fingertips touched her shoulder, then fell
away. "We still have some unfinished business. After we
leave here I won't be seeing Suzanne again. That's a dead
end. But I still want to see the Halverson book completed.
Have you given any thought to where Tillis might have
hidden her research material?"

Steven spoke in his publisher's voice. Nothing in his
tone hinted that Meg meant anything more to him than any
other author or business associate.

"I'll start searching for the notes tomorrow," she answered without looking at him. She watched her fingers
clasping and unclasping her purse.

"I'd like to help," Steven said. When Meg didn't speak,
he added, "It's a big house, I imagine you could use a
hand. You don't object, do you?"

"Is that a good idea?" she asked around the lump in
her throat.

"Why not? We're friends, aren't we? And I'm your
publisher." He smiled, moving firmly into his publisher-
encourages-the-author role. "I'm going to publish your
next bestseller..."

So that's how the future would be. Friends. Business
associates. Meg hurt inside, she felt herself dying by
inches.

"I'm going to beat this, Steven," she said in a low grim

voice, speaking between her teeth. "I'm not going to live the rest of my life driving away the people I love."

"Good," he said finally. For an instant his business facade cracked and she heard pain in his voice, too. "I hope you do. I don't see how you can have a successful relationship until you learn to believe in your own worth, Meg."

She squeezed her eyes shut. "I don't know how or when, but I'll recognize the moment when it happens. One day the jealousy will be—gone." Please God, let the sick helpless feelings go away. "And I'll be free."

"I hope you're right." He cleared his throat. "Well. I'll see you in the morning, then."

The awkwardness of the moment hurt as much as the words still ringing in her ears. She and Steven had never felt awkward with each other before. There had never been uncomfortable silences between them. Until now.

Blindly Meg reached for the door handle, then drew back as a shadow darted toward the window. A flashbulb exploded in her eyes, then another.

The reporters had arrived.

MEG WATCHED through the living room windows as another media truck skidded to a halt in front of the house. A dozen photographers milled about in the driveway and on the veranda steps. Those who had been camped out on the veranda the longest looked cold and red cheeked and uncomfortable. Meg considered sending James out with coffee or hot cider, then decided the idea was crazy. Making them comfortable would only encourage them to prolong their siege.

And that's what it was, she thought as a photographer spied her at the window and dashed forward to snap her photograph before she jerked the draperies shut. A siege, an invasion. Trucks and cars jammed the driveway; people pounded at the door; the telephone hadn't stopped ringing since Steven brought her home from their disastrous lunch.

When James appeared to inquire if she wanted coffee or tea, his tie was askew and a sprig of grey hair stood up at the back of his head. A dozen shouting, pushy reporters had managed to accomplish what two murders had not. James looked harried and out of sync with himself.

He pressed his fingers together and drew a breath. "I've put the phone messages on Madam's desk, miss. News stations are calling from all over the country. One from England. I'm telling everyone we have no comment. Is that correct, miss?" After she nodded, he drew another breath. "I phoned Sheriff Conner as you requested, miss. He said we may clean Madam's and Mr. Parnham's rooms if we wish. But I haven't done anything yet."

"Thank you, James." Meg thought about it a moment. "I'd rather we didn't disturb either room until tomorrow."

"As you wish, miss." They both ignored the persistent pounding at the front door and the nonstop ring of the telephone. "They're at the kitchen door, too."

"Make sure the windows are locked and the draperies are drawn," Meg said, but she felt confident James had already secured the premises.

They discussed strategy, then James withdrew and Meg was left with the evening stretching before her. She warmed her hands in front of the fireplace, listening to the pounding at the door and the voices shouting in front of the house. Then, because she couldn't bear to think about the conversation with Steven, in spite of the fact that it kept intruding on her thoughts, she straightened her shoulders and walked toward the staircase.

Curiosity drew her upstairs and carried her to Aunt Tilly's bedroom door. For a long uncertain moment she stood in the dim corridor with her hand on the latch, asking herself if she really wanted to step inside, if she was ready for this. Finally she exhaled slowly, then depressed the latch and entered the room.

The first thing she saw was the outline chalked on the carpet beneath the window. A gasp caught in her throat. Then, blinking at the tears welling in her eyes, she made herself look at the chalky outline until it no longer possessed the power to upset her. That wasn't Aunt Tilly. Aunt Tilly was the vibrant woman dressed in the spider gown whose bright eyes had twinkled and flashed with impish pleasure. That was how Meg was determined to remember Aunt Tilly, not as she had seen her last.

When her nerves steadied again, she inspected the rest of the room, not hurrying. Candida's ring, Howard's smashed liquor glass and Dennis's cigarette holder were gone. The police had taken them as evidence. The poker was missing, too, and other items that might have served as a weapon. Here and there she spotted traces of graphite where the fingerprinting crew had performed a haphazard cleanup.

The manuscript pages of Aunt Tilly's novel, *First Guess,* were also gone. If Meg remembered correctly, the plot was based on a trick premise. There hadn't been a murder at all; the victim in the novel had died of natural causes. Now Meg recalled seeing Suzanne inspecting the pages on the floor. And now she understood why Suzanne had suggested Aunt Tilly might have died from a heart attack or a seizure. Apparently Suzanne had also read *First Guess,* and scanning the loose pages had triggered her memory.

For several minutes Meg stood in the center of the littered bedroom, slowly gazing around her, remembering how the scene had looked when she first saw it.

There were so many questions.

How had Candida's ring, Howard's glass and Dennis's cigarette holder gotten into this room? Why were pages from *First Guess* scattered about the carpet? She didn't understand why Aunt Tilly had the dead copy of an early novel in her bedroom in the first place. The dead copies of her books were in the supply room downstairs.

Why hadn't anyone overheard the struggle that took place in this room? Meg examined the overturned lamp and side table, the toppled chair. The chair especially would have made a tremendous crash when it fell over. Why hadn't anyone heard the noise?

And why had the window been opened a few inches?

Meg had asked herself these questions a hundred times. Closing her eyes in frustration, she raised her fingertips and massaged her temples. "Help me, Aunt Tilly," she whispered. "I have a feeling everything would make sense if I just looked at it the right way." Now was the most conducive moment. Finally she was alone, unhurried and able to concentrate.

As clearly as if Aunt Tilly stood beside her, she heard Tillis Morgan's voice. *Never overlook the obvious.*

Rubbing her arms, Meg walked to the window and stared down at the latch until her eyes began to water and smart. The open window was the key. Logic and intuition told her so. What was the *obvious* reason why someone would open a window in a blizzard?

Think, she commanded herself. Start with the premise that Aunt Tilly opened the window. Why?

All right. Pretend it's you. You're in this room; you're alone and dressed for bed. You think someone in this house wants to kill you. You pace awhile, maybe you think about dying. Then you walk to the window and you open it because... Meg rubbed her eyes, swore softly under her breath and tried again and then again. You open it because...

Because...

And then she had it. Suddenly the obvious answer was right in front of her. Of course. Eyes widening, Meg continued to stare at the panes as a sad smile touched her lips. Yes, that had to be the reason for the opened window.

Turning, she surveyed the room, seeking other obvious answers to test the theory slowly coming together in her mind.

Why had Candida, Howard and Dennis lied about leaving the ring, the glass and the cigarette holder in this room? The obvious answer? They hadn't lied. Why had Candida lied about being in this room? Obvious answer? She hadn't lied; Candida was never here.

Why had no one heard the terrible struggle erupting in Aunt Tilly's room? Obvious answer? No struggle occurred. It didn't happen.

And finally, the biggest mystery of all—how had the killer escaped from the locked room? The obvious answer? He hadn't.

"Oh, Aunt Tilly," Meg whispered, smiling through a shine of sad tears. "I wish I'd known you better. You and I could have been such good friends. I would have enjoyed you so much." After wiping her eyes, Meg glanced at the chalked outline on the carpet. "But didn't you know you'd be found out?" The question was foolish. Of course Aunt Tilly had known she would be caught.

When James spoke from the doorway, Meg jumped.

"I didn't mean to startle you, miss. Mr. Caldwell is on the telephone. He says it's urgent."

"Thank you. I'll take it in here." After James withdrew, Meg sat gingerly on Aunt Tilly's quilt and picked up the bedside telephone.

"I know why the window was open," Steven said without preamble. "I just figured it out."

"So did I." Leaning forward, Meg covered her eyes with her hand. Once again she and Steven were thinking along a parallel track. "Tell me why you think it was open." When he finished speaking, she nodded. "That's what I think, too. I don't know what we'll find yet, but I can guess."

"Are the reporters still there?" Steven asked. Impatience deepened his voice.

"I'm afraid so. I won't be able to verify our theory until morning. But I can go through Aunt Tilly's statements and receipts."

"Meg, I want to be there when you check this out."

She nodded and looked at the dark windows. "We'd better plan on doing it at dawn. Some of these media people are early risers."

Again an awkward silence opened between them. There was nothing more to say, but neither of them wanted to say goodbye. Meg thought about asking where he had gone to dinner, but she didn't. Steven would interpret the question as, "Who did you have dinner with?" And maybe he wouldn't be wrong.

"Well. I'll see you in the morning," she said softly, sadly. After she hung up, she looked at the telephone a minute, then closed her eyes. But before she left Aunt Tilly's bedroom, she lifted the phone again and dialed Adell, Iowa.

Her father picked up on the second ring. "I know your mother wants to talk to you, honey, but she's resting now. We were up late last night talking, then up early this morning to watch the news reports."

"Don't disturb her, I know she must be terribly upset. But please tell her I need to speak to her when she feels up to it. I have some questions I think Mom may be able to answer.''

"Helen's upset," her father agreed. "She's sad, of course. And furious and, believe it or not, amused. She's feeling all the confusing things Tilly must have known she would."

"Amused," Meg repeated. So she was on the right track. The obvious answer.

"Your Aunt Tilly sure was something." Her father paused to blow his nose, then she heard a moist chuckle. "She'll be missed. Tilly Morgan was one of a kind. There will never be another like her. She just couldn't pass up a good prank."

"There may have been another reason none of us knew about," Meg said carefully.

She didn't know if her father hadn't heard or if he chose to ignore her comment.

"All the news stories have picked up on *Murder at Eight*. I'll bet Tilly's books are selling like hotcakes. She would have loved it, wouldn't she? All the publicity, the speculation, the mysterious circumstances, all the book sales." Something that sounded like a strangled laugh came over the wires. "And don't you know Tilly had a grand time setting up Candida Ripley as one of the suspects. Yes sir, I'll bet she enjoyed that part the most. It's a hell of a prank."

"One of the awful things is that Aunt Tilly isn't here to enjoy the fuss she's causing."

"We'll have to enjoy it on her behalf, honey. You know that's what she would have wanted. Like all the speculation about Candida's ring being in the locked room. Tilly had a wicked sense of humor, didn't she?"

"That's one of the reasons I'm calling." Meg drew a breath. "How *did* the ring and the other items get into

Aunt Tilly's bedroom? I have a feeling you and Mom know the answer.''

"Honey, I can't help you. But maybe your mother can. She's been sworn to secrecy for years. Maybe it's time her secret came out—but she's the one to tell you. It's her and Tilly's secret. I'll have your mother phone you tomorrow.''

Meg agreed because there was no other choice. It was frustrating not to have the answers right now this minute, but the pieces were beginning to fall into place. And she could guess what the missing pieces were. If the situation hadn't been so serious and so sad, if she hadn't felt so furious with Aunt Tilly, she would have laughed out loud.

Chapter Nine

A frosty glow lit the dawn sky when Meg's alarm rang beside her pillow. Yawning and rubbing her eyes, she slipped out from under the quilt. She swiftly found the clothing she had laid out the night before and pulled on her jeans and a thick sweater. She eased a pair of wool socks over her sore foot, then quietly hurried downstairs to the foyer for her cap, parka and gloves.

When she heard the crunch of car tires rolling over the brittle morning snow, she peeked outside to make sure it was Steven and not an early-bird reporter, then stepped out onto the veranda.

"Hi," she said, handing him a mug of hot coffee. The steam rose between them.

"Thanks." He accepted the cup with a look of gratitude.

"How did you figure it out?" Meg asked. She was determined not to allow any unpleasant silences. "About the window?" They started around the house, following the trail originally made by Steven and James, widened by the police inspectors. They didn't stop until they stood directly beneath Aunt Tilly's window.

"I'm not sure," Steven said, looking up. "Maybe it was getting away from everyone. The idea just came to me, and then everything fell into place." He tasted his coffee. "Did you check the records in Tillis's desk?"

Meg leaned on her cane and looked up as sunlight shot over the mountain peaks and lit Aunt Tilly's windowsill. Following an imaginary line down the two-and-a-half story wall, she drew her gaze to the ground.

"I found the statements. But it was too late to verify anything. No one would have been in their office. I'll do it after we finish here. If we're right."

But she saw what she was looking for, and so did Steven.

Holes made by falling icicles ran in a snowy line parallel to the foundation of the house. But here, almost at Steven's feet, one of the holes was out of line, positioned nearer the foundation instead of directly beneath the eaves. The snowfall on the day Dennis was killed had partially filled the hole, and two days of sunshine had melted the sides inward. It was more a dimple on the surface of the snow than an actual hole at this point. But it was what Meg had expected to find.

With Steven's assistance, she kneeled in the snow beside the dimple and examined it for a long moment through the silvery haze created by her breath. Everything hinged on this hole. If Meg was wrong about this, then she was wrong about all the rest, too.

"We'll know in a minute," Steven said, watching her. He spoke in a quiet voice, going through it again. "Why would someone open a window during a blizzard?"

"There's only one reason that makes sense. To throw something out," Meg answered. It seemed so obvious now.

"Something Tillis didn't want to be found in the room later."

"I can think of only one thing that could be."

Steven met her eyes. "Go ahead. Let's find out."

After expelling a long frosty breath, Meg plunged her glove into the dimple and immediately her fingers struck an object. "It's here," she said to Steven.

Slowly she removed a brown plastic medicine bottle from the hole and brushed away the loose snow, then tilted the label toward the sunlight. Although some of the writing had smeared, she could read Tillis Morgan's name and make out the date of Aunt Tilly's last dinner party.

"She had the prescription filled the day she died." Sadness clashed with the exhilaration of being correct.

Taking the bottle from her hand, Steven removed the cap and looked inside. "It's three-quarters full of lead shot. I guess she wanted to make sure the bottle sank in the snow and didn't bounce over the drifts, then come to rest where it could be easily found."

"What was the medication?"

Steven squinted at the smeared label and read it aloud. The name of the medication meant nothing to Meg. However, she could guess the nature of the original contents, and knew how to confirm her conjecture.

Although snow was melting through the knees of her jeans and she had started to shiver with cold, Meg didn't immediately push to her feet. She took the weighted bottle from Steven and held it in her glove, thinking about Aunt Tilly's last evening. About the outrageous spider gown, the startling dinner conversation, the people Aunt Tilly had chosen to spend her last night with. She remembered Aunt Tilly's laughter and bright eyes, her obvious pleasure in her final dinner party. Finally Meg tilted her head back to see Aunt Tilly's window. She laughed out loud.

"She really was one of a kind. I still can't believe she did this."

Steven smiled, too. "When someone, maybe you, writes Tillis's biography, this is going to make a hell of a finish."

He helped Meg to her feet, and it seemed so natural to step into his arms. For a moment they stood together in silence, holding each other and thinking about Tillis Morgan. Then Meg became aware of Steven's arms around her and felt her heartbeat accelerate. She stepped away self-consciously and dusted her gloves together after she checked to make sure the bottle was in her pocket. "I think James has breakfast waiting."

After breakfast, they went to Aunt Tilly's office and Meg opened the top drawer of the desk. Removing the pile of bills and receipts she had separated last night, she withdrew two receipts. She then placed a call to Dr. Li at the Vail Valley Medical Center and followed it with a call to Presbyterian Hospital in Denver, finding the names and phone numbers on the medical receipts.

"It's all coming together," she said to Steven when she finished the telephone calls. He stood at the window, drinking coffee and waiting. "We were right."

"We have to call Sheriff Conner," Steven said, turning to face her.

Meg sighed. "I guess so." Reluctantly she reached for the telephone as it rang beneath her hand. She lifted the receiver and eavesdropped as James answered and stubbornly repeated, "No comment," to the excited reporter on the other end. The instant Meg hung up, the telephone rang again. The sun was up and so were the news hounds.

Leaning back in the desk chair, Meg pushed a hand through her hair and glanced at the TV Steven had snapped on when they entered the room. One of the Denver stations was delivering an hourly update on the locked-door murder case. As far as Meg could tell, there wasn't any new information.

But the sensational aspects of the case had captured America's interest. Every commentator across the country had developed a theory to explain how Aunt Tilly's murder had been committed and speculated on the list of suspects.

The reporters dredged up the old scandal about Tilly, Candida and Howard. Suzanne's past was rehashed. Dennis's famous clients were mentioned. Caldwell Publishing's stock repurchase agreement was dissected. Meg was named as Tillis's heir.

And through all the excited speculation, Tillis Morgan held center stage. She was the undisputed star of the nightly news; she was America's current sensation. Everyone tried to solve the locked-door mystery and phoned their theory in to talk-show hosts. Aunt Tilly would have been the first to clap her hands and crow about what fun it was.

Meg released a breath and looked at Steven. "What if we don't call Sheriff Conner?" she asked. "What if we just let him discover the truth for himself? And he will. He'll know as soon as he gets the medical examiner's report."

Steven was watching a television reporter demonstrate how an interior bolt might have been locked from outside the door. The demonstration was unsuccessful. "You mean just let the prank play out?"

Meg nodded. "I have this fanciful notion that Aunt Tilly is perched on the edge of a cloud somewhere, looking down and thoroughly enjoying the hullabaloo she's caused."

"Sheriff Conner will be furious when he discovers we knew about this and didn't call him immediately." Steven studied her over his coffee cup. "But it's your decision. I'll go along with whatever you want to do."

"Then we'll let Aunt Tilly enjoy her last moment in the limelight," Meg said softly.

Steven nodded. "I had an idea that's what you'd decide." They smiled at each other, enjoying this moment of accord. Steven set his coffee cup on the tray and cleared his throat. "Well. How do you want to organize the search for Tillis's research material. Any suggestions?"

Meg turned to face the window and bit her lip. Why couldn't it always be like this? She and Steven working together, thinking the same things, sharing the same feelings? Why did the outside world have to intrude? With a grimace, she realized she was copping out. The outside world wasn't the problem. Meg Sandler was the problem.

This line of thought depressed her. And it was pointless. The moment had passed for what-ifs and might-have-beens. Suppressing a sigh, Meg tried to decide on a plan for today that would keep them in different parts of the house. When she was near Steven all she could think about was the touch of his strong hands, the taste of his lips... She didn't need that kind of distraction. Or that pain.

"I'll take the attic," she said finally. "You start with the basement."

A look of relief crossed his expression as if he had been remembering, too, as if being together was as difficult for him as it was for her. "Sounds good. Maybe we'll get lucky and find the file before lunch."

But they didn't get lucky. At six o'clock they called a halt for the day.

"Would you like to stay for dinner?" Meg asked when they met for a glass of wine in the living room. She was tired, dusty and out of sorts. After spending the entire day in the attic going through trunks and boxes and rows of ancient files, she was convinced Aunt Tilly had been a pack rat. Aunt Tilly hadn't disposed of anything. What couldn't be crammed into the attic went down to the basement. Steven hadn't finished there until thirty minutes ago.

"Thanks, but I'll take a rain check. What I want right now is a hot shower," Steven said, stretching his neck against his hand. "You wouldn't believe the stuff that's down there. Old encyclopedias, boxes of clothing that must have belonged to your grandparents, broken garden equipment, furniture that's now being used by mice and chipmunks."

"Everything but the Halverson file," Meg said glumly, putting her feet up on the coffee table. She wasn't using her cane today and her foot had begun to ache. She also had a headache brought on by wondering what she would do with the items in the attic and the basement once she officially inherited them.

"The file is here somewhere," Steven said. He sounded tired. "We'll try again tomorrow." He glanced at his watch and Meg wondered if he was meeting someone for dinner. She bit her lip hard and didn't say anything. "Don't get up, you look tired," Steven said. "I know my way to the door."

"If there's something you'd rather be doing tomorrow, I can finish the search," Meg said in a tight voice.

He was standing behind her so she couldn't see his expression. But she imagined it. And she silently berated herself for asking to be hurt.

"I'll see you in the morning. Bright and early," Steven said finally. There was resignation in his tone. And somehow that was worse than anger would have been.

Meg stared into the fireplace and finished her wine. A tear rolled down her cheek.

STEVEN AND Sheriff Conner arrived at the same time, just as Meg was finishing breakfast. They elbowed a path through the shouting reporters and James let them in, then quickly shut the door behind them.

Steven stamped the snow from his boots and nodded at Meg's foot. "You're wearing shoes. That's great."

His hair, like hers, was still damp from a shower. He smelled like soap and frosty air.

Sheriff Conner removed his hat. "This won't take long, Miss Sandler. I've heard from the medical examiner and—"

"And Aunt Tilly's murder is a hoax," Meg finished. Sadness deepened the color of her eyes. "Aunt Tilly committed suicide."

The sheriff stared at her. "You could have saved everyone a lot of trouble, Miss Sandler, if you had told the truth the day I interviewed you."

"Steven and I didn't know the truth until yesterday. Not for certain." Meg led them into the living room and asked James to serve coffee. James leaned against the archway, a shocked expression pinching his mouth. Frowning, Meg placed a hand on his sleeve. "I thought you knew."

"In fact, we thought you were part of the prank," Steven added.

James stumbled forward and sank into a chair. He passed a hand over his eyes. "Good God, no. This is the first…" He swallowed hard and shook his head. "A suicide!"

"But the telephones. That had to be your work. You and Hilda were the only ones who knew where all…" Then it came to her. James and Hilda were not the only people who knew the location of all the telephones.

"Tillis," Steven said softly, following her thought. "Tillis knew where the phones were located."

"She must have disabled them." Meg stared at him. "No one suspected it was her. But of course it was."

"Okay, folks." Sheriff Conner pointed to the sofa. "Sit yourselves down. You've figured out the telephones. And the locked bolt isn't a mystery anymore. What else can we clear up here?"

Meg's thigh brushed Steven's and a tingle shot to the roots of her hair. Startled, she eased away from him. But the unexpected contact had rattled her thoughts. She looked at the sheriff and heard herself babbling.

"In retrospect, the whole thing seems so obvious that it's hard to see how we missed it. Aunt Tilly scattered clues everywhere. Do you remember the little speech she made in the living room after dinner?" She directed the question to Steven because she didn't want him to know that his nearness affected her. But it did.

He was studying her with a distracted expression. "What did you say?" After she repeated her question, he nodded. "I agree. I think Tillis was saying goodbye, but none of us realized it at the time." His eyes dropped to Meg's lips. "Later she also managed to speak to each of us individually. She told me how much she had enjoyed being published by Caldwell, that she knew Caldwell would flourish under my stewardship, that kind of thing. It was a private goodbye, I think."

"That's how it was when she spoke to me," Meg said. Knowing Steven was watching her mouth made her lips feel funny. It occurred to her that Steven's sweater was the same dark caramel color as his eyes. She found it increasingly difficult to concentrate on what she was saying. "I think Aunt Tilly couldn't resist leaving clues. She could have closed the window, but she didn't. I think she left it open to nudge us toward the truth. That's also probably why she scattered pages of *First Guess* around the room, to suggest that no murder had occurred."

"When I saw her alone, she mentioned she had a headache.'' Steven moved slightly closer to Meg as he spoke. His hand was less than an inch from her sensitive thigh. ''Did she say anything about headaches to you?''

''Now that I think of it…yes.'' Meg could have sworn she felt the heat of his hand on her skin. Responding to the near touch of his fingertips confused her. This sort of reaction shouldn't happen.

Sheriff Conner cleared his throat again and Meg gave herself a tiny shake. She had forgotten him. Sheriff Conner accepted a cup of coffee from the tray James offered before he withdrew, still white faced and distracted.

''What I want to know is how Miss Ripley's ring and the other items got inside Miss Morgan's bedroom,'' the sheriff said. ''Miss Ripley and Mr. Clancy aren't budging off their story. They say they did not leave a ring or a glass in that room. So—how did those items get there?''

''I don't know,'' Meg replied, frowning. ''I think my mother may have the answer, but I haven't spoken to her yet.''

''Your mother?'' Steven looked surprised. He glanced at Meg's shoulder, then withdrew his hand from the seat of the sofa.

''The ring and the other items aren't important anymore now that we're dealing with a suicide instead of a murder,'' the sheriff said. ''But they're still a mystery. I'd like to hear your solution if and when you figure it out.'' He leaned forward and placed his cup on the coffee table. ''There's no doubt that Tillis Morgan died of a massive overdose of prescription painkiller. We've checked with Presbyterian and her doctor there confirmed it was her medication.''

''Steven, I think you'd better tell Sheriff Conner about the bottle we found.'' After Steven finished explaining, Meg added, ''I kept the bottle for you. We were both wearing gloves so Aunt Tilly's fingerprints should be the only prints.''

''Well, that's it, then. Your bottle is the last loose end. I'd say we've got this one wrapped up.''

''Sheriff…'' Some questions were difficult to ask; some truths difficult to hear. But Meg needed to know. ''Is it true that Aunt Tilly had less than a year to live?''

''That was the medical examiner's best guess.'' Sympathy softened Sheriff Conner's expression. ''Your aunt had an inoperable tumor at the base of her skull. The cancer had begun to spread to other parts of her body.''

When Meg leaned forward and covered her eyes, Steven placed his hand on her back. ''Why didn't Tillis opt for chemotherapy?''

''She could have,'' the sheriff answered. ''But her doctors weren't optimistic. You and Miss Sandler probably know that the dangers and painful difficulties associated with chemo keep it from being a real cure. Miss Morgan chose to forgo that route. But without treatment, her deterioration would have been rapid. Your aunt faced a painful and unpleasant set of choices, Miss Sandler.''

''And a painful and unpleasant future no matter what she did,'' Meg said in a low voice.

Seeing her distress, Steven caressed her shoulder. ''But that didn't happen. Tillis left the world in the same way she lived in it. In high spirits and with a smile on her lips.''

''Apparently so.'' Sheriff Conner didn't look happy. ''The whole murder setup was a prank. And most of America fell for it.''

''Candida was right all along,'' Steven added. ''The setup was simply too good to be true. The business about being marooned, the dramatic announcement that everyone present had a reason to want her dead. All of it. From the very beginning the weekend read like a mystery novel. Tillis was setting us up.''

"If Aunt Tilly's cancer had run its course, Aunt Tilly would have died quietly and in great pain. Her death would have merited a couple of inches in the newsmagazines and maybe a column in the book section of the major newspapers." Meg looked at him, but she was seeing Aunt Tilly in her mind. "That isn't what she wanted. She wanted to end with a big splash."

"Well, she managed that all right," Sheriff Conner said with a grimace. "Miss Morgan had her little joke. But the prank backfired. Someone used the opportunity your aunt created to commit a real murder. Dennis Parnham didn't fake breaking his neck. Someone did it for him."

Meg swallowed hard. In the exhilaration of solving Aunt Tilly's "murder," she hadn't forgotten Dennis Parnham, but she hadn't given him much thought, either. Focused on Aunt Tilly, she had vacillated between sadness and amusement. Now the smile faded from her lips.

"Yes. Dennis," she said uncomfortably.

"Either of you folks have any theories about that one?"

Steven leaned forward, his elbows on his knees. "I don't think the body was moved. I think Dennis was killed in his chair, right where we found him."

Meg nodded thoughtfully. "It seems obvious he was killed from behind."

Steven turned to look at her. "If someone tried to assault Dennis from the front, he would have put up a struggle. Is that how you see it?"

Meg nodded, then glanced at Sheriff Conner. "Are we on the right track?"

Suddenly Meg had the uncomfortable feeling that she and Steven were *too* close to the truth. She imagined Sheriff Conner was studying them suspiciously. "So how do you experts account for the fact that the medical examiner places Parnham's death as happening between ten and eleven o'clock? Probably closer to ten than eleven. A time when you people swear it could not have happened because Parnham was outside wandering around in a snowstorm."

"I don't know," Steven said. Meg spread her hands in agreement.

The sheriff lifted one heavy eyebrow. "As near as I can figure it, Parnham has a window of about seven minutes during which he had to reenter the house, hang up his cap and parka, go upstairs, start reading, then admit his killer into the room and get his neck broken."

Neither Meg nor Steven spoke.

"The time window narrows even further when you consider the traffic in the corridor that night. Miss Sandler, you're in the hallway talking to James. After leaving you, James fetched a bottle of aspirin for Mrs. Halverson, so he's in the hallway. Then you, Mr. Caldwell, come upstairs and stop by Mrs. Halverson's room for a moment, then you go to Miss Sandler's room, so you're in and out of the hallway. Then Mr. Clancy and Miss Ripley are out there. Everyone was wandering around, but no one saw Parnham return inside, or noticed him upstairs."

Meg slid a look toward Steven. She hadn't known he had stopped by Suzanne's room before he came to hers.

Steven read her mind. He spread his hands and frowned. "Suzanne left her scarf downstairs. I returned it to her."

"I didn't say anything," Meg said in a tight voice.

Sheriff Conner examined Steven's expression. "If Parnham had acted on his threat to withdraw the authors he represented from Caldwell Publishing, you would have lost six of your top-selling authors. The loss would have dealt a blow to your company."

"It was an empty threat," Steven explained. "Those authors are under contract. But it's true Dennis could have caused a problem. Maybe some of his authors would have acted on his advice and reneged on their contractual obligations. Maybe they would have taken their next books somewhere else." He shrugged. "I would have been upset, but it wouldn't have ruined the company."

"Then you aren't having financial difficulties?"

"Hell, no." Steven frowned. "My bottom line isn't as strong as I'd like it to be. What company's is? But Caldwell Publishing is a healthy business. You're welcome to audit the books if this is an issue. I didn't kill Dennis Parnham. Your own timetable ought to tell you that."

"That's what makes this case so interesting," Sheriff Conner said, pushing to his feet. He settled his hat over a close-cropped head of sandy hair. "No one could have murdered Mr. Parnham. But someone did—didn't they?"

Meg and Steven followed him to the front door. "I think we've figured out that Aunt Tilly disabled the telephones," Meg said, "but what about the skis? Did Aunt Tilly hide the skis and flatten the tires, too?"

"I'm guessing your aunt disabled the telephones to heighten the immediate effect of the prank." Sheriff Conner peered out the side window at the reporters milling about the driveway. "But there wasn't any compelling reason to delay informing the authorities. In fact a delay might have caused the prank to fizzle. Therefore, I don't believe Tillis Morgan hid the skis or flattened the tires."

"You know," Steven said, leaning against the archway. "It occurs to me that killing Dennis required surprise, not strength."

"So the killer could have been a woman." A humorless smile lifted Sheriff Conner's mouth. "That's occurred to us. We aren't ruling anyone out, Mr. Caldwell."

Meg's eyebrows soared, then settled into a frown. She kept forgetting that she, too, was a suspect in Dennis's murder. Sheriff Conner's glance reminded her.

Sheriff Conner reached for the door latch. "I'm holding a press conference in about an hour to announce Miss Morgan's suicide." He raised his chin to the window indicating the noise outside. "I imagine most of the excitement will die down once the reporters understand there was no locked-door murder. No whodunit for America to solve."

"What about Dennis's murder?" Steven asked.

"With respect to Mr. Parnham, he wasn't a famous or eccentric mystery writer, and—there's no tactful way to say this—his murder is ordinary run-of-the-mill stuff." A shrug lifted Sheriff Conner's uniform. Then his gaze narrowed on Meg and Steven. "I'm guessing the reporters will be gone by supper time. But I'm not going anywhere. I'll be keeping an eye on everyone until Parnham's murder is solved."

Meg didn't like the way he was looking at them. Drawing a breath she stepped forward and gave him Aunt Tilly's medication bottle. "Thank you for stopping by."

"If you come up with anything else, or if you find any more evidence—" his gaze steadied on her face "—you don't wait for me to drop by, understand? You telephone immediately."

Color rose in her cheeks. "I will."

Meg watched through the draperies as Sheriff Conner crossed to the top step of the veranda and addressed the reporters, announcing his press conference. A few of the reporters spun to look at the house, their expressions drawn with indecision. Then most of them jumped into their cars and vans and followed the sheriff's car down the driveway.

When she turned from the window, Steven was watching her. "Are you going to make an issue out of Suzanne's scarf?"

"It seems peculiar that you didn't mention it," she said, passing him on her way back into the living room.

"Come on, Meg. It was a small thing. It never entered my mind that mentioning it was important." Thrusting his hands into his pockets, he walked to the windows and frowned at the departing cars and vans.

Meg walked to the fireplace and held her hands out to the flames. "I don't know what it is about Suzanne that brings out the worst in me," she said quietly. "She's just so damned beautiful, so perfect. When I think about her I feel dull and inadequate. I guess I had trouble believing you weren't involved with her because I couldn't imagine why you'd want me when you could have Suzanne."

Steven continued to gaze out the windows. He didn't turn to look at her. "You've met Suzanne. You've spent time with her. You have to recognize there's something inside Suzanne that doesn't connect. Okay, she's beautiful. But so are you." He paused, then turned toward her. "Look, Meg, I'm not the writer here, not as good with words as you are. But I can promise you there will always be someone out there who is prettier, smarter, richer or more successful than you are. And there are also plenty who are not as beautiful, not as smart, not as rich or as successful. If you want to, you can focus solely on the first group and make yourself miserable."

Meg lowered her head and covered her eyes. "I hate this," she whispered. "I hate it that I'm so damned insecure. Please, Steven, stop. Don't say anything more."

The irony was she had believed she had her feelings in check. Then she arrived at Morgan's Manor and was confronted with Steven and Suzanne. And all the old insecurities had flared to life. Suddenly Meg tumbled backward in time and was once again the devastated girl whose fiancé had eloped with her best friend, leaving her to face the humiliation of explaining to her family and friends what had happened. And, just as suddenly, she was flashing back on Steven and all the anxious moments she had experienced thinking the same thing was happening again.

"I *will* beat this," she whispered, feeling raw and vulnerable, needing reassurance that pride wouldn't let her request.

When she lifted her head, Steven had moved to stand beside her. The room seemed to spin as she stared into his brown eyes, eyes that reflected sympathy and regret.

"Oh, Steven." Her own gaze filled with helpless sorrow. "I'm so sorry. I ruined everything, and—"

Gently he took her into his arms and kissed her. This was not the angry passionate kiss they had shared a few days ago. His kiss was soft, almost tender. His arms closed around her and drew her close, cradling her against him as if she were too fragile to risk crushing.

When his mouth released hers, he continued to hold her, resting his chin lightly on top of her head. "I'm sorry, too, Meg. I wish things had worked out differently. There are hurts and regrets on both sides." In the following silence, Meg heard his heart beating against her ear. She swallowed the tears clogging her throat. "Well," he said finally, easing her away from him. "We have a full day ahead. Where do we search today?"

With all her heart Meg wished Candida had never said, "Ask yourself what you suddenly have that Steven wants." That statement cast a veil of doubt. Would Steven have been so gentle if they had the Halverson file in their hands? Would the sympathy and regret still soften his gaze?

What difference did it make? File or no file, their relationship was over.

"Please don't kiss me again," she said quietly, backing away from him. Anger flashed in her eyes. He should have known his kiss would only make it harder. Only make her want him more. Was he playing with her? Either the relationship was over, or it wasn't.

"You're right," he said. "I apologize. I shouldn't have done that."

"No. You shouldn't have."

Lifting her head, she marched out of the living room feeling confused, angry and utterly miserable.

Chapter Ten

Sheriff Conner was correct. The reporters didn't reappear at Morgan's Manor after Sheriff Conner's press conference on the courthouse steps. The emphasis in the case had shifted.

When Steven and Meg gave up the search for the day and met, frustrated, in the living room for a drink, they switched on the TV to watch the five o'clock news. It was preferable to talking.

The lead story on all the channels featured the hoax. In the excitement generated by this sensational development, no one appeared to remember Dennis Parnham or recall that a genuine murder had actually occurred.

"I didn't like Dennis," Meg murmured, "but there's something a little sad in seeing him dismissed so indifferently."

"Sheriff Conner isn't forgetting Dennis." Steven rested his head on the back of the sofa, crossed his ankles on top of the coffee table. "I had no idea there were so many rooms in this place. We've been searching for two solid days and I feel like we've only scratched the surface." He ran a hand over his face.

After switching off the TV, Meg resumed pacing in front of the fireplace. "There's something about that night that we aren't seeing. Something as obvious as the solution to the opened window.''

"If there is, no one's spotted it. And all the evidence is in." Steven rolled his head to one side to look at her. "Everybody's spent hours puzzling over Dennis's murder. And everyone's coming up blank. Are you seeing something no one else is seeing?"

"No...it's just a feeling."

Meg couldn't pin down her intuition. But she felt certain there was something odd connected to breaking up the bridge game that night, something wrong. Something so obvious and ordinary that she couldn't isolate it. Thinking out loud, she replayed the scene for Steven, hearing the conversation that night, seeing the people.

She pulled off her bandana and pushed a hand through her hair. "It's so frustrating. I have a feeling that I'm right on the verge of seeing it."

"Seeing what?"

"Whatever is wrong with that scene. And there *is* something wrong." But the tiny wisp of memory flickered enticingly, then swirled away. It wouldn't be pinned down.

"And there's something about that incident in the corridor with Candida and Howard." There, too, something didn't ring true. Meg had sensed it from the beginning. That's why she had been so interested in the sconce Candida stood beneath.

That thought led to the memory of being pushed down the staircase. Concentrating, Meg tried to remember the exact moment when she had felt a hand against her back. But too much time had elapsed for her to be absolutely certain that she had indeed felt a hand on her back or that someone had really shoved her.

She cast a quick look at Steven and decided against sharing her thoughts. By now it embarrassed her even to think about the icicle incident. The icicle incident was a good lesson to remind her how jangled nerves could affect reason.

"I'm too tired to speculate over who killed Dennis Parnham," Steven said. "I shoved around more furniture today than a professional mover."

"And we aren't making any progress," Meg agreed, taking the thronelike chair across from him. Whatever she was sensing about the night Dennis was murdered would have to wait. In time it would surface.

"At least you got the supply room put back together."

Though Meg had known it was a foolish wish, she had hoped the Halverson file would appear in the mess covering the supply room floor. But of course it hadn't.

She found files of clippings, files of scribbled ideas for future books, files for books already published, files of press releases and promotional material, letter files and agent files, and papers that didn't appear to belong in any file. But nothing even remotely connected to the Halverson case had surfaced out of the chaos.

"So why wasn't the file in the supply room?" she asked, glancing at Steven. Already he had the shadow of a new beard. Once she would have teased him about it. "That's where the file should have been. Nothing else seems to be missing."

"Okay, let's work it through." Sitting up, Steven freshened his drink, raised an eyebrow at Meg. She shook her head and declined another Scotch and water. "We know the file existed. Tillis asked me to come here and review it."

"In the meantime Suzanne unexpectedly appears. It's safe to assume the file was intact at that time. And it was probably in Aunt Tilly's office. That's where she would have been working on it."

Standing, Steven moved to the fireplace. "Suzanne and Tillis argue in Tillis's office until they're interrupted by the arrival of everyone else. During that time Tillis tells Suzanne the notes are destroyed. Later she indicates to me that the notes are intact. She's hidden them and pointed you toward their location."

Meg rubbed her temples. "Aunt Tilly didn't leave the house, so the notes have to be hidden inside. What rooms did she go into? Can you remember? Did she leave her guests for any length of time?"

"Not that I noticed. My best guess is the file is in Tillis's office or her bedroom."

"We'll tackle those rooms tomorrow. My guess was the wall safe, or the concealed rooms where she kept the silver and her furs." But Meg had been wrong.

The silver and fur storage rooms had, however, solved a small mystery. The concealed storage rooms had been added long after the original house was built, and from the first, those rooms had been intended as secret hiding places for valuables. Creating space for the secret rooms had required reducing in size several adjoining rooms. Thus a few of the uncommonly small-sized rooms were explained. Plus, Meg had run across a few more windows that appeared to be boarded from the inside. The secret storage rooms supplied the explanation. Once again her grandfather had done his remodeling the cheapest way, building interior walls over windows. Slowly Meg was unraveling the mysteries of Morgan Manor.

"The mystery of the missing file is going to look so simple once we solve it," Meg said, frustrated. She looked up with a frown. "Steven—do you think it's possible that Suzanne found the Halverson file? Maybe we're wasting our time. Maybe the file is gone."

James appeared in the archway. "Sorry to disturb you, but your mother is on the telephone, miss."

"Finally. I was beginning to think she'd forgotten." Standing, Meg turned to Steven. "I really do need to take this call..."

"No problem, I was leaving anyway." He met her eyes. "Meg, about this morning..."

"There's nothing to talk about." Heat flooded her face. "Look, I overreacted. I'm sorry."

"I was out of line. I apologize."

Oh, God. He was apologizing for kissing her. It occurred to Meg this was a new low in their relationship. Wincing, she tried not to think about it. "We're friends, aren't we?" she said, her voice falsely bright. "Occasionally friends exchange a friendly kiss or a friendly hug. It seems I forgot that for a moment or two."

He looked as if he wanted to say more, but James was waiting at the archway. They were both aware Meg's mother was holding on the telephone.

"I'll see you in the morning," Steven said, lifting his hand in a wave.

Meg watched him pull on his parka and gloves, then she walked into Aunt Tilly's office to take her mother's call.

"I'm sorry I haven't reached you before," her mother apologized. "I've tried to phone, but your line was constantly busy, I couldn't get through."

Meg explained the media siege. "The calls didn't begin to taper off until about an hour ago. But now that the hoax has been exposed I expect things will quiet down."

"I know this whole experience has been terrible for you, honey. Believing Tilly had been murdered, then following that shock, Dennis's murder."

They discussed the weekend ordeal, exchanged condolences, talked about the arrangements, spoke of the hoax with a mixture of sadness and fond amusement.

"Did you know about Aunt Tilly's cancer?" Meg asked.

"No." A muffled sniffle sounded on the end of the phone line. "In retrospect, I think Tilly phoned to tell me one night, then changed her mind."

"She said you were always able to see through her. She said you could always spot her pranks."

"Yes," her mother confirmed in a soft voice. "Your father and I spied the makings of a prank as soon as we heard the news reports."

Meg leaned over the desktop and drew a breath. "Mother, Aunt Tilly made a point of directing me toward you." When her mother didn't comment, she continued. "I think Aunt Tilly was telling me that you would be able to answer a few questions that no one else can."

Her mother didn't deny the possibility or seem surprised. She merely said, "I see."

Meg continued. "The only unanswered questions left are—"

"How did Candida's ring and the other phony evidence get into Tilly's bedroom?"

"Yes! Plus there's a missing file I'm hoping you can shed some light on." Excitement charged Meg's voice. Until now she had wondered if she were wrong about her mother having the answers she needed. If she was building something out of nothing. But it seemed her instinct was correct. "Mother? Are you still there?"

"Honey, there's nothing I can tell you."

Disappointment drained the sparkle from Meg's expression. "Mother! If you know how those items got into Aunt Tilly's room..."

"I can guess. But if I'm right—well, it's a secret Tillis

and I agreed never to reveal. We made a promise to each other years ago when we were children." A soft chuckle sounded in Meg's ear. "If Tillis wanted you to know the secret, she would have told you herself, at least she would have given you a hint."

"But she did hint. She referred to secrets. And she talked about you. I believe Aunt Tilly wanted me to know the secrets of Morgan's Manor, and she expected you to tell me."

"I'm beginning to understand. That rascal, Tilly, sent you to me instead of telling you anything herself so I'd be the one to break our promise. A last prank on me. Well, Tilly was wrong. I won't break our promise, either."

Meg hunched forward and covered her eyes with her hand. "Mother, please listen. You're thinking Candida's ring and the other items aren't important anymore. And—" she hated to weaken her position by admitting it "—I suppose you're right. How those items got into Aunt Tilly's bedroom is still a mystery, but no longer important to anyone but me. I think the sheriff has dismissed the items by just assuming everyone lied."

"Maybe they did."

"Maybe. But if I understand what you're hinting at, there's another explanation. Even if it isn't vital to the case anymore, I need to *know*. Can you understand?" Meg tried to sound persuasive. "I think I became a mystery writer because I don't like mysteries. When I write them myself there is no mystery, I know the answers before I put a word on paper. But these mysteries are real. And, Mom, they're driving me crazy. If you know how those items got into Aunt Tilly's room, if you know where a file might be hidden…well, I believe Aunt Tilly expected you— wanted you—to tell me."

"I don't know anything about a hidden file." Her

mother hesitated, then spoke in a gentle voice. "Honey, isn't figuring out the answers part of the fun and the satisfaction of writing mysteries? Didn't you feel a thrill of discovery when you figured out Tilly's murder was a hoax?"

Meg frowned at the darkness pressing against the office windows. "Yes," she admitted at length. "But, Mother, I can't even guess what your secret is. Whatever promise you and Aunt Tilly made so long ago, surely the deal's off now. I need your help."

Another silence developed.

Finally her mother sighed, then spoke. "Once upon a time two young girls lived in a stone house on the side of a Colorado mountain. The two sisters were very close because all they really had was each other. They didn't have a happy family." Meg heard her mother exhale slowly. "Their father was a brooding, obsessively jealous man who spied on his wife and family. His jealousy poisoned whatever happiness the family might have enjoyed."

Meg drew a sharp breath between her teeth. No wonder Aunt Tilly had said jealousy was poison, using almost the same words Meg's mother had used.

"Their mother wept constantly and spent most of her time in her bedroom, choosing to become a recluse rather than incite her husband or subject her friends to his insane jealousy. The two sisters seldom saw their parents. It was difficult and ugly when they did."

"Oh, God. I'm sorry. I didn't know," Meg said quietly, covering her eyes.

"One day the two sisters were playing where they weren't allowed. When the housekeeper appeared they hid, knowing they shouldn't have been in that room. After the housekeeper departed, the two sisters fought over who was to blame for their almost getting caught. While they were pushing and shoving, they made a discovery about the extent of their father's sick jealousy. They made a pact never to reveal the secret to anyone. Three years later both parents were dead.''

''What did they discover?'' Meg whispered.

''That is the end of the story, honey.''

Frustration wrinkled her brow. ''Mother—this isn't fair.''

Her mother's sad chuckle sounded as if she were standing in the room beside Meg. ''I know. If Tilly had actually been murdered, and if I believed our secret played a role in her murder, of course I would break my promise.''

''Mother—''

''Meg, the secret has nothing to do with Tilly's death or with Dennis's. The secret has to do with mental instability. Tilly and I agreed to keep our discovery secret because revealing it would have embarrassed the family. Do you see? It was a matter of family pride.''

Meg blinked at the bookcases lining the office walls. ''No, I don't understand.'' Determination entered her voice. ''But I promise, if the secret still exists, I'll find it.''

Her mother laughed. ''It still exists. And I hope you do discover it. Morgan's Manor belongs to you now. It's right that you should learn its secrets. Both Tilly and I have given you plenty of clues.''

''If you agree I should know, then—''

''I wouldn't dream of cheating you out of the pleasure of discovering the secrets of Morgan's Manor for yourself…without me having to break a promise that's older than you are.''

Meg sighed. She'd been right to sense that her mother had some of the answers. But it had never entered her mind that her mother would balk at revealing them.

''Mother—may I ask you something?'' She hesitated,

then plunged ahead. "Jealousy ruined the life of your parents. And it sounds like jealousy created a situation that eventually drove Howard to have an affair with Candida, which led to the breakup of Aunt Tilly's marriage." She tried to keep her voice light. "Is jealousy a family curse?"

"It doesn't have to be," her mother said after a minute. The line fairly quivered with a mother-daughter pause.

Meg resisted the invitation to explain. "Haven't you ever felt jealous?" she asked.

"Everyone feels jealous at one time or another," her mother answered. "Whenever I feel jealous about some woman paying too much attention to your father, I remember my parents' marriage and what jealousy did to their lives. I remind myself that I'm strong enough to handle the pain if something happened to my marriage. And finally I tell myself that if your father can find a woman who's better for him than I am—then she deserves him. But she better want him poor, because that's how she'll get him."

Meg laughed. "Have you told Dad any of this?" She couldn't imagine her parents discussing divorce. They were the most loving couple she knew.

"Never," her mother said promptly. "That's the speech I give myself, not your father. As far as your father is aware, I think it's terrific that Virginia Mason thinks he's as handsome as Don Ameche. And part of me really does think it's terrific. Virginia reminds me not to take your father for granted, to appreciate him and the life we've built together."

Long after Meg hung up the telephone, she continued to sit at Aunt Tilly's desk, thinking about her grandparents, her parents, Aunt Tilly and herself. And Steven.

WHEN THE TELEPHONE RANG the next morning, Meg was in Aunt Tilly's bedroom, systematically searching the room for an unknown secret, hot on the trail of a wild guess. She didn't know exactly what she was searching for, but she thought it might be a false drawer or a hidden safe large enough to hold the Halverson file.

She had assigned Aunt Tilly's office to Steven. She felt a little guilty about it, but after speaking to her mother last night Meg thought the best hiding place was probably in the bedroom.

Children weren't supposed to play in their parents' bedroom. And Aunt Tilly's bedroom had once belonged to Meg's grandparents. At any rate, that was her guess. But she wasn't optimistic about finding something the police had not found after going over the room practically with a magnifying glass. Or finding a secret hiding place that James had failed to discover after twenty years of cleaning this room.

Steven appeared in the doorway. "That's Candida on the telephone. She wants to speak to you, too."

"What about?"

"About a MAIMS meeting."

Meg sighed and picked up the telephone beside Aunt Tilly's bed. "Yes?" She listened a minute, then expelled a breath of irritation. "You insist on having a board meeting in the middle of a murder investigation?" She rolled her eyes at Steven and he grinned.

Candida's grating voice lifted in Meg's ear. "I've been in touch with the election committee and they're getting nervous that the election is looming on the horizon and we still don't have a slate of proposed offices. The bylaws can't be altered merely to suit our convenience. And the committee can't throw together an election at the last minute."

"Two of our board members are dead." Meg didn't

apologize for her tone. "I'm sorry if that 'inconveniences' anyone, but that's how matters stand."

Candida's reply was as sharp as Meg's. "There are alternatives to allowing the organization to fall apart. We can appoint Steven to take my seat until after the election and the board can appoint me to fill out the remainder of Tillis's term."

"At the moment, you and I are the only living members of this board to do all this appointing."

An annoyed sigh sounded in Meg's ear. "What's the problem here?" Candida asked. "Why are you being difficult?"

Aware that Steven was watching her from the doorway, Meg bit her tongue and stared at the carpet. James had cleaned the room, but she imagined she could still see the chalked outline. "Right now I don't care about MAIMS. I have other things on my mind."

"I regret that you have 'things' on your mind, but so does the election committee. When you accepted a seat on the board of directors, you accepted the obligations that came with it."

"I'm in no mood for a lecture, Candida." Anger pinched her expression. From the corner of her eye, she saw Steven's grin widen.

"Well, maybe you need a lecture. Look, Steven has agreed to accept an interim seat on the board and he's agreed to an immediate board meeting. You seem to be the only problem here."

"He has?" she asked, swinging around to stare at Steven. He shrugged.

"There's a meeting room off the lobby at the Poles. Where Steven and Suzanne are staying," Candida added. When Meg didn't react, she continued in a brisk tone, "I'll expect you to be there at two o'clock. We have the room for an hour.''

Feeling outflanked, Meg hung up the telephone and glared at Steven. ''Why did you agree to this?''

''Why not? We aren't making any progress here. I thought we could use a break. If you agree, we could go out for lunch, then stop by the Poles for the board meeting.''

Suddenly the idea of getting way from Morgan's Manor even for a short while sounded appealing. But Meg was uneasy about the idea of having lunch with Steven. There were a lot of things she hadn't yet sorted out. One of them was how to be ''just friends'' with a man who made her feel weak inside whenever she looked at him.

''I'll pass on lunch,'' she decided, pulling off her bandanna. ''I still have some things to do here. You go ahead and I'll meet you at the board meeting.''

He studied her expression. ''Having a bad day?''

''I've had better.'' Hands on hips, she gazed around Aunt Tilly's bedroom. ''Aren't you getting a little discouraged, too? We're running out of places to search.''

''The truth? I'm starting to seriously wonder about what you said yesterday. I'm starting to wonder if someone else found the file first.''

Suzanne's unspoken name hung between them. Then Steven left, and Meg returned to her room to do something with her hair and stare into her closet in hopes of finding something she hadn't already worn a dozen times since her arrival.

BEFORE MEG LEFT for the Poles, she gave James and Hilda the afternoon off and apologized that she hadn't thought to inquire earlier which days they had off each week.

''If I'd been thinking clearly I would have realized

sooner that you must be desperate for a few hours away from here," she said.

James smiled. "Not at all, miss. This is our home."

"Of course." She returned his smile. "Still, I suspect a free afternoon would be welcome, wouldn't it?"

An hour later she slid behind the wheel of her rental car and followed Aunt Tilly's vintage Cadillac down the twisting road to Breckenridge. James drove the pristine old car like the treasure it was and Hilda sat beside him wearing her Sunday hat. At the base of the road Hilda turned to wave at Meg through the rear windshield, then they turned left on the road leading to the highway.

As it wasn't two o'clock yet, Meg continued past the Poles and turned onto Main Street, driving slowly past the shops, boutiques and restaurants.

Years ago, Breckenridge had begun as a gold-mining town, but now it mined its gold from the tourist trade. Charm, stunning scenery and fabulous ski runs were the primary attractions. Glittering snowcapped peaks soared above Victorian restorations. Skaters flashed across Maggie Pond. Smiling, bright-cheeked shoppers waited for the light to change at the town's only stoplight. Meg half expected to see a Victorian lady emerge from one of the stained-glass shop fronts on the arm of a turn-of-the-century cowboy.

She could understand why Aunt Tilly had fallen in love with the Kingdom of Breckenridge, as the locals referred to the town. Everything from the ice sculptures lining the streets to the old-fashioned street lamps had a way of seducing visitors and leading them toward daydreams of owning a nearby cabin in the pines.

A person could build a satisfying life here, Meg thought. Even Morgan's Manor was beginning to grow on her. It no longer seemed the oppressive pile of stones she had initially thought, but was in actuality rather quaint and possessed a unique fascination. How could one resist a place where rabbits scampered across the veranda and deer offered a passing nod as they meandered through the backyard? Where mountaintops appeared in every window, and the air was crisp and clean and tasted like cold honey?

When she realized what she was thinking, Meg laughed out loud and shook her head as she turned onto the road to the Poles. She had never felt entirely comfortable living in Manhattan—who did?—but until now she hadn't thought about retreating to a mountainside, either.

She parked the rental car in the Poles lot, then paused beside the car door to look at the hotel and wonder which room was Steven's. And which was Suzanne's. She didn't see the car Suzanne had rented. Could she hope Suzanne had returned to New York? Surely Sheriff Conner didn't seriously consider Suzanne a suspect in Dennis's death. Suzanne had hardly known Dennis. That is, as far as anyone knew.

Sighing, Meg fluffed her hair around her face, then entered the Pole's lobby. Steven and Candida were waiting for her beside a massive moss-rock fireplace that soared toward a two-story pine ceiling.

"I just realized," Steven said when he saw her. "You aren't using the cane anymore."

"Some friend you are," she said lightly, making a joke of it. "I haven't used the cane for two days now and you haven't noticed."

"You're right." A flush of discomfort darkened his face. "I'm sorry."

Meg didn't know what to say. There was nothing worse than an attempted joke that fell flat. She bit her lip and looked around the lobby. "Where are Howard and Suzanne?'' She hoped either Steven or Candida would tell her that Suzanne was on a plane back to New York City.

"Suzanne is skiing Keystone today," Steven said. He didn't explain how he knew. "I haven't seen Howard since lunch."

"Never mind them, we're here to have a meeting." Candida led Meg and Steven into a room off the lobby and seated herself at the head of the table. She rapped a gavel on the tabletop and Meg made a face. Where on earth had Candida located a gavel on such short notice, and why did she think she needed one?

In less than five minutes, they agreed to a new slate proposing Candida Ripley as the new MAIMS president. Meg noticed her own name among those listed on the page Candida passed to her.

"I'm not interested in serving another term," Meg said.

"Of course you will." Dangling magenta earrings swung against Candida's cheek when she lifted her head to scowl at Meg. "I want people on my board who aren't afraid to speak up and state an opinion. And I want you where I can keep an eye on you."

"Believe me, I have no political ambitions. I'm not sure being on your board is a good idea, Candida. For a time I thought we might become friends, but I don't think so anymore."

"Friends?" Candida's eyebrows shot toward her hairline. "My dear child, I'm not looking for another friend. I neglect the friends I have. What I need is a worthy enemy to replace that hack, Tillis. You could grow into the job. If you win the Macabre Series, you'll be halfway there."

Aunt Tilly had been correct. Candida was unique.

"I don't think I have the energy to be your pet enemy," Meg said. "But I certainly wouldn't rubber stamp all your opinions."

"Weren't you listening? I don't want a parrot. Your silly arguments will keep the meetings interesting and challenging."

Meg rolled her eyes toward the ceiling. "After such a gracious invitation, how can I refuse?"

"Excellent. Then it's settled." The gavel banged on the table with a nerve-rattling noise. "We are adjourned."

Howard poked his head in the door. "All finished? That didn't take long." Stepping inside, he gave Meg a hug and inquired about her ankle, then told Candida he had made dinner reservations for six o'clock.

"What have you been doing?" Candida scooped her papers into her arms and peered at Howard's wet pant legs. "Were you out wading in the snow?"

He laughed. "I walked down to the Bell Tower Mall to buy the New York newspapers. Took a shortcut through an unshoveled area." He said to Meg and Steven, "I think most of the excitement has died down. There was only one back-page column about the case."

"Good. Maybe we can leave this Podunk town and go home," Candida said as they reentered the lobby. "I'm sick and tired of that good-old-boy sheriff. We've been over the details in this case so many times I'm reeling them off in my sleep."

"You've talked to the sheriff again?" Meg asked in surprise.

"Again?" Candida made a face. "Hardly a day goes by that Sheriff Conner doesn't turn up for 'one more question.' He's worse than Columbo!" She lifted an eyebrow. "Are you saying the sheriff isn't bugging you?"

"No, he isn't."

"That's interesting." Candida looked at Howard. "I don't think he's pestering Suzanne, either. "Good God. Do you think he suspects us?"

"I can't imagine he would." Howard ran a hand over his bald head. "I'm not sorry to have Dennis out of our lives." He winked at Candida. "But I am sorry he was murdered."

The statement reminded them why they were still in Breckenridge. Candida broke the silence by lifting her arm and casting a hurried glance at her watch.

"I have to be running along. The election committee is waiting to hear from me." She patted Meg's sleeve. "Thank you for inviting Howard and me to breakfast tomorrow. Unless something comes up, we'll be there."

Meg released an exasperated breath. All she had said was she thought they should get together sometime before everyone left Breckenridge. Candida had translated a polite comment into an invitation for breakfast.

"I hope you'll come, too," she said to Steven. She didn't mention Suzanne Halverson.

Steven was facing the elevator. "Candida and Howard seem to be getting along better. That's a pleasant surprise."

"Let's hope it lasts." Meg remembered Candida saying she needed drama and lightning in a relationship. As far as Meg could tell, Howard was as nice now as he had ever been. No lightning flashed around his bald head.

"Meg, let's have dinner out tonight."

She looked up at him. "Is that a good idea?" she asked in a quiet voice.

"I don't know." The intensity in his gaze made her feel shaky inside. "I do know there's a strain between us. You and I are going to be business associates for a long time and I'd like that relationship to be comfortable for both of us. Maybe we need to practice being friends. Does that make any sense?"

Practice being friends. The phrase broke her heart. "We

are friends, Steven. We were friends before we were anything else."

"I've discovered an Italian restaurant I think you'll love. They have the best veal marsala you ever tasted."

What would they talk about? Against everything sensible Meg heard herself agreeing. And immediately regretting it.

"Good. I'll pick you up about seven."

They gave each other polite smiles, then Meg left the lobby and walked back to her car. After she slid into the driver's seat, she sat for a moment, drumming her gloved fingers against the steering wheel and cursing herself for agreeing to dinner with Steven. Then she drove to Main Street, parked and entered Myrna's Boutique.

When she emerged, her arms were overflowing with parcels. She was the new owner of a long leather skirt, a silver-and-turquoise belt and a silk turquoise blouse and coordinating suede jacket. She had even found a pair of stylish calf-high boots to complete the outfit.

The ensemble didn't carry a designer label, but it was more stylish than what she usually purchased. And it suited her. She drove back to Morgan's Manor and used her key to open the door. "James?" But James and Hilda hadn't returned yet. She really hadn't expected them. In fact, she had suggested they have dinner out and take in a movie if something was playing that they wanted to see.

Humming under her breath, Meg stopped in the kitchen to plug in the coffeepot, then she carried her packages upstairs to her room and arranged her purchases across the bed. When she stepped back to inspect her new outfit, she noticed something out of the corner of her eye.

One of the drawers on the bureau dresser was not pushed all the way shut. Meg disliked open drawers and always closed them firmly. Frowning, she studied the drawer a minute, remembering that she had pushed it shut this morning. Slowly she scanned the room.

There was nothing obviously out of place, nothing she could put her finger on. But something didn't feel right. She distinctly remembered, at least she thought she did, that she had left the new P. D. James novel on the bedside table facing her pillow. Now the cover jacket faced into the room. One corner of the dust ruffle was disturbed as if someone had tipped it up by running a hand between the mattresses. The closet door stood slightly ajar.

Heart hammering, Meg bit her lip, then tiptoed forward and yanked the closet door open. To her vast relief, there was no one hiding inside.

But someone had been in her room, she thought, feeling goose bumps rise on the back of her neck. Someone had been in the house this afternoon and had searched her bedroom. There was no doubt in her mind.

Chapter Eleven

Steven and Meg were shown to a linen-draped table in front of a leaded-glass window overlooking Maggie Pond. Bright lights rimmed the frozen pond illuminating pink-cheeked skaters flashing and whirling across the ice.

Raising his drink, Steven offered a toast above the candlelight flickering within a red hurricane lamp. "To solutions and new beginnings," he said, smiling at her.

New beginnings. Friends instead of lovers? Meg touched her glass to his. "You were right. I love this place." The savory fragrance of garlic and Italian sauces perfumed the air. Opera music drifted from strategically placed speakers. A romantic halo of candlelight glowed over the silver and the rose-colored linen.

"Did I mention that you look sensational tonight?" Steven cast a slow, appreciative gaze over her new turquoise blouse and suede jacket. Meg felt a blush of pleasure appear on her cheeks.

Steven looked wonderful himself. Tonight he wore a herringbone jacket and a navy-and-maroon tie against a dazzlingly white shirt. Meg recognized the familiar scent of an expensive English after-shave.

"Well, what shall we talk about, friend?" Her voice sounded artificial and overly bright. But suddenly she couldn't think of a thing to say. She looked at him and her mouth went dry.

"Your choice," he said, smiling. And she wondered if he couldn't think of anything to say, either.

The one thing Meg did not want to talk about was their changed status. She wanted no references to their past relationship, that was too painful. And she didn't want to think about their altered future. That was also painful.

"What do we do if we can't find the Halverson file?" she asked. "Maybe we should discuss the possibility that Suzanne already has it. That she found the file first."

"I've thought about that, and I really don't think Suzanne found the Halverson file." Steven examined her expression. "I do think it was probably Suzanne who trashed the supply room, but I don't think she found what she was looking for. If she had, I think she'd be asking Sheriff Conner's permission to return to New York."

"How do you know she hasn't?" Meg asked.

Steven met her eyes. "I had dinner with Suzanne last night. She talked about how bored she is. She complained that none of us can leave yet. But she didn't express any urgency."

Meg waited for the familiar stomach roll, the grip of jealous pain that accompanied any mention of Steven and another woman. She felt sorrow and regret, but not the deep, racking emotion she expected. Not trusting the delay, she let herself picture Steven and Suzanne sitting together over a candlelit table like this one, speaking intimately, easily. And still the hideous debilitating jealousy did not bite into her system.

She didn't understand. And then she did. Somehow, without realizing when it had happened, she had accepted that her relationship with Steven was truly ended. Her mind was letting him go, accepting there would be other women in his life. Meg no longer had a claim on him.

"Are you all right?" Steven asked, still watching her.

"Yes," she said, waving a hand and blinking at the moisture in her eyes. She trusted Steven with Suzanne because he was lost to her. Why couldn't she have trusted him when it would have made a difference? "I just realized—we will be able to be friends." There was sadness in that statement, and an aching sense of loss. And the realization that she loved Steven enough to want him to be happy, even if he couldn't find that happiness with her.

"I hope so. Meg, are you sure you're all right? You have a peculiar expression on your face."

There was no way to explain that she was letting go, that right now she was loving him as much as she ever had and at the same time she was setting him free. And feeling a new freedom herself. Maybe the loose ties Aunt Tilly had talked about were the ties of friendship. That was a concept she would ponder later.

Leaning forward into the candlelight, she looked into Steven's puzzled frown and managed a sad smile. "I'm sorry, I was thinking about that old adage, we're too soon foolish and too late smart." If she thought about too late, she would weep. "What were we talking about?"

"The Halverson file."

"Have you considered the possibility that Aunt Tilly did indeed destroy the file as she claimed she did?"

"Meg, what were you thinking about a minute ago?"

She tried to keep her voice light. "I was thinking how often people focus on their own selfish fears instead of focusing on happiness, their own and that of the people they love."

"Do you want to explain that a little more?"

"Steven, please don't ask me to go into this. I'd embarrass us both by breaking into tears. It's simply too late.''

"I wish to hell I knew what you were talking about." His frown deepened.

"I know. But it's better this way." She didn't trust her feelings enough to share them. What if these insights were transitory? What if tomorrow she couldn't love him enough to let him go? "Tell me what will happen if we don't find the Halverson file."

For a long moment Steven didn't speak. He studied her with those wonderful brown eyes. Finally he leaned forward, speaking in a low voice.

"All right, let's assume the worst. Let's assume Suzanne was indeed involved in Whitney's murder. Let's further assume she was feeling safe, believing she had gotten away with it. Then Tillis reopened the investigation."

"Go on," Meg said, gazing into his eyes above the hurricane lamp.

"We don't know that Tillis's new evidence implicated Suzanne. That was the suggestion, but Tillis did not confirm it. We could be wrong on that point. It's entirely possible I let my imagination run away with me. It's possible Tillis's new evidence focused on someone else or something else, that it had nothing to do with Suzanne."

The wine steward appeared beside the table to inquire which wine they preferred with dinner. Steven ordered a Chianti, then returned to the subject.

"I'm beginning to think I may have overdramatized Suzanne as a danger."

"Have you decided Suzanne had nothing to do with Whitney's murder?" Meg asked.

Steven didn't answer immediately. "There's no evidence tying her to Whitney's death. Until there is…" He shrugged. "As to Suzanne's interest in Tillis's file, frankly that strikes me as understandable. Of course she would be interested in how Tillis portrayed her. She would be curious about any new evidence. And it seems reasonable that she wouldn't want the case dredged up again."

Briefly Meg considered revealing her uneasy certainty that someone had been in Morgan's Manor while she was at the MAIMS board meeting and shopping. But there was no evidence to support her suspicion. She thought Steven might place the incident in the same category as the icicle incident, merely a case of an overactive imagination.

"On the other hand," she said slowly, "if Suzanne was involved in Whitney's murder and Aunt Tilly found something that proved it…it would be a miscarriage of justice if we didn't locate that file."

"Where else can we search?"

Meg turned her gaze to the window, absently watching the ice skaters glide in and out of the lighted areas of the pond.

"I don't know," she said finally. "We've almost reached the end of the line."

The last sentence stayed between them, carrying a personal charge more potent than any speculation about the Halverson file.

Meg was glad when the veal marsala arrived. The fragrance was a delight and so was the first heavenly bite. "This is wonderful," she enthused.

"Remember the marsala at Il Cantorini?" Steven looked as if he immediately regretted the reference.

"I don't think it was better than this. Honestly."

The next time Steven went to Il Cantorini he would take someone else. No, the jealousy was not dead. Meg felt it stir in her breast. But the green-eyed monster had lost its talons. She felt sorrow, but not the claws of jealousy. Jealousy was the fear of losing something one loved. Meg had already lost.

When she looked up, she caught Steven in an unguarded moment and his expression caused her to catch a quick involuntary breath. Candlelight shadowed his eyes, making them appear almost black and darkly intent. He was looking at Meg, but his gaze had turned inward. He, too, was remembering Il Cantorini. The wonderful food, the teasing touches beneath the table, laughing as afterward they ran hand in hand to Meg's apartment breathless with the anticipation of each other.

"Steven?"

"Sorry," he said, giving his head a shake. "I was daydreaming." After pushing at his veal, he gave it up and put his fork down. "Have you given any thought as to what you'll do with Morgan's Manor? Will you put it on the market?"

The food was wonderful, but Meg, too, was having difficulty swallowing. "I haven't decided yet. But I've made up my mind that I won't do anything until I've discovered all the secrets of Morgan's Manor."

"There are more?"

Speaking slowly, expressionlessly, she told him the story her mother had told her. "It seems jealousy runs in the family," she finished, trying to make a joke of it. To her relief, Steven didn't comment on that part of the tale.

Intrigued, Steven asked several questions, most of which Meg couldn't answer. "What do you think your mother and Tillis's secret is?"

"I'm not even sure if the secret is theirs or grandfather's. I don't know what I'm looking for." She smiled and spread her hands. "I hope I'll recognize it if and when I find it."

"If it's a hiding place, maybe that's where Tillis hid the Halverson file." Fresh enthusiasm lit his expression.

"That's what I was hoping. But I'm beginning to think this secret is something I'll stumble across by accident. Apparently James hasn't discovered it in twenty years."

Steven smiled, too. "So you may have to keep Morgan's Manor for a long time."

"This might sound odd, but Tillis hinted that the place might grow on me, and it's beginning to." She met his eyes. "I've been thinking about keeping it and living here."

For a moment he didn't say anything. "You're considering moving to Colorado?"

She turned to look at the skaters spinning on the ice. "There's really no reason to stay in Manhattan," she said quietly. "I've been thinking it might be—easier—to live here." She drew a breath. "Like Aunt Tilly said, what better place for a mystery writer than Morgan's Manor?" She continued to gaze out the windows rather than look at Steven. "Of course, I'd want to do some extensive remodeling..."

"It's odd to think of you living so far away," Steven said after another silence.

Meg ran a glance over the spectators standing in the snow beside the pond rink. As she watched, one of the men stepped back onto the sidewalk and stamped the snow from his wet cuffs. Suddenly she saw Howard in her mind, standing in front of her, his cuffs wet from melting snow.

She sat up straight and blinked.

"Oh my God! That's it."

"What?" Tilting his head, Steven looked out the window, trying to see what Meg was seeing. "Meg? What's wrong?"

"Wait a minute." Staring into space, she ran the memory through her mind, testing it. "Wet pant cuffs. Yes, that's what must have happened. Wait. We were playing bridge, then we heard a noise. You were going to investigate, then…"

"Meg? Talk to me. What are you thinking?"

"Oh, Steven." She raised her head and stared at him, speaking in a voice that was barely audible. Tears filled her eyes and glistened in the candlelight. "I know who flattened the tires and hid the skis. And I know who murdered Dennis."

"You do?" Steven studied her pale expression, then he put his napkin on the table and started to rise. "Stay put. I'll telephone the sheriff."

Meg placed her hand on his sleeve. "No, wait." She pressed her fingertips to her eyes. "There are a couple of things I'm not sure if I'm remembering correctly." She spoke in a soft voice filled with regret. "One more night won't hurt anything. Our murderer isn't going anywhere."

Concern filled Steven's eyes and he took her hand. "Does knowing the killer's identity place you in any danger?"

The warmth of his fingers enclosing her hand shot through her body. For a moment she closed her eyes. "No."

"Do you want to talk about this? With a friend?"

The story didn't take long to relate. Before their after-dinner coffee arrived, Meg had explained her theory to Steven.

He still held her hand, absently rubbing his thumb across her palm. "I think you're right," he said finally.

Without making a point of it, Meg withdrew her hand. She knew he didn't realize how erotic his stroking was. To focus her thoughts, she said, "We still have to check with James and Suzanne before we'll know if we're right."

"Everyone's coming for breakfast, correct?"

"They will be if you'll invite Suzanne and I invite Sheriff Conner."

Steven studied her expression. "You want me to invite Suzanne?"

"Yes, please."

He smiled at her. "This sounds like the old gather all the suspects, then announce the killer's name."

Sadness tightened Meg's throat. "I guess it is, isn't it?" She tried to smile. "Writers always go for the dramatic ending."

After Steven drove her back to Morgan's Manor, he walked her up the veranda steps and faced her under the old-fashioned porch light.

"I'd invite you in for a nightcap," Meg said, starting to shiver in the cold, "but I'm afraid I wouldn't be good company. My mind is racing a mile a minute."

"I understand. I'm as upset as you are."

This was the moment for a good-night kiss. Without it, the moment was awkward and uncomfortable.

Steven placed his large hands on her shoulders and looked down into her eyes. "Is a friend permitted to kiss another friend on the cheek?"

She managed a pale smile. "I think cheek kissing is in the rules, friend."

His warm lips brushed her cold cheek and a shiver rippled through her body.

"You're cold. You'd better go inside." Leaning, he opened the door for her. Then, although he didn't look much like smiling, the corners of his lips turned up. "You might think about this arctic cold before you decide to abandon balmy Manhattan."

"Sometimes," Meg said, trying to keep her voice level,

"distant friends are the best friends." Briefly she touched her fingertips to his cheek, then she quickly fled inside.

As PLANNED, Sheriff Conner was first to arrive. He appeared at Meg's door at eight-thirty. After hanging his hat and coat on the foyer rack, he entered the dining room and glanced at the breakfast buffet laid out on the sideboard. "Do you think anyone's going to be hungry once they discover why they were invited?"

"I don't know." Meg smoothed her hands over her red sweater and dark ski pants. "I might be wasting your time," she admitted. "I could be wrong."

"We have a few minutes before anyone arrives. Why don't we go through this, and you tell me what you've discovered." When Meg finished explaining, Sheriff Conner gazed at her with a thoughtful expression. "That's where I was headed, too. Only I couldn't prove it. I figured that's the only way Parnham could have been murdered."

"Steven and I didn't remember the wet cuffs until last night. I mean, I guess I did remember, I just wasn't seeing the forest for the trees."

"How and when he got back inside was a problem. I wish you'd told me this before."

"I didn't realize what I was seeing before." They turned toward the door as everyone arrived at once.

Candida swept into the dining room, then stopped so abruptly that her jersey skirt flared around her legs. Her eyes widened, then narrowed in irritation. "What are *you* doing here?" she said to Sheriff Conner. "Don't tell me you want to go over Dennis's murder *again!*"

Sheriff Conner did not smile. "One more time, ma'am."

"We can't even have our breakfast in peace." Candida sank into a chair and her bosom lifted in an exaggerated sigh. "You might as well buy that condo you were looking at, Howard. We're never going to get out of this place. Six months from now, Sheriff Conner will still be telling us he'd prefer we didn't leave quite yet. He'll still be popping up wherever we go, asking the same repetitious questions.''

"Good morning, friend," Steven murmured, stepping up beside Meg at the coffee service. "Are you all right? You look tired."

"I didn't sleep very well." She glanced at Suzanne and nodded a greeting. "I thought I'd go skiing when this is over. I have a feeling I'll need something that requires concentrating on nothing more than staying upright. I need a break from mysteries." A touch of pink lit her cheeks. "I was wondering if you'd like to join me…"

"I'd love to."

Howard appeared at the sideboard. He dropped his arm around Meg's shoulder and gave her a hug before he placed a muffin on a plate. "You're prettier every time I see you. This climate agrees with you."

Before Meg could reply, Sheriff Conner carried his coffee to the end of the table and rapped a spoon against a glass to get everyone's attention.

"As some of you may have guessed, this isn't entirely a social gathering. Miss Sandler and Mr. Caldwell believe they know who murdered Dennis Parnham. As it happens, I agree with them." A moment of surprised silence followed, then James started for the door. "No, James, we'd like you to stay."

Candida narrowed a cool glance on Meg, watching the color rise in Meg's cheeks. "I find it somewhat incredible that you believe you've solved this when no one else could. But if you're determined to make a fool of yourself, let's get on with it. Who are you accusing of having killed that slug, Dennis?"

"There are a few points I need to confirm." Meg remained standing while the others found seats at the table. "Suzanne, the first question is for you."

Meg looked at Suzanne directly, anticipating a twinge of jealousy. But nothing happened. Suzanne was as beautiful as always, as coolly superior, but her beauty and patrician attitude did not diminish Meg as before. Meg had her strong points, too. Her strengths were different from Suzanne's, but no less worthy.

"Ask away," Suzanne said indifferently.

"When you saw Dennis pass through the foyer that night, then out the front door, did you get a good look at him?"

Suzanne frowned. "I'm not sure I understand what you're asking."

"Would you describe exactly what you saw?"

Suzanne shrugged. "I saw Dennis pass the living room archway. By the time I looked up from my cards, he was reaching for the doorknob. He was dressed to go outside and he was smoking. That's about all I can tell you."

"He was wearing a ski cap and parka?" Meg asked. When Suzanne nodded, she continued. "Where did Dennis get the ski cap and parka? The coatrack is beside the door. Yet you say he was dressed for outdoors when he passed the living room archway. He didn't stop to put on his cap or parka. You're certain that's what he was wearing?"

"Yes. He had the cap pulled down over his ears, the collar of the parka was turned up. It was a blizzard out there. It didn't seem strange at the time."

"Would it be accurate to say that all you really saw was one quick glimpse of Dennis from the side and behind?"

"I suppose so." Suzanne frowned. "But I know it was Dennis. He was smoking. The rest of you also saw the smoke in the foyer."

She drew a breath and turned to James. "When you went outside to fetch the ladder to climb up to Aunt Tilly's bedroom, Howard accompanied you, didn't he?"

James lifted both eyebrows. "I was upset. I'm not sure—yes, I remember now. I believe you're right. I think Mr. Clancy followed behind me."

Meg didn't look at Howard. "But Howard didn't leave the garage when you did, did he?"

James darted an uneasy frown toward Howard who slowly peeled back the paper cup from his muffin and reached for the butter.

"I don't remember, miss. I pulled the ladder down from the hooks and rushed outside. I forgot about Mr. Clancy. I don't recall seeing him again until he came into Madam's room with everyone else."

Now Meg made herself look at Howard and her eyes were sad and filled with regret. "I think you stayed behind in the garage long enough to flatten the tires, Howard, then you noticed the skis and hid them in a snowdrift." When Howard raised his head, Meg said in a low voice, "I'm sorry, Howard. I'm so sorry. But I believe you killed Dennis Parnham. You're the only person who could have done it."

"*What?*" Candida half rose out of her chair. "Are you crazy? Howard didn't murder Dennis! Howard wouldn't hurt a fly!"

"I'm sorry, Candida," Steven said with genuine regret. "But Meg's right."

Meg held Howard's gaze. In the morning sunlight, he looked ruddy faced and as innocent as a baby. He looked like the nice man that he was. Anyone meeting Howard Clancy today would have seen a good-natured, balding middle-aged man dressed in a green sweater and dark slacks, who might have been on a second honeymoon with a wife whom he adored.

"Oh, Howard," Meg whispered.

"It's all right," he answered softly, then he looked away and reached for the raspberry jam to spread over his muffin.

"What?" Candida said again, swiveling toward her husband. "Howard! Aren't you going to deny this outrageous accusation? We'll sue, we'll—" When he said nothing, she fell backward in her chair and stared. A gasp strangled her voice. "Oh my God. No, it can't be! I don't believe this!"

Meg couldn't bear to watch. She turned to Suzanne. "You didn't see Dennis. You assumed it was Dennis because of the cigarette. But the person you actually saw leaving the house was Howard. Dennis was already dead." The room was absolutely silent. Meg's voice sounded overloud in her ears. She shook her head, unable to continue and gave Steven an imploring glance. He took up the explanation.

"Howard suggested bridge," Steven said. "When Dennis declined, Howard declined also. Both men went upstairs. I'm guessing Howard had been waiting for an opportunity. He had already disabled the cars and hidden the skis to give himself time to find that opportunity. He must have taken Dennis's cap and parka to his room earlier in case he found a use for them."

Howard didn't speak. He applied himself to buttering another muffin.

"Howard probably went directly to Dennis's room. Dennis's contempt was so great, he didn't feel himself to be in any danger. Very likely he opened the door, then returned to his chair. Howard moved behind him..."

There was no reason to describe the actual murder. They could all imagine it.

"Then Howard took a cigarette from Dennis's pack," Steven continued, "lit it, pulled Dennis's cap over his head, walked down the steps and out the front door. Because of the cigarette smoke, we all believed we had seen Dennis."

Suzanne stared at Howard. "How did Howard get back inside?"

Meg answered. "I think he walked around the house and climbed in Aunt Tilly's office window." She told them about the tracks in the snow that widened beneath the office windows. "He could have opened the window latch earlier in the evening."

"The noise we heard at the bridge table was Howard climbing in the office window," Steven added.

"When Howard appeared in the living room a minute or two later, we assumed he had come from upstairs. Except…his pant cuffs were wet. If Howard had really been upstairs as he said he was, his cuffs would have been dry."

"Oh my God," Candida said in a choked voice. Her rings flashed as her hands flew to her mouth. "I remember, too. But I didn't make the connection…oh, Howard!"

Meg sat in her chair, unable to say anything more. Deep sorrow constricted her chest. She hadn't wanted the murderer to be Howard. In truth, she hadn't wanted it to be any of them.

Sheriff Conner tied up the loose ends, watching Howard. "The ski cap and parka were a problem. Clancy had to get the cap and parka back on the coatrack to establish that Parnham had returned inside. Most likely Clancy left the cap and parka in Miss Morgan's office until he could retrieve them. He did this near midnight by telling Mrs. Clancy he was going downstairs to get another drink. He asked her to accompany him as far as the landing so she could swear he did not enter Parnham's room at that time.''

"He also instructed Candida to stand directly under the sconce," Steven added.

The sheriff nodded. "From that position Mrs. Clancy could not observe the bottom of the staircase. She couldn't see Clancy dash toward Miss Morgan's office, then hang the cap and parka on the coatrack."

"Oh, Howard, tell me this isn't true." Candida's voice was thick with shock. Her hands trembled.

Howard leaned back in his chair and closed his eyes. When he opened them again, he looked at his wife. "I hated the way Dennis talked to you," he said softly. "He didn't treat you with the respect you deserve. He wouldn't release you from his agency agreement, and he wasn't helping your career. Dennis Parnham was a nasty-mouthed, unpleasant man. I never understood what you saw in him, sweetheart." Howard lifted apologetic eyes to the others who watched with sympathy. "I'm sorry for... for everything. I'm honestly not sure how this happened. I guess I went a little crazy. I was jealous and—and Dennis just pushed too far."

Suzanne broke the silence. "Well, if you ask me, you deserve a prize. Parnham was a crashing bore."

Sheriff Conner reached for his handcuffs. "Mr. Clancy, I'll have to ask you to come with me."

"Cuffs?" Meg whispered. "Sheriff, is that really necessary?"

"Standard procedure, Miss Sandler."

Candida stumbled to her feet. "You killed Dennis for me." She stared at Howard, her eyes huge and filled with awe. "Howard, do you realize—this is a crime of pas-

sion!'' Her mouth fell open. "Imagine. I just can't believe it!''

Meg followed them to the door and watched as Sheriff Conner led Howard and Candida to his car. In a moment the car turned down the driveway. Suzanne departed, too, following the sheriff down the twisting road.

When Steven placed his arm around her shoulders, Meg turned blindly and pressed her face against the folds of his warm wool sweater. "Oh, I wish it wasn't Howard," she murmured, feeling the scald of tears against her eyes.

"I know." Steven stroked her hair, watching the cars disappear down the driveway. "Come on. You and I are going to get out of here. We'll ski until you're too exhausted to think about all this.''

MEG CONFINED HERSELF to the intermediate slopes as she promised Steven she would to protect her ankle.

At the top of a gently sloped incline, she pushed back her sunglasses and paused to catch her breath. The day was perfect for skiing. A single cottony cloud enhanced the beauty of a frosty blue sky. The snow was deep and sparkling white. Gaily colored parkas flew past Meg, sunlight flashing from poles and bindings. Laughter and cheerful shouts surrounded her. But every time she thought about Howard Clancy, tears glistened in her eyes.

When she reached the bottom of the run, cutting to a halt beside Steven, she looked up at him with an expression that blended confusion and bewilderment.

"I thought we were supposed to hate the bad guys, the murderers. I didn't know it could feel this awful.''

Steven removed his glove and cupped her cold face in his hand. "I like Howard, too," he said gently. "But it's over now, Meg. Don't dwell on it.''

"No," she disagreed softly, looking at the snow capping the far peaks. "It's not over. Not yet."

There was one more mystery to solve. The ordeal that had begun with Aunt Tilly's dinner party would not truly be over until Meg found the Halverson file and uncovered the final secret of Morgan's Manor.

Chapter Twelve

Meg and Steven had dinner together at Morgan's Manor and carried their brandy into the living room afterward. They sat on the sofa before the fireplace, pleasantly tired from the day on the slopes. Outside, snowflakes floated out of the night sky.

"Now that we're discharged as suspects and free to leave Breckenridge, will you be returning to Manhattan soon?" Meg asked.

She felt comfortably relaxed for the first time since the ordeal had begun. And she had begun to think about the future. Despite the terrible events that had occurred since her arrival at Morgan's Manor, a few good things had also resulted.

Now she was free to engage an agent with whom she would feel more compatible than she ever had with Dennis, and this time she was seasoned enough to make an informed choice. She had inherited Aunt Tilly's sizable estate and presumably would not have to worry about money for a very long time.

And she and Steven had put the bitterness of a failed relationship behind them. She no longer had to dread a chance encounter with him or wonder what they would say to each other in that event. But she had replaced an old pain with a new pain. She still loved him. There was no bitterness now, but there was loss.

Leaning forward, Steven refilled their brandy snifters. "I do need to be getting back. Dick Hines is doing an excellent job of taking care of business—so good, in fact, that I need to return before anyone notices they don't really need me. How about you? Are you still thinking about staying here?"

Meg turned her gaze to the flames dancing in the grate. "I've never really thought of my apartment in Manhattan as home. Adell, Iowa, was always home. Lately I've begun to realize Adell is my parents' home. I haven't made a home of my own yet. Maybe it's time."

Steven stretched his arm along the back of the sofa, his fingertips almost touching her hair. He, too, watched the fire flickering in the fireplace. Occasionally he glanced toward the fat snowflakes melting down the windowpanes.

"I'm beginning to suspect you're falling under the spell of Morgan's Manor." He made a face and smiled. "What's worse—I think I understand it. On a night like tonight the real world seems very far away. It's hard to remember the frantic pace New Yorkers set." Meg felt his gaze shift to her profile. "Do you really think you could live here, Meg? Aren't there things about New York that you would miss?"

She wanted to tell him, yes. She would miss him like she'd miss her own right arm if it was removed from her body. But the pain of saying goodbye to Steven couldn't be any deeper, any worse than the pain of losing him the first time. And she had survived. She was stronger than she had believed. Plus, life would be easier without worrying that she might run into Steven unexpectedly and be reminded of all she had lost.

"Writers can write anywhere," she said slowly. "I'm

not tied to a particular place, like a cramped one bedroom in Manhattan. Depending on the size of my inheritance, I may decide to keep the place in New York, though. For those times when I crave the big city, the restaurants, the theaters and all the rest. There are several options."

"I understand the appeal of two residences. In the past day or so I've been pricing condominiums in this area." When Meg shifted on the sofa to look at him, he smiled. "The skiing is terrific, I like the town." His eyes held hers. "And I have a friend here."

"It isn't necessary to buy a condo. You could stay with your—friend—when you came to ski."

In the firelight his eyes looked like warm chocolate. "That's what I was hoping you would say." His voice dropped. "But suppose I wanted to stay longer than two weeks…"

Meg's gaze moved to his lips. "Well, there are some business opportunities in Breckenridge that might interest you."

One of his fingers curled in her hair. "Is that right?" Somehow they had moved closer together. What Meg had mistaken as heat from the fireplace was Steven's thigh pressed against hers.

"Yes," she said, trying to remember what they were talking about. All she could think about was Steven's nearness and the feeling that something important was happening. "I haven't seen any Greek restaurants here."

His dark eyes seemed to caress her face, traveled to the pulse beat in the hollow of her throat, then back up to the tremble at the corner of her lips. He smiled. "Are you saying there is no place in this town where a starving tourist of discriminating taste can enjoy a decent lamb stew?"

His breath flowed over her lips, and Meg felt the resistance drain from her body. She tilted her head to look into his eyes and her mouth moved within an inch of his. "No Greek restaurants," she whispered.

"Beautiful Meg."

Then he kissed her, a slow deliberate kiss that explored her mouth with tender care, building, lingering, until they were both breathless when they eased apart to stare into each other's eyes.

"I don't think you and I can be friends," Steven murmured, his fingertips on her cheek.

His kiss had left her shaken, and she wet her trembling mouth with the tip of her tongue, then heard Steven's groan. Leaning forward, Meg rested her forehead on his chin. Tears sparkled in her eyes.

"What are you saying?" She didn't understand. "You kiss me, then announce we can't be friends?"

His arms enfolded her and he held her close. "I can't be near you without wanting to touch you and hold you. That's more than friendship." His fingers tangled in her hair and he gently pulled her head back until he could look into her eyes. "I love you, Meg. You drive me crazy, I get furious with you. You're stubborn and unreasonable sometimes, and I don't always understand you."

"I think I would like that speech better if you had stopped right after 'I love you.'"

Meg's heart pounded crazily, but she was afraid to let herself hope. Steven had said the words she longed to hear, but he didn't look happy. Confusion flickered in her eyes. Whenever she believed she understood their relationship, it changed. She had arrived at Morgan's Manor believing Steven had betrayed her with Suzanne. Then she learned the truth and realized he had not. But they had not returned to the relationship they'd had before. They had decided they would be only friends and business associates. Now, if she understood correctly, Steven was saying they couldn't be friends because he loved her.

"Do you mean previous lovers can't be friends?" she asked, staring into his eyes. With his face an inch from hers, she could see the green flecks in his warm brown eyes.

"To be honest, I don't know what I mean." Confusion troubled his gaze, too, and frustration. He framed her face between his hands and frowned. "I feel like we're trapped in some kind of emotional limbo. I love you, and I hope you still love me."

"Oh, Steven," Meg whispered. "You know I do."

"The question is what do we do about it? We can't go back and we can't go forward."

Meg drew a deep breath. "I know you've heard this before, but I believe we can be together without me driving both of us crazy with my insecurities." Was that true? Could she trust that the green-eyed monster wouldn't rage back to life, talons extended? "I've witnessed firsthand the destruction jealousy can cause. I know what I've done to us, Steven. I know that jealousy drove Howard to kill Dennis." She touched his lips with her fingers. "I can't blame you if you don't believe this time is any different from the other times I've promised to control the ugly feelings. But it is different. I hope you'll give me a chance to prove that to you."

He stared into her eyes. "I want to believe you. But you weren't the only person who was hurt when you and I couldn't work it out before. I don't want to go through that again."

"Oh, Steven, neither do I."

James cleared his throat behind them and smiled when they hastily broke apart. "You asked me to remind you when it was time for the news, miss."

Before he withdrew, James looked back over his shoulder and smiled again. Meg suspected it had been a long time since lovers exchanged kisses in front of the fireplace at Morgan's Manor. She had an idea James and Hilda were pleased by the thought.

Steven switched on the television and they settled back to watch the ten o'clock news. Actually Meg welcomed the interruption. It gave them both a few minutes to think about what had been said.

Howard's arrest made all the Denver channels. They watched as Howard and Candida stepped out of Sheriff Conner's car and were escorted up the steps into a brick building.

A moment afterward an interview filmed later in the day rolled across the screen. Candida wore what Meg referred to as an "author suit," except Candida's author suit was a violent lemon shade trimmed in black mink with a cape and mink hat to match. Diamonds flashed at her ears and wrist, and only her thumbs were bare of jewels.

"My husband is an extremely passionate man," Candida gushed into the camera in response to the reporters' questions.

"Howard?" Meg repeated. "Passionate?" She and Steven smiled at each other, then turned back to the television.

Candida listed Howard's virtues in such a way that no one who followed the eventual trial could look at Howard's benevolent expression and bald head without wondering and recalling the old platitude about still waters running deep.

"Listen to her," Meg marveled. "Candida believes every word she's saying about Howard being a passionate and possessive lover. Suddenly she's seeing Howard in a wholly different light, and she's enchanted!"

Shaking his head, Steven smiled. "Human nature is filled with surprises."

Candida flirted with the cameras. She batted her false eyelashes and gave the viewers a misty-eyed promise that she would stand by her man. Then she briskly reminded everyone that her next book would appear on the shelves in two months, and she hinted she was already discussing a blockbuster exposé of the hoax and Dennis's murder with her publisher. She gazed squarely into the camera and lifted an auburn eyebrow that seemed to say, *Steven, are you listening?*

There was a message for Meg, too. Before Candida concluded the interview, she announced she had withdrawn from the Macabre Series competition. She gave Meg an arch look from the television screen. "I have more pressing and more important matters to attend to than writing a series. Miss Sandler is welcome to it." Candida left the distinct impression that the Macabre Series, which had been so important to her a few days ago, was actually a trivial project of little consequence.

After Steven turned off the set, he returned to the sofa and gave Meg a thoughtful look. "She's right, you know. The hoax and the murder will make a hell of a book."

"Candida's the perfect choice to write it. I imagine you'll be hearing from her the instant she obtains a new agent." Meg rolled her eyes and smiled. "Meanwhile, I'll be occupied wasting my time writing the insignificant Macabre Series."

Steven returned her smile. "You won't think the series is so insignificant after you see the size of the advance." He paused. "You know we haven't really talked about what will happen to the Halverson book. It's my impression that Tillis expected you would finish the project. Have you thought about it?"

"Some," Meg admitted. "But right now there is no project to complete. No manuscript, no notes, no nothing. I'd say discussing the book is a moot point until and if we find the file. And frankly, that possibility is looking dimmer every day. We're running out of places to search."

Standing, Meg followed him to the door, watching as he pulled on his parka and red ski cap.

"Thank you for dinner and a pleasant evening." Lifting his hand, he stroked his thumb across her lips.

Tilting her head, Meg gazed up at him. "Steven, what are we going to do about us?" she asked in a soft voice.

His arms closed around her waist and he pulled her tight against his body. "I don't know." A sigh stirred the hair on her temple. "I feel like an idiot saying something so trite, but I can't live with you and I can't live without you." He grinned at her. "You'd think a publisher could come up with something more original, but there you are."

Stretching to meet his lips, Meg kissed him. She meant the kiss to be light, a good-night kiss, and that's how it began. But the chemistry she had cursed a few short days ago ignited and their kiss turned passionate and demanding. She felt Steven's urgent need and responded to her own need.

When they pulled apart Meg's heart was hammering and her body was hot and shaking. Feeling the heat pulsing in her cheeks, she cast a meaningful glance toward the staircase and the bedrooms above. "You could stay..." she whispered.

Indecision deepened his intent expression. Then he stroked her throat, his hand coming to rest just above her breast. "I'd love to," he said in a thick voice. "But each of us should think about the next step, Meg, and decide if we want to take it. This time is for keeps. This time we know what to expect. If you and I make a commitment to each other we have to do so knowing you are going to drive me crazy with your jealousy and knowing that I'm going to drive you crazy by refusing to justify every moment I spend away from you. Are you ready to accept that kind of relationship?"

"Are you?"

"That's what I want both of us to think about." He kissed her nose and held her tightly. "I'll see you in the morning."

MEG ROSE EARLY the next morning and watched the sun rise over the mountain peaks as she sipped her first cup of coffee.

Even if she had known where to begin today's search for the Halverson file, she wasn't sure she was in the mood to continue the search. She was thinking, as she had been most of the night, about Steven and everything he had said.

He was right, of course. And he had put his finger on the basic problem between them. In their previous relationship, Steven had wanted Meg to change, and she had wanted him to change. He wanted her to stop driving them both crazy with her jealousy and she wanted him to stop making her jealous. She smiled at how dumb it sounded. In the end neither of them had changed. She had driven him away.

Now they had a second chance. And Steven was suggesting that instead of trying to change each other, they try to accept each other, problem areas and all.

But that wasn't good enough, Meg thought. Steven shouldn't have to accept a destructive element in their relationship. Both of them deserved better. Sighing, she tilted her head back and gazed out the dining room windows at the peaks in the distance.

Jealousy had played such a large role in everything that

had happened since she arrived at Morgan's Manor. If losing Steven the first time hadn't been enough of a lesson, she had been surrounded by additional proof since her arrival here. Candida and Aunt Tilly's jealousy of each other had crackled between them. As had the jealousy between Dennis and Howard. And her own jealousy of Suzanne Halverson. Jealousy had almost destroyed her relationship with Steven. It had wrecked Aunt Tilly's marriage. Jealousy had led to Dennis's death. And there was the tragic story her mother had related about Meg's grandparents.

Oh, yes, Aunt Tilly had been so right: jealousy was poison.

If Meg hadn't learned that by now, she never would. But she had learned. Never again was she going to let jealousy get a grip on her emotions. Never again was she going to allow that kind of poison into her life. If her old enemy began to stir, she would remind herself of what her mother had said, and of all that had happened here. And she would remember how strong she had become. Strong enough to withstand the pain of loss if it came to that. Strong enough to believe in herself and in Steven no matter how hard that sometimes seemed.

Feeling better, she tied a bandanna over her short dark curls and turned her attention to today's search for the elusive Halverson file. For a while, at least, she needed to take her mind off personal considerations.

At this point they had searched every room in the house. Steven had torn apart the suit of armor beside the living room door; Meg had pushed a broom handle up the chimney flues. They had pulled the books out of Aunt Tilly's library and searched through them and behind them. Meg was ready to swear she had explored every inch of Morgan's Manor, and the Halverson file was not here.

Except it was. Logic insisted and so did instinct. When

all the rhetoric was brushed aside, Candida was right. Writers did not destroy their research notes. If the Halverson file had existed in the first place, then it existed now.

Before she left the dining room, Meg rang for James. "Are you absolutely sure there are no more hidden rooms in this house, like the liquor room, or the fur and silver storage rooms?"

"I've been pondering that question since Miss Ripley raised it." When Meg lifted an eyebrow, he hesitated. "And, well, this is going to sound silly, but..."

"We've already eliminated logical and reasonable," Meg said with a smile. "I'm ready to consider silly, so go ahead. No matter how wild, your suggestions can't be any crazier than some of the things I've been thinking."

"Hilda and I talked about it, and there's something— well, the thing is, sometimes Madam would just—well, it seems that sometimes she would just disappear."

"I beg your pardon?" Meg lowered her coffee cup.

James tugged his collar and looked distinctly uncomfortable. "I would arrive to announce lunch or dinner or a telephone call and Madam would not be in the room where I felt certain she had been just a moment before. Then later she would walk out of the same room. It was enough to make a man think his eyesight or his wits were failing."

Meg stared at him. "How did Aunt Tilly explain this disappearing act?"

"Madam would laugh and say, 'James, you need glasses.' Or she'd say, 'Of course I was there, where do you think I was?' Once—" he looked embarrassed "—she explained quite seriously that she had climbed out the window and gone for a walk. And I can't claim that she didn't, miss. Madam had some unique ways about her."

"How often did this vanishing routine occur?"

"Not often, miss, not often at all. It happened maybe ten or twelve times in twenty years. The last time was about a year ago."

"That you're aware of," Meg said, frowning. "How odd."

"The thing is, neither Hilda nor I ever thought about the possibility of additional secret rooms. But if more secret rooms exist they would explain where Madam disappeared to. So you see, I can't say there are other secret rooms, but I can't say for certain there are not. I can say this. The idea isn't as farfetched as I first thought when Miss Ripley inquired."

Meg poured more coffee, then paced in front of the windows. "Which rooms did Aunt Tilly vanish from?"

James smiled. "Madam could vanish from just about any room in the house, miss."

"Oh." Disappointment diminished the excitement in Meg's eyes. For a moment she had thought they were on to something. But she couldn't accept that every room in Morgan's Manor had a secret room attached into which Aunt Tilly could have vanished.

"It's peculiar that Aunt Tilly vanished on occasion, but I can't believe she disappeared into a dozen secret rooms." She thought James must have erred as Aunt Tilly suggested. Perhaps he did need glasses. She sighed. "It seems likely you would have discovered any additional secret rooms during twenty years."

"That's what Hilda and I concluded, miss. I found the rooms we know about almost immediately after beginning my employment here. If others existed I feel certain I would have stumbled across them, too."

Meg agreed. For a moment her hopes had soared, but it was just another dead end.

"Will you be needing Hilda or me this afternoon, miss?"

"I don't think so," Meg said absently, her mind jumping ahead to Steven's arrival.

"Hilda needs to go grocery shopping for the company we're expecting." This referred to Meg's parents who would arrive late this evening. "And we'd like to stop by the funeral home and pay our last respects to Madam."

"Take the whole day," Meg urged. "Mr. Caldwell will be here soon. We'll manage fine. Take Hilda to lunch and relax a little."

"Thank you, miss. We'll return in time to prepare dinner for you and Mr. Caldwell." He smiled when he mentioned Steven's name and Meg blushed.

Steven arrived an hour later, passing James and Hilda in Aunt Tilly's old Cadillac. Meg offered him a cup of coffee before they resumed the search.

"I have a plan for today," she said, not mentioning any of the conversation from last night. "It's flimsy, but at least I have a plan. Today we concentrate on Aunt Tilly's bedroom. We tear the room apart, and we don't stop until—"

"Meg, we need to talk."

The morning sunshine revealed circles under his eyes, suggesting he was as tired as Meg was. She suspected Steven had spent most of the night, as she had, thinking about their relationship and where it was heading. She looked at his handsome face, at his intense dark eyes, at the mouth she loved, and the Halverson file fell away from her mind.

"I wasn't out of your driveway before I was regretting that I didn't chase you upstairs the minute you suggested it." His lopsided grin made Meg smile in return. "And once I got back to the Poles I could hardly think of anything else.''

"But you did," she said softly.

Steven took her hand in his. "I sat up last night and listed all the pros and cons of our relationship. Finally I realized how stupid that was. How do you weigh 'her possessiveness drives me crazy' against 'I love the way she looks in the morning'? How do you balance 'she's the most stubborn woman alive' against 'I want so spend my life with this woman'?"

Meg laughed. "I don't know. How do you?" Happiness lit her eyes.

"You can't." Leaning forward, he kissed her smile. "The bottom line is I love you and I want to be with you. And that outweighs everything else."

Meg put down her coffee cup and sat in his lap, winding her arms around his neck. "Now this is a speech I like." She covered his face with small damp kisses until, laughing, he caught her hands and made her stop.

"So. What are we going to do about this?"

"I don't know," she said, leaning forward to kiss the top of his ear. "For starters, why don't you move in here?" A rush of color fired her cheeks.

"That's exactly the sort of brazen suggestion I was hoping you would make." Catching her chin, he gave her a long kiss filled with promise. "Look, Meg, you and I aren't going to have an easy relationship."

"You might be surprised."

"But that's okay." He looked deeply into her eyes. "I accept that we're going to experience some difficult moments. But I also believe we'll find a way to work things out if we don't lose sight of loving each other."

"I do love you, Steven," Meg whispered against his throat. "I love you so much. I know I have some proving to do to show you that things are different now. Something will happen and you and I will both recognize the moment. We'll understand the jealousy is under control and it isn't going to be a problem for us. Never again.''

He tried to look as if he believed her, but Meg knew he didn't. But he loved her and accepted her anyway. Knowing it made her heart soar. They stood and he held her in a loose embrace as if he didn't trust himself to hold her tighter.

"I'm going to drive back to town, check in with my office, fax a copy of the Kowalski agreement to the contracts department, then I'll check out of the Poles and bring my luggage back here. I saw James and Hilda leaving—shall I pick up some lunch?''

"You bring lunch." Meg grinned and kissed his jaw. "And I'll provide dessert.''

Steven laughed and patted her on the bottom. "Great. I'll see you in a couple of hours.''

In a daze of happiness, Meg stood on the veranda and watched until Steven's rental car curved out of sight. After the car disappeared, she gave herself a shake, then returned inside.

Because she needed something to do to fill up the next two hours, she prepared a coffee tray and carried it upstairs to Aunt Tilly's bedroom. She threw open the curtains to the bright morning sunshine, then turned Aunt Tilly's clock radio to a station that played classical music.

Her plan had been to search every inch of this room, but the truth was she had already searched every place she could think to search. Standing at the window, listening to Mozart, she tasted her coffee and let her mind drift, occasionally glancing at the sepia-toned photographs of her grandparents that hung beside Aunt Tilly's closet door.

Meg's grandmother had been a pretty woman with large

sad eyes and a mouth that looked as if it had been trembling seconds before the shutter snapped. Her grandfather didn't look happy, either. He peered out of the portrait frame as if he suspected the viewer of something suspicious. Meg sighed, feeling pity for them both.

She started to turn from the old photographs when a thought struck her and she turned a reflective stare back to her grandfather's wary expression.

"Mother said you were so jealous you resorted to spying on your wife and family," she murmured aloud. She turned in a slow circle, studying the bedroom where her grandmother had retreated in tears. "Now how did you do it?" she asked when she faced her grandfather's stare.

He couldn't have spied through the windows. They were two and a half stories off the ground. The time period precluded listening devices. There was no peephole into the corridor. And the walls were too thick to hear through.

Puzzled, Meg tried to figure it out. For spying to be effective, the person being spied upon couldn't know they were being observed. Her grandfather had to have hidden himself. But where?

A leap of excitement stirred in her breast and Meg sensed she was close to the secret.

All right. The secret was tied to her grandfather's jealous spying. That's why exposing the secret would have embarrassed the family and that's why Tilly and her mother had promised never to reveal whatever it was they discovered. And the secret had to be the method their father used to spy on their mother. How it was done.

Once again Meg turned in a slow thoughtful circle, inspecting the room, dismissing the windows, the door to the corridor, the wall that backed the outside stones. Her gaze came to rest on the closet door.

The closet was the best choice. Her grandfather could

have spied from that location. Plus the closet fit her mother's story about two children hiding from the housekeeper.

Meg walked to the large walk-in closet and opened the door. The small room smelled faintly of cedar paneling and of Aunt Tilly's perfume. Meg had searched the closet previously, but she had been looking for a missing file. This time she saw it differently. This time she was trying to solve the family mystery. How had her grandfather spied on her grandmother?

On a hunch, she pulled the closet door shut, then stood in the dark closet feeling a thrill of discovery. A pinpoint of light shone through a tiny hole that she had not noticed previously in the closet door. By lifting on tiptoe, she could peek through the hole and view the bedroom on the other side of the door.

Meg dropped down on her feet and pressed her forehead against the cool wood. It was so sad.

But discovering her grandfather's peephole didn't solve the mystery of how he concealed himself in the closet without her grandmother's knowledge. For his spying to be effective, he had to be able to enter and leave the closet without his wife knowing.

Meg opened the closet door and flipped on the light switch, frowning at the racks of clothing. Then she lowered her gaze to the floor. Maybe a trapdoor? On her hands and knees, she explored every board. And found nothing. But she was convinced she was on the right track.

Next, she pushed Aunt Tilly's clothing this way and that, looking behind the rows of sparkling gowns, looking for a door.

She didn't find a door, but she did find a row of old-fashioned clothing hooks placed about waist high from the floor. A summer belt hung from one of the black hooks. A scarf was tied loosely around another.

Meg pushed down on the first hook, then pushed harder. Nothing happened. She pushed down all four of the hooks and nothing happened. Next she tried pulling up on them. And nothing happened except she almost pulled the last hook out of the wall.

"Okay," she said aloud, squinting at the row of hooks. "We'll try sideways."

The effort felt foolish, and she began to think the whole idea was nonsensical. She didn't even know what she expected to find. Maybe she was wrong entirely. Maybe her grandfather had sat on the side of the mountain with a pair of binoculars or a spyglass or whatever they had in those days.

She pushed the last hook sideways and started to turn away. Then she heard a tiny click. Holding her breath, Meg turned back, then gasped. The wall behind the row of hooks had opened a crack along one of the cedar boards. A steady stream of cool air flowed from the opening.

"Good God," she breathed, feeling a burst of excited astonishment. "There *is* another secret room."

Because Meg possessed the kind of mind that insisted on knowing how things worked, she grasped the old-fashioned clothing hook and pulled the secret door shut. Then she moved the hook sideways again, pushing hard.

The hook did not move easily and she understood why James had never discovered the mechanism. First the hooks were concealed behind Aunt Tilly's clothing. Second, the last hook was the important one and it had to be pressed hard.

Eagerly, heart pounding with excitement and curiosity, Meg pushed the door open wide enough to step through, noticing the hinges didn't make a sound. Either the false wall was built exceptionally well or, and this struck her as more likely, Aunt Tilly had found it useful to keep the hinges oiled.

Meg couldn't believe what she found on the other side of the door. Not in her wildest dreams had she expected anything like this. It was not a room behind the secret door, but a passage. Far ahead shafts of light fell between the boards nailed over an outside window, dimly revealing a passageway.

Heart beating wildly, Meg dashed back into Aunt Tilly's bedroom and jerked open the drawer of the bedside table. Yes. The flashlight was where she remembered.

For a moment she paused and looked at the bedroom door, then she glanced at the clock on the radio. She should wait for Steven. He would be disappointed if she didn't.

She looked back at the door to the closet, biting her lip in indecision. The secret within drew her like a magnet. And Steven wouldn't return for at least another hour.

Curiosity and impatience won out. Steven would understand why she hadn't been able to wait for him. She snatched up the flashlight and ran back into the closet, then stepped through the cedar door and switched on the light.

The first thing she saw was a thick accordion-shaped file on the floor just inside the door. Smiling, Meg bent and directed a beam of light over the file cover. Halverson was written in large block letters across the side. A quick glance confirmed the file was stuffed with manuscript pages, notes, official papers and two video tapes.

She was relieved and happy to find the file, but at the moment the file didn't interest Meg nearly as much as the astonishment of discovering a hidden passageway. She simply could not believe her eyes.

After tucking the file beneath her arm, she trained the

flashlight on the dusty floor and followed Aunt Tilly's footprints. Almost immediately Meg lost her bearings as the passageway curved away from the stone outer walls and she realized another passage veered off from the one she followed.

"Amazing," she murmured out loud, shaking her head. "This is simply unbelievable."

Returning to the passage that followed the outside wall, she continued until she reached a short flight of steps that led up, then along a narrow corridor banked on the outside wall by a row of boarded windows. The passage ended at what looked like an ordinary door from Meg's side.

Feeling like a junior sleuth in a Nancy Drew novel, utterly astonished by the stunning maze of passageways she had discovered, Meg pressed the latch on her side of the wall. When she eased the door open, she was looking into a closet at a row of winter coats.

Knowing she was intruding, but unable to resist confirming her guess as to where she was, Meg pushed aside the coats and stepped into the closet, then opened the closet door and peeked out. This was a part of the house she had not seen before, but she could guess that she was standing in the hallway of James and Hilda's third-floor apartment.

A few steps to the left and she peeked into a tidy small bedroom. A few steps to the right and she was standing in a comfortable living room. She spotted the telephone at once. Aunt Tilly could have reached this telephone easily, pulled the wire from the wall and ducked back into the passageway in less than a minute.

Flushed with the pleasure and victory of unraveling secrets, Meg returned to the passageway, pulling the closet door shut behind her. Then she followed the footprints back down the interior staircase and down another flight of stairs. This set of steps took her to the first floor. She discovered a peephole that overlooked the living room and another that looked into one of the oversmall rooms. The only door she located opened into Aunt Tilly's supply room.

Meg leaned her head into the supply room and grinned at the old-fashioned clothing hook on which Aunt Tilly's sweater hung before she went back into the passageway and returned to the second floor.

She felt a little like a voyeur, but Meg couldn't deny that she was having a grand time exploring. It was like being a kid again and living out a childhood fantasy, discovering a labyrinth of secret passages that twisted through an entire house. The concept staggered her. No wonder there were so many odd-shaped rooms. Accommodating hidden staircases and concealed corridors had practically required rebuilding the house.

It was no longer a surprise to discover the passageways provided access to each of the closets in each of the second-floor bedrooms. It would have been ridiculously simple for Aunt Tilly to slip into Candida's room and take the ruby-and-amethyst ring from the bureau top. Candida had been right when she said a thief would have to possess the ability to walk through walls. But Aunt Tilly had that ability.

Maybe Aunt Tilly had planted the phony evidence for a second reason, to pique Meg's curiosity and lead her to discover the passageways and, with them, the Halverson file. But Aunt Tilly, being Aunt Tilly, hadn't revealed the existence of the passageways directly. She had left the excitement and fun of discovery for Meg to unearth on her own.

Reminded of the Halverson file and the final mystery, Meg moved down the dusty corridor toward a pair of boarded windows, hoping a peek through the slats would restore her sense of direction. It was time to examine the file under her arm.

Halting before the rotting boards, Meg wiped away a lacy design of cobwebs and felt her initial excitement begin to fade. The hidden passageways were fantastic and amazing, but there was something sad and depressing about them, too.

The elaborate infrastructure was a hidden monument to one man's sick jealousy. Jealousy had driven her grandfather to enormous expense and extraordinary lengths to satisfy his suspicions. No area of Morgan's Manor was truly private. No one in her grandfather's family had been able to evade surveillance.

Suddenly and with some regret, Meg made a decision she knew she would follow through. The first thing she would do once the paperwork was complete and Morgan's Manor was truly hers would be to tear out the secret passageways. She would obliterate this sad evidence of so much misery and heartache.

Placing her eye to one of the cracks between the boards over the dusty window, Meg discovered she was again on the third floor. Behind her was a staircase that would, if she calculated correctly, carry her over the ceiling of the second-floor bedroom corridor to the bedrooms on the far side of the house.

The boarded windows she peered through faced the front of the house. As it didn't matter anymore, Meg tugged at one of the rotting boards and it came away easily. Midmorning sunshine streamed into the passageway for the first time in nearly half a century.

Now she could see the back of a car parked in front of the veranda. By leaning to one side she glimpsed the trunk and taillights. A smile curved her lips. Steven was going

to be astonished. Then she remembered the door was
locked and turned to go downstairs and let him inside.

"Stay right where you are. Don't move."

Meg jumped. Her hand flew to her throat and she
whirled around from the window, her heart thudding
against her rib cage as she peered into the shadows.

Suzanne stood at the top of the stairs leading down to
Aunt Tilly's closet. She held a purse-sized .25 caliber au-
tomatic in her left hand. And she was pointing the gun
squarely at Meg's chest.

Chapter Thirteen

"How did you get in here?" Meg gasped.

Suzanne's smile held a superior edge. "With a key. When I was in the kitchen giving my statement to the deputy, I noticed an extra set of keys on a hook by the back door. I just helped myself."

That explained the afternoon Meg had sensed someone had been in her bedroom. But she wasn't thinking about that experience now.

During the course of her mystery-writing career Meg had written a dozen scenes in which one character aimed a gun at another. What she had failed to comprehend until now was how huge the barrel of even a small gun looked when one was standing on the wrong side of it. The gun Suzanne pointed at her was small, it would easily fit into a purse or a pocket. But Meg stared down the barrel and the opening looked as enormous as the mouth of a cannon. Her throat tightened and she felt her pulse hammering in her temples.

"I let myself in and followed the music upstairs and—" Suzanne shrugged "—discovered the secret door in Tillis's closet. You left it open." She glanced at the narrow passageway, nodded at the staircase visible from where she stood. "I wouldn't have believed this if I hadn't seen it myself. If Tillis built these hidden hallways, she was crazier than I imagined."

Meg wet her lips. A chill tightened her spine. "Put the gun down, Suzanne."

Suzanne moved forward a step and Meg could see her face in the shaft of light falling from the window. Suzanne's gaze was cool and expressionless. Her lack of emotion was almost as terrifying as the gun.

"I want the file. Give it to me, Meg."

"Aunt Tilly's notes? Is that what this is about?" Meg feigned surprise. She glanced down at the heavy file tucked under her arm, then back at Suzanne.

"Don't play stupid. We both know what's in that file."

"You're wrong. I haven't examined the file. And I don't think you know for certain what's in here, either." Meg stared at the gun, then wrenched her gaze up to meet Suzanne's eyes. "It's possible there's nothing in this file to warrant this kind of melodrama. Please, Suzanne. I think we can talk without threats. Put down the gun."

"I know Tillis discovered something important enough that she insisted Steven fly out here and review it with her. I'd have to be an idiot to imagine it didn't have something to do with me." A cold smile curved Suzanne's mouth. "Tillis couldn't resist insinuating that she'd been clever enough to find evidence the police hadn't discovered. But when she realized I was snowed in along with the rest of you, she tried to backpedal by claiming there was no new evidence, after all, that she'd abandoned the book and destroyed her notes. I didn't believe that nonsense any more than the rest of you did." She glanced at the file and moved forward another step.

Meg pressed back against the boards covering the window, dimly hearing the boards creak and crack beneath the strain of her weight. Frantically she darted a quick glance to either side, measuring her chances of escaping and out-running Suzanne. Such an attempt meant she had to dodge past Suzanne in the narrow passageway, race down the staircase to Aunt Tilly's bedroom and then...and then what?

Every time she looked at the gun it seemed to have grown in size. Perspiration dampened her palms and her jaw clenched. She might outrun Suzanne, but she couldn't outrun a bullet.

"You sent the death threats to Aunt Tilly, didn't you? And you pushed me down the staircase." The accusations blurted out of nowhere. But instinct ordered her to stall, to try to gain a minute or two to think. Fighting panic, Meg tried to imagine what one of her own heroines would do in this situation. Nothing leaped to mind. It was one thing to leisurely plot a heroic escape while safely seated in front of her word processor. It was another thing alto-gether to instantly create a workable plan when she was staring down the barrel of a loaded gun.

"Give me the file, Meg."

"If I give you the file, what happens to me?"

Even as she asked the question, Meg understood it was rhetorical. They both knew Suzanne intended to kill her. Suzanne would not risk that Meg had examined the Hal-verson file and knew what it contained. Once Suzanne chose to reveal the gun and aim it, Meg's fate had been decided.

And it could not have happened in a worse place. Biting her lips, Meg darted a glance at the dim passageway and her heart plummeted toward her toes. If Suzanne murdered her inside the passageways, it was unlikely anyone would discover her body. As far as the world was concerned Meg would become an interesting footnote to the hoax and Dennis's murder. She would go down as a missing person. And Suzanne would get away with another murder.

"I think you know what happens to you," Suzanne said softly, confirming Meg's fears. In the shaft of sunlight falling through the dust motes, Suzanne's hair resembled a golden halo. If one didn't notice her emotionless cold eyes, she looked like a lovely young woman enjoying a winter holiday dressed in expensive wool slacks and a cashmere sweater. The gun in her hand was chillingly irreconcilable with the rest of her image.

"Disposing of you will eliminate several small problems." Suzanne's satisfied scan of the passageway suggested she, too, recognized this was an ideal site for a murder.

"You did kill Whitney, didn't you?" Meg forced her gaze up from the barrel of the gun. Her heart was pounding so loudly she had to strain to hear Suzanne's reply.

"With you out of the way and the file destroyed, that damned book will die a natural death and there will be no more talk of reopening the investigation." Suzanne's slate-colored eyes swept Meg's slim figure. "And Steven will be free. You don't know how tired I am of hearing how wonderful you are, how talented, how beautiful, how intelligent, how everything ad nauseam."

Steven. Where was he? What was taking him so long? But she couldn't depend on Steven to arrive on the scene like the mythical hero and rescue her. It wasn't going to happen.

What on earth was she going to do? Just stand here and let Suzanne murder her? But what were her options? Meg's mind whirled in a dozen directions at once.

"Put the file on the floor and slide it over here." Suzanne gestured with the barrel of the gun.

"And if I don't?" It was a stupid question, but Meg felt

partially protected, holding the thick file in front of her chest. As if a few inches of paper would stop a bullet.

"No more conversation." Suzanne had advanced until they stood about three feet apart. Her eyes narrowed to slits. "Give me the file, Meg. Let's get this over with."

Meg had read that a person's life passed before his eyes when he was drowning. She discovered the phenomenon also occurred when one was staring down the barrel of a gun held by someone who had pulled the trigger before.

Except what passed through Meg's mind were not the things she had done, but all the things she wanted to do. She wanted to marry Steven and make a home and have children. She wanted to write a bestseller that swept all the lists. She wanted to own a red sports car at least once in her life. She wanted to wake up every morning with Steven's head on the pillow next to her and know he would be there for the rest of her life.

And that might have happened except Suzanne was taking her dreams away from her.

No.

Meg drew a deep breath. She had to believe she deserved her dreams. She had to believe she deserved Steven and a second chance at happiness. She had to find enough confidence in herself to believe she could get through this and that she could win.

Before she could talk herself out of believing, before she could think of all the reasons why she would fail, Meg hurled the Halverson file at Suzanne's face, then leaped forward, her eyes fixed on the gun, her hands extended.

She caught Suzanne's left wrist at the same moment Suzanne clawed at her hair, jerking her head back. The gun fired in the passageway, the sound deafening, blotting the noise they made as they struggled for the weapon.

Suzanne was taller, but Meg was more athletic and her

body was charged with adrenaline. The struggle was evenly matched, conducted in desperate jabs and blows. Suzanne slammed her fist against Meg's jaw; Meg flailed with elbows and knees, trying to grab the gun and falling frustratingly short. The gun waved in the air and fired again. Her ears rang as she and Suzanne twisted and fell against the rotting boards covering the windows. Meg saw the sudden cracks running up and across the boards, but she didn't hear the wood splinter because the gunshots had deafened her.

Slowly, teeth bared, Suzanne brought the gun down between them. Meg battled to prevent the terrifying descent, but Suzanne held the advantage as she was braced against the boarded windows. Panicked, Meg felt the gun dig into her ribs before she mustered a burst of strength and shoved hard to turn the barrel away from her body.

The noise of splintering wood and breaking glass tore through the sound of panting breath. Then, so close together that Meg could not separate them, she heard the blast of another gunshot and a scream. Then she felt a searing, burning pain so intense that it dropped her to her knees.

FOR SEVERAL HOURS Meg remembered nothing but fuzzy gray shapes. Only vaguely did she recall dragging herself to the telephone in Aunt Tilly's bedroom where she managed to phone 911 and mumble, ''Morgan's Manor. Send ambulance,'' before she fainted.

The next memory was that of being carried down the staircase on a stretcher and then outside. She saw flashing red bubbles spinning on top of police cars, saw another ambulance pulling out of the driveway and, as her stretcher was tilted up for an instant, she saw a jagged broken window on the third floor. Then the doors of the ambulance closed and she was driven to Vail for emergency surgery. She had a dim recollection of Steven's worried face hovering over her in the ambulance.

Steven was there again when she emerged from surgery, and Sheriff Conner. She thought they might have talked for a few minutes before she drifted into a drug-induced sleep, but she wasn't sure.

By the time Meg struggled awake again and was conscious enough to grasp where she was and to recall part of what had happened, she became aware that her right thigh was heavily bandaged and it hurt like hell.

Steven was sitting beside her bed, holding her hand. When he realized she was awake, he murmured something, then pressed her fingers to his lips. "If you ever again even hint that you lack confidence in yourself, I'm going to shake you until your teeth rattle!"

She gave him a drowsy smile. "Whatever happened to 'Hi, there, I'm glad you're alive'?"

"Hi, there. I'm glad you're alive." He stared at her as if he wasn't sure she was real. "When I saw you—covered with blood..." He covered his eyes and didn't speak again for a moment.

Meg squeezed his hand and looked away. Sunshine glowed on a half-dozen baskets of flowers.

"It's morning?" she asked when Steven raised his head. "How long have I been asleep?"

"Since yesterday afternoon." He stroked her hand between both of his, carefully, as if she might break. Now she noticed his beard and guessed Steven had been at her bedside since yesterday. "You lost a lot of blood."

Despite the growth of beard, and the exhaustion in his eyes, he was the handsomest man Meg had ever seen. It didn't surprise her when a nurse looked in her room and smiled. Every nurse in Vail would be dropping in for a second look at Steven Caldwell.

"I was shot," she said suddenly, trying to sit up. The memory fell on her like a stone. "Steven! Suzanne shot me!" Throwing aside the sheet and blanket covering her, Meg stared down at the bandages wrapping her thigh. A tremble swept her body and she started shaking. She lifted wide dark eyes and spoke in a whisper. "Am I going to be all right?"

"Shh, darling. It's over now," Steven said in a soothing voice. Gently he eased her onto the mound of pillows and pulled up the blankets. "The doctors removed the bullet yesterday. You were lucky. Another fraction of an inch and your thigh bone would have been shattered. The most serious problem was the loss of blood. You're going to be weak for a while, but you'll be good as new in no time."

Twisting, Meg stared up at the IV bottles on the rack over her bed. It was starting to come back to her. "We... we struggled for the gun, and..."

"I know. I was present when you gave your statement to Sheriff Conner."

Meg frowned at him. "I gave a statement to Sheriff Conner?"

"You don't remember? Yes, darling, you did."

She stared at him, but she was reliving that scene in the dim hidden passageway. She saw Suzanne's bared teeth. Heard again the blast of the gun in that confined space, inhaled the stinging odor of cordite, felt a sudden searing pain. And she remembered the blood on her hands, on her leg. The amount of blood had surprised and frightened her. She was light-headed and reeling long before she managed to drag herself into Aunt Tilly's bedroom.

"The passageways, did you...?"

"I saw them." Steven shook his head and smiled gently.

"Your parents arrived last night." Before Meg could say anything, he leaned to place a light kiss on her lips. "They were here, but left a few minutes ago to get something to eat. They'll be back soon."

Another thought caused Meg's muscles to tense painfully. Disconnected scenes flashed through her memory. "The file! Steven, I found the Halverson file."

"Shh, try to relax and don't worry about anything, just rest. Sheriff Conner has the file. I'm meeting him in about an hour to review the material."

"Aunt Tilly said something about photos," Meg whispered, her eyes closing.

"Just rest, darling, and get well."

Before she drifted off to sleep, Meg's eyes blinked open and she scowled at him. "I distinctly remember you telling me in the restaurant that you didn't think Suzanne was dangerous, after all."

Steven's fingers caressed her cheek and he smiled. "I remember, too. I'll spend the rest of my life making that up to you."

Meg smiled, leaned her cheek against his hand, then floated away.

WHEN SHE AWOKE again Meg felt rested and alert, relieved to notice the pain in her thigh had diminished to mere discomfort. The shadows lengthening across the room suggested it was late afternoon. A nurse brought her fresh ice water and mentioned that Meg's parents had left five minutes ago without waking her. "They didn't want to disturb you. They said to tell you they'll be back this evening."

To Meg's surprise, Candida had sent a bouquet of roses. Her parents had left magazines and a box of her favorite chocolate creams. James and Hilda had brought a small suitcase of toiletries, one of her own nightgowns and a change of clothing.

After dinner Sheriff Conner arrived with Steven a step behind him. Steven had shaved, showered and changed clothes, but he still looked tired. He bent over her bed and kissed her forehead.

"How are you feeling?" the sheriff inquired.

"Well enough to wonder why Jessica Fletcher never gets shot on *Murder She Wrote*," Meg said with a rueful smile.

Steven laughed and took the chair beside her bed. "If you can joke about getting shot, I'd say you're on the road to recovery."

The sheriff pulled up a chair on her other side. "Caldwell said you didn't remember giving a statement, so I thought we'd better go over it again in case you've remembered anything you didn't mention before."

Meg pressed Steven's hand, then frowned at Sheriff Conner. "There's something I have to know. What happened to Suzanne?" She touched her temple with her fingertips. "I remember fighting for the gun. I remember hearing the gun fire. Then crawling to Aunt Tilly's bedroom to the telephone. But there's a gap where Suzanne is…" Meg spread her hands. "She's just not there."

"Mrs. Halverson went out the window," the sheriff said in a matter-of-fact tone. "The wood over the windows was rotten, so was the window frame." He watched Meg shudder. "According to your statement, during the struggle Mrs. Halverson was pressed up against the boards." He shrugged. "They gave way and she fell out."

Meg stared at him, then wet her lips. "Did I…did I push her?" she whispered.

"Maybe." A sympathetic smile touched the sheriff's

lips. "It wouldn't surprise me. You were fighting for your life."

"We were on the third floor." Meg lifted her face. "Is she...did the fall kill her?"

"She's still on the critical list. By tomorrow the doctors hope to have a better idea if she'll make it or not. She sustained massive injuries from the fall."

"Oh my God." Horror widened Meg's pupils.

Steven took her hand again and held it tightly. "Don't blame yourself. Suzanne was trying to kill you."

The sheriff nodded. "After reviewing your aunt's file, there's enough new evidence to assume Mrs. Halverson was involved in her husband's murder. There's no doubt in my mind that she would have murdered you, too, Miss Sandler."

"I have to know," Meg whispered. "What's in the file?"

As Aunt Tilly had hinted, the new evidence was in the photographs and videos. When Whitney Halverson's body was found, he was clutching a silver earring of an unusual design. A transcript of the inquest revealed Suzanne had sworn she had never seen the earring before. But Aunt Tilly had unearthed a society photo published in a 1987 issue of *Town and Country* that showed Suzanne in profile wearing the same earring.

Steven stroked her hand. "Tillis made another discovery that neither Suzanne nor the police were aware of. The Beverly Hills Hotel, which Suzanne swore she checked into, the Royal Palms, maintains a video file of all registrations. Tillis uncovered that piece of information and obtained a copy of the video showing Suzanne at the registration desk. The video is in the file."

Sheriff Conner took up the story. "There's a full face shot of Mrs. Halverson checking into the hotel, picking up the pen to attempt to sign the register—which she didn't do—and paying for the room. What's interesting about the video, aside from the fact that the woman only marginally resembles Suzanne Halverson, is that the woman checking in is clearly right-handed. As you know—" he nodded to Meg's bandaged leg "—Mrs. Halverson is left-handed. I think a voice print taken from the video will be equally damaging. It should prove Suzanne Halverson did not check into the hotel. I think we'll discover it was her maid."

"The earring places Suzanne at the scene of the murder. The video breaks her alibi," Steven said.

"My office faxed the material to NYPD," the sheriff added. "They're checking it out now, but an early off-the-record opinion says there's enough new evidence to reopen the Halverson case."

"If Suzanne lives," Meg said slowly, "she'll be facing a murder trial."

"You can count on it," the sheriff agreed. "Plus we've got attempted murder right here."

After opening his notebook, he took Meg through her statement again. While she talked, Meg watched a nurse enter her room for no other reason, it appeared, then to flirt with Steven. Steven seemed oblivious to the nurse's attempts to attract his attention.

"Three shots were fired?" Sheriff Conner asked.

Meg nodded, watching the nurse rearrange Meg's flowers and try to catch Steven's eye.

Finally Meg leaned to whisper in his ear. "Oh, for heaven's sake, will you at least smile at her, so she can go check on someone else?"

Steven blinked and became aware of the pretty young nurse for the first time. "What?"

"She's pining away for you. She isn't going to leave

until you notice her. So give her a smile." Meg turned back to the sheriff. "What's the next question?"

"Wait a minute." Steven sat up straight and stared at her. "Meg Sandler. Are you urging me to flirt with another woman?" His dark eyebrows lifted. "Maybe you're in worse shape than the doctor said. Are you sure you didn't get hit on the head, too?"

When Meg understood what had just happened, she stared at Steven and her mouth dropped open. A look of recognition dawned on her expression. "The moment," she whispered. "This is the moment. I'm free."

"Uh-oh," Sheriff Conner said. "I think this is my cue to leave." Standing, he closed his notebook and reached for his hat. "If you're feeling well enough to be jealous, I'd say you're going to be up and around very soon now."

"You don't understand," Meg said, looking at him with surprise and joy. "I *don't* feel jealous! I asked him to smile at her!" She turned to Steven with a radiant smile. "I *asked* you to flirt with her." She shook her head and laughed out loud. "I can't quite believe this myself. But it's wonderful!"

The sheriff rolled his eyes, then followed the nurse to the door. "I am never going to understand women. Crime, yes. Women, no. Women do not make sense." He winked and closed the door behind him.

Steven sat on the edge of her bed and smiled down into her happy eyes. His own eyes were warm with love and amusement. "Does this mean you want me to carry on a flirtation with all the nurses in the Vail Medical Center?"

Meg wound her arms around his neck and smiled. "Easy, fella. I'm new at this. I don't think we have to carry it quite that far." She didn't remember ever feeling this happy, this free or this certain of herself, Steven and the future.

She wasn't so naive as to believe there would not be relapses. There would be moments ahead when the caged monster would waken and test her. The difference was Meg now knew she was in control. Trusting Steven had never been a problem. The problem had been believing in herself.

But if she didn't believe in herself after solving one murder and thwarting another, she never would. If she couldn't believe in herself after winning Steven back and caging the green-eyed monster, she was hopeless. But she did believe in herself. And in Steven. And she believed in the future that stretched in front of her like a dream come true.

"I love you, Meg."

She framed his face between her hands and gazed up at him with tears of happiness glistening in her eyes.

"I love you so much."

Tomorrow she would find an architect to redesign Morgan's Manor. By spring the labyrinthine monument to destructive passions would be gone. She would open Morgan's Manor—and her new life with Steven—to sunshine and love.

She felt certain Aunt Tilly would have approved.

**She'd survived when the plane went down—
but after one night with the gorgeous pilot,
she knew she was beyond rescue.**

ON A WING AND A PRAYER

Jackie Weger

1

"SANTEE, YOU HANG ON to Nicholas," Rebecca ordered as she lined up the five orphans just inside the hangar door. She had an instant sensation of space and unfamiliar shadow. The building, huge and poorly lit and smelling of grease, much like a mechanic's garage, intensified the sensation. Rebecca shivered. She'd had misgivings about this trip from the start, but her arguments against it had fallen on deaf ears. In her heart she felt the children would end up being disappointed yet again. Too, she wasn't certain of her ability to handle the five on her own. The orphans seemed to have an instant affinity for troublemaking.

"I'm hungry," said Jonesy. "We should've stopped at McDonald's for breakfast."

"They aren't open this early, it's barely dawn. Besides, you had breakfast."

"I'm cold," said Yancy.

"Swing your arms. I'll be right back. Don't anybody wander off. And hang onto your totes—I mean it. I'll go find the office."

It really wasn't much warmer inside the monolithic Quonset than outside, but at least they were out of the wind and sleet, thought Rebecca. She turned and studied the shadows.

She could make out the nose and propeller of a small plane and what seemed to be the dismantled parts of another. At the far end a beacon of light slanted from a pair of windows. She admonished the children once again not to wander, then negotiated the length of the building.

She stopped in the beacon of light and stared through the dusty windows.

As her brain registered the airline office her disquiet grew. There were furnishings of every kind that had nothing in common with each other but their infirmity and a dusty, dilapidated air. An oil heater was turned so low it had no effect on the thick rime of frost at the outside windows, where the curtain rods were bent and barely hanging on.

Amid all the clutter a man sprawled in a chair, asleep. His head was tilted back revealing a jaw covered with beard stubble, several days thick. His arms were folded across his chest and his booted feet were crossed and propped on the desk. He looked like a scruffy bag of assorted human parts loosely held together by army-surplus specials. He was a living reproach to manhood, Rebecca thought uncharitably. But then, she was intolerant of men. There wasn't a man in her life and she wasn't anxious to include one. If it meant lonely nights, well...her days were full.

But it saddened her that this was what the foundering Tynan Foundation had come down to; begging favors for the children from those who appeared least able to afford them. If she had one whit of sense, she'd grab up the kids, return to the orphanage and tell the director they'd missed the plane. She could practice the lie all the way back to Boise, then perhaps it wouldn't show on her face.

A yelp echoed in the dark vastness. She glanced at the orphans. They were arguing among themselves already. She expelled a sigh. They would put the rout to any lie about missing the plane. With a sinking feeling, she tapped hard on the metal door and moved across the threshold.

The man opened his eyes. Rebecca could see him trying to shake the dregs of sleep. Once his gaze seemed focused on her, she spoke, "I'm looking for Mr. Stillman."

He came alert, his lips thinning as suspicious eyes darted to appraise her.

"You a bill collector?"

"Rebecca Hollis, from the Tynan Foundation. Abigail Tynan booked us a flight on the mail run. To San Francisco," she added, since the man looked blank. "We're a bit early, but if you could just direct me to Mr. Stillman, I can let him know we're here."

"Captain Stillman."

"Captain Stillman, then."

The man dragged his feet from the desk, stood and stretched, which had the effect of making his shirt collar poke up like limp flags from beneath the crew neck of a British commando sweater. When he came out of the stretch, the gleam in his eye was still guarded. "You're looking at him and, I'm not."

"But..." Rebecca began. She caught herself before she blurted that he couldn't possibly be the pilot. She took a step back. Standing, the man was taller than she'd supposed. And given the slothful way his clothes hung on his frame, he appeared even more disreputable. The kind of man one either crossed the street to avoid, or if one were kind, dropped a quarter into his cup.

"You're not what?" she said, in no mood for benevolence, telling herself she'd misunderstood him.

"Not expecting you."

"You can't be Captain Stillman then, I assure you, we're expected." She was in no humor for charades. She'd spent the better part of last evening packing, managing only several hours' rest before she'd had to roust the children from their beds, after which she'd spent a tension-filled ninety minutes on slick and unsafe roads to reach the airfield on time.

"You hard of hearing or something? I'm Stillman." He was fully awake now. Irritably so. There was only the woman, but she was talking in plurals.

"We. Who's we?" he demanded.

Rebecca answered his hostility with what she considered to be more pleasantness than the situation required. "Myself, and the children. From the Foundation, the foundling home."

"Children!" Parnell Stillman yanked a clipboard from the wall behind him, flipping rapidly through it. "I got a group of social workers booked, going to a convention."

"I'm the social worker."

"There're six of you."

"One of me. Five children. I'm sure Abigail didn't say we were all social workers," ventured Rebecca. But she knew in her heart that the Foundation's director had probably misled the man with her use of sly and creative dialogue. When it came to bargaining, creative dialogue was Abigail Tynan's stock in trade. But bargaining with the likes of Stillman? Yes, Abigail would do that, too. She'd often said she'd bargain with the devil if it meant something good for the youngsters in her care.

Parnell Stillman consulted his notes. "Abigail said, 'important personages, big favor, cheap price.'" He remembered now. The old biddie had also reminded Parnell of her association with his Uncle Henry. "I wrote it down."

"Well, that's us," Rebecca said airily, offering a weak smile.

"Forget it. I'm not hauling you. That's final. No women or children. They make too much fuss. Everybody this side of the Continental Divide knows it. I don't even like being nice to women and children. Makes my stomach hurt. You can just take yourself out of here. Tell Abigail the deal's off."

It was just the out she was looking for. Now she could return to the Foundation and tell Abigail an honest truth—they'd been turned away, bumped from the flight. On the other hand, Rebecca thought indignantly, the pilot was being underhanded, unfair and rude. It made her mad. "I will not take myself out of here. You've been paid. You agreed." She hoped the check Abigail had sent hadn't bounced. Otherwise...

"I'll have my accountant send the Foundation a refund."

There was something in the way he said "my accountant." Rebecca eyed the stack of unopened mail on the desk, the disarray of paper in the In-Out basket, all of which was layered with undisturbed dust. Accountant, my foot, she thought. His tone held the same touch of superfluity that Abigail Tynan used in promising payments when she knew very well the Foundation's bank account was overdrawn. Rebecca knew just how to counter the pilot's maneuver.

"I'm afraid that won't do," she said. "We have to have the refund at once, in cash, so we can make other arrangements. It's urgent that we get to San Francisco."

"Can't. It's against my policy to give cash refunds. Besides, I don't keep cash on hand. Too dangerous. I might get robbed."

"You must not worry about getting robbed too much," Rebecca cooed, skepticism in full flower. "The gate at the entrance was open, your doors were unlocked. There's a plane sitting on the runway with no attendants that I could see. Security appears awfully lax. How many times have you been held up?"

Parnell scowled. The look she was giving him made him

feel like something one scraped off a shoe. He didn't like it. "There's always a first time."

"No respectable burglar would be out in this weather," Rebecca said lightly. "Anyway, isn't there some sort of government rule that if passengers are bumped, the airline has to pay double the cost of their tickets?"

The belligerent expression on Parnell Stillman's unshaven face told Rebecca she'd hit a sore spot. "Who cares about government regulations? Paper pushers one and all," he sneered.

"You won't have to be nice to us, Captain Stillman. I wouldn't want to be the cause of inflaming your ulcers. The children and I are used to managing just fine without ordinary courtesies."

He glared at Rebecca, desperately intent. The way she talked reminded him of a bitter mistake he'd once made. "I had a wife like you once," he divulged, tight-jawed. "She spent the whole of our marriage intent on vexing me."

It was incredible, Rebecca thought, how full of himself the man was. She reminded him of his wife? Well, he reminded her of another who'd also been full of himself, shallow of heart and mind. A riposte came to the tip of her tongue, slid off with ease. "Oh? And how long did your marriage last, Captain Stillman. Twenty minutes?"

"Just like her," he muttered.

"I'm honored you think so," Rebecca replied so reverently her tone couldn't be taken for anything except what it was—unveiled sarcasm. She moved outside the office proper and called to the kids. Once they had all trooped the length of the hangar, she directed them to a bench along the inside office wall. "Sit there. Don't get up. You might—"

"I have to wee-wee," said Molly.

Rebecca's face flushed with chagrin. With no other source

to ask, she had to direct the inquiry to Parnell. "Where's the ladies' room?"

Displaying ill-concealed annoyance, he pointed with a pencil, then sat down behind his desk and pretended his unwelcome passengers didn't exist. Though he did surreptitiously watch Rebecca remove her head scarf and overcoat. She looked young, vibrant, with her dark hair released, cascading in a froth about her shoulders. And much more shapely with her coat off. Much more. She was short, too. Women like her always tried to use that to advantage. Trying to make a man feel big, protective. Well, he didn't give a hoot in hell. A woman's shape, size and beauty no longer swayed him. They hadn't in years.

He knew all about womanly ploys—those provocative games of revealing a little here, a little there until a man was panting like a thirsty pup. He'd suffered the misfortune of becoming easy prey once. It would never happen again.

Back when he'd been stupid over women, he'd been in the Navy, stationed at the Pensacola Naval Air Station. The vamp that snagged him had made herself out to be a poor little widowed thing, all alone and with two darling children to raise. Just the memory of it made him sick to his stomach. He'd swallowed every honey-dripped word and married her. All she had done was raise one ruckus after another, and the darlings had turned out to be manipulative brats.

The marriage had spoiled the last three years of the twenty he'd spent in the Navy. At thirty-seven and at loose ends he'd made his way to Idaho where Uncle Henry had settled into crop dusting and hauling cargo. Two years ago Uncle Henry died. Parnell discovered the flying service had been bequeathed to him. The flying service and its mountain of debt.

What he needed, Parnell knew, was a sharp secretary-bookkeeper. But the salary he could offer wouldn't appeal to a man with a family to feed. That left hiring a woman and he couldn't make himself do it.

He counted himself among the honorable group of men who liked dogs, was kind to the elderly and had immense control over the needs of the flesh. Control was easy—his failed marriage had left him with a lingering animosity toward women. He didn't want anything in skirts hanging around the airfield. Secretary or passenger.

His self-imposed celibacy was annoying, but not earth shattering. On the infrequent occasions his flesh drove him to seek out a woman, he went where there was no romance, just bonhomie, crude jokes, loud laughter and inane conversation. If any woman mentioned marriage, he hightailed it on the double; if she mentioned kids, he disappeared faster than a jet stream in a howling wind. He protected himself from female wiles as best he could. His dimples had attracted the widow. Now he kept them concealed behind beard stubble. And he knew for a fact you couldn't be nice to a woman. First thing you knew she'd attach some unintentional sentiment to word or action. He had it in the back of his mind that women had been molded just to keep a man in misery. It was ironic that God had shorted men a rib just so he could create women. Parnell had decided long ago that he'd just as soon have his rib back.

His introspection was diverted to two of the boys edging crabwise off the bench. The control he had over his libido didn't extend to his disposition. He glared at them. "Get away from my desk."

"We're orphans," said Jonesy.

"Tough."

"What's he look like?" Nicholas whispered.

"Like that hobo old Abigail let sleep in the kitchen last week," Jonesy said.

"Hobo!" Parnell bristled. "Get back to that bench like you were told, you cheeky brat."

Jonesy didn't budge, but he kept a wary eye on Parnell. "Nicholas is blind," he volunteered. "He can't see nothin' but shadows."

"That's too bad," said Parnell, shocked and trying to sound mean. "I don't look like a hobo. I'm an aviator."

Nicholas squinted. "Can I feel your hands and face?"

"Hell no! Back up!"

Jonesy put a retraining arm around the younger boy. "We're goin' to San Francisco to see if we can get somebody to adopt us. There's a big meetin' with all these people who take handicapped kids."

Parnell's gaze took in Nicholas, Jonesy, and the two boys on the bench. Curiosity got the best of him. "What's wrong with you?" he asked Jonesy.

"I'm fat. Nobody wants a fat kid. Cost too much to feed."

"What about him?" Parnell nodded toward Yancy.

"He's got a friend named Scrappy."

"So?"

"Scrappy ain't real."

"Oh."

"Santee's got Indian blood. He won't stay in the city. Folks won't take him cause he runs away and lives in the woods. Molly has club feet. You got any kids?"

Parnell's curiosity dried up. "No, and I'm not looking to get any. Move out. Don't you know how to follow orders?"

"We've never been on an airplane before."

"I wish you weren't—" An idea flew into Parnell's brain. "Is that so? You scared to fly?"

Jonesy shrugged. Nicholas asked, "Is flying dangerous? What's it feel like?"

"It can be dangerous." Parnell's mouth compressed into the thinnest of smiles. "Yep, it sure can." The idea took solid root. He examined it from every direction and decided he had nothing to lose by trying it on...on...he glanced at the manifest on the clipboard...Rebecca Hollis.

"Miss Hollis," he said as soon as she and Molly emerged from the bathroom, "I need to go over the flight with you." He unfolded a pair of charts, topographical and meteorological, over the clutter on his desk. "It's a cold, bumpy ride. No frills, no food—"

"I know, we brought our own snacks."

Parnell withheld a sigh. "You're missing the point. Look here. See this chart. This is the flight path from Boise to San Francisco. We'll be flying over some of the most desolate terrain in the country—"

"What does that matter? We're not walking."

Parnell dropped into his chair like a deflated balloon. His idea wasn't working. He shot her his best scowl. "That's true, but we got crosswind, maybe even wind shear, sleet, snow. The weather isn't good—" Of course he planned to dip down and fly south of it, but he wasn't telling her that.

"Are you canceling the flight?"

"Can't. It's a mail run. You know the old saying, 'Neither rain nor sleet—'"

"If you feel it's safe enough to fly the mail..."

"I'm paid to take chances," Parnell said modestly.

"You were also paid to fly us to San Francisco. And back."

All the curses he could think of glowered in Parnell's dark eyes. "I don't want a woman and kids aboard my plane. Women are a jinx! Kids are nothing but trouble."

Rebecca shooed Molly back to the bench, out of earshot.

She lowered her voice. "I'm sure you've been told this before, Captain Stillman. You're acting like a horse's rear end. I'm willing to accommodate you. Just refund double our money and we'll make arrangements elsewhere. The truth is, you don't look as if you could fly yourself out of a paper bag. It makes me nervous—"

Parnell's lithe frame went rigid. "You hoity-toity broad! What do you know about what flyers look like? I suckled in a cropduster, barnstormed at fourteen, flew jets at twenty-two. Lady, I was raised on a wing and a prayer in the literal sense. Don't look as if I could fly myself out of a paper bag! Maybe I ought to tell you what you don't look like."

"I didn't mean to insult you," Rebecca replied so sweetly it gave the lie to her words.

"You sure as hell did."

She glanced over at the children. One and all wore pensive expressions. The conclave in San Francisco meant hope. A hope of finding parents to love and be loved by in return. She couldn't take that away from the children. Even if it meant they had to tolerate an insufferable prig of a pilot. She turned back to Parnell and met his angry glare.

"All right, I did mean to insult you. I'm sorry. We'll just sit here quietly until it's time to board. If that's all right with you."

It wasn't, but Parnell knew when he was hoisted on a cleft stick. He knew it because he'd never been any other place in his life.

Flying was his freedom, flying ennobled his actions, and he was inseparable from it. But flying also distanced him from the business side of trying to run an airline single-handedly. Oh, he was a likable man when he wanted to be liked, usually when he was negotiating for freight or mail contracts, but he didn't like the paperwork. Somehow, when the money came in, it got spent in the wrong order. Like the fares from the Tynan Foundation which had gone to pay his relief pilot who had refused to climb into the cockpit yesterday until he'd had cash in hand.

He should never have let that old bat, Abigail, talk him into flying her "clients." But she'd once been a good friend of Uncle Henry's, bless his debt-ridden departed soul, and they'd done a fair amount of crop dusting for her before Abigail had sold off most of her land and turned what was left of her estate into a foundling home. Parnell eyed Rebecca with an expression longer than a mournful bloodhound's.

"I'll send one of the ground crew to tell you when to board. You'll have to carry your own luggage. Stillman's doesn't provide porters."

"We'll manage our own luggage. Thank you," Rebecca said, feigning congeniality.

Parnell shoved himself into a sheepskin jacket and stomped out of the office. They could hear his booted footsteps echoing long after he'd disappeared from sight.

"Bet he takes off without us," said Santee.

"Don't worry, he won't." Rebecca didn't know just how she knew that. Instinct, she supposed. Santee's olive complexion was pale. Afraid to fly, Rebecca knew, he was trying not to show his fear.

"He won't make me leave Scrappy behind, will he?" asked Yancy.

"Oh, I'm sure not. There'll always be room for Scrappy."

Rebecca wasn't supposed to encourage Yancy concerning the pretense of Scrappy even though Scrappy was Yancy's best friend. But everybody needed a best friend, she thought. It was a measure of her empathy that Yancy had been willing to introduce her to his imaginary playmate.

Each of the children had taken a hard blow, some more than one, which had taught them to keep a low profile, to keep heads tucked down, to harbor only meager expectations. In the year that she'd been working for Abigail Tynan, working with the children, they'd come to trust her, as much as they allowed themselves to trust any adult. To Rebecca's way of thinking, that trust was a measure of progress.

She gave a moment's thought to the conclave. Months of bickering, bureaucracy and red tape had gone into the planning of it. More than five different state agencies and a dozen private placement centers had pooled resources to bring it off. She hoped it worked. She hoped... She glanced at her charges...society's rejects—lame, blind, unloved.

A sudden whirlwind of memories and emotions whipped through her mind. Unloved. Perhaps, Rebecca thought, the reason she had such an affinity for the children was that she too was a reject.

But she had learned to love herself. No easy feat since she hadn't thought there was anything lovable about herself. And working with the orphans had filled some deep biological need.

Once the Foundation had found homes for these remaining five children though, Abigail was going to close its doors. Too bad, Rebecca thought, she couldn't find someone to adopt herself. As it was, after the first of the year she'd be on her own again. No job, no home, no kids.

No man in her life, either.

She didn't want a man, she reminded herself. Truth was, she'd been weakening on that score, especially in her dreams. Meeting the pilot strengthened her. He was a good representation of the opposite sex; arrogant, slothful, insensitive. She was always telling the children to let the past go, to learn to depend on themselves, accept reality. She needed to take her own advice.

Her thoughts ebbed, her gaze focusing on the present. Santee was beginning to fidget. Rebecca gave him an encouraging smile.

An elderly man, his wrinkled face pinched against the cold, entered the office. "You can git aboard, the cap'n says."

"Where's Captain Stillman?" Rebecca asked.

"Doin' preflight check."

"Well, here we go, kids. Our great adventure."

"Scrappy's afraid to get on a plane," said Yancy.

"He can go with me," offered Molly. "I'm not."

Yancy scowled. "He ain't that afraid."

"What's flyin' look like?" Nicholas wanted to know.

Rebecca sorted totes, handed them out and picked up her suitcase. "I'll describe it once we're doing it. Santee, guide Nicholas. Molly, Yancy, Jonesy, stay together."

The old man opened his mouth then closed it. Rebecca had the notion that he wanted to offer assistance, but had orders to the contrary. He gave an embarrassed nod and held opened the hangar door as she and the children filed out.

The tarmac was slick with crusted snow and ice, the wind and sleet shoving at them, taking their breath away. Landing lights guided their way. Just as she reached the foot of the gangway steps, Molly slipped, her balance undone by the heavy corrective shoes she wore.

Parnell, watching from the plane, sidled down the steps past the boys and snatched Molly, slinging her over his shoulder as he might a hundredweight sack of grain. "I'm not responsible for accidents," he yelled above the storm.

"Nobody said you were!" Rebecca yelled in return, exasperated and fighting to keep her own balance. From her shoulder perch Molly lifted her bonnet-covered head and grinned. She liked being the center of attention.

Unaware of Molly's delight, Parnell mumbled to himself. The flight was jinxed for certain, he thought. The kids would probably be airsick all over his plane.

Rebecca dragged herself, the suitcase and tote out of the stormy darkness. The old maintenance man—a frozen shadow—drove a forklift that would pull the loading ramp away from the plane. She shifted her gaze from the ghostly scene to Parnell. "Are you sure you can fly in this kind of weather?"

"You want to change your mind?" he said, all hope. "I'll have Amos—"

Rebecca pursed her lips. "If you're flying, we're flying."

"I gotta deliver the mail." With no snarl-ups, he thought. He'd landed a plum contract for December. Parcel post and the military APO San Francisco mail that was distributed to service personnel in the Pacific. If he met the deadlines and kept his planes in the air, the money from the APO mail alone would pull his bottom line out of the red. He slid the door closed and secured it, then looked at Rebecca, at the ménage she had in tow. His stomach began to hurt. "Stow your gear," he said.

As he buckled himself into the pilot's seat, he decided he was going to stop being nice to elderly people. He'd been nice as pie to old Abigail Tynan and look at the trouble that officious, frumpy, octogenarian virago had bestowed on him. Soon as he got back from this run, he was going to buy himself a dog and be done with it.

That decided, Parnell preoccupied himself with what made him happy—flying airplanes. He scanned his flight plan and charts though he'd long since committed them to memory. The first engine turned over and sputtered to life, followed by the other three. He got the signal that the chocks holding the wheels were pulled. He released the brakes and shoved the four throttles against the stops. Then he aimed the nose into the blowing sleet and began rolling down the long ribbon of tarmac. Windshield wipers worked furiously, runway lights blurred past the wing tips, their luminescence fading behind the curtain of falling slush.

The weather didn't bother Parnell. He had the ability to fly through anything except solid mountain and he knew it. He expelled a satisfied smile. Flying was the high road.

2

"But you don't need a window seat, Nicholas," Jonesy argued. "You're blind! You can't see anything anyway!"

"I got here first!"

Rebecca jumped into the verbal fray. "Listen you two, you can take turns sitting by the window."

"But Nicholas could sit anywhere. It won't make any difference!"

"He has just as much right to a window seat as you do."

Jonesy sulked. "Everybody picks on me 'cause I'm fat."

"I don't!" cried Nicholas. "I can't see your old fat. I'm just takin' up for myself. Like I'm supposed to."

The plane shuddered, the boys quieted. Rebecca sighed. The plane staggered aloft.

The only light in the cabin was an eerie green glow spilling from the instrument panel in the cockpit, and the cold seemed to be seeping up from the steel deck. Rebecca pulled her coat collar up around her neck. Surely they weren't expected to suffer this debilitating cold the entire flight!

She was responsible for the safety and well-being of the children. What if they came down with the flu? A fever? And had to stay in bed during the conclave. It would break their hearts. Holding that thought, she kept her eye on Parnell, waiting for the right moment to approach him. Regardless of how cheap the fares, a little heat wasn't too much to ask.

The landing gear thumped loudly inside the wheel wells.

The pilot was talking on the radio. When he seemed finished with the conversation, Rebecca got out of her seat and
leaned into the cockpit. A welcome furl of warm air brushed
her cheeks. It galled her that he was all nice and cozy while
not giving a thought to the comfort of his passengers. She
tapped him on the shoulder.

"Is there any way to give us some heat back here?" she
asked, raising her voice above the harsh whine of the mo-
tors. "Our teeth are chattering."

Parnell twisted in his harness. He already knew the flight
promised to be a rough one. Even the takeoff hadn't been
exactly a garden-variety liftoff what with crosswinds and
sleet bearing down on the overloaded plane. He wanted to
concentrate on his flying, not pesky passengers. He displayed a mouth turned down in fixed antagonism. "Next
you'll be asking when cocktails are served."

Hackles rose on the back of Rebecca's neck. She'd had her
fill of the man's arrogance. "Look, all we've done is hire you
to fly us to San Francisco. You're acting as if we're criminals
or something. It's cold back here. And dark. A couple of the
children are afraid of the dark."

"I'm a flyer, not a nursemaid," he said, but he touched a
switch and a row of dim lights came on down the length of
the ceiling throwing the children in the single row of seats
and what appeared to be row upon row of carts stamped
U.S. Mail into shadowy relief.

"Thank you," Rebecca said with unctuous civility. "Now,
the heat?"

"You want heat? Open the vents next to the seats."

"Excuse me for disturbing you."

Suddenly there was a lurch of the aircraft. Rebecca fell to
her knees. She grabbed the back of his seat and hung on.

She'd argued against attending the conclave and lost.

She'd argued against flying. But the flux of December storms blanketing the West had finished that argument for her. The Foundation's old stationwagon was in too sad a shape anyway. Besides that, travel advisories had indicated that many of the main arteries were closed. She wished heartily that she had been more persuasive. Now there was nothing for it but to pray. A quick glance behind her revealed all the kids sitting straight and stiff, looking at her with frightened eyes from pale faces.

"Quit hanging on me and go sit down," Parnell shouted while his hands flew over the control panel.

"You're beyond belief!" she said, seething. But she managed to gain her feet and stumble back to the row of seats. Abigail must've been out of her mind when she booked their flight with Parnell Stillman! she thought crossly. In a brief moment of stability she found the heat vents, directing the warm jets of air across the seats.

"Ask him does he have parachutes," whispered Santee.

"Don't be silly," said Rebecca. "We're perfectly safe. I've flown on several occasions in worse weather than this." Not that she could think of one at the moment, but she did recall that the cabin attendants had always walked up and down the aisle reassuring passengers. Sometimes the pilot got on the intercom and explained what was happening. It was obvious Captain Stillman had a passengers-be-damned! attitude. He wasn't going to explain a thing.

"Scrappy doesn't like flying," whimpered Yancy, clutching at his imaginary friend. "He's afraid he's gonna fall out of the sky."

"Well, he isn't and we aren't!" was said firmly to reassure herself as much as the children.

When finally the plane seemed to level out she turned her attention to passing out scrambled egg sandwiches.

The plane jerked, then began to slew sideways. For long seconds the engines sounded strained. They bounced, fell back, were buffeted severely. Screams erupted from the smaller children.

"You can have the window seat now, Jonesy," Nicholas wailed.

"Keep those brats quiet," the pilot shouted over his shoulder. "They sound like a bunch of banshees going to slaughter!"

Rebecca stared at the back of his head with defensive hostility. "Take us back to the airport!"

Parnell turned around and grinned. "Can't turn around, but I'll be glad to let you out at the next corner."

Rebecca listened to him laughing at his own joke. "You have a sick sense of humor."

By the time the engines sounded normal again, Molly had turned pale. Rebecca made her put her head down, cautioned the others to do the same if they too, felt ill. She continued to reassure them as best she could. She did this quickly, efficiently, lest the captain turn and again shriek some sarcastic remark at them.

Outside the windows the sky lightened from black to gray. They had a few minutes of smooth flight. One by one the children relaxed in the pale-gray hush and ate their sandwiches. Rebecca passed out juice, then opened her own thermos and sipped from it.

Parnell sniffed. He smelled coffee. He'd meant to grab a cup before he started preflight, but what with the hassle in the office, he'd forgotten. He took a quick look over his shoulder. The Hollis woman had a thermos. It stuck in his craw to ask, but—what the hell—the coffee smelled good. "Hey! Can you spare a cup of that?"

"Actually, no. But if you want to pull up to the next coffee shop," she replied sweetly, "we won't mind the delay."

He twisted around to face her. "Okay, I deserved that. We're even."

Rebecca opened her mouth to spew another rejoinder, but thought better of it. Why bring herself down to his uncouth level? Still, when she'd poured coffee into the lid that served as cup and handed it over his shoulder she had to say, "I'm not a stewardess, you know."

"You distracted me or I wouldn't have forgotten to grab myself a cup."

"You distracted yourself." She looked at the empty seat next to him. "Shouldn't a plane this size have a copilot? What if something happened to you?"

"You should've worried about that before you came aboard." He drained the cup, returned it to her. They hit another pocket of rough air. Used to it now, Rebecca placed a hand against the low ceiling and braced herself. Parnell tensed, manipulated the controls.

"Is something wrong?"

"Just turbulence, I warned you." His face clouded. The weather was more unstable than the forecast had predicted. And the plane was gathering weight. Amos had de-iced the wings, but Parnell could tell that ice was again forming on the plane. He was losing airspeed. He adjusted the power to compensate.

"You didn't really talk about danger," Rebecca accused. "You were trying to get us not to fly because you don't like us."

"Still don't," Parnell said, but his mind was on the worsening weather conditions. The storm front had leapfrogged down into the south-by-southwest course he'd plotted. Nature was never to be trusted and it had sure tricked him this

time. A worried expression came over his face, which didn't
go unnoticed by Rebecca.

"You're concerned aren't you? Can we go back. I mean
that seriously."

Parnell shook his head. "We'd be flying right into the
storm." But perhaps he could fly a more southerly route,
ride the Nevada-California line. "We're only twenty
minutes or so flying time out of Reno. I can put down there
until the weather breaks. Then we'd just have a quick hop
over the Sierra Nevadas to San Francisco."

He began the slow turn that would put him on a southern
course. "Go sit down and buckle up," he told Rebecca.

Before he could complete the turn, the plane started to vi-
brate. Rebecca lost her balance and was thrown to the steel
deck. The children sent up a collective squeal.

The plane felt like it was shaking itself to pieces.

Rebecca dragged herself up, her elbow feeling as if it'd
been stung by a hundred wasps. The pain made her eyes
water. With a heart-thumping feeling of menace and dread,
she clung to the copilot's seat. "What's happened?"

Parnell's hands flew over the control panel, then he held
the wheel until his knuckles turned white. The way the
plane handled confirmed his worst fear. "One of the engines
threw a propeller," he said, his face stark. He feathered the
engine and soon the vibration ceased. He tested the controls
again. His heart sank. The ailerons and rudder wouldn't respond. The plane was losing altitude at a rapid rate. "I think
the damn thing has cartwheeled through a wing, maybe
even sheared off part of the tail."

Rebecca swallowed back the panic that threatened to
overwhelm her. "What does that mean?"

"It means we're losing airspeed, altitude."

"But...you can make it to an airfield? Somewhere?" Her tone begged him to say yes.

With the loss of the rudder and ailerons Parnell could go up or down, but he couldn't complete the turn and bank. The more altitude he reached the worse the weather, and in any case the weight of the ice was pushing them down. Even now he could feel the remaining propellers clawing at the rarified air. The best he could hope for was a glide path that didn't end in the face of a mountain. He muttered an epithet. "I'm going to have to set her down," he said.

Dread mushroomed inside Rebecca. "In the Rockies?" She could barely form the words.

"The Sierra Nevadas," he said grimly and turned all his concentration to keeping the plane level. He put on the radio headset, calling up Reno. Static hurt his ears, but he kept talking, giving his position, his glide path. If Reno was listening, static drowned them out. He tried Boise control, then Sacramento. But he was out of Boise airspace, Sacramento didn't respond. Parnell glanced at his altimeter. They were too low on the eastern slope of the Sierras. Sacramento didn't even know they existed.

For a moment Rebecca was mesmerized by the amalgam of green lighted dials, the pinpoints of red light. She jerked her gaze away from the instrument panel. "Can we dump some of the cargo? Can—"

Parnell shook his head. "You've been watching too many movies. Open a cargo door and we'd all be sucked out."

"Can you call somebody?"

Parnell almost laughed. "Sure, 911 to the rescue." They were already in the dead zone, at an altitude that wiped them off any radar that might have been tracking them.

"Damn you! We're going to die and you're being cute!"

Rebecca gasped. As if in a nightmare her entire body felt leaden and immovable.

Parnell looked into her face. "Do you feel like your number is up?"

Rebecca was numb. "We're going to crash into the side of a mountain."

"I don't feel like my number's been called. I've been up against it before. You just got to have faith."

"In you?" she choked.

He gave her a thin smile. "I'm afraid I'm your best hope. Now go back there and quiet those kids, check seat belts and strap yourself in. Heads down." He gave her a sudden look of compassion. "Just leave the driving to me."

He knew he couldn't stop their descent. If a mountain didn't stop them, they had a chance.

Rebecca wanted to take each of the children in her arms, hold them, croon to them. Oh, to end their lives like this, she thought miserably. Pride. That's why she was on this plane. Trying to outsmart Parnell Stillman. Her pride was going to kill her, the children. And they'd never even had a chance to live. She forced a rising panic out of her voice. "We're going to have to land," she said. "It may be bumpy, so we have to put our heads down."

"Are we going to die?" Jonesy asked.

"Nobody'll miss us if we do," added Santee.

"We're not going to die! Put your heads down or I'm going to switch some behinds." It was an idle threat, but the children complied.

No one cried now. They were too frightened. They just waited.

Parnell worked the controls. After one minute, two, the plane leveled out, the three remaining engines strained to keep the heavy plane airborne. He marked a glide path and held the wheel. The plane shot out of the overcast. The altimeter dipped below the ten-thousand-foot mark. He flicked on the landing lights and strained his eyes through the windshield.

Rebecca and the children sat frozen, tensed for the inevitable crash. Above the ragged whine of the engines, Rebecca could hear Parnell talking to the plane, as if it were a woman, sweet-talking to get what he wanted of her. At one point he sighed like a satisfied lover.

Out the window Rebecca could make out trees poking through the snow covering the mountains. As the plane dropped lower, she could make out the jagged summits rising above the wing tips. Her mouth went dry. She prayed. She could hear herself murmuring assurances to the children. She ached for them. Too young! Please God, spare them. A belly-hollowing fear overwhelmed her, took away her ability to think or speak.

"Hallelujah!" Parnell breathed. He found what he'd been looking for as he'd jockeyed the plane through a valley; a flat, snow-covered meadow. It was going to be a do-or-die approach and he knew it. Landing gear up. No time for the formality of a checklist run-through, no time to reassure Rebecca Hollis or the children. He yelled for them to keep their heads down.

The sea of trees disappeared beneath the nose of the cockpit. Relying greatly on his depth perception, Parnell cut off the ignition and stalled the plane a scant fifteen feet above the ground. The plane fell, its underside hit the snow—a belly whop that jarred teeth and bones—it bounced, then took to the snow like a ski, yawing and pitching, picking up speed as if the meadow were a giant slalom course and the best time to beat was Time itself.

The nose cone plowed into the snow, spewing it out of its

path, into the slowing propellers, onto the wings until the whole of the plane became one giant snowplow. The meadow rose into the treeline. Parnell blanched, threw his arms up to protect his face. He had never decided whether he was Episcopalian or Presbyterian. He covered himself, decided he was both. He prayed his passengers survived, hoped God was noticing his last prayer was for others, unselfish. The nose cone lifted on the incline of the meadow's end, the plane slewed, fishtailing, pointed itself at the forest. Then it came awkwardly to a stop, shuddered and slowly slid back down the incline. Parnell lowered his arms.

A sudden deep silence engulfed the plane.

Santee was the first to react. He let out his breath. It sounded loud in the silence.

Parnell turned slowly and stared at Rebecca, ashen-faced. His voice cracked. "We made it."

"Thank God," she said.

Molly threw up.

"ARE WE DEAD?" whispered Nicholas. His unseeing eyes
were wide, his hands going up to touch his nose, his ears,
his neck.

Rebecca discovered that tears were coursing down her
cheeks. She swiped at them. "No. No, we aren't." Thank
you, Heavenly Father. Her elbow ached fiercely. She savored the pain. It meant she was truly alive.

Santee remained rigid, but stoically he was sitting up, as
were Jonesy and Yancy. Molly had stopped retching.

"Anyone hurt?" Parnell asked.

Rebecca's eyes eyes met his. "I don't think so."

Parnell had regained about half of his composure, about
eighty percent of his legs were back under him. All of his
senses went into emergency mode. He sniffed for smoke,
the smell of aviation fuel. The snow must've acted as a re-
tardant, he thought, else they'd have already burst into
flames.

Rebecca wanted to ask, "What now?" but she didn't.
Somehow it seemed enough for the moment that they had
all survived the harrowing drop from the air. She got out of
her seat, teetered to a standing position. Had Molly not urgently needed looking after she would've sat back down.

It was dim and shadowy inside the plane. Except for the
cockpit, most of the windows were blocked by the snow the
plane had displaced as it made its terrifying slide. Rebecca
coaxed Molly to her feet and down the tilting aisle to the

rear of the plane. The cargo had shifted, they wove in and out of mail carts to get to the lavatory. No water came out of the pressurized faucet, she used paper towels.

"We almost saw God, didn't we?" said Molly.

"Almost," Rebecca replied, amazed that her voice sounded so normal.

"I wish we had, I want to talk to Him."

"He hears your prayers."

"No, He don't," Molly said with the utter conviction of a five-year-old who determines all in black and white and nothing in between.

Excitement had activated the children's kidney's, one by one they trooped to the rear of the plane. Rebecca gathered up their scattered totes into a pile and sat down. Parnell was struggling with the door.

"Can I help?" she asked.

"It's coming." He was met by a wall of packed snow. Rebecca breathed deeply and shivered from the sudden chill that permeated the cabin. Parnell went to a box anchored to the cabin wall. From it he took a hatchet and shovel, the kind that folds neatly into itself. He snapped it open and attacked the snow. It took ten minutes for him to hack out a hole large enough to squirm through.

"Damnation!" he groaned. Going headfirst was a mistake. The outer edge of snow was soft and he tumbled fifteen feet down snow banked against the plane.

He clawed his way up again, made his way onto the wing and gaped at the wake the plane had created the length of the meadow. In some places the meadow shimmered darkly where the heavy plane had skimmed down to frozen earth.

A vibration suddenly shook the plane followed by a sharp cracking noise. Parnell was thrown off balance. He lay flat on the ice-encrusted wing, then raised his head. The ground beneath the damaged fuselage was shaking, opening! He couldn't make his brain believe what his eyes were seeing. The hole in the ground enlarged, began to slowly swallow up the tail. Parnell clawed his way back inside the plane.

"Out! Everyone!" he shouted.

"But—" Rebecca began.

Jonesy came out of the bathroom. "That toilet flushes up," he said. The deck tilted and he tumbled backward.

"We've landed on a frozen lake. The ice is breaking up. The plane's sinking!"

Rebecca was nearest Parnell. He yanked her and shoved her out the door.

"The children!" she screamed as she fell down the snow-drift.

Parnell pushed them out so fast one tumbled atop the other into a heap. Jonesy was the last to come flailing down.

"Move!" Parnell yelled as he dove out the plane. He gained his feet and grabbed the nearest youngster. "The treeline," he huffed. They made it to the safety of solid ground and huddled together while their legs twitched and trembled.

Parnell counted heads. Satisfied there were no stragglers, he turned and watched gloomily as the tail and fuselage of his plane sank beneath the cold black water. The water sloshed up to the hole he'd hacked in the snow and began to pour into the cabin. He couldn't understand it. God had let him live only to allow nature to thwart him. He waited for the entire plane to disappear into the black hole. It didn't. But three quarters of it was submerged. The nose cone jutted up looking like the snout of a silvery shark, held there by an air pocket or submerged ice.

"That's the end of Stillman's," he said morosely. When he

got back to Boise he'd have to tolerate one investigation and inspection after another to qualify for government contracts again. It might take years. He gave Rebecca a dark look. She was bad luck, a jinx. If he hadn't allowed her and those mini-monsters on his plane he'd be landing in San Francisco right about now.

"Is that all you can think of? Yourself?" Rebecca asked, torn between anger and the lingering relief of having survived more danger than she'd ever faced in her life.

"Don't speak to me," Parnell growled.

Rebecca's eyes blazed. "I will speak to you. We're in this together whether you like it or not. Now, how long before we're rescued, do you think? What are we supposed to do? We can't just stand here, we'll freeze."

"There's an ELT, an emergency locator transmitter in the tail. It trips in the event of a crash. Signals are picked up by SARSAT, the Search and Rescue Satellite-Aided Tracking system."

"You mean it's like a radio beam that says where we are?"

"Something like that. *If* the batteries are working, *if* it transmits underwater, *if* the signal is strong enough."

Parnell didn't mention that ninety-seven percent of ELT signals were false alarms. ELTs were never ignored, but it might take time to run down which plane, from what airport, might be missing. If the ELT was working, a ground crew could take a precise bearing from sixty miles away— under ideal conditions. Unfortunately nothing about their situation was ideal, not the weather nor the fact that most of the plane was under water and ice. And even under the best conditions, it would take days to coordinate rescue efforts. He scrutinized the formidable chunk of rough terrain that surrounded them on all sides. At least days, he thought grimly. A glance at Rebecca's face warned him not to mention that, either.

It was taking Rebecca a few seconds to register his words. Blood drained from her face. "You mean nobody knows where we are?"

"Not precisely. I guess we're about a hundred or two land miles off course. But somebody will," he added laconically. "Eventually."

"Do *you* know where we are?"

Glumly, Parnell hunched deeper into his sheepskin coat. "Roughly. I could plot it within a few degrees." They were probably forty miles from civilization in any direction, he thought. Which in this desolate wilderness might as well be a thousand. He looked up at the sky. The opening he'd found in the overcast had closed. It was cold. And was going to get colder. "We'll stay near the plane," he said. "On the off-chance Reno control locked in where we went off radar."

Yancy wiped his runny nose on his sleeve. "Don't do that," Rebecca chastised, rummaging for a tissue in a pocket and handing it to him.

"This is good country," announced Santee.

"Stay where I can see you," Rebecca warned him. To Parnell she said, "We at least need a fire."

Leave it to a woman to state the obvious, Parnell thought. "Right. Do you have any matches?"

"No, do you?"

Parnell sagged. It sure as hell wasn't his day. He knew he was going to have to get back inside the plane, retrieve his charts, maps, flares, dye, survival kit, and anything else that might be of use. Muttering a string of expletives he stared dourly at the open stretch of water between the shore and the plane.

"Please don't use that kind of language around the children," Rebecca said.

"Well, geez! Pardon me." He looked down his nose at
her. "You got any better words that fit our predicament?"
The thin-skinned goody-goody, he thought, and was reminded more than ever why he didn't like women. What
grievous error in life had he ever committed to earn himself
this kind of punishment? Stuck out in the wilderness with a
woman and a bunch of kids who needed mollycoddling! He
believed in God, didn't he? He paid his taxes, didn't he?
Hell, he even put on a tie and went to church on Christmas.
He didn't deserve this kind of misery. He shrugged deeper
into his jacket.

"I'll tell you something, Miss Hollis. Don't goad me. If I
was by myself I'd already be hightailing it out of here. If I
hadn't had to worry with your safety, I'd've had time to
grab my kit and maps."

Rebecca put her arms protectively about Molly and Nicholas. "A comment like that doesn't deserve a response. If it's
any consolation to you, I can't imagine what I've ever done
to end up plane-wrecked with the likes of you."

"Yes, well, you could be worse off."

"I don't see how."

"We could be dead," offered Jonesy.

The truth of that could not be contested. "Button your
jacket," Rebecca told him sharply.

Jonesy shared a glance with the other children. Who understood grown-ups? it signaled.

Rebecca slipped inside herself, wondering how she was
going to cope. She'd suffered emotional and financial set-
backs in her life, but those paled in comparison to what she
now faced. Every icy breath was torture to her lungs. Menace seemed to breathe through the whole vast stillness of the

forest that rose at their backs. The long and short of it was their very lives now depended upon an obnoxious, disagreeable, self-centered bully.

Parnell had turned his attention to the lake, anticipating his dunking in the frigid water. He was having to dig deep inside himself to muster all his inner fortitude. Shoot! He didn't even like taking cold showers in ninety-degree heat. At the edge of his awareness he sensed Rebecca's eyes tracking him. She was looking at him as if she'd been eavesdropping on his thoughts. Which she probably was. With a woman you could never tell where danger lurked.

"What're you staring at?" he asked, scowling.

"Nothing! I was just wishing you'd been able to get the plane all the way onto solid ground."

"Would the face of a mountain have been solid enough for you?"

"I wish you'd quit taking everything I say the wrong way."

"I take it like I hear it."

"Well, hear this: don't you think you should quit taking potshots at me and figure out how we're going to get out of this mess?"

Parnell clicked his heels together and gave her a parade-ground salute. "Why, most assuredly, ma'am. At once, ma'am. You just leave every little old detail to me. Why, I'll just jump through that hoop you're rolling, like the cavalry to the rescue." He relaxed his stance and shoved his hands into his pockets. "What do you think this is? A John Wayne movie?"

Rebecca restrained a sudden urge to slap him. "I won't be put off by a display of silly sarcasm. You're the one who put us down in this...this wilderness. Now, if you don't have any suggestions, at least point us in the right direction. We'll walk out of here by ourselves."

"That's the stupidest thing I've ever heard. Look at the sky. Those clouds are fixing to dump snow like you've never seen. You and those kids would get maybe a mile. You'd freeze to death. What do you know about survival?"

"Enough to know that we can't just stand here and argue."

"True enough," he relented, facing once again his own truth in the matter: the icy water between the shore and the plane. He'd have to try it. He was probably going to die. He'd be lauded a martyr, a hero even, if any one of his passengers got out alive to tell the story. He'd be admired for his skill in getting the plane down without running into the face of mountain, too. He would be awarded a tiny, but indelible place in aviation history.

Posthumously.

However, if God decided to take him into His fold he didn't want an audience of children. He called to the boy who appeared the oldest, least scared and most alert. "What's your name?"

"Santee."

"You're the one with Indian in him, right?"

"One-quarter Sioux," Santee said, his dark eyes shuttered.

"Good. It's time to make your ancestors proud of you. See that tree? Using it as your center I want you to count off loud and clear a hundred paces in the snow. Turn around and follow your own tracks back, then do it again, like making spokes in a wheel. You get about a dozen spokes, you tramp along the outside of 'em forming a circle. Then you put everybody to work finding wood, logs and so on, for a fire. Drag it back to the middle of the circle. And, nobody goes outside the circle. Got that?"

All eyes were on Parnell. He felt the weight of them.

"I got it," Santee said.

Rebecca protested. "They might get lost in the forest!"

He sighed. "I just told them how not to."

"I'm responsible for them."

"There can only be one person in charge—me." Unless I'm dead, he thought.

"I'm better able to deal with the children."

"You want to be in charge?" Parnell fixed her with a malicious glare. "I'll tell you where the matches are and you go get them."

"I'll be more than happy to," Rebecca replied in kind.

Parnell pointed to the submerged plane.

"But..." Rebecca slumped against the cold bark of a tree. "There's no way to get aboard."

"Yes, there is. Swim."

Her hands went limp at her sides. "I couldn't. I don't know how."

"I guess that decides the issue on all fronts, doesn't it?" Parnell waved to Santee. "Get on with it." The children lined up single file. Nicholas brought up the rear, his hand on Molly's shoulder for guidance. They tramped off, making a game of it.

"I'll go with them," Rebecca said.

Parnell grabbed her arm. She yelped.

He jerked his hand back. "You hurt?"

"I hit my funny bone."

Parnell took her measure. It was good that she didn't complain about every little bump and bruise. But still, in his book it was too late to allow himself to be friendly. "I'll check it later." He told her what he expected to retrieve from the plane. Told her what to do if he didn't make it.

Rebecca blanched. "Please, don't attempt it if you think you can't make it." The idea of suddenly being alone with only the children, the idea of not having a man to take charge, to save them, caused her rib cage to contract painfully.

The winter-gray clouds were lowering. Parnell looked from the sky to Rebecca. In an offhand way, her concern made him feel good. Except for Uncle Henry, nobody in the world had ever cared whether he lived or died.

"If it goes against me, just remember that in a week, maybe less, the lake will refreeze. Then you can just walk out to the plane."

"A week?" Her voice was almost nonexistent. "How would we survive a week?"

His smile was a grim expression of forbearance. "Well, that's the problem, isn't it?"

The wind was picking up. Rebecca turned her collar up and held it closed. Snow devils swirled, disappeared into the rippling surface surrounding the plane. "What do you want me to do?"

"Follow orders."

"I'll try."

"All you have to do for the moment is spot me. And if...well, you be sure to tell old Amos I said—" Parnell embarrassed himself by almost choking up. "Ah, hell!"

Rebecca swallowed on a dry throat. She realized instinctively that she could not afford to let reality beat her down. Death as a possibility she couldn't consider, not the pilot's, hers, or the children's. She had to cling mindlessly to the idea that rescue was not beyond hope. She had to be practical. "Can you get our totes, you think? My suitcase?"

"You want a change of clothes and lipstick?" Parnell bellowed. "What's it going to take to make you understand the seriousness of our situation!"

"There're some sandwiches in one of the totes. And the thermos."

"All right." He forced his tone to a normal level. "I'll try to find them." He moved to the edge of the lake. Rebecca followed.

In the distance they could hear the children's voices, led by Santee. "Twelve, ho! Thirteen, ho!"

Parnell began to unlace his boots. He stripped down to his long underwear, handing each piece of clothing to Rebecca as he disrobed. Then he hesitated. His toes were already turning blue. Goose bumps covered his flesh. If he made it back, he'd need the insulating qualities of his long johns. "Turn your head," he said to Rebecca.

"You aren't...?"

"I have to." He looked at the deadly water. He hoped the lake was truly that and not some wide stretch of river or stream boasting strong currents that would drag him from the open water and thrust him beneath the ice. Rebecca closed her eyes and held out her hand to receive his underwear.

Like all pilots, most of whom were closet romantics, Parnell had daydreamed of himself in the role of rescuer. Now that the opportunity was thrust upon him, he wished he could take back every one of those dreams. He put a toe tentatively into the frigid water. The shock of it shot up into his chest and made his heart skip. But it was too late now to weigh his chances of success. "I hope my pecker doesn't freeze off," he said dolefully. Then with bravado summoned strictly for Rebecca's benefit, he cast his naked, goose-bump-crawling body full tilt into the lake.

The scream in his throat was seized up by the icy water.

Rebecca had a glimpse of wide shoulders, knobby backbone, tapered waist; registered, too, that his lean posterior was somewhat lighter than the skin on his back, a telling reminder of a once-bronze summer tan. She kept her eyes riveted on him, praying desperately that he'd make it. He was kicking his feet, sending up geysers of water, flailing the surface with his arms. He can't swim, either, she thought, yet he was making progress and she realized that his actions were probably designed to distract him from the freezing water and to keep his blood circulating. She felt impotent, standing there, just watching.

She draped his coat over her shoulders, glad of the extra warmth, then feeling guilty that she was warm and he wasn't, she opened her coat and pressed the rest of his clothes to her body. It'd help some when he donned them again, she thought. It wasn't much, but it was the best she could do. As the cold went out of his sweater, the faint man smell of soap and oil clung to her.

Parnell's head bobbed, his arms seemed to be tiring. He went under the water. Rebecca held her breath and when Parnell didn't reappear she let it out in a scream.

There was a sudden silence at her back, the children had left off chanting. They straggled out of the trees and joined her on the shore. The frightened look on Rebecca's face stifled their questions.

Parnell's head suddenly surfaced, they could hear his sputtering, his gasping. Impulsively, the children applauded, yelled. For one brief moment the captain turned in their direction. Then he hooked his hand over one of the flaps and moved along the wing until he was at the body of the plane. Water flowing over the threshold and into the cabin when the fuselage sunk had knocked away the snow.

Ice was forming on every surface. It took him two tries to lift himself into the cabin.

Rebecca could imagine what strength it must have cost him, for he no more gained his feet, silhouetted in the door, than his naked body seemed to shiver uncontrollably. He stumbled out of their sight.

"What's happening?" Nicholas pleaded.

"Captain Stillman's got inside the plane."

"He took off all his clothes," said Molly. "He's blue."

Santee, counting himself in charge of the fire brigade, ordered the children back to work. "There're some fallen trees," he said to Rebecca. "We can scrape the bark off, to have it ready."

"That's good, Santee."

"You want me to stay with you instead?"

She shook her head. "I'll yell if I need you. Firewood is more important."

"We'll need a shelter, too."

Rebecca smiled. "You're thinking ahead, but one thing at a time." And because she needed reassurance, even if it came out of her own mouth, she added, "We'll wait for Captain Stillman to direct us on the best place to build it. I believe he wants us to stay near the plane."

Santee hurried to catch up with the others, walking, Rebecca thought, as if he knew right where life was leading him. She watched him join the others. Molly, in her heavy shoes and Yancy in her footsteps were straggling. But it was something for them to do. They were participating in an adventure. She envied them their activity. She turned back toward the plane, pacing up and down the shore to keep warm, her eyes locked on the door for a glimpse of the pilot.

PARNELL WAS STANDING in icy water, thigh-deep. He had tried to drag one of the mail carts uphill in the aisle, but it was so water-logged its weight was beyond his strength. He couldn't get to the locker where the raft, its pockets filled with rations, was stored. He was sucking breaths of cold air that made his teeth stab with pain. Think! he told himself. Grab what you can for now. The plane isn't going anywhere. Matches. Don't forget matches. Totes. Suitcase.

The carts had wooden lids. He hacked one loose with the hatchet. He sloshed through the water and carried it back to the door. He loaded it up, then discovered the folly of that. He couldn't shove it out of the plane without tilting it and everything sliding off. Not thinking straight, he thought. His brain was responding sluggishly.

He made himself stop, plan.

Pile everything by the door. Put the makeshift raft in the water first and load it while he kept it balanced with his feet. That would work. Then he'd push the raft off and lower himself into the water after it. Yes. That was better. He'd have more control.

For an instant his eyes fastened on Rebecca as she paced the shore. Not a mirage, he thought, not a bad dream. He blinked. Faintly, he could hear the high-voiced chants of the kids. He hoped he could make it back to them. If not, maybe the raft would float toward shore where Rebecca could reach it. His teeth began to chatter uncontrollably.

THE COLD WAS NOW almost beyond his endurance, his toes so stiffened he couldn't curl them to grasp the decking. Painfully he made his way once more to the cockpit for his maps, his personal survival kit, anything else that might be useful.

He stubbed his toe, the pain was excruciating. He lifted the foot, lost his balance, fell and began to slide backward down the tilted aisle. The steel floor was roughly made, full of burrs, they cut into the flesh of his backside like hundreds of tiny sharp razors. The downward slide carried him into the sloshing water; he slammed into one of the submerged mailcarts. He yelped. Too late he realized the folly of that as the dark icy water filled his mouth and nose. He raised his head, coughed and sputtered, gasping for breath. He used the mail cart for a brace to push himself up the aisle until his head was above the water.

He lay there limp and knew he was freezing. He could just stop here, he thought. They'd find his body. Naked. He didn't like the idea of that. Too undignified. Dying naked in bed was one thing, but elsewhere, a man ought to have his boots on. Or at least his pants.

He thought about Rebecca. When the lake froze she'd walk in and find him. The sight would probably make her go round the bend. He'd be blamed for that, too.

He forced an arm behind his head, felt for the leg of the row of seats, closed his fingers around it and began to pull himself up until he was entirely out of the water. Then, on his hands and knees, he crawled back to the cockpit.

He lay on his stomach to load the raft, then gently pushed it away lest his own drop back into the frigid waters topple it. He gathered his energy, braced his feet against the plane and pushed off.

He gasped, gagged, ground his teeth until his jaws ached but he managed to push the raft ahead of him. His course was erratic. And then he felt the soft thump as the wood slab scraped the shore.

He had made it! A sense of physical release surged through him. He slid back under the water.

Rebecca almost cried with relief when the pilot came back into view. His absence had seemed endless to her. But then his head and shoulders were framed in the opening and she'd watched him loading the raft. After he'd slid into the water he was again lost to her sight behind the loaded makeshift raft. She watched the board bobble, bump ice and slowly come towards her.

When it hit shore, she expected the pilot to rise up. He didn't. Beyond the raft she saw his head slip beneath the surface. She splashed into the shallows, felt the shock of the water as it poured in over the tops of her boots. How could he have borne this cold! Twice! Her stock in him went up. She grabbed him by his hair and backed up, dragging the limp weight of him until he was stretched out in the snow.

4

REBECCA'S THROAT CLAMPED DOWN to hold back a wail of hysteria. She didn't know what to do first. The pilot lay in the snow at her feet, his skin an unhealthy color. Yet even in the extremity of the moment she could not help but glance down at the wide plain of his chest, the concave of his belly and the dark hair at the juncture of his thighs. His was a good body. A body that a woman... She caught the drift of her musing and stopped in mid-thought. Her feet were so cold and wet she could hardly think straight!

The man needed immediate attention. But the raft was floating off! She covered him with his own coat then raced again into the water and pushed the raft until it was lodged firmly in the slush.

The children had gathered round Parnell. Their faces, flushed from exertion, wore stunned expressions.

"He's dead," said Yancy.

"No, he isn't!" Rebecca's voice sounded strained and unnatural to her; her heartbeat seemed to be forcing all the air out of her lungs. She wouldn't let him die. And if he did, she'd resurrect him. She had to. How else were they to live? She couldn't manage on her own. "Santee," she rasped, "unload that board. Find the survival kit, the matches. Can you build the fire?" She had no idea how long before they'd be rescued. "Be careful with the matches."

She bent over Parnell. His pulse felt weak. His eyelids twitched, there were no obstructions in his windpipe as far as she could tell, and he was breathing. She placed her hand on his chest, felt it rise and fall. She pressed her ear to his heart. It sounded strong. So what was the matter with him? Suffering from shock? Exposure? Hypothermia? It didn't matter. In any case, he needed warmth. She knelt down beside him. It was then she noticed the snow around him turning a deep red.

"I think he's bleeding," said Jonesy.

Fighting down her panic, Rebecca made a quick inspection. With Jonesy's help she turned the pilot over.

"Ooooo," Molly exclaimed.

For a moment Rebecca couldn't think, she was cold and numb. The pilot's lower back and rear were shredded and raw, oozing blood. She pushed Molly out of the way. "Go help Santee."

She got her own coat under Parnell. Kneeling in the snow she tried to dress him. It was like trying to drape clothes on a dead bear. The body that had seemed all loose bones was now too long of arm and leg, too broad of chest and had feet that defied even a pair of socks. Then she realized it was her own trembling hands that were defeating her. She instead wrapped him in his clothes, first the longjohns, then his shirt, sweater, his pants. She managed to get his socks on, but still his long legs were bare, thrusting out of the cocoon of clothing. She tore into her suitcase, found her flannel nightgown and wrapped his legs in that. "Oh, for a blanket," she moaned.

"I found the matches!" Santee shouted, holding up a waterproof tin.

"Thank God," Rebecca breathed. She lifted one of Parnell's hands and placed it in Nicholas's. "Rub his hands, Nicholas. Jonesy, you and Yancy each take a foot. Don't stop. It's important you keep his blood circulating. I'll help Santee get the fire going."

"I don't want to do anything, I'm tired," said Molly.

"I know you are sweetheart. We all are. But you'll have to do your share. You rub the captain's other hand. I've got to help Santee, and then we'll have a nice warm fire to cozy up to."

"When are we gonna eat?" called in Jonesy. "I've worked up an appetite."

Food. Hunger. Rebecca saw all of them starving, dwindling to skin and bones. Frozen to death in grotesque shapes. There were only a few of the egg sandwiches left, a six-pack of juice and the odd one from another pack, because she'd had coffee instead. She quickly went through the totes that were now scattered in the snow. She found the blue one that held the food and slipped the strap over her shoulder. "Once we have the fire going and the captain settled, we'll eat."

Our last meal until we're found, she thought.

It was a pitifully small heap of wood that the children had gathered.

"There's a big fallen tree we could make camp under," Santee said.

"Under?" Rebecca puzzled.

"It didn't fall all the way down. It's caught in the crook of another tree. We could use it as a lodgepole to lean branches against."

"Show me," Rebecca said. To her eyes it didn't look promising, but Santee was full of enthusiasm.

"We could build the fire here," he said pointing to a depression in the snow. "And I can chop limbs off the firs with the hatchet to make the sides of the shelter."

"First the fire," Rebecca said. She felt the stealthy invasion of the cold through her wet boots. If she suffered frostbite, she knew that she was doomed, the children along with her, notwithstanding Santee's knowledge of the forest. Suffering such discomfort made her estimation of the pilot go up. That he had had the courage, the wherewithal to brave the frigid water, to withstand... She wanted urgently to return to his side, check on him, see if he had yet regained consciousness.

A snowflake landed on her face. Rebecca looked up through the trees at the muted gray and dreary light, the low-sagging gray clouds. The true horror of their situation came over her again, filling her with an urgency unlike any she'd ever known.

The fire didn't come easy. She and Santee scraped away snow down to the frozen earth. He drew from his pocket scraps of dry twigs interwoven with down and feathers. "And old bird's nest," he said proudly. "It's dry."

Rebecca managed a smile. She knew his Indian folklore came mostly from books for he'd never lived on a reservation; his forestry skill came from one summer that he'd been with a family that had enrolled him in Boy Scouts. His dream was to be adopted by someone who loved the outdoors as much as he.

It took four matches, persistence and long agonizing minutes before a wisp of smoke rose from the ball of kindling. Santee blew it into a tiny flame. He fed it with bark chips and finally, a branch impregnated with damp. "Don't worry, it'll catch," he said. After a moment, it did. Rebecca exhaled a tension-filled sigh.

With careful placement Santee began to build the fire with somewhat larger pieces of wood. "You have to keep it stacked so there'll be a draw," he explained.

Snow around the edges of the depression began to melt. It trickled into the fire, made it hiss. Rebecca's heart lurched.

She and Santee worked frantically to push back the snow with their bare hands. They managed to expose a ragged four-foot circle of earth. The flames leaped higher, the wood burning above the ground.

"I think it's okay for now," Rebecca said. She knelt a moment longer and put her palms toward the flames.

Fire was a human need so basic, so taken for granted in her life. She had never realized that lack of its comfort could be such a deprivation. Her mind flashed to a recent newscast about street people, about their plight in winter-whipped cities; scenes of men and women wrapping themselves in newspapers and sleeping in cardboard boxes. Bless them all, she thought.

She realized how rich in life, how privileged she'd been. So what, if she had not been well loved? Had had a miserable youth, an unhappy marriage? Her thoughts had often turned inward, she had revelled in self-pity. Never again, she thought.

Her feet began to ache, the pain a reminder that she was alive. She meant to stay that way. She'd be strong for all of them. She looked about for a branch from which to hang the food tote. She knew little about camping, but she recalled that on a school field trip all their lunches had been put in a box and stored in the crook of a tree against small and curious animals. Ants had gotten to them, but she supposed ants hibernated in winter. Like bears. Bears. Wolves. Stop it! she told herself. It was stupid to be inventing dangers when there were real ones yet to be dealt with.

Leaving Santee to tend the fire she went out of the forest and down the hill to the lake. Molly was sitting on the suitcase, her thumb in her mouth. Yancy sat next to her, crooning to his friend Scrappy. The pilot was folded into the fetal position.

"He started shivering and curled up," Jonesy said. "We couldn't stretch him back out."

"He said he wanted to sleep," informed Nicholas.

"He talked?"

"I just told you."

Rebecca kneeled down and shook Parnell, calling to him softly.

"Leave me," he groaned. "Save yourself."

"We're all saved," Rebecca said. "We have a fire built. Can you walk?"

Parnell's lids blinked open. Rebecca could see him struggling to focus, to drag himself from some deep lethargy. "Walk?" his voice cracked. "Can't walk out..."

"Just up the hill," she encouraged, putting an arm under his shoulders and tugging him into a sitting position. The weight of his body shifted to his backside. The howl came from far back in his throat. Rebecca was certain that he'd uttered a vulgar epithet, but it had come out garbled, and anyway, now was not the time to chastise him. Pain seemed to make him more alert. Perhaps he could help dress himself. To the children she said, "Each of you grab a tote. Jonesy, maybe you could handle the suitcase? Go on up to the fire, the captain and I will be along in a few minutes."

The falling snow was beginning to thicken. The wind was colder, stronger, whipping down the valley and across the frozen lake. Rebecca looked longingly at the plane. If only they'd been able to use it as shelter! On every side of the lake the forest stretched away in sweeping upward curves; up, up until peaks disappeared into a sodden gray. It seemed to Rebecca to be the picture of desolation. No bird fluttered, no animal moved. And yet, on a Christmas card it would be a winter scene, a thing of beauty. But it wasn't a mere scene. It was a harsh and uncompromising landscape. She felt small, a helpless speck of human matter. Her throat was dry. She realized she was thirsty. She turned to Parnell and began to unwrap the cocoon of clothing.

"Hey!" he protested, brushing weakly at her hands.

"I couldn't get your clothes on you before. You'll have to help me."

Parnell attempted to maintain a modicum of modesty, but he couldn't stand alone to step into his longjohns and pants. His hands shook as if palsied and he had to suffer the mortification of Rebecca zipping up his pants.

"Oh, hell," he said despairingly.

Rebecca looked into his face and smiled. She'd had another glimpse of his buttocks. More than a single layer of skin had been torn away. She could never have done what he had done. He had put his life on the line for her, for them all. He could've stayed with the plane, inside it. "I've never met a man so brave as you," she said shyly.

Parnell's blue lips suddenly flushed with color, as did the flesh beneath his beard stubble. No one had ever thought him brave before, not even when he'd been in the navy. Flying, surviving, those were things every pilot had to do. If one got out of a tight spot, why, one was just lucky. Nobody thought it brave, except maybe one's mother. He'd had Uncle Henry for a mother. And the old coot never recognized fear, much less bravery. Few other emotions, either. "It was nothing," he mumbled.

"It was everything," she replied.

It took some tugging to get his boots on. He leaned heavily on Rebecca and every struggling, uphill step caused pain. He had to clench his teeth to keep from groaning. By the time they reached the welcome warmth of the small fire perspiration was beading on his forehead. He dropped down to his knees, then lay on his side, crooking an arm beneath his head. His eyes closed. "Truth is, I'm beat," he said.

"I'm getting hungrier and hungrier," said Jonesy.

"Me, too," came the chorus.

Santee had dragged up a log. Rebecca sank wearily onto it. There wasn't enough food to really ration, but she wanted to wait as long as possible before they ate what was left of their snacks. Better to be hungry during the day, sleep on a full stomach. Then tomorrow...no, she couldn't deal with tomorrow. Each minute had to be dealt with as it came. She picked up a pinch of snow, put it on her tongue.

"You aren't supposed to do that," Yancy warned. "Santee said so."

"It cools your inside temperature," Santee added.

"Well, we have a fire, so let's agree that we only quench our thirst with snow if we can stay warm." Her feet were stinging. Frostbite? And snow was finding its way through the thick overhead foliage. "Let's all of us change our socks. Then we have to put up a shelter—"

"We can make a fort!" exclaimed Nicholas who was big on warfare. At the orphanage he played often with a set of carved wooden soldiers, their painted surfaces faded into pale replicas by his fondling to discern every tiny feature.

"Let's eat first," Jonesy persisted.

"We'll eat after we've got a roof over our heads, not before," Rebecca said firmly.

Yancy was rummaging through his things. "Everything in my tote is sopping wet!"

They each had only one change of clothing, for the conference was to be only a single day—tomorrow. They were supposed to fly back to Boise on the Sunday morning return mail flight. But now...

Nicholas said, "I wonder if everybody thinks we're dead."

"Who would care?" came from Santee.

Privately Rebecca wondered the same thing. She had been little more than an inconvenience to her parents. Her former husband? He'd be thankful that there was no longer a reminder of his first and failed marriage. "I care! Abigail cares. I'm sure we've already been reported missing. We're going to get through this."

"I'm tired of getting through things," said Yancy. "So is Scrappy."

Molly took her thumb out of her mouth. "Is somebody going to come get us before it gets dark?"

"I don't know." Rebecca glanced at the pilot. It wasn't fair that he was leaving all this to her. She wished she too could sleep, blot it out of her mind. Wake up and find it all a nightmare. "Let's hope so, but we have to prepare against the possibility that we won't be rescued today. Probably tomorrow." She rummaged in the suitcase, gave Yancy her only other pair of socks. "Put these on." She rolled the log closer to the fire. "We'll dry out the others on this." She tried to shake Parnell from his stupor.

"In a minute," he muttered gruffly.

"You wanted to take charge," she said into his ear. "Wake up and do it!"

He nodded his head slightly, but refused to be roused. Bravery notwithstanding, Rebecca began to thoroughly dislike him again. He was like every other man in her life who'd meant something to her—her father, her brother, her husband. Each of them had looked to his own needs before deigning to consider her own. Even then she'd had to suffer their condescension, victimized by their male attitudes and her own feminity.

Her feet hurt, her elbow hurt, she had to build a shelter while the pilot got his beauty sleep. They were lost in the wilderness and she was scared! It wasn't fair. Life wasn't fair! She shook her head as if to jar the thoughts. She'd learned that about a thousand years ago hadn't she? Why so disappointed now? Because she felt so isolated, that was why. She wanted someone to care about her, to be upset that she was lost. She wanted a champion out there in the civilized world telling the authorities to find her!

She started guiltily. She was drowning in self-pity again.

It would be nice to be at the center of someone's life. There! That was better.

She looked down at the pilot. But not the center of his life, the skinny, selfish, thoughtless worm. As she turned away to help Molly with her clumsy shoes, a contradiction popped unwillingly into conscious thought. He wasn't all that skinny. If anything, he was... No! She wouldn't get caught up in that kind of thinking. Not even if he was the last man on earth.

Then it came to her. The pilot might be the last adult man she'd ever see. For her, he might be the last man on earth. The idea of that caused renewed energy to surge through her. Be damned if I'll settle for the likes of him, she thought.

Still, she was ashamed of having tried to awaken him. He deserved a good sleep after what he done for them, after what he'd been through.

A sudden gust of wind soughed through the treetops. A shower of snow fell from the swaying branches. A chunk fell into the fire, hissing as it melted. "All right, Santee, let's get this show on the road. C'mon kids, we've got a shelter to construct."

It took two hours to locate enough of the evergreen firs small enough in diameter to attack with the small hatchet.

Rebecca took turns with Santee lopping off branches on the sides of the young trees that would serve as "walls." The hacked-off branches were used as thatching. In a gully they discovered a bed of black crowberry shrubs and these they chopped for bedding to keep them off the frozen earth.

Molly had long since given up and stayed by the fire, as had Nicholas, for without a guide, he kept wandering into trees and falling down gullies. They were within several yards of camp when Rebecca heard Molly's wail.

"It's not my fault!" the child was keening over and over.

Rebecca dropped her load of branches and raced into camp.

Parnell was outside the meager green bower swaying on his feet, but seeming to lord it over Nicholas and Molly. "What's going on?" Rebecca shouted. "What have you done to them!"

Eyes watering, he whirled about on unsteady legs, waving a rough hand toward the shelter. Smoke was pouring out the opening, gray wisps trailing skyward. "They set the damned thing on fire."

"We didn't," snuffled Molly. Rebecca pushed that log up to the fire, to dry our socks on."

"I could've burned up!" Parnell said succinctly.

"I wish you had," Rebecca cried. "You've left us to— Oh!" She swiped at a tear with a dirty knuckle, the tears provoked as much by anger as fear and frustration. "Our socks burned up?"

Parnell was spoiling for a fight. The choking stinging smoke had awakened him from the best dream he'd had in years. He'd gone to sleep on the words that Rebecca had found him brave and he'd enjoyed seeing himself in the noble role of a champion, however meaningless and futile and unreal. From pleasant slumber he'd leaped confused to his feet, hit his head on the lodgepole, fallen to his knees and crawled in ten different directions before he'd found the way out. Now he was hurting so he wasn't sure if he was on the stony road of life or the path to hell. Did Rebecca Hollis care? Hell, no! All she cared about was socks. He gave her a look of utter ill favor.

"We can manage without a pair of socks," he snarled. Her coat had spilled open, her sweater was unbuttoned, a gap in her blouse revealed a view of great aesthetic interest. Hah! He was a man who could rise above that trick. The tears, too.

"You can say that because yours are dry. Mine aren't."

"Well, have mine!" He plopped down and wished immediately that he hadn't. His backside felt on fire.

Rebecca saw the wince of pain move across the pilot's features. "Keep your old smelly socks on," she said.

The children exchanged cautious glances. Nicholas couldn't share their looks, but the discord between the adults affected his sensitive instincts. "I think we're in big trouble," he whispered behind his hand.

"I guess I'll just put out the fire before the whole thing goes up," said Santee, which brought the two adults back to sanity of a sorts.

"I'll help," said Rebecca.

"So will I," said Parnell, stiff of lip and body. "But we'll leave the fire going, rebuild the lean-to."

He directed them to dismantle one whole side of the lean-to.

Rebecca had longed for Parnell to give them some direction, but now that he was actually doing it, she considered him a villain usurping her authority. "All that work for nothing!" she snapped, eyeing him with one in her arsenal of deadly looks.

"If you're going to do something, you should do it right the first time," he replied loftily. "That's what my old Uncle Henry used to say. Bless his departed soul."

"We're not any one of us interested in Stillman family platitudes," said Rebecca, calling to the fore all the sarcasm she could muster.

Parnell stopped piling snow on the smoldering limbs. "You're ungrateful, you know that? I almost died for you." His fanny stung like crazy, a constant reminder of how unselfish he'd been. He threw it in. "I left some of the best skin I own out on that plane. What more do you want?"

"To be in San Francisco would be nice."

His lips curled down. She was still trampling on his sense of heroics. "I'll bet all your life you've been told you're unreasonable."

"I most assuredly have; mostly by overbearing despots who were forever trying to convince me that they were always right. Just like you're doing."

Parnell's stomach drew up into knots. He'd have bleeding ulcers before he got them back to civilization, not to mention his arse was probably scarred for life. "I'm right because I know more than you."

"You do not!"

"We'll see," he said, turning away to bark out orders to any of the kids who'd listen.

"Lift bale, tote barge, bully-bully," Rebecca said to his back. Her anger diminished when she glanced at her hands. All of her nails were broken. But not her spirit, she thought. In her life she'd survived far worse than broken nails and a grubby face. She'd survived a lifetime of Parnell Stillmans. This adventure—she wasn't going to name it a tragedy—was just going to make her stronger. Give her insights into herself that she hadn't had. She could hold her own. Above

On a Wing and a Prayer

all, she wasn't going to allow fear or Parnell Stillman to rule her.

The lean-to was reconstructed with a small gap at the top to carry out the smoke. The brush collected for bedding was hauled inside. The wood gathered to feed the fire was stacked around the inside edges of the shelter.

Finally, with the storm swirling full force upon them, there was nothing left but to crawl inside and crouch by the fire.

IT WAS CROWDED AND DIM inside the shelter, the only light coming from flickering flames. Rebecca felt almost suffocated by the greenery and shrubbery. It was above her head, at her back and beneath her hips. Small limbs and knotty wood poked up through the cushiony brush to stab her derriere. She sat lotus fashion and stared with dismay at the meager supply of food and drink which she had spread out on the ground before her.

"Everything's frozen," she said forlornly.

Parnell went outside and brought in a small log, placing it strategically near the base of the fire.

"Line everything up on this. We'll watch it. This time."

Rebecca glanced up from her dismay. "Stop baiting me. Burning up the socks was an accident."

"So was losing my plane," he snapped, aggrieved.

He was envying Rebecca her ability to sit. He could not at the moment absorb the torment of sticks and twigs jabbing into his posterior. The children had taken the snug deep end of the shelter, which left him to arrange his lanky frame laterally near the opening, the coldest spot.

Rebecca felt she had aged ten years since that morning. Exhaustion and stress were taking its toll. She felt as limp and ragged as the pilot looked. Had she been certain of rescue within a few hours, even a day, she wouldn't back down. But a wreck in the wilderness was a far cry from a flat tire on the highway where help was as near as the first cruising highway patrol. Even with her limited knowledge, she knew the snowstorm would hinder search planes. They were locked together in a life-threatening situation at least until the storm abated. If they were to survive she and the pilot would have to come to terms, somehow.

"Don't you think we need to stop going for each other's throats? I know the crash was an accident. And...and it was a brave thing you did—swimming out to the plane for matches and all."

"Well..." said Parnell, somewhat mollified, redeeming a speck of his battered ego.

"And truly," continued Rebecca placatingly, "I wouldn't have made any cracks at all if you hadn't been so obnoxious from the very first."

"You just had to say that, didn't you? You can't say one nice thing and leave it alone. You're persecuting me on purpose."

"You're the one! You badger and bully all of us. You can't expect me to just lie back and take it."

They argued another thirty minutes.

Arms hugging their legs and chins propped on knees, the children stared at the adults stolidly with expressionless faces and glazed eyes.

"When can we eat?" injected Jonesy in a small voice when Parnell paused to inhale, Rebecca to form a sharp riposte.

With a last look of umbrage, Rebecca turned from Parnell and attempted to pass out the sandwiches. His hand shot out and closed over her wrist.

"Not yet!"

Rebecca jerked loose. "Keep your hands off me."

A pocketknife materialized from his pocket and he thrust the point of it into the log. "Don't touch the food."

"I suppose you want it all for yourself. Survival of the fittest and all that."

In his indignation Parnell virtually gargled his words. "We have to satisfy our craving for food as well as our hunger. You put a piece on your tongue and hold it there for the count of ten. Then you chew." He cut the sandwiches into bite-sized pieces, dividing the portions into seven.

"Chew egg?"

"Chew! Like this." He demonstrated, exaggerating the movement of his jaw. The kids laughed. "It's not funny." He glowered until they produced solemn expressions. "Chew twenty times before you swallow."

"He's right," said Santee. "It makes the food last longer, makes it satisfying. That's what it said in one of my books."

Parnell beamed at him in approval.

"I can't hold it in my mouth," Jonesy said around the morsel of bread. "I have to swallow."

Parnell reached over and clamped the boy under his jaw. "Count! Now chew...now swallow!"

Jonesy began to sniffle.

"Did you have to do that?" Rebecca yelled. "Can't you be kind? These children have all been hurt at the hands of adults. They're orphans!"

Parnell moved to sit on his buttocks and grimaced. He couldn't seem to come out ahead lying on his side, with his head propped in the palm of his hand. "They can either be dead orphans or live orphans. You pick. And another thing, stop shoving that down my throat. Just because a person is an orphan doesn't mean he gets the world on a string to dawdle with. Or goes around making people feel sorry for him. An orphan's gotta learn to handle it. I know—from experience."

Firelight flickered, casting shadows across Rebecca's delicate, albeit dirty, features. "You were an orphan?"

"Damned right! And I turned out just fine."

"I see." Her voice was carefully leached of expression. She reasoned that disputing his idea of how he had turned out would carry them far into the night.

"Common sense, that's all we need," Parnell said. "Not bellyaching."

Rebecca nodded and picked up a tidbit of sandwich. She held it on her tongue to the count of ten, then chewed. It tasted as good as anything she'd ever eaten in her life.

5

AT DUSK, or what Rebecca supposed was the hour of dusk—her watch had stopped after plunging her arm underwater to grasp the pilot—the sky seemed to open, dumping great swirling drifts of snow. Outside the shelter the dark became oppressive, the snow appearing not white but purple. She estimated that they had been plane-wrecked for eleven or twelve hours. It already felt like days.

Inside the shelter each of them had a space near the fire, taking warmth from it and from each other. But it wasn't at all like sitting in the parlor after supper at the orphanage. There was no Abigail to chat with, no television to watch, no book to read, no toy to occupy an hour. Conversation was mostly among the children. Listening to their low excited voices, she could tell they found their situation to be high adventure.

The surge of adrenaline that had kept her going was draining away. She felt wobbly, fatigued. She wanted to sleep, but didn't dare close her eyes until the children fell soundly asleep. As yet, not one of them seemed inclined to do so.

"I have to go to the bathroom," said Molly.

"So do I," said Nicholas.

Parnell had been delving into the first-aid box, his personal survival kit, and lamenting the fact that he hadn't been able to launch the rubber raft in which was stored several days' food rations, water and most important, a thermal-foil survival blanket. He looked up and his gaze encompassed them all. "You should've emptied your bladders before it got dark and the storm got worse."

"Now you remind us," Rebecca said with unalloyed sarcasm.

"Common sense should've—"

"Well I don't have any common sense!" she cried. "Who would in a situation like this?"

"Cripes. You don't have to have another tantrum."

Rebecca expended great effort to withhold a reply.

"I really have to go," warned Molly.

Parnell dragged himself to his feet, stooping to keep from thrusting through the roof. He ducked his head out the opening. Wind-driven snow stung his face. Visibility was about five yards. He expelled a dour sigh. "All right, bundle up. It's best if we all go at the same time."

Rebecca was momentarily flustered. "We'll need some privacy."

Parnell shook his head. "Damn it, this ain't the Waldorf. Follow me and stay close. I know people who got lost in snow storms and froze to death ten feet from their own front door." He didn't actually, but he'd read about them. He didn't believe in lying unless the lie benefitted all concerned. Or saved his own neck. In this instance he figured both eventualities were covered.

"I take back every nice thing I said about you," Rebecca said as she leaned into the wind.

"I never pay any attention to female chatter anyhow." Parnell was stung. In swimming the lake he'd been gallant, selfless. And almost froze his pecker off. It just went to prove what he knew all along. Women were inconsiderate, insincere and rude.

Rebecca fell in line last. It was a most unpleasant experience. The boys had an easier go of it than she and Molly did. They, at least could lean into the shelter of a tree. The design of the female body precluded that. But because of the dark and the thickness of the forest, she did manage a modicum of privacy. It was too cold to dawdle.

It seemed they had no more gotten settled around the fire again when the storm rose in pitch. The trees surrounding the shelter blunted the wind, but still it whistled a steady discordant note, and above their heads the flimsy limbs creaked.

"Tomorrow I'll fix up a latrine of some sort," Parnell mumbled.

"Thank you," Rebecca replied stiffly, averting her gaze. The snow and forest had not hidden her as much as she had thought! To keep him from dwelling on it she asked, "Can we sleep without our shoes, you think?" She was concerned about Molly. The corrective shoes the child had to wear were heavy. Taking them off was always a relief.

"I wouldn't recommend it." Who knew what would happen during the night, Parnell thought. The shelter might fall apart, or catch fire. In a race for safety, shoes would be left behind. He wouldn't want to put odds on their survival if they had to go barefoot.

Rebecca searched through Molly's tote for the Lubriderm lotion then pulled Molly into her lap and began unlacing the unwieldy shoes. "A few minutes won't hurt. I'll massage your feet."

"Scrappy! I forgot Scrappy!" Yancy yelped. He scrambled over several pairs of legs and past Rebecca. Parnell caught him as he tried to lurch through the opening. He counted heads.

"We're all here."

"Not Scrappy," wailed Yancy. "I tied him to a bush while I was—"

Parnell was nonplussed. "Who the hell is Scrappy?" He looked at Rebecca. "Don't tell me, you smuggled a damned dog or something aboard."

"Scrappy is—"

"He's gonna freeze!" the child cried hysterically.

"I told you about Scrappy," Jonesy reminded.

"I'll go get him," Santee volunteered.

"Stay put!" bawled Parnell. "Just calm down. I'll get him." His eyes rested on Rebecca. "What am I looking for?"

She took a deep breath. "A horse."

Parnell was certain he wasn't hearing right. "A who?"

"A horse."

Jonesy leaned over and whispered in Parnell's ear. Rebecca watched the pilot. He seemed to sag. His face took on the look of a starving man invited to dine on boiled sheep's eyes. His gaze shifted from the panic-stricken Yancy to lock on her. Silently she implored him to accept the idea if not the fact of Scrappy.

"You see why I don't like women and kids?" he groused convincingly. But in a far corner of his mind was the vague remembrance of his own youth and the friendly cowboy warrior he'd often conjured up as a playmate. Though he'd sure as hell never told anybody about him! The little leg he grasped in his hand was thin as a stick. The youngster's eyes were rounded like a soulful puppy's, tears wet on long lashes. The expression on Rebecca's face was no less appealing. Shoot!

He crawled out the opening, stomped around the shelter once and reemerged. Agitated, his face flushed and feeling utterly the fool, he passed imaginary reins to Yancy.

"Here!" he choked. "In the future...in the future, act more

responsible." Sensing everyone's undivided attention, he said, "Hell!"

"Thank you," Rebecca told him, deciding it was just possible to like the man—though she knew there was a degree of rationalization in her thinking.

"Don't thank me! I don't like doing things to get thanked for."

"Yes, Captain," she answered, lamblike.

He gave her a dirty look, then settled himself on his side, and began rooting through the kit once again.

Rebecca watched him for a few seconds. No man that she knew would have indulged a six-year-old and gone out in the midst of a snowstorm to pretend to find an imaginary creature. She decided there was a kindness in him that was not readily apparent. True, he was bossy, he could turn the air blue with pungent language and he found fault with all that she said or did, but if one weighed all that against his actual deeds, he presented an entirely different picture. For all his bluff and bluster he was simply a macho romantic, she reflected, and scared to death he'd be found out.

"What are you smiling at?" Parnell snapped.

Rebecca jerked. "Who, me? Was I smiling?"

"Yes, at me," he accused, all male suspicion.

"An oversight on my part. It won't happen again."

"You looked happy." He didn't want to let it go. He thought she was laughing at him.

"I'm not happy. I'm miserable." She tried to fit her features into an acceptable image of wretchedness, keeping her eyes downcast lest the pilot read the truth in them. For a moment she was tempted to tell him she had his number. That she saw right through his facade. Better not, she thought. He might fall apart.

FINALLY, ROLLED UP in their coats and huddling together for warmth, the children slept. Totes were used as pillows while extra clothing was used to soften the knobby brush bedding. Nearer the fire Rebecca sat Indian-fashion upon her own coat.

The shelter smelled of wood smoke. Under other circumstances, she thought, it would've been pleasant with the wood crackling and the coals glowing red.

The pilot was still awake, his eyes narrowed to slits. Rebecca sensed his gaze upon her. She suddenly felt that awkwardness of being in a small elevator and unable to evade scrutiny by the only other occupant. Which made her wonder what she looked like.

The empty juice cartons were lined in foil. She tore open two, filled them with a handful of snow and put them near the fire. When the snow had melted she used her scarf to dip into the lukewarm water to wash her face and hands. Her hair was a mass of tangles. She brushed it. There was something so normal, so everyday in the act that Rebecca lost herself in the pleasure of it.

From across the fire pit Parnell watched her with a set, tense expression on his face. The flames cast patterns of golden flecks in her eyes so that he could not tell exactly their color. After several brush strokes, her lids fluttered and her long crisp lashes closed, leaving him guessing still about their color.

Each time she raised and lowered her arm one voluptuous breast rose and fell with it. He could tell she was voluptuous because she had buttoned her sweater and the outline was there for any but a blind man to see. The way she sat, the lift and fall of her arm hinted at a languid sensuality that burned just beneath her surface. A weak man would challenge that sensuality, Parnell thought. But not him. He was strong. Then he discovered he was holding his breath; his heart was jumping against his ribs like a caged animal. Cripes! She was getting to him. Before he could force himself to look away her eyes opened and she looked directly at him. She lifted her chin and held his gaze for just long enough and then turned her head unhurriedly to set aside the brush. Before he could decide whether her look was invitation or disdain, she spoke.

"You don't have anything for a pillow. Want to use this?" She passed him a folded garment out of her suitcase.

He debated acceptance. If he refused, no telling what she'd think. First rule in war games was never let the enemy know he had gained an advantage. "Thanks," he muttered and jammed it under his head. Immediately her scent filled his nostrils. Body musk and something flowery, lilac maybe. He hadn't smelled a woman's scent since he couldn't remember when. It conjured up all sorts of erotic images in his mind's eye.

"Good night," Rebecca called softly from the nest she'd created for herself next to Molly.

"Same to you," Parnell replied tersely, promising himself that the next time she began preening for his benefit, he'd ignore her entirely. His rear ached. He welcomed the pain. It kept him distracted from the woman smell lodged beneath his head.

THE SOUND, thick and gravelly, came coiling into her sleep. It continued for some time before Rebecca paid any attention to it and realized that it was a voice, and that she had slept through a night she had expected to be sleepless. Then she also became aware of the stab of cold and the buzz of numbness in her body. For an instant she felt the weight of a huge stillness. The wind had stopped.

The gravelly noise started again. She opened her eyes in the shadowed dimness.

The children lay body to body, not stirring, but snuffling softly so that she knew each was alive. The noise was coming from Parnell. He was on his feet, but bent over. The smoldering coals gave off little light. She had to raise her head to get a better view of him. His pants were down about his knees, and he was plucking at his underwear. All the while issuing low guttural moans.

"What's the matter with you?" she whispered.

Parnell jerked, straightened. His head hit the lodgepole. "Oh, damn! Ouch. Cripes. Mind your own business."

Rebecca sat up. "Why are your pants down? Were you doing something vulgar?"

"That was nasty and uncalled for." He stopped struggling with his pants, dropped down, rolled on his belly and pulled his coat over his head. The noises low in his throat began again, but were muffled somewhat by the coat. Rebecca crawled around to his side. She lifted a corner of the coat.

"I didn't mean to accuse you of anything. Why are you making those terrible sounds?"

"Leave me alone."

"Are you hurting?"

"I'm fine," came in a strangely anguished tone.

"Are you coming down with the flu? Is it your fanny? Let me have a look."

"Hey!" But Rebecca had already lifted his coat. The lighting was too shadowy for her to see much. She put her hand on him and trailed it cautiously over his backside. At her touch she felt his muscles contract, which in turn caused a gruff moan to escape his lips.

"Your underwear got stiff and stuck to you."

"Tell me something I don't know."

"Will you stop being a smart ass? Suppose this becomes infected and you die of blood poisoning?"

"Right now, dying looks good."

"Oh, hush and let me think."

Her hand was under his sweater, resting on the small of his back. It was cool on his skin. He could pick out its shape. Despite the pain radiating out below it, he felt an involuntary tingle of rising pleasure and anticipation.

"I'll heat some water like I did earlier," Rebecca decided. "Then pour it on warm and peel your underwear back. At least far enough that I can—"

"No." There was no doubt in Parnell's mind of the sense of what she was proposing, but he just couldn't see himself lying there, allowing her to administer to him. When he'd been unconscious, he hadn't had a choice. But now... If she was a nurse, it'd be different.

"Now, see here..." Rebecca projected the tone she used with the children when they were being stubborn.

"I don't want you fiddling with me," Parnell said.

His words sank in and registered. After a moment Rebecca trilled, "Fiddling with you? Fiddling with you...as in 'fooling around'?"

"It's been known to happen."

Rebecca leaned back and rested her derriere on her heels. "You're undoubtedly the most arrogant, the most vile, the most unhinged man I have ever met. I wouldn't be interested in you if you were shaved and dressed in a tuxedo!"

Parnell tried to discern her features, but her back was to the fire and he couldn't. She sounded serious enough. There was some comfort and safety in that. "You might change your mind," he suggested, probing the depth of her sincerity. A man had to be on guard against the fickle way a woman's mind worked, or else find himself committed to a life of misery without even opening his mouth!

Rebecca was dumbfounded. The man was so dense he couldn't even be insulted. "I don't even want to be friends with you. All I want is for you to get us back to Boise. Then I hope I never see you again in my life!"

"Oh, well, that's all right then." Satisfied, he laid his head back down on the makeshift pillow. The smell of it haunted him but he was certain of his resistance now. "There's some salve in the first-aid kit. And, be careful."

Rebecca built up the fire, repeatedly filling the juice packs with snow. The first that was melted, she and Parnell drank. The thermos had not been among the things he had retrieved and she mourned its loss. It still had several cups of coffee in it.

Bit by bit she dampened the longjohns and separated the fabric from his flayed skin, rolling it down inch by inch. Parnell put a twig in his mouth to bite down on against the pain. He kept biting it in two and finally just gave over to issuing small gasps.

Rebecca's fury at him stayed with her until his buttocks were revealed. They were so flayed, so raw that unbidden compassion rose of its own accord. "This will probably sting," she said quietly, her hands poised to lather him with the ointment.

"I can handle it."

"Here goes," Rebecca said and began to massage it in.

"Cripes!" Parnell yelped. Her hands were small, yet strong at kneading his flesh and there was that lingering womanly musk smell in his nose. After a minute he began to groan softly.

There was something in the sound of his "oohs" and "aaahs" that made Rebecca stop. She looked at his face. His eyes were closed. His full lips had lost their tenseness. The salve was a topical anesthetic laced with an antibiotic. It was supposed to relieve his pain, but still…the look on his face gave her pause. Testing him, she spread another layer of the salve, softly stroking his lower back and buttocks. "Does that feel better?" she cooed with artificial sweetness.

"Wonderful," he breathed, mesmerized by the first thrilling shock of stimulation.

"I'll just bet it does! You pervert."

Parnell's eyes flew open. He looked at her guiltily. "It was the pain going away. I swear!"

"Men! You're all alike. I dare you to turn over and pull your pants up in front of me."

Parnell cursed his body and stalled for time. "You have a dirty mind."

"I recognize arousal when I see it!"

"Is there anything for breakfast?"

Rebecca spun around. All five of the children were sitting up, eyes round. Her face flamed.

Parnell used the distraction to yank his underwear and pants up.

The survival kit held hard bars of bittersweet chocolate. He rubbed his hands with snow then broke the chocolate apart. "We'll wash these down with hot water," he said.

"I wish we had scrambled eggs and big thick sausages," said Jonesy.

"Shut up," said Santee. "That's the worst thing you can do when you're hungry. Anyhow, wishing ain't never got us anything, has it?"

"Stop being so cynical," Rebecca told him. The bit of chocolate melted on her tongue. It was old, terrible tasting. But as she washed it down she felt energy renewed. She straightened her legs and arched in a slow catlike stretch to release the stiffness in her body. Parnell's eyes swiveled toward her. Her gaze struck his, her brain named the expression he wore as a cow-eyed leer. She held her head at a haughty angle which emphasized the strong independent line of mouth and jaw.

"Wipe that idea right out of your mind," she said, voice clipped and dry as dust. But a small voice at the back of her mind was reminding her of how his hard-muscled back had felt beneath her fingers, how the fright within her had been comforted by the intimate, physical contact.

Parnell looked hastily away. To his dismay, the image of her stayed with him. He muttered something indecipherable, shrugged into his jacket and lunged out of the shelter into the grainy silver light of predawn.

"Are we gonna be rescued today?" asked Yancy.

"I hope so," Rebecca replied fervently. "Oh, I hope so."

"A smart person could make out fine in these woods," said Santee. "There're wild animals to trap and skin and eat. Probably fish in the lake..."

Rebecca started to remind him that they weren't on a scouting trip, but changed her mind. If his ideas occupied him and the other children, that was all to the good.

"I guess I'd better figure the place out," said Nicholas. "I was too tired last night." He engaged Santee in his clock routine to define the outline of his temporary home from where he sat.

Parnell appeared in the shelter. "Everybody out," he ordered, stooping to bank the fire. "It's stopped snowing. We can stamp out an SOS down by the lake." He reached for the survival kit and withdrew the spray can of orange fluorescent paint. Fluorescent had been Uncle Henry's idea. "Better than dye," he'd once said. He'd thought if ever needed, it'd at least carry some shine beyond dusk and be visible from the sky. Parnell hoped the man was right.

"You think somebody's out looking for us now?" Rebecca asked hopefully.

"I know they're looking. Let's just hope they look our way."

"Which is?"

"I'll figure that out later."

Mittens and caps had been left behind in the urgent exit of the plane or lost in the rush. Now the morning air chilled their ears and scalps, chapped their hands and made their lungs ache. The snow was deep, piled in drifts, knee-high on Rebecca, but almost waist-high on the younger children. Already Rebecca was anticipating having to dry them out, warm them. As if to enhance her dread Molly gave forth a phlegmy cough.

When they came out of the trees atop the incline that led down to the lake, Rebecca gasped. "Where's the plane?" Somehow it was a link to rescue, to her past, to the future. She couldn't bear its loss.

"Snow's covered it," Parnell told her, pointing.

Rebecca followed the direction of his arm. She saw it then, the ungainly shape. The nose looked only like a giant snow-covered rock, the wings barely discernible. "Will anyone be able to tell what it is from the air?"

The dawn light cast pearly highlights on her skin and shaded the hollows of her face. Her hair was loose, falling about her shoulders. There was a look on her face of unadorned vulnerability. It was something new for Parnell to think a woman vulnerable. He knew it was a vital ingredient in men, albeit a thing to be hidden at all cost. A too-vulnerable man in the clutches of the wrong woman was a goner. Yet, recognizing the unguarded emotion in Rebecca made him shiver. She was very pale, scared. Whether she wanted it or not, he decided, she needed his protection, from the elements, from fear.

"From the air, it'll look like just what it is," he lied. "Any pilot worth his salt will be able to pick out that nose cone from five thousand feet. Don't worry."

There was an element she had not heretofore heard in his voice. Rebecca glanced at him quickly, but he'd already turned away and was directing the children. "The incline works to our advantage," he was saying. "The SOS will stand out like a sign on a barn."

Nicholas kept marching out on the curves. "Damn it!" Parnell yelled, looking behind himself to view their progress. "Stay inside the line."

"Well, I can't see, you know," Nicholas yelled back. "Get onto Molly, it's her coattail I'm hanging on to."

"You better not fuss at me. I'm the littlest. And anyhow, I'll cry." Then she sat down in the trampled snow and did just that.

"Oh hell!" He signaled to Rebecca. "Do something."

"Well, we're all freezing. Can't we have a fire down here?" Her feet were so cold she couldn't keep her mind on anything else.

Parnell glanced at the early-morning sky. It was a sullen gray. Somewhere to the south or east of them air-rescue teams were reviewing the weather window, charting search grids. The smoke from a small fire would dissipate, be invisible. Once the air grid was flown it might be days before the grid was checked again, if ever. The bright orange SOS might be their only chance.

"After the signal is laid out, I'll build a fire, not before." He stomped his way back to where Molly sat. "Stop sniveling and get back in line." He searched for something to threaten her with. "If you don't, you're going to turn into a wart."

The other kids giggled. Molly began to wail in earnest.

Rebecca rained verbal abuse on Parnell for raining verbal abuse on Molly. Santee crabbed back to the girl and talked to her quietly. Molly's eyes got huge, her tears stopped. She got to her feet.

When the four-foot-high, two-foot-deep SOS was finally completed, Parnell insisted the sides be pounded into a hard icy surface. In the event it snowed again, he believed he'd be able to shovel out the new snow, preserving the signal.

"You did good," he told them all when they were warming their hands at the fire he'd promised to build.

Rebecca surged with hope. The bright orange letters looked so reassuring she silently forgave Parnell the roughshod way he'd hounded her and the children. She moved to his side and touched him on his arm. "What now?" she asked.

The weight of her hand was featherlight. Parnell felt a sudden warmth that she'd touched it. As casually as he could manage, as if it were the most natural thing in the world, he placed his own hand over hers while he searched the leaden sky. It was empty of bird, fly or plane.

"We wait," he said.

6

"YOU KNOW WHAT I wish I had," Jonesy said with a sigh. "A foot-long hot dog. Fried crisp and dipped in mustard and covered with so much chili it dripped out both ends."

"My mouth's watering for cinnamon toast," said Yancy.

"Double-stuffed Oreos!" piped Molly.

"I'm so hungry I'd even eat oatmeal," said Nicholas. "And, I hate the stuff!"

Rebecca visualized the food. Her throat convulsed in a spasmodic swallowing reflex. Hunger was quickly becoming a relentless enemy. Lunch had consisted of a tiny bit of hard chocolate. And they'd sucked the last of it for supper. To fortify themselves against the lingering sense of emptiness, the children had drunk so much warm water their stomaches bulged. Afterward Molly had complained. Rebecca suspected colic. Yet the warmed water in her own stomach seemed to drug her.

"If there's fishing line in your rucksack," Santee said to Parnell, "I could set rabbit snares tomorrow."

"There's some in the plane. Maybe we'll be able to get it in the morning."

Rebecca didn't like the implication of their conversation. "Surely we'll be found tomorrow."

"Weather permitting and depending on how they've set up search grids," Parnell replied. He'd studied his charts. He had the terrible suspicion that the storm had pushed them much father south and east than he'd first thought. He

knew the air rescue teams would chart search grids working
from his filed flight plan. But the skies had remained empty
all day. The logical conclusion was that he had landed entirely outside the far reaches of any supposed coordinates.

He suspected the frozen lake was little more than a shallow sink; dry some years, wet others, for there was no creek
or river feeding into it. Nor could he locate the lake on the
charts.

He caught Rebecca staring intently at him. She'd have to
be told the situation sooner or later. He decided on later,
warned off by the emotional intensity of her expression. He
gave her his most winning grin.

"Get some rest," he suggested.

His attempt at a lopsided smile startled Rebecca. It
changed his whole face, taking the menace out of it and
somehow making the formidable features in his bearded,
craggy face appear aristocratic and sensitive. Had the man
been clean shaven, she might even find him attractive. Now
that was a stupid irrelevant thought, she chastised herself. It
was only that hunger was so unspeakable. It was making
her imagination soar.

"Santa Claus will find us for sure," said Molly. "Santee
said he'd see our SOS and bring our presents here."

"Santa Claus!" Rebecca put her arm around the child.
"Christmas is two weeks away yet. We'll be home long before Santa arrives."

"But if we're not," the child insisted.

"We will be," Rebecca said tersely, and looked to the pilot
to back her up. But his face was hidden in the shadows and
he said nothing. To keep her uncertainty at bay, she kept
busy; she added wood to the fire, massaged Molly's feet, in-
vented a word game to occupy the youngsters for an hour.
They became drowsy and slept. Rebecca tucked her own

coat around Molly. The child's cough had worsened in the afternoon. She didn't want her chilled during the night when the fire burned low.

But Rebecca couldn't sleep. She felt the need of assurance, had an urge to talk. She moved to sit nearer the fire next to Parnell.

"Back at the orphanage," she said conversationally, "if I'd ordered them to bed this early, I'd've had to field twenty different excuses."

"They're tired."

"And you?" she questioned. All through the long gray day, the pilot and Santee had kept a vigil near the SOS. She and the others had been driven back to the shelter in the early afternoon by the sudden drop in temperature. As if nature meant to remind her of the cold, she felt a sudden draft on her cheek.

"I'm used to long hours," Parnell answered.

He was melting snow in the foil boxes and leaned forward to turn them. The foil was wearing out, Rebecca noticed. Managing the most mundane ablutions took extraordinary measures. She had tried to brush her teeth with snow and toothpaste, and found it too painful. A flimsy three-sided lean-to had been slapped together to serve as a bathroom, tissue from her cosmetic case used sparingly. Still, they had very little of anything to go on with. And no food at all now.

"What're we going to do?" she whispered. She knew her voice quavered, knew it revealed her fears. She couldn't help it.

Parnell reached behind him and tugged his kit forward. "I was saving this, but I think you need a nip." He dug around inside and brought out a pint of whiskey. "Not the best," he said of the Jim Beam, "but it'll help you sleep."

Whiskey! The sight of it brought back old memories, reminders of bitter disappointments. Her father's indulgence had been the bane of her childhood. He'd been a charming drunk, but a drunk nevertheless and not dependable. It frightened Rebecca to think that the pilot had that same flaw. In their circumstances a mind dulled by liquor would be disastrous.

"If you'd had food in that kit," she said pointedly, "if you'd been more responsible... You should've had—"

A strange gleam of belligerence began spreading in Parnell's eyes. He held up a protesting hand, "Spare me the lecture. There're some sea rations in the plane. I couldn't get to them. This is my private survival kit so to speak." He tore the seal on the bottle and took a long swig. Rebecca heard him swallow. Ten seconds ticked by in utter silence before Parnell said, "If it's food you want, then food you'll have. I'll go after it in the morning."

The rush of anger died in Rebecca. "You think the lake will be frozen over enough to hold you?"

"Hope so."

"Wait a minute," she said, clarity dawning. "You can't be thinking about swimming again. It's colder now than when we... Suppose... You can't. No! I won't let you."

Warmed by the whiskey, he mocked softly. "There're some things you might stop me from doing, but that's not one of them." His eyes changed to shrewd reflection as he held out the bottle toward her. "Have a sociable drink."

"No thank you," she said stiffly.

"Suit yourself." He put the whiskey away.

"What else is in that kit?"

"A blister pack of painkillers." He paused. "A gun."

Rebecca sucked in her breath. "With bullets?"

"Wouldn't do me any good without them."

"But, why?"

"Fear of fire, I guess."

"You're not making any sense. You're already drunk." She remembered he hadn't shared in the last bit of chocolate. "You shouldn't drink on an empty stomach."

"Rebecca," he said softly, using her name for the first time and liking the shape of it on his lips, "if you have a problem with liquor, don't lay it on me."

She stiffened and paled. "I don't have a problem, but swilling whiskey never solves anything."

"You have a husband who gets drunk and beats you?"

"No. I had a father who was drunk the first twelve years of my life."

"And then?"

"And then my brother was born."

"I guess I'm dense, but I don't see the connection."

"My father stopped drinking because he had a son to raise."

She had never resented her brother, but he had grown up in a charmed environment, exactly the opposite of her own youth. The sad thing was that whatever he asked for, he got. Now at twenty, he had the idea the world owed him. It wasn't until she began to work with the orphans that she'd realized how spoiled he'd become.

"Ah. Your father didn't appreciate you. He hurt your feelings and you blame it on the liquor. Women think crazy. I've known that for a month of Sundays." His expression changed, as if he'd had a sudden anxious thought. "You got anybody back in Boise who'd be raising heck with the authorities to get on with the search?"

"Just Abigail."

"No husband?" He paced his tone with a feigned hopefulness.

Rebecca took the bait. "No. I had a husband. But he was selfish. He found me boring. Anyway, he's married again. He couldn't care less. He'd probably be thrilled with the prospect of my...disappearance. I was his biggest mistake. He doesn't like being reminded."

There was a cunning satisfaction in Parnell's expression, as if he'd known all along which layers to peel back to reveal an inner core. "I don't think you're boring. Quarrelsome, maybe."

She'd said too much, Rebecca realized, and on all the wrong topics. What her life had been was none of his business. "We were talking about your gun."

He shrugged out of his jacket, stretched languidly to take his weight on his hip, wincing as he crossed his legs. "One thing a pilot doesn't like to worry about is being trapped in a cockpit fire. Fire's a terrible thing—not exactly quick, if you know what I mean. That's the reason for the gun." He checked the foil boxes, sipped from them. Held the last one out to Rebecca.

Rebecca scrutinized Parnell, but saw nothing behind the veil of his dark eyes. "You mean it's to kill yourself?"

"To end a horrible misery should the occasion arise."

Rebecca glanced down at the length of him. She didn't know if what he proposed was a strength or a weakness. She drank the water, gathered up the boxes and cached them. "Suppose the plane had caught fire when we crashed?"

"It didn't."

"But if it had?"

"It didn't. And anyway, we didn't crash in the literal sense of the word." With the hope that she'd recognize the skill it had taken, he added, "It was a textbook gears-up landing."

"But then the plane sank."

Effort wasted, Parnell decided, disconsolate. He wadded up the flannel gown of hers that was serving him as pillow. "In case you're still worried, I never drink to excess."

Rebecca averted her face. "I guess I was out of line."

"You're different, I'll hand you that."

The comment begged her curiosity. "What do you mean?"

"You're the first woman I've ever met who almost apologized for being wrong."

"You're the first man I've ever met who looks like a derelict, but isn't—almost."

Parnell grinned. "Comments like that might drive me to shave."

"Why don't you?"

"Couldn't bear up under the adoration."

"You're sick," she said, her tone as chilly as the fingers of cold creeping into the shelter. "All you are is another arrogant male, full of himself. You need a lesson in humility."

"I suppose you're just the person to give me the lesson."

"Not me, I couldn't care less."

"You're breaking my heart." He yawned a long comfortable yawn.

"As if you had one."

"Now that hurts. You don't hear me saying I couldn't care less, do you?" He reached up and put his hand on her shoulder. She tensed, but did not pull away.

"Lie back," he coaxed, arranging the brush and bracken to accommodate her. "You're getting cold. I can see you shivering."

"I'm all right." He was just feigning compassion, she thought.

"You look a bit unstrung to me." Then, softly, as if it were an afterthought he said, "You did pretty well handling things today."

His praise was so welcome that she did not resist when he tugged her down and covered her with his jacket.

Parnell wondered at the gentle streak that had surfaced in himself. He'd never known he possessed it. On the other hand, there'd never been anyone in his life to encourage it or draw it out. "How's your elbow?"

"My what? Oh. Oh, it's fine. How about your—you?"

"Better, much better."

When he thought she was soundly asleep he cautiously slipped beneath his coat next to her. She didn't move; he felt absurdly pleased with himself. After ten minutes he inched his arm across her abdomen. Her head was just beneath his chin, and even with the thickness of clothing her slender body seemed to fit exactly right with his own. But hell, he thought, that didn't mean anything. Except maybe that the whiskey had gone to his head.

He felt a stirring of life in his groin. Cripes! That was twice in twelve hours she'd caused his libido to act up. For a while he basked in the sensation. When it got too much for him to endure he spent a woesome twenty minutes overruling it.

IT TOOK ALL HER SELF-CONTROL for Rebecca to pretend sleep. She didn't dare move, yet her senses were uncommonly alert. The fire crackled as the wood turned to ash, she picked out the soft uneven snores of the children, and in the greater silence beyond the shelter, she could hear snow-laden limbs creaking beneath the weight.

She breathed in the oil and soap and sweat scent of Parnell. When she'd had her fill, she eased her throat and let her breath out slowly. A glorious glow suffused her tired body and lightning quivers ran to the tips of her toes, her fingers, and she thought, I can't let this go on. But it did, and she liked it.

On the face of it she couldn't understand how she'd let the pilot maneuver her into lying beside him. The universal need for companionship in a crisis, she supposed.

No, that was a lie. The touch of another human being, the fact that he wanted to touch her was exhilarating.

Oh, she thought, unreasonably near tears, she'd had such a small, dull life. Thirty-two years of it. She ached for affection. She always had. It was her Achilles heel.

Since her divorce she hadn't looked at or encouraged any man's attention. She missed the sense of belonging, missed having someone to love, someone to fuss over. To fuss at. If a woman had a natural inclination to nag, and Rebecca was sure she did, the pilot was a wonderful target. He had so many flaws, you could pick a different one for each day of the week and not run out for months.

And, he'd never change his ways, he was too lackadaisical. She was as certain of that as she was of her propensity for scolding.

In spite of the wretchedness of the situation, perhaps even on account of it, maybe Destiny was playing her a fair hand for a change.

Listen to yourself, you idiot! she mused. What happened to a brain when the body was starving? Did an empty stomach make for crazy ideas?

She felt the sudden swell of Parnell against her hip and bit back the gasp that rose in her throat. There was that to consider, too. As if they didn't have enough problems!

Crazy or not, it was nice to know she could stir a man to passion. Oh! It was lovely to cuddle, be comforted and feel protected. There was a humming in her breasts, a heat in her thighs. Dear God, she thought prayerfully, how she needed someone who needed her.

Ingenuously, as though shifting in her sleep, she fitted herself more snugly into the curve of his body. She felt the whole of him go rigid, sensed he was holding his breath.

First thing in the morning, she decided, she'd insist upon checking his injuries. It was the least she could do.

"NO THANKS, I'm fine," Parnell said, refusing to look at her. "How about letting me borrow that toothpaste. My mouth tastes like a stable."

She squeezed the paste onto his finger. "You don't have to act shy, not now."

He shot her a glare of high suspicion. Rebecca countered it. "Look, the sun is shining. I'll send the kids outside. It won't take a minute. Supposing you get an infection?"

Oh, yeah, he thought, but supposing he got something else? Like a pecker that stood up and waved like a flagpole. He couldn't take the chance. She was already bringing something out of him. Something he'd never felt before. A tug in his gut. In the light of day, he remembered he didn't like women. And why. Anyway, she'd made him miserable all night what with her hair tickling his nose, and smelling like shampoo and wood smoke. Not to mention curling up against him like she had. "My drawers go up and down like a snap," he said. "I don't need doctoring."

"Hey, Rebecca! Look at this," Jonesy said wonderingly. "I had to tighten my belt a notch. I'm shrinking."

"Yeah, well," Parnell shot at the overweight youngster, "you can afford it." He glanced outside. The sun was casting golden fingers on the snow, chasing the shadows back.

"I found some rabbit tracks out by the lean-to," Santee said as he emerged into the shelter leading Nicholas. "If we get that fishing line, I can set a snare. Roasted rabbit sounds good, don't it?"

"Roasted anything sounds good to me," said Jonesy. "My stomach's growling so much I could eat a horse."

Yancy screamed. "No!"

"Geez, I didn't mean Scrappy," Jonesy said.

"You're not supposed to eat horses," wailed Yancy.

"Hey anybody, my zipper's stuck, my fingers're too cold to get it uncaught," said Nicholas.

"My throat hurts," whined Molly.

"Let me outta here," said Parnell, exiting so fast he knocked over two of the foil boxes.

"Look what you just did, you clumsy ox!" Rebecca hollered after him.

Parnell bent down and talked through the opening. "We're going to be found today. We have to be. Another twelve hours of this and I'm going to be a basket case. Quiet down those kids before you let them come anywhere near me."

Rebecca crawled through the opening and stood to face him. Her breath misted the air. "There're just being kids. Good ones, I might add. They've hardly complained. Whose fault is it that we're cooped up here anyway?"

"Your own. I told you, you're bad luck."

"I don't know how I could have possibly thought you're anything other than what you look like: an unkempt Neanderthal with an underdeveloped brain."

"Oh, we're into name-calling again. Well, lady, have I got a name for you. Tease! Cuddling up to me last night. I know what you're after."

Rebecca's eyes went stony. "You don't have anything I want. I've seen you, remember? Besides, you insisted I lie down beside you."

"I had a weak moment. I felt sorry for you."

"Just go on down to the lake and drown yourself. See if I miss you."

"Stick it in your ear," he said, and stalked off.

In various states of undress the children had lined up outside the shelter to listen. Their expressions were wary. Facing them, Rebecca felt a stab of guilt. They were all from broken homes, abandoned by family or circumstances. She was supposed to be doing better by them than what they'd come from. "I'm sorry," she said. "The captain is just a bit upset. Inside, all of you. Let's get cleaned up and bundled up. I'm sure we'll be rescued today. We'll want to look neat."

She made everybody brush their teeth and hair, switch socks from one foot to another, put on a clean shirt. She fed them warm water and made Molly take a pill out of Parnell's kit. The gun was gone. At least he wasn't stupid enough to leave it lying about, she thought. But he was stupid in every other way. He thought her a tease. Well, he was right. But he'd started it.

"If we weren't already lost," said Yancy forlornly, "me and Scrappy would run away."

"I wish my mommy was here," said Molly.

Rebecca kneeled down by the girl. "She's in heaven, sweetheart. You know that."

"I know God took her. But he can get his own mommy. I want mine back."

Santee hefted the hatchet. "Me and Jonesy can chop wood, Rebecca. Okay?"

"Don't go far, I don't want you two lost."

"We already are that."

"No. The searchers know we're out here."

"Not for sure they don't. They probably think we're

dead." He sounded as if being lost forever suited him just fine.

"Well, we aren't and we're not going to be. Stop talking like that. You want to chop wood, go do it. But Santee, be careful!"

"That toothpaste tasted pretty good," said Nicholas.

Rebecca closed her eyes. Please let us be found today, she prayed. Please.

She kept the younger children with her as long as she could. But the glistening light of the weak sun drew them outside. And once outside, they wanted to play; make snowballs and snowmen. Yancy hit upon using the mail cart lid for a sled. They yelled and squealed up and down the incline, too often getting perilously close to destroying the SOS. They left their shirts and sweaters buttoned up to the top to ward off the cold, but left jackets open for better movement. They were far more durable than she, Rebecca mused and gave up trying to keep them bundled.

Parnell had built a small fire down close to the lake edge by a jumble of bulky rocks that had many ages ago tumbled down from a higher point on the mountain. His company she didn't want, Rebecca told herself, but the fire beckoned and she walked toward it. Studiously ignoring Parnell, she warmed her hands.

It seemed to her they were on the floor of the world, the curve of the land was upward, upward, upward. No birds flew, deer had moved to lower slopes, bears hibernated. Lucky bears, Rebecca thought, sleeping through winter on full stomachs in some warm cozy den. She listened for the sound of the hatchet. It came faintly, muted by the forest and the snow.

Parnell was backed up to the fire, his hands clasped behind him, his head tilted skyward.

He was very much aware of Rebecca's nearness, but he was determined that she, not he, would break the silence.

Rebecca's eyes kept straying to Parnell's wide back. It occurred to her that she wasn't as fearful as she might have been had she been in the wilds with a lesser man. In spite of their differences she was beginning to trust the pilot. Actually, trust!

Perhaps she was even falling for him. What a stupid idea! Just look at him. His beard stubble had grown thicker, his hair was in wild disarray and he still slouched inside his clothes as if they were old friends fallen on hard times. She had to keep reminding herself that they were thrown so intimately together by an unforeseeable event; that the sensation of wanting to cling to him was only natural. Fear was as much her constant companion as the bitter cold.

And the fluttering in the pit of your stomach? a small voice asked. Hunger, Rebecca answered. Still, she couldn't bear his silence another moment.

"Do you think they'll come today? The rescue planes?" she asked.

Parnell turned and gazed at her. He felt his resolution sway slightly. Her eyes were huge in her face. Gray. He wouldn't forget. The cold put color in her cheeks, highlighting the fine structure of cheekbone and brow. He felt again the strange tugging in his gut that had nothing to do with lack of food. If the feeling crept any lower he was going to be in big trouble. Cripes! He was turning into a mewling seventeen-year-old.

Rebecca misread the signals he was sending. "You think we're going to die here, don't you?"

"No, I don't think that at all. There may be no planes though. Sometimes everything is done by computer."

"What?"

"If the ELT is working they'll take a fix, estimating latitude and longitude, then send in a ground crew."

"A ground crew? From where? How long would that take? Parnell, we're hungry."

He didn't miss the use of his name. He liked hearing it. To hide his pleasure, he glanced at the sky. The sun would be at its zenith in a few hours. "It could take a few days, but it's a sure thing." He hoped.

"What about the rations on the plane? The ice? Have you checked it? Will it hold you?"

"Not yet. By midnight maybe." He watched her face crumble. She looked so small and defenseless standing in snow up to her knees, the mountain at her back dwarfing her. He couldn't help himself. He went to her and folded his arms around her.

She let her weight sink against him; felt the warmth of his embrace and buried her face in the shoulder of his jacket.

"I suppose you're just feeling sorry for me again," she said.

Parnell cleared his throat. "Well—no. Not exactly." He noted she fit in his arms standing up as well as she had lying down. Was that an omen?

She moved her head; he could feel her breath on his neck. "What then—exactly?" she said.

"Hell, I don't know." He didn't have any words for it. She was happening to him. He didn't have any explanation for it. But she was looking up at him. He had to say something. That was the way it was with a woman. You had to give her reasons, logic. A reason came to him. "I think it's sex."

She jerked away.

"You asked! I told you. What was I supposed to say?"

"Nothing. Just nothing."

"Damn it! You get stiff-necked over every little thing. If I was married to you, which I'm not, but if I was, I'd quit you, too. You'd drive a man to it! I have a lot on my mind right now. I need cooperation, not a short fuse!"

"That's unfair! I didn't drive my husband away. He ran—as in after every skirt that swished by his desk! He's remarried and he was unfaithful to his second wife within six months of marrying her."

"Came back to familiar ground, did he?"

"Oh, that's low. But just what I'd expect of your type."

"What's my type?"

"Pompous, inconsiderate, vain."

Parnell wished he hadn't asked. "It's obvious you only look at the surface. I'm more than that."

"More of it, you mean. You can just consider us finished."

Parnell gaped. "Finished? What've we started?"

"Everything, and you know it!"

He backpedaled as fast as a frightened man could. "I haven't said anything. Have I said anything?"

Rebecca replied haughtily. "Body language speaks volumes." Her gaze tracked him to mid-thigh and stopped, a gesture that was allusive and unadorned.

Parnell got the message. His eyes went flat, like a cat's. His cheeks went hollow, the ridge of bones beneath his dark eyes appeared suddenly too prominent. "You felt me up when I was asleep."

The accusation rendered Rebecca speechless.

"Well c'mon," he egged, jaw thrusting. "Give it your best shot."

"You're gauche!"

"I don't know what that means."

"Low-down reprehensible worm!"

"Not bad," he mocked. "Not bad at all."

His tone seeped through Rebecca's frustration. Oh, he

was a sly one. Well, she saw right through his ploy. He wanted sex. It was clear to her now. In the business of love, he was just as vulnerable as she. She looked him up and down and nodded. "I see right through you, Parnell."

He eyed her warily. She'd gone calm too quickly to suit him. She had a coy smile on her lips that made him stare at them, note how full they were, which made him think about kissing her.

"What does that mean?" he asked balefully, certain that somehow in the past few minutes he'd managed to shoot himself in the foot while his foot was in his mouth.

"Nothing," Rebecca replied airily and put her hand out to the fire.

Parnell pondered body language. His stomach began to ache. And anyway, he told himself, what did she know about men? She'd had a lush for a father and skirt chaser for a husband. She wouldn't know a good man if he fell into her lap. Saw through him! To hell in a basket. Just because there had been a bit of heraldic activity in his libido didn't mean anything. Considering the condition of his arse, he was lucky to have any! He was just about to tell her so when Jonesy burst out of the forest and tumbled down the snowy incline.

"Hey! Hey, Rebecca! Captain! We found a house!"

7

"WE'RE SAVED!" breathed Rebecca, stunned.

"Don't be too sure about that," Parnell warned in his rich careless voice. "We landed practically on their doorstep. You've noticed no one's come rushing out to greet us."

"Don't be so negative! Every time something good happens you knock it."

His eyebrows shot up. "What good happenings? You mean losing my plane? You mean taking a dip in ice water? Starving to death? Meeting you? Or maybe you mean 'good' as in putting up with the rowdy urchins you can't seem to control?"

Color deepened in Rebecca's cheeks. "You only think in terms of yourself—"

"That's not true. I'm responsible for—"

"A responsibility you'd rather not have—"

"There's no sin in that! I like—"

"I don't want to hear it!" She latched on to Nicholas and huffed her way up the incline where Santee waited and was urging them to hurry.

"I was just going to say I like a bit of peace and quiet," Parnell said soulfully into the empty air.

Molly tugged at his sleeve. "Will you carry me up the hill?"

"No. Stop hanging on me."

"If you don't, I'll start hollering and screaming. I'll tell Rebecca you hit me."

"Why you little twerp..." He watched her poky little face twisting, saw the intake of breath. "Don't you dare, you pint-sized witch!" He snatched her up. Grim-faced and thoughts black, he stalked after Rebecca with Molly riding happily on his shoulder.

The sight of him carrying Molly warmed Rebecca, dimmed her anger at him. "A house!" she cooed when he was in step beside her. "Oh, I hope they have coffee."

"I hope they can point me to the nearest road out of here."

In truth, he had no hope of that, much less coffee. It was possible, though, that he'd put the plane down in a national forest, which meant the house could be a ranger station of some sort; well-stocked with food, cots, blankets. Reasonably, it could be situated on a well-beaten path. If so, he could leave Rebecca and the kids while he hiked out. He might even meet the ground crew coming to rescue them. The rescue team could take over. They'd all be saved. He, in more ways than one. The thought cheered him immensely.

Santee, Jonesy and Yancy trudged eagerly ahead, retracing the footpath made in the snow. Rebecca judged the boys literally were leading them through dell and over hill. After a quarter mile she stopped to catch her breath. "How much farther?"

Santee pointed. "Just around that outcropping of rocks."

There was a scramble to be first around the ice-slick gray boulders. Rebecca skidded to a halt and gazed into the clearing.

Parnell lowered Molly to the path of beaten snow and came up behind Rebecca. "Well," he drawled, "I don't think you'll get a cup of coffee out of here." He surveyed the small dell in which stood a cabin that had long since seen its better days. Long since, he thought, like maybe a hundred years ago.

"The door's gone, and some of the roof," announced Jonesy excitedly. "But Santee and I figure we can fix it."

"I thought you said a house," Rebecca appealed, not wanting to believe in the dilapidated structure before her eyes, unwilling to give up hope of other people, food, immediate rescue.

"C'mon," Jonesy urged. "It's got a stove and bunks all around the walls and a bathroom even."

"An outhouse," Santee corrected.

"We're here, we might as well have a look," conceded Parnell.

Molly and Yancy, with Nicholas between them, raced to explore the new territory.

Rebecca's shoulders sagged as she watched the children run ahead. "I was so hoping..."

Parnell hesitated. She appeared unhappier than he felt. He knew it was a leader's responsibility to keep morale up. He wasn't certain of the best approach. After a moment's hesitation he put his arm around her. Her frown remained, but his own disposition improved at once. "We might find something we can use and who knows? Even from here the place looks sounder than the lean-to."

"Don't go getting cheerful," Rebecca touted, allowing him to propel her forward because she liked the feel of his arm across her shoulder. "I won't know what to make of it."

It impressed Parnell that she didn't make any effort to shrug him off. He tried not to read anything into it. That business down by the lake. She was beginning to like him. She had admitted it—in a vague way. In which case...in which case...he slewed away from the idea before it could make sense and brought his arm back to his own side like a shot. He wasn't about to improve her morale that much!

"An old trapper's cabin," he pronounced, his voice only a

little thick as he began to reconnoiter. He pointed out the rusted remains of traps hanging from pegs on the wall behind the ancient wood-burning stove. The stove too had a layer of rust. Parnell tapped it. "Bet it took a half dozen mules to drag this thing in here."

Rebecca had not missed the sudden change in his decorum, the way he snatched his hand back. She had the presentiment that he had taken flight from a sense of some preordained mystic junction point, a line over which he'd decided he'd never cross. She recognized that there was an elemental force working on both of them. He was fighting it. Well he could battle it all by himself. Falling in love was hard enough— She caught the clarity of her thought and gasped.

How ludicrous.

No, it wasn't.

Yes, it was.

Imagine falling for a man about whom she knew so little and who by his own lights disliked women and children. She was being irrational because she was hungry and tired and scared. That was it. Yet...a very important part of her wanted it to happen.

Parnell touched her arm. "You're not listening to a word I'm saying," he said crossly. "I might as well be talking to a tree."

"I was dreaming of coffee."

"I told you not to get your hopes up."

"I won't ever again."

The tone of her voice put Parnell on alert. "Are we having two different conversations here?"

"Don't be silly," she said and began another inspection of the cabin.

In addition to the stove in the first room, a smaller second room had a stone-built fireplace. There were bunks on two walls. Built head to head. She tested one. It was still sturdy. Near the iron stove was a shelf of sorts on which stood an old wooden bucket, empty tin cans, a cast-iron pot, a fork with bent tines. A rough-hewn table with a leg missing leaned askew upon a planked floor ankle-deep in debris. Rebecca saw the cabin through her dismay. "It's a mess. And there's a smell."

"Want to look at the next house on our list then?"

"Very funny."

Parnell wrinkled his nose. "Probably some wild animal has used it as a lair." He looked up at the holes in the roof that could easily be covered by brush. "I agree with the boys. We ought to move in here. I wouldn't mind having a solid roof over my head tonight. The temperature's dropping. I can feel it." He tapped on a mud-chinked wall. "We'd have more protection from windchill."

"I wouldn't mind having some solid food," Jonesy said pointedly as he picked up and inspected bits of flotsam from the floor.

"Why move?" Rebecca balked. "We'll be out of here today, tomorrow at that latest. Where'll we get the energy to—"

Parnell shooed the kids outside. "Now look. We don't have any idea when an air or ground crew will show up. It might be today, it might be a week from today. We'd be better off here. Besides, in the event that I have to walk out of here to get help, I'd feel better knowing you had some protection from the weather."

"Walk out?" Rebecca swallowed on a suddenly dry throat. "You wouldn't. Not and leave us. Suppose you died of exposure? Or got hurt?"

"What do you care?" He told himself he only wanted to know out of curiosity.

She assayed his tone, the implication; her heart tripped.

She felt suddenly shy of Parnell, yet the very vulnerable side of her craved him, craved a strong man to protect her. Parnell had proved his strength and stamina time and again. She couldn't discount it. She now found him exciting and appealing and having substance beyond the surface. It did no good to attribute the thoughts to hunger or exhaustion. She and he were becoming united in more than the cause of survival. She wondered if he guessed.

"Care?" she replied evenly. "Of course I care—about all of us."

Parnell didn't like her answer. It was too generic. Perversely, he pushed for one more to his liking, one to soothe his vanity. "But earlier you said—"

"No I didn't."

"Yes, you did."

"You misunderstood."

"You're playing games with me."

"Surviving a plane crash and being lost in the wilderness is a game?"

"Now you sound combative. I don't understand you. We were getting along good."

"When?"

He looked at her through slitted lashes. "Have it your way. Just remember, I'm in charge."

"How can I not? You remind me with every other breath."

Parnell ignored the dripping sarcasm. "We're moving in here."

"Whatever you say."

"Good. I say swab the decks."

"Swab the who?"

"That's Navy lingo," he said snidely. "It means clean the place up. Make everything shipshape."

"You're insufferable. I'm more than a housekeeper, you know."

"Really? Like to prove it?" He dealt her a fraudulent grin that stretched to reveal strong teeth made whiter by contrast to his dark beard stubble.

She looked at him from beneath her lashes and disposed of his leer. "Why certainly, Captain Stillman. Right after high tea."

"Cripes. A guy can't even make a joke around you," he complained in an attempt to save face. "I'm the boss, see. I'm supposed to have the last word."

"Well, all right. Have it."

He couldn't think of one. Instead, he focused on her wide, full-lipped, unlipsticked mouth. It entered his mind that a man could go to heaven nibbling on her lower lip. It also entered his mind that either you got them, or you let them get you. He had the unhappy feeling he was on his way to being had. And he was hardly putting up a fight. Two females in the group, he thought, and both of them had outmaneuvered him. He made a derisive noise. "Never mind."

"Your problem is you think a woman ought to fall over at the knees every time you open your mouth."

"Boy, are you off the mark!" He turned away and yelled for Jonesy and Santee.

"Stop screaming at those kids."

"They're out of sight. What do you want me to do, whisper?"

"Don't bully."

"Next you'll be insisting I walk around on my tippy toes."

"You're hopeless," she said. Leaving him standing on the threshold she moved deeper into the cabin to see what could be salvaged.

Parnell slipped around to the side of the cabin and leaned against it a moment, in hopes of retrieving his mental bearings.

He had never been more nervous. He hadn't spent so much time in a woman's company since he couldn't remember when. It was telling on him. He was feeling things. Like protective. Like, maybe Rebecca needed him. He was thinking about have sex with her all the time now. He tried to shy away from the idea. His feet were cold. His bum hurt. Think about that. No, better not think on any area below the belt. It was all her fault. She should never have snuggled up to him last night and stuck her head under his chin. She did it on purpose.

Nicholas came around the corner and plowed into him.

"Hey! Watch where you're going."

"I can't."

Parnell winced. "Sorry."

"That's okay. I'm just getting the feel of the cabin. What side am I on?"

"East."

"Front door faces north then?"

"Right."

"Where's the bathroom?"

Parnell judged the distance. "Twenty-five paces downhill on the diagonal from the southeast corner."

Nicholas looked confused. "Tell me on the clock."

"Oh. From the corner of the cabin the outhouse is at eleven o'clock."

"Got it," Nicholas said.

Parnell took the child's arm. "C'mon, I'll take you."

The boy jerked away. "I can do it myself."

"Independent little bugger."

"Have to be," Nicholas said with brevity. He groped his way to the corner and began slowly counting off the steps. Parnell watched until he'd reached the outhouse and disappeared inside. Poor little sod, he thought with a bit of grudging admiration, wishing he could do something nice for the boy. Hell! Now even the kids were getting under his skin. No doubt in some sly way, Rebecca put them up to it.

He spied the older boys horsing around atop the boulders and whistled for them.

As DARKNESS APPROACHED Rebecca wondered, not for the first time that day, how the pioneer women and settlers had managed day in and day out. It wasn't so much the loss of plumbing and electricity she missed, though she longed for a bath, it was the small everyday items one took so much for granted, like brooms, dustpans and toilet paper. She was improvising, but not without hard thought and some difficulty.

A small tree with a wealth of bare limbs had been made into a sweep to clear sixty years or more of spider webs, mice and bird nests from the chimney in the smaller room. A cheery fire burned now and the younger children sprawled drowsily in front of it. Santee was out with Parnell gathering more wood.

And they were going to need it. Little of the warmth from the fireplace penetrated into the room in which she worked. The temperature had continued to fall all afternoon and sullen clouds scudding out of the north had blocked out the sun. Parnell had forecast more snow. Already scattered flakes had begun to fall.

The busy work had a side effect in that it had kept them

all from thinking of hunger. And of a rescue that had never come. For a moment Rebecca stood in the open doorway. Nearby was a pile of leafy cedar limbs set aside to fill up the opening once they were all in for the night. She enjoyed the fragrance of the freshly chopped wood, but the air chilled her ears and scalp and drove her back inside. At full dark Parnell and Santee returned.

"There's nothing like coming home to a snug house," said Parnell approvingly as he warmed his cold-reddened hands at the fire.

"We saw a deer," said Santee. "It came down to the lake to drink where we'd chopped a hole in the ice to put the wooden bucket to soak. The captain thinks he can get a shot at it if we build a blind."

"Kill a deer?" Rebecca said, not liking the idea. Putting the wooden bucket in the lake to swell the wood and make tight against its wooden straps had been Santee's suggestion. Rebecca did approve of that. And she was proud of Santee. He was proving himself as he'd never had the opportunity to do in the city. He needed a woodsman for a father, she thought. She'd put that in his file when they got back. When they got back. She found herself wondering, what if no one comes? Impossible. Someone has to come. But what if no one comes?

"He's stringy lookin'," said Parnell. "Probably an old bull that was turned out of his harem. And don't count on it. I'm a better pilot than I am a marksman."

Then the import of what Santee had said struck Rebecca. "You had to chop the ice? Is the lake frozen solid again?"

"On the surface. Not solid. But it's getting there. I think in a few more hours."

"But it's pitch black out there!"

"I've given some thought to that." If he broke through the

ice and went under it...he didn't like the odds, but all of them were becoming lethargic from lack of food. The faces of the younger children were pinched, even in sleep, he thought, as he gazed at the two who were snoozing under Rebecca's coat upon the bunk nearest the fire. "We can build up a bonfire near the lake edge. That'll help guide me."

"You're certain you have food on the plane?" she asked, needing reassurance, aware of the fact that he was less confident of early rescue now and was planning for a longer duration.

"Positive," he replied trying to recall the list of rations. He'd glanced at them once before he'd deflated and stored the Air Force surplus A-3 raft. The labels on the food packets then had sounded dry and repulsive. "I remember malted milk tablets, powdered eggs, bacon paste, instant coffee—"

Rebecca's face lit up. "Instant coffee? Really?" In her sleep, Molly coughed. Rebecca went at once to feel the child's brow. "I think she's running a temperature." She moved Yancy to another bunk, lest whatever Molly might have was catching.

"Keep her warm and dry," Parnell offered. "Especially her feet," he added, thinking of his own. The cold and damp had crept through his boots. He was going to have to borrow his socks back from Rebecca to make the attempt to reach the plane tonight. Aching and trying not to show it, he sat down in front of the fire. He wished now that he'd let Rebecca medicate his arse that morning. It was prickly as heck again, shooting pain up his spine. Just thinking of her hands touching him caused a pleasant shiver; an antidote to the pain.

Rebecca urged the older boys, not without some argument, to lie down on the bunks and rest. Santee balked until she assured him she'd wake him when it came time to hike down to the lake. For a while she sat in the shadow of Molly's bunk, listening to the girl breathe.

Once all the children were asleep, the cabin offered more privacy than Rebecca anticipated.

Alight by the glow of the fire, Parnell seemed an island to himself and very much alone. His movements were stiff as he bent to unlace his boots. He was in pain. She could tell. She couldn't bear it that he hurt.

That decided it. She settled the matter in her mind's eye. Settled it in her heart where her realistic dreams and aspirations lay. She was falling in love with an unkempt, cynical, nettlesome rogue who was still hung up on the ache of old wounds from a long-past failed marriage.

But then, if she suddenly became sweet and lovable, he'd confront her with a dense intractable funk as he had earlier. Her only course was to keep an acid tongue until he was caught beyond defense. But not too acid. He was bound to have weak moments during which the right words, the right kind of gesture would not go amiss.

And one of those moments was now.

She glided quietly to him and knelt down. "Let me help you."

Parnell, tired to the bone, acquiesced. "Might not be a pleasant sight," he warned.

"I know. I made the boys dry out their shoes and socks this afternoon. Their feet were wrinkled from wet snow." Parnell's feet, without the protection of his woolen socks, were far worse; frozen and bloodless. Rebecca swallowed back a lump in her throat. "You should've said something! Damn you! You don't have to be brave on my account." She took the T-shirt that now served as washcloth, rinsed it in the cast-iron pot of warm water and began to wash, then massage his feet.

"This is embarrassing," Parnell told her; it was almost Biblical. On the other hand, he found it highly erotic.

When feeling began to surge back into his numbed limbs an involuntary groan escaped him. Rebecca glanced sharply at him, then softened her expression, deciding she needed to use every wile she possessed to get inside him. Her hand moved above his ankles to his calves.

"Better?" she asked.

He sighed. "Truly, that feels wonderful." Her fingers were magical. There was a tingling throughout his body. His heart thundered. But he couldn't accustom himself to the sudden excess of emotion. "Maybe you ought to stop," he said, voice thick.

"Why don't you take off your jacket and lie down on it?"

"Then what?" He gazed at her with a varlet's eye of suspicion.

"I'll massage your back and neck. You have to be sore from sleeping on brush. I was," she added to make her suggestion appear ordinary and plausible. She wished to touch him all over; an impractical wish at the moment with all the children sleeping nearby.

"Why do you want to do that for me?" No one had ever paid him such intimate attention.

"Oh," she replied, presenting an arabesque of indifference. "To pass the time, to keep my mind off of how hungry I am."

Parnell told himself he would get up later feeling unaffected, feeling right and sane. He lay down on the sheepskin lining. But when Rebecca's cool hands slid under his shirt to knead his flesh, all he felt was short of breath and giddy.

He bit down on his tongue to keep from emitting exclamations of pleasure. Rebecca leaned so near his ear that he felt her warm breath. The giddiness increased. "Do relax," she urged in a whisper.

Not in a thousand years, Parnell thought. Not with this coming down on him. His response to her was visceral. Lust, not love. A familiar panic rose in him. He knew all about love and loving. It left you open for rejection, not to mention domination. And the more you loved somebody, the more those things hurt. Damn! What was she doing? Kissing his ear it felt like. Goose bumps erupted along his arms. "Hey!" he crooned, fighting the quaver in his voice. "Stop...that."

To Rebecca his protest sounded as if he were begging her to continue. Her tongue darted in his ear. "You don't like—"

"I do, but—" He was breathing heavily.

"But what?" she asked, and trailed her fingertips down his spine. He shivered.

"I'm getting excited. That's as nice a way I can think to put it. A certain part of me is about to explode."

"I don't mind," Rebecca said, driven by the desire to experience the full gamut of feelings that went with having the man she wanted wanting her.

Parnell twisted slightly out of her reach. Firelight tinged her flushed complexion a burnt sienna, her hair was in a tangle. It made her appear exotic and lush. He glanced quickly about the cabin. Every last one of the barbarians was soundly asleep. Just when he'd welcome an interruption, an argument or fisticuffs. Undependable little beasts.

"Listen," he said, "I don't think what you propose is ethical. Under the circumstances, I mean."

"I'm not proposing anything," returned Rebecca innocently. Retreating somewhat, she wound her arms about her legs and rested her chin on her knees. "You felt good. I got carried away for a moment—"

Parnell's skepticism knew no bounds. "In my book what you just did is called foreplay. Sexual foreplay."

A telltale blush colored Rebecca's cheeks. She had to rein in. "You misunderstood."

"Signals like that I don't misunderstand."

It was bluff or bait. She baited. "You must admit, you're a fine figure of a man. I imagine you get a lot of attention and flattery."

He never got any. He shrugged. "Sometimes. When I get away from the airport." Which was seldom. Or when he shaved and revealed his dimples, a thing he wasn't inclined to do until his beard got itchy. He looked at her soberly. "You weren't flirting with me?"

"No. Oh, no. I didn't mean to. I was admiring you."

His ego caught and flared. "Well, that's all right, then." He felt a sudden obligation to return the compliment. "You're not bad looking yourself."

Rebecca lowered her lashes, her smile, a mixture of seduction and reticence. "Thank you." She stretched, arms high, back arched; a shamefully provocative display of herself. And she knew it. But in the past she'd overthought scores of decisions, missing opportunities. Parnell was the man for her. No wiffle-waffling about it. Therefore it followed, didn't it? He had to fall in love with her. That meant she'd have to make a lasting impression upon him. Very lasting, so lasting that once they'd returned to Boise, his impressions of her would intensify, not wane. "We'd better get some rest, don't you think?" She lowered her arms and began to remove her boots.

Parnell was reluctant to agree. She might want to lie

down next to him. He wouldn't be able to keep himself under control after the way she kept flaunting herself.

"You're not thinking about taking off your clothes...?" he blurted.

"What's wrong with you? I'm just going to dry your socks! You'll need them out on the lake. I have some knee-high nylons I can wear instead." There were iron hooks embedded in the mud mortar between the stones of the fireplace, she hung the socks on them.

"I'll just stay here by the fire and snooze," he said, fishing for where she meant to sleep.

"I'll bunk down with Molly, make sure she stays warm. You'll wake me when it's time to try the ice?"

"Right."

Rebecca got as comfortable as the hard slats allowed. She'd done it, she thought. She'd been more forward and brazen than she'd believed possible. She had Parnell's attention now. She was certain of that.

But was it a forever kind of thing? she wondered. She was under pressure and people who were under pressure did crazy things. As for all their fussing back and forth—well, when one is scared, as she was, one took that fear out on whomever was around. Parnell was around. Eyes shuttered, thoughts growing vague, she watched him at the hearth until at last she slept, disturbed only by the rumblings of her empty stomach.

LYING ON HIS SIDE in front of the fire with his head resting on his bent elbow, Parnell's mind was busy looking for a reasonable explanation for Rebecca's behavior. She could deny it into the hereafter, he thought, but she must've felt him up while he slept last night. Must've! He couldn't figure anything else for the sly change in her attitude toward him.

He knew one thing as fact: women were the strangest creatures God had a hand in making. One minute they hated you and the next... He caught his breath. He wouldn't consider that even if she hired a skywriter to tell the world!

Just to indulge himself, he closed his eyes and tried to imagine what his life might be like with a woman as comely as Rebecca at his side. No mental picture materialized. The idea was so foreign, so beyond the realm of possibility, so frightening, his mind stayed blank.

He'd have to watch what went on, he decided. He'd handle it with a bit of himself, but he'd keep the rest of himself in reserve. Any woman who took his attentions to her as something more than a willingness to pass a short time pleasurably had another think coming.

Including and most especially, Rebecca Hollis!

8

IT HAD BEGUN TO SNOW in earnest and there was no moon. Parnell walked ahead, bent low into the wind, and Rebecca could only just see the outline of his figure against the snow. Santee brought up the rear. Rebecca measured her steps. She was weary and weak from hunger. The deep winter darkness enclosed them. It was an eerie feeling. She shivered as much from the odd sensation as from the cold. She guessed the temperature was well below zero.

At the lake's edge Parnell stirred the embers of the fire and after some coaxing, brought it to life. The wind blew away its warmth. Rebecca beat her arms and stamped her feet to keep warm, but again, the howling wind blew away any warmth she managed to work up. "I'm freezing!"

"I warned you," Parnell said. "Go back to the cabin."

"I'm staying."

"You don't have to be gutsy to the point of death, you know."

"I couldn't bear the suspense—waiting in the cabin. The not knowing if you made it or if you didn't."

He pulled her closer to the fire. "I just might get used to you worrying about me."

His nearness reminded her of what her healthy body yearned for. She smiled and shook her head. Parnell moved off to inspect the ice.

Santee took the wooden bucket from the lake. In the firelight, he examined it, pronouncing it free of leaks. "Now we can haul water from the lake instead of melting snow."

"That's good, Santee. You've really come into your own. I don't think we could've made it this long without you and your smart thinking."

"The captain's pretty smart—"

"It was your idea to soak the bucket. He said to burn it."

"I just read about it somewhere," he mumbled.

"I guess I'll try it," Parnell said.

"I'll go with you," Rebecca said.

"Like hell. Suppose the ice doesn't hold?"

"Two have a better chance. We'd have each other's help."

"Yes, but if we were both drowned, the kids couldn't make it alone." He glanced at the SOS. It had lost its luminosity. Snow flurries were beginning to dim the orange-painted troughs.

"Let's wait until daylight. A few more hours of being hungry won't hurt. We're getting used to it."

"There's a blizzard coming, Rebecca. Look at the way that wind's gusting. It's picked up a few knots just since we've gotten down here." He suspected a few more hours without food would weaken him beyond measure. The warmed water they'd been drinking offered no sustenance from which his body could draw energy. It'd been more than three days since he'd had a hot meal. He turned his collar up. "I'm going."

"Wait!" Rebecca insisted.

"For what?"

She reached up and hugged his neck, buried her face in his chest. "Good luck. Be careful."

He held her tightly for a moment, thinking how nice it was to have someone worry about him. "I'll be fine. Look, if the lake's frozen all the way out to the plane we're only talking about twenty minutes. No need to make a big deal out of it."

Rebecca and Santee followed him a few feet onto the ice. Parnell, gesturing with the hand axe, made them turn back. The wind sang, the snowfall thickened, visibility dropped to a few yards. He was soon out of sight. Rebecca and Santee were soon forced to move from the ice and hunker down by the fire on the embankment.

Snow swirled and piled up around them. The fire hissed. More and more snow fell, blowing into their eyes and ears and down their necks. In half an hour they were both shaking with cold, teeth rattling.

"Oh, why doesn't he come back?" Rebecca wailed.

"We need two fires," Santee said, teeth chattering. "We can sit between them."

It wasn't the cold so much that slowed the building of the second fire, but hunger. She imagined she could feel the blood slowing in her veins. She crawled around on all fours gathering the wood, dragging it back for the second fire. *If I can barely move*, she thought miserably, *how must it be with Parnell?*

PARNELL WAS ELATED. The ice was holding.

The jutting nose of the plane had long since been covered with ice and snow. White against white, it had no definitive shape. When the wind whipped up snow flurries and tossed them about the frozen surface of the lake, the plane became almost invisible. He stumbled over the wingtip, which led him to the plane's bulk.

A vague smell greeted him as he stepped inside, but his brain didn't go so far as to identify it. He was preoccupied with trying to discern shapes in the pitch-black of the plane's interior. Wishing he had a flashlight, he moaned.

The emergency generator! He felt his way into the cockpit, found the switch with numbed fingers on the control panel. The lights came on. He sat in the pilot's seat for a moment. It was like coming home. He tried the radio. Nothing. The lights flickered, dimmed. He moved quickly to reconnoiter the cargo hold.

On the row of passenger seats he saw the thermos, a pair of gloves... He marked them for retrieval on his way out.

The view of the cargo made him sag. Mail carts were piled atop one another. The ones on the bottom were locked solidly into ice. The same water that had frozen to allow him safe passage was also frozen inside the plane. He could just make out the top portion of the locker where he'd stored the raft. Straining, he pulled several carts from atop one another, lined them up and crawled on top of them, going as deep into the rear of the plane as he could.

The wind battered the downed plane and whistled through the interior, the frame creaked. The lights flickered again. He held his breath. They stayed on. He wedged himself close to the walls and peered down. The bottom half of the locker door was blocked by submerged mail carts that were frozen into place. It'd take hours to hack through the ice to dislodge the carts and free the door. He shook his head. Outside the storm was increasing in intensity. Time was of the essence now, for Rebecca and Santee were exposed to the elements.

Quickly he rummaged through the twin overhead lockers. The first gave up his navy flight bag, two rolls of toilet paper, a stack of one-ounce bars of lavatory soap; the second, a jar of salt tables, a grease gun, a screwdriver. No food. But he had a change of clothing and his own toothbrush in the flight bag. The glum thought came that if he starved or froze to death, at least he could be buried clean.

He shoved everything into the bag and crawled back the way he'd come.

He switched off the emergency generator and was debating whether or not to close and latch the door when his brain recognized the smell.

HE REACHED OUT and tugged at Rebecca's arm. There was no response. He tugged again and she didn't move. "Rebecca!" he yelled, shaking her.

She hardly stirred, but mumbled something he could not hear for the wind. Parnell went on shaking and yelling until Rebecca woke up, angry.

"Leave me alone. Leave me alone."

"What're you trying to do? Kill yourself? Get up!"

"I'm sleepy," she insisted.

"You should never have given in to the temptation to sleep!"

Santee had been more easily aroused, perhaps because of his youth, or excitement that kept adrenaline pouring into his system. Parnell turned on him. "You were supposed to keep each other awake, keep the fire going." He kicked at the embers. Sparks flew, then scattered in the face of the blizzard.

"We didn't mean to sleep. We were just trying to keep warm."

Parnell found his heart pounding in panic. If Rebecca died... The thought wasn't one he cared to dwell on. He brushed snow from her face, her hair, then dragged her, protesting, to her feet.

"I'm terribly hungry," she said, slurring her words.

"I know. I'll help you walk." He put an arm around her, lifted his flight bag with the other. "Santee, you take that box."

Uphill and against the wind, progress was slow. They kept sliding back. Parnell drew upon language like the Navy wordsmith he was. The growled epithets had an effect on Rebecca. She moved her feet. In the shelter of the forest, drifts piled up against rocks and trees. Parnell lost the path. Half-carrying, half-dragging Rebecca, he crashed through undergrowth. It took most of an hour to locate the cabin. Santee collapsed at the base of the great gray boulders in the clearing. After Parnell placed Rebecca on the hearth and shoved new wood on the fire, he went back for the boy.

Stumbling blindly he made a second trip for the box, then forced himself to take time to pull the branches back over the opening. He knew the blizzard would soon pile snow against them and seal the cabin off from the world.

REBECCA WOKE UP with a start. "What's wrong?" she called out.

Molly bent over and whispered into her ear. "The captain's mad. He's trying to fix the stove. I want to sit next to you."

"Mad?" Not yet alert, Rebecca coughed and dragged herself to a sitting position. "Mad at who?"

Parnell materialized before her. His face and beard were streaked with soot. "I see you decided to join us," he said with mournful sarcasm.

Rebecca took note of his tone. It all came rushing back. The storm, the vigil at the lake. "Oh! I must've—"

"Must've, my foot! You went to sleep in the face of a blizzard. You have about as much sense as a flea's tit. I thought you were dead."

"Santee?"

"He's fine. I'm the one who's not fine. I'm the one who's been baby-sitting! I'm— Don't tell me. You're gonna start crying again." He knelt down in front of her. "I could throttle you! You scared the hell out of me."

Molly scampered away. Whatever room the captain was in was not the room for her.

Rebecca said slowly, "Parnell..."

"Don't make eyes at me."

She sat unmoving, letting his full gaze rest upon her, then she reached out and lay her hand on his chest. "I'm sorry."

"You should be. The elements are nothing to fool around with. For the kids' sake, if you want to pretend this is a picnic outing or an adventure—okay. But the dangers are real. One careless move and we could freeze, starve, get hurt. When you're up against what we're up against, you don't get second chances. Don't forget it."

"I won't, not again."

"Hell!" he said and moved away before he did something disastrous, like take her into his arms and smother her with kisses.

Rebecca thought it was a good thing he moved away. She was about to throw herself at him. After a moment she said, "Did you get the rations?"

"No, but I found some apples. Somebody was shipping a crate to a sailor stationed on Guam." Christmas apples, the letter accompanying the crate had said, picked from the sailor's favorite tree. The one he'd fallen from and broken his arm when he was seven. The letter was signed 'Love, Mother.' Shipping fresh fruit was against postal regulations so he didn't feel too badly about confiscating the parcel. "We've eaten two apiece. I thought that was enough for the time being."

Rebecca's mouth watered. "No!" Then she sniffed, and because she couldn't keep from it, began to sob quietly.

Parnell sagged. "Damn! I knew it."

He went to the iron pot at the fire and withdrew the thermos where he'd stashed it to defrost.

"If apples make you whine, no telling the flood this'll bring."

He handed her a precious cupful of the coffee.

"Oh!" Rebecca's hands trembled as she sipped.

Yancy brought her two apples. Rebecca hugged him tightly, which had the effect of sending him scurrying back into the other room.

"Eat slowly," Parnell warned when she'd finished, suggested a third. Rebecca refused it.

"If two is all you ate—" She refilled the thermos cup. "I feel I've just dined at a banquet." She was almost to the point of crying again. When she was certain her voice was stronger, she said "You saved my life. All of our lives, again."

"I was saving my own neck, too." But he would never forget that sinking, stabbing feeling he had felt when, arriving back at the lake's edge, he had found her circled into a ball, asleep—nearly frozen. Another thirty minutes and she would've been lost to him forever. Had he stayed in the plane to chop through to the locker... For some few seconds a surge of emotion raged through him. It must be more than sex, he thought. Maybe it was love. But he didn't see how it could've crept up on him without him noticing. Anyway, they were strangers. Thrown together by happenstance. When they got out of this, she'd go her way, he'd go his. He'd be a fool to consider a woman like her doing otherwise.

Suddenly very formal, he said, "I was getting that old stove going, I'd better finish it. As for saving your life. We're even now."

Rebecca puzzled over his sudden coolness. Reluctantly, she let him go.

THE STORM RAGED for three days. The wind sang around the corners of the cabin, the noise becoming a constant.

To Rebecca's dismay, Parnell continued to maintain his distance. For hours on end she was pressed into thinking *What have I said? What have I done?* When she wearied of guessing, she tried to engage him in conversation. Beyond extreme politeness, he had nothing to say, nothing to volunteer.

During the times the blizzard seemed to lessen, he alone gathered wood out of the forest.

Excursions to the outhouse were sheer torture. The children were all for an indoor chamber pot. Rebecca refused on the grounds that some privacy and a modicum of modesty should be maintained.

The water well on the woodburning stove was filled with snow to melt. To make a hot meal, Rebecca boiled apples into sauce. They ate it, dipping into the iron pot with the thermos lid and the old tins and a chipped enamel plate.

She passed the time rooting in her suitcase and all the totes, setting aside items they could make use of.

It took more hours than she dreamed possible to keep the children and herself as clean and neat as circumstances allowed. The bars of soap Parnell had discovered were a godsend.

The boys plagued Parnell for tales of flying. At first he only told them skimpy stories, but one thing led to another and he found himself regaling them with how a plane is catapulted off a carrier, the dangers of flying into a hurricane... Soon he saw hero worship glowing in their eyes. He had never been worshiped before and found it a most gratifying experience. It almost put him in a good mood.

Once Rebecca caught him surreptitiously staring at her. She tried to approach him, but as if she were a blot on his well-ordered life or as if he were in a panic—Rebecca suspected panic—he moved off the bunk and went to help Santee. With the screwdriver and grease gun the boy was trying to rework one of the old rusted traps.

Each time she even looked as if she meant to speak to Parnell he found something that needed doing that took him from her presence. Snow had to be knocked off the roof lest the rotten timbers fall in; over her protests he replaced the brush pile with the door from the outhouse; snow had to be hauled in to melt for water. He was so polite and correct there was no doubt his was purposeful behavior.

She dallied with her cosmetics, considered applying some but thought that might be too obvious a ploy to garner his attention. She was as enthralled with his stories as the children. When one of them raised a question, he answered it. When she did the same, he raved, ranted and sulked to the extent that she'd been obliged to make the noble gesture of keeping her mouth shut lest he go mute and deprive the children.

On the third night of the storm, the wind died and the sudden silence woke her. As always, she listened for a moment to Molly's breathing. She'd been doling out the aspirins to the child in halves. Now Molly sounded fine. Rebecca sat up on the side of the bunk. No one else had awakened. The four boys shared two bunks to leave one free for Parnell. She glanced at him. In the light from the fiery embers she could only make out that he slept with his elbow crooked over his eyes.

Because it seemed the thing to do, because it created a

semblance of normalcy, she had insisted that everyone sleep in their pajamas. Coats were used as blankets. In spite of the primitive conditions, the cabin was "home."

She shoved her feet into her slippers and glided across the room to add a small log to the fire. She then went to do the same in the front room. Keeping the fires going had proved the most arduous of tasks, second only to attempts at keeping the kids clean. They were surviving in a civilized manner—but only just.

She returned to the hearth and sat down, hugging her legs, chin resting on her knees and wondered if the outside world had given them up for dead. Please, she prayed, let them keep looking.

She felt a twinge of hunger, but took her restless mind elsewhere. Be grateful for this bit of peacefulness, she told herself. Enjoy the privacy...privacy! She had been longing for a good wash.

PARNELL WAS WIDE AWAKE. Curious about Rebecca moving about in the middle of the night, he adjusted his elbow so that he could watch her.

He no longer used her nightgown as a pillow; she was wearing it. But the scent of the gown stayed with him, filled his head. Wanting somebody so bad it hurt was something else, he thought. Having to keep up the pretense that he didn't want her was driving him crazy. Not only that, he was having a dreadful time making his genitals behave. It kept seeping into his brain that he was in love with her. Real love. He held his breath and struggled with that utterly paralyzing thought as he watched her poke around in her suitcase.

She took up something, tucked it under one arm, then using the hem of her nightgown, removed the iron pot from the hearth and disappeared into the other room. He'd gotten a glimpse of her legs when she raised the gown. Very nice legs made copper-colored by the firelight.

After a few moments he heard water splashing. He'd just see what she was up to. He wouldn't speak to her. She might misunderstand, think he was suggesting something, seeking her out for reasons other than simple curiosity.

The firebox door on the old stove was open, throwing off a feeble, flickering light. In that light Rebecca stood, naked. She was pouring water over herself. Dipping it can by tin can out of the iron pot, reaching above her head, letting the water sluice over her body. Parnell inhaled deeply and held his breath.

Her name escaped his lips.

She did not turn around, but her heart began to beat hard in her chest. She could feel it hammering, and feel the rise and fall of her breasts. "I'm bathing," she said.

"Yes, I heard you."

She hoped he'd approach her, and told herself hope was pointless. But now... "I didn't mean to wake you." Her voice was tremulous. She dropped the can into the iron pot, moved to reach for the gown that she'd hung on a wall peg. Her fingers poised there she waited for some sign that Parnell wanted her. Loved her.

His need for her grew, becoming more savage and immediate. "You didn't wake me. I couldn't sleep."

"Oh." Rebecca felt deflated. Her fingers closed over to gown.

"You're beautiful." It wasn't what he wanted to say. It sounded lame, but flowery words didn't come easy to him. Curiosity and courage meshed. His muscles were quivering with tension. The pressure building inside him had to be released. Either he must do what his entire being demanded or leave the cabin. Without warning he closed the distance between them, placed his hand over hers. "Don't cover yourself."

All at once the tension between them was a tangible thing. She was aware of a stillness of emotion, as if all thoughts, sensations were in abeyance, locked in the eye of a storm, a lull before another onslaught. If not that, whatever it was had a physical presence of its own, stronger than her own will. The puddle of water she stood in began to cool; she hardly noticed. She didn't speak, but touched his face with the tips of her fingers. His lips were taut and cool, the tactile contact with his beard—much more than stubble now—gave her a tingle of pleasure.

Parnell lifted his hand and touched her damp hair. "I want you very much. I've wanted you for a long time. Unless you go back in the other room right now, it's going to happen."

Rebecca didn't move. Go! she told herself.

The seconds went by, marked only by their strained breathing. When at last she felt Parnell pull her body against his own, she was ready to yield. Her breasts trembled and the nipples were swollen and hard.

"A moment," he whispered and went into the other room, returning with an armload of clothing. He spread his coat on the floor near the side of the stove and led her to it, then he quietly closed the firebox.

"Perhaps we..." Rebecca whispered. She was having second thoughts. "Suppose one of the children wakes?"

He stretched out his hand and touched her cheek. "They're sound asleep. I checked." He removed his clothes and layered them with the others he'd brought. "Tuck these around you. I don't want you cold."

Rebecca almost laughed, caught herself in time. "I'm not

cold. I'm not at all cold." The degree of her desire was frightening. She wanted to talk, perhaps lessen it, but was conscious of the silent sleeping cabin that prevented voice above a whisper. Sex! she thought. It was taking her over, running her body, dictating to her. Oh! She wanted it to be so much more than that.

At first he only put his arm across her; their bodies touched. That was all. It was the only important thing. Slowly he drew his tongue along her lips. He bulged hot and tumescent against her thigh and she thought of tasting him, but not yet, not now. Such sensitivities were no part of this particular moment. Then his strong sure hands began to explore her, know her.

They had both lost every vestige of fat. Rebecca thought herself too thin. He cupped her breasts with his hands, she felt a surge of pure pleasure and her concern about thinness faded.

The bits and pieces of fabric bunched beneath her, a soft pallet. There was a building frenzy in her loins. She had been married yet she had never been touched so, never been made to feel as if she could sense the blood coursing through her veins and pumping life into her heart.

He spread apart her flesh and entered her, the penetration slow and purposeful as if he were only now arriving at some shrine at which he meant to worship.

Her hips rose, straining to take him completely inside her, and she rose and fell to his rhythm. She could feel him swelling within her, filling a hollow depth; could sense the ending coming upon her much too soon. She was held in his grip, powerless to halt her movements, or his.

Outside a sudden wind gusted. It had the sound of a roaring cataract far away. Then Rebecca realized the roar was inside her head, pulsating. His beard brushed her cheek.

"Parnell..." she said between gasps.

He increased his tempo. The breaking, tidal release closed over them both in great looping gusts.

THE STRAIN OF FINDING himself in love was too much for Parnell. He looked for a way to shake it off, disavow it. "You seduced me," he accused.

He sounded so lachrymose Rebecca realized it was going to take him some time to come to grips with his emotions. He was arguing against Destiny. He'd have to find out for himself that warring against Fate was a losing battle.

She said, "Funny isn't it? How you're only now complaining?" Despite his gloom he had not yet loosened his hold on her. The room was becoming cool. She felt a draft whip across her feet.

"We can't let this go one bit further. You might as well know. I'm a coward."

She laughed. "There are cowards and there are cowards."

"I'm not good at word games either. All I know how to do is fly."

"You sure had me soaring."

"I did?" He tripped over his ego. "I mean, so what?"

"So, nothing. We don't have to do this ever again." Her hand rested on his chest. She let it slide down his abdomen, drawing her fingertips down and up the inside of his thigh.

His voice thickened. "Well, that's all right then."

"Besides, it was just a fluke, wouldn't you say? We're adults. I guess the strain of being lost, hungry and in each other's company for days on end got to us." He shifted his hips as if to make himself more comfortable. Her fingertips brushed his growing erection. In the dark, Rebecca smiled. "I'd better finish rinsing my hair. If there's anything I hate, it's shampoo-sticky hair."

Before he could do more than issue a low groan, she moved off the pallet, opened the firebin door to the stove and added a stick of wood.

Parnell sat up. His enlarged shaft ached for what her caressing hand had promised. He wanted her again. But how could he admit that now, damn it!

"There's plenty of warm water left if you want to bathe," Rebecca told him as she pulled her night gown over her head. "You'll have to stand over here though. There's a crack in the floor where the water runs out." She retrieved a shirt from the pallet makings and began to dry her hair.

"You're teasing me," Parnell said. He couldn't seem to control the thing between his legs. He felt it waving like an unstrung flagpole.

"I'm not. I'm just respecting your wishes."

"I hate women who do that."

"Oh. Well, what would you have me do?"

"Nothing." It was too monstrous an idea to change his stand. Let a woman find a man's weak point and the rest of his life she'd make a man miserable. Wheedling this and that until she got her way on everything.

The sticks Rebecca had put in the stove caught and flared. In the sudden spark of light she glimpsed the engorged length of him. She had thought to use a woman's subterfuge, to go back to her cot, leaving him with an ache that would keep her in his mind. She couldn't make herself do it. She knelt down on the pallet before him. "Would you like for me to sit on that for a minute?" she asked softly, reaching for him.

The words were feathers that raced down his backbone and lodged firmly between his legs. "You're seducing me again," he moaned, trying to keep the delight out of his voice.

Rebecca took a deep breath. "It'll be the last time," she whispered. "I promise." She positioned herself as she guided him fully inside her.

He was conscious of her weight, felt her pelvic muscles contract. A band of tenderness encircled his chest and tightened on his heart.

"That's...all...right...then..." he said and began to knead her buttocks. Rebecca moved and found her rhythm.

He was helpless against the crazy way his heart was acting now. He was sure it was affecting his brain, the way he saw things. But tomorrow he was going to purify himself of certain impulses. Then he'd be straight again. Normal.

Rebecca leaned forward and nibbled on his earlobe. His thoughts faded.

Something stronger prevailed.

9

REBECCA STARTED to say something, but Parnell wouldn't let her.

"Just keep unloading those mail carts," he said, turning away to continue hacking at the ice-bound locker. The sound of the hatchet cracking ice reverberated throughout the plane and echoed the breadth and width of the frozen lake.

"That noise hurts my ears," bewailed Molly. "I wanna go make a snowman."

Rebecca acquiesced, and watched the child scamper as freely as her heavy shoes allowed across the frozen lake to shore.

Wind had swept the surface clean of powdery snow, the ice gleamed with an iridescent sheen of sunlight being fed through a prism. Landward it was much different. The drifts were high and almost impossible to negotiate.

The younger boys were making a game of scooping snow from the SOS. Santee had begged permission from Parnell and was in the forest setting the two traps he'd managed to reclaim from rust.

The contrast between the boys' laughter on the shore and Parnell's mood was obvious. No wonder Molly wanted to escape. Inside the plane was about as cheerful as a morgue.

From the moment they'd awakened and faced each other, Parnell had worn the look of a man who'd suffered a great injustice and couldn't figure out who to blame for his misery.

The Morning After Syndrome, Rebecca thought. Women suffered it, but it surprised her to think men did. Especially Parnell. Maybe there was something to the suggestion that the American male was the Great Pretender of the twentieth century!

Watching him swing the hatchet gave her insight into why his clothes seemed to misfit him so. He worked with his entire body. His sweater had ridden up, his shirttail escaped his belt, his cuffs, neatly rolled earlier, now drooped.

The poor darling, Rebecca thought. His face drooped, too. He had dark circles under his eyes.

He straightened a moment to release tension from his cramped muscles and out of the corner of his eye saw the hint of laughter about her mouth. "What're you smiling at?" he said, glaring at her.

"I'm happy. I feel wonderful. Don't you?"

Parnell thought, *She's gloating*. She had her claws into him, but good!

Last night after she'd gone back to the bunk she shared with Molly, he'd gotten up and actually teetered, his legs were so weakened from lovemaking. He'd splashed water on himself, called it bathing and worried the night away on thoughts that she'd wormed her way into his psyche so that he couldn't do without her. The idea had clung to his brain like a bloodthirsty leech. He'd spent hours envisioning her living with him in the house trailer behind the hangar. Most of the daydream had taken place in the bedroom. And somehow without him even saying it, she knew. She was evidently plumbing new ways to make him miserable.

"You're supposed to be salvaging the mail, not standing around grinning."

"Right." She kept on smiling. "What if nobody comes back to get it?"

"You don't know postal inspectors. If it's got a stamp on it, they'll get it."

Rebecca glanced at the packages stacked in the cockpit and along the walls above the frozen water line. "You think there might be other foodstuffs in any of those?"

"If we run out of food again, we'll look." He needed to get away from her, get his thoughts clear. "I want to tell you something. I'm hiking out of here as soon as I can."

"No!"

"I am."

"You can't leave us to fend for ourselves!"

"I'm going after help. We've been here six days. No, seven. Don't you understand? They've stopped looking. They wouldn't expect that we've been able to survive the storm we just had. They probably don't even consider we survived the crash."

"But you said—"

"Now I'm saying different."

"It's me you're running from. It's me you want to escape."

Parnell couldn't form the words to deny the truth of that. Rebecca seemed like almost a part of him now. Yet it was irrational to believe their relationship would go on once back in Boise. If he got in deeper, he'd just be setting himself up for heartache. "I'll make sure you have plenty of food and wood before I go."

"With plenty of food and wood we could last here indefinitely! All of us."

"I have an air freight business going to pot, Rebecca. We're prisoners here, not pioneers. There's a difference."

"The difference is that you made love to me. Now you wish you hadn't!"

"I got carried away. If you hadn't pranced around naked, it wouldn't have happened. But this morning I remembered why I don't like you. Loving a woman wrecks a man."

She didn't know whether to laugh or cry. "You were a wreck when I met you. You still are. I can't see that making love has improved you any."

The sinews at the side of his neck moved slightly, tightening. His narrowed, unsmiling eyes bore down on her. "It hasn't. But I see that look in your eye. You're figuring ways to make me over. You're not gonna get the chance."

"As it happens I like you just the way you are."

"I've heard that tale before."

"I'm in love with you." He went pale so suddenly, Rebecca knew she'd crossed a boundary he wasn't yet ready to recognize. She hurried on. "However, that's not your problem, it's mine. I'll deal with it. The psychologists will probably come up with a very good explanation. We were thrown together by unusual circumstances, cramped quarters, lack of privacy.... But I'm warning you, I'm not some little annoyance you're going to be able to forget."

His stomach knotted. "It was lust, plain and simple. You ever heard of lust?"

"Call it by any name you like—sexual static, lust, whatever. We both enjoyed it."

"I got ice to chop." He went to do it. He wasn't about to give her an open hold on him. She had it. But what she didn't know was better for him. After he'd positioned himself he glanced back at her. She appeared more disconsolate than he felt. "If you start crying," he yelled, "so help me, I'll throttle you!"

"Why should I cry? I don't have anything to cry about.

Unless being lost in the wilderness with a horse's ass quali-
fies. I'm going to check on the kids."

Parnell stared unseeing at the ice-encrusted locker. There
it was. She didn't really love him. He could tell. She was
calling him names. "People in love don't fuss and fight," he
bellowed.

Hearing his outburst, Rebecca stepped back inside the
plane. "How old are you, Parnell?"

"Forty-two."

"Incredible," she said.

There was a look of knowing instinct and intuition on her
face. Parnell felt his palms dampen. He sensed he'd somehow just destroyed his own defenses. But he couldn't
fathom how. He took the whiskey flash from his back
pocket and downed a long draught. "See," he muttered, as
if responding to a second self, "now she's driving me to
drink."

Rebecca opened her mouth to protest his imbibing. She
stopped herself. Perhaps the liquor would cushion the
shock of reality. "Lovers most certainly do fuss, fight, battle,
make up and begin again. Your idea of love and being loved
is an illusion. Grand passions are not like they are in story-
books."

"You're right as rain on that," he said morosely. "They
put a good man through hell." And rendered a man not responsible for his actions. That's it! he thought. He wasn't so
muddled after all. He stared at Rebecca, and as she stared
back he was aware that she was seeing a spectrum of reality
entirely beyond his field of vision. But there was a side to
passion even she hadn't considered, he decided. The very
definition of the word implied the impulse to freedom. He
damned sure meant to keep his!

Rebecca correctly read the expression on his face and

countered it. "You have a lot to learn, Parnell. Love is the pinnacle of human achievement. You're behaving as if it's some terrible affliction."

"I'm not interested in silly female claptrap. Let a man pay just one little bit of attention to a woman and first thing she does is dissect every little word and goings on."

"One little bit of attention? Is that what you're calling it? Well, I suppose you can't do otherwise and keep the image you have of yourself intact."

He turned away. Thwack! went the hatchet.

Rebecca left him to it. If ever there was such a thing as woman's rites, she was in the throes of it—with a man who was a particularly reluctant participant. He was discounting factors such as the irresistible chemistry they shared, that sex between them was good, that—well, there hadn't actually been that breathtaking meeting of minds. Warlike and crashing was more the description. Perhaps if she could see things more from his point of view.

Halfway to shore she turned about and retraced her steps. "Give me that flask," she demanded. He put his hand protectively over his back pocket.

"Nix that. This isn't the African Queen, you know."

"I want a drink."

"Oh yeah? And I'm the president's personal pilot."

"It's true. I do. I want to see what it does to my mind."

"In that case..." He unscrewed the top and handed her the flask. "I'm all for any improvement in the female mind."

The whiskey trailed fire as it slid down her throat and settled on the quarter slice of apple she'd consumed for breakfast. "Thank you."

"My pleasure. Notice any improvements?"

"Quite a few." She felt a burning behind her eyes. "One of which is a clarity of mind. I see things so-o-o clearly now.

You're a disagreeable, obnoxious, insensitive snake-in-the-grass. You took advantage of me."

"I knew that was coming! By God, I knew it." He snatched the flask from her hand. "That was a waste of good whiskey."

Rebecca stared him down before she stalked out of the plane and headed toward the slew of gray boulders behind which she disposed of the apple and Jim Beam into the snow. So much for looking at issues from a man's point of view, she thought. Head aching, legs trembling, she hailed Nicholas and Molly. Together, the three of them staggered up the mountain to the cabin.

THE SEA RATIONS came with all sorts of wonderful things, the best of which were collapsible utensils from forks to frying pan.

Rebecca prepared a feast.

There was powdered milk, powdered coffee, powdered eggs and tubes of bacon paste to cook them with. There were sugar packets, salt packets, chunks of hard and bitter chocolate that she shaved and melted into hot milk. There were also packs of dried beef strips, malt tablets and several unlabeled boxes she meant to experiment with later. There were only four tin cups. She sipped boiled coffee laced with milk from the thermos cup.

Parnell drank his coffee from a tin can. He had laced it with the last dollop of Jim Beam, which was not enough to dull his senses. The earlier exchange with Rebecca had left him emotionally flattened. She was behaving as if everything was hunky-dory. Laughing, even. As if diddling with him had only been an amusing little whim.

Well, she wouldn't get another rise out of him! Of any kind. He was keeping to the edge of the activities, staying si-

lent and looking inscrutable. It was only in the odd quiet
moment that he was deluged with the memory of her strad-
dling his groin and purring with pleasure.

Rebecca brought him a plate and sat next to him on the
bunk to eat her own.

"There's no need to sit on top of me," he said.

Rebecca turned on him a lovely, wicked smile. "If I were
on top of you," she said sotto voce so that it didn't carry to
the children, "you wouldn't be interested in food."

"It's unseemly for a woman to brag about her sexual ex-
ploits," he said, then spent an uncomfortable moment dealing with the images her pithy remark evoked.

Though her cheeks were hot and flushed, as were unseen
parts of her body, Rebecca's smile widened; her voice
stayed low. "You mean it's okay to talk about sex while
we're doing it, but afterward or before, you'd rather not?"

"Only certain types of women discuss—"

"What type is that?"

"You know."

"I don't. Perhaps after the kids are asleep you could en-
lighten me."

All of Parnell's prudence couldn't keep the words from
his tongue. "Okay," he said, and delved into the food.

Every mouthful of food was savored, rolled on the
tongue, swallowed with reverence.

Jonesy noisily scraped his plate. "I guess you could say
this is our very first meal in our very own house."

"This isn't our house. We're only borrowing it," Rebecca
said.

"We decided," said Nicholas. "We want to stay here."

"Yeah," put in Yancy. "Scrappy likes it here. He has lots
of room to gallop."

"You could go get Abigail, couldn't you Rebecca?" Molly

said. "You could bring her here. It's cheap. She wouldn't have to worry about money. We haven't had to spend any. Have we?"

One by one Rebecca took in the serious expressions on the young faces. "I'm proud of all of you," she said slowly. "You've faced up to adversity much better than I imagined you could. You've been a team and we've survived. But we have to go back. This isn't—"

Santee shifted on his haunches to face Rebecca. "Why do we have to go back? No one wants us. We could stay here. We could get books and teach ourselves. We could live off the land. I know we could. I'll bet there'll be rabbits in my traps in the morning. And that deer is still out there. I saw his tracks."

"And I'm getting around real good," announced Nicholas. "I know my way from the cabin down to the lake and back, by myself."

"I haven't wet the bed once since we've been here," reminded Molly. "Don't forget that."

Rebecca looked to Parnell for help. But he just sat cross-legged, pretending invisibility. He did lift the tin can perceptibly, as if in salute. Oh, great! Rebecca thought. Was she the only one among them with any practical sense left? Parnell expected romance to be all champagne and roses, man's finest hour. Now, the children, too, were playing at fairy tales.

"Listen to me, all of you. We're going back to Boise. If we aren't rescued by others, then we'll have to find our own way back. Captain Stillman is planning to hike out. We'll be going with him."

"No, you won't," he said, coming alive.

"You can't stop us. We'll follow you."

"I'm not going anywhere until after Santa comes," said

Molly, defiantly. "If we keep moving around no telling where he'll leave my presents! Santee said if hasn't seen the SOS, his elves probably have."

Rebecca's face tightened. "We'll be back in Boise for Christmas. We're staying together. We got into this together. We'll get out together."

Santee was stoic. "We like it here."

"Perhaps one day we'll be able to come back," Rebecca offered.

"We won't," Jonesy said. "They don't let orphans have reunions. As soon as we're separated, that's it."

At the orphanage, Rebecca wore a number of hats, but in truth she wasn't a licensed social worker, only a housemother, an aide. Having been in the system most of their lives, the children knew more of the legal machinations than she. She sighed, defeated. "Under the circumstances, considering what you've all been through, that rule might not apply. Now come on, cheer up."

"How many days till Christmas?" asked Molly, her face recording her anxiety.

Rebecca looked to Parnell.

"Five," he said. He reached under the bunk and pulled out the rolls of maps and topographical charts.

Rebecca began to gather the dishes. "Think how sad Abigail must be, thinking we're all lost or dead," she said of the old dowager. "It's not fair to her that we stay here one minute, one day longer than necessary. Think how unhappy her Christmas would be."

Yancy stretched out on his stomach. "She was sending us off to find parents. She has to get rid of us. She doesn't have any money to keep us anyhow."

"That doesn't mean she doesn't love you."

"Nobody loves us," said Jonesy. "We're just commodities."

"I love you," Rebecca said.

"You get paid to."

"No, I don't. You can't put a price on love."

"Well, if you loved us," observed Molly, "you'd let us stay right here until after Santa comes." She stuck her thumb in her mouth and stared at the fire. Rebecca set aside the dishes and gathered the child into her lap.

"I do love you. If ever I have a little girl I'd want her to be just like you. Maybe not quite so sassy."

"Even with crippled feet?"

"One day your feet will be fixed."

"Would you let her suck her thumb?"

"I suppose."

"She'd have to watch out. It's not much good being somebody's little girl. God might take you."

Rebecca discovered her headache was returning. "There are worse places to be than with God." A platitude, she thought, ashamed of herself.

Molly sighed. "Yeah, and one of them's where Santa isn't."

THE LOPSIDED three-legged table now had four uneven legs. Parnell had hacked the three down and used one of them to create the fourth. The table was low, Chinese-style, and wobbly. But it created a surface for his unrolled maps. The boys hunkered around him. He found himself thinking aloud for Nicholas's benefit. The other boys easily followed the path his finger traveled over the charts.

"Where are we on the map?" Santee asked. Parnell pointed. "Somewhere in here, above forty degrees latitude and one hundred twenty degrees longitude." Which was twenty ground miles from the nearest highway in mountainous forest so thick the map only showed it as the Sierra Nevadas.

"How do you know for sure?"

"I don't," he answered and let his fingers trail down to Desolation Valley Wilderness. Not possible, he thought. Too far south.

"How are you gonna know which way to walk out?"

"If I head southwest, I'll come on a highway, eventually. North might take me deeper into the forest."

"North is where I'd like to head."

Parnell met Santee's dark eyes. "Don't even think it. I expect you to stay with Rebecca until I bring help. She won't be able to manage without you."

"I don't want to go back. Abigail can't keep us anymore. I've run away so much, I'll have to go to a juvenile home."

"Now's the time to stop running." Santee didn't appear convinced. Parnell heard himself say, "Look, when we get out of this mess, I'll look you up, maybe even teach you to fly. I've got this crop duster I've been meaning to put back together, you can help me."

"Then what?"

"I don't know." He was out of his depth and knew it. "Nobody can foretell the future."

"I can," snapped Rebecca as she carried a dozing Molly to her bunk. "The immediate future is everyone gets ready for bed. Adults excepted," she added icily. "The later future is we stay together, here or marching out."

Parnell jerked his thumb at the boys. "Hit it. I'll take care of this."

"I don't see how," said Jonesy. "Rebecca thinks she's the boss."

"Don't be a poop-head," said Yancy, willing to take his

hero at his word. "If the captain said he'll take care of it, he will."

Beneath his beard, Parnell's cheeks felt parched. "I'll give her something else to think about."

Rebecca had no intention of debating Parnell while the boys kept their ears open or at her own expense. It was an hour before she was ready to give him the opportunity to "give her something else to think about."

The cabin reeked of wet wool and the tiny bar of Camay soap she'd put in a can of water to soften for morning ablutions. It went farther that way.

As she scraped the plates with snow by the door, stacked them on the counter and filled the water bin on the stove with snow to melt, she was aware that Parnell was watching her.

While his impatience grew she washed her face, brushed her teeth, tossed that water out and hung the shirt-cum-towel on a peg. From her cosmetic case she retrieved an emery board and when she finally sat cross-legged on the floor before the fire, she began filing her nails.

To Parnell the scrape of the nail file sounded like chalk screeching on a blackboard. It drove him nuts.

"Do you have to do that?"

"My nails are a wreck."

"It's putting my teeth on edge." He wanted to argue, but the expression on Rebecca's face was one of innocence—almost. Her hair and eyes seemed to suck up all the firelight, so that all else seemed dim. Her skin, he thought, was the rich color of cream, and he began to imagine kissing her on her neck. He raised his eyes and she was looking at him. He was afraid that she had a complete grasp of what was on his mind. Too quickly he lowered his head and tapped the chart, "I can't concentrate with that racket."

She put the nail file aside. "Get on with your bravado." She could see the comb marks in his hair where he'd wet it and slicked it down. He'd done a bit of preening when he thought she wasn't looking. "What is it you want me to think about?"

He stiffened. "That was just boy talk."

"How indifferent you men are."

"I don't know what you're accusing me of now, but if you want to fight, let's!"

"Wake the kids, why don't you?"

"I'm trekking out of here and you're not going!" he said in a hoarse whisper.

"In the interest of fairness I'll hear you out on the reasons why not."

"Alone, I can travel faster. And, have you noticed the snow. It's layered, the kind avalanches are made of. Who knows how high up the mountains I'll have to climb before…there aren't any sidewalks you know. A couple of the kids couldn't hack it."

"You can mark the path. We can keep up."

"It's impossible to talk any sense into you."

"I just have this feeling we should stay together. And we have to get back to Boise by Christmas. We just have to."

"What's Christmas? Just another day."

"You remind me of the boys. They pretend Christmas is nothing to them, but just watch their faces on Christmas morning when they're unwrapping presents. Up until the moment they have their gifts in their hands they're scared they won't get a Christmas. Many years they haven't."

"That's not me."

"Oh, I think it is. You want good things, you're just scared that when you get them they'll be snatched away."

"That's crazy."

"Tell me, how were you orphaned."

Parnell shrugged. "Same as a lot of kids. My dad was killed in the Korean conflict, my mother kept...following the troops, so to speak. One day she followed and left me behind."

Rebecca winced. "How old were you?"

"Thirteen."

She put her hand on his knee. "I'm sorry."

"Don't be. I made it."

"How?"

"Took to the road. It was easier to do back then. There was always a commune of flower children willing to take in a stray. Uncle Henry caught up with me a couple of years later." His voice softened. "He taught me to fly. We did mostly crop dusting, a few air shows. I wanted more and joined the Navy when I was seventeen. I mustered out after twenty years. Had no place to go except to Uncle Henry. He died and dumped the airfield in my lap."

"Dumped? You love it."

"Belongs to creditors now."

Her hand was still on his knee.

"You can make a go of it, if you want to bad enough."

"Oh, I want all right." Much more than the airfield, he thought, keeping an eye on her hand, watching for any perceptible movement. He lifted his own leaden hand and placed it atop hers, casual like.

Rebecca took the gesture much to heart. The glint in her eyes was as if she knew of something exceedingly satisfactory. Very softly, she said, "Shall we make up a pallet in the other room?"

Parnell started, his heart leaped.

"Well, all right," he said. "I guess we could."

10

ONE OF THE MOST USEFUL ITEMS out of the locker was a thermal foil survival blanket. Parnell had pegged it over the doorway separating the rooms. One effect it had was keeping warmth in the bunkroom; the other was the privacy it afforded to anyone in the front room of the cabin. Rebecca wallowed in that privacy, not that she could speak above a whisper, but the blanket did afford the comfort of making the pallet in front of the stove. The woodbox door left open gave feeble light; it was enough by which to see Parnell's face.

"You look quite nice with a beard," she said, stroking it with her fingertips.

The compliment was heady stuff. Parnell was in bliss. "It's nothing but a flea catcher."

"I noticed there's some gray in it."

The bliss went.

"You're not one of those men who worries about aging are you? I think gray-streaked hair is distinguished looking."

He ran his hand down her naked back. She was so slender. He was enchanted by the svelte length of her, fitted next to him. A perfect alignment, he thought. He felt so relaxed, stretched out on the pallet. Her cheek rested on his chest. He stroked her shoulder and leaned down to kiss the top of her head, murmuring, "You make me crazy, Rebecca. You undo me. I can't even figure out who started this. Was it you?"

"I suppose it was a combination." She put her arms around him and kissed him. "So distinguished."

"A combustion, you mean." He massaged the delicate vertebrae that protruded down her back. "If you kiss me like that you're only going to get me started again." There was a slight but obvious movement of her hips against his thigh.

"Oh? Well how about if I kiss you like this?" She buried her face in his chest, her tongue flicked out, touching his nipple."

"Hey!"

"Shhhh. You do it to me."

"That's...different..."

She drew the tip of his nipple into her mouth and sucked.

"Dear me," Parnell groaned. He loved how affectionate she was. The idea of having that, day in and day out, was beginning to have solid appeal to him. He imagined what she'd be like in a real bed, with true privacy. He didn't think he'd be able to stand it. It was the wrong kind of imagery. Wishful thinking. For all her "making do" since the crash, in his mind she was a champagne-and-silk kind of woman. He was Jim Beam and oily rags.

Her mouth left his nipple. He felt her tongue on his ribs. The hand that had been at his neck moved in a slow downward spiral until it reached the juncture of his thighs where he began to swell almost immediately. The philosophy of silk and rags left his mind. He made a noise in his throat.

Soft laughter erupted from Rebecca. "I thought that'd bring you back."

"I wasn't anywhere."

"You weren't here. Does my lovemaking bore you?"

"Bore me? You're the most exciting thing that's ever happened to me."

"What were you thinking about then?"

"I was asking myself how much of you I could bear."

Rebecca raised her head. "What was your answer?"

He pressed his arms about her. "As much of you as you'll give me."

"Suppose it's all of me?"

His stomach tightened in alarm. It was a question on two levels. He'd cut his tongue out before he admitted love. As soon as they got back to civilization she'd go off to silk and he back to oily rags. Then where would he be? Off in broken-heart land, that's where. As it was, he'd be months getting his libido under control again.

"Suppose?" he tossed back playfully. But to dissuade her of further talk he brought her face to him and kissed her, his tongue thrusting between her lips. Rebecca's breath caught in her throat. He was engorged and pressing between her legs. He pulled her body higher and penetrated her. For a long moment he held her there, unmoving.

"Something wrong?" she asked, voice thick.

"Enjoying," he whispered into her ear.

"We'll always remember this won't we?"

"I couldn't live long enough to forget."

"I love you," she said softly.

"I—I was talking about knee and elbow burns."

He sounded forlorn and vulnerable. Rebecca laughed, the sound of her laughter melded with the crackling fire, the winter wind bracketing the cabin, Parnell's involuntary intake of breath.

"Were you? Poor darling. You're body's really had the worst of it. Shall we stop?" She tightened her muscles; felt the length of him respond inside her.

"Don't tease me like that."

She rubbed against him, then leaned forward and kissed

him lightly on the ear, taking his earlobe between her teeth and gently sucking on it. "You're so strong…"

"Stop that. Keep still," he said, his voice huskier than before.

"But I want you so… Here, suppose I just do this?"

"Oh, Lord—" His back arched.

"We're meant for each other. You know that don't you?"

"I don't know anything. I can't think."

"Perhaps I ought to just let you get some sleep."

"Move off this pallet and I'll break your ankle," he muttered through clenched teeth.

She rose up on an elbow. "I'm not a violent person."

"Could you please just shut up?"

"But I thought you wanted to talk."

"This is what I want," he said, demonstrating.

REBECCA CAME AWAKE slowly. The smell of boiling coffee was in the air. For a brief drowsy moment she thought herself at the orphanage, imagined she could hear the chatter of the children down the hall in the great old farmhouse kitchen where so much of their living took place. Imagined she could hear Abigail chastising one child or another on table manners. The alien hardness of the bunk intruded, striking the chord of reality. The fragrance of the coffee remained, but the cabin was quiet. Too quiet. She raised her head and discovered herself alone.

She dressed, thrusting her arms into her coat as she went outside. It was easy to pick out Molly's footsteps in the snow. They lead up to the outhouse. "Molly?"

"Went all by myself," the child answered.

"Where is everybody?"

"I don't know. But nobody would let me go with them."

"What did the captain say to you?"

"He said, stay with you till you woke up."

"Then what?"

"Then I had to go to the bathroom."

"How long has he been gone?"

"You know I can't tell time. Are you gonna fix breakfast now?"

"In a minute. I'll walk you back to the cabin. If the boys show up, tell them I said stay put until I get back."

"I don't want to stay by myself. A bear might get me."

"All the bears are asleep."

"That's not what Santee said. He said only mother bears sleep all winter. Daddy bears don't."

"Santee isn't the last word on bears! Now please, I've got to find the captain." Suppose he's left us! Rebecca thought, recalling how he'd brushed aside her anxieties at being left alone in the wilderness with the children. She glanced at the sky.

The sun was shining, gray-tinted clouds hugged the mountain peaks. Nearby a pair of birds chattered. She settled Molly with a hard cracker in front of the fireplace.

"A bear is gonna get me and I'll be dead and you'll be sorry," she complained.

Rebecca dipped into the pan of coffee on the stove and took a sip to fortify herself against the cold, against the anxiety that was creeping up her spine. "I'm just going down to the lake."

It was a futile excursion. No one was there. The door to the plane had been closed. She couldn't get it open. Behind her the SOS glared bright orange in the snow. It did no good. There was only herself to see it.

When she returned to the cabin, the boys were clustered under the lintel. Santee was not among them.

"Rebecca, look!" Jonesy said. At his feet was the skinned carcass of a rabbit. "Santee must've trapped it."

"Where is he? Where's the captain?" She watched the boys exchange glances. Her heart slid into her stomach. "They've gone off together, haven't they? Left us here?"

"Santee said he wasn't going back, you'd have to find him first."

"And Captain Stillman? What did he say?" He had betrayed her. Used her! Made love to her and escaped while she was wallowing in the afterglow.

"That we'd all better mind you or he'd skin us alive," said Jonesy. He poked the rabbit with his shoe. "You think that's what we'd look like skinned?"

"He said he'd take Scrappy to the glue factory," said Yancy.

"And that he didn't have anything against whipping a blind kid," put in Nicholas.

Rebecca visualized Parnell lining up the kids, passing out orders, making threats, dishing it all up with a dash of bravado, then going off and leaving her with the consequences. He was probably laughing his head off.

"Do you know how to cook a rabbit?" asked Jonesy.

Rebecca looked down at the skinned pink carcass. She felt squeamish. "No."

"It's protein. We need protein, you said."

"I wonder what Santee did with the skin?" Nicholas said.

"He's probably gonna make himself a coat out of it," suggested Yancy.

"It takes more than one fur, stupid."

"Stop it!" Rebecca said, ushering them all inside. The rabbit carcass caused Molly to squeal and retire under a mound of clothes to her bunk, thumb in mouth.

"Fat lot of pioneers all of you would make!" Rebecca said.

She scooped up the rabbit, held it at arm's length. "We'll boil it."

"Roasted would be better. In cowboy movies they always roast it over a fire."

"Well, we're not in a cowboy movie. We're just lost." A sob broke from her throat. "We're lost and we're going to stay lost. We're going to die."

Alarmed, the boys backed away from her. Molly covered her head.

"Oh, don't pay any attention to me, I'm just scared. I don't know how I can find Santee. I'm mad at the captain for going off without us."

"He'll be back. He likes us," volunteered Nicholas.

"I'll hold that thought."

A half dozen times she scoured the area around the cabin and the lake trying to spot Santee. She visited the old campsite in hopes of finding him there. But the snow near it was virgin and untrampled. She told herself he'd show up by dark. Behind the cabin she found tracks leading upward to a southern ridge. The size of them suggested they were Parnell's.

At dusk the leafless trees were engraved in clarity; blue-black shadows. A northerly breeze whipped up the snow. Rebecca felt an ache in her throat. She missed Parnell. She'd taken so much strength from his presence that now she felt detached in some odd way. As if she'd been severed from all that was important to her.

The seemingly deserted winterscape was alive with night sounds she couldn't identify. She stared unblinking at the footsteps until shadows overtook them. She had a strange whisper of dread. She wouldn't allow her brain to tell her the feeling was for Parnell. He was fine. He knew how to take care of himself. His Navy training was bred into him. The dread was for herself, for the children.

She wrapped her arms around herself and waited for her life to pass before her eyes. Her only vision was those hours spent in Parnell's arms, the lovely way he made her feel so much a woman.

Just get us all out of this alive, she broadcast to Heaven, *and I won't ever complain again—at least not to You. When I catch up to Parnell Stillman I'll take care of him all by myself!*

Inside the cabin she hung her coat on a peg. "I think we're going to be all right," she said.

"What about Santee?" came the chorus.

"Him, too. He's smart. He can handle himself. I'm sure he'll show up soon. He knows I'd worry."

"What about Captain Stillman?"

Rebecca poked angrily at the rabbit with the bent-tine fork. "Nothing about him! He's the stupidest, most uncaring man I've ever met. I'm going to tell him so the first chance I get."

The first chance she got came as she was dipping up the first serving of rabbit. Parnell burst through the door roaring in fury and dragging an unhappy-looking Santee by the coat collar. The cabin echoed with his anger.

"This is the thanks I get! I promised to help this kid, teach him to fly. He gave me his word that he wouldn't slip off. Found him across the lake on that north ridge."

"I was tracking that old deer!"

"Bull-doody! You were setting up a camp."

"Tell him, Rebecca. I found droppings. I was building a blind! I told Molly to tell—"

"Don't blame me! I'm too little to remember everything. I'm only five."

Rebecca couldn't speak or deny or verify. The tube of her

throat had closed up. Relief was jackknifing through her, the sensation coming from far away, as if borrowed and unfamiliar.

She dropped the cup; it disappeared into the pot of thin rabbit stew. "Oh! Look what you made me do," she wailed.

Parnell took in her stricken expression: the eyes huge, the slender neck so taut the hollows at her throat deepened. He could see her pulse beating. He put his arm around her and led her to a bunk. "Hey! Calm down. We're all safe."

"I don't feel like calming down! I thought you'd left us."

He shook his head. "I scouted the ridges above the treeline. We'd feel pretty stupid if we walked out of here in one direction only to discover there was a highway or road beyond a ridge we hadn't checked.

"Was there?"

"Nope."

"You said we... That means we're not fighting anymore about who's going, who's staying?"

"You've convinced me. Staying together is the best policy." Staying together. It had been in his mind the entire long and tiring day. Rebecca was for evermore a part of the fabric of his life now. There was no undoing it. He looked down at her, smiling, conscious of his height beside her smallness. He wanted to tell her, watch her reaction, but pride held him back—and an awareness of the children standing in a semicircle, staring and listening to every damned word! Declaring himself in front of an audience was asking too much! Anyway, he didn't have the words right. And even if he had, Rebecca didn't look to be in a mood to hear them. "Well!" he said brightly. "I'm starved. What's for supper?"

SHE HAD A CHOICE, Rebecca told herself. She could start a fight and ruin what promised to be a nice evening. Or, she could just forget about being angry.

The rabbit stew had been a bit thin, but she'd picked the meat off the bones and seasoned it with the bacon paste. It had made even the hard crackers taste satisfactory. Not a drop was left and Parnell had been effusive with his compliments for both Rebecca and Santee.

Santee strutted with importance at providing the meal. He had managed to convince Parnell that he really had lost track of time, building the deer blind. The boy had gone off to his bunk weary, but happy. The other children had followed suit.

Parnell was studying his charts, plotting their passage out, but Rebecca knew he was keeping a wary eye on her.

And so he should! She was most annoyed with him for being gone all day, then treating her so cavalierly. She'd worried herself sick! But she could feel herself giving in. Her acquiescence made her angry at herself.

"You might as well spit it out," Parnell said, not looking up.

"Do you really want to know?"

"I asked, didn't I?"

"I'm angry, that's what."

"No foolin'."

"You're being condescending."

He decided to wait that one out.

"I'm annoyed at your attitude toward me, at the way you just went off today without telling me. That was inconsiderate."

"You were asleep."

"You could've awakened me."

"I started to. But you looked so..."

"So, what?"

"Fragile, I guess. And don't expect me to keep on saying stuff like that."

Fragile? She'd never been thought fragile or delicate before. It implied that she needed someone to take care of her. She'd always taken care of herself. "I was worried. I went looking for you."

"I'm not used to anybody worrying about me."

He stared at the fire a long time, the silence creating a strange nearness between them rather than a gulf. Rebecca watched him. She was suddenly afraid of what he was going to say next.

Finally, he looked at her; he smiled a little half-smile. "I might know a cure for worry."

"Oh?"

"I'll make us some hot chocolate."

Rebecca gazed at him in disbelief.

"We could drink it in there." He tilted his head toward the other room.

"You just want sex," she whispered.

"I just want to do something nice for you."

She let out a deep breath. "As it happens," she said slowly, "I'd like for you to do something nice for me, too.... But, Parnell?"

"What?"

"Forget the hot chocolate."

IT TOOK TWO DAYS to prepare to leave. All that they couldn't carry out had to be hauled down to the plane and stored. The children's totes were converted into backpacks in which to carry the sea rations. Walking sticks were cut and trimmed for each. The great yellow raft was laid out in the snow and painstakingly cut into rectangles for makeshift ponchos. Parnell instructed everyone to wear two sets of clothes. He gave up his socks once again to Rebecca and fashioned for himself foot wrappings out of a shirt.

The sun was only a pink glow in the eastern sky when the fires in the stove and hearth were put out for the last time. Parnell drained the dregs of his coffee and looked at Rebecca. He was in a lousy mood. "That's it, then," he said.

She took one last glance about the cabin. "In a way I hate to leave after we've finally caught the rhythm of living in the wilderness.

Santee hung the traps he'd brought in on the pegs. They'd been empty that morning. "I'm going to come back one day."

Rebecca lay her hand on his arm. "I feel the same way. Perhaps some summer…"

"If we're going, let's go!" announced Molly. "I gotta be somewhere Santa knows where I am before Christmas Eve."

"Fall in!" Parnell yelled.

Rebecca jerked. "Do you have to scream like that? We're none of us deaf, you know." His face was flushed, his dark hair curled over his forehead. "You feel all right?"

"I feel fine. Let's move out." He was anxious about the strenuous activity that faced them. He had the notion Rebecca was going to see him in a different light once they were back in their own lives, on their own turf. He suspected she wouldn't give him a second glance. All that night as he slept, he had dreamt of her…kissing her, lying at her side. He had awakened with a dull ache that refused to go away.

He could feel her eyes on him as he checked his pockets for folded maps, the compass, the tin of matches. The hatchet as well as the gun were tucked into his belt. "What're you staring at?"

"Nothing!"

"That's what I thought."

"Why are you trying to start a fight now?"

"We don't have time to indulge your whims. Let's get the show on the road."

"Whims?" she thrust at him, but he refused to be provoked.

Outside the cabin with the door closed firmly behind them, Parnell looked over his motley entourage. Santee's face was pinched. "You and I will take turns at leading and bringing up the rear. You take point first," he told the boy. "But set us a fast pace. I want to be out of this valley and atop the first ridge by nightfall." He turned to Rebecca. "You all set?"

"I look like a Laplander. I feel stupid," she said of the way she wore the only skirt she'd packed over her slacks.

"Leave it to a woman to worry about what she looks like in the middle of nowhere," he scoffed. "You'll be glad of the warmth later." He reached out to touch her. He would have to live with things whatever the outcome. No sense buying misery, he thought, dropping his hand.

Rebecca sensed the distance he was putting between them. He was having second thoughts about her! As she felt her heart sinking she turned away to touch the cabin door. It was forever shut on a part of their lives.

But inside the spare ramshackle cabin she'd found something she'd been looking for for a long long time. She wasn't about to let go of it so easily.

Molly skipped ahead, so she took Nicholas's hand.

"I'm set," she said and dug her walking stick into the snow.

STRUNG OUT YARDS APART they climbed, crawled and hobbled up the twisting course behind Santee. It seemed to Rebecca they had to stop every few minutes on the hopeless wild inhospitable mountainside to catch their breath in the thinning air. When Parnell finally called a halt, she collapsed in the snow. "My legs," she moaned. She stretched them out in front of her and watched them tremble.

His face inscrutable, Parnell knelt beside her and massaged first one leg, then the other. "How's that?"

It was the most impersonal ministration Rebecca had ever been subjected to. "Heaven," she cooed lightly. "Now if only there was a sauna!"

Parnell forgot himself. "You like all that fancy stuff?"

"It's nice if it's available. I can live without it. Why?"

He sat back on his haunches. "Just making conversation."

"Save your breath." When his brows knit together in a frown she started to smile to take the sting out of her words, but changed her mind. If he was going to revert to type, so could she.

"I think I'm gonna get rid of Scrappy," Yancy said with a long sigh. "He's a horse and I can't even ride him. I wish I had a real horse! Then I could go up and down the mountains faster 'n' faster."

"Scrappy's been a good friend to you," Rebecca said with caution.

"I know. But he's a lot of work. And anyway, can't anybody else see him but me. Abigail keeps saying I ought to put him out to pasture. If I get worried about anything I can always go and talk to him."

"When we get back you can talk to Abigail about it."

"I'd like to see the look on her face when she finds out we're alive," said Jonesy.

"I bet the whole world thinks we're dead!" came from Nicholas and was voiced with glee.

Molly started. "If Santa thinks I'm dead, he'll give my presents away!"

"Santa's like God," Parnell said. "He knows if you're dead or alive."

Rebecca's eyes widened. "Parnell! What a sweet thing to say."

His cheeks and brow flamed. "I was just trying to avoid histrionics. Get up everybody. March!"

Within two hours Molly's legs had given out. Parnell carried her on his shoulders. By dusk, their faces and hands were chapped by the cold dry air, their ears so frozen just to touch one brought tears. It took ten hours to crest the ridge Parnell had scouted in four.

They found shelter under a shelf of rock on the southern face of the mountain. It was not quite a cave; it was perhaps five feet from floor to ceiling at its entrance and eight feet deep into the mountain. The floor was free of snow, but littered with sticks and leaves. It held a vague scent of animal musk.

"Home for the night," groaned Parnell as he lowered Molly to the ground.

Amid ooohs and aaaahs of relief the boys flopped helter-skelter about the cave. "I knew it," moaned Jonesy as he peeled off his shoes and socks. "Blisters! And they're all raw."

As she let her makeshift backpack, which was Parnell's flightbag, slide from her shoulders, Rebecca peered into the gloomy depths of the shelter. "If I sit down I'll never get up."

"I can get a fire going," Santee volunteered, raking a pile of dry leaves with his hands.

"My nose is frozen," announced Nicholas. His cheeks were scarlet and wind-whipped. Rebecca put her hands to her own numbed cheeks. She longed for the warmth and primitive comfort of the cabin they'd left behind.

Parnell looked first at Nicholas then inspected Jonesy's feet. "We're going to have to find some way to protect ourselves better from frostbite."

"Is my nose gonna fall off?"

"I don't think so, sport." He motioned to Rebecca. "You think you can have a look at everyone's feet?" He tossed the first-aid kit to her. "Blisters are going to be as much an enemy as the cold."

It was an agony for Rebecca to bend her legs to squat. Her stomach griped from hunger. She squinted against the pain and drew cold air through her clenched teeth.

"I shouldn't have insisted we all go out together. I was wrong. I don't think the children have the stamina. I don't think I do. It's suicide."

"Belay that!" Parnell growled. "It was my decision. Mine alone. If I didn't think we could all march out of here, I would've insisted you stay behind." He watched her begin applying the antiseptic. "Use that topical anesthetic on everyone's feet, too."

Rebecca turned her face up to him. "But look at us!"

"I'll figure something out, a better way for us to travel."

"Like hitch Scrappy to a sleigh?"

"Not too much is wrong with you. Your tongue's still sharp."

Rebecca sniffed. "The tongue is always the last to go."

Parnell unzipped the flight bag, drew out the pans, the packets of powdered eggs, milk, chocolate. He moved slowly, his shoulders ached, a stiffness was settling in from the unfamiliar burden of Molly. "You rest for an hour. I'll see to the food."

Rebecca lifted an eyebrow, but called the younger boys

and Molly to lie down next to her. It was a measure of how weary they all were that no one complained of the way hard rough rock bit into elbow and hip bone. She unfolded the thermal foil blanket and spread it over them all. At the mouth of the overhang, the leaves and twigs flickered into flames. In the darkness beyond an owl hooted.

The firelight cast Parnell's shadow on the ceiling. For a moment Rebecca watched it. He was being only as nice as circumstances dictated—less, perhaps—reverting to the insensitive clod he'd been when she'd first laid eyes on him. She hoped he didn't carry it too far. She'd get mad. But at the moment she didn't have the strength to squeak, much less squawk. She closed her eyes and succumbed to exhaustion.

When she next stirred it was because Parnell was shaking her awake, roughly so.

"Let me sleep," she protested.

"Like hell! I did that once. You chewed me out." He grabbed her hands, pulled her to her feet and shoved her toward the fire. A plate of eggs, very browned, and a tin of coffee were on the rock floor. "Go eat."

The kids were sprawled every which way, curled up on the strips of yellow raft and covered with their coats. Rebecca picked her way over them. They've toughened, she thought, or perhaps they were more adaptable. Bones and muscles she didn't know existed within her ached from lying upon bedrock. She stepped beyond the fire, scooped up snow and rubbed it on her face.

While she ate, Parnell sat gazing into the fire, knees up, elbows resting on them with his hands hanging down between them. He didn't look happy.

"You're worried aren't you?" she challenged.

He didn't look at her. He felt like telling her, just to see what she'd say. He had one foot in paradise, one in hell and he didn't know which way to jump. But it seemed to him with every step away from the cabin she'd begun lapsing again into the kind of woman that made his stomach hurt. If only he could be more direct—but it just wasn't in him. He sighed glumly. Even knowing that, he couldn't help himself from being attracted to her. He could feel it between his legs.

"I was just thinking about the plane," he said when he discovered she was still waiting for an answer.

"Isn't it insured? I thought—"

"I'll replace her, but buying used planes isn't like going to your corner used-car lot. Boeing doesn't build her class anymore. She was a good airship. Amos and I reconditioned her ourselves."

There was something in his tone. Rebecca tried to lock onto it and couldn't. "I'm a little scared—about going back," she admitted.

"Why?"

"Won't there be publicity?"

"I imagine we're old news by now."

"Be practical. Five orphans, a single woman, a single man, we show up after almost two weeks in the wilderness..." Her voice trailed off.

He drew in a sharp breath. "If you're asked, just stick to the basics. Don't mention—"

"Don't mention what?" But she knew what he meant. Forget their relationship. Forget that they'd fallen in love. Forget the lovemaking. Don't mention... "Of course," she said.

"Well, it wouldn't look good, would it?" he said, filled with misery, aching to tell her he didn't give a hoot in hell if she shouted it for the world to hear.

Her mouth was suddenly dry. "No, it wouldn't," she said stiffly.

Their eyes locked.

Rebecca waited for him to say that it didn't matter what people thought, that they were going to get married.

Parnell waited for Rebecca to say that she loved him no matter what, that she didn't care whatever anyone thought.

He shrugged to accommodate the sore muscles in his shoulders. Rebecca read the gesture wrong. She looked away.

"Well, I guess that's it then," Parnell said.

Rebecca looked down at the empty plate in her hand. She'd eaten without tasting a thing. "I guess I'd better see to my own feet before I sack out," she said.

"I'll help you."

"That won't be necessary."

"I don't mind."

"I don't want you to touch me!"

Parnell winced. "Of course. I understand. *See?* he told himself. *Love hurts!*

11

PARNELL'S BETTER WAY to travel was for him to forge ahead. Where the rest of them were to stop at noon or as close as he could judge it, he would arrange firewood, ready for the match. Then he would move on until just before dusk to locate a suitable campsite for the night.

Rebecca suspected his reason in that method. He wanted to distance himself from her.

They weren't even looking at each other when they spoke now. Words were cast into the air at shoulder level or staring at the ground or while she helped this child or that adjust a backpack or tie a shoelace.

"Aren't you going to take some food?" she asked. It was an innocuous question and meant to engage him in conversation and put his leaving off.

"I filled the thermos with coffee. It'll do me until you catch up." There was a nervousness in his voice that she had not heard before. He seemed almost insecure. "You won't have any trouble following my trail in the snow."

"I don't like it. Suppose one of us gets hurt? Suppose you do?"

"Send Santee to get me."

"Well, suppose it's Santee who's hurt?"

"Listen damn it! Quit buying trouble. That's all you women do. You're making my stomach hurt."

Rebecca didn't like the slant of his innuendo. He was back to lumping her with other women he'd known; the ones who had made him unhappy. She summoned every ounce of self-control, forcing an attitude of amiable nonchalance.

"Well, by the time we catch up to you, I expect you to have the campsite ready, beds folded down, supper in the pot. We'll be worn out you know, tramping the forest."

"Very funny."

She couldn't just let him go like this. She had no idea what he felt for her anymore. A sense of terror overtook her. "Why are you doing this to me, to us?"

"You want to get back to Boise, don't you?"

"That's not what I meant."

Distractedly, Parnell turned away. She was tearing him up. Yet all he could think of was that once returned to their ordinary lives, she wouldn't give him a second glance. He remembered how she'd looked at him when he'd first encountered her. Like something she would scrape off a shoe.

"What did you mean?" he finally said.

Rebecca was afraid to put it into words. If she did he might distance himself even further. She felt as if a weight were crushing her chest. "You never tell me how you feel about anything."

"I feel like finding a way out of here. That suit you?"

"Why are you being so stubborn, so obtuse?"

"I want out of here." He was infatuated, he thought. That was his problem. Never before had he wanted to give so much of himself to a woman. Not only sensuality, but tenderness. It just didn't fit the image he had of himself. He was lean and mean and tough. He was forgetting himself because Rebecca was bent on captivating him. The way he was thinking, the airy sensation in his gut was all her fault.

Rebecca stiffened. To say more would be resorting to begging. She couldn't do that. Pleading had been too much a part of her earlier life. She hadn't liked herself then. She'd spent years building her self-esteem, learning to like herself, learning to become independent, and since the crash— strong. She picked up her walking stick, called to the orphans.

"Let's get out of here, then," she said to Parnell. "Do whatever it takes. Which direction are we going in today?"

For the first hour they trekked together. In some places the snow lay thigh-high. And though Parnell forged a path of sorts, it was hard work to force her body through it. Often, she leaned into a drift and fell rather than walked forward. But as Molly began to tire and Jonesy's blisters began to trouble him Parnell pulled ahead. When he disappeared around a heap of scree Rebecca called out to him. He turned back, lifted a hand, then disappeared again.

Rebecca sagged. That was it. He'd left them behind. "We'll stop and rest here for a minute," she told the others.

"I think I'd be better off walking barefoot," Jonesy said.

"Who's going to carry me?" Molly wanted to know.

"I'm scared," said Nicholas. "I don't understand why nobody found us."

Santee helped the unseeing boy to a downed tree. "Because they didn't look."

"Of course they looked," Rebecca chastised as she lowered herself to the log. "I'm sure when we get to a telephone, we'll discover that hundreds of people searched for us."

Yancy plunked down next to Nicholas. "They sure didn't look in the right place."

Rebecca smiled. "No they didn't. But we found ourselves, didn't we? We never really felt lost, did we? Anyway, it was an adventure. Just think of the stories you can tell when you go back to school."

Jonesy cried as he unstuck first one and then the other

sock from his heels. "I'll never make it. How far do we have to hike anyway?"

"I don't know. But you will make it. We'll all make it." Rebecca liberally applied the topical anesthetic to the broken blisters. "Put your shoes back on."

A dark cloud crossed the sun, the mountainside went suddenly dark. She scowled at the wintry sky. "Come on. Let's hurry."

As they moved up, following in Parnell's footsteps, the terrain became more formidable. Trees stood high out of the snow, bent and gnarled by the constant wind. Once they came upon where Parnell had backtracked, he'd drawn an arrow in the snow, pointing to the correct path. The link reassured Rebecca. Eventually they came upon a second snow-formed arrow. It pointed to a protective outcropping of rock. Behind it they found a small pile of brush. Rebecca fumbled with the precious matches, lighting the fire. They all sank about it wearily.

"Who's hungry?" she asked brightly.

Nobody was.

"Let's go back to the cabin," Yancy pleaded. "I'm cold."

Rebecca took out the thermal foil blanket. They all hunched beneath it. She put her arms around the blind and the lame. "We can't go back. We're going forward. There may be a road over that next ridge. The captain may be waiting for us this very minute."

When they caught up with him, she wouldn't let him go on ahead anymore. She didn't care about being independent. She couldn't do this, couldn't keep encouraging the kids, cajoling them, pushing them to take another step, then another. She didn't care about her pride anymore.

The fire died. There wasn't another piece of wood to add.

Parnell had probably judged the time it would take to burn down. She used her walking stick to drag herself to her feet.

Each forward step was a chore. Molly whimpered. The pain of it all emotionally, physically was nearly too much. Rebecca was so short of breath she kept having to take big gulps of the frigid air. When her voice gave out, Santee had to take over. She couldn't help being proud of him. He talked them up and around the mountain—always in Parnell's footsteps.

When it became so dark they could hardly see, she called a halt. Santee pointed. "Look! Look there!" he shouted, directing her gaze down the mountainside. "There's a glow. I'll bet it's a fire. The captain has set up camp there."

And then out of the darkness Parnell materialized. "I could hear you a mile off," he said.

"If it's another mile, none of us will make it," Rebecca choked.

"I found a road." He wore his face like a mask, but Rebecca heard an undertone of controlled excitement in his voice.

"Well...hooray," she said.

He stood mute for a moment, then hefted Molly, picked up his flight bag and strode off toward the camp he'd made.

"Hey, Captain," Jonesy called after him. "You gonna come back and carry me?"

"Afraid you'll have to manage for yourself, sport."

Jonesy sniffed. "Nobody likes a fat kid."

All their old fears and hang-ups were coming back, Rebecca thought. "Go ahead and take off your shoes, Jonesy," she said. "I don't expect you'll come down with pneumonia in the distance between here and camp."

"Okay," he said. "But I bet I'm the only orphan in the

world with blubber who's tough enough to hike through snow and woods."

"That's enough. All of you. You've survived an event other kids would give their eyeteeth to have experienced."

"You think so?"

"Of course. You're all heros."

"Hey!" said Nicholas. "Maybe they'll make a movie about us!"

Rebecca rolled her eyes. "I hardly expect we've caused that much attention." She hoped and prayed not. Some publicity was inevitable, but the idea of television crews and newspaper reporters made her shudder. Her face felt hot just under the skin, but icy on the surface. She'd have to bring up the subject of themselves with Parnell. Make sure they had their stories straight. She couldn't bear it if suddenly the whole world knew she'd been rejected by a man a second time in her life.

By the time they reached the campsite, Parnell was stirring an egg-snow mixture into a froth with a peeled stick. He'd constructed a simple lean-to on a small bit of level ground below a large overhang of rock. It sheltered their backs from the cold breeze. In minutes, with their faces leaning toward the cheery fire, they were warm and lethargic.

Rebecca forced herself to scoop up snow to melt for hot chocolate. "Seems like old times," she said.

"Meaning?" Parnell asked cautiously.

"This is how we started out, melting snow. I guess you could say we've come full circle." She felt his eyes on her, but she didn't look up to read what might be in them. Parnell's socks were much too big for her, and one had slipped down inside her boot and rode painfully against her ankle. She sat back down to remedy the problem. Suddenly the cold and her own bleak exhaustion overwhelmed her. She rested her forehead on her knee and squeezed her eyes shut tightly. Damn it! She loved him. He was being such an ass. Insufferable!

Parnell was trying to serve up the eggs and watch what Rebecca was doing at the same time. When she put her head down on her knees, prickles crawled up his neck. He squirmed inside. He knew what she was up to all right! She was trying to make him feel guilty. Every woman he'd ever known had a knack for doing that. They did it just to make him miserable. Get him to suck up to her. It wasn't him that had called it off. Rebecca had done it with all her screeching. Don't touch me, don't touch me! Hadn't he told her that he couldn't get enough of her? What'd she want him to do anyway? Beg? Get down on his knees? To hell in a basket with that! He was better off pretending nothing had happened.

Under self-inflicted duress, he shoved a plate of eggs at her. "You want to eat or what?

Rebecca lifted her head. "Don't take that tone with me. It's not my fault we've been stuck out here."

Hostility got the better of him, he slammed the plate at her feet. Eggs flew. "Seems like I've heard that song before."

"So have we," muttered Santee.

"Keep outta this," Parnell snarled.

"Why are y'all fussing again?" asked Nicholas.

Delicately, with her fingertips, Rebecca picked bits of egg out of the snow, arranging them on the plate. "We're just having a discussion. It has nothing to do with any of you. But in the interest of harmony, the captain and I will chat later."

"Suits me," Parnell agreed, his face filled with mistrust and apprehension. Overcome with a sensation of helplessness, which he didn't like, he built up the fire and sat opposite Rebecca. The flames towered so that he couldn't see across to her. Out of sight, out of mind, he told himself.

By the time the fire had died down, the kids had curled up to sleep in the lean-to. When Parnell raised his eyes he found himself faced with Rebecca's accusing stare. "Don't try to make me the scapegoat," he warned.

Rebecca glared at him, a good imitation of his own ferocious bulldog expression. "You mean about the crash?"

"I take full responsibility on that score. I'm talking about the other."

She felt bands tighten in her chest. The ache almost took her breath away. "I won't mention it, if you don't."

"The kids didn't notice anything." It was a statement, spoken to reassure himself that his tough exterior image would remain intact.

"Probably not."

"We were discreet." He watched her pupils contract into tiny black specks.

"Oh, shut up," she said, barely audible because she was on the verge of tears.

A cold sweat suddenly drenched Parnell's brow. He had a galloping urge to gather her into his arms, croon sweet things into her ear, put his hand under her sweater. He restrained himself, but he had to move. He stirred around, made up a brush bed for her next to Molly under the lean-to. "You ought to get some sleep," he said.

"You, too," she managed, and after a moment went to lie down.

"I think I'll keep the fire going for a while." It would cut down on dream time, he thought. No sense letting a fantasy get the best of him. Overhead a break in the clouds revealed a star-studded sky, a hanging slice of moon. The fantasy came anyway.

He could see himself waking up mornings, Rebecca's head on his pillow, her body arched, fitted into the curve of his. But he'd probably have to marry her to make that fantasy real. The first time he'd been married he hadn't had to raise the question. One night he'd gone over to Frieda's and she had told him she'd made arrangements with the chaplain. Most of his clothes and shaving kit were already at her place. At the time it seemed the right thing to do.

Somehow, he couldn't see Rebecca making such an assumption. She'd want it to be a joint decision. Hah! He could just see himself asking.

"Dear, how would you like to get hitched?" He shook his head. That sounded like he was trying to harness a horse to a wagon.

Maybe: *"Say Rebecca, since we've already been...you know— wanna get married?"* Not romantic enough, and above all women wanted romance.

"Darling...?" He couldn't even start the question out that way! He'd never called a woman darling in his life. She'd probably laugh him right out of the room.

Then what?

He stared down at his hands. They were trembling. Coward! Jell-O gut, he named himself.

Rebecca slept. He watched her, transfixed, until he'd convinced himself that the real fantasy had been the hours he'd spent with her on the pallet in the cabin.

THE SUN CAME UP all brazen and cheerful as if there wasn't a bit of misery or hunger anywhere in the world. Rebecca stared at the sky as if betrayed. When she turned that same stare on Parnell, he avoided looking at her. She just couldn't let him get off that easily. The good sleep she'd had renewed her courage. What had been done could not be undone.

Could not be forgotten. She opened her mouth to tell him, and finally she burst out, "It won't work, you know, pretending nothing's changed, pretending there's nothing between us."

His face went rigid with panic. "I don't know what you're talking about."

"Yes, you do. And that's the point I'm trying to make." She took off the overskirt and shoved it into a tote.

"You better keep that on."

"No, it hinders me."

"What you said a minute ago..." he began.

Rebecca smiled nervously. "Yes?"

"It was unrealistic from start to finish."

"So you've given it some thought?" He was silent. She went on in a chatty voice. "Well, so have I. And the way we took to each other, I don't mean at first—what we did— there has to be something there." She tried to look past his expressionless eyes. She saw him searching, asking himself if he believed her.

He hesitated for a moment. "It was like you said. We were thrown together by accident. Just lust."

"I never said just lust!"

"You made me think it. Same thing."

His stubborn tenacity was infuriating, especially since he was so wrong! "Can we agree to discuss it once we're back in Boise? We can meet for coffee or something." She just couldn't let him go out of her life.

"Okay," he said. He didn't go into Boise more than five times a year. Amos did all the grocery shopping. Sometimes business took Parnell out to the regional airport, but he bid contracts from his desk, or the kitchen table in the trailer out behind the the hangar. Everything else got done by phone. Hell. Rebecca had just let him off the hook.

The boys appeared out of the woods from the direction of the temporary latrine. "Molly wants you, Rebecca," Santee yelled. "Her zipper's stuck and she won't let me help. You better hurry. She's afraid a grizzly is gonna get her while her pants are down."

"A grizzly?" She headed into the woods. "No bear in his right mind would come within a mile of me today!"

"Amen to that," she heard Parnell say.

She dealt him a lofty smile over her shoulder. "Isn't it your turn to do breakfast dishes?"

"There really might be grizzlies or brown bears around here," he returned.

"Oh, great!" She took off at a trot.

Parnell stared after her, liking the way she moved. "But, not at this time of year," he muttered sotto voce, pleased with himself.

"What's funny?" Yancy asked.

"Nothing! Get your poncho on before I separate your head from your neck." In Parnell's estimation it was a good threat. In the past days he'd perfected several variations of it to keep the boys in line. But now Yancy just stood there aping him. "You deaf or something? Get with it. We're ready to haul out of here."

"Geez! I hate grown-ups. I hope I stay a kid forever."

"That can be arranged," Parnell said, warming up to a tirade. Being around the kids had given him an anxiety neurosis. If he believed in shrinks—which he didn't—he'd have to spend two years on a couch just to rid himself of it.

Yancy shuffled out of Parnell's reach. "You're an ugly old man."

Ugly didn't bother Parnell but *old* did. "I'm not old."

"You look old. You got wrinkles around your eyes."

"Those are laugh lines."

"You're not laughing now and they're still there."

Parnell scowled which added wrinkles to his brow. He could see Yancy counting them. "Your day's coming, brat. I hope you own a kid just like yourself someday."

Yancy drew himself up. "I am never gonna have any little kids. Intercourse is yukky. And besides, you'd have to do it with a girl."

"Intercourse? Intercourse!" Parnell was shocked. "Where'd you learn words like that?"

"In school."

"If we could spare it, I'd wash your mouth out with soap for lying. You don't learn that in school."

"Yes, we do, in sex education."

"In my day we learned that stuff on the street!"

"Now you have to read it in a book. You learned in olden times."

Parnell made some unpleasant hostile sounds.

"That kind of language indicates a very poor vocabulary," Rebecca said acidly, on approach with Molly in tow. "Yancy, get your poncho on."

Parnell faced Rebecca. First he had to put up with a kid calling him names, now Rebecca was attacking him. "I'll have you know I'm in my prime," he ground out in defense, which made not one whit of sense to Rebecca.

"Well...okay," she answered, taken aback.

"It's disgusting. Seven- and eight-year-olds discussing sex."

Rebecca clamped her hands over Molly's ears. "Have you lost your mind? Sex is not a topic for youngsters."

His lips curled in a smirk. "Just goes to show how much you know."

His sarcasm engulfed Rebecca. "You're worse than the kids. You're not happy unless you're stirring up trouble or fighting. I can't take any more! The sooner we part company, the better I'll like it. Direct me to that road."

"My pleasure," he said, bending over in an exaggerated bow.

"You should think twice before you present such a target, Parnell. Somebody might consider it the perfect opportunity to knock some sense into your head."

He snapped straight. "And you should keep your sweater buttoned up, Rebecca. Somebody might consider your display of flesh entrapment. That is, once he has some sense, however gained." Her face closed up. Parnell grinned inwardly. Goading, he thought, did have its compensations.

"YOU SAID A ROAD!" Rebecca wailed accusingly. The lane was narrow and in places wind-swept of snow, so that the dark earth and ruts were visible where the sun shone through a towering overhead foliage.

"It is a road. I didn't say it was the Los Angeles Freeway. What'd you expect?"

"Lines painted down the middle, road signs, cars, a motel, a bath, a telephone—a real road," she said lamely. "Not a path out in the middle of nowhere."

"Some people just can't be pleased," Parnell groused. "It is a real road. It was probably constructed by a lumber company to carry trucks, or maybe a parks department."

"At least it's flat," said Jonesy, dropping down on the verge. "I couldn't crawl over another rock or wade through another inch of snow for a hundred dollars."

"Well...?" said Parnell. "Do you want to stand here jawing and whining or get on with it?"

Pulling Nicholas along, Santee lurched through a drift and stood in the middle of the road. "Which way?"

"Just flip a coin," Rebecca said, dejected.

"We'll keep southeast," Parnell said, and directed Santee left. He started to take Rebecca's arm but stopped himself. Better not take too big a leap of faith, he told himself. "Give me your pack," he offered instead. "It'll free you to help Molly."

It was an offer she couldn't refuse. The makeshift straps were cutting into her shoulders despite her coat.

Parnell watched her face. She was keeping her thoughts to herself. He couldn't read anything into her expression. Maybe he'd gone just a bit overboard, carrying on as he'd been. If he knew for certain just what she'd say, he'd... But suppose she said no? Or just stared at him with those big gray eyes as if he were a candidate for a mental institution?

He tried to tell himself that the law of averages might be on his side. He was due some good luck. On the other hand, who trusted averages? If one believed in statistics, every human on the face of the earth was likely to die twice over of some terrible disease.

If only there was a way he could bring up the future in a roundabout way. After they'd trudged a quarter mile in silence he hit on it.

"Cheer up, Rebecca. You'll be back in Abigail's parlor before you know it. Tucked in front of that great old fireplace."

"I guess so." But the orphanage wasn't where she wanted to spend the rest of her life. Abigail had taken her in as a lost soul, much as she had the children. She didn't feel so lost now—at least in the literal sense. "I won't stay tucked for long. Abigail's closing the home. The foundation's out of money."

Every fiber in Parnell's being came alert. "Oh? What will you do then?"

"Find another job."

The wheels in his head began to spin. He looked at it from

every angle. Yep, he thought. Maybe there was a way. He'd think it out. "What about the kids?" he said, pouring sympathy into his voice.

"The state will find them foster homes."

"Poor tykes."

She glanced at him, taking in his profile as he matched her, step for step, in the crisp snow. "You're buttering me up for something."

He'd suspected it, but now he knew for sure. She could read his mind. "I'm not."

"You want me to tell everybody how thoughtful and wonderfully heroic you've been."

"Hell no!" Despite his protest, pleasing headlines popped into his head anyway. *Pilot saves social worker and five orphans.*

"When I came into your office and found you asleep, I should've turned around and left."

"Then I'd've been out here all by myself."

"Meaning?"

"Meaning?" Meaning! How'd this happen? He circled around it warily. "Well, I want you to know I have enjoyed your company. Some of the time."

"You sound like a thank-you note with reservations." She recalled the texture of his skin against her own when their bodies had been entwined. Recalled the feeling she'd had of being well loved, secure. And every step out of the wilderness was one step closer to being separated from him. She felt a dull ache in her heart.

He watched her out of the corner of his eye. "A person doesn't have to get along with someone every minute of the day. It's not possible."

"I couldn't agree with you more, present company included."

When he next glanced at her she was deep in thought. The delicate line of her jaw was tense. She stumbled. He put out his arm steadying her at the waist. When she didn't shrug him off he arranged a scowl on his face to mask his pleasure.

12

THE ADVANTAGE of following the road, beyond the promise it held out to them, was that they were all in view of one another at all times. Rebecca lagged behind, as did Jonesy, who was suffering terribly with his feet.

It was only when Parnell called for a rest that the tired little party cheered up, they straightened their tortured backs and ignored their sore feet. "On the whole," Rebecca complained, "we're in far worse shape than any time since the crash itself!"

Parnell held up his hand. "No nagging. It's disheartening and will only slow us down."

Rebecca burst into tears of rage and misery. "Why didn't they find us? Why didn't they keep looking?"

Parnell trooped to her side and hunkered down. "Come on, hush," he said softly, brushing gently at the tears on her cheeks. "You've done great. I just pick at you to have something to say. To reassure myself you're still with me. Right now all I'm asking from you is the will to survive a bit longer. You can't lose it now. We're close to getting out of this, I feel it."

The pep talk, along with his gentle manner helped. She nodded. "Okay. But couldn't we have a fire—just a small one?"

"All right. But we can't build one at every rest stop or we'll run out of matches."

While Parnell passed out some of the last malt tablets, Rebecca gathered moss and twigs, piling them at the roadside. The small mound was carefully lighted. They collapsed around it.

"We might as well check ourselves over," Parnell instructed.

Though the rigged pack straps had cut into shoulders, socks were wearing thin and pants were ragged, Jonesy's feet were the worse. He'd lost so much weight that his shoes were now too big. They kept slipping and rubbing his blisters raw. Rebecca peeled his socks away.

"He can have my socks," offered Santee.

"And, mine," Parnell said.

Once the exchange was made, they stumbled off again.

As they plodded on, their spirits lifted. In spite of their aching legs and arms, the walking was keeping them warm and they were making much faster progress than before.

At each bend in the road the anticipation grew that they would round it and come upon a house, a park station, or meet the rescue team.

"Are we nearly there?" begged Molly.

"Where is there?" said Santee.

"We're on a road," Parnell said, reassuring them as they trudged along. "Every mile we cover is one mile closer to somebody."

Rebecca sensed in Parnell an urgency that she didn't share. It was all she could do to coax one foot in front of the other and find voice to encourage the youngsters forward.

Lunch was a frugal affair, prepared right in the middle of the road. In any case, there was nothing left for supper except powdered milk and a handful of malt tablets. Parnell allowed them a longer rest. He spread the thermal foil blanket and the little group huddled together like puppies. Aching and uncomfortable they curled up and were all asleep within five minutes.

An hour later Parnell shook Rebecca awake and made her stand up. "We've got to keep moving."

"I don't know if I can!"

"Just a bit farther."

He wakened the kids. "Let's push on, boys."

They staggered forward. The sun weakened, their shadows grew longer.

They came around a bend; the trees widened out suddenly as if they had been pushed back for the express purpose of revealing a valley of snow-capped hills. A quarter mile farther and the trees engulfed the road once more. Rebecca gasped at the beauty of the panoramic view.

"God's work," she said.

"More like the devil's," Parnell muttered, taking in the sheer drop from the verge of the road. "You kids get back from there! Damn it! That's all we need, one of you to go falling off a mountain."

"Can't be much worse than falling out of the sky," Rebecca retorted.

"Keep moving!" he said. The road narrowed where snow had drifted against the cliff to the left. Parnell glanced up at the wall of snow. The look and shape of the ice sent alarm signals clanging through the back lobes of his brain.

Jonesy hobbled to the edge of the drop and issued an unsuccessful yodel. It came echoing back, reverberating off the mountain.

"Don't do that!" Parnell ordered so softly Rebecca caught his alarm. Her heart skipped a beat.

"What's wrong?"

"I don't know. Maybe nothing. I don't like the way that snow looks."

The late-afternoon sun was bathing the sheer upward slant a pinkish gold. "It's beautiful, though," Rebecca said.

"And dangerous." He yanked Molly off her feet and deposited her on his shoulders.

Down the road well within the shadows of the trees, a movement caught Rebecca's eye. The movement became a man who was waving his arms and shouting.

"Oh!" she cried. "We're found! Parnell! We're found!" Her knees buckled and she sat down.

He grabbed her arm and jerked her to her feet. "Keep moving!"

"It has to be the rescue team!"

But Nicholas, who had God's compensation of keen hearing, puffed, "He's calling us idiots."

A great rumbling sound overtook them. Parnell stopped and stared up the cliff. A great wall of snow seemed to erupt slowly from the top of the escarpment.

Now there were two men shouting at them. Parnell thrust Nicholas into Rebecca's arms. "Run! Everybody, run!"

Santee grabbed Yancy's hand and the two boys sprinted forward.

Parnell shoved at Jonesy so hard the boy lifted from his already loosened shoes.

At first Rebecca only heard the sounds of her tortured breath, the yelps of Nicholas, the thudding of boots pounding, but after a moment a greater sound seemed to burst the very air. Jonesy streaked past her.

The men were coming out of the forest toward them, their faces stricken, hands out. One of them jerked Nicholas from Rebecca. Breathless, sides aching, she collapsed and felt herself being dragged.

Behind her, the noise was as if the world was coming to an end.

She lay on the ground, lungs bursting, and lifted her head.

As it broke entirely away from the earth, the massive wall of snow sent spume shooting into the air. The sun penetrated it causing starbursts of color. Parnell was sprinting hard, Molly bobbing and screaming atop his shoulders.

"Man, he's not gonna make it," came a stunned voice from above her.

Rebecca scrambled to her feet, attempting to lurch forward. Strong arms held her.

The men were yelling encouragement to Parnell.

A huge chunk of ice slammed into his legs. He lost his grip on Molly and she flew through the air and then the miasma of snow swallowed them both.

Rebecca sagged.

It was a full minute before she realized the screaming in her ears was coming from herself. She choked it back.

Another few seconds and there was deep silence.

"They couldn't live through that," Rebecca said, almost inaudible.

"Don't give them up so easily, little lady," a gravelly voice said in an aside as he delegated a crew to begin searching with an urgency proclaimed by sharp staccato orders.

She looked at the men, a half dozen or more of them now. "Why couldn't you have come sooner?" she wailed. "Five minutes sooner?"

The man who had first spoken shook his head, and after a moment, Rebecca and the boys were ushered some yards along the road where a caravan was parked among trucks and oversized snow- and earth-moving machines.

Dazed, Rebecca let herself be helped into the caravan and seated. Blankets were brought and draped over their shoulders. Someone brought out a medical kit. Bruises and scrapes were inspected, cleaned, and Jonesy's feet were bandaged.

At the periphery of her consciousness Rebecca absorbed the dialogue directed toward her.

The men worked for a lumber company. They were opening the road to a camp deep in the forest. The avalanche had been man-made, activated by dynamite. And except for their presence, a perfect "blow." A mug of hot coffee laced heavily with milk and sugar was thrust into her hands.

"How'd you get into the forest," asked the crew foreman. "That road hasn't seen any traffic in three weeks."

Rebecca took a sip of the coffee. "Our plane crashed. I don't know where. We were walking out."

The foreman exhaled. "Dear God in heaven! When?"

Rebecca had to stop and think. "The twelfth. The morning of the twelfth."

"We have to get you to the authorities. Was there...how many?" He slapped his forehead. "You're the social worker with the orphans from Idaho aren't you? It was on the news."

Rebecca nodded. "I don't want to leave here until you've found Molly and Captain Stillman. I won't leave."

"Neither will any of us," Santee asserted. "We started together. We want to finish together."

He had said it as well as she herself might have. Rebecca lifted her ashen face and smiled her approval at the boy. Of all the children, he and Molly were the closest to each other.

"We'll give it until dark," said the burly built crew chief. "That's the most I can promise."

Rebecca met his gaze with a jut of jaw and a frosty look in her eyes that betrayed a certain hostility. "We've been through a lot together. We're not leaving without Molly and the captain. We can't."

"Ma'am, you don't understand—"

"It's you who doesn't understand! If it weren't for Captain Stillman none of us would be alive today. And if he's—" She couldn't finish.

"We're not deserting him or Molly," Santee said. "She'd be scared of strangers."

"We'd tell the police you were mean to us," promised Yancy.

"Right," the foreman grunted finally and stepped out of the caravan.

Rebecca heard him yelling for someone to scare up some sandwiches. Her adrenaline spent, she sagged against the plastic cushions. The sandwiches were brought, but she found she couldn't swallow. Nor could she stay snug and warm inside the camper while Molly and Parnell might be—were surely—struggling for their lives. She slipped outside.

SHE STARED OUT at the gathering darkness as she paced up and down the road. She could hear the search party calling out to one another, but she couldn't see them. The air was redolent with the smell of earth. She glanced once at the escarpment from which the wall of snow had been dynamited. It looked bleak and raw and rocky. It looked the way she felt. The fear that kept sweeping over her had settled into a tightness in her throat.

When she heard a commotion coming from far down the mountainside, her heart missed a beat. *Both of them, God!* she prayed. *Please, both of them.*

Santee came racing up to her. "It's Molly," he yelled breathlessly. "She's alive!" Rebecca didn't have the courage to ask about Parnell. It would be too much like bargaining with God.

Molly was more than alive. She was hoarse and furious. Inside the caravan Rebecca gathered the child into her arms. The tumbling snow had rocketed Molly into a small gully out of which she couldn't climb. She had yelled until her throat hurt she said.

"I didn't like it. I was by myself and I thought a bear was gonna get me and my clothes are all torn up and I went and wet my pants, but I didn't mean to."

Rebecca brushed hair back off the child's forehead. "It's all right sweetheart. We'll get you—" She looked up into the cratered face of the man who'd thrust Molly into her arms. "Thank you."

He left to rejoin the search for Parnell. Santee hovered. Reluctantly Rebecca relinquished Molly into his care; she could see he needed to touch the girl. To make the rescue of her real. As she needed to see and touch Parnell. She went back to pacing the road.

The moon came up, but was soon hidden by cloud, only a faint luminosity lingering. The heavy earth- and snow-moving equipment loomed up, dark shadows whose shapes seemed imbued with life. The torches and flashlights of the searchers were like pinpricks in the distance. They had sticks and were poking them deep into the snow.

The crew foreman approached her. Rebecca sensed what he was going to tell her. He wanted to stop the search. Night was hard on them, the wind had come up. It was cold down on the slope with no protection. He was thinking of his men. But she had to think of Parnell. If he were under the snow, what chance did he have of lasting until morning. When the foreman lifted the Coleman lamp it illuminated the tightness of her lips, the strained look in her eyes. She had death looking over her shoulder, she wasn't about to give in.

"If you stop now, you'd be killing him!" she shouted, depriving the man of a soft approach, the coaxing she was certain he'd attempt.

He hesitated. "Ma'am, you don't seem to realize, it was a miracle we found the girl. I've sent one of the boys to notify the authorities. We don't have a chance in hell now of finding your friend, at least—not alive."

"He's alive! He's been through worse! He's flown into the eye of hurricanes and survived; he's landed on aircraft carriers in twenty-foot seas; he's done belly landings and crashed into a corn field! Don't tell me he's dead!"

The man tried to put his arm round her. "You're upset. You have a right to be, considering—"

Rebecca jerked away. "Give me that lamp! I'll search for him myself!"

"For God's sake, lady—"

The shouting came from below them on the slope. Rebecca froze. "What'd he say?" she whispered.

Then she heard it clearly, the words echoing into dark. "We found him! He's breathing!"

Rebecca snatched at the foreman's coat. "There!" she said triumphantly. "You see?" Then she crumpled to the ground and sat there, hugging her knees, rocking, crying.

"The reason I like this job," the man said succinctly, "is because there ain't a woman within forty miles on any given day." He bent down and helped Rebecca to her feet, surprised to find that she was smiling at him through her tears.

"I know a man who holds those exact same sentiments."

The foreman's name was Edwin Salter, called Salty by friend and foe alike. The lamp dangled in his hand, the upward glow illuminating Rebecca's face which seemed bloodless to him. Her eyes were gleaming and feverish.

"Pull yourself together," he said, thinking how sad it was that after all she'd been through, she had utterly lost all her senses.

13

MOLLY CIRCLED AND DANCED around Rebecca like an excited puppy. "Is any of that mail for me?"

"We'll see."

"Pour it out on the table," said Abigail. "We'll sort it before supper."

"You're as bad as Molly," Rebecca chided.

The charming old wreck of a woman grinned and put her arms about Molly. "What're the most famous words in our world?"

"'Has Santa Claus come yet?'" Molly responded, collapsing into a welter of giggles.

"We ought to invite that reporter for dinner sometime," Abigail mused. "The story she wrote and photos she took sure wrung a lot of hearts."

Rebecca shook her head. Abigail had a tough dryness, a voluble energy, an inconsequent loquacity, a warm-hearted kindness illumined by a shrewdness one seldom gave the frail woman credit for. And all of that was dedicated toward the children's benefit, but still...

"Doesn't it bother you to keep exploiting the situation, the children?" she asked.

Abigail snorted. "Bother me? Where, my young friend, is your sense of justice? Here we were, the Foundation, out of money, trying to place the children in God knows what kind of homes and along comes this heavensent opportunity.... Look at all these letters! Most of them containing checks.

There's money for Nicholas to have eye surgery. Would you deny him the chance to see? Money for Molly to have her feet straightened. Money to buy food, pay the fuel bill. And money left over for trust funds for the kids. Every single one of them. College! Do realize what kind of future—"

"I know, but—" Rebecca was remembering the frenzy when they had deplaned in Boise, the rush of flash bulbs going off, cameras, microphones thrust into their faces, the questions screamed from every direction. She was remembering with mortification the photo of herself, too. Hair awry, eyes swollen, clothes bedraggled. She'd been carrying Molly, and the enterprising reporter had gone behind her back and asked Molly how they had celebrated Christmas in the wild.

Molly's shocked expression, the now famous words, had been flashed to television stations across the country.

It had been the day after Christmas. The idea that the orphans had missed Christmas had grabbed a nation by its heart and opened wallets when most people were still in the afterglow of a holiday spirit.

Offers to adopt the children had poured in. But Abigail was finding fault with each and every prospective parent. The Tynan Foundation could now afford to be choosy. After all, Abigail said over and over, what with their trust funds being established, it was as if the children would be taking dowries into their new homes. One couldn't be too careful.

Not to mention more practical matters. According to the Indian Child Welfare Act, Santee's adoption would have to be approved by Tribal Council. That sometimes took years. Nor could Abigail consider separating Molly and Santee. Santee would most assuredly have to be on hand to cheer Molly on during the girl's foot surgery next summer.

Nicholas was scheduled for cornea transplants. Abigail

was reserving for herself the joy of showing the boy the
wonders of the world. And it wouldn't be fair would it, to
send Jonesy and Yancy out of the bosom of the Tynan family
while all these exciting things were going on?

"I do wish you would give an interview," Abigail said,
momentarily drawing Rebecca out of her thoughts.

"The children have said it all. I'd be boring."

Parnell wasn't giving any interviews, either. He was refusing on the grounds of the ongoing investigation by the
Federal Aviation Agency and the postal inspectors. For a
time, he had hidden behind a hospital gown.

He'd been unconscious when the rescuers had brought
him up to the camp. She had neither seen nor heard from
him since he'd been whisked off in an ambulance. She knew
only what she'd read in the papers. He'd suffered a dislo-
cated shoulder, some terrible bruising. But he'd been out of
the hospital for four days now. Television cameras had re-
corded his discharge.

He'd had plenty of time to call her and hadn't. She had a
mental list of reasons why he had not.

He was busy filling out forms for insurance to replace his
plane.

The FAA investigators were grilling him.

The postal inspectors had him in jail for losing the mail,
opening the box of apples.

The press was sitting on his doorstep and he couldn't escape.

He had amnesia and didn't recall that she even existed.

His telephone had been disconnected.

With her very bright, sharp eyes Abigail was absorbing
every expression flitting across Rebecca's face. "Molly, my
sweet," she said. "I'm going to leave you the job of sorting
the mail. Put all the ones with your name into a pile by itself.

I'll help you open them later." She then took Rebecca's arm. "Come along, I think it's time you and I had a little talk. Let's have tea by the fire in the parlor."

The room was full of the scent of chrysanthemums, splashed with colorful poinsettias and a towering Christmas tree fully lit—a gift from an anonymous donor.

The position of the furniture had not been changed in forty years. The old sofas and chairs were elegant, shabby and comfortable. In another part of the old farmhouse was a den which held the television. The parlor's focus was a grand stone fireplace.

"I've always liked this room," said Abigail as she poured and passed Rebecca the delicate china cup. "It's just always seemed a room in which one could air one's problems, see them in a truer light."

"I don't have a problem," Rebecca said, regretting at once the telltale sharpness of her tone.

"My dear, Parnell Stillman is most assuredly a problem. You forget. I've known the boy since he was a teenager. I admit there was that gap of time when he was in the Navy, but his Uncle Henry talked of him often."

"I'm sure I haven't given you any indication—"

The elderly woman held up a care-worn hand. "Rebecca dear, you've spoken volumes by omission. Every time his name is mentioned on the news, you fly to the television. When the telephone rings, you tense, you hover as I speak. So distracting. You read and reread everything printed about him, then you look off into space.

"I may be old, but my eyes and ears are as sharp as they've ever been. You're in a funk. At first I put it down to the terrible ordeal you've suffered. But as I listen more and more to the children, I realize that though there was extreme difficulty and hardship, there was also a sense of adventure.

Santee can barely keep his mouth shut. Exactly opposite the way he'd been for months. That boy was almost a mute, except when it came to Molly. Well, that's neither here nor there. My point is, you've met your match in Parnell."

"That doesn't mean—"

"Pooh. You're in love with him. The Stillmans have always been a rogue species. Parnell's a bit of a mongrel. So was his Uncle Henry." There was a note of affection in her voice. The words almost an endearment. "That appeals to a woman. It most assuredly appealed to me. Getting one of them to marry is the problem."

Rebecca sank deeper into the overstuffed chair and with a weak smile, gave up all pretense. "What can I do?"

"I've invited him to supper."

An electric force shot through Rebecca. "He's accepted?"

"He could hardly refuse. After all, I did hire him to fly all of you to San Francisco. The detour was not to my liking. I suffered terrible bouts of depression. Not to mention how frightened I was for all of you. I never thought you dead, but I did imagine you maimed and suffering. He owes me."

"When?"

"Tonight. I didn't think it would be too troublesome, what with having the funds to recall the cook—"

Rebecca put down the tea cup with a clatter. "Oh!"

"My dear," Abigail said to Rebecca's departing back, "you must remember to be careful with that china. It was my grandmother's, you know. Irreplaceable."

SHE HAD TO LOOK HER BEST, smell wonderful, wear her frilliest underwear. Bathe and shampoo her hair. Those things accomplished, she demolished her closet. The ivory sweater dress, she decided. But the lack of color made her look drab. Anyway, it was too formal. She settled finally on a burgundy cashmere sweater with matching slacks. Not too much makeup. Mascara on her lashes and the barest hint of blush.

She knew he had arrived when she heard the excited squeals and shrieks of the children. The tapping on her bedroom door made perspiration break out on her palms.

"Rebecca?" came Abigail's voice. "Our dinner guest is here."

"I'm just coming," she said, and grabbed a tissue, drying her palms.

They were all gathered in the parlor. A log had been added to the fire. The Christmas-tree lights sparkled. The children were sprawled in chairs, on the sofa, on the floor.

Parnell was standing near the fire, a drink in his hand. He glanced up as she entered the room. Their eyes met.

Suddenly Rebecca couldn't swallow, couldn't breathe properly. She had absolutely no idea what he felt for her anymore.

"Hello," she said softly and her eyes took him in. She had spent hours going over the contours of his face in her mind, impressing it into her memory so she could always retrace it. It was different now. He had shaved. The beard gone, but a thick dark mustache held forth over the sensual curve of his mouth. He wore a suit and tie, cuffs perfectly shot. He lifted his drink in greeting, as if he, too, was at a loss for words.

"You two have met," Abigail said into the silence.

Thus prompted, Parnell found his voice. "How are you, Rebecca?"

"Fine, thank you."

"What wonderfully scintillating conversation," Abigail scoffed in disgust.

"Usually they fight," put in Jonesy.

Rebecca saw Parnell flinch then. She could see that his eyes were as bright as hers felt. She was afraid to say anything. It was useless to try to make small talk anyway, she thought, when the greater question loomed and filled her with tension. She sank down on the arm of a chair occupied by Santee, suddenly too weak to stand.

"Come along to the dinner table, children," Abigail said. "Let's leave these two to become reacquainted."

Rebecca protested. "I thought—"

"You got me over here on the pretense of dinner," Parnell said, his dark eyes glinting wildly, and his gaze touching on everyone in the room except Rebecca.

"I'm still indulging the children's appetites," Abigail returned airily. "It's hot dogs with chili for them. We adults are having rare roast beef. I'll send the cook for you. Thirty minutes."

She herded the children out of the parlor, down the wide hall and to the back of the house.

"Well," Rebecca said.

"I need a drink," Parnell said.

"You have one in your hand."

"Refill, then." He loosened his tie with a savage jerk.

"Am I such awful company that—"

He ran his fingers through his hair, disheveling it. Rebecca couldn't take her eyes from him. Closer inspection revealed his cuff links didn't match, the collar button beneath the tie knot was missing. He was almost the familiar Parnell she knew and loved.

"You're not awful company. What made you think that? It's—you look beautiful. I knew you would. I always thought of you as silk, imagined you—" Hell! He wasn't about to say that.

"You did?" When he stayed mute, she went on, found a safer topic. "How's your shoulder?"

He flexed beneath the suit jacket. "A little sore, not enough to keep me from work."

"How is it? Work? The airfield?"

"Paperwork has me snowed under. Twenty-five different forms to fill out. I have depositions running out my ears. Don't think I'll ever wreck a plane again."

Rebecca took a deep breath. "Could you use some help?"

"You?"

She nodded.

He looked at her for a long moment, then shook his head. "I don't think it's the kind of job you'd like. No excitement."

Rebecca felt her heart seize up. He didn't mean doing office work. He meant in his life! "If you'll excuse me," she said utterly calm, "I'll just go see if Abigail needs—"

"Wait!" He moved across the room to her, grabbed her arm. Touching her sent a jolt to his head. He had promised himself he wouldn't get near her. Now he was breathing in the scent of her, his nerve endings recording the feel of her skin. "Rebecca..." His voice cracked, both his arms went around her.

She bent her head, let it rest on his chest, doing nothing more than absorbing the essence of him, afraid to move, to speak lest she awake and find herself only dreaming.

"Damn! But I've missed you. I've been feeling as if I left a part of me back in those woods."

"Why didn't you call me, you sorry lout?"

"Why didn't you come to the hospital?"

"I was afraid to."

"Afraid? You? Of what?"

"I thought you might not want to see me. What we did, the circumstances..."

"Same here," he said. He bent his head, nuzzled her ear, her brow. "You smell good enough to..." His libido was in a frenzy. "Let's get out here!"

He pulled her along, stopping in the foyer only long enough to grab his overcoat, a wrap for her.

ABIGAIL HEARD the front door slam, heard the heavy motor of Parnell's truck chug to life. She hurried into the foyer, peered out the window.

"A perfectly good roast gone to waste," she said with a sigh. Then she began to think of all the publicity a wedding between the two would garner. Molly as flower girl, Santee as best man. And there was that lovely offer from that magazine tucked at the back of her desk drawer. Not that Rebecca and Parnell would agree. Therefore, she wouldn't ask!

Abigail, my dear, she chided herself, *you're a nasty, interfering old fool. Make that an old avaricious romantic fool,* she amended. A twinge of guilt weighed upon her thin shoulders as she returned to the kitchen. She looked about for some small penance with which to assuage her conscience.

"Pass the mustard, Santee," she said. "I think I'll try one of those dreadful wieners."

14

HE WAS STROKING her hair, her face, kissing her neck, her ears, her lips, as though he would starve without her. He hadn't let her go since they entered his trailer. He had led her to the bedroom, turned on a lamp and undressed her.

"I knew it would be like this," Parnell said. "I kept dreaming how it would be in a bed, not having to worry about anyone listening." He drew his hand down from her shoulder to her thigh. "You've gained back some weight."

"Not romantic," Rebecca murmured. She reached up and traced his dimples. "I never knew you had these."

"I keep 'em in reserve. When all else fails...."

"Did you think you were going to?"

"I didn't know what to think."

"Now you do?"

"I only know I've been miserable."

That seemed about as far as he meant to take it. He was doing things to her with the tips of his fingers, making it hard for her to concentrate beyond the excitement, the swelling in her body.

Her eyes feasted on his muscular arms, the wide shoulders, the narrow hips, savoring him piece by piece. Against her pelvis his erection pulsated with a life of its own. She ran her fingers over the throbbing vein.

Parnell moaned, bruising her lips with furious kisses. Her lips were as hungry as his. Rebecca ached with happiness.

This was how it would be between them forever, she thought.

She hadn't known what to actually expect after the wild drive out to the airfield. He hadn't told her that he loved her. She hadn't told him, either. But then, in that first rush, that first desperateness, the only thing that had seemed important was to be in each other's arms, to satisfy the deep visceral craving.

As his hands played over her, Parnell watched her face with pleasure. He felt so drawn to her, as if she were a refuge where he belonged.

"Do turn off the light," she begged.

"Not a chance." He flicked his tongue in the hollow of her neck, felt the pulse beating fast and hard.

"At least close your eyes."

"Can't. I'm afraid you'll disappear. I have to keep my hands on you. I have to... Damn! I've never *needed* anyone so much!"

He moved atop her then, spreading her legs with his knees, but pushed into her slowly, deliberately giving her time to feel him inside her, as if entreating her to surrender more of herself. When she felt him barely inside her, she held her body taut and poised. Their hands and mouths stroked, touched, searched. He burrowed his head between her breasts, his mouth lingering on one nipple, pulling in and releasing. Then he was greedily penetrating her thighs. "Hold me, Rebecca," he whispered as he thrust deep into her. "Hold me."

"Parnell, let me up. I have to get dressed." There was little conviction in her voice, she felt relaxed and dreamy.

He draped a terry robe about her shoulders. "Hate like hell to have you covered up, but here—put this on."

"I can't go back to the orphanage wearing your robe."

"I want you to stay here. You're kidnapped."

She drew a shaky breath. "Don't joke." But she slipped into the robe and belted it.

"What do you think of the trailer?"

"All I've seen is the bedroom. The bed's nice."

He ushered her from room to room until the tour ended in the surprisingly roomy kitchen. "Well? What do you think?"

"It's bigger than I expected. Cleaner, too. Considering what your office looks like."

"This is where I live! You wouldn't expect me to wallow in dirt."

"Hate to tell you, but I did expect it." He was leading up to that wonderful something—marriage. She couldn't bear him dragging it out, teasing her. "Give me a hint. Why do you want my opinion?"

He hesitated. "Did you mean it—your offer to help with my paperwork?"

Casually, she pulled back a curtain, gazed out the window. Halos surrounded the vapor lights on the airstrip. All else was dark. "Of course. The Foundation has an unexpected cash flow now. Abigail is looking for more help. She can replace me. I can still help her out, though, on a volunteer basis."

"That's great. I need a bookkeeper in the worst—"

She whirled to face him, her gray eyes blazing. "Bookkeeper? *Bookkeeper?* That's why you dragged me here?"

"You know that's not the only reason—"

"Right! You wanted a little on the side! Well, no thank you!"

"Wait a minute!"

"No! You wait. You need a bookkeeper and a live-in piece

of flesh, too? What were you going to offer me? Bedroom gymnastics between accounts receivable and payable? Just to sweeten the offer?"

"I know what you want! You want to tie me into knots. Give me ulcers. Turn me into a wimp. 'Do this, honey. Do that, honey.' I'm not a man to rush into things!"

"Oh, I can think of any number of names to call you besides 'honey.' Like, lowlife, two-faced, vulture—"

"Hold on! Are you perfect? Look at the way your nose is going up."

"There's a bad smell in here. Excuse me, I have to get my clothes on."

THE TELEPHONE BEGAN RINGING at two o'clock in the morning. Not yet able to sleep, Rebecca hurried to answer it. Abigail switched on the hall light.

"We both know who that is," the old woman said. "For heaven's sake, answer it before he wakes the whole house!"

"It's me," said Parnell, his voice throaty, irritable. "I can't sleep."

"So you want to keep the rest of the world awake?"

"We're not going to let the sun set on our little differences, are we?"

"The sun's been down for hours."

"I'm not giving up wanton women and lost weekends for this kind of misery."

"What wanton women?"

"Don't you want to know why I can't sleep?"

"I couldn't care less."

"My pillow smells like your shampoo. My sheets smell like your perfume. It's driving me crazy."

"I'm surprised your stomach doesn't hurt."

"It does. I ache all over. I wish you could see what else aches."

Rebecca remained silent, the telephone clenched in her hand, pressed to her ear.

"Rebecca?"

"I'm listening."

"I can't live without you."

Her legs were suddenly weak, air disappeared from her lungs. "You can't?"

Parnell felt the collapse of his vocal cords. The most important words he'd ever have to speak in his life and he couldn't get them up. He inhaled, spinning words out in a rush on the exhale. "Damn it! I love you." There was such silence from Rebecca it scared him. "Did you hear me?"

"Yes. Was there something else?"

"Else? What else could there—oh." His heart was pounding in his ears. His eyes closed for a moment, his breath stopped, he was sure he had died. "You want to—" his voice faded "—get married?"

"Yes."

He held the receiver away from his ear and stared at it. "Did you say yes?"

"A thousand times—yes!"

Parnell sighed heavily. "That's all right, then."

"Very much all right," Rebecca whispered.

"I can be there in forty-five minutes," Parnell said, all hope.

"There's only the sofa."

"Better Abigail's sofa with you nearby than my bed without you."

ABIGAIL WOULDN'T STAND for the wedding to be held in the office of the justice of the peace. "I feel responsible. We'll have the wedding here in the parlor. I'm sure my old friend, Judge Stanley will preside. Besides, you can't leave out the kids. They were part and parcel of the whole affair."

Parnell looked at her. "No reporters, Abigail. I know how your sly mind works. I won't have you turn this into a circus."

"Just a photographer? You'll want pictures, won't you?"

"Of course we will," Rebecca agreed, slipping her arm through Parnell's.

THE BRIEF CEREMONY was over. Parnell looked dazed. Rebecca smiled. "That wasn't so bad was it?"

"I hope not. It's for the rest of my life."

"Mine, too."

His arm snaked about her waist possessively. "Let's go somewhere. I want to get a head start on what grooms do on their wedding night."

"What's that?" asked Jonesy. He, as did all of the boys looked trim and neat in their new suits.

"You'll grow up and find out one day," Parnell said. "Unless you keep eavesdroping, in which case, you'll be dead."

"Time to cut the cake," Abigail announced, ushering the bride and groom into the dining room. The cake was cut, champagne poured, pictures taken, with Molly somehow managing to be in every shot.

"Okay. It's officially over. Let's go," Parnell said.

"Don't be in such a hurry," Abigail admonished. "I haven't given you your wedding present. I've been saving it for a surprise." She handed Parnell a thick envelope.

"I can't accept any of the loot you've been dragging in."

"Don't be nasty, dear boy. Open it."

"Parnell!" Rebecca breathed looking over his shoulder. "Those are airline tickets."

"To Hawaii," put in Abigail.

"What's the catch?" Parnell asked, scouring the lace-draped Abigail.

"Don't be so suspicious. Your plane leaves in two hours."

"We can't—"

"We can!" Rebecca put in. "You've already arranged for four days away from the airfield. And I'm packed."

"So is Parnell." Abigail beamed. "I had Amos pack for him. The suitcase is in the hall closet."

"Oh, Parnell! Say, yes!" Rebecca pleaded. "Just think. Beaches, sun—look out the window and tell me no."

Outside it was snowing lightly. White flakes drifting lazily downward. Some of the flakes settled briefly on the windows, sticking for an instant before the warmth from inside penetrated, melting them.

"All right, you win."

"I have it all planned," said Abigail. "The children and I will see you off at the airport."

"Why do I feel I'm being taken?" muttered Parnell.

Judge Stanley pounded him on his back. "Because you just got married, my boy. The feeling never goes away."

At the airport the wedding group drew a crowd when the photographer began snapping pictures of the kids throwing rice and confetti at the newlyweds. Mortified, Parnell sought and received permission to board the plane early. He pushed Rebecca to the last row of seats in the plane. "Finally!" he exhaled.

"It was a lovely wedding," Rebecca said, putting her head on his shoulder.

Parnell stifled a yawn. "I think the champagne has made me sleepy."

Rebecca pressed her lips to his ear. "Close your eyes and rest if you like. I won't mind."

"You won't think I'm a bore?"

"Darling, you're many things, but never boring. No, I'll just consider you're getting rested for a late-night walk on the beach. I'm excited. It'll be so romantic. The moon, blue waters, waves lapping."

Parnell gave her a lazy grin. "Late tonight will be romantic, but I sure as hell am not spending my wedding night on a sand dune. And if you don't let me close my eyes for a minute, if you keep talking, we're gonna have to get off this plane and—"

Rebecca brushed confetti from his jacket. "Go to sleep."

While the rest of the passengers boarded, Rebecca watched Parnell and daydreamed. Once they arrived on the island, they'd have to buy swimsuits. She could almost feel the goodness of the sun on her body. Parnell stirred when the plane took off, but once safely aloft, his eyes closed again. Rebecca passed time reading a magazine and staring out the window. It was not unpleasant. The knowledge that she was Mrs. Parnell Stillman warmed her as much as she imagined the sun soon would.

"Hi," said a small voice.

Rebecca looked across Parnell and stared aghast. "What are you doing on this plane?"

Molly grinned. "We're in first class."

Parnell opened his eyes and glared at Molly. The photographer walked up and snapped their pictures. "Perfect," she said.

"HOW CAN YOU BE SO CALM!" roared Parnell. "The sly old biddie tricked us! Of course we'll have the wedding here," he mimicked. "Of course, no press. Just a photographer. You *do* want pictures? She *sold* us!"

Rebecca went to the window of their hotel room and

stared out. A golden moon traced a path on the blue Pacific, lacy waves curled onto the beach. The first night of her honeymoon! "Are you going to spend all night raging like a bull? I can think of something far more interesting to do. And anyway, Abigail had our best interest at heart. She finagled us a free honeymoon, didn't she? Had you thought of Hawaii? We were going to spend four days cooped up in a Holiday Inn."

"Free? She sold us and the kids as an exclusive! That's where the money came from. I should've guessed. And did you hear what Molly said? 'The captain took off all his clothes and went in the lake and hurt his fanny and Rebecca had to put medicine all over him without his clothes on!' What are people going to think! Our pictures are going to be plastered all— What're you doing?"

"I'm taking off my clothes."

"That chicken-necked old crone kept sneaking up behind me ordering me to restrain myself, keep my hands off you in front of the kids. As if I'm not respectable. To think I just let that go by without a word."

"Of course you're respectable," Rebecca said soothingly.

"Some honeymoon. A clutch of brats and a photographer following us everywhere."

"They're three floors below. You're not going to begrudge them a few days of sun and sand, are you? They deserve a bit of fun, too. Abigail had to go to great lengths to get permission for them to miss school."

Her dress fell at her feet. She was a mass of cream-colored lace, sheer fabric, glowing skin. Her smile was a smile of complete adoration.

"My permission is the one she should've sought."

"You wouldn't have given it. And you always find twenty-five different ways to argue a point."

"Then how come I never win?"

She began to loosen his tie. "You looked so dashing at the wedding. I'll bet the photos of you will make the cover. I'll be the envy of every woman in America." Her hands slid down his chest.

Parnell began to bask in pleasant sensations to which he tried not to give a name. "I'm never going to win an argument with you," he said. "Your tactics are too distracting. What was I saying?"

"You had to restrain yourself."

She stood before him naked, solemn and clear-eyed. His wife. His woman. Offering herself wholly and without conditions.

"Shall I put my clothes back on?" she asked.

He reached out and touched her smooth sleek body, circled her waist with his fingers and drew her close. "Nope, if this is the way I'm bested, I can probably bear up."

His lips went to her breast, his teeth gently touching her nipple. In the sweet taste of her flesh all else was forgotten.

At length he said, "I just want to lose myself in you."

Rebecca's arms enveloped him.

"That's all right, then," she said and gave herself up to being possessed.

HARLEQUIN®

AMERICAN ✦ ROMANCE®

LOOK FOR OUR FOUR FABULOUS MEN!

Each month some of today's bestselling authors bring
four new fabulous men to Harlequin American Romance.
Whether they're rebel ranchers, millionaire power brokers
or sexy single dads, they're all gallant princes—and
they're all ready to sweep you into lighthearted fantasies
and contemporary fairy tales where anything is possible
and where all your dreams come true!

You don't even have to make a wish...
Harlequin American Romance will grant your every desire!

Look for Harlequin American Romance
wherever Harlequin books are sold!

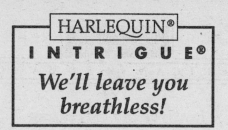

HARLEQUIN  PRESENTS®

HARLEQUIN PRESENTS
men you won't be able to resist
falling in love with...

HARLEQUIN PRESENTS
women who have feelings
just like your own...

HARLEQUIN PRESENTS
powerful passion in
exotic international settings...

HARLEQUIN PRESENTS
intense, dramatic stories that will keep you
turning to the very last page...

HARLEQUIN PRESENTS
The world's bestselling romance series!

Harlequin® Historical

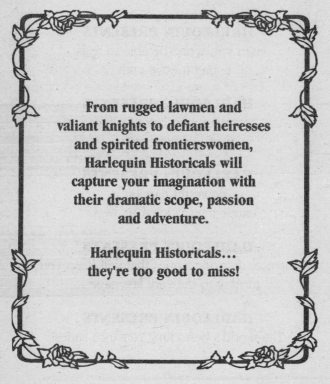

From rugged lawmen and
valiant knights to defiant heiresses
and spirited frontierswomen,
Harlequin Historicals will
capture your imagination with
their dramatic scope, passion
and adventure.

Harlequin Historicals...
they're too good to miss!